CW00798331

The Break of Civilisation

The Restoration Legends, Volume 1

Rob Bleckly

Published by Rob Bleckly, 2024.

This is a work of fiction. Similarities to real people, places, or events are entirely coincidental.

THE BREAK OF CIVILISATION

First edition. September 24, 2024.

ISBN: 979-8223746003

Written by Rob Bleckly.

Part I: The Test of Reason

Prologue

Hedley sat facing the sea, his legs crossed, his lined hands resting lightly on his knees, palm up, thumb and forefinger looped, but the quietude he sought would not come. Despite the intervening centuries, whenever he contemplated the devastation, the lives lost, both down here and in the orbiting station from which he and Jorgena had escaped, it brought tears to his eyes. He felt a desperate need for someone to understand.

A mellifluous female voice gently invaded his mind. [I understand.]

Hedley wiped his eyes with the back of his hand. [I doubt it Severne,] he thought back, his implant rendering his synaptic pulses machine-readable before transmitting the thought to the orbiting artilect originally called seven. He'd been using Severne, her, and she, for seven's pseudo personality as the self-styled Goddess of this blighted planet since before his and Jorgena's escape from the orbiting station.

[Typhon's course remains unchanged. If you wish to avert the coming tragedy, you will need to do more than sit and meditate. We have limited generations in which to breed a host and wake the colonists or we will lose all that remains.]

Typhon, he thought, Severne's name for the asteroid it had detected. According to its calculations, Typhon's orbit would eventually intersect with New Earth and wipe out the last remnants of this once great colony. Perhaps it was time he tried to help.

[What do you need?]

[I need you to go to Deep Creek.]

[Why?]

[My projections indicate Jorgena will soon have another child, perhaps more.]

[Not with me, she won't.] They had co-habited after landing but It hadn't worked.

[She will use her partner's sperm. Her children will make suitable candidates.]

Hedley rose in a single fluid motion, turned and walked toward the squat stone complex that dominated his high plateau. Massive doors slid soundlessly apart at his approach. Brilliant white light rushed out as if to beat back the coming darkness.

• • • •

Hedley arrived in Deep Creek as an ordinary server and settled into the small community. Years passed before Severne provided him with a name and a terse description of a woman she considered suitable: Eliza Wainwright, thirty-eight, devout.

[She's a bit past her prime breeding years.]

[She is however quite capable, and in the right place at the right time.]

Severne paused where he expected continuation.

[But?]

[Nothing is certain. Childhood is fraught with danger particularly for boys.]

[Eliza will accept?] he asked, noting Severne had already decided the gender of this latest attempt to breed a host for its consciousness.

[Eliza would otherwise be barren. She is also unmarried and will need a father for the boy. You will need to broker an arrangement between Eliza and Arthur Forrestor who needs a mother for his orphaned grandson.]

Severne then added in a seductive tone of thought, [by the way, I have suggested she name the boy Willard.]

Hedley felt flattered, though somewhat surprised at her suggesting his middle name for her most promising candidate. His pleasure soon fell to suspicion. Severne did nothing without reason. [You're not using my genetic ...]

[Of necessity, my selection criteria emphasised survival traits.]

Chapter 1

Fools!

Why do they do, it thought Willard, watching the long line of Penitents at the Public Arch, waiting patiently to put a question to Our Lady's oracle. He hadn't been for a telling since his eyes began changing, exactly as his mother hoped, and Ser Hedley predicted. The change in his eyes already mapped out a destiny he would never have chosen, didn't want, and now actively shunned. As he told Kezia, "If the Goddess can foretell what's going to happen to me, what's the point of living it?"

It surprised him to see several deep blue uniforms in the queue. Watcher veterans who followed the ancient Aithist creed. Why would those who professed not to believe in Our Lady of the Towers queue for a telling? He tried to imagine what questions they might ask. 'Will the Wall hold?' or perhaps 'What happens to me if The Wall falls?'

That thought automatically drew his gaze to the top of the tower. Like the opaque lenses of a blind beggar, Severne's Ears stared silently out at the horizon, sending petitioners' questions to Our Lady, the Goddess Severne.

Maybe I'm the fool.

Then again, how could Our Lady, floating somewhere high above, ever receive their questions when her 'Ears' pointed at the horizon?

A flash of light at the tower's base pulled his attention back. Deep Creek's new server, Ser Hedley's replacement, emerged from the shadows of Pauper's Arch. He stood in the arched doorway, shielding his eyes from the glare and gazed across at the public queue.

Willard moved to put the stonework of Paupers Gate between him and the server. Too late. The server was already striding down the short path to the gate. Willard watched in fascination as sunlight shattered into a myriad of tiny rainbows where it stuck the server's talisman.

While Willard was still thinking about whether to slip away, the new server stooped under the stone arch and said, "Forewarned is forearmed. There is no need to fear a telling. Our Lady's answers are never sinister."

"Yes, Ser," Willard said, keeping his eyes downcast. He kicked idly at a tuft of grass, shifting uncomfortably from one foot to the other, not wanting to appear rude, simply wanting the new server ignorant of his candidacy for as long as possible. One look at the colour difference of Willard's irises is all it would take. Most likely it was already too late. Surely Ser Hedley, who had coached Willard from birth, would have told his replacement about Deep Creek's prime candidate.

It soon became obvious the new server would not take the hint, and the prolonged silence was making Willard uneasy. He glanced up one eye closed as if sensitive to the glare. His gaze fell on the server's badge of office dangling from the lanyard around his neck. Up close the server's talisman looked quite ordinary and dull, a flat oblong card that in shadow lost its iridescence.

"Unusually hot for this time of year," the new server said, smiling down at him. "I'm Ser Tomas, Willard." His smile widened at Willard's resigned sigh, "Ser Hedley has told me all about his 'special' candidate. You were easy to spot. The difference in your eyes is as he said, quite striking, more so than your friend Wylie."

He spoke casually, as if to a long and trusted friend, while occasionally nodding a greeting to those passing along Ring Road.

"Yes, Ser," Willard said with resignation and tensed, waiting for the inevitable next question.

Ser Tomas wiped his brow with the sleeve of his black robe. "Yet here you are, a patron's son, lurking around Pauper's Gate? One might think you had better things to do on your birthday. I suspect you are here, because your less well-off friend and fellow candidate, Wylie, who has presented for the test you refuse, is soon due back."

"Yes, ser."

A week ago, Wylie had gone into Our Lady's Tower through Paupers Gate and out through Parsons Gate, the private entrance at the back, for sers, sevs and warriors, often derided as Priests Gate. A closed carriage had whisked him away to the Pillar's servatory for his test. The sequence would supposedly reverse when he returned. He'd enter through Parsons and re-emerge here.

With no reason to hide his eyes now, Willard stared back. Ser Tomas had dark eyes, blue and brown, the difference minor; the eyes of a failure.

"If we all became warriors, there would be no servers. I assure you Willard it is quite an honour to fail."

The fine hairs on Willard's neck stood up.

Ser Tomas sighed. "To have been born such a strong candidate is a rare privilege. It comes with obligations, but I suppose Ser Hedley has made you aware of this."

"Yes, ser," Willard said, repeating his singular reply, unwilling to venture any information about himself, despite that Ser Tomas probably knew it all, anyway. Why is the man still here? He should be back in his tower, supervising his acolytes.

Ser Tomas persisted. "Why then, such reluctance? You not only refuse to take Our Lady's test, but you do not even consult her oracle to find out why Our Lady needs you."

'Yes, ser' wouldn't work this time, but before Willard could form a suitable reply, someone pushed between them. Ser Tomas grunted and put his hand to his chest as if someone had punched him.

"You there, no running in the grounds," Ser Tomas said and with a quick apology to Willard, turned and hurried after the runner. Within a few steps he paused, looked down at his chest, then back at Willard his expression changing to one of disbelief as he held up the dangling ends of the lanyard that had held his talisman.

• • • •

Averil Leach passed a hand over her short-cropped hair and wiped the collected sweat onto her alpine jacket. Fate had conspired against her. The first day of bud was unseasonably hot. The New Year's Day show, always a Satelday, was in full swing around her. Averil, trapped in the stifling air between two show stalls, had only worn her alpine jacket because it had a hood. She was boiling. The thud and clatter of the knock-em-downs on one side and the cloth merchant spruiking his wares on the other, wasn't helping her already taut nerves. As she scanned the tower entrances for the server, doubts crept in about what she was attempting. Despite mother's assurances and her own careful planning, the opportunity might not arise.

She felt relieved to see the flash of a talisman as Ser Tomas, Deep Creek's new server, emerged from the tower. Fate had turned her way at last. Too late for doubts now. She pulled the hood of her jacket forward and reached for her knife. The new server strode down the short path to Paupers Gate and started a conversation with someone standing just outside it.

Averil burst from between the stalls and ran at full speed towards them, nearly stumbling when she saw it was Willard in conversation with the server. Severne's tits; why did it have to be someone who knows me? She barged between them with her back to Willard and thumped the server in the stomach. Gasping for air, he bent forward. Averil grabbed the dangling talisman and sliced through the lanyard.

Still breathing hard Ser Tomas straightened. "You there, no running in the grounds."

Ignoring him, Averil sprinted up Paupers Path and plunged into the tower's cool interior. She pushed her way through the queue of startled penitents, navigating from memory while her eyes adjusted. The acolyte regulating traffic was so astonished he failed to protest and in that brief hiatus, Averil felt Ser Tomas enter behind her. She glanced back, saw him silhouetted against the glare, an accusing finger stretched towards her, trying to pin her in place, his voice changing from disgruntlement to anger.

"You! Stop right there. In the name of Our Lady, you must stop. This is sacrilege."

Tightly clutching the borrowed talisman, she jumped down the first steps. His words hunted her as she hurtled around the stairwell, her thoughts bitter. The all-male serverhood treated female candidates as breeders for the next generation of male candidates.

At the bottom, she cut across the lower foyer and slipped through heavy drapes into the Penitent's Waiting Room. As she jogged down the central aisle, puzzled frowns tracked her passage, but no one interfered. Averil's thoughts whirled as she broke into a run for the shimmering curtain, her eyes on the shaved head of an acolyte up front speaking with a penitent. This had better work, mother.

"Wait your turn," a voice challenged.

An acolyte she hadn't seen stepped into the aisle behind her. Severne's tits; there goes my retreat. I'm committed now. Then she remembered where she was and mouthed a quick apology for her language. If the Goddess truly could listen in on her thoughts, here would be the place for it.

Alerted, the acolyte in front moved to intercept. Penitents stirred as Averil lunged, the talisman firmly clutched in her hand. The acolyte ducked as she surged up and over him, pulling her body in a curve, tucking her head inside the line of her shoulder as she hit the floor behind him and rolled to her feet, straight through the sparkling curtain that covered the Audience Chamber entrance.

Only her ragged breathing broke the silence. None of the uproar she had created in the Penitent's Waiting Room penetrated the shimmering curtain into this sacred space.

"It worked," she yelped.

She was as much astounded at it working as at her own audacity in attempting it. Thank you, mother, she thought, as she scanned the chamber for the oracle's guards, surprised not to see a single snake. Maybe the Goddess sensed she meant no harm, or maybe, as her Watcher instructors said, her reptilian guard were like most of the tower's assertions, pure invention.

The sweat cooled on her face. Small sounds arose in the silence: moisture trickling over rough-hewn rock walls and down between patches of dark green moss. In the background she could hear a gentle hum of power, builder magic. Vapour rose from a long crack in the floor, yet despite all the moisture, the stone underfoot was dry and, thank Goddess, free of snakes.

The server's tripod, a wooden three-legged stool, stood empty directly in front of the equally empty oracle. The huge crystal cube on its polished altar hummed and emitted a bluish light shot through with coloured sparks, but Our Lady was as absent as her reptilian guard. This was not good. Maybe there's more to consulting an oracle than I thought.

Averil hesitated and was, as the saying went, lost, unable to transgress another step, clutching the talisman so hard the faceted edge cut into her palm. When she tried to speak, she found her tongue uncooperative. She licked dry lips swallowed hard and tried again. "Dear Lad ..." she croaked and the sparks inside the oracle swirled, increasing in frequency and intensity. A radiant image coalesced inside the crystal. Our Lady of the Towers, the Goddess Severne, familiar from countless statuettes, sat, and settled her long white robe. The image was ghostlike, almost see-through, an appearance that could well lead to the belief the Watchers held, that she was an illusion.

"Averil, how nice to see a new face. What can I do for you?"

The voice of the Goddess was, as expected, soft and rich, but the content and delivery astonished her. It was one thing for servers to say 'Our Lady cares for each and every soul', quite another for her to recognise and address Averil by name. It should not have come as a surprise, but it did; the price of growing up in a household of mixed beliefs was uncertainty.

"You have a question, Averil."

Averil did, but was speechless. For a long while, she stood mute in front of the oracle, breathing rapidly, strangely inarticulate. She still found it hard to believe she was here, inside the Audience Chamber for a private telling.

She swallowed, then blurted out, "Where are the snakes?"

The Goddess smiled. "Is that what you really want to know?"

"No, Lady."

"Relax, Averil, have a seat."

The offer dazed Averil. Plain speaking was no way for a Goddess to talk. Where was the majesty in a conversational utterance like 'have a seat'? Worse still, the only seat available was the server's tripod. Heart pounding, Averil took the two uneasy steps required to reach it. Illusion or not, the Goddess tracked her, watched her, as Averil carefully seated herself and became enveloped in the vapour. It had an odd smell, like a struck flint, and made her feel light-headed.

"Ask."

"Will the Wall hold?"

The question was important to her but nothing like the question she had intended to ask. Now that she was here, that question was simply too hard.

The Goddess shimmered, became transparent for a moment. "I do not know. The probability is ..."

"But you're the Goddess, you have to know," Averil interrupted, forgetting whom she addressed.

"If that is what my servers teach, they misrepresent me," the Goddess said. "The future is uncertain. I cannot control every aspect of Nuaith, but I have plans for you Averil, and I will do all I can to see they bear fruit."

Averil's private telling was freaking her out. The Goddess could not control everything but had plans for her. The Wall might fall. Averil didn't know whether to feel happy or scared. She had a thousand more questions, but didn't know if Our Lady would allow her to ask them. Servers only allowed one question per telling and she had already asked two.

"Let me sum up your situation," the Goddess said, crossing her hands at the wrists draping them over a knee. She leant forward. "The Academy has rushed your training and you are being sent to the Wall early. You fear the Federals, those you call ferals, are about to overrun it. You want to know what will happen to you."

Averil nodded dumbfounded, knowing now she would never ask the real question. Unanswered, she could hope. A refusal would be final. As Willard would say, better not to know.

"Again, I can only reiterate I do not know, but I will be there to protect you as best I can."

"Why?"

"I want you to survive to have offspring."

Averil's response was automatic, out before she had time to think about it. It was the sort of question frequently asked of the oracle but rarely answered, "Who with?"

"Willard Forrester."

Averil nearly fell off the stool. No way, she thought, not in a hundred years. Willard? "I can't. He's oathed to my sister," she said, finally finding her voice, objecting, arguing with the Goddess, marvelling that she could, knowing it was futile.

"Nuaith is at a crossroads, Averil. You and Willard have vital roles to play. You can refuse to cooperate as Willard continues to do, but it is not a wise course for you, Willard, or Nuaith."

The Goddess stood, her robe gently falling around her bare, perfectly formed feet. "The choice is yours. I have my eye on you Averil," she smiled, "give it some ..."

'Thought,' Averil completed, but the crystal was empty. Just when Averil thought nothing could ever surprise her again, the Goddess had snapped out of existence. One second, Our Lady was there smiling casually as she delivered one shock after another, and the next the oracle was empty. The soft bluish light and swirling sparks that had greeted Averil's entry were gone, sinking the Audience Chamber into semi-darkness. The big crystal cube, devoid of life, was featureless grey. Blank too, were the walls of the Audience Chamber, as blank and as bland as the outside of the tower. The Watchers are right. It's all illusionary, builder magic.

Bedlam poured in through the now uncurtained doorway. "Tits," Averil whispered. This isn't supposed to happen. The server's tripod fell as she spun and stared into the enraged face of Deep Creek's new server.

"What have you done candidate?" he hissed, his differently coloured eyes flicking around the chamber's walls widening when his gaze came to the dull oracle. His mouth opened and closed to a thin, angry line.

"This isn't my fault," Averil said, knowing no one would believe her. Someone parted the drapes, allowing a ray of daylight into the waiting room. Averil let out a paralysing scream and ran for it. Ser Tomas stepped back nearly falling over one of his acolytes. She dodged around him, tossing his talisman toward the ceiling. "Catch," she yelled and while the server tracked his precious badge of office, she sprinted back up the waiting room aisle between stunned penitents.

• • • •

"It's me," Kezia said in Willard's ear.

Willard's thoughts, dwelling on the daring talisman theft, scattered and his heart raced. "Don't sneak up on me like that. You scared the ..." He left off when Kezia's eyes blazed.

"How are you, Kezia? Good to see you," she mocked. "What were you staring at kiddo?"

He glared at her. "Don't call me that," he said. Immediately he felt the need to apologise, amazed at how quick they were to argue. "I'm sorry Kezi, how are you?" he leaned over to kiss her, but she turned aside at the last moment.

"Fine thanks, kiddo, and you?"

Willard steamed silently. From his point of view, while he'd been at the Pillar Servatory for the last three years, a training school for candidates, Kezia had matured from the sixteen-year-old girl he'd oathed into a somewhat perplexing young woman. He loved her, or at least he thought did without really knowing how to define what he felt, only that he wanted to be with her all the time. He didn't think he had changed much, but she certainly had. Increasingly over the last two years since returning, he often caught her with a troubled expression. Something had happened to her that stood like a wall between them. He never knew quite what to expect; could not really relax in her presence anymore. He still enjoyed her company, but sometimes she could be so—exasperating.

"You haven't done it, have you?" she said, stating the obvious.

"No," Willard said, looking away.

"So why the interest?" Kezia asked. "You do know Wylie won't come back through Paupers. He'll come out through the Public Gates, so we can all celebrate our first warrior."

"You're probably right," he said, and to get away from the subject added, "Someone just stole the new server's talisman."

Kezia arched a neatly trimmed eyebrow.

"It's true," Willard said, his circled thumb and forefinger, invoking the Goddess as witness.

"Well, I'm not letting it spoil my day. Are you coming kiddo?"

Willard bristled at the taunt, but forgot his retort when he saw the harsh line of her mouth had softened and an amused look had replaced the troubled one. She was teasing him now, paying him back for his less than enthusiastic welcome. He returned her smile as she led him away. All would be well again; for now, anyway. He looked back once at Paupers Arch, through which the thief and the new server had vanished, with a sense of foreboding, but saw neither them, nor Wylie.

Chapter 2

Averil pounded up the stairs into the light, the server's wail chasing her once again.

"Stop him. Stop the blasphemer."

Him, thought Averil, peeved he should think her a boy. She pelted out through Patrons Arch, and barrelled into the crowd. Fate dealt her another blow when she burst through a knot of people right in front of Willard and her sister Kezia. He barely had time to pull her sister out of the way before she slammed into him.

They tumbled together, rolling into the feet of the people too slow to get out of the way. Willard ended up on top and she saw recognition in the disconcertingly different eyes, pale blue and deep green, the reverse of her own, like looking into a mirror.

"For Goddess' sake, hold him," she heard Ser Tomas shout as he pushed through the crowd, his face shiny from his exertions and the heat. Legs parted, making way for their new server.

She saw Kezia tug urgently at Willard's sleeve and bend down to plead in his ear, "Let her go, Will."

Willard glanced up and Averil grabbed the opportunity, rolled him off and catapulted to her feet in a single practised move. She soon lost herself in the gathering crowd.

"Why didn't you stop him," she heard Ser Tomas shout and after a long moment, Willard said, "He was too fast."

Averil grinned, noting that no one in the milling crowd heeded Ser Tomas's plea to 'stop him'. They stepped around her, more intent on the altercation behind her, loud and clear in the still hot air.

"Rubbish, you had him on the ground," she heard Ser Tomas say as she slipped between stalls.

The loud dispute was never out of earshot. Averil walked briskly behind the stalls, between overflowing rubbish bins. She returned to where she had left her backpack. Quickly, she jammed her jacket under the flap, wiped her face free of sweat, and fluffed her short hair.

On impulse, she returned to the fray, careful to stand at the back of the crowd now four deep. She arrived in time to see Ser Tomas carefully scrutinising Willard.

"You again, Hedley's 'special' candidate," Ser Tomas said.

That and the way he'd invested the word 'special' with derision gave her chills. She wouldn't want to be Willard just now.

"You were right there when he stole my talisman," Ser Tomas continued, and in the brief silence that followed, Averil could see him putting unrelated facts together.

Nobody noticed her. Two years at the Academy had obviously changed her enough that even Willard, who'd been courting her sister before she left, hadn't recognised her until she was in his face. This was the man the Goddess wanted her to have children with, her sister's betrothed, Deep Creek's number one candidate.

"Accomplice," Ser Tomas accused. He pulled a handkerchief from his robe and mopped his face, staring at Willard as if he'd had a sudden revelation. The accusation hung in the air like the smell of the bins behind the stalls. The trio, Willard, Kezia, and Ser Tomas, stood suddenly isolated like a contagion. The crowd stilled, fascinated but not wanting to be involved.

"No, ser. It's nothing to do with me," Willard said politely.

Averil admired his defiance. Challenging one of Our Lady servers could lose you your head. Poor Willard, I'm sorry it had to be you.

"You just happened by, and ..." Ser Tomas stopped and glanced back at the tower, his finger tracing the symbol on his tightly held talisman in unthinking ritual.

She saw Willard tense. "No, Ser, I have nothing to explain."

Ser Tomas reddened and blustered. "Better you come now, than I send the militia to arrest you."

In the abrupt silence, she heard Kezia's sharp intake of breath just as a new voice confronted the server.

"What's all this about priest?"

Averil, recognising Willard's brother Aldus, shifted to put someone between them, thinking she should go before anyone else who knew her turned up. She saw Willard and Kezia exchange a brief smile and Ser Tomas stiffen at the ancient derogatory term, priest. He flexed his fingers, smoothed down his robe and turned to meet this new challenge to his authority.

"This is no business of yours, Aldus."

"Is that a fact?" Aldus spoke with an air of assurance Willard's defiance had lacked. "Does not article three say, 'Each man shall watch for his brother'?" He nodded at Willard. "So, what do you want with mine?"

Ser Tomas seemed puzzled. "Your brother," he said, glancing sceptically from one to the other.

Averil, who had grown up with the Forrestor brothers, looked at them anew, seeing them as Ser Tomas might, the tall fair-haired Willard with the startlingly different eye colouring and the short dark-haired Aldus with perfectly matched brown ones. It wasn't at all obvious that they were brothers.

Aldus took a step closer and Ser Tomas, despite being head and shoulders taller stepped back, defensively.

"You have no business quoting Our Lady's Articles. You never set foot in her tower. Besides, one can't just choose the articles that suit one's argument." He fidgeted with his talisman, glancing back at the tower.

Aldus poked him in the midriff. "And one can't just choose to ignore the articles that don't suit one's argument, like me looking out for my brother. It's a simple question priest, what do you want with Willard? Our father, your biggest patron, will want to know."

"If you must know," Ser Tomas said, squinting down at Aldus, anger hardening his response. "Your brother was lurking outside Paupers at the precise moment the blasphemer stole my talisman, and just moments ago he let the miscreant go. You work it out."

He turned on Willard. "Admit it, you know the thief."

Willard flushed and Ser Tomas pounced. "See."

"What's that in your hand priest?"

Ser Tomas looked down. "Getting it back does not excuse the theft. Besides, it's much more than mere theft. The culprit used it to break into the Audience Chamber and stopped our oracle. Your brother knows him."

Averil, suddenly aware of her surroundings, knowing she should leave while she had the chance, stood mesmerised. Ser Tomas looked anxious.

"Do you have any idea ... no you wouldn't? Now I really must go and if your brother doesn't come with me then 'special' or not, patron's son or not, it will go hard for him. Stopping the oracle could bring a warrior down on us."

He turned abruptly and pushed into the crowd, seeming to have forgotten all about her and Willard. Moments later, he was through the public gate, hurrying past the stalled queue into the tower.

As the crowd dispersed, Averil at last slipped away. She didn't go far though, lingering in Severne's Wood on the path she knew

Willard would take to get home, curious to know what he would make of Our Lady's plan for them. Besides, given the delay her private audience had caused, she would need a horse and the Forrestors had plenty.

• • • •

With dusk already shrouding Severne's Wood in gloom, Averil was about to give up when she spotted Willard on the path. He walked slowly, deep in thought, oblivious to his surroundings. Voices reached her ears. Willard might be unaware, but the militia was right behind him. With no time to warn him, she slammed him off the path into the undergrowth face down, and lay on top of him, whispering a warning in his ear. He lay still. When she relaxed, he threw her off and sprang to his feet.

Averil, seeing him ready to sink in a boot, scrabbled out of reach, and rolled to her feet, her whisper ferocious. "What were you going to do, kick me to death?"

Willard snapped back, "You started it."

"You earned it."

"What? How?"

"I would have got away clean if you hadn't tripped me."

"Trip you? You barrelled into me."

"Severne's tits will you keep it down? The militia is not far behind you," she whispered, holding a finger to her lips frantically motioning him to squat. He stood staring at her until she grabbed his hand and pulled him down. As children, they had probably held hands a thousand times without thinking about it. It's different now, she thought, glancing sideways at his face. If it came to it, at least he wasn't ugly or short.

Two militia passed within inches of them hurrying towards Eldwin's Ford, muttering about a fool's errand.

"I need to borrow a horse," she said, dropping his hand, wiping hers on her pants as if his touch had been offensive.

"Why are you asking me?"

"Who else but your old man would have a spare?"

"He won't listen to me."

"It's only a loan."

"You'd have better luck asking Aldus."

Shoulders hunched and fists clenched, Averil stomped away. Behind her, she could hear Willard following as she headed towards the pool. As children, the foursome: Aldus, Willard, Kezia, and Averil had on a dare, skinny-dipped here. The short walk calmed her and the pool brought back pleasant childhood memories of a time less complicated, before Willard's eyes changed and then hers; before she knew Our Lady's plan.

"Do you believe in the Goddess?" she asked suddenly. "Our all seeing, all knowing, all caring Lady of the Towers."

"I hadn't really thought about it except for the Test. Aren't the warriors' swords proof enough? They're named by Our Lady and their power comes from her."

"It's Builder power," she said, before adding, "How about her oracle's tellings?"

"Depends," Willard said.

"On what?" she challenged.

"On the server, I think her oracle is always right, but servers' interpretation of what she said, is sometimes wrong."

Averil studied him closely for a moment, wondering if she could trust him.

"If they do, it's deliberate. She talked plainly to me, just like I'm talking to you?"

"How do you mean?" Willard asked.

"Face to face," Averil replied, agitated now. "She just sat there and told me she has plans for me—and you."

"Me? Why would she talk to you about me?"

"I told you. She has plans for us."

Willard placed his hands over his ears. "I don't want to know."

Averil glared at him, drew a deep breath, and waited until he took his hands away, "If you're not going to the take the test, why don't you do something useful and sign up for the Wall."

"I've thought about it," Willard said.

"Thought about it," Averil shrieked. "Severne's tits Willard there's a war on. Why do you think I finished training a year early?"

"No idea," Willard said,

"The Wall's in trouble, I'm supposed to train a whole bunch of new recruits on the way to the Wall. I need to report to the assembly point in Grundston by this time tomorrow, but ..."

"Grundston, you haven't got a hope."

Averil glared at him, drew another deep breath, and spat a tirade in one long steam, rising almost to a shout at the end. "Look, they won't leave for a couple of days, but if I don't make it, they'll think I've deserted. Why do you think I need a bloody horse? Are you going to lend me one or not?"

"They're not mine to lend."

"Thanks for nothing, you useless prick," she spat.

"Break it up," said a voice behind them.

Averil dived into the thick undergrowth, leaving Willard to deal with the militia.

· · · ·

Bastard.

As Averil slammed through the bush, ignoring the scratches from hard twigs and thorns. She imagined every footfall treading on Willard bloody Forrester's head, pounding his face into the ground.

Bastard.

There is no fucking way we are having 'offspring' she thought. She hated him. First, he almost foiled her escape from the tower, then he wouldn't lend her a horse. I hope they lock him up and throw away the key. Small creatures scurried from her path.

Bastard.

I should've just stolen a bloody horse, but a quick mental calculation showed Willard was right, that even if she had a horse, and even if they delayed, she could not make Grundston before the contingent had left for the pass. If she went south, however, she could intercept them. It would take the fully laden contingent three weeks to reach Rivers Junction. Once I get out of Deep Creek, I can do that without a horse, except the militia, having sighted her leaving Willard, had formed a cordon through Severne's Wood and was now herding her in the opposite direction.

If only I hadn't dallied. She was still fuming at her own stupid sentimentality when she reached the edge of Severne's Wood. She had arrived at the twin ramps leading down into Eldwin's Ford, the cordon closing in behind her. The ford was twenty yards wide and a hundred long. The Builders had cut deep excavations through the banks so long ago that the trees seeded on the raw cuts now joined overhead. Local history credited the cuttings to Deep Creek's founder, Eldwin the Forrestor. Averil disagreed. The scale of the earthworks and the placement directly in line with the Arch of Restoration, described in *Legends*, as the Builders' most significant artefact, made it obvious the Builders did the excavation.

Slightly out of breath, Averil peered down the shaded corridor to where the road crossed the creek and swore silently. At the bottom of the far ramp, a squad of militia was stopping pilgrims, pulling back hoods to check faces. Five militia to stop a single fugitive whose only crime was to borrow a talisman, seemed excessive to Averil. Five in front and who knows how many, behind? *They must blame me for the oracle breakdown,* she thought, on seeing a pilgrim's expression of shock and a ritual pressing of a circled thumb and forefinger to head and heart. *How do they know who to look for when the damn server thought I was a boy?*

"You up there show yourself," someone called out as two of the five militia started up towards her.

"Give me a break," Averil whispered. She backed away, quickly melding into the bush, turning upstream, mindful of the tightening net. Away from the ford, she slithered down the steep bank and waded forcefully but slowly across the creek, constantly watching over her shoulder. Fortunately, it was shallow because Averil had never learnt to swim. At a flash in the bush over her shoulder, she plunged into the reeds. A moment later, two militia stepped out of the bush up to the edge of the bank she had just left. After a token survey, upstream and across the creek they turned toward the ford.

Averil waited and then clawed her way up the far bank, freezing in the evening breeze. An hour later, legs aching and clothes steaming from her uphill jog from the ford to the high plateau, she left the pilgrim's narrow path and crossed to the farm road. She paused there to read the messages flashed from signal tower to signal tower along the face of the foothills, catching the last rays of the setting sun. YOUTH - SLIM - BLONDE - FIVE NINE - WANTED FOR DESECRATION. *At least youth is neutral. Any desecration wasn't my fault. The Goddess must have* just quit, or had she? Thinking back, Averil remembered the Goddess had stopped in mid-sentence. So who? She doubted the new server had anything to do with it. He was as shocked as she had been.

She resumed jogging before she started shivering again, her thoughts spinning in circles. Who could stop an oracle, except an Arch Server or a warrior? Perhaps the breakdown was one of those things the Goddess couldn't control. That was a scary thought.

The glow on the snow-capped peaks faded as Averil crested the edge of the Forrestor plateau. Forrestor ancestors had farmed this fertile but unnatural plateau since Eldwin's time. Most now believed there had once been a natural valley, like those on either side, that material from the mountain the Builders decapitated to make a platform for the Arch, was what filled the valley. The resultant plateau and the flat-topped peak on which the Arch stood were unique to the island, perhaps the world.

Averil immediately felt safer. The Forrestor farm had been like a second home during childhood. She stopped to listen, silence. The militia had abandoned the chase for the night. She left the road, jumped the fence, and made her way towards the homestead across a ploughed field. She grinned. "Sorry Mrs Forrestor, Willard's gonna be late."

She put on her jacket as she recrossed the headwaters of the now ankle-deep creek. Looking up, she drew her bearing from the softly glowing outcrop behind which her escape route lay, a fissure that ran right through the ridge into the next valley. The hard beaten path up to it, a record of their youth, was hard to find even when you knew where to look. In the dark, she would have to feel her way around the granite base to where it started. With thick scrub at her back and her hands on the hard rock, she worked her way along until she found the gap, an old animal tunnel, long disused. The brothers had found it by accident, looking for an easier way down after climbing the sheer face.

Averil made her way to the cave behind the outcrop, itself an anomaly that had become the foursome's secret place to escape the adult world. About twenty paces high and thirty deep, it was smoothly cylindrical, one more builder relic in this odd valley.

The fissure, which ran through the valley's western ridge, was at right angles to the cave. It would cost her a day, but she had to avoid having the militia, drag into one of her father's cells; She had been calling Deep Creek's Magister, by his title since she was twelve, to remind him she could belt him one if he tried it on again. That first time she had grabbed the nearest thing to hand, a cast-iron frying pan. He'd left her alone after that and went after Kezia again, a more pliant target.

Having Averil locked in one of his cells, might embolden the bastard. Then again, she was now eighteen and Watcher trained in hand-to-hand combat. She shuddered at what Kezia must have endured. Willard was bloody clueless, and Mother, for all her witching ways and her vast storehouse of working builder artefacts, refused to acknowledge what was happening.

Lying back on the still warm granite she looked up at the emerging stars for Severne's Eye, wanting reassurance, wondering if the Goddess's need for her and Willard to have 'offspring' meant she already knew she wouldn't find a host this generation? I should have paid more attention to *Legends*. When nothing moved in the twinkling canopy, Averil gave up, fetched the pile of dry leaves and twigs always left ready in the cave. With her uniform hanging between bushes in the entrance, she sat by her small fire, her jacket around her bare shoulders, listening to the lid of her billy rattle.

The contents of her backpack were meagre provisions meant for a couple of days. It would be easy to eat everything she had. She opted to eat only a thick slice of cheese, washed down with billy tea. She had been counting on people's natural generosity to Watchers to supplement her provisions, but with her description flashing up and down the entire Aldgate-Meander basin, she couldn't chance it, she would have to live off the land.

After repacking, she settled down behind the dying fire. Tomorrow she would have to wind her way down the adjacent valley, which would bring her out on the southern outskirts of the town close to the Rivers Junction road. A hard walk would get her there before the contingent. No worries, she thought, watching the sky through the cave entrance.

A tiny moving light waxed bright and Averil, feeling lucky to have seen it, was at peace. 'I have my eye on you, Averil,' the Goddess had said.

Chapter 3

Kezia Leach sat alone at the kitchen table finishing breakfast when creaking timbers overhead alarmed her. She held her breath, waiting to hear if it heralded someone rising. The sound of a trickle followed by a light thud and a scrape reached her, a twin taking a pee. Bedsprings creaked and went silent.

Kezia relaxed and hastily finished eating, but before she could get out of her chair a familiar odour, a mixture of old sweat and new beer, warned of her father's silent approach. She tensed. Surely, with everyone at home, he wouldn't dare.

She was wrong. A wet kiss landed on her neck. His arms reached down, encircling her from behind, his hands fondling her breasts. She went rigid. As his lips worked their way across her cheek, she turned her face and desperately sought to wriggle away.

"Come on Kez; give your poor old dad a kiss."

Despite the early hour, he'd been drinking, yet his voice was smooth and his embrace lingered. Then he pulled out the chair next to her, sat, and reached out to stroke her thigh. "There, there, Kez. You're safe with me. You know I wouldn't hurt you."

A loud knocking startled him. His dark eyes suddenly cleared. He withdrew his hand and placed it on the table. Kezia jumped up and was out the door, heading for the front gate before he realised it had been her knocking on the underside of the table.

After yesterday's heat, Serverday had dawned with a brittle chill in the air. Kezia walked briskly and was halfway along the esplanade towards Eldwin's Ford when she spotted the tiny speck wending its slow way down the long brown strip from Forrester Farm. Willard, she thought with mixed feelings, the desperate ones she suppressed, promising herself today would be a good day. She would buy him something in Arthurton to make up for forgetting to wish him a happy birthday.

Across the creek, Our Lady's Tower shone in the first rays, as the sun topped the Lesser Range. Severne's Ears flashed like signal tower beacons. People were already crossing the bridge. Stallholders probably; going to pack up after the show and what a show. What was Averil thinking breaking into the oracle? She was still supposed to be at the Academy, yet Kezia had clearly seen those unmistakable eyes. Thank Goddess only Willard and I recognised her.

Light crept swiftly down the Barrier Range ahead, touched the tiled rooves and then suddenly flooded the town. The sun was warm on her back. Her mood lightened when she spotted the dray climbing out of Eldwin's ford, passing a squad of militia checking pilgrims. Averil must still be free. Her mood darkened again when Aldus hailed her from the dray.

"Couldn't wait, eh," he said, grinning down at her.

The tension from breakfast burst forth in an angry curse that Aldus, busy driving over to the wrong side of the road, missed. He pulled back hard, turning the pair in a tight circle around her and making deep ruts in the wide verge. Arthur Forrestor's prize pig squealed in protest as his crate bounced across the dray. Kezia winced at the strain Aldus put on the horses.

"Don't tell me, let me guess," Aldus said as he drew alongside. "Our Lady has called you in for a private audience. Since yesterday, they've become quite fashionable."

Kezia grimaced. He doesn't know how close that strikes. She found it incongruous that, unlike Willard, Aldus always lifted her spirits. She loved Willard, but his brother was more likeable.

"Where is he?" she asked.

Troubled eyes made his grin seem false. "He wasn't back from the Watchhouse when this pig to market must go, so I'm here instead."

"The Watchhouse?" Her stomach churned. Yesterday's confrontation with Ser Tomas over Averil's stupid oracle break-in still haunted her.

"The militia nabbed him in Severne's Wood." Aldus paused, watching her face, "with the oracle breaker. Averil eluded them yet again."

Kezia's earlier misgivings turned to alarm. "Averil," she squeaked her voice off key. "How do they know it was Averil?"

"They don't. I was guessing, now I know."

Kezia stifled any further reaction, cursing inwardly. At least only Aldus knew—besides Willard and me. Damn. Curiously, she found Aldus knowing a comfort, the four of them sharing a secret like an echo of childhood. She glared up at him and silently cursed the brothers Forrestor. Her chance to make it up to Willard was gone. Still, without him along, she could avoid his disapproval if she had a telling.

"Help me up," she said to Aldus, hitching her skirt and placing a booted foot on the axle's hub.

"Certainly Mrs Willard, anything you say," Aldus joked as he reached down and gripped her wrist, "Up you come."

Kezia found herself almost catapulted into the dray's seat. A long moment later, Aldus let go of her wrist.

"Come on, let's go. I don't want to waste the day."

"Yes ma'am, right away," Aldus said with a mocking salute. "Yup," he shouted at the horses, "Mrs Willard has a day not to be wasted." Deftly slapping them into motion, Aldus wheeled the dray back across the road, completing the circle with a lurch neither the horses nor the pig appreciated, and headed back the way she had come.

Kezia felt her smile widen. His antics were just the antidote she needed after her father's unwanted attentions. They were soon out past Martha's bridge, dropping in quick swoops through the foothills, the tree cover giving way to rolling pasture. Conversation dried up. Aldus seemed to be content just to drive the cart. Except for the creak of the springs, the clopping of the horses and an occasional grunt from the pig, the ride was peaceful.

Inevitably, Kezia's thoughts returned to Willard, her way out, and ... Averil. The more she thought about it, the more she saw how Ser Hedley, their previous server, had constantly pushed Willard and Averil together. He must have known, as he had with Willard, that Averil would be a candidate and I wouldn't. That's so unfair. I never had a chance. Ser Hedley never mentioned it and I wouldn't take his hints. If only I'd had been a girl candidate like Averil, Our Lady might have seen me as breeding potential for Willard.

Pastures dwindled as they emerged onto the plains into the full midday sun. Streets and houses began invading the pastures. Other carts and drays, loaded with, or trailing livestock, joined them in the general movement towards the Arthurton Sale yards.

"Aldus," she asked suddenly, "why don't they test girls?"

"Why test a girl, when you're looking for the Man Who Will Be Face?" He stressed the word 'Man'.

"That's self-fulfilling," Kezia retorted. "It can't be anything but the 'Man' if the tower never tests girl candidates. It doesn't even make sense that Our Lady wants to come down to Nuaith as a man."

"Who would believe a woman?" Aldus said with a grin. After a long thoughtful silence, broken only by the continuing sounds of the cart, he added, "Still, you may have a point. Article Five, in *Legends,* says something like, 'By their eyes, you will know my candidates', nothing about gender in it."

"Then why aren't girls tested?"

"Because the damn priests say so." Aldus spat the word priests. "Who's going to argue with their Goddess-given authority? Even the Watchers who don't believe a word of it are cautious around servers these days for fear of attracting a head-lopping warrior."

He went quiet again for a few moments before saying, "Actually, the early Watcher histories mention a female warrior. Medora, she called herself, born way back, became a warrior at twelve. She defended those building the Wall. Without her, they couldn't have finished it. Imagine that, your Goddess has been looking for her Face for three hundred years. I'd love to have been there when Averil broke into the oracle," he finished and Kezia blanched, wondering if Averil's secret was safe with him after all.

"Imagine fronting the Goddess personally instead of wondering if the damn priests gave you the answer Severne wanted you to have," he added, his voice wistful. "I'd sooner trust a warrior; at least they passed the test."

Kezia, noting his tone, realised with an unexpected insight that part of Aldus's antagonism towards the towers could be jealousy of his brother's candidacy. She saw now that Aldus, unlike Willard, wanted to have a go at the test, had maybe dreamt of becoming a warrior until it was clear he had passed the age at which his eyes would change.

The dray slowed to a walk near the outskirts of Arthurton, the number of travellers swelling with carts from the hamlets of Briarfield and Walker North.

"And speaking of the test, there are worse fates than failing. Just taking it can fry your brain."

"What!"

"I'm not surprised you don't know. I'll bet Willard doesn't either. I should warn him. It isn't something Our Lady's tower-full church likes to advertise," he chuckled. "And in the absolute worst-case, it can kill you stone motherless dead. I always start wondering when candidates like our Wylie don't come back. It is to be hoped that he is now about Our Lady's business, but who knows? The ways of the tower are exceedingly mysterious."

Kezia shuddered, unsure whether to believe all Aldus told her. What if Willard went in but never came out? What if he passed, or Goddess forbid, he ended up disabled or dead? How would she escape home then?

When she looked up, they were in Arthurton and the dray had slowed as carts and drays jostled for shady parking spots close to the Saleyards. Beside them, Deep Creek had become a wide river.

"You can drop me here, I'll find my own way home," Kezia said and Aldus dutifully reigned in. Impulsively, she reached over and kissed his cheek. "Thanks for the lift, brother."

In quick succession, Aldus's expression cycled through surprise, hope, disappointment, and resignation. He helped her down in silence, turned away and picking a break in the traffic whipped the horses into a canter, upsetting the blue-ribbon pig and drawing angry shouts from other drivers.

Kezia stared after him. *What does he expect? I'm oathed to his brother.*

• • • •

Kezia arrived home late, having walked all the way, mulling over the oracle's foretelling. A visiting Arch Server, Sev Miller, had taken her aside to give her the oracle's answer in person. Our

Lady had confirmed to him that Willard would fail. The Sev hadn't put it quite that way; he'd been more cruelly detailed and emphatic than her worst suspicions, saying the Goddess needed offspring from Willard and Averil, which amounted to the same thing. He had to fail. He couldn't be a warrior and marry Averil. Warriors never married. Mother is so right. The Goddess is very choosy about whom she helps. Perhaps if I were carrying Willard's precious 'offspring', Our Lady would take better care of me.

Wearily and warily, Kezia quietly entered through the back door and found her mother at the kitchen table kneading dough.

"What's wrong Kez, bad telling?" Jorgena Leach said not stopping or turning around.

"It's not ..." Kezia's throat went dry and her lips seemed stuck together. How could she possibly know?

"I've joined Medicorps," Kezia said, finally able to get the words out, leaving her mother's intuitive question unconfirmed. Her telling had been devastating.

Jorgena nodded as she rounded the lump of dough then pressed it flat with the heels of her hands. "Good for you. You're as well qualified as any can be, these days," she said, sounding relieved, not the reaction Kezia expected. No surprise, no remonstrations, but then her mother had always been—different.

"It means a tour of duty on the Wall," Kezia added, to be sure her mother had not missed the point.

"You'll be better off," Jorgena said.

Better off on the Wall? It's the front line. People die there. The only thing good about it was escaping father.

"I leave first thing tomorrow," she said, hiding her turmoil. "They're sending our group by coach from Walker. We'll join them in Everild. They've had so many late joiners they're delaying a day or two in Grundston."

"Same trick every year," Jorgena said. "I should have told Averil."

"You've seen her?"

"She dropped in a couple of days ago. She finished training early. The Watchers have assigned her to get this year's contingent to the Wall. I would have told you, but lately you've been gone before I'm up." She turned and beamed at Kezia. "You'll be together."

Two days ago, thought Kezia. She stopped the oracle yesterday. A barrage of thoughts struggled into line. "You told her how to use a talisman," Kezia said in wonderment, "and she broke the oracle. If they catch her, you'll be under suspicion again."

Jorgena paused, wiped the flour from her hands on a tea towel and picked up the rolling pin, using it as a baton to emphasise her argument. "All I told her was the truth. The cards, everyone calls talismans, work for whoever holds them." She turned back to roll the pastry. "Did she get a private audience?"

"I don't know. We bumped into her but didn't have time to talk."

"How is Willard?"

"Fine," Kezia said, her tone betraying her anguish.

"I like Willard. For such a strong candidate, he has a healthy scepticism. Does you joining Medicorps mean you and he are not ..." a quick glance at Kezia and she left the rest unsaid. "Pity, but it's probably for the best."

Best for whom, Kezia wondered.

For the next few minutes, Jorgena busied herself shaping the pastry, rolling it, cutting it, and laying it in a pie dish. With sure and practised moves, she added the partially cooked meat and vegetable filling, rolled on the top, then brushed it with milk, pricked it, and placed it in the oven.

Kezia watched with fascination, absorbing the sights, sound, and the smell of it all, storing memories against a bleak future.

"That's tea ready," Jorgena said turning, "now, come on down to the potting shed. I have some things that may help keep you alive."

"That isn't reassuring, mother."

They left the warm kitchen through the back door, stepping into the cool of the evening. The first stars were just becoming visible. Kezia found Severne's Eye immediately, always a good sign, but as she watched, it faded out. She waited breathlessly, exhaling her relief when it brightened again. All would be well so long as the Eye of Our Lady watched over them. Except now that Our Lady had snatched Willard away and given him to her sister, Kezia was less sure Our Lady's intentions were all good. The sudden mournful pealing of chime birds from Severne's wood made her shiver. She looked up to find clouds had obscured the stars. Severne's Eye was gone. Quickly she touched a circled thumb and forefinger to head and heart as she hurried to catch her mother.

An earthy smell assailed her as the door to the potting shed creaked opened. The shed was about twelve feet square, its walls made from dressed stone with a single opaque window for light, and a bench under the window stacked with ceramic pots. All of it was a clever disguise for mother's refuge, an inexplicable builder vault that lay beneath the potting shed.

Their steps sounded hollow and rattled the pots. Together they heaved the trap door up against the wall and descended narrow stone steps into the cellar. Slivers of light, bleeding through the gaps in the planking overhead, drew soft lines on the hard packed dirt floor. A muffled fifth bell rang out the day's end as Jorgena lit a candle.

The cellar was a windowless replica of the potting shed above, deliberately bland to forestall idle curiosity. The shelves lining the wall opposite the stairs were empty except for dust. The only relief to the room's sparseness was a recessed niche in one wall, containing a hand painted statuette of Our Lady. She stood with her arms outstretched in a gesture of welcome. Her eyes, brightly painted in different colours, glowed in the candlelight.

Jorgena put the candle on the floor and stood before the niche, placing her hands on two well-worn blocks. A thin beam of blue light jumped from the mouth of the statue and briefly struck Jorgena in the eye. Although Kezia had seen the ritual many times, even done it herself, she flinched, but the fine hairs on the back of her neck only stood when the shelves disintegrated. The tiny pieces fell to the floor and burrowed into the dirt, disappearing as if they had never existed.

Hidden behind the disintegrated facade was the outer wall of the huge builder vault that mother called her refuge. The smoothly curved outer wall, built of similar material to Our Lady's Tower, glowed in what little light the candle gave. An oblong crack, rounded at the corners, appeared in the smooth surface. Alongside the crack was a picture of a bird Jorgena said was a Kestrel. With a hiss, the outlined door swung inward. Kezia squinted as strong white light poured into the dismal cellar along with the quiet hum of builder power.

Mother's refuge was a world apart. The walls, floor and ceiling of the entry room were all made of the same smooth builder material. Already the outer door, which had to shut completely before the inner would open, was closing. Kezia stepped over the threshold through the invisible barrier and paused. She watched as dust particles on the sleeve of her coat sparked, crackled, and disappeared.

"Hurry up."

Kezia did, but as quick as she was, the hem of her Medicorps greatcoat caught on the edge as the door slammed shut. She felt a tug, heard the material sheer. "It's not even a day old."

Jorgena gave her daughter a speculative look as the inner door opened and the background hum, augmented by multiple soft clicks and whirrs, peaked. It faded again as her mother led her down a passage with closed doors on every wall. Sealed to protect their contents mother said and, Kezia knew without doubt, they hid a treasure trove of working builder artefacts, hidden because owning them was not just sacrilegious but illegal.

Despite being underground, the refuge was always light and airy, its thick walls comforting, a place where Kezia felt safe. The refuge was an Aladdin's cave of illegal riches and a true haven from the outside world, especially when father ... she pushed the thought back. I'm leaving tomorrow. It can't ever happen again.

They eventually entered a room about as big as the potting shed. On one side were racks crammed with an assortment of twinkling artefacts. A bench on the other side had cupboards above and drawers below. Jorgena pulled open a drawer and withdrew several objects, placing them on top while she rummaged deeper. The only object Kezia recognised was a small flat box, shaped like twin joined circles. Containers for the eye-covers her mother had given Willard and Averil to make their pale eyes match their dark eyes. Averil had declined the offer, but not Willard. Why he bothered was beyond her. Everyone already knew.

From the back of the drawer, Jorgena pulled out a heavy-looking box and heaved it onto the counter. When she opened it, Kezia's eyes bulged at the heap of old golden Roos, silvery Koalas and other coppery coins, builder money still in use a thousand years after their demise. These were still shiny, unmarked, as if freshly minted. Jorgena counted out a small fortune, dropped them into a black drawstring purse, and handed it to Kezia.

As Kezia hefted the bag, thrilling at the weight of it, Jorgena selected a small round jar from a stack of similar jars in an overhead cupboard. She unscrewed the lid, showing Kezia it was full of the healing dust, profound aithcraft. A pinch of the silvery stuff would heal the worst of wounds. The gifts stunned Kezia. Her mother only used the dust in critical cases, always ensuring the patient was never aware of the process. Kezia had assisted from an early age, frequently on Averil who often came home bruised or bleeding. Compared to what a grain of this builder magic could do, the healing arts taught at the Institute were antiquated.

"On second thoughts, take several," said Jorgena, pulling down more of the squat jars, "you will no doubt put them to good use on the Wall but please take the same precautions I do, or you'll have servers hounding you." She screwed the lid back on the one she had opened and Kezia stuffed the jars into pockets in the Healer's shoulder bag Medicorps had issued her.

Realising this was her best chance to say goodbye, Kezia opened her arms. Mother and daughter stood hugging for several minutes, Kezia letting remorse wash over her, for all that might have been.

"One more thing," Jorgena said, producing a small paper packet. "I made these for you and Averil. I forgot to give her hers."

Kezia squeezed the side of the paper sachet, opening the mouth. Inside were two rings, intricately carved silver bands. She shook them into her palm, where they refracted the refuge's light into filmy rainbows like a server's talisman. "They're lovely," she exclaimed.

"They'll help me ..." Jorgena stopped. "Give Averil hers when you see her."

Before Kezia could respond, Jorgena placed both hands on her daughter's shoulders. Kezia was instantly alert certain something dreadful was coming.

"Look, I'm truly sorry Kezi. I let you down. I should have had it out with your father at the start." She paused, concentrating on Kezia's eyes, waiting for the information to register.

"You knew!" Kezia shrieked, outraged at all the times she had tried to say what had been happening to her and her mother had ignored her. She tried to pull away.

"Yes," Jorgena said, hanging on to her, "but Kezi, please understand the circumstances, had me scared."

"Of what? You weren't the one suffering."

Kezia saw her mother wince and knew her remark was wrong. In some unknown way, her mother had suffered.

"Your father saved me. I owed him my life. Then you came along, and I needed the protection ..."

What her mother was saying so shocked Kezia, she failed to make sense of it. Tears blurred her eyes.

"I was watching him. I wouldn't have let ... It's more complicated than you can imagine. He's never been down here, but he knows about it and this must never fall into the wrong hands." She made an all-encompassing gesture.

"You knew and you did nothing," Kezia cried.

"That's not true, I warned him ..." Jorgena's denial fell away. In a barely audible whisper, she said, "Yes. I'm sorry." Her head dropped. "I hope one day you'll understand."

Unexpectedly, Kezia felt as sorry for her mother as she felt for herself. Laying blame would reverse none of her suffering. She was suddenly glad to have joined Medicorps.

"What about the twins?" she asked.

"Seven will take care of them," Jorgena said. "Their eyes are changing."

"What?" Kezia cried.

"It ... she takes care of Averil. She will look out for Sarah and Lisa, too."

Kezia's mind whirled as she tried to understand, focussed on the statement that because the twins' eyes were changing Our Lady would take care of them, as she does Averil.

Jorgena pulled back, gently wiped the tears from Kezia's cheeks and her own. "Come on, it's time you packed."

In a daze, Kezia allowed her mother to lead her back into a dark and starless world, the sky now overcast and the air chill. A cold drizzle struck her in the face like an omen of her future.

• • • •

Averil found the bird song that woke her unfamiliar, which struck her as an odd way to feel about her home environs. Three years at Fort Ricco, in the empty south beyond Port Calder, had tuned her to a different set of sounds. The overnight mountain chill rapidly dissipated and the morning promised a repeat of yesterday's unseasonal heat. She rose, packed, tidied the camp, and then sat cross-legged on top of the outcrop. For breakfast, she ate an apple while watching Deep Creek stir.

Light from the rising sun poked through scattered clouds and bounced off the shingle rooves and wet paved roads of Deep Creek. The town, just visible over the lip of the plateau, looked peaceful, even beautiful, and the tiny people in the town square, like so many twigs blowing in the wind. She had mixed feelings about leaving: sadness that her relatively carefree childhood had gone, but excited that she was going to the Wall as a captain, with a chance to make a name for herself.

The increasing sunlight highlighted both Eldwin's statue and Our Lady's Tower across the creek. The tower dwarfed the statue, dominating the town as much as her servers and their tellings dominated their lives. Her gaze continued to drift as she munched. Opposite the outcrop, the Builders' enigmatic arch, many times higher than Our Lady's tallest tower, overshadowed the town. Behind the arch, the snow-capped peaks of the Barrier Range soared past the clouds. Her gaze continued upwards to where Severne's Eye had passed over last night. To the Eye of the Goddess, somewhere in the distant blue, even those towering peaks must look small.

This new perspective caused her to feel as tiny as the stick figures in the town square, strangely forming into lines like a militia squad. Her consternation grew when the lines became a column and moved off towards Eldwin's Ford. Severne's tits. She must have really pissed off the new server.

With determination, she settled the pack on her shoulders and looked at the fissure, as narrow as her options. Turning for a last look at Deep Creek, Averil cursed them all: her father, Ser Tom, and Willard too. Poor Kezia. Get out sis, don't wait for Willard, he's next to useless and ... the Goddess has plans for him.

In parting she stood up on the outcrop and with middle finger extended, raised her fist to the little black figures marching through the rain to the ford, a scurrilous Watcher salute handed down from antiquity. Some even said it came from Aithe with the Builders. Its significance now lost to history, but considering its use at the academy, Averil surmised it to be rude and insulting. For some inexplicable reason, performing the small gesture gave her an inordinate sense of satisfaction.

Averil paused briefly at their cave. In daylight, the initials W
F loves K L scratched into the wall inside a heart shape stood as
stark denial of the ludicrous plans the Goddess had for her and
Willard. The irony of her situation made her spit and forced her
to admit she was jealous, not of Kezia but of Willard. When her
own eyes changed, revealing a potential she could never realise,
the hopelessness of her dreams bordered on despair.

Watcher officer was the closest she would ever get to warrior.
She had trained with determination then risked it all to put
her dream to the Goddess, but the reality of her audience had
made it impossible and the question had remained unasked. She
had wasted the chance and now she would pay for making the
attempt.

In memory, the fissure had been wide and easy to navigate,
not the overgrown rock-strewn sliver she found, which narrowed
in some places to a body width. It could take her most of the
morning just to thread her way down through the trackless bush
of the adjacent valley.

The day heated rapidly. Her small canteen ran out of water
at midday. The rocky creek in the centre of this valley only ran
with snow melt during fall. Still, she would be out of here
mid-afternoon. She picked up a small rounded stone from the
creek bed and put it in her mouth.

A flock of corellas burst from the bush and screeched
overhead. Averil, wondering what set the birds off, stopped, took
a deep breath, and waited for her heart to stop hammering so she
could listen. She heard voices.

Severne's bloody tits. This is getting ridiculous. How had the
new server forced Magister into pursuing her, or had he guessed
who'd broken into the oracle and had plans of his own? Magister
was a nasty piece of work, but not stupid. She doubted he knew
about the fissure, which meant he was being thorough covering

all possible exits from the plateau. Her only hope was to slip through the approaching cordon.

"Stay in sight of each other," said a disembodied voice. With the sudden gust of wind that brought those words, Averil realised how close they were; almost on top of her. She cast around for a way out and spotted an animal trail burrowing into a dense blackberry thicket. On elbows and toes, she crawled along it into the centre, pushing her pack ahead of her to avoid most of the thorns. The newer canes lashed back viciously, and her uniform provided only limited protection. She closed her eyes against the pain and waited, felt blood oozing from the scratches and trickling down her arms. Sweat poured off her face. She wished they would hurry. They were being careless, chopping the bush with swords that could slice through canes with ease, and severely damage an arm.

As the slashing came closer, she heard them laughing, exchanging jokes most of which she had heard at the Academy. The man closest to her position stopped and she could hear him pop the cork of his canteen, the splash and gurgle as he drank. Bastard, she thought, and with her tongue pushed the small stone to the other side of her mouth.

They were well up in the valley when she wriggled backwards out of her burrow, gathering more thorns and cuts, and headed on down. She had gone maybe a hundred yards when she ran into the second line.

Chapter 4

Sleep eluded Kezia. She stared up at the cracks in the wooden ceiling. That Mother had known all along filled her with disappointment and a sense of betrayal. Why Dear Lady, she prayed, why me? Have I not always believed? Why did I not deserve the same protection as my sisters? I needed it more than Averil did.

Turning over, she again checked the pack under her bed. She was ready to go. Her Medicorps uniform lay on the dresser. She had said her goodbyes to mother and the twins and she would soon be with Averil. There was only Willard. She couldn't just leave without letting him know. Then she could put it all behind her: home, parents, sisters, and dreams, all because her eyes hadn't changed. It's so unfair. Why hadn't Our Lady mentioned she wanted Averil to have Willard's offspring until now? What good were the oracle tellings when they missed such vital detail? Huge tears welled in her eyes. She soaked them up with the top of the sheet. If only she and Willard were already married. If only Willard would take the test. If only Deep Creek did not consider mother an Aithist witch. If only her father ... If, if, if.

The back door banging shut sent a shiver up Kezia's spine. Her eyes snapped opened to find it was already light, that she had slept after all. Damn. She had wanted to be long gone before anyone woke. Was the door bang, someone going out or coming in, mother or father? Not mother, she would have gone to her refuge after father took the twins to Petitions. Her father insisted the twins get a good Severnian upbringing so they didn't turn out like Averil. He must have come back for something. Oh shit, not now. I'll be gone shortly.

Risking an arm to the cold, Kezia reached under the bed and grabbed her backpack. If she stayed still, he might think she had gone. A light tap on her door made her jump. She looked at the door, wondering if she had latched it. The handle squeaked, the door opened and the dark brown eyes she had inherited focused on her.

"I heard you joined Medicorps Kez," he said, then nodded at the uniform. "You'll look smart in that. I came to say goodbye."

Kezia stiffened, shivering even inside her woollen nightshirt. If only I hadn't fallen asleep, she thought as she pulled the covers up to her neck with one hand and gripped her backpack with the other. The long surgical knife jammed in under the top flap seemed to jump into her hand.

• • • •

When Kezia finally pushed through the back door, she ran into the twins. At twelve, Sarah and Lisa were at that precocious stage of self-discovery that Kezia wished she could relive. From their expressions, Kezia's fright must still be clear even though she had deliberately calmed herself, washing and dressing with care, then quickly making her bed, all the while cautiously stepping around her father. Bryant Leach, Magister of Deep Creek, lay unmoving on her bedroom floor. Why today of all days?

"What's up Kez?" said Sarah, the elder twin, by a few minutes.

Kezia snapped back to the present, "Sorry?"

"You look like you've seen a ghost," Lisa added.

Concerned they not go inside before she found mother, Kezia improvised. "I ... I want you to do me a favour. Find Willard. Tell him to meet me at the outcrop. He'll know where that is ..." Dear Lady, help me through this, "... by third bell. Tell him it's urgent."

"It's a long walk," Sarah said.

"To the Forrestor farm," Lisa completed.

Both had fair hair and blue eyes like Averil, and now that mother had mentioned it, she could see their eyes were changing.

"Take father's horse, ride double," Kezia said and reached into her coat. Her fingers felt as thick as sausages as she fumbled with the bag's drawstring. She gave each of her sisters a copper emu, which quickly disappeared into matching shoulder bags. In unnerving synchronism, the twins turned without a word. She watched them as they headed to the stable.

Averil's eyes had changed at thirteen. The twins would turn twelve in a little over two weeks. She would miss their birthday. She waited until they rode out of sight before setting out for the outcrop, hoping to reach it by the third bell. She might need to dodge the twins on their way back, but she had to see Willard one last time, wish him a happy birthday for yesterday, no, the day before. He might even come with her. If he joined the Watchers, he could travel to the Wall with her and Averil.

As she slipped out through the gate, Kezia glanced back at the potting shed. Mother, forgive me.

• • • •

Willard was not happy. Thanks to Averil his birthday had been a disaster, that landed him gaol overnight. His father hadn't bothered getting him released until after Aldus had gone to the Arthurton Markets in his stead, and Kezia had gone with him. As if to add to his misfortune the twins had brought him a message. 'Kezia says to be at the outcrop by the third bell.' Willard had sensed an unspoken 'or else' at the end of the message, but that could be the twin's delivery, rather than Kezia's intent.

The first inclination he had, that something beyond their usual argument was amiss, was the light grey Medicorps uniform she arrived in. *She's given up on me, she's going to the Wall.*

"I'm leaving kiddo," she said, coming towards him, her voice strangely subdued, as if worn out. For once, there was no sting in the annoying nickname. He held out his arms. Kezia rejected the offer and sat.

Willard sat beside her. They stared out over the valley together, drinking in the view, the silence more companionable than giving voice to turbulent thoughts.

"When?" he asked absently.

"Today. Now."

Willard felt his knees shake as he turned towards her. She fell into his embrace, burying her face in his neck, hugging him fiercely.

He could feel her shuddering. As gently as he could, he pushed her back a little and looked at her face, shocked at the absolute misery he saw. Dark, puffy skin surrounded the red-veined eyes. "Good Goddess Kez, what's happened?"

Kezia looked away. "Nothing," she said quietly. "I just wish ... it's too late. I need to leave Deep Creek. Will you come with me? I won't make you take the test."

Willard, staggered by her offer, thought she seemed bitter and realised that if he didn't front up right now, he would lose her. She had dressed to go. She would leave no matter what he said or did. He could feel her waiting patiently for him to make up his mind, hope battling with expectation. She had never looked more beautiful or fragile. He wanted to reach out to assure her it would be all right, but he couldn't. He didn't think it would. Fate held him fast. There was no way to unmake his candidacy. He wanted her so much, yet felt powerless to act.

"I didn't think so," Kezia said, watching him, disengaging.

"You're going then," he said, a statement of resignation.

"I have Healer training," Kezia said. "They need me on the Wall just as much as they need Averil."

She reached into a shirt pocket and all Willard could see was the breast beneath, remembering all the times they had been naked together, her creamy white skin glowing in the starlight, the dark pubic triangle every bit as mysterious as the massive Arch opposite. The first time they had done nothing but hold each other, flesh to flesh and he had ached all the next day. Each time since had been more urgent and more passionate, as their mutual exploration went further than either expected, yet neither wanted to stop.

"Here," she said, and Willard blinked.

She handed him an intricately carved ring, as highly refractive as a server's talisman. He grasped it tightly. They stood facing each other, eyes restless, memorising.

"I'm sorry Will, there's nothing for me here. I'm ..." A tear formed at the corner of her eye and she slumped into herself. Willard went to wipe it away, but she forestalled him.

"Don't," Kezia said, then kissed him, "forget me, kiddo."

The last Willard saw of her was the red-flecked brown hair bouncing around her shoulders as she stumbled away and disappeared among the bushes covering their secret trail. She did not glance back, and he remained absurdly silent and immobile. The pressure of the ring in his palm was reassuring, a link to his shattered dreams.

Her last statements on either side of kissing him reverberated in his mind. Had she meant, 'Don't. Forget me,' or 'Don't forget me'. It hardly mattered now. Her kiss lingered on his lips and the image of her face as she did so, remained indelibly etched upon his mind. He had no hope of forgetting her.

He went straight back to work after she left, throwing himself into the planting, as if her going didn't matter to him. Row after row, hour after hour, trying to bury his thoughts in mindless, repetitive activity. It didn't work. Once he found his rhythm, it freed his mind to wallow in regret and self-pity. Stupidly, he had let her go with hardly a protest. Too bloody late now. His brother scooped out a hole and pressed in a small green seed potato that Willard then covered, tamped down, and watered in. He focussed on Aldus's boots a few steps ahead, one on either side of the furrow.

The handmade Henry Burton boots were a gift from their father for Aldus's birthday. Willard had expected similar but got an embroidered shirt from their mother. Fine needle work, but nothing like the magnificence of those boots. It was as if he didn't exist for his father and although he loved his mother; he didn't like her. She was always going on about how special he was to the Goddess. Willard spat. If I'm so special, why did Aldus get the Burtons?

As the brothers neared the end of the paddock in late afternoon, a faint metallic jingle, like a wind chime in a gentle breeze, caught Willard's attention. He stretched his aching spine and scanned his surroundings. Uphill beyond the fence was the silent bush and the towering builder Arch backed by the snow-capped Barriers. Downhill the rest of the farm: the neat paddocks, the creek, the dam, and their homestead.

He could find nothing to account for the sound. The air was still. He must have imagined it. Tiredness brought on by the turmoil since his birthday.

The jingle came again, closer.

Willard wiped the sweat from his eyes and gazed in the sound's direction. As if by magic, several mounted horsemen had appeared on the other side of the creek. Ferals, he thought immediately, his mind still turning over images of Kezia on the Wall.

Aldus moved on unconcerned. Willard rubbed his eyes and looked again, unable to comprehend what he'd seen. He counted seven. His mouth went dry and his palms moist. Either the Wall had fallen or he was having his worst nightmare, in broad daylight, and couldn't wake up. I should have gone with Kezia, he thought, as he closed the distance to grip Aldus's shoulder, trying to give voice to his alarm.

Aldus shrugged him off and the drinking gourd he carried dropped from his shoulder. The cork popped. "Now look what you've done," said Aldus as water washed over several uncovered seed potatoes.

Still desperate to transmit the danger to his older brother Willard tightened his grip, but his frantically working mouth could only grunt. Aldus glanced up in annoyance, then quickly followed Willard's frightened stare. He tensed and put down the bag of seed potatoes.

"It's a drill," he said calmly. "Mind you, seven to two is a bit rich. Rule one little brother; we're outnumbered, we run."

Willard nodded, trying to remember what the militia taught. He had paid scant attention, because, as everyone knew, ferals this far behind the Wall could never happen. While Willard was thinking how good their costumes were, Aldus, a volunteer with the militia, must have been studying their faces as the line moved towards them.

"Funny, I don't know any of them. They're not ours."

Willard's glance switched between the advancing line and Aldus. "What are you saying?"

"I'm saying, let's not take any chances." He stepped in front of Willard and together the brothers edged back towards the fence, and the uncleared scrub on the other side.

Willard's gaze never left the slowly advancing line. It bristled with spears, swords, and bows. They looked so real. His stomach cramped recalling the gruesome tales veterans told of ferals on the Wall. The brothers were at the fence line when the rush came, signalled by an ear thumping ululation.

Placing a hand on a post, Willard vaulted over the barbed top wire and sprinted into the bush. A quick glance back showed Aldus was heading the other way, towards the homestead, splitting the pursuit. The riders had dismounted at the fence. He had drawn two pursuers.

Willard pelted up the slope, leapt over roots, and dodged around blighted trunks. The slope became steeper. The scrub thinned and the shale increased. He sometimes slipped on the pebbly surface underfoot. Maintaining his balance became ever more difficult. He was off the arable plateau, heading up the sacred mountain. Where's the bloody pilgrim path?

He risked a glance behind to get his bearings and felt a moment of panic to see his pursuers so close, one had stopped to take aim. With renewed energy, Willard sprinted in a new direction, ignoring the momentary pain of an arrow nicking his calf. Changing course again, he headed for a patch of denser scrub. The pounding behind him felt closer and another arrow narrowly missed him, striking the ground ahead, almost tripping him.

Were they deliberately aiming low, he wondered, or just having trouble firing uphill on the run? Now the archer was so close he had stopped firing. Willard had the insane idea they wanted to bring him down without killing him.

Blood trickled down his leg. His calf muscle cramped, twisting him sideways. A thrumming spear that might have skewered his shoulder passed under his arm, sliced his biceps, tore skin from a rib and pinned him to a tree by his shirt. The lead feral, the spearman, caught up as he was trying to work the spear out of the hardwood.

When he saw Willard's predicament, he slowed and levelled his sword at Willard's throat. In clear, slightly accented Islander, he said, "Don't move, Forrestor."

How does he know my name?

The spearman smirked and glanced back. Willard took a chance and launched himself forwards, ripping his shirt over the head of the spear, and realising too late that he wouldn't make it. The sword was so close to the end of the short spear, and with his shirt guiding him down the spear he would impale himself on the sword. At the last second, the spearman looked back, twisting the sword point away. Willard came off the shaft and fell, his shoulders slamming into the spearman's knees, who toppled forward, his own weight forcing the slim haft of his embedded spear through his neck.

Blood oozed down the shaft and dripped off the end. Willard rolled out of the way, trying not to vomit. When he looked back, he saw the spearman's startled expression fade with his life. The thought tormented Willard. If this was only a drill, he was a murderer.

The archer caught up, and ignoring his comrade, stood over the still shaking Willard, his bow slung across his shoulder, smelling as if he hadn't washed in weeks. The huge double-edged sword he raised had dark streaks on it, dried blood.

Oh fuck, it's not a drill.

Frightened for his life, Willard scrabbled with his good hand for a handful of the gritty shale. He threw the pathetic handful straight into the looming face and was up on his feet, running before the archer had cleared his eyes.

Heart pounding and legs aching Willard scrambled upward over the edge of the decapitated mountain. He staggered on across the flat grassy top towards the distant fabled Arch towering above the trees, shrouded in mist and mystery, the archer not far behind.

Up close, the Arch of Restoration's true majesty become apparent. From its vine-covered base, it ballooned outward as it soared upward for a mile and a half, its apex lost in the clouds. Behind him, the archer slowed. Despite the impossibility of ferals being thousands of miles behind the Wall, Willard was now convinced they were real and out to kill him. *Damn my eyes.*

He cursed himself for a fool as he limped towards the Arch. His leg was killing him and his side ached from more than a stitch. *It might need a stitch. Why did I come this way? It's not safer here than anywhere else.* The mist wasn't thick enough to hide him. There were no pilgrims today absorbing its healing power or tending the huge meadow in which the Arch stood. The precipitous far edge, fenced to stop pilgrims falling off, only led deeper into the Barriers.

With nowhere else to go, Willard staggered on, tiring fast, the litany his mother had instilled in him as a child surfacing. The words told of Our Lady's benevolence, of her Eye watching over them. *Just words,* Willard thought, glancing skyward. In daylight, Severne's Eye was invisible. He slowed as he approached and looked back. The archer stood staring up at the Arch as if unsettled by it. *Who knew what ferals believed?* Willard stumbled on at the limit of endurance with renewed hope.

As he passed into the shadow of the side of the arch, heading for the nearest corner, rising into the mist like a colossal tower, his skin tingled and the hairs on his arm stood up as they sometimes did close to Our Lady's Tower. 'It's a by-product of builder power', Ser Hedley had told him. Willard had never felt it at the Arch before, despite having been here many times to graze their horses. He turned the corner, thinking to put the massive arch between him and his pursuer, and run to the side edge bush to hide. Instead, he collapsed in a rasping heap at the base of the ancient monument. He couldn't take another pace, let alone five hundred plus to get to the side edge. It was just too damn far. Another verse of the litany sprang to mind. According to *Legends*, the arch was critical to the restoration. Again, the words were no help against his pursuer. The feral archer caught up. Barely able to move, Willard closed his eyes, blotting out the raised sword, bothered by the thought that he would never know if he could have passed the test. Except for Kezia, everyone assumed he would, but only in taking it would he know.

When nothing happened, Willard opened an eye. The archer standing over him had not moved, the hairs on his arms standing like the bristles on Kezia's hair brush. He also had his head cocked to one side like a warrior, as if listening. Willard felt the earlier tingling intensify and hum in his ears. The poised sword appeared to be vibrating in sympathy with the tingling. The archer shook his head and focussed his eyes on Willard, but as his sword descended, the humming in Willard's ears skipped up several octaves until it became a vague pain behind his eyes.

When the tip of the sword was closest to the Arch, a bolt of blue-white energy leapt the gap. The blade crackled along its edges like a named sword. For several seconds, the Archer jerked as a man possessed, his bow slipped from his shoulder, his sword dropped from spasming fingers, he went rigid and fell leisurely backwards. Wisps of smoke curled upwards from the toes of his boots.

Willard felt his sphincter relax. He didn't know whether to laugh or cry. He was alive beyond reason. He had seen his imminent death twice in quick succession and survived both. He wondered if he owed thanks to the Goddess for the last. Perhaps his mother's beliefs had more foundation than either he or Aldus …

He had to help Aldus. The thought brought a wave of panic that had Willard back on his feet, leaning against the Arch for support. Ignoring the smell of the sudden deluge down his pants, he tried to think. Aldus had headed towards home.

The darkening twilight didn't bother Willard as he stumbled towards home; he knew every inch of this plateau. Various scenarios played through his mind; what to do if he met the ferals before he found Aldus. He couldn't stop dire thoughts that Aldus may not have been as lucky. *One of my ferals killed himself and the Arch scorched the other. Who'd have thought the Arch was anything other than a dead monument?*

A hundred yards from home, Willard figured the likelihood of catching Aldus had passed. He was so tired now he could hardly walk and he felt an urgent need to get clean before he went inside. He angled off towards the dam and slid down the grassy embankment straight into the chill pool. Above him, water was already trickling through the large upper pipes in the dam wall. The smaller ones below were in full flood with premature snowmelt from the early bud heat.

The smell when he removed his pants was ugly. He thrashed them against the dam wall, watching with relief as the brown stain flowed away through the pipes on its way down to Deep Creek. He hoped no one used the old swimming hole for a couple of days. Cold but clean, he started back up the embankment. As he passed one of the large upper pipes, he glimpsed something bulky blocking it. He later wished he hadn't looked.

What little light penetrated the dark interior showed him the familiar tooling of a Henry Burton boot. The discovery threatened to crush him. 'Please Severne, not Aldus,' he screamed silently. He refused to believe it, his mind tossing augments back and forth. Many people have Burtons. But no one except his own family came up here. The ferals had, but ferals don't wear Burtons.

Even before he forced himself to crawl into the pipe, Willard knew whoever lay there was dead, the dark lump attached to the boot, lay face down in the water. The lack of smell other than the stagnant water suggested the body was recently dead.

Bloody ferals.

Eyes brimming, Willard edged up to the lump not wanting to touch it, wanting but not wanting confirmation, steeling himself against the possibility it really was Aldus. Before he reached shoulder level, he recoiled in horror and his stomach lurched. In the wet shadows, he could see there was no head. A warrior execution. Oh shit, all those times Aldus baited the servers finally got him killed. He instantly revised the thought. Warrior executions were public. Pushing the body into the overflow pipe so it stayed hidden until heavy rains flushed it out, was more like the ferals covering their tracks.

As Willard backed out, he heard feet stamping on the road above, then voices. He opened his mouth to yell 'down here', but vomited instead. He was about to try again when an underlying jingle caught his attention. Suddenly, he was no longer cold.

The stamping stopped and Willard heard scrabbling sounds, someone making his or her way down the embankment. With two dead at the arch, there would be five above. He was way outnumbered. Flight or fight? Except with neither possible, he just lay still, turned away from the tragedy beside him, bitterness and anger overriding the taste of vomit.

"It stinks down here," an accented voice said. "The water is safe, yes?"

"Yes," replied a quiet voice, strong and deep with only a slight accent, muted by the rushing water.

Drink deep, Willard thought.

"Be quick, we have not the time," a higher voice said, the tone commanding, the accent heavy.

Willard twisted his head for a look and instantly closed his eyes. A feral, crouching on the bank filling a gourd, was staring straight into the pipe.

A new voice spoke, no accent, his tone nervously friendly. "Unless he slipped past you, he must come this way, don't you think?"

Chills that had nothing to do with his wet clothes ran up Willard's spine. He knew that voice, that odd expression. He trawled his memories for a location, and the answer staggered him. The servatory! He tried to match a face to the voice.

The deep accented reply was full of menace. "We need not think. We pay you to tell us."

Willard could only think about that voice. Someone at the servatory had sold them out and it had to be someone intimate with the layout of the valley to know he would come back this way. A server who regularly visited the farm but not Hedley; Willard knew Hedley's voice, nor Ser Tomas; he was too new. whoever it was, had helped the ferals kill Aldus, and now he wants me dead. He clamped his mouth so tight his jaw ached as he memorised that voice.

A change in the tone of the deep voice had Willard straining to hear over the noise made by the feral scrambling back up the bank. The traitor was objecting to something. A loud smack cut his protest short. Willard, picturing the blow whispered, "Hit him again. Use your sword."

"Speak only when the prince asks," said the deep voice, cool and unruffled.

Prince, Willard thought, a feral Prince?

"If he is not the one, your birth you will regret," the high voice said, the prince?

There were low chuckles amid the metallic jingling and the slap of leather as the group moved off. The thud of falling hooves grew fainter.

Willard waited for what seemed like hours. He'd heard three feral voices, the two above and the gourd filler. Where were the other two? When he started shivering uncontrollably, he backed out of the pipe, careful not to disturb his brother's body. Dusk enveloped the valley, bringing an evening breeze. Willard, in wet clothing, felt chilled to the marrow.

No one challenged him as he stumbled on towards home, struggling with emotions he barely understood. Poor Aldus got in the way when they came for me. Seven of them, a full warband, a thousand miles behind enemy lines looking for him, added significant weight to Hedley and Mother's claim that he was 'special'. He searched the sky but could not find Severne's Eye and felt abandoned. The cost of his refusal to take the test weighed on his mind. Poor Aldus. Hedley and his mother would be so disappointed that their special candidate had offended the Goddess.

In every sense, darkness was falling across the plateaus. That she had saved him and let Aldus die was a lesson that caused a sudden of burst anger and spurred him on. He had to let the militia know, had to find the bastard who had betrayed them to the ferals. He was almost home, could see the homestead lights when he fell and found it impossible to rise.

Chapter 5

Kezia tried to look inconspicuous as she descended the Forrestor Valley Road. Aware she had left Willard bewildered; she chewed her lip. It was over, done, ended. She had wanted to tell him everything, but found it impossible. Instead, she had gambled on one last desperate offer for him to join her. As she expected, for Willard to leave, as she was doing, was too much to ask of him. Once again, she had forgotten to wish him a happy birthday.

She hurried on, already knowing she wouldn't make Arthurton today but compelled to get as far from Deep Creek as fast as possible. She might have to spend a koala or two, buy a horse from a farmer, and intercept the contingent. From Eldwin's Ford, she chose the old road, now called Pilgrims Way, through Severne's Wood. The road ran along the north bank of Deep Creek above the town that bore the creek's name. Our Lady's Tower was the only structure on the high side of the creek. Pilgrims from the remotest parts of Preservation Island started their pilgrimages to the sacred Arch at the tower. The few Kezia met, intent on their own purpose, some on hands and knees, ignored her.

Pausing at the Public Gate, she gazed briefly across Tower Bridge to Eldwin's statue in the town square. The statue's uncanny resemblance to Willard was a final reminder of all she was leaving. Only two days ago, oblivious to the changes about to overtake them, they had argued on this very spot, until Averil ran into them. Damn her, thought Kezia, looking back along Pilgrim's Road. Willard would have come this way to get home from the show. Averil must have deliberately waited for him. She choked back a sob and walked on, upset by how easy it was to imagine Willard and Averil having sex in their cave. It seemed foolish now. Two days ago, she had been desperate for change. Now that she had it, she hated it.

Twilight beat her to the picnic grounds at Martha's Bridge, on the eastern outskirts of Deep Creek. Gently she stuck her thumbs under the backpack's straps, eased them off shoulders unused to such loads. Tears of guilt, tiredness and frustration streaked the dust on her cheeks. She scanned the area for a place to hide in case someone had found her father.

Thankful that the picnic grounds were empty, she ran over the bridge and across the oval, into the thick undergrowth bordering the creek. Thorns plucked at her clothing as she forced her way through. But a vision of becoming entangled, unable to break free, and the militia dragging her back to face her crime, induced mild panic. Ignoring the pain from cuts and scratches, Kezia renewed her push and found the creek was closer than she imagined, and the bank steeper. In two steps, her frenzied rush broke through the undergrowth. She stumbled forward at a run. Something snatched at her pack, but she had no time to think, no time to take a breath before plunging into the icy water. Her lungs ached and she thought of letting go, of finding peace, but then her hand touched bottom. With renewed vigour, she got her feet under her and pushed up, bursting through the surface into even colder darkness. She gasped as the icy water cascaded from her head. To her relief the water only came to her waist. She stood as immobile as Eldwin's statue, ignoring the stream rushing around her and the hidden tears in the water streaming down her face.

The chilling breeze on her upper body made her teeth chatter. Then something in the water brushed her leg and Kezia bolted for the shore, scrabbling for finger holds among the moss-covered rocks as she clambered up the slippery bank, sobbing when her nails tore. Over the lip, and away from the edge, she rolled on her back and lay exhausted looking up, but there was no friendly Eye in the overcast sky, and no one came to help.

As her clothes dried, the shivering eased, and her eyes gradually closed. She drifted off into a semi-conscious nightmare: the face of her father leering, the flash of the surgical knife, his shock when she stabbed him, his leg giving way as he sprang back. Then the sickening crunch as his head hit the marble-topped washstand followed by a deathly stillness as she dressed, tidied up around him and let herself out.

• • • •

Warming sunlight dragged Kezia from her nightmare into an even weirder reality, where she had no idea where she was, or how she got here. A whip-crack over her head made her jump in fright. She dared not move. The second whip crack, dreadfully loud in the still morning air, seemed right on top of her. Between whip cracks, the creak of loaded wheels underscored the bullocky's call to his team.

Memory struck so hard she started sobbing again. She had hoped to be halfway to her unit by now, and here she was still on the outskirts of Deep Creek. Too much time wasted in the forlorn hope that Willard might come with her. Kezia wiped her eyes. *This is no time to be feeble. Mother always said I have father's brains.* Though she hated to acknowledge the relationship, it was time she put his contribution to work, and deal with whatever life Our Lady had mapped out for her. With a moan, she pushed herself into a sitting position and cast around for her pack, remembering that last night it had caught as she fell. For a terrible moment, she thought it lost in the creek, torn off during her plunge. Then she saw it dangling by its strap in the tree overhanging the water's edge, the buckle jammed in a fork.

"Thanks be, Lady," she whispered automatically, relieved it was safe. The pack seemed in better shape than she was. Besides stiffness, she had scratches, bruises, broken nails, and her hair matted with creek muck. The unwanted dip had ruined her newly issued Medicorps uniform. Only the pack, dangling from its buckle, remained unscathed.

Kezia waited for the sound of the dray to recede before moving. Using the tree for support, she forced herself upright against protesting muscles to recover the backpack. With care, she removed a jar of healing dust and unscrewed its lid. Even before she had sprinkled a pinch of dust on her knee, she felt a warm tingle run up her arm. As it spread, her tentative smile broadened. Mother's builder magic always healed fast. Before screwing the lid back on, she gently shook the jar to settle the silvery grey dust mother had said were micro-injectors, a term with no meaning for her. The dust moved as if alive.

'It's not,' she heard her mother say, the words appearing in her mind like an echo of a remembered phrase.

Dismissing the thought as wishful, she washed herself and her clothing, brushed her hair and ate the now stale sandwich. Rain started falling, another light shower like last night, a promise of cool relief from the heat of the last few days.

A short time later, as she headed downstream from Martha's bridge, she noticed that although her legs ached a little; the cuts had scabbed and her bruises had yellowed. Elation, tempered by guilt, suffused her; she was finally free of father. But with no way to find out if he was still alive, she decided her safest course was to assume his death. It was an accident, but it was still her fault.

By late afternoon, she began thinking she was going mad. A voice screamed in her head 'please Severne, not Aldus'. She spun in terror, clapping her hands over her ears, the scream loud and close. Her surroundings were empty. Impossibly, it had sounded like Willard's voice, but that was probably because it said Aldus. As the scream tapered off, she closed her eyes, tried to hold on to the lingering echo of his voice. Heart pounding against her ribs, she opened them again on the same empty paddocks. Too long without food. I'm hallucinating. Earlier she had felt a sharp pain in her ribs quickly followed by nausea. She had rested on a boulder until the feeling went away.

Where the road forked, Kezia stopped. She had passed this spot countless times and always gone straight ahead without reading the signpost. Straight ahead went to Arthurton and then Walker, to her appointment as a Medicorps Healer. The road curving away to the south went to Crossroads, and beyond, to places she had heard about but never thought to see. Both directions led her away from everything she had ever known.

The Walker recruitment office expected her, had arranged a fast coach to Everild for her, and three other late recruits from the area. There was no comfort in the thought that she could still make it. Yesterday would've been fine, but not today. Stabbing her father changed everything. If they didn't know about it yet, they soon would. A Magister was always in demand.

Feeling she had no choice, Kezia turned south and within a few steps, she was crying uncontrollably. She had no idea where she would end up or what she would do when she got there, except she would start from nothing. Only now did she realise just how much of her future she had taken for granted.

Having her dreams swept away was heartbreaking, but not as tragic as trying to construct new ones without Willard.

• • • •

A second line meant the new server had somehow convinced Magister to take Averil's capture seriously. Now caged in Magister's cells, she couldn't sleep, and was still awake near midnight, looking at the stars framed in the high window, hoping to see Severne's Eye. This set off a chain of thoughts that led to Willard, so that when she did eventually sleep, he haunted her dreams. The idea of them having offspring was insidious. Like a worm in an apple, it burrowed away below the surface. She wished she had asked the real question, the one she broke in for, and not asked 'who with', or heard the answer. She wished it as hard as she had once wished the Goddess would test her.

When Marketday dawned, Averil was already up and pacing her cell. The Watchhouse, like most of the town, was old but not ancient, not a builder structure, but locally built of stone and iron. Four cells, two on each side of a wide corridor, and she was the only inmate. Not much crime in Deep Creek. Not much here worth fighting over. The ceiling of the cellblock was a foot above ground level, allowing light and air through barred windows too narrow even for her. It sometimes flooded when it rained. She had a bucket for clean water and another for ablutions.

The only way out was the way she came in, the door at the top of the stairs into Magister's office. For all that Our Lady has her eye on me, she is not helping—unless this is where she wants me? Shit, Willard must still be here. It wasn't past Magister, despite his lack of belief, to help Our Lady if it served his purpose. Was the reverse true? Was Our Lady helping him fulfil her plan, despite me telling her Willard and I having offspring would never happen?

A scuffle at the door just after breakfast heralded a bellowing voice she now recognised as Ser Tomas. "I need to see if you have the right lad."

Averil bristled.

"You'll have to wait until Magister Leach returns," she heard Granger say.

"I am Our Lady's representative. You cannot stop me."

"Wanna bet."

Averil heard another scuffle, then a cry of pain.

"How dare you," Ser Tomas wheezed. "You will never reach her Eye. Our Lady will not revive you at the Restoration."

"Like I care, get lost priest."

A door slammed.

It amazed Averil that a bastard like Magister could inspire such loyalty in a Watcher veteran that he would send a server packing.

She should never have come back. She'd lost another whole day. Granger, the Wall veteran in charge during Magister's absence, told her he had orders to keep her here until her father returned. But nobody could tell her when that would be, and she needed to get out of here. Probably some young girl's father has caught up with him.

• • • •

Noise from upstairs jolted Averil from her doze. The orange glow of late afternoon dripped through the high windows. Feeling guilty for another dream in which she betrayed Kezia with Willard, she sat up and listened. Those above were arguing over who should replace Magister. Shit, he's still missing. The contingent and her recruits would have now left Grundston. She had until they reached the first checkpoint in the pass to join them or lose her captain's commission.

Her first thought, when the door opened, was that at last Magister had returned, which might be good or bad for her. Having her in his cells might tempt him. If he tried it, he'd wear the ablutions bucket. Mother was the last person she expected to see. Jorgena Leach stood on the landing, smiling at Granger as she thanked him. He left, and as Jorgena descended the stairs, the door closed behind her with a click, but, noted Averil, no key turned in the lock.

"What brings you here, mother?"

"You, of course," she said, looking around, "I haven't been down since we ... have you seen Kezia?"

Before Jorgena changed the subject, Averil had the impression she was going to say—since we built it—but that would make her over two hundred years old, simply impossible. Despite she had to be over forty, she looked no older than Kezia. She could be our sister.

"She's joined Medicorps," Jorgena added.

"Tits," said Averil, the expletive automatic. Kezia was off to the Wall and won't be marrying Willard, so he's free and still here. Our Lady's plan progresses. Bugger that.

"Is that a problem?" Jorgena asked. She unlocked the cell door and stepped inside to give her daughter a big hug.

"No mother, it's just that ... have a seat," Averil said. And nearly choked on the memory of Our Lady saying the same thing in equally bizarre circumstances.

They sat on the narrow cot. "Where's Magister?" Averil suddenly asked.

"He's gone and he won't be back. I've seen to it."

"About bloody time," Averil said, wondering how she'd seen to it. If it was that bloody easy, why hadn't she done it before Magister damaged Kezia?

Her mother seemed shocked at her vehemence, then sorrowful. "Truly, I am sorry I didn't stop him sooner. I have told Kezia the same, but I couldn't explain it to her, so I won't bother explaining it to you. When you see her, tell her he's alive. She may think she killed him."

Averil stared at her mother as if she was speaking feral, "What are you saying?"

"From what I could see they had a tussle. She stabbed him in the leg and he hit his head when he fell. He's had worse in the militia before he became Magister. I patched him up, brought him round, and gave him his marching orders. Oh, and ask for the ring I gave her. I made one for each of you."

Jorgena stood up walked to the door of the cell before turning to face her. "You're free to go."

"How in the ..."

"I made Granger an offer he found appealing, although he needed little persuading, he likes you. The charges stand. They're a tower matter neither of us could fix. Granger's taken the militia on a fruitless search for your ... for Magister. When he returns, you will be gone. Whoever replaces the Magister might resume the hunt, but I doubt it. I suggest you get as far away from here as you can, as quickly as you can."

Averil did as her mother suggested, opting for the most direct route to Rivers Junction, if not exactly the quickest. To avoid the militia, she walked cross-country through the isolated farms scattered along the Barrier foothills. It was slower and harder than by road, all up hill and down, and splashing through creeks. She crossed the infant Wanetta River, knowing in the back of her mind she would have to recross it later, but pressed on through the rain; it cut miles off her journey.

By pushing hard, she covered close to forty miles. Hours after dark, she collapsed in an abandoned goatherd's hut, discovering too late she had pushed too hard for too long, and with too little sleep last night. She was exhausted.

Chapter 6

Creaking timber woke Willard. The nightmare broke apart: ferals on the plateau drowning him in a foul stream, a faceless black-robed man repeating 'don't you think', and Kezia laughing as she ran away, hand in hand with a headless Aldus. He stretched and a band of light moved across his closed lids. It was all a bad dream. He was home in his own bed, warm and comfortable.

Rolling over to see if Aldus was awake, he felt a sudden sharp pain in his thigh. His eyes sprang open to find Aldus's bed empty. Memory overrode the remaining fragments of sleep, leaving bleak reality.

"You're awake."

Willard turned at the voice. His father sat on a reversed chair, brown forearms resting on the chair's back, his gaze fixed on Willard. Sunlight haloed Arthur Forrestor's head, casting his face in shadow making his expression unreadable.

"How did I get here?" asked Willard. He couldn't remember much after crawling out of the drain where he'd left Aldus. It had been dark and raining, and he had stumbled on in fear of his life, weary and bleeding, relying on memory and instinct.

"You collapsed out by the front gate late last night with this in your belt." His father's hand came up holding the gemmed blade. "It's feral, and going by the gem belongs to someone of rank." Willard swallowed hard as his father continued. "Among other mutterings, you talked of Aldus in your sleep. The fact that he hasn't returned worries me. Do you know where he is?"

Severne help me, how do I tell him? As if seeing his father for the first time, he noticed the deep lines in the tanned face, the white strands that had replaced the grey. Both parents had always been older compared to the parents of his peers. Lately, it had become more obvious. *This will kill him.* Tears started in Willard's eyes and he saw the life go out of his father. *He knows what's coming.*

Willard turned away from his father's piercing gaze, said what he had to say to the wall. "I took that off the feral that tried to kill me. Aldus wasn't so lucky." He didn't mention that someone from the servatory had helped the ferals kill his brother. Nobody but Aldus would believe it.

Arthur tapped his son on the shoulder, waited until Willard faced him. "Where is he?"

Willard shrank before the tone in his father's voice. *It would have been better for everyone if they had killed me.* "One of the overflow pipes, we got separated. They must have caught him at the dam ..." Willard stopped. He couldn't tell his father they had beheaded Aldus. He heard the chair scrape across the floorboards as his father got up and left the room. Even in their mutual grief, they could not get close. He had always envied Aldus his easy rapport with father, but then Aldus was like that ... had been like that, with everybody except servers.

With mounting dread, Willard realised nothing would ever be the same. The two most important people in his life were now gone, Aldus forever. He stared at the ceiling, imagining Severne's Eye somewhere above and cursed the Goddess. *Your plan for me sucks.*

Rising voices penetrated his introspection, disjointed segments of conversation between his parents overlaid with his father's pacing.

"He's only a boy and ..."

His father cut off her plea. "For fuck's sake, he's twenty-three. He's been back a year, and still refuses to take the bloody test, as promised."

The outburst shocked Willard. Father never swore. The pacing stopped and his father's next words were quite clear. "Aldus is dead. It's over Eliza."

He heard his mother sob, his father's striding footsteps, and a sharp screech of hinges followed by the bang of the back door as it slammed shut.

Willard could not believe his father had broken such news so harshly. He dressed quickly and escaped out the back door for urgent bladder relief.

As he dried his hands, he stared at his reflection in the mirror above the basin, at the differently coloured eyes that dominated his face. He closed one eye as he straightened his hair with his fingers, wondering what life might have been like if his eyes had stayed the same colour.

Not that it mattered anymore. With Aldus dead, the Forrestor farm would be his whether he wanted it or not. Any thought of taking the test, or chasing after Kezia had died with Aldus. Full of bitter resolve, knowing his first task was to report the ferals to the militia, Willard strode back into the kitchen wondering what his father had meant by, 'it's over'. What was over?

His mother sat, head in hands, at the long table.

"What did dad mean, what's over?" he asked, as gently as he could.

Eliza Forrestor stood to greet her son with a strange air of resignation. "He wants you gone."

Willard stared at her in incomprehension. Surely, that wasn't what he meant. Aldus was always his favourite, but that didn't mean ...

"Sit down Willard. What I have to tell you may be painful."

• • • •

Willard watched as his mother sat opposite, carefully placing her forearms on top of the table, fingers alternately spread then clasped. He waited while she tried, several times, to start. An accumulation of nuances sparked a horrible thought that gnawed its way into his consciousness. *If candidates run in families who gave me my eyes?* Neither parent, nor Aldus were candidates. He had always pushed that thought away. *A family trait had to start somewhere,* but with his life crumbling, the anomaly took on a disproportionate significance.

"Could you get me a cup of water, please?"

Willard rose, saying nothing, and took a jug to the sink. *So what if father prefers Aldus, and mother likes me? Why would he want me gone, especially now?* Yet he had never seen his mother more serious or more at a loss for words. *Still, what more could she possibly say that could be more painful than losing Kezia and Aldus in quick succession? She'd better be quick. The ferals won't wait.* He returned to the table with the filled jug and poured her a cupful.

Eliza took a few grateful sips. "I did not mean it in the way you might think, although he really does want you out of here."

Willard stared at her none the wiser. Like his father, she seemed to have aged overnight. Her hair was white, not grey, something he hadn't noticed until now. *Maybe she was senile. Where was I when all this happened?*

"I'm sorry Willy, there's just no easy way to put this."

Willard blinked. *She hadn't called him Willy in years. Was that a sign of senility? She seemed all right, but she was over sixty.*

"Your father ... my husband ..." Eliza doggedly pushed on. "Arthur is not your father."

Willard treated her with a look of forbearance, and the resultant outburst floored him.

"I may be old, but I'm not crazy. I asked Our Lady for a child and she agreed but I wasn't married. Your father ... Arthur needed a mother for Aldus after Jocelyn died. We made a pact."

The words bounced back and forth in his mind, 'a mother for Aldus after Jocelyn died'. "Who is Jocelyn?" he asked.

"Aldus's mother, Arthur's daughter, she died giving birth to Aldus. Aldus is his grandson."

Willard clutched his head as he tried to grasp what his mother was saying. I'm his uncle. That didn't make any kind of sense.

"We adopted Aldus, so he could inherit. It was part of our pact, but with Aldus dead our pact is over."

"Why adopt if he was already blood?"

"Only through his mother, he was not a Forrestor until we adopted him. You are by marriage."

"Oh," Willard said, trying to understand. "I was born after you married." In dizzying confusion, Willard latched on to the singular fact that although he had been born a Forrestor, he was, in one sense, less of one than Aldus. Eldwin, despite the uncanny resemblance was not his ancestor. Aldus was the blood heir.

"Yes. We always thought your destiny was with Our Lady. I promised Arthur you would leave when your eyes changed."

"And he believed you?" It astounded Willard that she could promise his eyes would change before he was even born.

"Ser Hedley arranged a private audience with Ob Walker for Arthur. Our Lady confirmed it."

"Is Hedley my father?" he asked.

"Good Goddess, No."

"Then who is?"

"I don't know."

"Beefshit. How can you not know, mother? Were there so many you ..." He saw her shocked hurt and rushed to apologise.

"I'm sorry, mum. I didn't mean it like that. I have no reason to think ... I mean ..."

Eliza's shock dropped away. "You're ..."

"Special?" Willard said, cutting her off. "I know. You've told me often enough. I just had no idea what it meant." He paced the short side of the room kicking at the chairs, the table the stove anything in range, pounding the wall with his fists, letting out days, weeks, years of pent-up anger and frustration. "All this time," he muttered, shaking his head.

Eliza's eyes followed him as she pleaded for him to understand. "You're a gift from the Goddess. I was nearly forty when I asked the oracle for a child. Our Lady took me to the Eye and I came back with you."

Willard glanced upward, a reflex action. "That's lame, mother," he said, trying to make sense of nonsense.

"I've wanted to tell you for years. It might have made things easier, but Our Lady swore us to secrecy."

Of course, Willard thought, bitterly. "Then why tell me now?"

"You need to protect yourself from the ferals."

"I know. They tried to kill me. They got Aldus instead."

"They don't want to kill you. They want to capture you. They know how special you are to Our Lady."

Willard's groan was automatic. Yet he vividly recalled the death of the first feral, skewered on his own spear when he twisted his sword away. *Was he trying to avoid killing me?*

His mother retreated into a look he knew well. "Your eyes have become so very different," she smiled. "You could be much more than a Restoration Warrior. You could become the Face of Our Lady."

Willard sat, too stunned to reply.

Eliza became serious again. "Go to the servatory Willard. Ask for Sanctuary. Ob Walker will know what to do."

"You're not joking. You truly believe it all."

Eliza rose and moved to embrace her son. He held her at arm's length. "Please trust me, Willard. I don't want you to go, but you must start for Grundston tonight before the ferals come back."

"I doubt they will. Two are dead already. Once I tell the militia, the rest won't be going anywhere but the gallows. That's what father ... should have done instead of going after ..." Willard said, glancing out the window. The day was ageing fast, and he had yet to sound the alarm.

"If these fail, more will come. You will not be safe until you take the test."

A knock on the door disrupted his mother's argument.

"Militia. Open up."

Willard stood, and Eliza frantically pushed him towards the back door.

"Go," she said, "Please."

Willard easily resisted. "What are you doing, mother? I have nothing to fear from the militia." Gently, he disentangled her grasp and headed back towards the front door. "I'm coming," he shouted. Out through the window, he could rain falling from an overcast sky. The unseasonal weather was getting worse.

"Please Willard, you don't understand. Kezia is missing."

Willard stared back at her as he pulled the door open. "She's not missing. She's joined Medicorps."

"Willard Forrestor," the man at the door asked, and Willard turned to him.

"You know it is, Samals. Come in. I have lots to tell you."

Two more militia were stamping on the veranda, brushing drops from their uniforms.

"I'm sure you do lad, and you'll have plenty of time to tell it. Willard Robert Forrestor, I am arresting you in connection with the disappearance of Kezia Anne Leach." He stepped aside with an apology. "Sorry Will. Bring him."

The militia on either side of Samals stepped forward. Willard bellowed with sudden pain when they grabbed his arm, pulled him onto the verandah, and force-marched him down the steps. Two more militia waited at the bottom of the verandah steps. The five of them propelled him down to the homestead gate where a captain and sergeant waited. A full squad just for him made Willard nervous. The sergeant sat him in the cart and tied his hands.

In flashes of bewilderment, Willard saw his mother fall to her knees in the doorway and clasped her hands together in the attitude of a pilgrim, the light behind picking up motes of dust swirling around her head. As the cart clattered down their drive towards Deep Creek, a figure in crimson robes stepped out of the shadows on the verandah and reached down to comfort his kneeling mother. The face was familiar from his days at the servatory, but he barely had time to wonder what brought an Arch Server to the farm before he lost sight of the house.

• • • •

After yesterday's exhausting push, Averil had overslept and by the time she exited the hut, the Middleton Signal Tower was already flashing out the morning's signals towards Signal Tower Three, high in the Barriers. It did not surprise her to read that Magister was still missing; she already knew he would stay that way. The next flashed messages she decoded stopped her. The militia had caught two ferals and arrested Willard in connection with a missing Kezia.

Ferals this side of the Barriers she could understand. It suggested, as the academy predicted the invasion was imminent. She also knew why Kezia had disappeared. According to mother, she thinks she killed Magister, but I can guarantee Willard had nothing to do with it.

Having started walking, Averil almost missed her own name and description at the end. I'm now famous, no longer just an anonymous youth. The mention gave her a tingle of pleasure until she thought about it. The only people who knew the fateful audience had been hers were Mother, Willard, and Kezia. None of them would have given her name to the militia, would they? Willard might if tortured, but the militia under Magister didn't use torture?

"It's a bloody mess," she said aloud, her voice drowned out by the Wanetta River running alongside.

At dusk, as Averil crossed the road up to Signal Tower Four, she briefly contemplated leaving the hills. There was a bridge on this road that serviced signal towers three and four. It would get her across the Wanetta but take her twenty miles back, and she had barely managed thirty miles today. Even at its slowest, the contingent could now be five days out of Rivers Junction. More likely it was four, but she was a week away. She couldn't afford to backtrack. Thinking to cross at Wisemans Ferry she set off again into the dusk.

As night descended on her, a chill breeze caused her to glance back. A huge storm was lashing the mountains around Deep Creek. Significant rain might stop the ferry. She would be stuck on this side while the contingent rolled on past the other side. She hurried on through the night in light drizzle, the outer edges of the storm. Eventually, giving up around midnight, she bedded down under a small rock overhang.

In the morning, after wading across a knee-deep tributary, Averil paused and read the day's dispatches flashing along the signal line to Port Calder. The militia had replaced their missing Magister and were again hunting her.

By midday, the rain had cleared and as the sun touched the snow-capped peaks, a change in the wind brought her the sound of racing water. She walked toward it with a sense of foreboding that manifested itself the moment she saw the river. The Wanetta's flow had grown too strong for her liking any thought of crossing that, even on the ferry, scared her witless. During training, a much smaller stream had swept her off her feet and nearly drowned her. Her fellow trainees, after pulling her out, had found the incident enormously funny. The only cadet who couldn't swim became the source of many jokes.

With a sense of hopelessness, she saw the river, now too broad and too fast, would be impossible to wade across. Tits, she cursed, knowing now she should have backtracked to the signal towers' bridge when it was only a half-day back. Now it was two days back. She had no option but to go on. Crossing at Wisemans Ferry would make it possible to reach Rivers Junction before the contingent left, but it would be close. Despite painful fatigue, she redoubled her effort and jogged on, hoping any further runoffs were not too bloated.

Averil stumbled into the terminal area at dusk and cursed her luck. The ferry had moored over the other side, and the pilot had locked the hut on this side. Not wanting him offside, she decided not to break in. As she bedded down on the verandah, she wondered about how her narrowing choices helped the plan the Goddess had outlined. *Is she trying to stop me from going to the Wall as a way of keeping me here for Willard?*

Chapter 7

As Kezia walked on through the soft heat of bud, she re-evaluated each event in the sequence that had led her here, trying to see if she had somehow inadvertently offended Our Lady of the Towers. But there were blanks in the disconnected nightmare that was yesterday, or was it the day before that? Whichever day that was, had also given her swollen feet, hunger, and a raging thirst, which at one point forced her to drink from an animal trough. She had gagged and gone into paroxysms of dry retching before she saw the floating ball device that kept it filled. She pushed on the ball and drank greedily from hands cupped around the spigot.

The days had blurred into sameness. Worse were the sleepless nights out in the open. She tossed and turned, walled in by unknown animal sounds and constantly harassed by insects. Fortunately, it had stayed warm enough to ignore the light rain. She regretted discarding the torn greatcoat as too hot to wear and too heavy to carry. It would have made a great blanket.

And today was not much better. She stank. She hadn't washed herself or her clothes in days; her hair was a tangled mess and the bitter berries, plucked from a roadside bush and swallowed, had given her a bellyache. As she trudged on, she wondered where all the people were. Since her decision at the fork, she hadn't seen another living person, yet there was evidence of activity all around her, fields of wheat and barley, all too young and green to be edible. She had not reckoned on this being a back road. It had looked normal at the junction, but had now narrowed to twin wheel ruts through spiky grass.

Mobs of sheep and occasionally a small dairy herd, scattered as she passed. Empty sheds were plentiful, one of which drained into a small tank with a cup chained to its outlet. Climbing over the fence, she quickly slaked her thirst, rinsed her hair, armpits, and groin with nothing better than a wet hand. What she really needed however was food. She hadn't eaten since Martha's Bridge. Although there was nothing edible here, water was plentiful. She poured several cups over her head to rinse her hair and in doing so, noticed with shock, her arms were bright red. She determined to treat it with mother's dust when she found a place to stop.

Hoping the track she blindly followed was going somewhere, Kezia plodded on. The last junction was miles back and the signpost had showed Walker was seventy-five miles behind her, which meant she had only come about thirty up this track; disappointingly slow progress. Clouds gathered and the wind picked up. The rain was cooling on her sunburnt arms. It also gently combed out the tangles in her hair and soaked through her ragged clothes. Not wanting to spend a wet night in the open she increased her pace. She needed shelter.

On both sides of the road, dark fields stretched as far as she could see. The glow outlining the black horizon to the east could be a town, but she couldn't trust they hadn't heard about her crime. Tired, gritty eyes, tried resolving any dark shapes in the dark fields, but nothing looked promising until she saw a flicker of light appear from behind a tree. Further along, a gap in the fence showed where her track turned in towards the building. A farmhouse?

Cautiously, Kezia made her way between the sagging posts that had once held a gate. It soon became obvious the building, though not deserted, was derelict. The flickering light from a fire glinted off the jagged edge of a broken pane. Someone had beaten her to it. She continued up the now slippery track; shelter was imperative, company would be nice.

The closer she came, the more dilapidated the building appeared. Every window had jagged fragments reflecting the flicker, the door hung askew and the roof sagged like an old nag's back. She glanced up at the chimney, also broken, but it was now too dark to see if the smoke she could smell issued from it. She peered in through the broken window. As she had thought, the flicker came from a fire in the hearth, but other than that the room appeared to contain nothing but flickering shadows and night sounds.

Kezia's skin prickled. Someone must have set it. She reached for the long knife, hesitated, and drew back a trembling hand. She was a healer. With quiet deliberation, she put the pack down on the verandah and knocked. The cricket song went quiet and her knock echoed preternaturally loud. She waited in breathless silence, ears straining for the slightest sound. The gradual return of circadian clicking subsumed the light crackle and hiss of the fire. She called out, then gently pushed open the front door and stepped inside.

She looked again at the fireplace and saw a neat stack of kindling on one side and two larger logs on the other. A big log in the grate was only now catching. Whoever set it must still be around, but where? On the one internal wall, a doorway into a second room stood open. Perhaps in there, maybe hurt. I should go in and see. Despite the warmth, goose bumps rose on Kezia's arms as she crossed the main room and peered into the second.

All she could see from the doorway was a ragged black patch in the ceiling, flecked with stars. The rest of the room was in shadow. Severne's Eye, this has gone far enough. With purpose, she walked to the fire and picked up a piece of the kindling. Her eyes constantly scanned both doors while she held it in the fire until it was well alight. Then, torch first, she stepped into the second room. It was also empty. Where in the Eye are they? Not knowing made her scalp crawl.

Holding up the tiny torch to dispel the shadows and her fear, Kezia scanned the bare second room. The dust covering the floor was undisturbed. Whoever had started the fire hadn't been in here. They must be outside or gone. She didn't believe they had gone. The tension in her shoulders ached and her sunburn itched. As she turned back to the main room, a large shadow blocked the flickering light from the fireplace.

Frightened beyond reason, Kezia brandished the torch like a club as she ran for the main door. A hand flicked out and grabbed her torch wielding wrist. Another hand smelling of eucalyptus clamped over her mouth.

"Don't scream," said a young male voice.

Kezia turned, instantly attracted to his eyes, one dark brown and one light green. A quick glance at his brow ridges confirmed she was in the grip of a Restoration Warrior. She shook uncontrollably as childhood stories flooded her mind, stories of green-robed warriors with dazzling swords spoken of in whispers; Severne's executioners. Escaping them was not possible. Wherever and whenever they showed up, someone died, publicly beheaded without warning or trial. Kezia quailed, Dear Lady, why me? She felt warmth flow down the inside of her legs, but she refused to faint.

"If you promise not to scream, I'll release you. My ears are sensitive." The skin over one hairless eyebrow ridge rose as if asking for acknowledgement.

Kezia nodded, unable to take her eyes off his face. So young. The hand on her mouth came away grabbed the torch, taking it from her before releasing her wrist. With a flick, he sent the torch spinning across the room into the fire. He didn't even look. Then he stepped back, glanced down fleetingly at her embarrassing puddle.

"Our Lady does not want your death," he said evenly. "What makes you think she should?"

"Why," Kezia swallowed, "why else are you here?"

"It's been a long day. I needed a place to rest for the night." His odd eyed gaze scanned her from head to toe. "As do you, apparently?" He shook his green cloak and it was suddenly dry, the floor wetter.

Aware of her drowned, dishevelled appearance, Kezia subjected him to an awed, but searching look. Wispy hair sparsely covered his head. It had to be only days since his test or he would be completely bald. Total depilation *Legends* called it. The test removed hair, roots and all. Willard's fate, if he ever took it. This was probably why the warrior's ears were sensitive, unless he's an impostor with plucked eyebrows, and natural balding. If it was an impersonation, it was a damn good one, right down to the gemmed hilt showing above his left shoulder.

His left eye reminded her of her own, the brown so dark that in this dim light it looked to be all pupil. It was possible to fake the eyes as mother had done for Willard, but in the end, his eyes convinced Kezia he was genuine. The depth of knowledge and understanding she saw in those eyes went far beyond what his youthful, unlined face indicated. She was past fear now. If he had come for her, then so be it. She no longer cared. She knew Our Lady wanted Willard for Averil, and she suspected the Goddess was making sure he never heard from Kezia again.

The warrior frowned in an expression of dismay. "How does one so young become so ready for death? Where is your faith?"

Kezia stared up into the ancient-looking eyes. Did he just read my mind? "An Arch Server has betrayed my faith," she said though she left unvoiced her reasons.

"I'm sorry I frightened you. I was out getting more wood."

Kezia looked at the fireplace saw he had indeed added more split logs to the pile. How long was he in the room without me knowing? Her senses had been at full stretch and she had heard nothing? Her gaze returned to his face.

Dear Lady, he's the genuine article. Her legs gave way as the events of the last few days caught up with her in a rush. The warrior reached out to steady her as she crumpled, gently helping her over to the wall.

"I suggest you rest. I need to prepare. Our Lady says there's a storm coming, a big one."

Kezia, grateful for the extra time to recuperate, drifted in and out of sleep while the ever-resourceful warrior fetched and carried and battened down the hatches. Strangely, even when he was absent, she felt secure. Perhaps Our Lady had sent him to help, perhaps she cares for me after all ... sort of.

• • • •

Willard lay on his side in the cart, the pains in his arm, chest and thigh feeling every jolt.

"Why don't you sit up, let your backside take the pounding," said Samals, the only one on his escort Willard knew.

"I did that. It went numb."

He had sat up but with hands still tied, fallen into the same position when his backside lost all feeling. The layer of wet straw under him smelt of manure. This was his second arrest, first for helping Averil, which he hadn't, and now because Kezia was missing, except she wasn't. If it wasn't so serious, he might laugh. Ser Tomas' accusation of accomplice he understood, but not Kezia's father blaming him for her disappearance; he knew they had oathed. Perhaps he didn't know she had joined Medicorps.

"This is a mistake," Willard told him. "Everyone knows I'm a ..." special candidate, he thought, and the thought put a sour taste in his mouth. Can't you see how special I am? Futile, only Hedley and mother believe it.

Samals gave a throaty laugh. "Your name is the problem. Our Lady's servers don't like their Arch being on Forrestor land and access to it subject to Forrestor whim."

"So what?"

"So it was our acting Magister, not Leachy, who signed your warrant." Light from the next flash overhead caught Samals' grim expression as he spat a brown wad into the bush. "Sev bloody Miller. It ain't right. An Arch Server running the militia is like a feral running the Watchers."

Willard stared at Samals in surprise, remembering a Sev Miller from his time at the servatory, and suddenly he could match the remembered voice and expression with the man on the dam wall who betrayed them. Sev Miller was probably also the man on his mother's porch, a man who knew the farm. The only thing Willard didn't understand was why.

The cart bounced around like his thoughts. So many things he had accepted on faith now made little sense. His mother's claim that her birth resulted from her journey to Severne's Eye disturbed him. Why it did so, he couldn't quite say. The notion was as preposterous as his arrest for Kezia's disappearance. Certainly, the supposed abode of the Goddess moving across the sky was an oddity among the fixed stars, but the notion of anyone other than the Goddess or the spirits of the dead could go there was plain silly. More likely, mother never left the servatory and if she came home pregnant, then Ser Hedley and/or Ob Walker had a lot to answer for.

When his escort turned aside after Eldwin's Ford and took the old road through Severne's Wood, anxiety replaced nervousness. Where in Severne's name are they taking me? The tower? When they passed the tower, his anxiety rose to alarm. The manure he was in was obviously deeper than he thought, but as the day wore on and they showed no sign of stopping, his alarm eased. If they intended to kill him, they had missed plenty of deep gullies on this back road where a body could disappear forever. He relaxed.

• • • •

The storm that had begun around the time she turned in here steadily strengthened to a squall that rocked the old building. Wind-driven rain battered against the warrior's repair work. Only once did an errant gust cause the fire to splutter and a ball of smoke to puff into the room. Kezia, snuggled into the bedding, watched the warrior brush his head, stare for a few seconds at the handful of light hair and throw it on the fire where it crackled and burst into flame.

She woke in the middle of the night, shivering in nameless dread, feeling that Willard was in trouble. "I'm going to die." she thought she heard Willard say, the sudden thought so apt she was sure it was hers. She was equally sure she hadn't really heard him; the thought was just there in her mind; her thought in his voice.

Fully awake now she strained to hear it again, but only the storm raged in her ears. I'm imagining things. I must stop thinking about him. She felt for the comfort of the ring mother gave her. She had given Averil's to Willard in their intense final moments together, after she realised, he wasn't coming with her. If Our Lady has anything to do with it, he'll see Averil before I do, except he won't know to give it to her, I didn't tell him.

Despite the constant howl, the drumbeat rain and the creak and squeal of moving timbers the warrior slept. She could see the ember lit outline of his back rising and falling in a steady rhythm. Scratch one more myth: warriors sleep. As Kezia's mind drifted, she fell to wondering where Willard truly was, what he was really doing.

• • • •

The sudden lurch of the cart, caught Willard unawares and his ribs banged on the plank floor with a crack. He felt the spear wound open. "Keep her safe," he whispered, holding his shirt against his side to soak up the blood. A chill wind had risen and the sky had grown dark. The unseasonal bud weather had become even more unseasonal.

"Kezia isn't even missing," he said to Samals, walking in the rain behind the cart. "She joined Medicorps. Ask them."

"I'd be careful what you say, lad. Her signing on, voids your oathing. Some might see you as wanting her to go missing, if you get my drift."

Samals had tilted his hat forward to shed water from the dent in the crown. Willard couldn't make out his features, couldn't tell if he was serious.

The escort moved on through the late afternoon downpour, the cart now slip-sliding on the increasingly muddy road. Cut from the side of the hill, the road had a steep drop on one side and a steep rise on the other; at least it was flat.

"Shouldn't we be stopping Sarge," Samals called out, "can't see the bloody edge back here, sir?"

The voice of the sergeant called from the darkness up front. "Shut your trap Samals and get a move on."

"But Sarge ..."

"Captain says no. Break out the lanterns."

"Yes, sir," Samals said, his tone as derisive as his quiet laugh. "Stupid flatlander will get us all killed."

Flickering wicks disrupted the darkness as drumrolls of thunder, closer with each flash, lumbered overhead.

Eerie disembodied faces emerged from the gloom. Willard heard Samals mutter to himself, "first the heat now this. It ain't bloody right for bud."

Someone called softly from across the other side of the cart, "Captain's in a hurry to see a couple of heads roll."

Willard swallowed hard. "Whose?"

"Don't fret lad," Samals said. "We caught a couple of ferals yesterday, public execution in Walker tomorrow. And we don't roll heads, they'll hang."

Willard's relief choked on the sudden vision of Aldus in the pipe. Simple arithmetic held his attention. Two dead up by the arch, two caught made only four. "What happened to the other three?"

"What other three?" Samals said.

Willard swallowed. "When you arrested me, I was coming to you to tell you we, my ... brother. A full warband attacked me and Aldus. They killed him."

Though he could not see Samals' face in the darkness, Willard heard the intrigue in his question. "Two from seven is five. You asked about three."

"I ... saw two dead up by the Arch."

"Have you reported this?"

"You arrested me before I could."

Shod hooves clamouring on the planks of Carters Bridge drowned further conversation. The escort had descended to the floor of the valley. Before them, a series of short, steep switchbacks climbed up out of the valley to Upper Walker Road on the next ridge. As they climbed, Willard wondered why they chose this route rather than back through town. The road was a nightmare in good conditions and seldom used except for emergencies when Martha's bridge was out.

The escort halted. They had reached the first and worst bend, which turned around on itself like a hairpin before it clawed its way up the other side. Willard heard voices up ahead arguing.

"The cart is too long to get around the elbow."

"I don't need excuses, Sergeant Ashley. Get Dalton to lead the horses, and put the rest of them to lifting the back away from the edge. The prisoner can walk."

"But, sir."

"You have your orders sergeant, see to it."

"Yes, sir."

"Stupid bloody orders," Samals said as he stepped back from the cart into the gloom.

In the steadily increasing rain, Sergeant Ashley dumped his lantern on the wet straw at the back of the cart, then leant over the side to drop a noose around Willard's neck.

"Just so you don't nick off while I sort this," he said, tying the other end to a tailboard clamp. "Out," he barked, his breath sour smelling as he jerked Willard into a sitting position.

Instinctively, Willard slipped the fingers of his bound hands under the noose as Ashley grabbed his arm and dragged him off the back of the cart into the mud. As soon as he got to his feet, the tension on his neck eased. Willard hoped Samals might intervene, but the sergeant had disappeared.

The rain strengthened, more felt than seen, and a lightless miasma enfolded the escort detail, the lanterns highlighting only their immediate area.

"Smith, you take the inside wheel," Ashley ordered. An 'Aye' came from behind a lantern glow and Willard recognised the voice as the man who told him about the captured ferals. "Keep testing the edge. Leave yourself enough to stand on so we can lift the cart around. Samals you're on the middle."

Samals did not answer; the only sound was the drumming rain. "Where the fuck is Samals?" Ashley whispered. The circle of lamp-lit ghosts shrugged.

"What's the holdup Sergeant Ashley?" The irate voice of the captain called from up front.

"No hold up, I'm on it," Ashley shouted back at the bobbing lantern, swearing as he stepped up to the middle of the cart. He called to the driver, "lead 'em off Dalton. Slowly dammit."

The cart moved, jerking Willard forward. In the dark, no one noticed him widen the noose and lift it off his head.

The rising wind drove the rain harder, plastering strands of Willard's hair over his eyes. He held onto the rope and strained to see where they were going. The lantern in the cart blew over, spluttered, and went out. Ashley swore and somebody replaced it, this time hooking the handle over a peg in the side.

"Hold it!" Smith shouted. "We're too close to the edge."

Ashley jerked Willard. "Feel your way to Smith's corner and give him a hand."

Willard moved to comply. Smith was barely visible in the downpour. Something about the storm unsettled him. As Samals had said, this was not right for bud. What might normally be a trickle in the elbow's crook was a flood that poured over the road, turning the already sodden ground to slush.

"Useless trying to do this in the dark," Smith said

"Right," yelled Ashley. "Everyone set, on the count of three, one, two, heave."

The cart moved easily at first, lifting on its springs, but stopped when Smith and Willard had to shoulder the full weight. Unable to lift it from the sucking mud they gave way and the cart settled again, slipping closer to the edge. With the sludge

---

moving under their feet, it took all their effort just to hold the cart in position.

A sudden howl, punctuated by sharp cracks of splitting timber, seemed out of place in the steady downpour. The canopy of a huge tree, fully as wide as two carts, whipped past Willard's face. He dropped the rope and jumped back. The cart tilted on its side crushing Smith as it slid over the edge, inexorably dragging the kicking, squealing horses backwards over the precipice. A loose strap snagged Willard's leg and he went over with them, cursing the Goddess.

The cart paused on the slope, briefly held by straining saplings. Willard freed his leg and scrabbled sideways across the steep slope, blindly grasping at small bushes, one after the other, as each lost its hold on the soaking ground. In a flash of lightning, he saw four militia, two on horseback, standing at the edge looking down at the cart. Abruptly, they disappeared, blotted out by a large bulk looming unseen behind them.

Willard yelled up at them as he struggled to his feet. Then he was labouring across the impossibly steep slope, slick with runoff. "I'm going to die," he screamed, but the roaring in his ears eclipsed his scream and those of the men and horses as the mass of mud rushed past him, whipping his feet out from under him. He pitched forward, curling up into a ball as he smacked through shrubs and over rocks in a mad tumble down the ravine. The last thing he recalled was slithering into something a lot more solid than a sapling.

Chapter 8

C old and stiff from her night on the wooden planks Averil woke to rain beating on the verandah roof.

Dawn broke with a roar. The Wanetta had risen dramatically to become a raging torrent. It tore relentlessly at the already soaking banks. The storm Averil had seen around Deep Creek must have been widespread. She did a quick exercise routine to restore her circulation and warm up. Hunger gnawed at her, but she had already eaten all her provisions. She returned her attention to the dimly visible far shore and the still docked ferry, wondering if it could even operate in this torrent. She would have to wait and see. How long was another question?

Originally, the Watchers set up ferries to service their signal towers, scattered along the Barrier Range foothills. Farmers saw they could farm that side if, for a fee, the Watchers made the service available for transporting their produce. The Watchers agreed provided signallers got priority; the fee would help fund the service. The fertile western foothills blossomed with crops.

The glint from a wet cable lifting out of the water as it came taut brought Averil alert. At last, the ferry was pulling away from the opposite bank. She had to suppose the operater knew what he was doing and thanked the Goddess for this small mercy. The pilot came into view about once a minute as he led the mule around the windlass on the lower deck. She couldn't see any passengers on the upper deck. Guessing that reading signals was likely a job requirement, she hoped the pilot had taken no notice of the signal describing her. She would be gone before any image of her arrived on a wanted poster.

Relieved that the signal towers were quiet, Averil studied the far bank, planning for a hasty exit just in case. The distant terminal building, shadowed by the sun rising behind it looked tiny against the high cliffs. The roadway to the top was a long dark slash, cut into the escarpment at a low angle to allow passage for carriages and drays: another bottleneck like Eldwin's Ford, another potential trap. Averil weighed up alternatives: slip aboard unnoticed, bribe the pilot, or bluff her way past him if he showed any sign of recognition?

If only I had learnt to swim. Not that anyone could in this torrent. She stood at the landing ramp, watching the ferry, now halfway across and well downstream, pushed off its path by the savage flow. The creaking, which had previously blended into the background, became an ominous groan. The ferry's slow creep towards her halted, but the groan of protesting timbers continued, interspersed now with the snap and shriek of splintering wood. Averil looked back in alarm as the huge stanchion, anchoring the main cable, tilted towards the river. At its base, through the soft blackness of rot, she could see the sharp edges of raw wood.

She watched in fascinated horror.

The pilot led the protesting mule around the capstan oblivious to his danger. It's not my problem, she thought, except that I need the ferry. The cable snapped taut as soon as the capstan took up the slack from the tilt. The ferry jerked. The stanchion splintered further. Soon, if nothing else, it would tilt so far over, the cable would slip out of its groove and over the head of the post.

Damn it all the way to Severne's Eye, thought Averil, as she sprinted twenty yards up the bank, towards the terminal hut, estimating distances, working out a solution as she ran. The nearest tree in any reasonable line behind the stanchion was thirty feet away. She needed long, strong ropes. On the assumption there would be spare cables in the hut, Averil bounded up onto the verandah, glancing through the window as she went for the door. She was right. There were plenty of them neatly coiled in one corner. Glass tinkled in a shower about her feet as she smashed the legs of the chair through the window, running it around the edges to remove the jagged remains.

The pilot must have seen her. She could see him shouting, but could not hear his words. Stepping to the end of the verandah, she tried to indicate with gestures that the stanchion was breaking, that he should stop hauling, but he couldn't hear her either. From his angle, looking straight down the cable, the stanchion might look fine. In fact, the pilot seemed enraged by her attempts to communicate and urged the mule to greater effort. Averil gave up, regretting the time wasted.

She climbed through the window and fetched the longest rope she could find. After throwing a loop over the stanchion, she played out the coils as she ran for the tree. Before she reached it, the stanchion gave a nerve-crawling squeal and snapped at the base. The current immediately tugged the unsecured ferry downstream. Averil grabbed the rope burning through her hands and it instantly pulled her off her feet. The jagged remains of the stanchion loomed in her path as the rope dragged her over the uneven ground. She rolled aside at the last moment and let go. The freed tail, still partly coiled, bounced and by the greatest good fortune snagged in the splintered stump.

Everything stopped. In the hiatus, despite her arms feeling as if dislocated from her shoulders, Averil quickly threw two coils of rope around the stump and gingerly tied off the end with a couple of hitches. Breathing hard, she surveyed the damage. Her torn clothes, aching shoulders, bruised and scraped arms were minor. Her hands on fire and weeping were not. At least it isn't my feet. I can still walk. I might still make it.

The ferry listed. Its lower deck, on the downstream side, was under water. The mule was gone and the pilot was in the river, clinging to a broken railing that played him in the water like a fish on a line.

Averil groaned as she climbed wearily to her feet and placed her bleeding palms in her armpits. Why is this happening to me, dear Lady? You're supposed to be looking out for me. She hobbled down to the river, passed the broken top of the stanchion, acting like a turnbuckle between the rope and the cable. It might hold for a while, but the ferry would not survive. The Signal Service would have to replace everything. Hang on, pilot, I'm coming. She reckoned if she could make it to the ferry on the cable, she could make it all the way across after she rescued the pilot.

With trepidation, she waded into the water. It eased the fire in her palms as she pulled herself along the cable by her fingertips. Terror struck when her feet lost contact with the bottom and she went under. She surfaced long seconds later, spluttering and fighting down panic, crabbing backwards until she could feel the slimy mud with her toes. Elbows hooked over the cable; she hung there coughing for several minutes. At least it was better than the sinking feeling of nothing underfoot.

'Fear can kill you quicker than a feral arrow,' her drill master had said. 'Not that we expect you to be fearless. That will kill you just as quick. Be afraid, face it, conquer it.' She began chanting the ancient Aithist maxim, 'Nothing to fear but fear.' The chant calmed her, allowed her to edge her way out to the ferry. Although the cable sank when she lost the bank underfoot, her arms hooked over it kept her head above water.

By the time Averil climbed aboard and made her way down the sloping lower deck, the flow of the river had increased. Close to exhaustion, she stopped at the break in the railing, looked directly into the lined face of the pilot, and wondered how to reach him. The current kept him at full stretch on the end of a swinging gate, his arm hooked around a slat. He, too, was close to exhaustion.

"Hang on pilot."

Puffy eyes opened and fixed on Averil and he mouthed what looked like the word 'tired'. The gate swung from a single hinge. He probably grabbed it for support and it broke when the stanchion gave way. Sheer, stubborn tenacity was all that kept him hanging on. Averil clung painfully to the railing and leaned out as far as she could, but was still an arm's length short. The one remaining hinge looked old and worn and with the combined weight of the gate and the pilot, was already tearing. There was no way it would support her as well. She cast a glance around the deck, but there were no ropes in easy reach. Then a log slammed into the cable. The gate bucked and the hinge tore a little more. There was no time.

Averil eased herself into the river, feeling the increased weight of its pull, even in the short time since she had clambered aboard. She clung desperately to the railing as she let her feet trail in the current towards the pilot. "Grab my legs," she shouted over the torrent. She felt first one hand, then the other grab her right leg. With every muscle in her arms screaming, and her palms on fire, she pulled herself back towards the deck. Temporarily letting go with her one hand she hooked an elbow over the railing and lay there a while, panting from the effort, stretched as taut as a bowstring. Then, in a last gasping effort, leg muscles straining she drew the pilot towards her outstretched hand. As she gripped his wrist, the railing broke.

In absolute panic, she held fast to the pilot as the torrent tumbled them. She shrieked at the Goddess for abandoning her, sure that she was going to drown in this whirling world of water. A piece of flotsam hit her in the head and as consciousness slipped away, her final thought was, I should have learnt to swim.

· · · ·

"Breakfast," a voice said.

Kezia's mouth opened to respond and caught the cooking aromas wafting through the room, reminding her she hadn't eaten in days. She felt refreshed from a long and mercifully dreamless sleep. From the short shadows in bright sunlight, seen through the open door, and the angle of the thin beams that wavered through the drifting smoke it was around noon.

She sat bolt upright, clutching the blanket to her chin, the material unlike anything she knew: soft, warm, and so smooth to the touch it positively slid over her bare skin. Bare skin. A quick peek confirmed she was naked except for the ring. Her burnt arms had tanned and her feet were no longer swollen. Had he treated her, or was this a residue of the dust used earlier? Her face was red though, at the thought of a young man she hardly knew, undressing her while she was not conscious.

"I can assure you, as lovely as you are, Our Lady's plan keeps me fully occupied. My mind has little time to dwell on anything else." The warrior spoke without turning around, his uncanny perception into her thoughts producing a sudden chill.

If it's true that even this young, he no longer thinks about sex, then maybe Willard was right not to take the test. For the first time, Kezia admitted to herself, the difference in Willard's eyes indicated he was likely to pass. If he did, this would be his lot. In leaving, she had made the right decision, albeit for all the wrong reasons.

"Your clothes needed attention," the warrior continued.

He was right. Since leaving home Kezia hadn't been out of them, had crashed through brambles, fallen in a foul creek, walked miles on hot dusty roads and last night had pissed herself. The floor was now clean. Her undamaged and perhaps unopened pack hung on a nail. Her clothes lay across a rack of lashed branches by the fire.

"Hungry?" asked the warrior rising. He brought over her clothes.

"Famished," she said. Good Goddess I'm about to have breakfast with a Restoration Warrior.

Kezia waited until he returned his attention to the fire then dressed quickly, thankful he did not look around. Her clothes were clean and felt unusually soft. As soon as she could, she checked her pack, relieved to find the bag of coins and the jars of powder intact. So far, he had proven as trustworthy as he was polite. She wondered how she should talk to him.

The warrior himself sat on a stool made from three lashed branches tending several pots, which stood on stones inside the fireplace next to the small fire. Positioned on the other side of the fireplace was a second tripod chair, apparently made just for her. It had a woven grass mat across its splayed legs as a seat. In daylight, the room seemed almost homely. How did he do all this?

"What name did you choose?" Kezia marvelled at being able to speak at all, and glad that she knew something she could ask. Willard and Averil knew more; Aldus knew just about everything.

"Howard," he said.

"Pleased to meet you Howard, I'm ... pleased." She should choose a new name. Kezia Leach would soon be infamous in her own right, not just the oracle killer's sister, but a Medicorps absconder and killer of Deep Creek's Magister.

"Our Lady has sent me to Port Calder," Howard said, seeming to ignore her failure to provide a name. Kezia stared at his back with suspicion. His statement made little sense. This was a private road that ended here. That he still had hair was evidence of how recently he'd taken the test. From *Legends* she knew only a servatory could test a candidate; the nearest being on the Pillar in Grundston. If he was heading to Port Calder, then he had gone about two hundred miles out of his way to end up here. She shuddered at what the Goddess planned, if not her death. Obviously, she doesn't want me anywhere near Willard and Averil. Howard's job is to shunt me into a siding while they have offspring. This was a telling without benefit of an oracle; stay out of the way and I'll help you. She didn't want to think about what rebelling might mean.

• • • •

Without opening his eyes, Willard sensed how the mud slide had deposited him, spreadeagled on his back, with his feet down-slope. Daylight filtered by the gently moving canopy, flicked at his eyelids. Awareness of his surroundings came suddenly. He could feel pain throughout his body and ants crawling over his skin. Frantic, he went to brush them off and found his arm wouldn't move. Oh shit, I've broken my back, he thought, panic rising. He tried to scream for help, but his mouth would not cooperate. He could feel everything but move nothing, muscles frozen, nerves very alive. Kezia had told him there were animals that could numb their prey. He shuddered at the thought the ants might be slowly devouring him. Tears of relief coursed down his cheeks when he felt a tingling warmth in his fingers and could flex them. He now took stock of his actual circumstances rather than his imagined ones.

He opened his eyes. He could see trees rushing into the sky all around him, but couldn't move his head to see the ants. Curiously, warmth came and pain eased wherever the ants went. It felt like the healing powder Kezia's mother had once used on him. Maybe crushed ants are the main ingredient in the healing powder. He closed his eyes again when they crawled on his face. They aren't ants at all he decided, but little creatures of the Goddess. The tower had dismissed such rumours, saying Our Lady's magic came only from her towers. All else was aithcraft and thus inherently evil. Aithcraft or not, Willard thought, the ants were helping. His whole body, including his head ached less. How could that be evil? Perhaps the Goddess had not deserted her 'special' candidate after all.

Except for his hands and feet, he was still immobile, almost as if the ants needed him to be still to do their work. Fine by him. He didn't want to move. Even small movements brought pain. He had no idea how bad his injuries might be. He gave a small cheer when he found he could lift his head, but the movement bought such pain he let it fall back and the jolt caused him to black out.

He regained consciousness with no idea of how long he had been out. The ants were gone. Warily, he turned his head. His arm showed yellowing bruises and multiple clean cuts, some of which looked stitched closed. The Goddess made manifest. Wait until I tell Averil ... and Kezia. It surprised him that his first thought had been to tell Averil but then it had been Averil who had challenged his belief in the Goddess.

Feeling returned as the sun warmed him. The light, scattered by foliage, gave soft illumination to the hardening mud. Small birds hopped across the surface of the slide, pecking out an easy breakfast. The peace and tranquillity of the freshly washed and glistening forest belied the mayhem and death of the previous evening. He saw no sign of any other survivors.

Why are you doing this to me, Severne? The answer he gave himself made his stomach churn. The Goddess was clearing obstacles from the path of her special candidate. A path he had rejected. He wondered whether he could have prevented this, if he had gone to her oracle and received foreknowledge of it. Perhaps if he had followed the path Our Lady had chosen for him from the very start, then everything that happened after Kezia left might not have. His next thought was even less comforting. What if Our Lady wanted him in her debt? Silently, he bemoaned his fate. It's not my fault, I didn't ask to be special.

As movement returned to his legs, he sensed advantage in his special status, a way to bargain with Our Lady. His concern however was her help, both at the Arch and here, had come too late and others had paid the price. Under that bland surface must be the bodies of his entire escort, seven men and eleven horses together with a wagonload of supplies. Some names, those called out in the darkness: Smith, Ashley, and Dalton, echoed in his mind. Samals, how prophetic he had been when he'd said the flatlander would get them all killed. All but me, he sobbed, and felt the stirring of an emotion he didn't like—hate.

He turned his head easily now and lifted his body, supporting his weight on an elbow. The wide brown swathe that stretched from his fingertips right across the gully and all the way back up to the road was shocking. He closed his eyes against the absurd sight of a horse's foreleg sticking out from the fresh brown scar. He rolled over, gently pushed himself to his feet and began the long climb back up to the road, using the trees and bushes at the edge of the slide for support.

I must get help.

But as he climbed, he knew he could not go back. There was nothing in Deep Creek worth going back for: Kezia was gone, Aldus was dead and his father had disowned him. He need only send word to his mother to stop her worrying. He paused, looking at the all-concealing mudslide. What would the militia do when they missed the escort and their search found this?

Would they assume them all dead and mark the spot, or dig it all up to identify the bodies, probably the latter?

Special or not, his singular survival on top of Kezia's disappearance would not go down well. He needed to find Kezia to see she was alright and at least clear his name of that charge. Absently, he rotated the ring around his little finger as he worked out how. She had joined Medicorps. Walker then. The contingent had been gone maybe four days, a week at most. Their office in Walker would have a record. Once he knew she was with them, he could head off towards Rivers Junction. He could even volunteer, as both Averil and Kezia had suggested. Together, they could work something out.

The sky was cloudless, the air fresh and warming. Birds chirped, whistled, and chimed as they flitted through the trees, promising a lovely bud day. The vicious storm must have been a freak of nature. The slide it caused had swept a large section of road on either side of the elbow into the gully, making it impassable. His decision to go on, not back, found him on the wrong side of the slide; he would have to traverse it. He dragged his eyes away from the fly encrusted horse's leg, the only sign his escort was ever here, and clumped across the crust, staring straight ahead. It broke easily under his weight, creating a trail of footprints. That might lead the militia to speculate on survivors.

Samals, he thought. Samals had been absent before it happened. Maybe he'd survived. That left, six or seven dead here, two at the Arch, and he had walked away both times. He had killed none of them, yet he felt responsible for their deaths, and indirectly for Aldus's, the brother who wasn't his brother, grandson of the father who wasn't his father. Who in the name of the Goddess am I, besides her 'special' plaything?

Willard pushed down the thought to focus on finding Kezia. In assessing himself, he found his appearance tidy, belying his less than graceful descent down the gully. As well as his body, Severne's ants had repaired his clothes. It seemed the what the Goddess took with one hand; she gave with the other, just not in equal measure.

Almost immediately, he reached the end of the old forest road and stepped out onto Ridge Road. A hail from a passing dray was hardly surprising.

"Going to be tested?" the driver asked, spitting a desiccated morsel of the wad he chewed over the side.

"Yes," Willard lied, not surprised by the question but wishing he had his eye cover. Lying was easier than trying to explain the complexities of his predicament. The driver wouldn't believe it, anyway. Willard didn't believe half of it himself. It didn't add up, or maybe the problem was it added up too well and that didn't bear thinking about.

"I can't pay you; I have only what I'm wearing."

"A strong candidate like you need only remember who helped him when he was just a candidate," the driver said. "So that you know, the name's Tolbert. Climb aboard."

As they moved off, Willard looked back over his shoulder, but could not see the scar for the trees. Despite his escapes, Our Lady had fallen in his esteem. Like Aldus, he had learned to distrust first her servers, then the Goddess herself. They and she had deceived his mother, and coaxed her into lying to him about his father. His desire to avoid the test became a commitment. He would find Kezia and they would go somewhere where the Goddess couldn't reach them. Kezia's Aithist mother would know if such a place existed. Willard looked up from his thoughts, smiling. For once in his life, he was following a plan of his own, rather than simply avoiding the plans of others. It felt good.

As Ridge Road wound its way across the hills, Willard had glimpses of the plains through the trees. Tolbert stopped the dray soon after they rounded the last bend, and the vast expanse of the Aldgate-Meander basin spread out before them like a painted landscape. Willard shielded his eyes from the bright sky, amazed he could see all the way to Grundston, the Pillar, and beyond them to the endless ocean. Somewhere, a long way to the southeast beyond the Lesser Range, this year's Wall Contingent was making its slow way toward Rivers Junction, taking Kezia away from him—he hoped. If she made it to the wall, Averil would take care of her. Averil would have made it. She always achieved what she set out to do. Once he knew for sure, he could join them.

"No matter how many times I come this way I never tires of this sight. It changes with every season and every passing year," said Tolbert. "Was a time, when I was about your age, that Walker was no bigger than Deep Creek. Now look at it. It'll soon swallow the entire riverfront from Ferntree to Swamp Gully. Bloody shame when there's all that empty grassland t'other side of the Barriers." He spat over the side slapped the horse into motion, and they began the long descent into Walker.

Tolbert's comment set Willard thinking. On the servatory's maps, the Great Plains were five times the area of the entire east coast. He couldn't envisage what they might look like, but surely, somewhere in that vast expanse he and Kezia could find a place, away from towers and warriors and the plans the Goddess had for them.

Tolbert set him down in the main street of Walker. Willard thanked him for his hospitality.

"No offence, mind, but I hope we never meet again. If we do, you just remember it was Tolbert gave you a lift."

He drove off whistling.

Chapter 9

Replete in body if not in mind, Kezia sat sipping Howard's coffee, looking at the gemmed sword resting in its scabbard against the wall. The name tooled into the leather read *Firebolt*.

Intercepting her glance, Howard gave her a boyish grin. "It isn't true," he said. "We do not keep count. Our Lady's justice is not a game, nor is it our only purpose, just all anyone hears about." He reached out and handed her the scabbard, sword, and all.

Except for the name, the supple leather was unblemished. It should be, thought Kezia. He's hardly had time to kill anyone yet. His hair is still falling out. "I've heard no one say different," she said, fingering the unworn letters, enjoying the smell of new leather.

The term 'Our Lady's Executioner' did not fit Howard. He was younger than she was, barely out of his teens and balding. When he scratched his scalp, hair fell away in clumps. Despite his youth, he was an excellent host and provider. Breakfast had been a banquet: eggs, mushrooms, tomatoes, fried vegetable patties—mostly potato—and fresh cream to go with the coffee. Where had the cream come from? She had seen cows, but fresh cream took time. Did he threaten a farmer? He wouldn't need to; just arriving at the farm would be threat enough.

When she hesitantly questioned him about it, all he said was, "For those who choose her way, Our Lady provides."

Kezia grunted; her scepticism fuelled by experience. She had believed, yet Our Lady had provided her with nothing, had instead taken everything. She held out her cup for another coffee and as Howard refilled it; she pondered the calm she felt, drinking coffee with a fabled warrior who could lop off her head at any moment. And talking to him as she would to Willard, well maybe not Willard but Aldus. Talking to Willard had often been hard work.

She suddenly found she didn't care anymore.

"The stories about us are mostly wrong, but hard to put down. You've heard the expression, 'A warrior is the last person you are likely to see.'"

"Hasn't everyone," Kezia said, shuddering at hearing him say it.

"It started after an execution in 843FD of an Arch Server who murdered three candidates."

"That's over a hundred years ago," said Kezia, wondering why he was telling her this.

"The story handed down is that Warrior Baxter had killed them, and then executed the Arch Server to cover his crime. Neither Our Lady nor some very able warriors since have been able to repair the damage to our reputation. The real story, recounted in *Legends*, is one of many that most servers don't mention. Trust me, executions do not happen every time we appear."

Howard captured her gaze. "Your fear has dropped noticeably since our first unfortunate meeting, no doubt dispelled by personal experience."

Kezia handed back *Firebolt*. As she made the bed he'd constructed, so some other itinerant might benefit, she wondered if perhaps she was being unfair. She was alive, rested, and well fed. Besides, she had only consulted Our Lady about Willard, after they had oathed. Yet she still felt poorly treated, singled out, the only one of her sisters not a candidate. Until that last telling, Kezia had believed as Howard said that Our Lady's plan benefited all, except where is the benefit for me, Willard, or Averil? None of us will get what we want. If my eyes had changed, it might have been different.

Howard shouldered *Firebolt* over his cloak. Unlike the scabbard, which seemed ordinary, the long green cloak made her Medicorps uniform look like rough homespun.

"Where are you headed?" he asked, breaking into her thoughts.

"South," she said, away from Deep Creek.

"I would be happy for company."

Kezia studied his face to see if he was joking or hiding something in the offer. She was certain he had come for her, just not to kill her. Why then, after years of neglect, was the Goddess now taking an interest in her?

"Why are you here?"

"I have a task to perform for Our Lady."

Kezia blanched. She found she wanted to live after all, and since he wasn't after her head, she should stop worrying about it.

"Well?" he asked, interrupting her dread imaginings of what his task might be. "Might I have the pleasure of your company?"

"Why not," she answered. Travelling with him would be safer than alone. Port Calder would be as good a place as any to start again; provided Our Lady's plan allowed it.

• • • •

They reached Crossroads around the middle of the next day after another night in the open, but so much better than her other nights in the open. Howard had provided, including a shelter. It was now Satelday, a week since Averil broke the oracle on Willard's birthday. Kezia closed her eyes. Stop it, she told herself, just stop.

Howard suggested she go alone into the town to purchase any personal supplies she needed and to hear the latest news.

"Why alone?"

"As we've talked about, reputation. I don't want to frighten anyone. I'll meet you on the other side."

Without him, she felt free. She hadn't felt free when she left home, but with restored health and a full belly, she had the luxury to feel free. One bit of news surprised her; Palma, on the Aldgate River the other side of the Lesser Range had just given the contingent a big send-off. She realised she was about the same distance from Rivers Junction as them. If she wanted to, she could buy a horse and reach Rivers Junction in time to re-join her unit.

She didn't want to; she wanted a new life.

After re-joining Howard, they continued south towards Wiseman's Ferry, passing through the rich agricultural land beside the Wanetta River. Kezia, looking back for the Arch noticed flashes from the Crossroads signal tower. Shielding her eyes, she shifted her gaze to find the Arch, surprised she couldn't see it. Less than a week from home and she had lost all contact. In her imagination, she could see the outcrop where she had told Willard to forget her. She couldn't forget him. In fact, now she had lost him, her feelings for him had intensified.

"Want to talk about it?"

"No," Kezia said brusquely before adding, "Do you know what the signals are saying?" It baffled her how anyone could read the flashes.

Howard turned and studied the tower for several minutes. "Two ferals hung in Walker ... and Deep Creek's Magister is missing."

Kezia looked back towards Deep Creek in alarm. What were ferals even doing ... then the message about her father registered; not dead, missing. Dead, she would have understood. Mother must have found him and is covering for me. Tears formed and she turned from Howard lest he see. I must be stronger than this. I must forget.

They walked on in silence for a while; Kezia frustrated knowing Howard from his pause he hadn't given her all the news.

"How long will it take us to get to Port Calder?" she asked, impatient to put distance between herself and her past.

Howard considered for a moment, "At this rate, twenty-seven days, give or take a day."

"That's nearly five weeks," Kezia exclaimed. She hadn't thought of her journey as a major expedition, anticipating a few of days, one week at most.

"It's roughly five hundred miles. Don't they teach geography in Deep Creek?"

"What are we going to do for food?" She held up her hand to forestall Howard's reply. "I know. Our Lady will provide; right?"

Howard grinned and nodded, but said nothing. He'd lost more hair after washing this morning, and the youthful face under his pale clean scalp made him look childlike. His grin irritated her.

"Ask her to provide a horse then," quipped Kezia, knowing warriors never rode. "My feet are sore."

Howard looked pensive. "It would cut our time in half," he said, softly as if thinking aloud or perhaps, as most people held, communicating directly with the Goddess.

Kezia wasn't sure whether this appeased, offended, or just scared her. She was travelling with someone who would one day be a legend, like Baxter and Fletcher, talking back to him, asking questions, and now making demands. If she didn't shut up, she might end up headless. She knew that wasn't true anymore, but the ingrained beliefs of a lifetime were hard to break.

Instead, Howard seemed to be seriously considering her request. There was hope in that thought. The ways of the Goddess are every bit as mysterious as our Arch.

· · · ·

The pain in her chest and stomach caused Averil to double up as she rolled to the side and retched. A putrid combination of bile and brackish river water dribbled from her nostrils.

"You'll live."

Averil coughed, spat, coughed again. She felt her stomach leap up her throat as it tried to turn inside out. She could concentrate on nothing but taking in great racking gulps of air.

"Lie still and try to steady your breathing," said a deep voice.

Good advice, she thought, but her lungs ached with the effort while her mind exalted at the reprieve. Plain, ordinary air had never tasted so clean, so fresh, so breathable.

A strong arm slipped under her shoulders and lifted her to a half sitting position. "Here, drink this."

A cup of warm broth touched her lips. She took a mouthful, rolled it in her mouth, and spat it to the side. Her mouth clean, she let the next sips trickle down her throat. She felt herself relaxing, a feeling of lassitude spreading through her body. She took a bigger sip, laid back, closed her eyes, and drifted off.

· · · ·

When next she woke, she felt remarkably well, for someone who nearly drowned. The last thing she remembered was hanging onto the ferry pilot as the torrent swept them away, then the pain, then the voice saying "You'll live."

She opened her eyes; knew from the broken window she was inside the terminal hut. She was also on a bed, wrapped in a finely woven, dark green blanket smelling of lavender. How in Severne's name did I get here? She turned her head. Twenty yards away, out through the open doorway, down a gentle slope, she could see the river. It had gone down a little. The ferry's list was now hardly noticeable. Apparently, her impromptu repairs still held. The far cliffs were ablaze with golden light from the setting sun. Another day lost; another day closer to disgrace. She wondered if being alive was the best outcome.

"The pilot, what ..."

"Gone," said the voice behind her. Averil's eyes misted as he continued, "I could only save one. Our Lady chose you."

Unshed tears evaporated in anger. Damn your plan Severne. She was about to berate her rescuer as well, but her mouth went so dry her tongue stuck to its roof. Differently coloured eyes under hairless brow ridges, Severne's tits, she thought automatically.

The last person anyone wanted to see regarded her with what looked like concern. No strap crossed his chest. She scanned the room and found the sword propped up in the corner. Etched into the scabbard's leather was the name *Brimstone.* Warrior Gardner had rescued her. Only seven named swords existed and Averil knew every name and its owner. His words, 'Our Lady chose you' and the memory of her tragic audience dispelled the thought that he had saved her so he could execute her. Severne's tits, she meant it. She sent a bloody Restoration Warrior to babysit me.

Although grateful for her life, she hated it had cost the pilot his. I didn't even know him, but he's dead because Our Lady chose me. Why didn't you get here earlier, Gardner, she thought, but didn't say? Not much point railing against him for being unable to save them both. She took a deep, sad breath, coughed, and spat again, then closed her bandaged hands around the cup and sipped the delicious warm broth.

Goddess, it was good to be alive on such a fine bud morning. Dying would have been such a waste, all the academy's training for nothing. As she gazed through the door at the cliffs across the river, a sudden burst of bitter laughter tinged with hysteria caught her unawares. She was still on the wrong damn bank.

Her laughter eventually subsided, replaced by tears, strange tears of frustration at her lack of progress mixed with remorse for the pilot. *What is wrong with me? I never cry.* She had so wanted to be a warrior, but despite a strong difference in the colour of her irises, she had the wrong gender. She could not take the test and now her second choice, to become a Watcher Captain, was rapidly retreating from her with the contingent. She needed to get going.

"What day is it?" she asked Gardener.

"Serverday, you slept all day yesterday."

"That isn't possible?"

"It was necessary."

Necessary, it took her a moment to realise that her sleep had not been natural. He had drugged her; the broth. She stared at the warrior who stared back.

"You needed time to recover. Our Lady suggested sedation to ensure you rested."

"Goddess be damned," Averil shouted at him angry beyond reason. By her calculation, the contingent was already on the other side of Rivers Junction and she was still four days away on the wrong side of the river. Even if she had the fastest horse now, she wouldn't catch them. She would never get to the Wall. She would lose everything she had worked towards since her eyes had changed. There were limits to what the Watchers might overlook; desertion wasn't one of them. Her commission would go. They would outlaw her.

She stood and poked the warrior in the chest, safe in the knowledge the Goddess needed her as an incubator for Willard's offspring.

"You can tell Our ... your Goddess," she corrected. Our Lady now seemed too respectful for someone who had wrecked her life. "Her plan for me and Willard won't ever happen."

"Our Lady disagrees."

"Wanna bet? I'd sooner jump off the Wall."

The warrior drew a breath, stared at her with glazed eyes, and spoke quietly. "Your attempt to catch the contingent before the pass is misguided. The Watchers will hold your commission until the contingent arrives without you."

Her nape hairs rose, unsettled by the tone and pitch. It was as if the Goddess had replaced Gardner, and was speaking directly to her, yet still she answered back.

"You don't understand. If I'm not under Watcher protection, I won't get through the first checkpoint in Long Gully Pass. The militia will arrest me and return me to Deep Creek."

Gardner's eyes focussed on her; he was back. "There is another pass, a shorter route with no checkpoints."

Averil had to think for several seconds before a groan escaped her. "You can't mean Perisher. That's suicidal."

"I do."

"You know why it's called Perisher. It's a broken ledge on a sheer cliff, mostly above the snowline. If you don't freeze to death, the wind will pluck you off."

Gardner was unperturbed and imitated her as he had the Goddess. "You know why it's called a pass."

Bastard. Just thinking about it made Averil feel tired. She sat down on the bed. Maybe she hadn't fully recovered after all. As she sat, she noticed the bed as if for the first time and realised Gardner must have made it. He had stretched a mat of woven ferry ropes taut over a box frame made from freshly debarked wood, still shiny with sap. Between the rope and the blanket was a thick layer of grey-green stems tipped in purple flowers, lavender.

She looked up at Gardner with new respect and wondered if he had always been this resourceful, or had gained it from the test. Perhaps the Goddess trained them. A calculating thought she couldn't finish followed. If Willard turned out like this ...

Crossing the Wanetta turned out to be anticlimactic; scary and brutal but anticlimactic. Gardner, half-swimming half-pulling, hauled them through the torrent. Averil clung to his back, her arms around his chest holding *Brimstone's* strap, the sword pressed between her breasts, as he hauled them along the cable. They had a brief respite on the ferry climbing onto the deck, no longer tilted at an unnavigable angle. Then they were back in the river, the water bulging over the cable and their heads, soaking them, chilling them, buffeting them. Talking was impossible against the roar.

The smooth material of the warrior's cloak and clothing emerged dry. In contrast, Averil stood dripping. Gardner turned, drawing *Brimstone.*

Tits, I was wrong. This is it, she thought, as she considered her options: run, plead, or fight.

"Hold still. I'll have you dry in a few minutes."

Gardner held the sword horizontal, the gem glowing a dull red. For a few seconds, the blade crackled and sparked along its edge, then settled to a soft glow. As he swept the humming blade slowly across her body, she could feel her skin tingle and her clothes drying in a heat that warmed her skin.

Averil couldn't help staring at her dry clothes, at Gardner, at the sword he was now sliding back into the tooled scabbard. His use of it astounded her. It was tantamount to sacrilege, like wiping yourself with a page from *Legends*. She could now see how he might make good on his promise; until he spoke.

"Now I must leave you."

"What happened to helping me over Perisher? Was everything you said beefshit?"

Gardner's differently coloured eyes blazed, but he kept his voice calm. "Our Lady's tasks are many, we are few. You can make it to Perisher by yourself. I suggest you go via Light Pass." He pointed towards the Lesser Range, blue in the shimmering distance.

Averil pointed north. "Perisher is that way."

With slow deliberation, Gardner continued. "So is Deep Creek. My way you might just avoid recapture. I strongly suggest you cross the river at Paxton Bridge, head to Rizedon Vale and follow the Meander River. I will re-join you at Sandbank in two weeks, assuming you know where that is, and can get there by then."

Averil looked down to hide her growing anger at his humiliation of her and willed herself not to explode. Now was not the time to lose her head.

Briefly, his voice changed again to that of Our Lady. "Please try to stay out of trouble, Averil."

Gardner's voice was back when she looked up. "I have to see a man about a horse," he said and left at a fast jog towards Rivers Junction.

Chapter 10

Willard entered the Medicorps Office in Walker with trepidation. As the northern basin's regional centre, it was an imposing stone building by the river. Inside, the dark polished timbers and large windows with views of the water only enhanced his first impression. Tolbert was right; the town had grown. Having its own Medicorps office was testament to how big.

Willard stood at the window, pretending to watch the boats until he was the only customer, before he approached the orderly behind the counter. Her dark hair and the uniform reminded him of Kezia. Clinging to the slim hope that something had delayed her, that she might still be here, he grinned at the orderly, an image in his mind of Kezia's expression when she saw he'd come after her.

"Can I help you?" asked the orderly.

"I'm looking for my ... sister. She joined," he thought back, trying to work out how long ago it had been, "about a week ago." He realised then he was too late. It was more like a week and a half.

"You've missed her. The Everild coach got there yesterday. She will be with the contingent now. What's your sister's name?" she added, watching Willard's eyes.

The tacked-on question caught him unprepared. "My sister?"

"The one you're looking for. I'll see if she got on the coach," prompted the orderly. "There was one no show."

"Kezia ... Kezia Leach," Willard stammered not liking the direction this was taking.

"Ah," the orderly said, pulled out a register and flipped the pages, "Kezia Anne Leach?"

"Yes," Willard nodded.

"From Deep Creek?"

Willard nodded again as the orderly looked up at him her expression full of pity.

"What?" Willard asked, shaky with premonition.

"Your sister is in big trouble candidate Leach," she said, closing the register. "She signed articles, took her uniform and kit, but didn't show."

Willard didn't know what to say. Kezia was the Corps' no show. Then where in Severne's name was she?

"She was in uniform when she left me to come here. She even told me she felt needed on the Wall. Maybe she had an accident on her way here."

He heard the orderly murmur something about him waiting while she went to check with her superior, but when she turned her back, Willard slipped out. He needed to think.

How, in the name of the Goddess, am I going to find her now? Had she had an accident, as he first thought, or considering her distress when they last met, had she decided at the last minute to disappear? It wasn't really like her, but then joining up wasn't like her either. He brooded over where she was likely to go.

"Hey, watch where you're going."

Willard looked up.

"Er, sorry candidate," the man who bumped into him said. Then he looked harder. "Pale blue, deep green. You're the one they're looking for." He grabbed Willard's arm as he turned and began shouting for the militia. "I found him. I found Forrestor. He's over here."

Willard chopped down on the arm holding him. The man swore and let go. Willard ran, skidded around the first corner he saw, pelted down the street and turned again. He attracted curious glances as he alternated left and right, only slowing when he ran out of breath. He paused in a quiet cul-de-sac, a part of Walker unknown to him. The man who grabbed him had known his eye colours and his name. Clearly, the militia had found his escort and identified who was missing.

He stilled his rasping breath to listen. He couldn't hear any sounds of pursuit, but that didn't mean there wasn't any. What he could hear was the river still in full flood. Head down to hide his eyes he walked towards the sound, fearful now that finding Kezia had just become harder. He had to vanish and search for her simultaneously, with no idea where to start. He might need something he had assiduously avoided, a telling but not here, not even near here. In Grundston, he would be just one candidate among many. Decision made Willard closed one eye and asked the next person he saw for directions to the sale yards. He was soon in familiar surroundings.

Stable Master Hartley greeted him warmly. "Willard my boy, how goes it? How are the folks? When's your dad bringing me his latest yearlings?"

"Soon," Willard said. Thank Severne, Hartley didn't know the militia were hunting him.

"I hear you had some trouble up at the farm," Hartley said, twitching his large moustache.

Willard tensed.

"Ferals, I heard. Who would credit ferals in Deep Creek?"

Even as he relaxed, Willard had to suppress an image of Aldus lying in the overflow pipe.

"I need to borrow a horse," he said, grimacing. Averil had asked the same of him and look how that turned out. "Just a few hours, I have an errand to run for ... dad. He's so busy I had to get a lift here."

"Aye bud is a busy time on farm. A few hours, you say?"

"Just this afternoon," Willard said, the lies getting easier.
"Take the black. His owner won't be back until morning.
Treat him gently. He's one of Arthur's finest. See he comes back
in good nick or he'll hear about it."

· · · ·

The closer Willard got to the Capital, sprawled across the
confluence of the mighty Aldgate and Meander rivers, the more
chance he had of anonymity. His eagerness to find Kezia before
her trail went cold intensified. It had taken him three days solid
riding to get here and she had been gone for two weeks. She
could be anywhere between Sandbank up north and Port Calder
down south. The only sure way to find out which direction she
went was to consult Our Lady's oracle; use the advantage strong
candidates had of unlimited free tellings.

He found it easy to sell the thoroughbred. He went into a
pub and made it known he had a horse for sale. He settled for
half the stallion's worth. As a strong candidate, he had little need
for money. A flash of startlingly different eyes brought offers of
food or shelter. Often the offer of a bed came with broad hints of
someone to warm it, the family hoping to gain a candidate. The
coin he got might be useful to buy another horse once he knew
which direction to go.

Shit, if his father … Arthur didn't compensate Hartley, then
either Ser Tomas, or the Magister, would add horse stealing to
his crimes.

Willard worked his way back to the main avenue that
pointed like an arrow to Saint Jon's Tower. Everywhere he
looked, there was someone with unmatched eyes. His candidacy,
despite the strength of it went almost unnoticed. He skirted a
column of Watchers parading around the grand circle, all smiles
and crisp blue Watcher uniforms. Averil's by comparison had

looked faded and worn. Her warnings about the ferals massing for a big push seemed out of place here. The crowds picnicking in the extensive grounds around the tower watched the parade as if nothing was amiss.

Saint Jon's entrance was an imposing series of fluted marble columns two stories high, topped by a triangular stone lintel engraved with ancient builder symbols. It was not builder construction but after the style. The risk in coming here was that an Arch Server might force him to the test. Even though *Legends* said candidates must come willingly to the test, rumours of involuntary testing persisted. For Willard, the chance of finding Kezia was worth the risk.

He threaded his way up the broad steps for the first time. A plaque on the wall read, "St. Jon, First Ob server." Four years at the servatory, countless trips into Grundston and he had never been here. The foyer was much bigger than Deep Creek's. A couple of sparrows circled beneath the vaulted ceiling. The short stairs could take five people side by side. In keeping with the rest of St. Jon's, the scale and trappings of the Penitent's Waiting Room went way beyond Willard's expectations. He paused and gaped through the heavy drapes, wondering how to phrase his question, but the incoming throng soon jostled him inside.

The noise was unexpected. Deep Creek's waiting room was always silent, but St. Jon's auditorium had a more festive air. Penitents talked while they waited. A woman just ahead vacated an aisle seat and Willard gratefully slipped into it. Curved tiers of individual hide-covered seats had replaced Deep Creek's ranks of hard wooden pews. The focus of the semicircle was the Audience Chamber's five shimmering doorways. Five oracles or five entrances to one oracle, Willard wondered?

A scuffle broke out in the next section. Two acolytes held a struggling youth by his arms while a third poked at his face. An older woman screamed at them to leave him alone. Seconds later, the third acolyte stood, triumphantly holding aloft, what looked like the boy's eye. The woman hurried the youth away, huddled over and clutching his face to jeers and a ripple of appalled laughter.

"Does anyone need a glass eye?" the acolyte joked with the nearby penitents. The business of petitioning resumed. The background conversation settled back to its previous level.

Willard felt sorry for the impostor. It had once been commonplace. Unscrupulous parents, wanting their son to have a chance at the test, would poke out his eye and claim it had been different. To stop the practice, the towers refused to test one-eyed boys. Willard, using the colour changing eye cover Kezia's mother gave him, had no such trouble. No one expected a strong candidate to evade the chance.

At the front, queues of acolytes handed their tablets of petitioner's questions to servers stationed at each Audience Chamber entrance. The servers constantly disappeared and reappeared through the five doorways, their talismans flashing as they broached the power curtain.

After years of avoidance, Willard had multiple pressing questions: where was Kezia, did his mother go to the Eye, was Our Lady responsible for his birth, who was his father, and why would the ferals be after him? There were also questions he knew he couldn't ask. Had the Goddess killed the feral up at the Arch then wiped out an entire Watcher Patrol to set him free, or was he just lucky?

With a limit of one question at a time, Kezia's whereabouts took priority, but he would have to phrase it carefully. No good asking 'Where is Kezia?' His answer was likely to be 'Preservation Island', accurate but useless. He tried several ways of phrasing his question and considered his best to be, 'how can

I find Kezia?' That at least eliminated a 'yes/no' answer. Specific directions would be useful, but he could see 'by following her' might easily be all the acolyte brought back. He discarded the impulse to make it 'how soon can I find Kezia?' He didn't want 'never'. Maybe I should try Averil's approach and break into the Audience Chamber. He rejected that immediately. He didn't know how and besides what might be possible in Deep Creek had no hope here, too many servers.

He jumped when an acolyte thrust a tablet and stylus into his lap.

"Let me see if I can guess your question, candidate."

"Er ... I have lots," Willard stammered. His palms were suddenly sweaty and he felt as if everyone was watching him. He looked down at the tablet.

"Most do," replied the acolyte. "The trick is to narrow down your question to the most important one for now. You can always come back for another at a later session or try out of town. You, being a strong candidate, it might tempt you to ask, 'Am I the Face.'"

A shocked Willard stared at the acolyte. Nothing was further from his mind, yet it was the question they would expect of someone with 'strikingly different' eyes. The obvious answer would be 'take the test'. As Hedley had often told him, 'Even if you fail you will have all your questions answered'.

"I'm right am I not?" nodded the acolyte.

"Er ... I suppose so," Willard said, though his mind whirled with altogether different thoughts, and despite the cavernous surroundings, he suddenly felt claustrophobic. He wanted out. This had been a bad idea.

"Well, let me tell you, candidate, it's not a good question. If Our Lady knew that, we wouldn't need to test candidates, am I right? Better to ask something more useful like 'will I marry?'

Willard looked up into the earnest face not much older than he was. "How will that …"

"With your eyes, a yes would mean server, probably Arch Server. A no would mean Restoration Warrior." He was nodding vigorously again as if to compel agreement.

Just thinking about it made Willard tremble. It was exactly what he feared most. I don't want to be a bloody head-lopper he screamed silently.

"Are you alright candidate, you're shaking?"

"Just a chill," Willard said, thinking about what to ask. Extrapolating from the acolyte's idea, he scratched his question on the tablet, then signed it.

The acolyte beamed as he retrieved the tablet until he read the question, 'Will Kezia and me stay married?'

"An interesting way of putting it. I may be wrong, but I doubt you will fail. I'm Melvin by the way, Lord. Remember me when you make warrior," he said, winking. Then he strode off down the aisle as if he had recently inherited a fortune.

Willard watched him all the way to the short queue at the fifth entrance. A simple 'yes' to his question would be great, a 'no' would at least mean he and Kezia would be married or … shit even a 'no' might mean we never marry. He didn't want to think about the myriad of answers possible.

Melvin smiled back as he moved a step closer to the front.

Willard rubbed sticky palms together and looked around for the nearest exit, convinced now that any answer other than 'yes' would be useless. He'd blown the question. Part of his mind told him to wait in case it was 'yes', the other part told him to flee. Having this telling was wrong. He hadn't wanted his and Kezia's lives mapped out, he had only wanted to know her whereabouts.

Now was his last chance to cut and run. While Melvin handed the tablet to the server, his back to Willard, he stood and, in an unhurried manner made his way towards a side exit constantly glancing back at entrance five. The server quickly became embroiled in conversation with Melvin.

As Willard reached the exit, Melvin turned and pointed to where he had been. Even at this distance, Willard could see his dismay at finding the seat empty, watched him scan the near exits.

"There," Melvin shouted, his finger pointing.

A hush came over the vast waiting room as heads turned, following the pointing finger. The server motioned to several other acolytes as Melvin headed in Willard's direction. The whole auditorium seemed to surge his way.

Willard ran.

He ducked through the drapes and up the carpeted stairs two and three at a time. At the top, he ran straight into a server, automatically apologising for knocking him down as he raced through the majestic columns and down the wide steps onto the lawns. His destination undecided he plunged straight down the hill and burst into the crowds on the streets of Grundston. He was a block away when he paused doubled over, panting with the exertion.

When he looked up, it was straight into the 'strikingly different' eyes of a face he recognised at once, Ob server Rayburn Walker. His smiling countenance stared out from a poster, below a caption proclaiming 'Our Lady is with You Always'. According to pillar records, Ob Walker, a formidable warrior several hundred years ago, had been Our Lady's principal server for the last seventy years.

His mother's words came back to him with absolute clarity. 'Go to the Pillar, Willard. Ask for sanctuary. Ob Walker will know what to do.' Yes, Willard thought, only Our Lady herself would know more. Maybe his mother was not senile after all.

Maybe now was the time to take his questions right to the top. Strong candidates were always welcome at the servatory.

Although there was no sign of pursuit, Willard still had an uneasy feeling that someone was watching him. He looked out across the Meander River and up the tiered mountain to the servatory complex at its summit. The Pillar, marked on maps as Mount St. Pol overshadowed the whole of Grundston, including St. Jon's Tower.

Willard started up the ramp to the first terrace, knowing it would take him until dark to reach the top. The only compensation going up was the increasingly spectacular view and the decreasing time taken to make each circuit. He would find a billet in a Way Station and go to see the Ob in the morning.

• • • •

The Arch Server looked up from the table like a startled rabbit when Willard gave his full name. His glance raked Willard from head to toe before coming to rest on his eyes.

Willard cleared his throat. "I'm here to see Ob Walker."

The Sev hesitated, then nodded his head.

"Why?"

"Sanctuary," Willard said, recalling his mother's urgent plea.

"Wait here," he said, before disappearing through the carved doors behind his desk.

As soon as he spoke, Willard's hackles rose. The voice sounded very much like the traitor who got Aldus killed, but he couldn't be sure. If this was the man, it might explain his reaction. He would now know the ferals had killed the wrong man. *Thank the Goddess none of them saw me; he won't know I was there.*

"I cannot disturb Ob Walker for another hour," the Arch Server said on his return, then went and sat behind the sumptuous desk.

Willard covertly studied the man. His eyes were two shades of green, but like all Sevs, he bore a confident manner. The crimson robe warmed his rather pallid complexion. Willard tried to imagine that voice saying the phrase the traitor had used hoping to identify the man. He couldn't put the two together.

He gave up and spent the hour gawking at the huge reception room. In his time here, he had never seen this part of the servatory. 'Opulence' was the word that most readily came to mind: polished wooden floors, intricately patterned carpets, delicately carved furniture, and a lofty ornate ceiling, ablaze with light, a numbing display of builder power and of privilege.

Occasionally the Sev would look up to study Willard and although used to people staring once they saw his eyes this man's scrutiny made him nervous. He couldn't help wondering if the interest was more than casual, as if the Sev had divined Willard's suspicions.

At the tinkling of a tiny bell, he stood. "The Ob will see you now," he said, leading Willard through the carved doors and down a long corridor lined with portraits and busts of previous Ob servers. One that looked like Hedley made Willard stumble when he read the inscription, 'Ob Hedley Bakor FD 85-157. Commissioned the building of the Wall. One of Hedley's ancestors being Ob made sense; candidates ran in families.

Bald guards, either side of the door into the Ob's office came to attention, ornate swords held point down and hilt out from the body in a laughable imitation of a Restoration Warrior's stance. The Arch Server passed his talisman over a pedestal, and the massive doors swung silently inward. Impressed as Willard was by the smoothly functioning aithcraft, anger bubbled below the surface as he followed the Sev into the Ob's study.

The Ob sat with his back to them at a large polished desk in one of two bay windows bent over his work, his shock of wavy hair greying almost white.

Here sat the man who, with Ser Hedley, had organised his birth and promised him to the Goddess, losing him Kezia, and in Willard's opinion, indirectly getting Aldus killed. Through the other bay window, Willard could see all the way to the Barriers. He looked away when he noticed the Arch. There lay home and mother, and below it, Deep Creek, where he and Kezia had met and fallen in love. Along with childhood, it had all gone, and this man knew why.

Either the Ob hadn't heard them enter or he was reminding them of who was in charge. Why else did he ring to say he was ready and then continue working? He dipped his pen in his ink well and paused as if in thought. The drop of ink on the nib swelled ominously.

The homily giving you trouble, Willard thought. Can't explain why there are ferals up at the Arch.

The Arch Server cleared his throat, "Ahem, Willard Forrestor to see you Ob."

Ob Walker started, the drop dislodged and splattered across the pristine page.

"Goddess be," he cried, reaching for blotting material, and then noticing he had visitors, "Oh, it's you, Willard."

He finished blotting before turning.

"Yes Ser," Willard nodded, falling back into childhood habit.

"Yes, Ob," the Arch Server corrected.

The Ob's eyes sparkled, full of understanding, full of the ancient wisdom of one who has taken the test, pale blue, and deep green like mine Willard saw with a shock. Could he be my father?

Ob Walker picked up the cane leaning against his desk and came forward, hand extended, "Please, call me Rayburn. Come, sit with me."

Willard remained standing, hands at his side, balled into fists, inuring himself against empathising with this frail old warrior, preparing for a confrontation he could neither avoid nor win.

Ob Walker turned his outstretched hand into a gesture of dismissal. "You may leave us Nyle," he said as the Arch Server was positioning three chairs in the empty bay window. The Arch Server opened his mouth as if to protest, then walked stiffly out.

"Close the doors, please."

"Is that wise do you think, Ob?" Nyle asked.

Although not the exact phrase, the voice, the way he said it and his intonation made Willard certain the Ob's secretary had sold them to the ferals.

"Thank you, Nyle," The Ob said.

Speechless with the enormity of his discovery, Willard turned slowly as the massive doors closed. His smile was grim. He could now put a name, and a face, to that voice—Arch Server Nyle Miller. Once he had Kezia back, he would pursue justice for Aldus.

When he turned back, the Ob was fiddling with his talisman, tracing a circle on its surface with his index finger, tapping it as he sat down.

"I have put a seal on the door to ensure no one disturbs us," he said. "Nyle tells me you are here seeking sanctuary. Sanctuary from what Willard?"

"Sanctuary from the ferals your damned assistant sold us to. It got Aldus killed."

Willard's eyes bored steadily down into Ob Walker's, as if he could extract and unravel all the personal secrets this man held.

The Ob flinched. "Please Willard, sit down. I'm sorry about Aldus, I only heard last night. Your allegations against Nyle however are very serious. Tell me what you think happened."

"Think," Willard said, still standing, "I know what happened." He told the Ob everything he could remember, beginning with the raid and ending with the Arch Server's parting comment. "I recognised that 'do you think' expression he has," but even as he spoke, Willard felt his argument weak, his evidence flimsy.

"The expression is not uncommon. I use it myself sometimes," Ob Walker replied.

"It's not just that, it's his voice and the way he says it. I first heard it up here during training."

Willard wondered how the Ob would react to that. See, I was here right under your nose, without your knowledge.

"Ah yes, your server training," Ob Walker said, his eyes alive with mirth. "Hedley told me how and where you got the ... eye cover."

Willard's eyes narrowed.

"Tut, tut my boy, I know more than you can ever hope to learn while you continue to refuse the test. As for Sev Millar ..."

Willard glanced back at the closed doors. "It was Sev Millar, acting as Deep Creek's Magister, who signed the warrant for my arrest."

"Really? That I did not know."

"For a man who knows more than I can ever hope to, you know very little."

"Touché. Hedley kept me better informed than Ser Tomas. I shall investigate your suspicions as soon as your business here is over. But enough of that for now. How is your mother?" he asked. "Hedley told me she was quite distraught when the militia dragged you away."

Hedley, Willard thought, remembering the crimson robes of an arch server on the verandah consoling his mother. Arch Server is he now. Willard's ignorance was scaring him. He stared at the Ob in bewilderment. You and Hedley knew and did nothing. How am I supposed to get sanctuary here? The unmatched eyes regarded him with concern as he sat down somewhat wearily in the long ago offered chair.

"Why are they after me?"

"Why do you ask?"

"That's an evasion," Willard said. "I expected better. Mother said you would know why the ferals want me, and what to do about it."

Ob Walker smiled as he leant forward. "I'm sorry Willard, I didn't mean to be ... unhelpful. Let me be candid, the ferals ..."

Willard stopped listening. He had come for one reason, to ask the one man who most had the ear of the Goddess, where Kezia had gone. He found a helpless old man, knowledgeable but so powerless, he couldn't even control his own staff.

"Are you my father?" Willard interrupted.

Again, the Ob started, as if his question was completely unanticipated. As an afterthought, Willard added the other possibility.

"Is Hedley?"

"Neither I'm afraid, but I'm not surprised you might think Hedley could be. He has been coaching you since birth but no, he is not, and although you and I have identical iris colouring, I'm not either. I would guess that your mother has now told you Arthur's not. You are a rather special gift from Our Lady."

The Ob spoke so earnestly Willard was ready to believe him, almost did.

"As I was trying to explain before you interrupted me, someone has convinced the Federal leader, Charismatic Doane, that you will become the Face of Our Lady. Doane believes it. He thinks to control the world by controlling the Face. He is wrong. Like us, the Federals believe in Our Lady. Doane however does not wholly believe in her Restoration."

"Neither do I," Willard said and for the first time saw the Ob's smile falter.

"You must if you are to pass the test. You, Willard, are our hope for the future, the best candidate Our Lady has ever produced."

Willard's eyebrows rose. 'Produced' made him sound like a product.

"You sound like my mother, Ob."

"I am proud of my and Hedley's association with her. You have a fine pedigree and ..."

"So you do know who my father is."

"Only Our Lady knows who your father is."

"A gift from the Goddess has always sounded like a way to avoid explaining sex to me. I know about the birds and the bees now, Ob."

Ob Walker winced. "Considering your less-than-ideal training it is not surprising you have lost faith. Look, I am not disputing the biology of procreation Willard, but, truly, you are a gift from ..."

Willard groaned and the Ob cut his explanation. "Hedley brought your mother here and Our Lady had her—I'm sorry there is no other word for it—inseminated."

Inseminated! produced! Our Lady inseminated mother like a prize pig to produce me.

"From time to time, Our Lady's plan has required her direct intervention to produce special children, which is how I can assure you of your pedigree without knowing who your father is. Only Our Lady knows. You must ask her."

"I might, if I could ask privately like Averil did."

The Ob chuckled. "I heard about that from a rather irate Ser Tomas, but you my lad, sorry, bad word choice. You won't have to break into the oracle. Our Lady has wanted to see you for some time. She hoped you would come of your own accord. If you're willing to talk with her now, you can use my private Audience Chamber."

It's come at last, Willard thought. Why fight it? Except that rejecting her plan was the only choice still his.

"Is there anything else I can help you with before you go in?" asked the Ob.

Willard drew his thumb and forefinger together across closed eyes. "There is so much Ob. I hardly know where to begin." Abruptly, he felt a need to get everything said while he had the chance. Who better to tell, short of the Goddess herself? "I don't like your Goddess. Her plan has ruined my life." He sat up straight in the chair and subjected Ob Walker to an intense scrutiny. "I can't prove she took Kezia from me but ..." He left the implication unsaid.

The Ob shook his head, a look of utter despair in the old eyes. "I hardly think you can blame ..."

"Did you know," interrupted Willard, "that in the last few days your Goddess has killed nine people protecting me?"

Willard watched horror play across the Ob's eyes as he stood.

"You know Ob, the more I think about it, the more inclined I am to have nothing more to do with her. Forget the audience, I'll find Kezia on my own."

Chapter 11

K ezia came to an abrupt halt. Grazing on the verge, hitched to a fence post, was a saddled horse. The surrounding fields were empty, not a house or animal in sight, yet here was a riderless horse, saddled, ready and waiting. *Yesterday I ask; today a horse appears.* Despite her astonishment, Kezia hoped this signalled a change in her fortune, but realistically it probably meant the Goddess was in a hurry to get her away from Willard.

The horse, a striking brown and white, raised its head, ears cocked forward as Howard approached. He reached out and let the horse sniff his hand, then rubbed its nose. He spoke softly as he unhitched the reins.

"What are you doing?" asked Kezia as he handed her the reins and cupped his hands to provide a step.

"Your ride ..." he started, then paused, an inquiring tilt to one bare eye ridge.

It took Kezia a moment to realise he was prompting for her name and another to know she couldn't tell him. She hadn't yet decided on one.

"We can't just take it. That's stealing."

Howard looked perplexed. "But Our Lady provided the horse at your request."

"Not possible. It's not a wild horse, it has a saddle."

"Would you prefer to ride bareback?"

"That's not the point. Someone had to saddle ... her," she said after a quick glance under the horse's belly. "Where's the rider? They might have fallen and lie injured somewhere."

"What you say might have happened, did not. Our Lady provided this horse for you. If you've changed your mind and want to walk, I can return the horse to its previous owner." Howard again cupped his hands. "The choice is yours."

Previous owner? Our Lady, or a believer, must have bought the horse. "In that case, thank you," she said, putting her foot in his hands. "I'll take your word for it and call her *Providence*." She mounted, gave a gentle squeeze with her knees, and the mare moved off.

Howard loped alongside. She had thought one horse would be useless, but Howard seemed indefatigable as he jogged along beside her hour after hour.

Naming the mare recalled her own need, a new name to match her new life. She had mulled it over for some time, rejecting her first impulse to call herself Kezia Forrestor. It would be a constant and painful reminder of all she had lost. Equally, she didn't want to lose all links to her true heritage, perhaps Jena after her mother Jorgena. For a family name, she wanted something extremely common like Setler. Jena Setler then. That had a nice ring. She would submerge herself in her new role; use her skills, her training, and mother's jar of magic to become a prodigious healer, perhaps even a doctor. As part of her new identity, she tied her hair back.

Kezia looked down at the upturned face of the warrior. "By the way, the name's Jena, Jena Setler."

"As you wish, Jena," Howard replied without the slightest hesitation, though he must know who she really was, or he would not be here.

To Kezia's surprise, having Providence doubled their pace. Her spirits rose as the miles fell behind. She rehearsed introducing herself: g'day, I'm Jena Setler, healer.

Her first chance came when they paused for lunch at Wiseman's Ferry, and Howard helped the Watcher squad repair the storm damage. Nobody recognised her, or if they did, said nothing. They probably only glanced at her because of Howard. Given everything she knew, she would think the sight of a warrior with a travelling companion was far more noteworthy. Howard might be the first.

As the sun slid towards the Barriers, Howard told her they would stay would the night in a settlement called Woodbridge. An elated Kezia looked forward to a hot bath and a warm bed. The new sense of freedom she felt struck her as quite perverse. While she had obeyed the rules, her life had become steadily more unbearable, but as soon as she rebelled, it improved. Not that there wasn't a downside. She had lost Willard, mother, and her sisters. Then again, what had she really lost? She would lose Willard anyway, when he took the test. She had already lost mother to the mystical world of her builder refuge, and like Averil, the twins were candidates, lost to Our Lady. All Kezia had really lost was her father and all the problems he had created. Looking forward caused her less distress than looking back.

Kezia's first sight of Woodbridge enchanted her, a fairy tale village in a quiet valley reminiscent of home. With a whoop, she urged *Providence* into a canter, ignoring Howard's shouts of caution. As she pelted down the road, her only thought was of a bath and a bed. She waved at a sentry as she clattered across the wooden bridge into the town and reined in, looking around for a pub or a boarding house. Her eyes widened with wonder at all the novelty: the buildings, people, sounds, and smells now seemed exotic. It was totally unlike Deep Creek.

Then she noticed the faces were less than friendly. Those who stopped to stare quickly looked away when she waved or nodded. Kezia was wondering at their manner when she spotted the militia heading her way across the cropped grass, a heavily tanned young man in a faded Watcher uniform and a boy, a cadet half her age. She dismounted while she waited.

"Nice horse," said the older Watcher. His oddly accented voice held no menace. His eyes were grey, his dark hair straight, and pulled back into a strange club affair at the back.

"Yes, she is," said Kezia, unaccountably nervous. As she reached for her pack, her fingers touched a sharp edge. Relax she told herself, Providence is mine, bought for me by Our Lady.

The speaker leant back against one of the short stone pillars, squat replicas of Our Lady's Towers, and watched her, his directness unsettling.

"Pity it isn't yours."

I knew it. Damn you Howard, I told you we ... Kezia took a deep breath, forced herself to remain calm as she searched for a way out. How could she prove to them she didn't steal the horse? For Goddess's sake, Howard, hurry up.

"It is actually. A warrior gave it to me," Kezia said without turning, not knowing how they might greet such an outrageous statement, hoping it gave them pause, in case her claim was true.

Someone in the growing crowd laughed.

They're gathering like vultures only I'm not dead yet. Beyond them, she spied the black robe of a server, hurrying down the street from the tower, the person limping beside him talking rapidly. She was simultaneously aware the Watcher had stopped his amiable lean on the pillar.

"Can we talk about this after I find a place to stay?"

"You have a place to stay," he replied carefully, "the Watchhouse."

Without warning, the cadet snatched Providence's reins and the Watcher reached for her. Kezia felt panic rising. After tasting freedom, she had vowed never to allow anyone to manhandle her, especially someone wearing that uniform.

"Get your hands off me," she screamed as she spun, whipping the blade from her pack so fast it caught everyone by surprise.

The Watcher gasped and clamped a hand over the bright red line that appeared on his inner forearm.

"You cut me," he said in wonder, his eyes flicking from the cut to Kezia.

The cadet dropped the reins and backed away wide eyed.

"Sorry, I didn't mean to," Kezia said, brandishing the knife awkwardly in front of her. She winced in sympathy at the pain she had inflicted. She had only intended to make them back off, but he had been too close when she turned.

The stunned Watcher stared at her. "Why?" he asked, shaking his head. "What did I ever do to you?" Then his eyes rolled up and his knees buckled.

"Wesley's hurt," someone said, breaking through the crowd's trance. Others murmured, the crowd rousing like an angry beast. It horrified Kezia to see how much blood welled out between the fingers of the man they called Wesley. She must have accidentally cut an artery. Dear Lady, help me. I never wanted to hurt anyone.

"I'm a healer, I can help him," Kezia shouted, remembering her mother's jars of dust. She dropped the knife, turned quickly, and lifted her pack down. The small jar was out of her pack and she was desperately trying to unscrew the lid when the crowd rushed her.

"Let me go. I can help him."

The crowd bellowed in disbelief.

"Grab her."

"Don't let her near Wes."

"She's trying to finish him."

Kezia pleaded as she struggled, but the numbers were against her and no one was in a mood to listen. In their effort to keep the stranger away from their injured Watcher, they punched or kicked her every time she made a move towards him. The hail of blows and curses forced her to her knees. She was dimly aware of the black-coated figure striding through the crowd, of a new outraged voice shouting above the angry clamour.

"In Severne's name stop, what kind of animals are you to attack a defenceless woman?" he asked.

"Defenceless, she had a knife."

"She slashed Wesley."

"Who's helping Wesley while you beat her up?" Woodbridge's server stood protectively over Kezia and glared at his flock.

"I can help him," whispered Kezia through swollen lips, as she again strove to reach the fallen Wesley, crawling towards him on hands and knees, every movement a slow agony, the precious jar clutched tightly.

Once the blows had stopped, she could feel a warm tingling sensation in her own limbs. The healing effects of the dust I used days ago. It surprised her it kept its power for so long.

Wesley still bled profusely. His tanned skin had taken on a greyish pallor. A woman alongside, trying to stem the flow, had tied a piece of cloth hastily torn from her under garment, now soaked and dripping, around his arm.

"If the flow doesn't stop soon, he could bleed to death," the woman said.

"I'm a healer," Kezia said again. "Please let me help him."

The crowd paused, waiting on their server as Kezia carefully unscrewed the jar's lid. The silvery dust looked as if it was moving of its own accord.

"Aithist magic," someone shouted.

Damn, I should have remembered.

"Our Lady's magic," a commanding voice boomed from the back of the crowd before the server could respond. Howard had caught up.

The crowd suddenly went quiet when they saw who spoke. A hairless young man in a green cloak with a gemmed sword strapped across his back. Some took hurried steps away from Kezia, the Watcher, and their server. The number of onlookers thinned rapidly. Kezia watched Howard assess the situation. There was nothing boyish in his manner now. He looked straight at her.

"Do it."

Kezia pulled the soaking cloth away, pinched some dust between thumb and finger and sprinkled it on the bloody gash. Against Wesley's pallor, the dust was invisible.

The server tried to re-assert his authority, "You ... I am Our Lady's representative here. I must protect my petitioners from Aithist magic."

"Did you not hear me Ser Hagen? Healer Jena uses builder magic sanctioned by Our Lady."

The server paused, swallowed. "But what of the horse she stole conjured from a locked stable? Surely that's Aithist magic."

Howard's voice deepened, then rose to level those at the back of the crowd would hear. "You surprise me Ser Hagen. Would a locked stable trouble Our Lady? However, it did not happen. Our Lady paid Bramwell more than the horse was worth." He said, demonstrating he knew who had made the accusation.

"Water," Kezia said. "He's lost a lot of blood. He needs to something to drink. A broth would be better, but water will do. Lukewarm is best."

Wesley's wellbeing focussed their attention. The blood had stopped flowing within a minute of Kezia's treatment and as she gently sponged away the mess around the wound; the crowd gasped. Although still angry and swollen, neat stitches held together the puckered edges of the long gash.

The townsfolk peering from windows and from around buildings muttered, the predominate phrases being 'builder magic' and 'Our Lady's magic'. Ser Hagen, his eyes darting everywhere, fingered his talisman.

"If Wesley dies," he argued, "I cannot allow this to be seen as Our Lady's magic."

"Our Lady will tell you what you can and cannot allow, Ser Hagen."

Wesley moaned and some of the less timid townsfolk, presumably with nothing to fear from a warrior, ventured out and carried Wesley off to the hospital.

Kezia was still sitting on the ground, too weary to move. The cadet tugged at the server's sleeve in a way that was both familiar, yet respectful.

"Is she still under arrest for stealing the horse?"

Ser Hagen stuttered into silence, his hands trembled as he traced the paths on his talisman, his eyes on the Restoration Warrior.

Perhaps he now wonders, as I did, if his time has come, thought Kezia. But unless Howard lied to me, or Our Lady has given him new orders, his business is not in Woodbridge. The half-hidden fearful faces around her were an insight into why the execution rumours persisted. These people fear what they might have done. Few are innocent enough not to feel it when faced with ultimate authority. Anyone who really had done something against Our Lady would be long gone and wouldn't return until Howard left, as if that could save them.

Howard reached down to help Kezia to her feet as the Ser Hagen looked around at the emerging townsfolk. "Anyone see where Bramwell went? I was talking to him only minutes ago."

Kezia suspected he had been the man with the limp and probably the one who had called her Aithist. Bramwell was missing and no one had seen him go.

Howard turned and spoke to the server. "My friend and I require lodgings for the night."

Kezia's feeling of wellbeing was not entirely because of the residual magic of her mother's dust. One of the mysterious, often feared Restoration Warriors had just called her 'friend'. With a friend like Howard, enemies would be few.

The server bowed. "Please, warrior, you shall be my ... guests in Our Lady's Tower," he said, looking from one to the other, his hands never still, "er ... you warrior are not long to your calling, how are you and you companion called?"

"I have chosen the name Howard. My friend is Healer Jena."

• • • •

Averil soon established a routine, rising and bedding down with the sun, alternately walking and jogging for about ten hours each day, quickly devouring the miles. Where she could, she scrounged from the isolated farms, a bath, a bed, or a breakfast, rarely all three together. In most places, her uniform, neither helped nor hindered, but as with any potential Man Who Will be Face, country people were just as generous to a potential Mother of the Face. They soon paraded any sons before Averil, who politely declined.

When she couldn't scrounge, she went hungry or lived off the land, wild fruit, and the occasional rabbit. She had long ago burned off her humiliation at Gardner's hands. She consoled herself with the thought that she would only allow a Restoration Warrior to get away with it. This warrior was the reason she continued to push the pace. She wanted to arrive at Sandbank before him.

Unfortunately, getting to Paxton Bridge took longer than expected. Four creek crossings, while still recovering, had cost her five days of the two weeks. With only seven to go and not even halfway, she couldn't suppress a wry smile. Gardner had precisely weighed her ability and calculated how long she would take. A horse would have ensured victory, but the Goddess speaking through Gardner specifically warned her to stay out of trouble; no horse stealing.

His advice had been to follow the Meander River, from Rizedon Vale, but for Averil the Meander did too much of what its name suggested. Instead, she opted for a more direct route cross-country, estimating it would save her a day and a half. She might just make it.

Her second day out of Walker North a swollen tributary, thirty yards across, depth unknown and flowing rapidly, exposed Averil's mistake. *Bloody Gardner must have known I'd come this way, but the bastard hadn't bothered to tell her.* As she pondered the flow, she saw a wide swathe of churned mud on the far bank. She found a similar well-trod mud flat, bordered by close-cropped grass on this side, and figured she just got lucky. Where animals crossed, so could she.

At the water's edge, among the animal tracks going down the bank, Averil noticed five, maybe six, sets of footprints and a large churned area of hoof-prints in the damp sand. She went down on one knee for a closer look at the footprints.

Ferals!

She quickly scanned her surroundings ears straining for the slightest jingle. With nothing seen or heard, she returned her attention to the three sets that had every hallmark the Watchers had taught her to look for: rounded edges, wide at the front, snicks on the outside at the heel, soft soles—ferals. The other three sets were boot-prints with very Watcher-like sole patterns.

The hoof-prints, too many and too churned to separate showed only shod horses. Did that mean Watchers with feral prisoners, or ferals on stolen horses with Watcher prisoners?

A memory surfaced, a signal about the militia hanging ferals in Walker two weeks ago. But the ferry disaster and Gardner's arrival had pushed it from her mind.

The confusion of prints fascinated her. Whoever they were, they had paused and watered their horses before crossing. Further scrutiny made it clearer, in every case booted prints overlaid the soft soled prints; Watchers following ferals. Why were the ferals here? There was nothing here but scattered farms and signal towers. Averil swore. The signal towers were a vital link between the capital and the Wall. Thank Goddess, the Watchers already knew and were tracking them.

She contemplated the river again. The rapid flow suggested it was shallow, and since both groups had crossed here, it must be doable. The large clearing on the other side was a concern, but considering the Watchers were chasing the ferals she felt it was probably safe.

"I don't have time for this. I have an appointment to keep," she said aloud, and after a quick glance at the far trees, started down the bank. She was still uneasy about the freshness of the tracks, and not having seen or heard anything of those who made them.

Trying not to think about current or depth, Averil splashed into the river, her focus on beating Gardner to their Sandbank rendezvous. As hoped, the river was swift but not deep and she emerged without mishap on the other side. She broke into a trot towards the trees which seemed unnaturally hushed; no birds taking flight or animals scurrying from her approach.

A spear thudded into the soft mud several yards to her right before she had taken three strides. A quick glance confirmed the design on the quivering haft was feral. Averil leapt sideways and sprinted, hoping the density of the understory would give her a sporting chance. Simultaneously, she glanced back along the spear's flight path to find the thrower now intent on riding her down. Severne's tits, that's not fair.

After an already strenuous day, running was hard. The crossing was at the bottom of a bowl. Everywhere away from the rider was uphill. A second spear sliced her shoulder. Averil barely noticed; the pain would come later. Whoever it was, had found her range. The trees that had seemed so close were taking forever to reach. It surprised her when she again glanced back that her assailant had slowed to retrieve his spears. Arrogant bastard. He could've ridden over me if he hadn't stopped.

Averil abandoned her erratic course and threw all her energy into a single, straight-line burst to the trees. Forearms up for protection, she plunged headlong into the dense bush, not caring where she headed, simply putting distance between herself and the mounted spear thrower.

As she pelted through the undergrowth, the fatigue in her legs screamed at her to stop. She was on the point of collapse when she tripped. A hand snaked out and grabbed a handful of her jacket as she fell. It ripped as the hand pulled her down to the decaying forest floor. She could see nothing and had trouble breathing. More hands reached out, big muscled hands, blacksmith hands, pinning her wrists and ankles.

Out of the frying pan and into the fire. She struggled, and her attempt to free herself was far from silent.

"Be still, you're making too much noise," said a voice in her ear as a harsh breath full of onions washed over her. The voice was not feral, merely coarse. Averil bent and bit into the back of the hand holding her wrist.

"Fuck," Onion-Breath whispered, smacking her ear with his other hand. The grip of the hand she bit remained rigid on her wrist, an admirably tough nut.

"Keep it down," another voice whispered, slightly further away.

"Trying to," said a third voice, belonging to the other hands that held her, short stocky arms covered in fine orange hair.

"Shut him up, they're coming," said the more distant voice. She sensed authority in the last voice as a blade point pricked her cheek and knew instinctively that Onion-Breath wouldn't hesitate to cut her throat to keep her quiet.

The surrounding voices fell silent. She lay still, listening for the horses, stolen Watcher horses, no jungle. Her breathing was rapid and shallow, blowing dead leaves away from her mouth with each exhalation. Now I know how Willard felt.

Faintly through the ground, over the blood pounding in her ears, she heard the drumming hooves recede. A horse snorted. It was close. Then she heard it clopping slowly and two ferals arguing. The first voice was a woman, the second deeper, commanding. Both voices had surprising little accent, obvious choices for work behind enemy lines.

"The Uplander peasant ran well," said the female.

"A peasant doesn't run so. This was a Watcher, one of those trailing us. You should have killed him first throw."

Him again, thought an irritated Averil, surprised her attacker had been a woman.

"Where is the sport in that?"

A bitter male voice, not the deep voice Averil thought of as their leader, added, "We're not here for sport. We have lost too many for this one and he is not the man Miller promised."

The deep voice and the female chuckled. Averil desperately wanted to get a look at 'this one' who was not the promised man, but their horses were almost on top of her. She held her breath as the voices passed. Hooves stamped the ground a few yards away, picking a path through the undergrowth. The animal smell was now stronger than the sweat and breath of those holding her. That the passing horses didn't shy, confirmed for her they were Watcher horses, quite used to such smells.

"They must still be here. We should find them and kill them," the woman said.

"We don't have the time. Darkness comes and Padget will not wait," the leader said.

The bitter second male voice then spoke with a sense of panic. "Who is going to tell the charismatic?"

"Take heart, Oswell, that task won't fall to you." The leader's voice was full of contempt.

The female was more conciliatory. "Why do you think Doane sent Durward, if not to be rid of him? He was totally unsuited for this expedition. Besides, we may not make it back. Their signalling tower can alert this entire area."

"We will be gone before they repair it," the leader said as their horses clomped away. The conversations soon faded to nothing, replaced by the distant sound of horses milling, forming up, and then breaking into a trot.

While she waited on her captors' next move, Averil thought about what the second male feral had meant. *Is the entire world going mad, or just me?* He implied they had come for the Face, but 'this one', the one they had, was not the man that Miller, whoever that was, had promised.

Night was falling fast as the forest sounds resumed. The knife at her throat withdrew and she heard Onion-Breath sheath it.

"That was close," said Orange-Hair.

"Let him up," the authoritative voice said and the hands that held Averil gradually released. She flopped over on her back enraged but thankful she could breathe freely again. From their uniforms, her captors appeared to be Watcher like her, but you could never tell these days. They could be deserters or bushrangers in scrounged clothing. Besides, what would Watchers be doing here trailing ferals rather than killing them or taking them prisoner?

Using the manoeuvre that had twice freed her from Willard, Averil arched her back and sprang to her feet, snatching Onion-Breath's knife from its sheath as she did so, landing upright beside the leader, a captain like her. She held the blade to his throat as she spun him around, a barrier between herself and two corporals.

"It's a girl," corporal Onion-Breath said.

At last, Averil thought. "Tell them to back off or you're going to have breathing problems."

Onion-Breath and his short red-haired companion paused, but only after she scraped the edge upward over the captain's neck, removing a few hairs, drawing a bead of blood. The captain didn't speak, but his careful hand signal had the desired effect.

"Now I have your attention. Let's all calm down and introduce ourselves shall we, assuming we are all Watcher." "Sit," she said, pulling the knife away to show goodwill.

The corporals sat.

"Is that all of you? You're a few short of decent patrol, especially for chasing a warband."

"Ha," said Onion-Breath, "them ferals are a few warriors short of warband."

"So I noticed. Who are you?" she asked.

"Brande, Captain Brande. Wall Watch five."

"You have ID?"

"Do you?"

Averil touched the blade to his neck. "In my jacket, right pocket," he added quickly, then went on. "Look, whoever you are, I don't have time for this. If we lose them, I'm in deep shit."

"Then get a move on, pull it out with your right hand, toss it to Red."

Brande withdrew a small leather folder and lobbed it toward the short redhead. The corporal picked it up and opened it, showed Averil the flat rectangular card with rounded corners.

"Hold it up to the light."

Where the sun caught the Watcher logo, it flashed with iridescent colour. It looked authentic, but was it his? Averil took the chance. She removed her knife, stood up, withdrew a similar folder, and flashed her own card. "Captain Leach, Wall Watch Seven. Sorry about any misunderstanding."

Captain Brande stood, moistened his fingers, and rubbed the nicks in his neck. He looked from the card to Averil obviously still sceptical. "You're young for a captain," he said.

"Rushed training, I'm heading to the Wall to take up my commission."

The captain studied her for several seconds. Averil's grip on her knife tightened as she watched his eyes, certain that he knew all about her. My eyes and the signals, she thought, as he wiped his bloodied finger on his pants.

"Kingsley," he said, nodding at the redhead and Onion-Breath, "Hollis and Dean."

The corporals getting to their feet and dusting themselves off nodded to her as he introduced them.

"And you, Averil Leach, our candidate captain, are going the wrong way."

I was right, thought Averil, unable to hide her smile as he continued.

"You're the reason I got this detail. You didn't turn up and the contingent couldn't wait. The major wanted you chasing this lot so you'd recognise the bloke they snatched in Deep Creek."

Averil instantly thought of Willard but rejected it. They knew they had the wrong man. Wylie? Her turmoil went unnoticed. "Why haven't you freed the captive?"

"Major wants to know how they got here ..."

"They don't have the man they wanted, and they won't need a hostage when they leave. Are you going to rescue the poor bugger before they kill him?"

"In the end, but first the Major wants to know how they intend to get away. I would like to know why a blonde youth wanted for desecration is so interested." Captain Brande wasn't smiling, but his eyes were alight.

Averil grinned. "I'm from Deep Creek."

"Ah. So where's your horse, Averil? They scattered ours. One of us will have to ride over to Meander Bridge and commandeer three more."

Averil took a deep breath. "I'm on foot."

"Fuck."

Kingsley stared at her with despair and frowned as he looked north. Suddenly his eyes widened and Averil nodded, knowing he was smart enough to have worked out she was attempting Perisher Pass. He won't know about Gardner and I can't tell him.

"Right guys, we're on foot. We better get a move on and hope the fucking ferals keep going the same way."

"If you make it to the Wall, save me a place at the bar. I'll shout you a beer. I might be a corporal again after this."

"You're on."

"In fact, Averil, we might meet again sooner than you think. The ferals were heading the same way you are." He touched his cap in a loose Watcher salute. He was looking at her as Willard had in Severne's Wood, as everyone used to look at Kezia. At least he no longer thought of her as a boy.

Averil straightened as she returned the gesture. "Thanks ... Kingsley. See you on the Wall," she said, feigning a confidence she didn't feel.

Chapter 12

Willard strode towards the doors of Ob server Walker's private suite, having just said he didn't need an audience; he could find Kezia on his own.

"I'm sorry Willard, we can't allow that," Ob Walker said.

Willard strode back to the bay window, reached out and grabbed the Ob's talisman. He jerked it sharply and the Ob rose, allowing Willard to drag him to the doors. Strangely, Willard felt no fear, confident now the Goddess would not harm him, despite knowing she could.

"It won't work without my cooperation," Walker said.

"Where does it go?"

"It doesn't go anywhere. I simply wish to go out and the doors open. I could demonstrate, but I won't."

"I saw you trace a circle and tap on it when you locked us in."

"A worthless observation," the Ob said somewhat breathlessly.

Willard jerked the chain again. "Does her plan include your imminent death?"

"Does yours?" countered the Ob, and Willard's resolve faltered, his bluff hollow. He released his grip on the talisman and resisted the intense temptation to shove the old man.

"You're just a spent warrior living out your old age in luxury," he said, indicating the surroundings with a quick wave, surprised to see Walker stung by this.

The Ob rubbed the back of neck and straightened his collar. "You have no idea, Willard. Your ignorance puts you in a position where you cannot make an informed judgement." He picked up his fallen cane. "Follow me. Our Lady will be happy to tell you all you need to know."

Occasionally leaning on his walking stick, Ob Walker led Willard from his office through a maze of servatory corridors. Eventually they arrived before a glass wall, ablaze with light, which Willard could only describe as awesome. The room behind it looked more like a storehouse of working builder artefacts than an Audience Chamber.

Such power, he thought, but to what purpose? Who benefits? Willard recognised only two objects, the crystal cube from storybook images of oracles, and a door sized replica of the Arch, as he imaged it would be, if they excavated the earth covering the base.

The Ob lifted the talisman from around his neck and placed it in the slot on top of the pedestal then glanced up sheepishly, aware of Willard's scrutiny.

"There really is no need. I do it out of habit as I am often in the company of servers who do need to use one."

As he spoke, the whole glass wall in front of them shimmered like an Audience Chamber curtain. "After you," Ob Walker said, pointing at the effulgent wall.

Willard stepped through into a jumble of unnatural sounds. The Ob stepped through behind him. In a builder sense, the inner sanctum was more lavish than anything Willard had ever seen. If Our Lady's plan was to restore this to everybody, he might have to change his mind. It was as if the room was a living thing. The flickering of tiny multi-coloured lights mesmerised him. The clicks, whirrs and swishes blended into a pleasant sleep-inducing hum.

"Willard, how nice to see you again," a female voice said. An image of the seated Goddess, depicted in countless statuettes, coalesced in the oracle. "I haven't had the pleasure of your company since you were a small child."

Willard froze, surprised the Ob had not needed to perform some litany to invoke her presence, he simply acknowledged her with a nod. The image sparkled and danced, became translucent, then transparent and again opaque as the eyes of Our Lady turned on Willard.

"Why do the people I need most fight so hard against me?" She turned to the Ob. "Send him, Rayburn."

"At once, Dear Lady."

Ob Walker, chuckling as he dropped the cane, grabbed Willard's wrist, bent his arm up his back and propelled him towards the scaled down Arch. Willard struggled, but couldn't halt his rush toward the replica. The Ob was not the frail old man he had supposed. The arch abruptly came to life, if one could describe as life, the unremitting matt black surface that suddenly filled the space inside the ellipse.

"Close your eyes."

Willard barely had time to register Ob Walker's shouted warning, as he stumbled and fell headfirst into the impenetrable black. For the briefest instant, as Willard's head broached the surface, he felt he was nowhere and everywhere at once, compressed to a point and stretched to infinity, utterly swallowed by a void and unbelievably cold. Then he was stumbling forward, trying to regain his balance.

He failed, and lay where he sprawled, powerless to move. His breathing was raspy, his heart pounding, and his body wrapped in incredible lethargy. In the name of the Goddess, what just happened?

Warm air settled the goose bumps on his bare arms. His nose wrinkled at several unfamiliar smells. He opened his eyes and saw the soft floor on which he lay was blue. His head jerked up and he eyed the soft blue ground critically. Material; he was lying on a finely woven mat, finer than any he had ever known.

Where am I?

He looked up and across a wide plain of the soft blue matting. It curved gently upward as it rolled away through a cream-coloured canyon studded with multi-coloured boulders. No, he thought, not boulders, bags like flat-bottomed teardrops. It's a room. The canyon walls were just the walls of a long room with a curved floor. A curve that continued up and up, until it met the ceiling a long, long way in the distance. He closed his eyes and rolled onto his back. For no reason, he could fathom he had expected going through the Arch would lead outdoors.

"Where am I?" he reiterated aloud.

"If I told you, you would not believe me?" said the Goddess her voice so rich and full he felt sure it issued from a real throat.

Not wishing to embarrass himself in her presence Willard clenched his sphincter hard and opened his eyes. Our Lady of the towers, the Goddess Severne looked down at him, a solid-looking image unconstrained by her oracle. It must be a statue he thought. Please let it be a statue, but the statue moved as he hoped it wouldn't. With fluid grace, the Goddess sat on a bag which re-formed to accommodate her.

This can't be happening, Willard thought, closing his eyes against the incomprehensible. I must be dreaming. The Goddess isn't real. Tangible Goddesses belong to the myths of old Aithe, brought here by the Builders. Aldus had told him the image she projected in the oracle was an illusion to give the faithful a focus.

His mind rolled around the well-worn thought patterns of his upbringing. He hadn't meant she wasn't real; she was, but only in a spiritual sense, not flesh and blood real. Tentatively, he opened one eye. She was still there. The mouth in the exquisite face formed words. Words reached his ears.

"A first portal experience is often disorienting, but we had no time to prepare you. Come, sit with me. We have much to discuss."

Though he would have liked to test her reality, he couldn't bring himself to reach out and touch her. Averting his eyes, he hoisted himself up onto his elbows, then to a sitting position.

"There is no need to fear me, Willard. I won't hurt you. I need you."

Entranced by the cadence of her voice, Willard, only slightly reassured, forced himself to look up, but instantly shied away. The physical presence of the Goddess was too much to deal with. The details, however, remained etched on his retinas, the wavy golden hair that danced around her shoulders, the perfect unblemished face and the dazzling eyes that drew him against his will.

Fascinated by the intensity of her eyes, he watched them change colours independently, flashing rapidly through every combination he had ever seen, his own, Averil's, Ob Walker's, Hedley, server Tomas and then on through iridescent colours he could never have imagined. They stopped at deep brown, almost black. Willard blinked. Kezia's eyes.

"That's better. Now that I have your attention, tell me why you, my most promising candidate, have not sought my advice?"

Acutely aware the Goddess was waiting for an answer Willard remained mute, awed by a presence, so much more alive than the image that had greeted him in the Ob's Audience Room.

"Where am I?" he asked again.

"It is difficult to explain to an untested candidate, but let me assure you, this is not a dream. All you see and feel is quite real."

Willard felt too bewildered to reply.

"I'm glad Averil wasn't this reticent. We sorted out ..."

"What did you tell her?" Willard exclaimed, her jibe breaking his trance. He trembled immediately afterward, expecting the Goddess to strike him down.

"The truth. I want her to have your offspring."

Willard's mind whirled. It was true. She'd spoken to Averil. *The plans for us that Averil mentioned. How can Averil and I have children when I'm oathed to Kezia?*

The Goddess seemed to read his mind. "You do not need to marry Averil. You need not even have sex with her if that offends you. If you would trust me like your mother did. I could ..."

"Inseminate me ... I mean her, Averil ... inseminate Averil."

Once again, Willard had interrupted the Goddess, the words escaping as soon as she triggered them. *I'm as bad as Averil*, he thought, but once started he couldn't help himself; he needed to know.

"What have you done with Kezia?"

"I am assisting Kezia to follow a path of her own choosing."

"But you know where she is."

"Yes."

"Then where?"

"Take the test and you will know."

Take the test to find her and if I haven't already lost her, I will when I pass it. Severne's words that Kezia was following a path of her own choosing troubled him.

"Who is my father?" he said, trying another tack.

"Ah, so Eliza has told you that Arthur is not. Does that bother you?"

The response showed the Goddess hadn't known his mother had told him. It made her seem less Goddess-like. He felt the beginnings of panic. So many beliefs had crumbled in the last few days. He wondered if he was going insane. He shrank back as the Goddess rose and walked towards him. She stopped and crouched before him, so close he fancied he could feel her scented breath.

"Not everything you believed is untrue. You, of all my candidates must learn to trust me. You must understand and come to believe that my plan for you will benefit us all."

Her statement had the opposite effect. It convinced Willard that Ob Walker had shoved him into a secret room in the servatory complex, with someone pretending to be the Goddess. Not a bad performance, but she wasn't fooling him. He scanned the big room with its gently curving blue floor and found the Arch through which he had come.

"Then why not answer my questions?"

"I would if I thought you could comprehend the answers. You could be the one. You have the blood of the Builders in you."

"The real reason is you don't know," Willard said, emboldened by the realisation this Goddess wasn't real. She sounded just like Hedley. It's all an elaborate tower hoax, he thought, Ob Walker's magic-show.

"You're a fake. If I'm the one, why do you need my offspring?" he asked, pleased to have spotted a flaw in her argument.

"Nothing is certain. I cannot predict the future. I project likely outcomes by studying past and present information."

That was enough for Willard. The idea struck him he could use this imposter as a hostage to bargain his way back past the Ob server and deal with the treacherous Sev Miller. He reached out to grab her wrist and his fingers closed into a fist right through her. In disbelief, he tried to grasp her by the shoulders. His hands banged together through her breasts.

Willard almost screamed.

The Goddess seemed amused at his shock. "So many have lost faith. I have only my powers of persuasion, occasionally backed by a warrior, to sustain my search for a host. Are you not yet convinced I am who I say I am?"

Willard sat open-mouthed. He had never felt so stupid. She must be the Goddess but she can't be the Goddess. At least not the Goddess he had grown up with, unapproachable, aloof, remote, dispensing wisdom and foretelling futures through her servers. This Goddess was, in an extraordinary way, too ordinary,

"I think," she said quietly, "it would be best if we saved our discussion until after you've rested."

"Yes, Lady," he replied, head bowed. He felt mentally exhausted. "That would be best." He was thankful that when he looked up, she had gone.

· · · ·

Willard woke in fright, not knowing where he was. He had dreamed, of going to the abode of the Goddess, the otherworld, a strange bowl like world with soft blue grass and giant people-swallowing rocks, of walking through the Goddess and merging with her as expected of the Man Who Will Be Face.

Opening his eyes made it real. It wasn't a dream. He was lying where he had fallen, sat talking with the Goddess, then fallen back, asleep almost instantly. Hesitantly, he sat up and moved to a teardrop bag, softly textured like the blue matting. He went to sit on it and instantly jumped to his feet again when it tried to mould itself around him.

His thoughts circled around last night's startling interview with the Goddess, assuming it was last night. He knew he had slept and woken, yet he didn't know how long. It was dusk when the Ob pushed him through the arch thing. The long room's windows seemed to be in the ceiling. Oblongs of some paper like material that let in the light. At least he knew it was daytime. Or was it? The light didn't look quite right. It was too even. More aithcraft, more Goddess illusion. Damn, I can't even assume it's a new day.

After a while, the functions of one item became apparent, a water spigot over a shiny bowl, set in a recess. Once he understood its purpose, like the boulder chair he sat on, the items were less threatening. What he couldn't identify was a toilet, to ease a desperate need.

"Finding an interface is taking longer than I anticipated."

Willard spun to confront his Goddess. She had dressed in a loose, flowing silvery gown that hid little. His gaze shied away in embarrassment. At the back of his mind, under the turmoil, he wondered what she had meant by finding an Inner Face. Surely, the candidate who passes will be the Outer Face of the Goddess.

The room you need is through the opening a few feet from the water fountain. What opening, he thought, looking around at the spigot and seeing that an opening had appeared in the previously blank wall.

· · · ·

"Time is running out Willard," the Goddess said, on his return, much relieved. "Are you ready to be tested?"

Willard swallowed hard and did not look up. "What choice do I have?" he muttered, curious that she had phrased it as a question. Who was he to deny the Goddess?

Severne exhaled softly. "Your attitude saddens me. It demonstrates that some I have empowered to instruct candidates have distorted my message. Let me set the record straight. The deciding test will test your faith. It is essential that you choose to take it willingly and whole-heartedly. You must have absolute certitude. Any doubt, no matter how small, even an unconscious hesitancy, will spell failure. Is that now clear?"

Willard's eyes had glazed over, trying to extract meaning from the words swirling in his mind. He felt he was missing something vital, but what?

The Goddess had stopped. He refocussed and she continued. "I need help to save New Earth, but I see that despite Hedley's teachings you are unconvinced. Lamentably, it appears as if the twin characteristics I require are incompatible. I need someone of both high intelligence and strong faith, sufficient to see the necessity and then surrender their will to achieve it. My expectations of you, Willard, remain high, but the choice must be yours."

Fascinated, Willard asked, "What do you mean surrender their will?"

"If you pass the Test of Faith, we will be one. Together, we can accomplish what neither can do alone. Will you at least allow me to test your reason?"

Willard shook his head in frightened wonderment. "What happens to me if we become one?"

Severne was silent for several seconds as if she hadn't heard. "I don't know. If it had been done, you would not be here."

Willard was not the least encouraged. The Goddess didn't know something, hadn't done something, yet still demanded his absolute conviction. He found it impossible to have faith in a flawed Goddess, let alone one who killed to get what she wanted. There were no answers for him here. If she would not tell him where Kezia was, or who his father was, he may as well go back and make the best of the world he knew.

Thank Goddess ... he stopped. Why was he thanking her? The phrase was automatic, part of the language. Everyone said it, mostly with no real meaning. The expression now irked him. He had absolutely nothing to thank her for. Time to rid himself of the expression. He began backing away from her towards the Arch. In an eye-blink, the Goddess vanished.

"I take it, your answer is no," her voice said in his ear. He spun, then snatched his hand away when he saw it was inside her left thigh.

"Yes ... my answer is no. I'm not ready to give up on life. I've hardly had one yet. I'm going after Kezia, even if I have to go all the way to the Wall."

"I am disappointed, Willard, but the choice really is yours. I will do all I can to keep you safe while I try to change your mind. The Wall is a dangerous place. At least take a talisman." With a nod, she indicated a wall recess next to the Arch. Shiny rainbow hued cards dangled from several hooks in the niche. "Use it at any of my towers or shrines whenever you need me."

Humouring her might make leaving less of a problem. He carefully lifted a talisman from its hook. He looked at the iridescent oblong with awe. He never imagined he might get one without taking the test. It crystallised the realisation that he was, as his mother had always said, special. That sent a shudder through him. Special was the trap he wanted to extricate himself from.

He would still need to get past Ob Walker and out of the servatory complex. The possession of a talisman would help. Briefly, it crossed his mind that, in giving him the talisman, the Goddess might not be helping him, but he couldn't see how it could further her plan.

"Give my test some thought, Willard. I await your return."

The Goddess vanished, leaving Willard staring at the replica Arch. If return was a prediction, Willard felt confident in it being wrong. He had no intention of ever returning. After one last look at the strange pastel abode of the Goddess, as he vowed to get Kezia back, or die trying, Willard grasped the talisman, closed his eyes, and stepped back through the incredible blackness.

He shivered at the thought of what the aithcraft might have done to him in transition and from the cold of this new place, not the Ob's Audience Chamber but similar. He turned back to the arch ready to step through and demand the Goddess return him home. He found that on this side the arch was a rectangle, like an ordinary doorway, and he could see straight through it to the wall behind. The blackness was gone. He walked through, knowing nothing would happen and nothing did. When he thought about it, he was glad it hadn't. He didn't really want another confrontation with the Goddess, or Ob Walker.

Well mother, he thought, as he surveyed the room, I went to the Ob and look where it got me. "Is anyone there?" he croaked. His throat was dry and his stomach ached. He hadn't used the Goddess' water fountain, and she hadn't fed him. He felt as if he hadn't eaten in days.

The room remained silent. No one came to either greet him or challenge him.

Willard looked down at the talisman. Its edges and the chain had left deep indents in his palm. He placed the chain over his head so it hung down his chest inside his shirt, turned stepped off the raised platform on which this rectangular arch stood. Seeing it worried him. Straight lines and square corners had no place in the builder architecture familiar to him.

Wherever this servatory was, it was also less active, almost quiet, and probably a long way from home, perhaps beyond the Wall in feral territory. Yet for all he knew, he could be in the room next to the Ob's audience room, or still in Severne's Eye, just a different room from the one he left. He had to get out of the building to see where she had sent him. Until he knew that, it was pointless to make any definite plans. He headed for the shimmering section of the transparent wall. Beyond it, the corridor was empty.

This time, he kept his eyes open as he stepped through. He wished he hadn't. Solid darkness greeted him. Oh shit, it's made me blind, he thought, snarling at himself for being so stupid. I should have known there was a reason the Ob shouted, 'close your eyes'. Then his eyes adjusted and he saw to his relief he was in the corridor as expected. His exit must have somehow turned off all the lights in the room he'd left. What light remained filtered down through dust and cobwebs from a hole in the ceiling. With a fright, he realised the corridor he had viewed from inside had not been real. Aithcraft in the walls had provided an illusion. What strange people the Builders had been, only seeing what they wanted to see.

In the actual corridor, small, unseen things scurried away at his feet across a rubble strewn floor. Willard found it sad that this once great builder servatory was falling into ruin. He picked his way through the rubble toward the shaft of light falling from the ceiling. Aldus was wrong. As contradictory as it sounded, the Goddess existed, but she wasn't real. As he sneezed on the dust he kicked up, he imagined the ensuing argument when he ... except he couldn't. Aldus was dead.

Willard suddenly choked up with more than dust. He wiped his eyes with the back of his hand and spat. "Bloody ferals," he'd thought after discovering Aldus' corpse had no head until he realised decapitation was also how warriors carried out executions. Back then, he had thought Aldus' server baiting might have got him killed, but what if the Goddess had another reason—to kick start him on this journey? That was a thought he refused to think.

Reaching the pool of light, Willard looked up, squinting at a patch of bright blue. A fringe of grass softened the hole's ragged edge. Now and again a gust of cold of fresh air seeped through with the light. It smelt of home. Perhaps she had sent him back to a servatory buried under Deep Creek? He shook his head, knowing it was beefshit. To get out of this, he would have to think, not wish.

The hole, though small, was probably wide enough to crawl through if he could reach it. He needed something to stand on or another way out. He looked away, closing his eyes for a while to readjust to the dark. Dimly he saw closed doors at the end of the corridor and two sets of tracks in the dust, two people going to them and one coming back. The sweeping pattern in the dust showed the doors did open and had done so recently, but when he tried them, they refused to budge. For all the apparent disrepair, the doors were so solid all he got was a bruised shoulder. At the side of the door was a pedestal, its small square top covered in dust. It would give him the boost he needed if he could drag it back under the hole. Like the doors, it refused to budge.

After a time, he gave up the struggle and slumped down the wall. He was tired now, as well as hungry, and so parched by his exertion, he could feel tiny cracks in his lips. He might have to go back after all. He was silently cursing the Goddess for dumping him here, and trying to scratch an itch on his chest, when he found the talisman.

Idiot, he thought, laughing at himself. Then he remembered Ob Walker had used it 'out of habit' to enter the Audience Chamber because servers needed to. The talisman I have might only be for servers. He tried to remember all the Ob had done.

The cloud of dust he blew off the pedestal made him cough and stung his eyes. He waved it away with impatience. Etched out of the top, he found a rectangular indentation with rounded corners that matched the talisman. He took it from around his neck, folded the cord on top, and laid it in the inset. Something clicked.

"Yes!"

With a powerful hum, the doors parted and swung inward, renewing the twin arcs swept out in the dust and debris. Light and air flooded into the corridor from an empty-looking landscape.

Chapter 13

Kezia was as glad to see the last of Woodbridge as she had Deep Creek. She wondered why people around her so often ended hurt? She didn't start out to hurt anyone. At least this one had ended better.

She had stayed at the hospital with her patient - the Watcher called Wesley, to monitor what the staff called his remarkable recovery. Her polite refusal to reveal her healing methods the Woodbridge locals took for modesty. They called it a miracle, and her, a Goddess inspired healer. Together with Howard's continued insistence that servers treat her with the same deference as they did him, had forged a solid link between her and the Goddess. That linking was what made Kezia eager to move on.

Away from Woodbridge Kezia promised herself, she would stick close to Howard from now on. The world at large was so much more dangerous than Deep Creek. She didn't want a repeat of the beating she had before he turned up.

In late afternoon they topped the last bridge over the Wanetta River and Kezia caught a glimpse of Rivers Junction. At first glance, it appeared to be on an island, but a second look showed it to be a bulging peninsular between the Wanetta and the Aldgate. North of the town the rivers came close, but didn't meet. As usual, Our Lady's Tower stood on the highest hill and dominated the town. Kezia looked away.

The town square, festooned as it was with colourful awnings, told her it was Marketday. This time last week, she had just said goodbye to Willard and was heading to Walker to join Medicorps. So much had changed, not the least being her decision to abandon her assigned unit.

"Has the contingent passed yet?" she asked Howard.

"Two days ago," Howard said after briefly tilting his head, no doubt consulting with Our Lady.

Good, Kezia thought, I'm safe.

Howard, as was his preference, went straight for the tower. Kezia would have preferred a pub. She dismounted at the Public Gate and Howard had a trembling acolyte stabled *Providence*. Kezia kept close behind him as they entered and he introduced her to Ser Lyman. The moment her eyes adjusted to the gloom a sense of déjà vu overwhelmed her. She clutched Howard's arm for support as she cast a quick glance over her shoulder to a reassuringly different view out through the Public Arch.

"What is it?" asked Howard.

"Nothing," she replied, not wanting to discuss her fears of a forced return to Deep Creek. "The foyer's familiarity disoriented me. For a moment, I thought I was back in Deep Creek. Are all her towers identical?" she asked. When the apparently preoccupied server did not reply, Howard prompted him.

"Well, Ser Lyman?"

"Pardon?" The Sever glanced up and focussed on the Warrior, frown lines on his forehead.

"Healer Jena asked you a question. It would be polite to reply."

Ser Lyman blushed, "Sorry Jena." Then his eyes widened. "Our Lady's healer?"

Kezia blinked. How had the rumours beaten them here?

"Er ... sorry Healer, what was the question?"

"Are all the towers identical?" Kezia repeated.

"Oh ... not really, but there are quite a few like this, scattered around the country." Ser Lyman said, his speech halting, as if he constantly lost the thread of what he wanted to say. "The ... er ... layout is basically the same, though the details may vary."

It intrigued Kezia to see him constantly glance at Howard, as if expecting contradiction. She hadn't thought of the warriors as tower experts. Nor had she thought of warriors having friends, despite what Howard had told her. Ingrained beliefs nurtured by her mother said warriors brought only death. Perhaps Ser Lyman was wondering who of his flock was about to die.

"St. John's in Grundston, as one might expect, is ... er ... much larger. It has five oracles I'm told." He paused and absently rubbed his hands together. "This way warrior ... and um ... Jena."

Kezia almost looked around for an extra person before remembering she was Jena. Answering to Jena would be as important as not answering to Kezia.

The server turned to the acolyte who had stabled *Providence* and clipped him behind the ear. "Well, don't just stand there, Willard. Pick up the healer's belongings. We haven't got all day."

Kezia blanched so much anguish in that name. She diverted her thoughts by repeating her new mantra. I'm Jena, Jena Setler, healer. The torment she had felt at Woodbridge, which had faded with distance, returned. I'm a healer who will slash you if you get too close.

Ser Lyman led them straight past the stairwell, between a pair of folding screens, and around to the back of the tower's central column to Parson's arch, which was not an arch at all, but a locked door. Priest's Arch, Aldus would have called it. She missed Aldus's ability to make her laugh.

Ser Lyman passed his talisman across a panel on the column wall and an oblong section parted to reveal an empty closet-sized room.

"You can leave us now Ser Lyman. Healer Jena needs rest. She has had a harrowing few days."

"Um ... yes, warrior, I have had rooms prepared for you and ... um, your companion." Ser Lyman swallowed, "Level Two."

Kezia glanced at Howard. Unlike Woodbridge, Rivers Junction had expected a warrior and companion. In Ser Lyman's manner, however, Kezia sensed an undercurrent to his preparations and in his calling her companion.

As if privy to her thoughts, Howard said, "My friend is to be addressed as Jena or by her title Healer. She is beloved of Our Lady."

Kezia wished he'd left out 'beloved of Our Lady'. She was suddenly full of questions but constrained by Ser Lyman's presence.

"Of course, warrior, we had heard. I meant no offence," Lyman replied, bowing. "Would either of you care for some refreshment before you ... retire?"

Howard caught Kezia's gaze and shook his head slightly.

She took the hint. "No, thank you, Ser Lyman," she replied with as much authority as she could muster.

Howard and Lyman stared at each other, a contest of wills which excluded and alarmed her. That servers had failed as warriors did not explain the interactions she was watching. She was out of her depth with these two. Ser Lyman was no more afraid for his head than Woodbridge's Ser Hagen had been. Perhaps warriors visited towers all the time, perhaps even in Deep Creek, and we just never heard about it.

Lyman broke first and hurried away.

Howard ushered her into the closet and turned to face the doors. Kezia followed his example. "The ancients called this a lift," he said. "It will take us up to our room." He pushed a small roundel, one of six, set vertically in a panel by the door.

The doors shut by themselves reminding Kezia of Mother's refuge. The instant they clicked together; the lift jerked upwards.

"My apologies Jena. I suspect the headgear needs oiling. Our Lady trains all servers in tower maintenance; some do it better than others."

As the lift rose past the closed doors, Kezia's eyes came level with the floor above. Then she was looking across a magnificent rug at the legs of a bed and still rising. It made her feel woozy.

Howard steadied her. "I should have warned you; this tower's lift is open above the foyer."

As he was speaking, the lift floor came perfectly level with the room's floor and stopped. Kezia remained focussed on the bed, which appeared luxurious and inviting. She surmised it was probably better than she could have got in the pub, and free. It irked her how well servers lived. She could have been a server's wife; except as she now knew, with eyes that different, Willard would not have failed the test.

"Do all towers contain such marvels?" Kezia asked.

"Yes and no," Howard said as she stepped hesitantly into the room.

"What does yes and no mean?" Kezia asked.

"All towers contain what you call marvels, but not always the same marvels. We make repairs where we can. In the past we used to install new artefacts, and get them working, but that hasn't happened in a long time."

"We?" asked Kezia.

"The Brotherhood of Restoration Warriors, my brethren," Howard said proudly, as if he had been with them for years. Perhaps he has, thought Kezia, in a surrogate way. The test was supposed to confer great knowledge. Perhaps it also gave them shared experiences, a communal consciousness.

He reached out, gently grabbed Kezia's hands, and spoke to her as she might to dying patient, full of earnest intent. "The main purpose of Our Lady's Towers is to sift acolytes and prepare them for the test. Only finding her a Face will allow the Goddess to return to us, restore the full power of the Builders and stop a repetition of the Days of Fire."

Howard suddenly stopped talking and tightened his grip.

Kezia recoiled. He was staring straight at her, but his gaze had no focus. The furrowed lines across his brow and between his eyes deepened, giving him an expression of either pain or malice. Frightened, Kezia tried to withdraw her hands, but his grip held firm.

"Yes, Lady," he said.

It seemed to Kezia his mind abruptly snapped back to the present and looked out at her. This scared her more than his vacant look.

He squeezed her hands again, gently this time. "As we suspected, Ser Lyman has broken faith. We must leave."

"But we just got here. I'm tired."

"Quick. Take the lift, hold your finger on the top button, and don't let go until after you step out at the top," he said, pointing to the ceiling, turning her around, picking up her pack and thrusting it at her.

"What about you?"

"Now," he shouted at her.

"No need to shout," she shouted back, as she pushed and held the top roundel, assuming that was what he meant by button. The last she saw before her head broached the ceiling was Howard drawing *Firebolt,* the gem in the hilt pulsing yellow.

The lift jerked as it ascended through the next room, fortunately empty, and kept going. Shouts reached her from below. How many more, Kezia wondered as they passed through the next empty level, gawking in wonderment at each room. One floor, full of working artefacts, that rivalled mother's horde.

Her finger was getting sore, but she dared not let go, despite not knowing what might happen if she did. She might not trust the Goddess but she trusted Howard. The floor of the next room Kezia breached was in semi-darkness. She could see stars; she must have reached the top. Cold air struck her as she ascended further. A wide-eyed Acolyte Willard stood against an open lattice wall, arms in the air as if surrendering.

"What do I do now?" she said to herself.

"Hold on until you get out," the acolyte said.

The lift stopped as he spoke and Kezia twisted around so she could step out. Her fingers slipped as she was twisting and the lift started going down.

"Jump," Acolyte Willard said, and reached out both hands as Kezia jumped, grabbing the outstretch hands. The acolyte pulled her forward. Her shins hit the edge. Searing pain exploded in her head as the acolyte fell to a sitting position against the lattice, still holding her hands.

"Pull your feet up," he screamed, and the terror on his face frightened her into instant compliance. Seconds later, as she looked back, the top of the lift dropped past within inches of her shoes. Kezia stared at the rattling cables in horror. But for the young acolyte named Willard, the lift would have taken her feet off.

The lift descending left a trembling Kezia, in shock and pain, trapped amongst Severne's ears on the summit of the Rivers Junction Tower, in the company of a brave but scared acolyte. She closed her eyes and took several calming breaths, willing her trembling to stop. Then she turned to the acolyte. "Thank you, Willard," she said, the familiar name bitter on her tongue.

The acolyte seemed pleased she had remembered his name but said nothing and didn't move, simply watched her. Opening her pack, Kezia retrieved a jar and sprinkled a pinch of Mother's healing dust. The pain in her weeping shins eased. As she forced herself to stand, the rattling of the lift cables paused. Whatever was going on below was beyond her control. She and young Willard would have to wait on Howard.

After helping the lad to his feet, she looked around her elevated cage. The summit was circular, about fifteen feet in diameter, surrounded by a metal-like lattice. The lattice held several outward facing ears of the Goddess. The structure whistled in the bitter breeze. This close, the scale of the bowl-shaped ears became apparent. They were twice as wide as her height. Thick black cords ran from the centre of each into holes in the floor's perimeter. Seeing the details disturbed Kezia, it demystified the sacred, reduced part of Our Lady's mystique to nothing more than a working builder artefact. It irked her even more that this lost ignorance was irrevocable. The cables rattled again. Kezia shivered with the thought that this day, already long, showed no sign of ending.

"I guess we just have to wait now ... Willard," she told the acolyte.

As the top of the lift poked above the floor, Kezia stepped in front of young Willard, determined to protect him. It was a relief to see Howard's head appear. The acolyte raised his arms again, his eyes fixed on the gemmed hilt in the warrior's hand.

Howard, his finger still on the button, dumped a large sack on the roof, then raised Firebolt. The gem glowed red and lightning crackled along its edge. He let go the button and stepped back. As the lift descended, *Firebolt's* tip touched its control panel. Kezia's eyes recovering from the blinding flash, saw the lift had stopped and acrid smoke emanated from where the control panel had been.

Howard stepped up out of the lift. "Locked," he said, as he coiled a shiny rope he had withdrawn from the bag.

"Put your arms down, he won't hurt you," Kezia told young Willard as one set of fears replaced another. "You won't hurt him, will you Howard?"

The warrior looked up and shook his head.

Behind him, Kezia saw a prayer-bowl with its back open, revealing a compartment stacked with unknown objects. Howard withdrew several, placed them on the coil, and closed the compartment. Kezia blinked. The back of the bowl now looked no different from any of the others. As with the door to mother's refuge, any sign of an opening had vanished. aithcraft, thought Kezia, and turned away, focussing her attention on the young acolyte.

"What were you doing up here, Willard?" she asked.

The boy looked down.

Howard answered for him. "Lyman sent him up to spy on us. The outside emergency ladder runs past our window."

The boy nodded. Kezia quailed at two thoughts, one that this boy had climbed up the outside of the tower and two that she might have to climb down it. "Have you been in the tower long?" she asked.

"Only this year, Healer," the boy replied. Her manner had relaxed him. He now looked at her instead of maintaining his fixation on Howard. "Arch Server Barclay is training me for the test," he said with pride.

Kezia cast a glance at Howard. "Really? I didn't know you could train for it. I thought you had to be born to it."

The warrior paused, stepped down off the framework, and looked sharply at the acolyte. The acolyte cringed under the intense stare. "Training you how?" he asked, cocking his head to one side, an attitude Kezia now associated with him listening to the Goddess, or perhaps letting her review what he was hearing.

The acolyte turned and parted his locks to reveal two cleanly shaved circles on the back of his skull.

"Our Lady thanks you," Howard told Kezia. "Your simple question has exposed Sev Barclay's purpose and method."

Kezia was none the wiser.

"You will come with us, Willard. Our Lady has need of you," Howard said.

The boy nodded in awe as the warrior threw the coiled thread out into the darkness. Kezia couldn't help noticing the two small circles of pale scar tissue on Howard's newly balding head. Easy when you knew what to look for. She had no time to wonder further. Faint sounds of hammering floated up from below. The lift jumped and buckled. Alarmed, Kezia looked at Howard, shocked to see him ruffled.

"You will pay for this," he roared, and the hammering stopped.

Both Kezia and the young acolyte backed away.

With visible effort, or maybe help from above, Howard calmed himself. "Let's go. I must get you two to safety."

"How?" asked Kezia, already dreading the answer?

"Up here," Howard answered.

He climbed the lattice framework that supported the Petitioning Bowls then sat astride it and helped her up.

The view was spectacular even by the limited illumination of starlight, the town below defined by twin strips of warm yellow lights.

Fascinated and appalled, Kezia looked at the slim, taut thread tied around a bowl support. Her eyes followed it out and down into the darkness until it disappeared. She judged it would reach the ground at the ghostly line of trees, well beyond the familiar path around the tower's perimeter wall. How did he secure the other end? Aithcraft? No, an accomplice was more likely. Another warrior would be too much.

"Don't look down," Howard said as he clipped a small buckle over the thread. A leather loop dangled from the buckle.

Kezia stepped back to the roof. "Oh no, I'm not sliding down that. I'll take my chances with the server."

"He will kill you," Howard stated flatly.

"So will the fall from that."

"This wire is builder material. It won't break and the slope is not steep."

"For you maybe."

"It will be almost horizontal for half the journey, still fast but controlled by an automatic brake on the pulley wheel. Even if you let go ..."

"Why will he kill me? I'm beloved of the Goddess you said," interrupted Kezia and stepped down to the tower roof.

"Lyman is in thrall to Sev Barclay and you know too much," Howard replied, indicating the acolyte.

"But you're here," Kezia snapped, scared, and not just at jumping off a hundred-foot tower suspended by a simple hand strap on a slender thread. What scared her more was that the highest authorities in the land, both claiming to be servants of the Goddess, had turned on each other. Scarier still, Our Lady's much-feared Restoration Warrior wanted to avoid the confrontation.

"What kind of warrior are you? Why don't you stand and fight? Why aren't you using that?" She pointed to the sword, now back in its scabbard, across his back. Even without Goddess power, *Firebolt* looked like a formidable weapon.

"Despite the damage Ser Lyman is doing he is not the problem. Sev Barclay holds his wife and candidate son hostage. We can't afford to lose either of them. Now come on."

"I'll go first," young Willard said into the tense silence.

"Good lad," Howard said as he helped him up. "Put one hand through the strap and grab it above, then your other hand here." He demonstrated, cupping his hand over the top of the buckle. "That's it, well done."

Acolyte Willard beamed.

"When you stop at the bottom, support your weight with the hand on the buckle, then you can slip out of strap and drop off. Your height and weight will put you about four feet off the ground. Now go."

The acolyte's legs bent at the knees as his hands pushed forward out over the abyss. Then, with a rasping hiss from the buckle, his feet left the rail and he was gone, falling away at speed, into the starlit night.

Bloody little show off, thought Kezia.

"Now you," Howard said gently, as he clipped another hand strap to its buckle.

Kezia stepped up without a word, slipped her hand in, gripped the strap as Howard had shown, put her other hand on the top of the buckle, closed her eyes and jumped.

She wobbled for a second or two before acceleration took hold. Then she was flying. Her hair streamed back from her face. She held on desperately as the rush made her stomach lurch. She was travelling horizontally before she looked. Her immediate reaction was fright. She was hurtling towards a giant tree. The hand on the buckle came free. An instant later, she was glad her other hand remained trapped. The ground was still twenty feet below and she was spinning. Frantically she tried to re-grab the buckle, but her hand closed over the wire. She screamed with pain at the sudden loss of several layers of skin across her palm, even as the slope reversed and she slowed. A jerk on the wire as she stopped told her Howard had started down. *Oh shit, he'll slam into me and crush me against the tree.*

"Let go healer."

The voice of the acolyte came to her out of the darkness and she nearly kicked him in the stomach when he grabbed her legs to hold her steady.

"Free hand on top," he whispered, and she felt an uncharitable urge to throttle the brat.

"I can't I've hurt my hand," she said but already the fire was gone from her palm; her shin treatment. As she went to reach up, Howard suddenly loomed out of the darkness and lights came on around the tower. Kezia, mentally prepared for a crushing blow, as she freed her hand from the strap and dropped to the ground as Howard pelted past, using the tree to end his run. In his hand was a small, bent rod.

Good Lady, he came down on that. Even as she admired the feat, it dismayed Kezia to note the acolyte looked at Howard with adoration.

"I want to be a warrior," he said.

"Why are you still here?" Howard asked urgently, helping her to her feet. "We have to run."

"Run where?"

"Over here," a voice called from the darkness and Kezia whirled. She could just make out two horses standing in the shadow of overhanging branches. The voice came from the person leading them, the Watcher she had slashed in Woodbridge; Wesley someone. *Providence* nudged her affectionately.

"Hey, I wasn't expecting two," Wesley said.

"Only Healer Jena is going with you. Our Lady needs Willard and I elsewhere."

"You're not taking him back to ..." Kezia stopped, unable to voice what she was thinking. You can't let him watch an execution.

"I'm taking him to Woodbridge," Howard said. He looked at Kezia with what she thought was amusement, though in the dark it was hard to tell. "Our Lady's justice will soon catch up with Sev Barclay but not today and not by me."

It mollified Kezia to see Howard get down on one knee to look acolyte Willard in the eye. "Do you accept Our Lady's plan for you, Willard?"

The acolyte looked briefly up at Kezia who remained blank. She had no wish to encourage another Willard down that path, but unlike hers, this Willard immediately agreed, grinning, and nodding vigorously.

Howard stepped past him and overwhelmed Kezia with a crushing hug. Severne's eye, she thought, he's almost human sometimes.

He took the boy Willard's hand and spoke to Wesley. "Healer Jena Setler is beloved of Our Lady, take care of her. I suggest you bypass Aldgate Bend and wait for me in Fishmarket." Howard and young Willard then faded into the night, the acolyte struggling to keep up.

Though Kezia said nothing, the remark had angered her. In the guise of care, at the behest of the Goddess, one man had just passed her off like a package to another man. While they arranged her future, Kezia decided she had had enough. She sent a mental apology to Willard, her Willard. His rejection of Our Lady's plan now made sense to her. She could feel the Goddess, through Howard, usurping her newly won freedom. To the Eye with that, she would find a way out even if it killed her.

She and Wesley were soon at the neck where the rivers almost met. The checkpoint was not on alert and Wesley's

Watcher uniform easily secured them passage through the grinning militia. Kezia was pensive. She hadn't known towns needed checkpoints, or that ex-Watcher could stay Watcher when they joined the militia. Nor had she known it seemed normal for a man of the Watcher, accompanied by a young woman, to ride out of town in the middle of the night.

Apparently, she knew very little about anything.

Hours later, when she looked back the way they had come, there was no sound of pursuit, nothing but the dark grey road winding through open-canopied trees, black silhouettes against innumerable stars. Severne's Eye was not among them. Probably the wrong hour, thought Kezia. Timing of the Eye's transit was just one more thing she didn't know.

Her unease about Wesley, a man she nearly killed, a man she knew nothing about except that Howard trusted him, matched her anger at Howard for handing her over. Her level of ignorance continued to appal her, but for the moment she would trust Wesley because despite everything, she trusted Howard, although now she no longer liked him.

Lulled by the soft rhythmic tattoo of hooves clopping along the road, Kezia nodded off several times. Her head falling forward brought her awake again. She could see no reason they shouldn't stop now that they were well away from Rivers Junction, except that Wesley seemed disinclined. She shook her head and blinked rapidly, trying to dispel her tiredness. Seconds later, she again dozed off and this time, did not rouse. The gentle movement gradually shifted her balance and she felt herself slip sideways. An arm snaked out and pushed her upright.

"Time to stop, Jena," said Wesley.

Kezia looked up at him with relief and dismounted stiffly. Thanks to Howard, Wesley accepted her completely as Jena Setler, a healer beloved of Our Lady. They walked the horses up a slight incline away from both the road and the river and made camp. Wesley scoured the immediate area for fallen branches and leaves and soon had a small fire going in a pit scraped in the earth with a folding spade. He had come fully prepared. Incredible, she thought. Why doesn't he hate me? Guilt prompted her to ask.

"How's your arm?"

"The scar itches, but it is healing well, thank you," he replied from the darkness.

"How can you thank me? I nearly killed you?"

"Were you trying to?"

"Well, no, but ..."

"Warrior Howard told me I have your great healing powers to thank for my life. So I thank you."

He said this with such earnest conviction she did not doubt him. "But if I hadn't slashed you, you wouldn't have needed healing."

"If?" he questioned. "If Bramwell hadn't reported the horse stolen, if I hadn't arrested you, if you had been less scared," he paused, took a breath, "if the warrior had come sooner, or with you. If, is a dangerous word."

Kezia knew he was right. She had already played that game with the events that put her here. She lay back against the tree and watched him fill a pannikin with water from his saddlebag.

With his hair pulled back to form a club and his dark skin he seemed alien, almost feral, but handsome, and kind of exotic.

"Where are you from, Wesley?"

He turned from adding tea to the boiling water, his face barely discernible in the flickering shadows except for the glint from his eyes. "Woodbridge," he said, handing her a pannikin of tea.

Kezia sipped it gratefully, feeling the warmth course down her throat. "I meant, where were you born?" she asked, stifling a yawn.

"I don't know. My first memories of growing up were in a Canalbridge orphanage."

"You're a long way from home."

The only thing Kezia knew about Canalbridge was it was close to the Wall. Her eyelids drooped even as Wesley answered. She snapped them open, took a big sip, and tried to pay attention.

"I guess so. I never considered the orphanage as home."

Kezia took another sip of tea, then placed the pannikin carefully on the ground, too tired to continue.

"Goodnight Wesley."

"And you, Jena," he replied softly. She liked the way he said her new name.

Chapter 14

Averil reached Sandbank a day early to find Gardner already there. Bastard. He rowed her across the Meander River, rowed back to return the boat then swam across to join her. He made it look so easy. She promised herself she would learn to swim as soon as she had the time.

The reason for her journey soon faded into the daily ritual: walk, eat, and sleep. They stopped each evening at dusk for a hot meal. Gardner would prepare some small animal Averil had caught, rabbit possum or small kangaroo, expertly eviscerating the carcass and paring back the skin. Averil meanwhile tended the fire steaming the edible plants Gardner had gathered, few of which she recognised. According to Gardner, they were the wild descendants of once cultivated crops.

In the mornings, Averil, wrapped in the soft waterproof builder blanket Gardner had lent her, would wake to delicious aromas. She would open her eyes to see Gardner hunched over a steaming cup of his seemingly inexhaustible supply of fresh coffee. A second cup would stand on a flat stone next to a small fire. No matter how hard she tried, he always rose before her and had breakfast ready. She wondered when he found time to sleep.

What a pity warriors didn't marry. If ever she trusted men again, he was the sort of man she might consider—resourceful and excellent company. Around the nightly fire, they engaged in interesting, sometimes frightening, conversations.

"Won't you be in trouble when you get back?" Averil asked one night.

Gardner replied without looking up from the rabbit roasting on the fire. "Why would I be in trouble? And back where?"

"For helping me when you report back to your servatory." Averil wasn't sure of her ground here. She just assumed the warriors had to be based somewhere; a servatory seemed the natural choice.

"We report to Our Lady not the tower."

"But you've seen what the towers are saying, my crimes against the Goddess." Even as she said this, she knew the Goddess didn't think so or she wouldn't have had him choose me over the pilot.

"Yes and no," Gardner said, removing the rabbit from the fire, tearing off a hind leg and handing it to her on a small tin plate. It was hot, juicy, and smelled delicious from the aromatic leaves he'd chopped and stuffed into the breast. After adding a wild carrot and an unknown green plant, he sat next to her.

"Crimes defined by those you offended: Ser Tomas, who knows as much as you do about why it stopped, and Sev Miller, who has a sudden deep interest in Deep Creek, but not by Our Lady. Sev Miller is being watched. The Goddess is not her tower, and her tower doesn't always properly represent her."

"That's what she ... the Goddess said. Before the oracle stopped cutting her off."

"That is being looked into. Breakdowns and loss of power are common. The builder artefacts are old and replacement parts scarce. We can't yet manufacture them. The knowledge needed to cut oracle power is only available to the brethren."

Averil tossed the sucked clean bone over her shoulder into the bush and wiped her mouth on her sleeve. "Which of the seven warriors, do you think, might have done it"

"Eight. None of us. Our Lady always knows each warrior's location. None of us were there."

"Eight? Who's the eighth?"

"Warrior Howard has recently joined us," Gardner said, his eyes alight and his grin wide, "And for that list you have memorised, Our Lady gave him *Firebolt*."

To hide her embarrassment that they knew of her list, for if one knew they all did, Averil posed another question, while thinking the new warrior must be our Wylie. "When she, Our Lady, said she couldn't control everything, I never thought she meant her towers. Everything they do is in her name."

"But not necessarily at her behest or in her interest, which is ultimately in everyone's interest."

"Why does she let them get away with it?"

He divided the breast, giving half to Averil before he continued, "because Our Lady must have someone administer the towers and even eight are too few brethren. Servers, having undergone the experience, are well-suited to prepare and present candidates for the tests."

"Why do you keep saying tests? I thought there was only one, those that pass become Restoration Warriors, like you, and the failures become servers."

"A common misconception. Because so few pass the first, Our Lady deemed it unnecessary to burden candidates with knowledge of the second, before knowing the result. The first, the Test of Reason is simple. Our Lady implants a communication device in the candidate's head. It may surprise you that the majority cannot accept her voice speaking directly to their mind. Our Lady turns their implants off. They can never be more than servers. The Ob selects his Arch Servers from those who accept her voice in their mind. Their implants remain on. A few of us go immediately to the Test of Faith. The brethren have all failed this second test."

"What!"

Averil, caught by surprise with a mouthful, swallowed a partly chewed lump of rabbit, almost choking on it. She felt the lump painfully descend as she searched Gardner's face, but his expression was quite matter-of-fact. Why had she not seen it before? Testing candidates would stop when the Goddess found her 'Face'. That much was simple and obvious, but without knowing there was a second test it wasn't clear that Restoration Warriors were those who failed to become Our Lady's Face. Severne's tits, is Willard ever in for a surprise.

Gardner pulled a morsel of meat from the remaining bones. "It's not that surprising. To fail the Test of Reason is to reject Our Lady as your guide, but to fail the Test of Faith is to reject her utterly. And yet, Our Lady rewards us for the attempt."

Finished, Gardner threw the bones into the fire, licked his fingers, and then cleaned his utensil set.

Averil digested the information without comment. If she could believe Gardner, much of what her schoolteachers and academy instructors had taught seemed like misinformation, at best, ill-informed. She felt she had learnt more about her world in the last few days than her entire formal education.

Averil wanted more. "How often do you talk to her?" she asked, as they settled down for the night.

"As frequently as I need."

"What do you ask?"

"I should probably ask, how may I serve," Gardner replied, gesturing with an open hand in such a way that Averil couldn't tell if he was merely repeating a litany or offering her his services. Then he grinned. "Mostly I don't need to ask, but when I do it's more like, what's next?"

Averil's grin matched his. She could not deny the feeling of security she derived from his presence, although she didn't know quite how far he would allow her to treat him as her own personal champion. She decided she would run it up the flagpole and see if he saluted.

"Get some sleep. We have a long way to go."

"As my lady wishes," Gardner said, with barely restrained mirth.

Averil didn't find it funny, not knowing if he meant her wishes or the Goddess's. Henceforth, she would shorten Gardner to Gard as a reminder that her protector was also her gaoler.

• • • •

The road stopped at Fort Blackstump. From there the path to the Perisher signal tower and on into the pass, was just a two-wheel track, through a pine forest with an understory of dense prickly shrubs. Hakeas, Gardner had told her. The track was barely wide enough for a cart with no place to turn around. Until it reached the Signal Tower, it ran westerly alongside an unnamed river, climbing steadily into the Barriers.

At the last moment, Averil turned to read the flashes from the Abbot Lane tower before she lost her view of it, still troubled by her overheard conversation about the ferals being gone before we could repair it.

"What do you make of that Gard?" she asked, her breath steaming in the cold mountain air.

"The Lane repeats. Perisher doesn't answer."

"Exactly. The ferals I told you about gave the impression they had taken out one of our towers. Perisher would be a good target."

Despite its name, the Perisher Signal Tower, a vital link between the Abbot Lane and Baldrock towers, was nearly a hundred miles from Perisher Pass. Baldrock Tower was on an island in the Pearl Chain, allowing the signals to bypass, rather than go up over, the Barrier Range.

"Will this alter your plans?" Gardner asked.

"No way. I still need to get to the Wall by the end of Bud. Besides, I doubt they left anyone there. They probably just smashed the mirrors. Nothing we can do about that," Averil said, making light of it.

Gardner was more concerned. "Still, we go right past it. We should proceed with caution."

As the track wound its way up the gorge, it frequently crisscrossed the unnamed stream. Averil watched as patches of melting snow dripped steadily into trickles and ran together under the simple plank bridge. She marvelled that such small beginnings could produce torrents like the one that nearly killed her. Walking across it in a single step, gave her a deep sense of satisfaction.

Gardner's hand on her shoulder broke her rhythm. She looked up with annoyance, then followed the warrior's pointing finger. Perisher Tower was a hundred yards away and as many above them. Five stories high, it towered over the levelled cut and fill, hacked from the side of the peak on which it perched. The giant mirrors looked undamaged, their shutters open and ominously still.

A familiar whistle made Averil cringe. With a grunt, Gardner pulled her backwards off her feet and she landed in his lap, sandwiching him against the wall of the cutting. When she tried to get up, he grunted again. She turned and saw an arrow standing out of his shoulder.

"Tits," said Averil, rolling away, staying low. Gardner's expression was one of displeasure, as if the fault was his, for allowing the arrow to hit him. Teeth clamped in a caricature of a grin, he reached up, grasped the protruding shaft, and jerked it out. The arrow, a plain untipped feral shaft, came free with a wet sucking pop. The warrior sniffed the tip and threw it away as he pulled back his robe to reveal a jagged-edged puncture.

As Averil watched, the blood oozing from the wound dried and scabbed just as if Mother had treated it with some of her healing dust.

"Our Lady's gift to warriors," Gardner said and Averil wondered how her mother came to possess such a hoard of Our Lady's gift to warriors. The scab shrivelled and dropped away, leaving a clean puckered welt.

"Neat," Averil said, holding back that such healing was not new to her.

"Our Lady takes care of her own," Gardner replied, tentatively flexing his shoulder. The puckered welt still looked raw, but it did not bleed.

"Now what Gard?" asked Averil, surprised to learn she already counted on his Goddess-backed judgement? Her masters at the Academy would not approve. Self-reliance was a core tenet of officer training.

"Tonight, they will not see us pass."

"Pass? We can't leave ferals up there. What if the signallers are still alive? We can't leave them hostage. Besides, the Signal Corps will send replacements. They don't train signallers to deal with ferals."

The warrior looked at her as if trying to discern what she wanted. She supposed his job was to dissuade her from foolhardy ventures just like the one she had in mind. If they passed in darkness, no one would ever know, but she was Watcher, and with warrior help it would be a piece of cake.

"We fix this tonight," she said, wondering what Gardner would do.

"As you wish."

His reply delighted her. Thank Severne the Goddess hasn't given him other orders.

They were days from the pass, yet the air was already chill. A biting wind hit them as soon as they left the shelter of the cutting and sprinted towards the base of the signal tower. Tiny lights winked on raced before them to highlight their path. Averil grinned at the clatter of arrows ahead, the ferals aiming at the firefly-like lights. They were at the tower's base before the ferals had worked out they needed to shift their aim.

Climbing the stairs, though it proved harder than Averil imagined, was warming after the chilly wait and a test of her stamina. Clouds obscured the stars, making the night as black as tar. Without the fireflies showing them where to place their hands and feet, it would've been impossibly slow. Gardner led, *Brimstone* slapping lightly against his back. If climbing gave his shoulder any trouble, he showed no sign of it. They found the hatch into the mirror platform, one level below the signaller's quarters, closed but not bolted.

There was no movement from above, and no sound except for the biting air whistling around the open superstructure. Muscles bulging Gardner silently lifted the hatch up and over, then lowered it gently to the floor. He paused for a quick breath, then scrambled up the remaining steps, Averil following seconds behind. The fireflies spread out, intensifying, highlighting two bodies in Signaller green. A bow and empty quiver lay on the floor, and a black-robed figure was turning from peering down into the darkness. The firefly light glinted off surprised eyes.

The server shouted a warning, his sword coming free of the scabbard at his waist. The blade hissed through the air inches from Gardner's chest, slashed deep into a support post and jammed. Gardner who'd stepped back into Averil, grabbed the server's wrist, and twisted. The man screamed as his wrist snapped, his sword clattering on the wooden floor. Gardner reversed *Brimstone* and hit him on the temple with the gem in the hilt. Blood oozed from the wound as Gardner lowered the unconscious body to the floor.

The fireflies massed into an intense ball, giving off a soft white light that illuminated the signal room. That the recovery of the signal tower had been easy, pleased Averil, but the culprit being a server, using feral arrows, soured the achievement. It also pleased her untrained eye that the shutter mechanisms, the pulleys, and the counterweights that turned the mirrors all appeared undamaged.

Then, as she saw all the cut ropes, her shadow on the workings abruptly changed. The ball of fireflies dimmed and Gardner turned her to face him, a finger to his lips, his eyes upturned to signallers' quarters on the floor above.

Averil had no time to wonder what he meant, before a figure came swinging in out of the darkness behind Gardner and booted feet slammed squarely into *Brimstone*. Gardner crashed into Averil, knocking her down. The man let go his rope and landed in a crouch. He wore only undergarments. Gardner rolled away, jerking each time his shoulder hit the floor. Flat on her back Averil slithered away, awkwardly drawing her sword, shocked to see the man she assumed was another server, had the skills of a warrior. Ignoring her, he went for Gardner, his sword poised in a two-handed grip for a killing blow.

With a supreme effort, Averil arched her back and leapt to her feet, landing clumsily, unbalanced by the sword. The server glanced over his shoulder, surprised to see her on her feet. He pirouetted with lightning speed. Averil swung, diving sideways. Her sword savagely slashed his shank. The man faltered. *Brimstone* flashed up through his arm. The weapon clanged on the floor still firmly gripped. The shocked man reached for it with his stump, collapsed with his first step, and toppled headfirst through the open hatchway. He bounced off the first landing and thudded with sickening repetitiveness into several crossbeams on his way to the rocks below.

Averil heaved and heaved again.

"The first one stays with you," Gardner said, "a pity yours was so ... untidy."

"I didn't kill him," Averil protested. Not directly anyway, but she knew he was right. This would stay with her.

Gardner went upstairs and reThe Blackwood Writers Group 3rd anthology turned with a black robe; not that Averil needed confirmation. Both men had genuine talismans around their necks. Gardner knelt and stared at the unconscious server's face. To Averil, he explained, "Our Lady can see through my eyes, and check, which Arch Server instructed him, away from the path."

"Someone attached to Walker's Tower," Averil said and Gardner looked up at her. "The arrows were feral and the militia hung two ferals in Walker."

"Our Lady thanks you."

Averil grunted. "I don't want her thanks. Her plan for me sucks."

Gardner insisted on burying the dead, and Averil could see no good reason to disagree. They ferried the bodies and the prisoner down in the supply cage signallers used to bring the giant mirrors up. During the descent, she noticed the two signallers had had their throats cut; feral fashion. She wasn't unduly worried that ferals would get the blame. What concerned her was a couple of Our Lady's servers had helped the feral group she encountered get away with an abductee from Deep Creek.

In the morning, once *Brimstone* had dug several graves, exploding the ground into neat piles on either side of shallow furrows, Averil again had to confront the server she killed. If she hadn't slashed his shank, he wouldn't have fallen. He would've had time to bleed to death from the handless arm, making it

Gardner's fault. But she couldn't. She was responsible; she had to
bury him. Her stomach rebelled when she properly positioned
the battered server's detached hand.

After they had mounded the stony dirt back over the bodies.
Gardner chanted a warrior ritual over the signallers.

We commit these lives to Our Lady, blessed be Our Lady.

Aithe to Aithe, dust to dust, blessed be Our Lady.

Until her Face, wakes the Sleepers, blessed be her Face.

At the coming of the Restoration, blessed be her Face.

Listening to the refrain raised questions Averil had never
considered. Did the Goddess also turn newly departed traitors
into sleepers, to await the Restoration? And what about ferals?
She asked, but on this subject, Gardner was reticent, and she
couldn't tell if he didn't know or just wasn't saying.

It was midday before they could get away. Gardner securely
trussed the now conscious server to the ladder, telling him,
"We're leaving. The militia and replacement signallers from
Blackstump will arrive tomorrow."

Once they were out of the server's sight and hearing, Averil
asked, "Why didn't you just kill him in the first place? The
militia will hang him as a traitor."

"Only after a trusted Arch Server Our Lady is sending has
questioned him."

"Are there any left?"

Gardner left that question unanswered.

· · · ·

The trail steepened as they headed towards Perisher Pass. Averil
constantly looked over her shoulder to reassure herself Gardner
was still following, and found, as always, her guard two steps
behind, ready to assist.

Brimstone was now over his right shoulder, and Averil saw him wince occasionally whenever he had to use his right arm. Climbing the signal tower, before it had healed, must have aggravated the damage. Externally, there was only the tiniest scar. She had watched him massage the muscle each night and practice manoeuvres as they trekked. Perhaps there were limits to whatever healing aithcraft warriors used.

Day by day, the forest thinned, trees giving way to bushes. Game became scarce, but Gardner still provided. Averil now realised she would not have made it without him. The narrowing trail eventually emerged from the last vegetation, and they were climbing across bare rock with occasional patches of snow. She was back into her alpine jacket, despite the return of bud's clear skies and sunshine. Thinning air slowed them down.

On the fourth day out from the signal tower, their midday stop found Averil dispirited. In anticipation of a hot coffee, she had searched both sides all morning, but the barren trail had yielded nothing of use for making a fire. Gardner's preparedness again surprised her; he produced a small burner that fitted into the base of a slender boiler and gave them hot water in seconds. builder magic, Aithe magic, or Goddess magic. It was all the same to Averil. She didn't care; she had her hot coffee.

She wrapped her gloved hands around the cup he offered and sipped, grateful for both the rest and the hot liquid coursing down her throat.

"Tell me something Gard, what is the Restoration really about?"

Gardner took a cautious sip before answering in a like manner. "Exactly as it says in *Legends,* Our Lady will restore the power of the Builders."

"I know the words, but what do they mean?"

"The Builders generated vast amounts of energy to power the artefacts they used. The towers have a fraction of what was once available."

"But didn't the power also cause the Days of Fire which destroyed them? So why does the Goddess want to restore it?"

"How people use the power is their responsibility." A moment later, Gardner cocked his head in an attitude of listening. "Drink up, we need to move on."

The Goddess has spoken, Averil thought, dissatisfied with his answer, but knowing it was all she would get. Sometime he was open and informative and at others, downright taciturn. It appeared the Goddess censored certain subjects.

Mountainside by mountainside, they trod the path as it wound its slow way around the slopes of the northern tip of the Barrier Range. The slopes varied from mild to precipitous, until they reached Mount Barren, which rose sheer from the high valley where the Mighty Muddy: mighty long, mighty wide, and mighty deep, began its long journey across the Great Plains.

Though it shortened the distance to the Wall by a thousand miles, Perisher Pass was not straight, nor level, nor uniform in width. In places, it narrowed to a goat track. In other places, rock falls had obliterated it and in other places great cracks had split the path apart. The lower ledges were inaccessible even to the short-horned mountain goats. Unlike the rest of the trail, the pass itself, known also as the Pipe, was a straight, concave indentation, obviously of builder origin. The once smooth pipe, after centuries of weathering, had made the only end-to-end navigable ledge across Mount Barren dangerous. It channelled the wind.

The thin air was freezing, breathing became harder and their pace slowed. Talking, already difficult in single file, became impossible as they approached the Pipe and the wind increased.

The transition was abrupt, one moment still, the next a howling gale.

Logically, Averil knew that body heat radiated outward, sucked away by the wind, but to her it felt as if the cold was a malevolent force, viciously attacking her with deadly intent. She tried to remember what the academy instructors had said about wind chill. Something like a fifteen mile per hour wind at zero degrees was equivalent to ten below. Fat lot of good the knowledge is when you're in it, and freezing.

Even light airs, when funnelled by the Pipe, had plucked unwary travellers over the lip of this precarious ledge. Averil wondered if a successful passage was possible. All the stories were about those who tried and perished. Why did I let Gardner talk me into this? I'll die with my commission unconfirmed.

Half way into the Pipe, Gardner tapped her on the shoulder shouting, "There's a storm coming."

Averil glanced up and sure enough, masses of dark clouds were gathering swiftly, the wind picking up. That's all we need. She looked back at Gardner only half convinced the Goddess had told him about it, anyone could read storm clouds. She upped the pace as much as possible, given the conditions. Gardner followed easily. She realised she was holding him up, but he never complained or pushed.

As the wind strengthened, it occurred to Averil, they might not make it. She had worked out the chill factor would now suck the heat from her body with the numbing equivalence of forty degrees below, and the constant battering sapped her strength to where she felt she was past her limit of endurance. The only way to stay warm is to keep moving, she told herself, but her reserves of will were running low, her ability to generate any warmth fading. She needed to rest, but knew stopping would be fatal. Already the tips of her fingers were prickly with the first hint of frostbite. She placed her hands in her armpits whenever she didn't need them for balance and trudged on.

A squall hit. The turbulence lifted Averil and coaxed her towards the edge. Gardner grabbed her jacket, pulling her back and down. He crouched against the sheer wall, his hand through a ring attached by a piton to the rock. He pushed her into the angle between the ledge and mountain and sat beside her, anchoring her with his legs across hers. Immediately, her backside and legs went numb. The rock under her was ice, the wind shrieked past her ear as she sat panting, the lip of the narrow path her only shelter. Icy needles of rain speared her cheek when she lifted her head, looking for the crack she had seen just before the squall. She had bemoaned it as an obstacle. Now it might offer a refuge. She tapped Gardner's arm and pointed. He nodded lifted his legs off hers and stood. A gust slammed him headfirst against the wall.

Dragging the unconscious Gardner, Averil crawled another inch along the frozen ledge, a constant stream of abuse hurled at the Goddess. With numb hands, she dragged the warrior into the crevice behind her. It was not deep, but the angle gave respite from the full force of the blast in the Pipe. There was just enough room for them to sit up, with Gardner in front, protecting her again, however unwittingly.

The squall died as fast as it had started and with the sudden silence, the rain slowed, gentling into flakes. Now, when they could and should continue, tiredness stopped her from moving. They sat close in the narrow crevice, Gardner between her legs, her arms around his chest, and her head on his back to stop the biting air slipping between them, sharing what little mutual warmth each had left. His cloak kept a lot from escaping, but it was not enough. Every breath seared her throat. Snow built up around them, walling them in. It helped a little.

"Why did you bring me this way?" she asked when Gardner finally stirred.

"Our Lady ..."

"Then she's killed us both."

"Faith Averil," he whispered back, "she will provide."

Unconvinced, Averil waited impatiently for the end, wondering why she was here at all. I'm only eighteen. I've done nothing, my entire life spent learning skills for a life I won't ever have. What's the point?

She felt an itch on her face and tried to twitch a cheek muscle, not wanting to withdraw her arms from the comfort of the warrior's cloak. The itch persisted, changed, becoming more widespread, akin to tiny pinpricks like ant bites. Something was crawling on her face. Averil cracked out of her frozen shell and clawed at her face.

"Get off me," she shouted, and plucked several in one handful, flicking them away. Gardner surprised her by reaching back and grabbing both her wrists.

"Stop."

Averil struggled in his grasp. The Restoration Warrior suddenly let go, turned swiftly, and kneeling in front of her, grabbed both wrists again. Winged beetles about a quarter of an inch long covered his face, leaving only his eyes and nostrils exposed. He spoke, and a thin slit magically appeared where his mouth should be. "Her microbots are here to help. I will let you go when you stop fighting them."

His mouth disappeared when he closed it. Averil, held by his eyes, felt she could read his thoughts, 'trust her Averil, she has a plan for you'.

She relaxed a little, wincing as she felt the beetles scurrying over her face. Still revolted, she closed her eyes and held her breath. Gradually, warmth suffused her. When she cautiously re-opened her eyes, black beetles totally covered her leggings. For the first time in a long while, she allowed herself to relax tense muscles. The beetles adjusted to her movements as she straightened her cramped legs. They had totally excluded the heat suck air. She was keeping all of what little warmth she had left. What took you so long? she thought, in silent admonishment of the Goddess. She was still not happy about Our Lady's plan for her and Willard, but at least she would live long enough to argue against it.

It was at that moment, with hope rekindled, that Averil saw a sight stranger than she could imagine. Drifting across the distant mouth of the pipe was a collection of twelve to fifteen red dots. She shielded her eyes with her hand to study the phenomenon. The motion caused a ripple as the beetles crawled rapidly into her exposed armpit.

"What the ..." Averil grimaced when the beetles adjusted to her moving lips. She tried again, attempting to speak with a minimum of movement.

"What's that?" she asked and pointed. The beetles adjusted around her straightened elbow.

Gardner must have misunderstood. Instead of looking, he grabbed her outstretched arm and began pulling her to her feet. She closed her eyes, hardening her herself against the delicate touch of tiny legs, scrabbling to adjust. When she looked moments later, only clouds remained. Whatever else had been out there was gone. At this distance, the dots must have been huge. She soon doubted what she'd seen. Probably it was just spots before her eyes brought on by fatigue. The sooner they were off this mountain the better.

"Let's ..." she paused, again startled by the warrior's appearance. The shiny, overlapping carapaces made him look like a badly hammered, black metal statue.

"You're a frightening sight yourself," Gardner said, as if reading her thoughts, a ripple of movement around the statue's lips.

Averil didn't dare laugh, thinking she might inhale one. Instead, she started up the narrow, now snow-covered ledge, in cautious good spirits. She would make it. Perisher Pass would soon be behind her, but she doubted anyone would believe how she did it.

Chapter 15

Willard stepped out through the doors of the abandoned servatory into an open meadow. Off to one side stood ruins of what had once been an outbuilding. Now only the stubs of walls remained, covered in earth and grass, the ground littered with fallen masonry. The view on the other side was immense. He could easily imagine why people considered high places sacred, why servers claimed it put them closer to the Goddess. He felt he was at the summit of the world, higher than he'd been in Ob Walker's office in the Pillar's servatory.

Invigorating as the cold air was, it rasped at his dry throat. He would have to find water soon. He turned to retrace his steps and noticed the faded sign on the doors: Mount Bakor Observatory. Two servatories when there is only one Ob Sever, Willard thought absurd. No wonder they had abandoned it.

The doors reopened at his approach, which was fortunate because he couldn't find a talisman pedestal outside. His search of the servatory found nothing to eat or drink and made him wonder why the Goddess had sent him here? What point did she want to make? Perhaps his refusal to take the test had annoyed her more than the disappointment she had expressed. His first thought was to find the settlement that had once serviced the servatory and hope someone had stayed.

Still thirsty, Willard headed back outside. The main doors closed behind him with a heavy thud and in the sudden quiet, he heard bleating. As he slipped the talisman back inside his shirt, a flock of goats topped the rise in front and split, bolting left and right, leaving the goatherd standing startled and alone, staring at him. His relief that he wasn't completely alone was heartfelt, but short-lived. Wherever this was, the Goddess ruled here.

The lad had fallen to his knees, stretched out his arms, and touched his forehead to the ground. From behind the scattering flock, an animal, more wolf than dog, emerged ran quickly to the boy and licked his ear. The boy rapped it on the muzzle with a gruff command. It lay down with its head on outstretched paws almost parodying the boy, except that its unwavering gaze remained on Willard.

Halting two paces away, Willard slowly squatted on his heels and reached for the bulging animal bladder on the ground between him and the boy. The wolf-dog bared its fangs and growled ominously. Willard changed his mind.

"Water," he croaked.

Without looking up, the boy urgently shoved the bladder towards him, and with another rap on its muzzle, admonished the wolf-dog to be still.

Carefully, Willard reached out, untied the knot, lifted the bag to his lips and slowly hoisted the other end. Water trickled into his mouth. Suddenly, he no longer cared about the wolf-dog as he fell back and took a large swig. He chewed the mouthful, forcing it up around his gums and making his cheeks bulge before slowly swallowing.

The boy remained prone; his attitude reverential.

Willard swallowed another mouthful before asking, "Where are we?"

The boy stared at Willard's boots.

"Look, I'm not the Ob, or even an Arch Server. In fact, I'm not any sort of server. I'm just lost. I have no idea where I am."

Dark eyes peeked out from under a mass of dark, curly hair.

"Can you understand me?" Willard continued clearly enunciating every word, wondering at the stupidity of his question. How can he answer if he doesn't?

"Yes Ser."

The timid voice shocked Willard, a girl. Willard immediately thought of Averil.

"I am not a Ser," he reiterated.

"talisman," she said, with a slight accent.

"Oh that," he said, looking down, finding it had somehow come out. "The Goddess gave it to me. She ..." He stopped.

The girl was looking at him quizzically.

This is going to be hard to explain. "Let's leave that for now. I need to find out where I am, and," he added as an afterthought, "I'm hungry. Can you take me to the nearest town?"

"Please. Have mine, Ser."

"And don't call me Ser. My name is Willard. What's yours?"

"Nelda, Ser Willard," she said, handing Willard her packed lunch. Then she whistled softly, a series of pulses of different lengths. The wolf-dog bounded away to round up the gazing goats.

After Willard had swallowed the last mouthful of Nelda's packed lunch, they headed down the mountain behind the herd, following a wide, gently sloping path. He felt guilty. It was only a couple of small round loaves and two thick slices of hard cheese, but it was all she had. Still, Nelda had insisted. His hunger overrode his qualms.

"What's his name?" Willard asked, scratching the behind the wolf-dog's ears.

"Bandit."

Willard chuckled, but made no comment.

As they wound their way down the mountain through a wide meadow, the scenery piqued Willard's curiosity. The twisted scrub which bordered the meadow, and the carpet of colourful flowers that the path bisected, were not familiar. Even the air smelt different. The cold suggested he might be further south towards Port Calder, but it could just be the altitude. He glanced up at the sun. With the Barriers behind and wide sweep of sea in front, East should be ahead, except the sun seemed to moving that way as well. Willard staggered to a halt.

"Where does the sun set?" he asked, dreading Nelda's answer, visualising the map of Preservation Island on the wall of the servatory's library.

"There Ser ... Willard," said Nelda, frowning, pointing.

He sat down in the dirt and held his head in his hands, shivering from more than the cold. He was facing west. Not wanting to offend Nelda, he cursed the Goddess silently.

From the height of the surrounding peaks, and assuming he was still on the Island, not dumped in the lowlands, this had to be the Hummocks. And if this was the Southern Hummocks, which he was sure it would be, then he was more than a thousand miles from both Deep Creek and the Wall; as far from civilisation as the Goddess could put him.

Willard's questions to Nelda when they resumed walking, drew cautious answers. She didn't know how many people lived here though she tried to name them all, from which Willard guessed her village was smaller even than Deep Creek. When he asked, "do you have a server?" Nelda looked embarrassed and didn't answer except to nod. He let that go, knowing he would find out soon enough. All he really wanted to know was the fastest way out of here and back across the Island to pick up Kezia's trail. That journey might take several seasons, if not years, a prospect that threatened to overwhelm him.

Nelda led him to a small round shepherd's hut made of stone with a single door, no windows, and a smoke hole in the shingled roof. Four yards across it contained a cot, a table, a small shelf above the cot on which rested a copy of *Legends*, a cupboard on legs with rows of fine holes punched in the sides, and a working artefact.

"What does that do?"

Nelda looked quizzical, as if not understanding how he could not know. "It cooks Lord." She opened a shiny metallic looking cupboard, unhooked a piece of raw meat, and placed it on the top of the artefact.

Instantly the light on the front blinked and the meat sizzled, smoke rising to the hole above. The unique smell of roasting goat made his mouth water. When the blinking light stopped, Nelda turned the slab over with a quick flick of her fingers. Willard had never tasted better more perfectly cooked meat.

Nelda insisted he sleep on the cot as befitted a Lord and she on the hard-packed dirt floor. He had thought once he rested, he might get up in the night and put her on the bed, but he never woke.

They started down the mountain at dawn and by midmorning had reached a wide, flat plateau. Willard was about to ask how long before they reached the town, when Bandit suddenly stopped snapping at the goats, turned and stalked towards a clump of reeds around a wallow.

Nelda froze. The goats turned to the clump ears erect. Willard felt helpless. He carried no weapons not even a staff. Reflecting on the Goddess's statement that she would help where she could, he touched the talisman through his shirt.

A soft whistle and Bandit crept warily towards the reed bed at the edge of the trees, ears forward, nose quivering. Whatever was in there gave no sign of its presence until it burst out.

The boar charged, head down, and long curved tusks wobbling from side to side. Goats scattered. Bandit jumped clear with ease and locked onto one of the boar's hind legs as it passed. The boar scarcely slowed, dragging Bandit along by its teeth as it barrelled towards its next target. Willard tensed ready to jump aside as Bandit had, but at the critical moment, a blurred motion to his right distracted him. Nelda, arms outstretched, dived for the boar's head, grabbing at the tusks.

"No," Willard screamed as he jumped clear, landed on loose rocks, skidded, and fell.

Nelda, who had misjudged and seized only one tusk, barely deflected the charge. With a powerful neck flick, the boar threw her away.

Willard struggled into a sitting position, snatched up the nearest rocks and hurled them at the boar, to no effect. He kept missing.

Bandit's tenacious grip finally got through to the boar. It twisted and turned, trying to snap Bandit against a tree, as it began circling back towards Nelda. Somehow sensing Nelda's danger, Bandit suddenly let go of the boar's leg and cut across the circle on an intercept course. Scrabbling to keep its feet, it spun in front of its mistress, then charged straight at the boar, diving between the tusks to clamp its jaws on the boar's snout.

The enraged boar twisted its head, threw his attacker high and hooked a tusk into its belly as it fell. It vigorously shook its impaled tormentor, continuing to eviscerate Bandit long after the wolf-dog was dead.

Nelda hadn't moved.

Willard, who had stopped throwing rocks when Bandit charged, was reluctant to restart. It would attract the boar's attention.

The boar, surprised by its success, appeared unsure what to do next. Willard held his breath. The small eyes cast around the battlefield then trotted off towards the reeds, favouring a hind leg.

Willard now cursed the Goddess, in terms learnt from returning Watcher veterans, alarmed that she had added Nelda and her wolf-dog to the increasing death toll attributed to him.

Nelda's moan brought tears of relief. She wasn't dead. Her scream ended Willard's inaction. He scrambled over to her. She was on her back, legs and arms akimbo, though none were in an unnatural position. The livid red streak across one hand turned out to be an old scar, so except for some superficial cuts he could see nothing wrong. Her eyes were alert but frightened.

"I can't move my legs," she whimpered.

Willard squeezed the talisman and prayed for help. He received no response, not even a sign. He felt rejected by the Goddess he had rejected. He would have to continue to the town.

"I'll get help," he said.

"Don't leave me Ser Willard," Nelda pleaded, her hand reaching out to him. "Help me up."

"I can't. It might hurt you more." What little Willard knew of the healing arts from Kezia said moving Nelda was probably the worst thing he could do; it might cripple her for life.

"The boar will ..." Nelda broke off to scream in pain " ... kill me if I am left here alone."

She had a point. Severne help me, he thought as he reached over, gently took hold of her hand pulled her onto her side. She screamed and passed out, leaving Willard to stare dumbfounded at the blood-covered rock she had fallen on, and the weeping bruise in the middle of her back.

Dear Lady, what do I do?

• • • •

After bypassing Aldgate Bend, as Howard suggested, Kezia and Wesley had crossed the river at Morgan to the less populated side. Now, as they approached the outskirts of Fishmarket, where Howard was to re-join them, they recross the river into the town.

Neither had realised how close they were when they camped last night.

"I could have had a nice soft bed," Kezia said.

"You did," Wesley replied.

Kezia had been so tired and slept so soundly the last couple of nights she couldn't remember a thing except waking in his embrace. Blushing, she shot him a glance as they walked their horses towards the bridge; two more travellers joining the throng in a country where everyone seemed to be on the move. The flow was constant in both directions, slowing where it concentrated to cross a massive stone bridge, three sweeping arches on squat pillars.

Kezia, wondering where all the people were going this early in the morning, noticed the inbound traffic had fully loaded carts and drays; the outbound traffic was mostly empty. "Market Day?" she asked.

Wesley considered this for a moment. "It is, but this looks more like their stocking up for a siege," he said, deliberately loud enough for people to overhear.

"Too right," said a listener, a small man with thinning hair and oversized boots, waiting patiently in the bridge queue. "Where have you two been?" he added and spat over the side of his dray.

"Woodbridge," Wesley said, while Kezia was wondering what to say that wouldn't bring trouble.

"That backwater. I'm not surprised you don't know," the man said, spat again and nudged his horse to take another step. "There are ferals this side of the Barriers, first time ever. The Wall must have gone." Murmurs of agreement and nodding heads rippled around him as the speaker stood on his seat to look over the heads of the drivers in front. "What's the hold up?" he shouted, having already forgotten Kezia and Wesley's presence.

If he thinks Woodbridge a backwater, what would he make of Deep Creek? His implied criticism of people from small towns stung. It was time to put her backwater days of ignorance, oppression, and hopelessness behind her. If she wanted her new life to have meaning, she would have to throw away more than just her name. Kezia turned her horse out of the queue.

"Hey," shouted Wesley, "where are you off to?"

"To Port Calder," she shouted back.

"But Howard said to wait here."

"You wait for him then. He doesn't own me."

She had reined in further back at a cart piled high with goods. By the look of it, the whole of a small general store heading for safety within the walls of the town. She hailed the driver. "How would like to make a sale while you're waiting?"

The large woman holding the reins, big arms, big bust, and a backside to match, eyed her thoughtfully. "How much you want?"

Kezia reached into her tunic and withdrew a single gold Roo from her purse. She urged *Providence* close to the wagon and reached out with the coin cupped in her hand to show the woman.

The puffy eyes bulged, then narrowed quickly. "I got no change."

"I'll take what I can get to the value of this coin."

"Then we can do business," the woman replied as Wesley drew up.

"Are you coming with me after all?"

"I have no choice?"

"Did Howard tell you that?"

"The oracle," Wesley said.

Kezia stared at him in disbelief as two of her assumptions collapsed: one, that Howard had conscripted him and two, that as Watcher he would follow the Aithist creed. It never occurred to her he could be Severnian.

"You're a believer?"

"Aren't you?"

"Hurry up you two, the queue's moving," interrupted the big round face.

Kezia turned back to the woman, "Sorry, I'll take a bag of flour, some sugar, tea ..." She rattled off a whole list of supplies. The big woman threw each item to Wesley who packed them into a couple of bags the woman had provided and he'd tied across their horses' backs. When Kezia started on fruit and vegetables, Wesley stopped her.

"Too heavy and too perishable," he said

Kezia wanted to argue. She didn't have full value yet, but when she saw the bulging bags, she gave in. "Keep the change," she said and they headed back along the waiting column, which had grown a mile longer, while she'd haggled.

"Maybe you should've bought the cart," Wesley joked as they cantered away south.

"I thought about it. But it would slow me down."

"You know that Fishmarket's Bridge is the last crossing point for a hundred miles."

"I didn't, but so what?"

"All the towns and most of the farms are on the other side. This road runs out before Port Calder. The river comes right up to the foothills."

"So? We have supplies for a couple of weeks, and it should take us less than one." She continued before he could answer, "and we'll have plenty of water if we stay close to the river."

Wesley's grin went unnoticed as Kezia began planning how she would use the rest of the money to set up her clinic in Port Calder. Jena Setler, healer, would look nice on a shingle.

They stopped for lunch on a grassy knoll overlooking a large loop in the Aldgate River. Kezia bit into the thin flat cake, freshly baked on a hot stone and spread with homemade apricot jam.

"So what exactly did her oracle tell you?" Kezia asked.

"Be ready to follow the healer."

"Is that it?" Kezia spluttered, nearly choking, spraying crumbs over Wesley. Good Goddess, did Our Lady know this was coming, or did she manipulate the process to make it happen?

Apologising profusely, Kezia looked for something to clean him up, but with nothing to hand used her sleeve. Wesley suddenly reached forward and kissed her and just as fast started apologising.

"I'm sorry. I don't know what came over me. Yes, I do. You're beautiful."

He stopped, and Kezia felt her face reddening. Will had never called her beautiful. He might have thought about it, but he never said it. She could remember kissing Willard goodbye, but not how it felt. Wesley's kiss woke a longing she hadn't felt for ages, and the memories of home prompted her to ask, "What day is it?"

"Aithday, the seventeenth of Barton," said Wesley, already up and repacking.

Kezia stood to hide her tears. Sarah and Lisa became teenagers yesterday. She had missed the twins' birthdays, the first of many family celebrations she would now miss. As she mounted, she had to suppress feelings of self-pity. She could not, would not go back.

She took a deep breath, drank in the open countryside through which they had been riding, the breathtaking natural beauty of the Aldgate River Valley. Although constrained between the river and the mountains, their path was still wide and the light breeze wafting up from the river was fresh. The sun shone and the river sparkled. Her new life was good, wasn't it?

• • • •

Almost a week later, as they set up camp a couple of hours short of Ogden, Kezia analysed her continuing sense of wellbeing, surprised to find the reason for it was she had a last freed herself of all shackles: father Willard and the Warrior Howard. The journey, a transition between where she had been and where she was going, had freed her from all obligations. Perhaps she should just keep moving.

In retrospect she realised Willard had been 'special' in every sense of the word, his brother Aldus fun, her father a beastly hypocrite and Howard safe, but none had been as Wesley now was, a friend. Until that kiss, he had made no demands and she had never given him a second thought, despite sleeping in his arms. Now she wondered if a friendship like this might be more important than love. Loving Willard had been fractious.

Kezia didn't want to be alone and she liked Wesley's company. He would certainly stick with her; the oracle had told him to. She could do a lot worse.

"A penny for your thoughts?" asked Wesley.

"Oh, nothing much," she said, treating him to a big smile as they bedded down.

Wesley was soon snoring lightly, unconcerned that in the height of passion, she had pushed him away. She sighed. *He's a good man, but he isn't Willard.* She knew it didn't need to be like this. *Before her father, she and Willard's explorations of each other's bodies had been a thrill with a dreamy aftermath. May the Goddess rot my father's soul, and not wake him in the coming Restoration.*

She rolled away from Wesley and watched her only remaining link with home transit across the sky. Severne's Eye faded, then brightened like a slow wink. Idly, she wondered if Willard, or Averil or anyone she knew, was watching the same blink at this moment. *Providence* whickered softly. She rolled on her side, eyes moist, pushed the past away. This moment, here and now, is all that is real. Good and bad, the past is dead and buried. No matter what I do, I can't alter it, or Our Lady's plans for Willard and Averil.

Wesley didn't stir and she rolled onto her back again and listened to the night sounds, cicadas chirping, the scampering of small nocturnal rodents, the croaking of frogs from the river. Restless, she turned again, concentrated on Wesley's sleeping profile. He was so different. She suspected mixed parentage, a touch of feral despite the taboos, which is probably why he ended up in an orphanage. He was also gentle and patient. She could learn to love him given time.

When she had started out, Port Calder had seemed impossibly far away, but tomorrow, after they re-crossed the Aldgate, it would be only a day or two away. She vowed that when Jena Setler set up her clinic in Port Calder, Kezia Leach would cease to exist and Wesley would be part of her new life.

As she drifted into sleep, her new dreams slipped quietly off the edge into the maelstrom of nightmare. The distorted face of Wesley leered and he held her down while her father repeatedly extracted his revenge. Howard stood in the background, pointing an accusing finger constantly repeating, "Fishmarket, Fishmarket, Fishmarket."

• • • •

Port Calder, my future home, thought Kezia, was flatter than any town she had encountered in the long journey from Deep Creek.

From the top of the bridge over the Aldgate River, she had seen right across the city to the distant harbour.

Hours later, she and Wesley were riding through a sprawling tent city outside the gates, mute testament to the port's inability to contain its burgeoning population. Plenty of work here for a healer, she thought. But in the back of her mind, she worried that someone might one day uncover Kezia Leach, murderer and Medicorps deserter, hiding inside the Healer, Jena Setler. She suppressed bitter memories. Running away made her look guilty despite her father's death being an accident. Doing so after signing articles and taking her Medicorps kit had compounded her error. And all because the Goddess had promised Willard to Averil. Too late now, she had passed the point of no return. She had to live with it; all of it.

They crossed the turgid River Lynn, western boundary of the city, flowing through huge pipes underneath the causeway. On either side of the road, gangs of workers stripped to the waist, sweated to crane large square blocks of stone onto new gatehouse towers. The gang's two supervisors stared at them, as if expecting trouble, and we could be it. Wishing Howard was here, Kezia whispered to Wesley. "The natives don't look friendly."

"So I see. We'll probably be alright though, they're mostly ex-Watcher, just don't look at them and don't stop."

Kezia did as Wesley suggested and looked straight ahead, but they were not alright, far from it. The attack came without warning as they passed between the half completed stone towers. A militia led crowd sprang from nowhere and pulled them from their horses. So savage and unexpected was it that Kezia and Wesley were on the ground, people kicking and punching them before they had time to realise what was happening. The crowd bayed at them, calling Wesley a feral and she a feral-loving whore. How stupid, Kezia thought, detaching her mind from her body as she had done with father, as if a feral would be in a Watcher uniform.

Her memory of subsequent events was hazy. That she was still alive meant someone must have stopped the crowd before they beat her to death. Hoping the same was true of Wesley, she lay still awhile, breathing as lightly as possible, trying to ignore the ache behind her eyes, trying to work out what she had done wrong this time.

Strangely, wherever she was now, was warm and comfortable. Her first thought was that perhaps she had died after all, and gone to the otherworld. If so, she had a few choice words for the Goddess. Her second thought was that it had been a dream, but no, she could recall with incredible vividness every detail of the attack. Besides, even the slightest movement brought pain to every part of her body, especially her head.

They had beaten Wesley harder and it's my fault. Whenever I care about someone, the Goddess separates me from him. First Willard now Wesley, perhaps I just shouldn't get involved with anyone whose name begins with 'W'. If not for the pain, Kezia might have laughed. Instead, she listened to her surroundings, wishfully hoping for the familiar creaking timbers of home as they warmed to a new day. Nothing but a gentle hum greeted her, reminiscent of being in mother's ...

"How do you feel?" a voice said.

Kezia's eyes snapped opened and she turned towards the voice in time to see a section of shimmering wall solidify. A tower? *Please no, not again,* she thought as her mind filled with memories of Rivers Junction. She was finding her constant reversals of fortune disturbing. *It's as if the Goddess can't decide what to do with me.*

"You're well I trust?"

The owner of the voice was a woman about her mother's age, a full face with undefined cheekbones, dark hair with a flinty hardness to her mismatched blue eyes. She wore a long translucent gown that showed to good effect a well-rounded figure. It gave Kezia the impression the woman was trying to emulate the Goddess.

"Fine," Kezia said, and despite the soreness of her bruises, she felt rather better than she would have expected.

"Good. I'm Lady Elmira. I rescued you from, shall we say, our overzealous militia, and you are?"

"K ... Jena Setler, I'm a healer."

Elmira eyed Kezia speculatively as she sat on the bed. "Look, I'm sorry for any injury or discomfort you may have suffered. Calder is a big port, and the times being what they are, overflowing with plains refugees, and wall wounded."

"What happened to Wesley, the Watcher with me?"

"He is being treated for his injuries. You will join him in the palace shortly." Elmira's sentiment was compassionate, but the hard eyes never warmed. Her words were like shards of ice. "These are dangerous times," she reiterated. "We tend to overreact to strangers."

"Like me," said Kezia.

"Mostly, the Watcher with you," Elmira said. "You must admit he is feral looking, and from the excellent condition of his uniform he was not returning from the Wall. Perhaps the militia was hasty. It was all an unfortunate misunderstanding. You will explain it to him, won't you?"

Kezia nodded, wondering why Elmira had rescued them.

"Now dress, you and your friend have an interview with Port Calder's Arch Server, Lord Tyrell, my husband."

Elmira helped the fragile Kezia into an extensive addition to the tower. The room had no parallel to any tower she knew of or had visited. Palace, Elmira had called it, and Kezia could see no reason to disagree. As big as her childhood home was, her entire house could fit inside this room. A carpet as wide as a road ran from the imposing doors, across a polished stone floor to a raised dais, on which stood a wide, high-backed chair that dwarfed its occupant. Shimmering curtains covered the Audience Chamber doorways on either side behind it.

Kezia felt herself shrink as Elmira led her towards the dais, one painful step at a time. The crowd milling around the fluted support pillars bowed as Elmira passed. Among them, she glimpsed the occasional black robe of a server, several brown ones, which Kezia had never seen before, and plenty of acolytes in white.

Wesley stood to one side, held erect by militia. He looked up as Kezia and Elmira reached the dais. Injuries hardly described his condition. His face was lumpy and he was favouring the arm she slashed when they met. *Poor Wesley. If not for me, you wouldn't be in this mess.*

Taking a chance on how far she could push the unknown advantage that caused Elmira to rescue them, Kezia whispered, "Get him a chair or I won't explain."

Elmira stiffened, then gestured. A chair appeared behind Wesley and as the militia lowered him onto it, Kezia automatically reached for her shoulder bag, but it and its contents were gone. She looked away unable to help him, turning towards Sev Tyrell, enthroned like the legendary Kings of Aithe, feeling a stirring of hatred.

Though dwarfed by his throne, Sev Tyrell was a big man, not fat, tall and broad shouldered like Wylie. His deep-set eyes peered out at her from the shadow of bushy eyebrows. He lifted his chin, his eyes coming out of the shadows, and Kezia noticed that milky cataracts covered them.

"This is the famed healer, Jena Setler," asked Tyrell, confirming Kezia's fear. Her reputation had raced ahead of her.

"So her companion claims," Elmira replied. "Though we have not yet verified this, my Lord."

'My Lord,' thought Kezia with a sudden pang of envy. This was my hope for Willard and me. Lady Kezia, if only ... Suppressing pointless thoughts Kezia realised the reputation she had feared may have saved them. She glanced across at Wesley to thank him.

'Sorry Jena,' Wesley mouthed and Kezia felt her eyes sting. I will repay you Wes, she thought.

"Come closer, girl, my eyes are not so good," said Tyrell.

With nothing to lose and hoping a good result with Tyrell might allow her to tend to Wesley, Kezia spoke up. "I could help you see again, if I had my bag."

"If she were really a healer, my Lord, she would know your sight is not restorable," Elmira sneered.

Elmira's alternating hot and cold attitude baffled Kezia.

"Pity," Arch Server Tyrell said, "with hundreds of Wall wounded coming here we have need of good healers."

A clamour in the corridor outside drew everyone's attention. Elmira froze and Kezia saw fear flash across her face. She gestured to a brown robe man and Kezia saw he held her shoulder bag.

"Can you see to that disturbance?" Sev Tyrell asked impatiently.

"It's all a misunderstanding my Lord," Elmira said above a loud sizzling crack.

Howard, thought Kezia, with relief. No wonder Elmira is so conciliatory. The rumours from Rivers Junction must have mentioned Howard. More likely, Ser Hagen sent a warning and Elmira 'rescued' us, just in case.

Elmira hastily continued, repeating to Tyrell what she had told Kezia.

"My Lord, there are so many refugees and we have so few militia to check for deserters and infiltrators. The Watcher looks feral. They erred on the side of caution."

Kezia's next thought caused her hand to fly to her mouth. Howard's destination was Port Calder. Elmira's fear is for her husband. Poor Tyrell, thought Kezia.

Lady Elmira suddenly produced Kezia's shoulder bag and held it out to her. "You will find the contents undisturbed, Healer." The hard blue eyes pleaded and pierced simultaneously, as if she hated handing it back but was desperate to have the gesture acknowledged.

To Kezia, the abrupt silence beyond the doors felt more ominous than the scuffle. Elmira must have felt the same. With quick movements, she untied a small black bag from the cord around her waist and placed it in Kezia's hand.

"Please accept this as compensation for any perceived injustice."

Kezia hefted the bag with astonishment.

"What about Wesley?" she asked.

"The Watcher is free to go with you," Elmira said, the words ground out through clenched teeth. "The sooner you accept our apology, the sooner this unpleasant business can be ..."

The doors exploded inwards before she could finish. The crowd jumped and scurried into the shadows. In a swirl of green robes, Howard strode through the doors, *Firebolt* already sheathed.

Elmira stepped aside, pulling Kezia with her as Howard strode down the red carpet and stopped directly in front of Tyrell.

"Your tower has wronged Our Lady. I am here to ensure it never happens again." His mismatched eyes blazed, his voice boomed deep and commanding. There was nothing of the boy left.

Lord Tyrell searched myopically for his wife. "As you can see warrior, no one has harmed either the Healer or the Watcher."

"The issue, Sev Tyrell, is the premature deaths of four candidates, the responsibility of your tower."

Kezia felt a chill down her spine when she heard *Firebolt* slither from its scabbard. So much for Howard's claim that executions didn't happen every time a warrior appeared. She pitied Elmira for having to witness this act of barbarism. The other onlookers gasped and edged towards the burst doors, black robes in the lead. *Firebolt's* gem glowed cherry red as Howard stepped forward, pirouetted like a dancer, *Firebolt* a blur as it sliced the air.

Tyrell sat up straight, staring eyes wide in what Kezia thought of as grand acceptance. She closed hers. The whispering whistle halted, and Kezia felt Elmira subside next to her. Instinctively, she reached out to steady the older woman and flinched. Something hard struck her arm. Her eyes flew open. Elmira's head landed at her feet. Kezia screamed, backed away from the falling body, bright blood covering her arms. Her temples pounded and her legs wobbled. Wesley stood and reached out to hold her up, and once again, even above the other screams, she heard Willard's voice ask. "Where are you?"

"Here", was all she managed before blackness claimed her.

Chapter 16

Surviving Perisher elated Averil. Been there, done that. The path now widened and had steps in the steeper sections and Averil almost danced along it, oblivious to the still precipitous drop. The trail was still hard yakka, and bitterly cold, but the wind had abated markedly, the moment they left the pipe.

Beetle by beetle, Averil's chitinous covering disappeared over the next several days. Thank Severne, she sighed, when the last one finally left her face and she could take stock. Incredibly, her Watcher uniform now looked as new as when the academy issued it to her. Gardner explained that most of the Goddess' microbots were multi-functional.

"Clever little beetles," Averil said, enjoying the journey again.

"How are you with heights?" asked Gardner, tapping her on the shoulder.

"The pass didn't trouble me."

"The pass is different. There you had solid rock beneath and beside you."

She was about to ask the reason for his question when they rounded a shoulder and came to the head of a rope bridge strung across a deep valley. Leading into the pipe, the bridges had all been wood planking across solid log beams. Averil studied the three cables arranged in a Vee. The thick greyish one at the bottom was about four inches in diameter. They ended around thick stanchions, held in place by several stays that ran from the top of the stanchion to large ground pegs. Her experience at Wiseman's Ferry had Averil checking the entire anchoring system.

"Feels solid enough," she told Gardner as she kicked a stanchion.

"Our Lady agrees, her microbots have checked it for rot," he replied. "Wait here until I signal you."

"As you wish, master," Averil quipped.

Gardner grinned as he unpacked a rope from his backpack. "Tie this around your waist," he said, handing her one end and tying the other around his own. He stepped onto the thick central cable, still instructing and even demonstrating. "Always keep three points of contact, move one arm or one leg, never two at once, and don't look down. Watcher."

The bridge swayed with each splayfooted step Gardner took. Averil fed out the rope that linked them, making sure it didn't tangle. At the far end, he tied it to a stanchion, then beckoned.

To Averil's surprise, the experience thrilled her. When she looked sideways into the breeze whistling up the ravine, she found it easy to imagine how a bird might feel. In the middle, she slowed to take a long look out to sea. Again, she briefly glimpsed red dots drifting across the gully. They were bigger now, closer, less round, more like an inverted droplet with a black design on the red. She was pleased she hadn't imagined them, but couldn't imagine what they were.

Gardner's tug on the rope brought her attention back to the bridge. It annoyed her so much she made an elaborate show of untying the rope and throwing the end at him.

Gardner immediately started towards her, but Averil waved him back and almost started running up the cable. It bounced and swayed alarmingly, but Averil, with uncanny instinct accounted for each change as she almost ran the uphill half of the bridge at a steady sure-footed jog. She was so delighted with herself she ran the last few steps without holding on. She beamed at the warrior as she jumped off.

"How's that?"

"So you're not afraid of heights," Gardner said, "but you can't swim." His face was in what she called his guard mode. Impassively, he coiled his rope, as if his task had been to evaluate her.

"Swimming, I can learn," she countered, but already the thrill had gone and she resented its loss. Damn all men, they never take me seriously she thought, stomping away. Well, I showed father, I showed Willard and I showed Captain Kingsley Brande. I'll show this Goddess-damned Restoration Warrior.

After the rope bridge, now several days back, the trail picked up the upper reaches of the Mighty Muddy, which they could follow all the way to Roden Crossing, four hundred and fifty miles downstream—a couple of weeks. Now that she might arrive before the Grundston contingent, hope quickened Averil's stride. Currently, the river flowed towards a northern coast gulf it would never reach. Large dunes would turn the fledging river south a couple of hundred yards short. It would then traverse the entire island to an immense delta on the southern coast.

They were soon out of the Barrier foothills, following a seldom-used trail that often disappeared in the scrubby bush.

"Time to stop," Gardner said, tapping her on the shoulder.

"What's the matter? Got no stamina?"

Averil strode on, obsessed with impressing him. His patronising attitude at Wiseman's ferry, Sandbank, and the rope bridge had inflamed her beyond reason.

"It's getting dark," he said.

"We climbed the signal tower in the dark."

"We had Our Lady's help."

"Call her up then."

"I do not command Our Lady. She provides as required."

"Then she bloody well better provide, or I might just fall down a gully," Averil said and strode into the darkness. I must be crazy, she thought.

Night descended and the fireflies appeared. Averil grinned at the tiny lights lighting up the path ahead. She was good at maintaining a rage. It had kept her father at bay until the Academy. It had kept the boys at the Academy at bay. It kept her going now, long after her body wanted to quit. Gardner quietly kept pace.

They walked all night.

As dawn approached, Averil smelt salt in the air. Then the ground beneath her became soft and difficult to walk as the gently rhythmic crash of waves on a beach reached her ears. She looked down and saw white sand. The mountain track had disgorged them onto the coastal dunes. How did that happen? Had she missed the turn or had the fireflies led her astray?

As a wave of fatigue suddenly hit, Gardner passed her, kicking up little piles of sand with each stride.

"Where's your stamina?" he called back over his shoulder.

"Bastard," she thought, and redoubled her pace, fighting down pain signals from protesting leg muscles.

She brushed past him, staggered over a low dune, and confronted a large strangely dressed company. The tableau was so unexpected it instantly and indelibly imprinted itself on Averil's mind.

Behind the company, billowing directly towards her, was a roughly circular expanse of crumpling red material. Thin ropes trailed from there, across the flat sand at the water's edge, to two small wooden boats. Three of the company were loading a large basket into one. Beyond that, standing out to sea, dazzling in the morning light was a small sailing vessel. Severne's sacred symbol, an eye, flapped at the masthead in black on red.

Mutual shocked recognition occurred simultaneously
"ferals," whispered Averil through a constricted throat.
"Grab 'em," one feral yelled.

Averil whirled to find a surprised Gardner. Either his
Goddess did not foresee this or she had and omitted to tell him.
She suddenly remembered the Goddess saying she could not
control everything. This might be one of those times.

Gardner drew his sword his head cocked to one side as Averil
tried to back up but found it impossible. She managed a single
step before sinking to her knees, automatically calling on the
Goddess.

Gardner stepped past her, and after sweeping his sword
through several preliminary arcs, took up the stance. The leading
feral was a big man with black hair and a full beard that covered
two-thirds of his face. The beard parted to reveal a huge smile
of straight white teeth. From his belt, he pulled something that
looked like three weighted cords tied together, twirled it around
his head twice and let fly at Gardner.

Averil watched, fascinated, as the whirling cords wrapped
around *Brimstone* and the weighted ends dropped to the sand.
She had expected the device to flash into non-existence. She
saw Gardner's knuckles tighten on the hilt but *Brimstone's* gem
remained dull and lifeless. A Goddess- named sword had no
right to fail and yet the blade's edge did not spark. Gardner
used the powerless sword to fling the corded device back at the
thrower who uncannily snatched it from the air and with wide
white grin said in barely understandable Aithish, "Just testing
warrior."

With a supreme effort, Averil got to her feet and stood
back-to-back with Gardner leaning on him for support as the
ferals encircled them. Even unpowered *Brimstone* was still a
formidable weapon in skilled hands. She hoped Gardner was

skilled. She had never considered she might die while under warrior protection.

Tossing her own knife from hand to hand, she tried to intimidate the surrounding ferals. The lifeless tip of Gardner's sword flicked into her peripheral vision at each end of the arc he weaved. The ferals outnumbered them four to one, with nowhere to run even if she could manage it.

The salt tainted air from the Dividing Sea was fresh, the rising sun gently warming. It flooded the bay, highlighted the beauty of the nearest of the mountainous rocky islands known as the Pearls. Gulls wheeled and cried on the breeze and wavelets toppled quietly onto the beach.

A morning to die for, not to die on, thought Averil. I'm too young and I haven't had Willard's offspring yet, have I Severne?

As she calmly prepared for what might be her journey to the otherworld, Gardner bent to whisper in her ear. "Let me do the talking."

"Talk fast," she said.

The Black-bearded cord thrower spoke first. "Give up your resistance, Gardner. *Brimstone* is useless here. We have no wish to harm you. We also serve."

"Then you should know that this young woman is special to Our Lady," replied Gardner.

Young woman, she liked that.

"We have no wish to harm her, but ..."

"Standing aside and letting us pass would please Our Lady."

" ... we cannot let her go," Blackbeard continued. "We serve Our Lady, not uplanders, who continue to exclude us from our birthright."

"Bastards," interjected Averil. Furious, she leapt forward and slashed with her knife, caught the nearest feral by surprise, and opened a long cut across his chest. The man cursed and clamped his free hand over the wound but didn't move as she stepped back fury spent, staring at him with grudging admiration.

Blackbeard spoke on as if nothing had happened. "We saw you on the bridge. We cannot assume you did not see us. If it was only you, Gardner, we would not be concerned, but we can't take a chance on your Watcher clad friend."

"But I saw nothing," Averil protested. What she had meant was she didn't understand what she saw. "Thanks for telling me there was something to see." As she spoke, she looked over at the basket in the boat, then at the mass of red material lying on the sand. Red dots that float in the sky. Her eyes widened. "Flying craft, you can fly ..."

She trailed off, Blackbeard watching her avidly. Oh shit! *Legends* spoke of flying craft returning to the skies, but it had said nothing about bloody ferals flying them.

"You see our problem, Gardner. You can come peacefully or chance having your fire-breathing friend harmed in the melee. We won't offend Our Lady by killing her, but she might lose a limb or two."

His broad smile was so at odds with his words, Averil couldn't tell if he was serious. All her training emphasised they were bloodthirsty savages you couldn't trust. Better to die than let them capture you. What was now obvious, they had no fear of warriors. Everyone she knew would have scarpered by now. She looked to Gardner for a lead and envied him when she saw his inward-looking expression as he talked to the Goddess. Slowly, Gardner raised his sword, tilted the tip back and sheathed it.

"You're just giving up?" Averil asked astounded. "It's only four to one. I thought she pledged you to die protecting me."

"How would my death protect you?"

"Ugh." Averil did not disguise the disgust in her voice. "To think I once wanted to be like you."

Blackbeard held out his hand for her knife. For a second Averil considered giving it to him point first, or take him hostage, as she had Kingsley, but who knew if he was important enough? Without Gardner's help, fighting was pointless. The ferals were closing in. She relaxed her stance, and threw the knife between his feet.

"Thank you," Blackbeard said.

"Sail," shouted a feral from a rocky outcrop further up the beach.

"Quick," Blackbeard yelled, and the beach was suddenly alive with activity.

One feral went to put a choker on Averil, but Gardner stepped in, "I will vouchsafe her conduct."

Traitor, she thought as he hastened her down the beach to one of the small boats. He could free them now while they were busy. That he didn't, meant the Goddess had other plans for her, or perhaps for him.

She glanced back as Blackbeard's crew gathered up the red material, folded it into a large bundle, then stuffed it into the basket, which, when loaded, took up half of the other boat.

Blackbeard stood in the stern, holding the tiller, issuing crisp orders. His remaining crew pushed the boat off the sand, scrambled aboard and bent to their oars.

Their flying craft staggered Averil. Having the use of a ship, she understood. According to the academy tutors, some island captains traded with, and for the enemy. The rewards were commensurate with the risk. If the Coastwatch caught them, they would hang.

The island's Coastwatch ruled the Dividing Sea. The ferals had few ships, and apparently no desire for more, making a seaborne invasion unrealistic. Every attempt made by Charismatic Doane, and his predecessors, had concentrated on scaling the escarpment known as the Break, and breaching their Wall.

Averil knew immediately why the ferals couldn't let her go. Their flying craft would shift the likelihood of a successful breach in their favour. For the first time in centuries, a feral invasion was a possibility. She had to get word to the Watchers.

The sailors chanted rhythmically in time with their oar strokes: dip, heave, raise, return. It was hard to see feral sailors as any different from a well-tanned islander sailor. In fact, anecdotally she had heard defections occurred both ways.

The boat picked up speed, buffeting through the waves. Seeing how quickly their distance from the shore grew alarmed Averil. When she looked over the side at the impenetrable frothy green, she felt stirrings of panic. The boat was small and unstable. Her fearlessness on the rope bridge and the beach vanished. She dreaded falling overboard, but it was more than dread that made her stomach lurch. Each big swell that hefted the boat high then dumped it in the following trough made her feel queasy. She closed her eyes against the feeling and felt worse.

"Ship oars," she heard Blackbeard call, and suddenly they were gliding through a flatter green, into dark shadow. Their run ended with a jarring thud and the small boat rocked violently as ferals jumped to a net hanging on the side of the ship, now so much bigger than it had appeared from the beach.

"Up," Black Beard shouted and Averil tried to stand, but her legs went to jelly. Gardner hoisted her to her feet, slipped a rope under her arms and tied it at the front. Before she could protest, the ferals hauled her up the side of the ship by the armpits. As she twisted and turned, her back elbows and knees found every knot in the net. Gardner climbed beside her.

The sailors, who hauled her aboard, rushed her across the deck to a hatch and manhandled her down a short flight of steps into dank semi-darkness. She regretted not having the time to get a good look at her first ship close-up. They forced her head down as she they jostled and dragged her along under the low deck to another hatch covered by a wooden lattice from which issued the most appalling stench. They removed the lattice and dropped her through. Her legs buckled and she sank into a pool of stagnant water, her pack catching, jerking her around the neck. She collapsed in a fit of coughing. Rats scurried and swam away from where she fell.

Gardner joined her.

"So much for them not wishing us harm," she spat at him between laboured breaths.

"You're alive," he replied. The warrior squatted to inspect his surroundings.

"You call this living."

"You need rest. There's a dry spot on those cables." He walked bent over, back through the stinking gloom to Averil and turning her over grabbed her pack and dragged her across to the coiled ropes. Averil was too weak to resist.

"Push with your legs. You need to get your body out of the bilge."

Averil was past exhaustion, too tired to laugh and though she tried, her legs had no power left in them. Marching hard for a day and a night on an empty stomach had finished her. She could not lift herself. Besides the small comfort of her back against the ropes and the rocking of the ship, while making her queasy also made her eyelids droop. She didn't even see the rats returning as she drifted into fitful sleep.

• • • •

Averil smiled in her sleep at the deliciously distinctive aromas of coffee and sizzling bacon. Our Lady's Restoration Warrior has been providing again, she thought as she rolled onto her side to enjoy the last remaining minutes of perfect warmth. Rolling over was difficult, constrained at the sides, and too flexible underneath. Something wasn't right. She woke with a snap to find herself cradled in the gentle swing of a suspended blanket staring at deck planking, a foot above her head. A hammock, he's made me a hammock, for Goddess's sake.

As her mind grappled, her eyes followed where her nose led. Gardner was sitting by the burner he carried, turning a small animal on a spit over it. Coffee steamed in the accompanying water boiler, now hanging from the spit's support. The fire, she noticed, burnt with a blue flame, and a thread of black smoke drifted up through the wooden grate. Averil's astonishment grew as she looked around the compartment, defined by the ribs of the ship and the deck above. It was clean and dry, the ropes neatly coiled in two tight piles.

The motion of the hammock showed they were still at sea. From above came the sound of footsteps, shouted orders, the snap of canvas, the slap of rope on wood, the crew working the ship, ferals or maybe not.

"What's going on?" Averil asked, swinging her legs over and spilling out of the hammock, landing in a heap on the deck.

"It takes practice. Care for some breakfast," Gardner said.

Though still fully clothed, the clothes themselves were again clean and smelt fresh. Is there no end to a warrior's talents or was this more of Severne's - what did Gardner call them - microbots? First fireflies, then beetles—her skin still crawled with revulsion at the memory—What next?

As she joined him, sitting on an unoccupied pile of coiled ropes, she looked askance at the small animal turning on the spit. After a moment's contemplation of its probable origins, Averil decided she was hungry enough.

"Thanks," she said, closing her eyes and taking a bite. The meat was tender and quite tasty. "Our Lady provides."

Averil looked sceptical. "She's not here. You did this."

"I can do many things you might think amazing," Gardner said, his wave encompassing the neat dry bilge. "But I cannot conjure material out of thin air. It bears repeating. Our Lady provides." He pointed at the spit and made little leg motions with his fingers. She stopped chewing and held up the leg bone she'd been stripping. He nodded.

"I figured it's what I'm eating, but I don't get what you're saying. Who helped you?"

He grinned. "Her rat provided."

Averil Looked closely at what she was eating, went to put it aside, then changed her mind and took a big bite.

"That one," he added.

She followed his pointing finger. Red eyes stared back from under the hatch steps, making the fine hairs on her nape quiver.

"Oh," she said, "except for the overly bright eyes, it looks like an ordinary rat. How can you tell it's a ... bot?" She stared back at the rat as if to say, red eyes or not, I'm still hungry, you're next.

"I asked. It's one of several bots aboard that monitor our world for her. That one fetched the ingredients of our meal; coffee, sugar, some spices, and the chicken you're eating." Gardner added.

Averil looked at the clean bone in her hand and laughed. The more she knew about the warrior brethren the more she liked their ways, if not their Goddess.

Her warrior dreams had begun long before the change in her eyes made it hurtful. When they did, her mother had immediately gone to extremes to hide her candidacy and warned her never to mention it to a server. That hadn't stopped Ser Hedley, who seemed to have known before they changed. In time, Averil learned that if she still wanted to become a warrior, her best hope was to join the Watchers, but wearing blue instead of green would always be second best. She should have asked the Goddess when she had the chance. Instead, she'd thrown it away, asking about the wall and then who would father her offspring, both at the prompting of the Goddess. Her stupidity in trying to impress Gardner had killed her second-best option. She was now unlikely to make it to the Wall in time, if at all. She would lose her commission. Is that one of those things the Goddess can't control or part of her plan?

The movement of the wooden grate brought her back to reality. Averil wasn't the only one astounded at the changes. The feral who came down the ladder took one look, dropped the bowls he was carrying, and scampered back up the steps, slamming the grate back in place and yelling for the shipmaster.

"Doesn't look as good as what we're having?" Averil said, eyeing the spilled contents of the bowls. She sipped her coffee, still incredibly reluctant to move.

The rat under the stairs emerged and lifted its leg over the spillage. Then it circled, using its tail to sweep the edges towards the centre. The once sloppy gruel coagulated into a flat round pat, which the rat turned into a compact ball and rolled away. The wooden grate moved again, distracting her, and when she glanced back, rat and ball had vanished.

Blackbeard, who Averil assumed was in control, if not the shipmaster, surveyed the hold with something more akin to speculation than wonderment.

"As you can see, Our Lady provides for those she favours. I would advise you to take good care of how you treat us, Padget of the Stones," Gardner said.

Averil's ears pricked up; 'Padget won't wait'. Did that mean the feral trio, and the man they abducted from Deep Creek, were also aboard?

Paget's black beard showed a large slice of white teeth. "When have I treated you badly, Warrior Gardner? It offends me, you think so. I put you down here for your own protection. We were much too pressed, evading the cursed Coastwatch to attend to honoured guests."

Padget let his eyes travel slowly down Averil's body. "Such a pity to be pressed for time."

Averil would have attacked him with her bare hands, except for the painful grip Gardner had on her shoulder. "Trust her Averil. You will come to no harm."

Padget turned back to Gardner, "Come, we must talk."

They left her to fume alone, except for the two red eyes under the stairs.

· · · ·

Averil's life became routine again. She could do nothing to change her circumstances, and Gardner showed no inclination to do so. He convinced Padget to allow her on the deck provided she didn't interfere with the working of the ship, didn't talk to the crew, and stayed in a specific area in the bow. Only once did Averil hear a voice she thought she recognised. The woman from the feral band. She wondered where they were keeping the Deep Creeker, but she never saw or heard any other passengers. She counted six days on the Dividing Sea, four out of sight of land. According to the sun's movement, they travelled northwest except on the last day when they turned north and sailed into a bay, landing on a bleak section of what had to be a feral coast.

After breakfast on deck, Averil went below to fetch her pack. Gardner joined her and she handed him the builder blanket. "Thanks."

"My pleasure," Gardner replied, stepping down. Then, as he sat on one of the rope chairs he had made, he looked at the pack she held. "What makes you think we're going anywhere?"

"They won't keep us aboard. Our Coastwatch might take them. In that case, we ... I would report what I saw." She avoided mentioning her speculations about the flying craft's potential. She was no longer sure the brethren and their Goddess were as neutral as they claimed. "How am I doing so far?"

"Fair to middling," he conceded.

"Equally, they can't kill us, because for some strange reason they think they serve the same Goddess and you've convinced them I'm a special case. We're at anchor on their side of the Dividing Sea. I figure they will hand me, us, over to their equivalent of the Watchers."

Gardner's eyes unfocussed for an instant while he concentrated. "Impressive," he replied, then paused, as if he had something more to say but didn't know how to continue.

"So, where are we going?"

"Not we, you. Our Lady has reassigned me."

"I thought you were supposed to protect me," Averil blurted.

"I have."

"But you're leaving me at the mercy of a bunch of ferals."

"You will be far safer in their custody than you were at home. Our unbelievers, some of them as high as Arch Servers, are far more dangerous to you than the ferals. They would kill you for who you might be, and for the same reason, your captors will only try to control you."

"Who I might be?"

Gardner cocked his head, probably asking what he could say before speaking. "The Man Who Will Be Face may not yet be born. His mother will probably be a strong female candidate."

"It won't be me." Especially not with Willard, she thought, inexplicably close to tears. She had grown attached to Gardner in a way she had not expected, had not looked for. She had thought herself immune to male dependency, unlike poor Kezia. If she had to breed with someone, Gardner would be a better choice, but that was hopeless. He was a Restoration Warrior, for Goddess's sake. She shook her head, a desperate effort to dislodge unwelcome emotions.

"Will we meet again?"

"If Our Lady requires it, we will." He reached out and brushed a lock of hair away from her eyes. "Protecting you was a pleasant duty, but I have dedicated my life to Our Lady's plan. I must be ready to go anywhere, anytime, as directed."

"So what's keeping you?"

"Nothing, I just came to say goodbye." He stood, crouched over, and headed for the stairs. "Come. They're waiting."

Averil spat, "Bloody ferals."

Gardner turned back to her as he ascended the stairs. "A word of warning Averil, you can forget most of what you think you know about the Federals. They have a place in Our Lady's plan, just as you do."

Averil snarled, "them trying to invade us is in her plan?"

Gardner bit back. "You'll never find out if you don't keep your eyes open and your mouth shut."

Averil looked incredulous, then followed the Restoration Warrior up two decks, blinking in the sudden brightness. Whose side is your Goddess on, she wanted to ask, but by the time her eyes had adjusted to the morning he was gone.

Chapter 17

Two men, running hard, found Willard kneeling over the unconscious Nelda. They headed straight for her, as if she was the sole reason for their coming. Perhaps the Goddess heeded my plea after all, Willard thought.

The younger one, about Willard's age, knocked him aside, putting him on his back. He stood glaring and frowning at him with equal intensity, as if perplexed. My eyes, Willard thought, dazed by the unexpected hostility. He stifled his protest, sensing the man would need little provocation to start a fight.

The older man bent to Nelda, put one hand under her head and gently stroked her cheek with the other.

"Nel wake up."

"I think her back's broken. She was ..."

A boot to the ribs, hard but not vicious, cut Willard short, "Shut your mouth."

Willard winced with the pain. My candidacy puzzles but doesn't frighten this one. I'm not so special here. Brutality he expected from ferals, not his own people. Maybe he'd made a mistake, maybe he was on the other side of the Wall. He'd had enough of this bloke and kicked out, hitting the man's knee, and bringing him down. The surprise on his face as Willard stood, their situation now reversed, turned to hate. The man regained his feet, wincing when he put weight on the knee. Willard watched him tense and ready.

The older man looked up. "Easy Thane, it is not for us to judge. Our Lady sent us for Nelda and she will know the how of it."

This didn't quell Thane. He stared straight at Willard. "If she dies, you die," he said. Didn't he know what befell those who killed a candidate, or didn't he care?

A grunt from the older man drew the attention of both. With quick gestures, he pointed at the tracks Bandit and the boar had made. Willard watched them work it out. The wordless exchange and pointed glances eased some of his fear. Ignoring him, they set to work constructing a stretcher from the staff each carried, slipped through the arms of their jerkins. Nelda remained comatose as they lifted her onto it and set off down the path. Willard had little option but to follow.

The two men easily carried Nelda on their makeshift stretcher. They did not run or jog, simply walked swiftly, ever mindful of their burden, and the pace was brisk until Thane's increasing limp nearly tipped Nelda on the ground, forcing them to stop.

Willard volunteered to take his place

"No, I won't allow it." Thane shouted.

"Then Nelda dies. Shouldering her will kill her, leaving her will kill her. She needs him."

Thane looked stricken. Brother or lover, Willard wondered?

"You, go on ahead. Warn Ser Langley."

Thane left at a hopping run.

Despite Nelda's reticence in saying so, they had a server, thought Willard, picking up his end of the stretcher. As they set off after Thane, walking briskly through the afternoon, the older man introduced himself.

"I am Edwy. Nelda is my daughter."

He didn't mention Thane.

Throughout the journey, Nelda did not stir, and Willard feared the worst. It isn't my fault, he thought, and decided he would have to trust the Goddess to save the girl and him. Nelda had thought him a server perhaps the town would too.

Gradually, as the terrain flattened, the first farms appeared and then abruptly they passing through wide terraces; the road maintaining a continuous, gentle descent. Although green, the land looked poor. Rocky outcrops abounded in the stubble of old crops. Ahead, the sun dropped steadily as they approached what seemed like the edge of the world. The town's tower stood on the brink with only the setting sun behind it.

A belligerent Thane greeted them and walked beside Nelda, anxious looks for her, dirty looks for Willard. Edwy threaded his way through a collection of flat-roofed buildings, each a different colour. Everyone in the crowd lining the street, while treating Willard to furtive glances, enquired after Nelda; clearly a favourite daughter.

As they closed on the tower, the western ocean seemed to rise behind it, and Thane went on ahead, and knocked on the door of the small adjacent house. When Edwy stopped behind Thane, Willard, his arms aching but unwilling to put down the burden he'd volunteered to carry, peered over the edge. It amazed him to find the town continued down a forty-five-degree terraced slope to a vast landlocked lake. Despite first impressions, the place was miles from the sea.

At Thane's insistent knocking, a bent figure opened what was to Willard, the Public Door. The bent figure, presumably Langley, straightened with obvious difficulty, and held the door wide.

"We found this one with my Nel," said Edwy as they carried the stretcher through the door, Thane following. Behind them, the sun dipped into the distant ocean, painting the town in an orange dusk.

The old server's pale eyes lighted on Willard and widened as he passed. He said something over his shoulder to Thane as Willard and Edwy carried Nelda inside, eased her onto a bed and Willard had his first real look at her since replacing Thane as bearer. Her pallor shocked him. Her feet and hands were grey, turning dark, the scar on her hand purple. Despite the care they had all taken, the mountain journey had not been good for her. At least she was breathing, but he doubted she would live if the Goddess didn't revive her. And if she didn't, he'd be lucky to get out alive.

Edwy approached the old man, with Thane close behind.

"My thanks, Ser, but my Nel does not look so good." His dark eyes glanced at Willard and widened imperceptibly, a flicker of recognition passing across his eyes.

"Thank Our Lady Edwy, she would not have sent you on a useless errand. It will be well."

Willard, absently fingering the talisman, wondered how the Goddess knew the boar attack would nearly kill Nelda and have Langley send someone up the mountain. How long had it taken Edwy & Thane to reach them, running uphill with only their staves? Could they have started after the boar attack? He couldn't work it out.

"What are you hiding in your shirt young man?" asked Langley.

Willard could see no difference in the pale eyes of the man Edwy called Ser as he slowly drew out the talisman. Its iridescence clear, even in the indoor dimness. Edwy and Thane took a step back.

The pale eyes blinked. "You found him at the mount's top?"

Edwy nodded and, as Nelda had done, dropped to his knees in the doorway and prostrated himself.

"My humblest apologies, Lord, in my anxiety for my Nelda, I did not recognise you." After a brief pause, he added. "Please Lord, can you help her?"

Behind him, Thane cringed at the words, as if shamed by her father's humility.

"I'll do what I can," Willard mumbled, not at all sure it was possible.

Thane sneered.

"I'll need to consult with Our Lady," he told Langley

"Of course Lord."

As Langley led him to the adjacent tower, leaving Edwy and Thane with Nelda, Willard speculated that Thane and Nelda had oathed. He now wished, having rated Nelda's chance of survival as thin to nil, he'd kept his mouth shut.

"Why is everyone calling me Lord?" he asked Langley.

"Is it not written in *Legends*, that the Goddess will send her Face to begin the Restoration?"

"What does that have to do with it?"

"Do you not wear her talisman, Lord?"

Willard recognised Langley's knack of making every statement a question as a hallmark of servatory training.

"I'm hardly her Face. Having a talisman would only indicate a server. I'm not even an acolyte." Willard pulled at a tuft of his hair.

"Did you not also come out of our servatory?"

"As do servers," or did, he thought, a long ago.

"But Lord, to come out of a servatory you must first enter. How did you enter, Lord?"

"You would hardly ..." Willard stopped with the realisation that the Goddess was attempting to cast him into a role far greater than the one he'd rejected. He had no one to blame but himself. It had been hypocritical to deny her plan and accept a talisman. I should have thought more before acting. He grinned at that. Kezia said he already thought too much.

"You are the server here, aren't you, Langley?" he asked.

"I act in that capacity, while we await Our Lady's pleasure, but I do not have a talisman. Is that not why have you come, Lord?"

Willard had no answer, did not even want to think about why the Goddess had sent him here.

Langley took his silence as answer enough and led him to the tower's spiral staircase.

As they entered the Penitent's Waiting Room, Willard, remembering the times his mother had taken him before he rebelled, noted differences. It was smaller than Deep Creek, with only two pews, one against each wall, which gave the room a friendlier feel, than the one at home, where everyone faced the oracle. He paused at the shimmering curtain across the entry to the oracle, wondering what these people would make of Saint Jon's.

Willard knew the talisman would get him through as it had Averil. This curtain appeared to be the same as every oracle curtain he had encountered: home, the Pillar, Saint Jon's and up on their mountain.

"Will you wait? I won't be long," I hope.

"With pleasure, Lord," Langley replied, staring at the power curtain as if he'd never seen it before. He seemed grateful for the opportunity to sit for a while.

Willard stepped through without apparent hesitation. Only he knew how relieved he was that the talisman worked. This Audience Chamber looked how children's storybooks always pictured it, a cave of dripping stone walls, a steaming crack in the floor under the server's tripod and snakes writhing in the corners. The oracle, however, was missing. No crystal cube, just an altar. Willard was at a loss. How does Langley consult her?

"Where are you ...?" He didn't quite know how to address her after his experience in the Eye: Our Lady, or Goddess, or perhaps just Severne.

"How nice to see you again Willard, and so soon too," the honeyed voice crooned in his ear. "I expected you to hold out longer."

He turned, startled to see a ghostly image of the Goddess standing beside the altar. "What can you do for the girl?" he asked peremptorily.

"What girl is that, Willard? Averil or Kezia?"

"Nelda," he snapped, "the girl who saved me from the boar on the mountain, where ... you dumped. Some choice. You said the choice was mine."

"It is. You are free to leave here."

"No, I can't, and you know it. I don't know where here is."

"Your lack of reverence is unbecoming of my strongest candidate."

Willard gulped, half expecting some sort of reprisal yet he knew she was right. He had lost his awe of her.

"I'm sorry. I didn't mean to be rude. I need you to help Nelda, if you can."

"I can, and will, as a demonstration of my faith in you."

Severne then proceeded with explicit instructions for Willard, most of which made little sense to him.

"Why can't you heal her here in the tower?"

"The healing must not only be done, but must be seen to be done."

"But it will look like I did it."

"How astute of you, candidate Willard."

"And if I refuse?"

"Then Nelda will die."

She had him neatly trapped, with no way out. She was taking advantage of his need to set him up, no doubt to further her plans for him. His respect grew as his reverence diminished.

"I have already prepared her. I put her in a coma."

"What? When did you do that?"

"On the mountain."

"Ants," he said.

"Microbots."

• • • •

News of Willard's arrival and Nelda's imminent death spread quickly through the village. By the time he and Langley emerged pushing a rolling altar Severne called a gurney, it was dark and the entire village, young and old, male and female, each with a blazing torch had assembled at the tower door. Willard removed the heavy package of folded material from the gurney and carefully unfolded the silver bundle in the middle of the Public Path. Once it was straight, he bent and pulled the marked cord. With a hiss, the silvery material rapidly expanded to form a dome. He was glad most of the village seemed to have adopted a wait and see attitude.

Only a few fell back muttering, "aithcraft."

Langley quelled the mutterers with a stern glance, telling them, "The ways of Our Lady are ever mysterious, but they are always beneficial."

He then spoke to Edwy and Thane loud enough for the assembled village to hear. "Fetch Nelda from my house, on Our Lady's rolling altar. Bring her here," he pointed, "to Lord Willard's healing station."

Oh yes, Willard thought, she's putting me right in it. If it goes wrong, I'm dead, but he knew it wouldn't; that wouldn't suit her plan.

"Our Lady wishes us of all to witness Lord Willard helping her restore Nelda. Blessed be Our Lady. Blessed be Lord Willard."

The crowd produced poles for their torches, placed them in two semi-circles on either side of the Public Path between the tower entrance and the gate. The village gathered outside the circle, sitting on the lawns, the wall, transit way and the steps of before Patrons and Paupers doors.

The gathering went quiet when Edwy and Thane returned with Nelda. A sheet like a funeral shroud covered her body, leaving only her white, still face exposed. As Edwy pushed the gurney through the silent villagers to the centre of the torch circle, Nelda's scarred hand fell out from under the sheet. The villagers who saw gasped. The scar was black.

Willard took over, pushing the gurney into the dome, which self-sealed after him. The structure was just tall enough for him to stand. As instructed, he removed Nelda's clothing, continually apologising to her inert form for any accidental intimacy. Many times, he wondered if the whole charade might be futile. He had seen no one less alive. Her skin was cold to the touch, and blotchy grey, except for the scar as black as the crusted blood on her back.

Worn out and sweating from his effort in the close confines, he went to sit on the floor, and a seat emerged from the wall. He sat gratefully and watched with morbid fascination as Severne's ant-like artefacts emerged from the gurney and crawled all over Nelda. He stopped watching when he saw one burrow in through the scab on her back.

The voice of the Goddess whispered from the walls. "You should sleep Willard. The damage to her spine is severe. Repairing it will take all night."

Willard thought about it, but after a glance across at the distorted, torch-lit shadows dancing on the inside of the semi-transparent dome, he decided against it. The crowd was settling in, preparing for an all-night vigil. Willard felt he could not do less.

He could hear most of what they said through the thin fabric. Nelda was, as he suspected, a favourite child, well-liked by everyone; no one had a bad word to say about her. Some, having seen how she looked, mourned already, believing her dead. The sentiment flowed around the structure like a river around a rock. Eventually the murmurs died away, replaced by a soft, melodic chant as her friends offered a combined prayer to Our Lady for a miracle.

Willard quailed as he thought back over how he came to be here at the centre of these people's hopes. He didn't need to ask why.

• • • •

When Nelda's sigh woke Willard, a cold grey light was seeping through the fabric of the structure. He had fallen asleep sitting up, cradled by the fabric. He opened his eyes directly into hers. What a beautiful face, he thought. Smooth, lightly tanned skin, framed by curly black hair, wide-set eyes, clear and alive. He felt his heart jump. Alive! For once, someone hadn't died to save him. He offered a quick thanks to the Goddess. "Keep it up and I might consider the test, which I suppose is one effect you want." He hoped it wasn't true that she could read minds.

"Ser Willard," Nelda said in a soft voice, "what happened? The last I remember was the boar flinging me away." She looked around at the enclosure. "Where are we?"

Willard blinked as he struggled to sit up. "How do you feel?" he asked, eyes locked on hers, noting the colour of her irises differed slightly.

"Wonderful."

He smiled at that. She looked wonderful. He felt around for the sheet. "Try moving your arms."

Nelda raised her arm languidly and a puzzled look came over her face when she saw her hand. Then her hand dropped and she sat up, her face reddening as she tried to cover herself.

"Here," Willard said, eyes averted, holding the sheet up like a screen between them. "I'm sorry, Our Lady insisted." She took and held it up to her throat and stared at him with wide eyes. "I'll leave you to get dressed," he said, adjusting his trouser as he got to his feet and pushed out into the dawn. He stood shakily at the entrance, tired and desperately needing to urinate. Those in the crowd, who were awake, soon roused the rest and they bunched up towards the entrance, watching his every move. The expectant hush made him self-conscious.

A boy at the back of the crowd, now four deep across the Public Path, disappeared through the Public Gate to Langley's house next door, and returned with him soon after. Rubbing his eyes, and leaning on his cane, Langley threaded his way through the crowd to Willard. Willard couldn't help wondering if his frailty, like Ob Walker's, was an act.

"All is well, Lord?" he asked quietly.

Willard nodded. "She's getting dressed," he whispered.

Langley shot him an inquiring glance and Willard quickly explained, then nodded towards the watchful crowd, "what do they expect?"

"A sign Lord," Langley said. "They see you have the eyes. You carry the talisman and you came from the servatory, so they hope you are the promised one. They wait, as I do, Lord, for confirmation."

"What would that be?"

With great solemnity, Langley said, "A miracle, Lord."

Willard almost laughed. "Nelda's revival isn't one. She was never dead." He shivered in the cold morning air.

"Where's Nelda?" someone shouted and he recognised Thane's voice. "Look at him," Thane continued. "He is not the Goddess come to life? Does he look like any sort of Goddess? He shivers in the cold like us."

Langley straightened into his accustomed role. "Your faith has shrivelled to less than your intellect. Come for a telling, Thane, Our Lady will cure your ignorance."

The crowd chuckled. Thane reddened. Willard suspected it was more anger than embarrassment.

"He can't have taken the test. He still has his hair. He's no more a server than you are." Thane shouted.

Willard saw Langley flinch, and the crowd rouse, their frowns directed at Thane. Langley shook off the jibe. He turned with a flourish to the crowd and raised both arms to embrace the dawn. Then slowly he turned to face the dome and pointed dramatically.

"Nelda lives," he shouted.

Heads swung back as one, just as Nelda emerged. Brilliant timing Langley, Willard thought. The crowd rose in tumultuous applause, roaring in unison, "Nelda lives."

Edwy immediately embraced his daughter and then Willard in a huge hug. There were tears in his eyes.

"Thank you," he said fervently and returned to Nelda. The crowd parted to make way but surged back, surrounding the pair. Thane was not among them. Nelda looked at Willard, then back at her hand as she engaged in animated conversation with her father and those around her who also occasionally looked Willard's way. In a brief lull, as Nelda made her way through the crowd, Willard heard her say, "Look, the scar is gone. Lord Willard has made my hand whole."

"Would that qualify as a miracle, Lord?" Langley whispered to Willard. "She's had that scar since she was three."

"A miracle," someone said, and that cry sped through the throng in an instant, morphing as it went: "The miracle man", "The Man Who Will Be Face", "The Face of the Goddess".

Heads bobbed in agreement and craned forward. Willard felt hemmed in. At first, few dared to get close. Most stood back in awe, or bowed. Several prostrated themselves, touching their foreheads on the ground at his feet. Thane, his face dark stood mute at the back, isolated, badly out of touch with the general mood.

Some of the awe-struck edged forward, reaching out to touch Willard, saying, "Bless me, Lord." The surrounding circle tightened as they jostled for position. He felt the crush and then a sharp sting on the side of his head; someone had pulled a hair.

"Stop this," Langley shouted. "If you touch the Man Who Will Be Face, Our Lady will be angry with you." He rapped a few knuckles with his cane and slowly the faithful backed away. A dumbstruck Willard was about to protest when Langley grabbed his elbow and urged him towards the tower.

"Not now Lord."

• • • •

In the days following 'the miracle of the hands', hands not hand, despite Nelda's singular scar, ardent followers besieged Willard whenever he left the tower. It took Langley a nearly two weeks to convince the village they needed to leave Lord Willard alone, insisting the miracle was only one sign, Our Lady had yet to test

Lord Willard. Eventually, he prevailed. Willard still drew furtive glances when he walked abroad, but they no longer mobbed him.

On his first day of pseudo-freedom, ten days since the miracle, Willard explored the limits of his prison. The combined upper and lower village was smaller than Deep Creek. With the abandonment of the servatory hundreds of years ago: the population collapsed, the traffic decreased, the roads became trails and the trails had overgrown until no one could remember where they led. The only exception was the path up the sacred Mount to the high pastures around the servatory.

On the far side of the lake, opposite the jetty where he sat in contemplation of his prison, the outflow disappeared into a sinkhole. The Goddess had him encircled by trackless wilderness, in an isolated village stalled in the past, waiting for the coming of the Man Who Will Be Face.

Without warning, a scream knifed through him. He was so certain it was Kezia he jumped up to help her, but the jetty was empty.

"Where are you?" he asked, and thought he heard her reply, "here", but it was quiet and faded so quickly he could not be sure. He strained to hear her voice, wanting to reconnect. A splash in the lake from a jumping fish broke into his intense longing.

Willard looked around uncertainly as sounds he hadn't previously noticed poured into the silence. Third bell ringing, an echo of his last meeting with Kezia; a loaded goat sled rattling up the steep cobbled path. The staff of the boy leading the goat tapping on the cobblestones beside the animal; a heated conversation between a couple standing outside their front door.

Disappointed, he rose and headed to the tower. He supposed that until he submitted to the test, and finally proved the truth or otherwise of everyone's conjecture, the Goddess would not let him go.

As he entered the Audience chamber, Kezia's scream was still raw in his mind. In front of him, an oracle he was positive hadn't been there when he came to plead for Nelda's life, sat on the altar which had. The blue-white crystal cube hummed with life, its glow throwing a shadow of the altar on the floor.

"What have you done to Kezia?" he said to the empty oracle.

Sparks like fireworks on a dark night swirled and coalesced into an image of the Goddess, more solid looking than her previous ghostly appearance but not as real as she had been in the Eye. Willard liked that the oracle now constrained her, made her unable to move about him. He felt safer.

"Willard, how nice to see you again." The iridescent eyes flashed at him. "Kezia is safe. She was witness to an event she found repellent." The engaging smile beguiled and distracted him. He sighed. Kezia was safe and he had other issues.

"I know you saved Nelda's life and I'm not ungrateful, but the removal of her scar makes them think I'm going to be the Face, your face."

"With a probability of ninety-seven percent, but to be certain you must take the Tests."

It always came back to the test. Tests, he corrected. Test was now Tests, as plural as Nelda's scar-less hand was hands. It was all one test to Willard and the constant push to have him take it had made him fear doing so. What if the conjecture was right, what if he became her Face? He shuddered at her ninety-seven percent prediction for him. Everyone from the Goddess to the lowest acolyte expected too much of the Man Who Will Be Face.

According to *Legends*, the 'Face' of the Goddess, would be both Ob server and brethren leader, required to rule Nuaith, above and below, secular, and religious, Federal and Islander, and that was only the start. He/she must then travel to the Eye to wake the Sleepers, who would help him/her save Nuaith from Typhon. There was no agreement among the Society of Scholars (SoS) on what some terms in *Legends* meant. Who were the Sleepers if not just dead patrons? Who or what was Typhon? Very few of the public and no paupers could afford an oiled casket. Only rich patrons and Arch Servers had a possibility of waking at the Restoration.

Willard's concern however was personal. He wanted to know if he would still exist, if he became the embodiment of the Goddess, and if so, who would have control? He glanced up at her, appalled she might one day be with him every time he took a pee or worse. No wonder Restoration Warriors didn't marry.

His 'No' was emphatic.

The melodious voice crooned, "Why resist when you have the potential to save your world and mine? If I could save our world without help I would, but my Builders restricted my access to the ..." For a moment, the Goddess seemed to struggle for words. "Without the means, I need a physical interface to do what must be done."

The Goddess stood shimmering and came to the edge of the oracle, a scant foot away, her mesmerising eyes now a reflection of his own; blue and green.

"The truth is Willard; you may not be the one. I may have to search elsewhere, but I cannot know until I have tested you."

"Why not assume I'm not and go on searching without me?"

"Because time is running out. I cannot afford to leave any possibility unchecked."

"But I'm not a possibility. You said yourself, you need someone willing and yet you don't even know if the outcome will be successful. I've never been willing and doubly so now because you can't tell me it will work, even if I make the sacrifice."

The Goddess swirled away in a shower of sparks and resumed her seat in the centre of the crystal cube. Her face remained pleasantly impassive, but her eyes coruscated. It was, Willard thought, the closest she had come to showing displeasure or perhaps frustration. He trembled at the thought, but remained resolved, clinging to the remaining three percent.

• • • •

The jetty quickly became Willard's favourite spot. He went there each day at sunrise and sunset, watching the light dance on the water. The rest of the time, he wandered the village, helping wherever they would let him, nervously waiting for another contact. He had no idea how it happened, but he was sure it was Kezia's voice. At night, he would reluctantly return to the tower to sleep.

Feet dangling over the end of the jetty, Willard absently fingered the ring Kezia gave him, and recalled her face on the day she left. Her last words 'Don't forget me', coloured as they were by the pause when she kissed him goodbye, still bothered him. He feared the likely interpretation of the pause, but then the two fleeting contacts, which had felt like he and Kezia reaching out to each other, kept his hopes alive.

The jetty timbers clacked behind him with Langley's easily recognised slow cane tap.

"A pleasant evening, Ser Langley," Willard said, using the honorific as a gentle rebuff to counter Langley's persistent 'Lord'.

"Langley will do fine Lord," he replied and eased himself down beside Willard. After a moment in which to settle, he sighed. "I have often wondered what power draws people to water when they wish to think on weighty matters; perhaps the uncluttered expanse or the calming sounds or perhaps identification with mysterious depths."

"Perhaps a little of each," Willard said, smiling. Matters of mysterious depth were indeed on his mind.

"So what troubles you, Lord?"

"I don't like what your Goddess is doing to me."

"Not my Goddess Lord? Our Lady belongs to everyone. She is your Goddess too. Her Eye watches over all, even ferals and unbelievers." Langley delivered his reply in what Willard thought of as fatherly tones, something he had rarely experienced at home. He turned to make sure Langley was listening.

"She doesn't just watch; she interferes. She took Kezia from me."

"Kezia is important to you?"

"We were oathed."

"Taken from you by Our Lady, you say?"

"We oathed against our server's advice, who else should I suspect?"

"Were this as you say, it would not be without good reason."

"Just not a reason I can understand. Averil, that's Kezia's sister, told me your Lady plans for Averil and me to have children, in case I don't meet expectations. The way my mother and Ser Hedley tell ..."

Langley interrupted with sudden interest, "Ser Hedley Lord?"

A cloud of waterbirds out in the middle of the lake rose in unison and whirled away towards the coast as Willard studied the old face, the bright eyes. "Yes. Ser Hedley was Deep Creek's server when I was born. He was more a father to me than the man whose name I bear, but isn't my father." Willard paused, took a deep breath of crisp mountain air, let the quiet rhythm of wavelets lapping the jetty's pylons soothe him. "Shortly after he left my life unravelled. Kezia left. Mother told me my father wasn't my father. Then your Goddess killed a couple of ferals that came after me, but let the rest of the warband kill Aldus, my brother who isn't really my brother either. Then she killed an entire Watcher patrol to free me so she could send me here. You think all this is coincidence?"

Willard felt his selection of events showed a clear pattern of Goddess interference in his life.

"Ah," Langley said, as if he now understood something that had troubled him for a very long time.

As Willard waited to be enlightened, the sun broke through under the mass of dark clouds. A dazzling golden line stretched across the water, pointing right at him.

Langley rolled his shoulders, then uncrossed his legs and like Willard dangled them over the end of the jetty. "I think you exaggerate Our Lady's part in those deaths, but your being here would make sense if my suspicions are correct," he said softly.

Willard stared at him.

"You may even be her Face, something only your test will reveal. To us, however you are the fulfilment of a promise made long ago." His eyes took on a faraway look. "I have a story to tell. If you have the time, it may help."

"I'm not going anywhere."

"When I was a young lad, younger even than you," he said, glancing at Willard, "a day came when our server, the man I replaced, told us he must leave. This astounded our little village, for strange to tell. He had been with us for many generations, from before our great grandfathers, grandfathers had been boys."

Willard raised an eyebrow. Not even Restoration Warriors lived that long.

"Which is fortunate," continued Langley, "for in all that time no candidate was born here, but I tell this badly, I have put the sled before the goat. You need to understand that I was a foundling left in the Penitents waiting room. Our tower has always been my home."

Langley chuckled at Willard's expression.

"I was playing in the Audience Chamber ..." Willard's eyes widened and Langley hastily added, "I didn't know I shouldn't. It has always been open to me. The shimmering power curtain only ever appears when others are present."

"Our server was often away for long periods and in his absence Our Lady told me things to tell the village. At first, no one believed me. Our custodian had me taken to a foster home and forbidden the tower. It didn't work, of course, because when our server was away, Our Lady would only admit me into the Audience Chamber. It became obvious to all that only I could give tellings and when they turned out to be true predictions, our custodian gave up."

Langley was silent for some time. The underbelly of the clouds blossomed in shades of purple and orange as the bright disc sank between two peaks. The light faded and a chill crept into the air.

"Why are you telling me all this?" prompted Willard.

"To help you understand, I hope. Help me up please Lord Willard."

They started back, the old timbers creaking under their feet as Langley continued. "One day, when I was about eleven or twelve, Our Lady appeared and told me that in two days, our server would be back for the last time. The entire village assembled, and as foretold, he returned. He officially anointed me his replacement and then said his goodbyes. As he was leaving, he gave us one last telling about the Man Who Will be Face. I have waited sixty-three years.'

Baffled, Willard turned to study the old man's face, trying to see what he was getting at, other than constantly painting him as the Face.

"I remember his exact words," Langley said. He took my young shoulders and said, "Your isolation here makes this the ideal place to instruct the candidate destined to be the Face of Our Lady. Watch for him to come from the mount."

Willard's thoughts groaned

"Fool that I was I asked him, but Lord, how will I know him?"

"He cannot come from the servatory unless I send him," he said.

Willard seized his chance to debunk the idea he would be Our Lady's Face. "Our Lady sent me here from the Eye, not your ex-server."

"But who sent you to Severne's Eye?"

"Ob Walker. He's old, but not enough to be your ex-server."

"All true physically, but who prepared your mind for your stay here?"

"Ser Hedley," Willard said, remembering Langley's interest when he mentioned Deep Creek's former server. "You can't mean him. He's younger than my mother."

They stopped where the jetty came ashore. "There should be a sign around here somewhere. I brought it up from the wharf when the port closed."

"What Port? You don't have access to the sea."

"We did once," Langley said, poking in the grass with his cane and mumbling. "It's been so long and our population has dwindled so much, I am the only one who remembers. Ah, here it is."

Willard bent down and rubbed the encrusted dirt away. The engraved letters, though faded and splintered, were perfectly clear: Port Hedley.

"Now do you understand, Lord?"

It must be another Hedley, Willard thought. His Hedley can't have been server here for generations, then Deep Creek's server. He looked up from the weathered sign with troubled eyes. "It can't be the same man."

"Our Lady can confirm it," Langley said, standing, his arms wrapped about his chest, his teeth chattering beneath his smile.

Willard diverted the conversation to think. "We should get you in out of the cold." He took off his jacket and wrapped it around langley's thin shoulders.

"Yes Lord, at my age I find the tower a welcome haven at night."

As Willard helped him up the steep path through the village, he asked. "Supposing I am the one that your server Hedley prepared, though I'm not convinced. What else did he say? What did he expect me to do here?"

"That is between you and Our Lady."

This time Willard's groan escaped his lips. The Tests, of course. Hedley prepared me, the Ob and the Goddess conspired to get me here. The Tests are my only way out. He had to see the Goddess again. And to keep alive the hope, however slim, of reuniting with Kezia, he would have to ask her about the future; a telling seemed unavoidable.

As they reached the tower entrance and passed through the server's Archway into the foyer, ablaze with light, power and warmth, Langley said, "trust her Lord, be proud to be a part of her Restoration."

"I wish," Willard started, but sensing Langley could hear the bitter resignation in his tone, he stopped. His wish, that he had never been born a candidate, went unspoken.

Chapter 18

P adget anchored his ship off a deserted stretch of the coast, and two of his crew rowed Averil ashore, the only passenger to disembark. It annoyed her not to have seen or heard anything further about Kingsley's quarry or the abducted Deep Creeker. It was, she thought, probably Wylie the only candidate other than Willard. If they'd had Willard aboard, the Goddess would have stranded him with her. She committed to memory the ship's name, *The Golden Pearl*, to give to the Watchers once she was free.

It also annoyed her that despite the promises of Our Lady and Gardner, she, as a Watcher captain, in a conspicuously new uniform, marooned on an unknown feral coast, was likely facing certain death. Even before the ship had sailed out of sight, a thrumming of hooves announced she would soon have company. She had to assume Padget had made arrangements to keep her from getting free. Moments later, a feral warband thundered into view around the headland. With nowhere to run or hide, Averil took off her shirt and turned it inside out to hide her insignia.

The warband came to a halt. Seven mounted warriors, two abreast behind a lead rider trailing an extra pony saddled ready, confirming her assumption. The feral on the lead pony, a wiry little man balding in front, glanced briefly at her, uttered a single word "Come" in perfect Islander, then rode off.

A hard-faced female at the rear tossed Averil the reins of the spare pony and like the rest of the band, rode off before Averil had mounted. Realising that on such a desolate unknown coast, she had no option but to follow, Averil mounted, dug her heels into the pony's flank and cantered after them. She had a ride at last, just too bloody late.

A hot sun burned from a pale blue sky, stinging her bare arms as the company of her sworn enemies rode northwest, the same direction *The Golden Pearl* had followed at sea. She found it ironic that at this moment she was closer to the Wall than the Contingent, with little hope of reaching either. She was on the wrong side of the Wall, travelling deeper into the feral lands, further from her commission, further from the plan the Goddess had for her and Willard. To the east, a range of Mountains, the ferals called the Shadows, rose abruptly from the rolling gibber plain. The range, an extension of the Barriers, crossed the Dividing sea as the chain of islands called the Pearls, controlled by the Watchers.

Her captors stopped only once that day, at a wide shallow stream, to rest the ponies and refill their gourds. In the half day since picking her up, they had not spoken to her or each other. Fine by me, she thought, deciding to take Gardner's parting advice, though it had hurt to hear it, to keep her mouth shut—unlike at school.

"The ferals are Goddess forsaken heathens," one of her teachers extolled. "They have been trying for centuries to scale the Break. Why?" he snapped, pointing a finger at Averil.

"They want what we've got," Averil answered.

"True but simplistic, what specifically do we have they want?"

"Power," said Averil, not at all sure of her answer.

Her teacher's gaze spread around the class. "Exactly, the power of the Builders that drives the artefacts, bequeathed to us by Our Lady through her towers, the power that will one day restore the Arch ..."

"But we don't have any," Averil blurted, emphasising 'we', meaning anyone outside the towers. What mother had under the potting shed was exceptional.

The class held their breath. The teacher's stare impaled Averil. "When did you last visit an oracle?"

The class tittered, and Averil flushed. "That's only a shimmery curtain," she said stubbornly. "My mother says ..." At the tender age of ten, Averil had gone on for several sentences about what her mother thought of the towers.

Despite the heat, Averil shuddered at the memory. The teacher had reported her comments. The circuit Arch Server had summoned mother to the tower. It had taken the combined efforts of Magister and Ser Hedley to free Mother.

Now that Averil thought about it, mother was always in trouble. She wouldn't stop helping people, and tales of miraculous cures had a way of getting back to the tower, yet she always escaped any punishment from either the law or the church of Our Lady. Ser Hedley seemed soft on her, fixed any tower problems and Magister dismissed any charges of aithcraft as nonsense, saying he ought to know he lived with her.

Averil looked ahead through the dust at the warband. Two loose files of three, one out in front, all oblivious to the heat. Their ponies all carried bulging leather panniers; hers did not. The members of this warband were both more and less than she expected, taller, thinner, but without the characteristics her Academy masters taught her to look for. True, their eyes were not as round as if they had permanent squint and their skin was much darker but she could easily imagine being the same after a couple of seasons in this landscape. As for the deformities her teachers had told her they possessed, like webbed feet, six fingers or furred bodies, they were simply not obvious. In fact, the only identifying feature was their clothes, including the soft-soled shoes and the tracks their unshod ponies left. Had they dressed in the fashion of home, they could've passed among us unnoticed.

Tits they already have, more than once.

Averil remembered the Academy had paraded a captured feral for their inspection. After carefully scrutinising the man, Averil had pointed out to her unit's combat instructor, "He looks the same as us."

"This one does. That's why they chose him to infiltrate."

"Then how do we tell?"

"Sniff them out, you can tell feral by their stink," he said.

Well, here she was now, surrounded by them and true they stank, but so did she, and so did their ponies. Who wouldn't after a long, slow ride through unrelenting heat and dust? We could all do with a bath. That thought made her intensely grateful to the lead feral when he called an early halt at a wide, shallow stream.

With a trained eye, Averil studied the terrain. A good campsite, on the other side of the river, suggested itself immediately. Flat and cleared, well above the high-water mark, good grass in an otherwise harsh desert. She watched with interest as the lead feral did a quick survey then urged his mount into the stream, heading straight for the spot she had picked out. Gardner was right. The ferals were nothing like the stupid ugly savages the Academy had taught her to expect.

Averil dismounted to attend to her pony, loosening the straps and removing the elaborate feral saddle, still amazed her enemies had allowed her to ride unfettered. She looked around at the others, hoping to borrow a brush.

"It is good to see you know how to care for your mount."

Averil jumped at the voice, strangely accented. Absorbed in the task, she hadn't heard the feral's approach and the unexpected sound of speech after so long in silence was startling.

"First rule of mounted troops, care for your animal or walk," she said, tensing ready for any eventuality.

The feral probably had ten years on her, taller by a head, with dark brown hair cut short like hers. The tanned face a myriad of fine lines radiating from the corners of his mouth and his eyes. "A wise rule you stole from us, Uplander," he said, hand her a brush, his mouth curling with suppressed laughter.

The way he said Uplander made the hairs on the back of her neck rise. She brushed the pony in silence, feeling she had heard the voice before. Her expression when she turned to give back the brush, must have shown she felt a connection.

The hazel eyes studied her. "Have we met?"

"The Meander," she said, thinking he must have been with the warband Kingsley was tracking.

"What is, the me and her?"

"A river at …" She choked off the thought. Home, a place she might never see again.

"I have never been to the Uplands. Why do you think you know me?"

"I thought I recognised your voice."

"I doubt that Averil Mary Leach."

Her astonishment took another leap as he looked her over. He knew her name, her full name. Few people outside her family would know she had a middle name. "How do you know my name?"

"Warrior Gardner wished us to know."

Bastard. Gardner must have met them before they met me. And if he trusts them, does that mean the Goddess also trusts them? It made little sense to Averil that Our Lady of the Towers was also the feral Goddess. A Goddess, yes, but it can't be Our Lady of the towers, the Goddess Severne, it just can't, and yet Gardner not only handed her over to them but gave them her full name; and what other details?

"I am Sumner of the Lakes," he continued, subjecting her to intense scrutiny. "Come, Averil of the Uplands, turn your jacket back the right way and put it on. It is almost dark and the nights here are cold. We must eat and prepare." His voice was deep and slow, his accent slight.

As Sumner led Averil to the fire pit, she tried to pin down where she had heard his voice. If he had been with the band Kingsley was tracking, then he had just lied to her. Never mind the lie. How did he get back here ahead of me? Could the flying craft travel that far, that fast? Is that why they had shod horses? They couldn't bring their own in the craft and had to steal their rides. But no, they came back by boat.

Averil felt dazed by her conclusions. The craft was wind driven and the prevailing wind only went one way, to our island, their uplands; that's how they think of our lands. To them we are up. But the island was only seriously up at the Break, the mile high rupture between the Pointing Finger Isthmus, an extension of the island, and the vast feral continent. No wonder they were so focused on getting 'up' to our lands. And we are the same, calling their continent the lowlands, when not calling it the wastelands. She must learn all she could before escaping back to the Watchers.

Seeing the deference afforded Sumner as they approached the fire, Averil came to realise. He led the warband, not the wiry little man who had been out front when they picked her up. All day, Sumner had been content to remain inconspicuous at the back, sometimes riding alongside her, and no doubt studying her, while she studied who she thought was a leader. He's a smart bastard.

Since she was stuck with this lot, she may as well keep it civil, if not friendly. "Good choice of campsite. Your lead rider did well in selecting it."

"Ambler of the Stones always does well."

"You also look well-organised," she added, surveying the purposeful activity around her. They had lashed a hitching rail between two trees and settled the horse, erected tents in an orderly pattern around the main fire, and though it seemed hardly likely to rain, had dug runoff trenches around them. In short order, the overnight camp looked like a permanent settlement.

"Thank you," Sumner replied with a touch of pride as he showed her to a place at the fire. "We like order. Each knows their duty and does it. Now I must leave you to do mine." He turned away, walked over to his pony, took something Averil couldn't see from his pannier, and then strode off along the river bank into the trees, soon disappearing in the dark.

Curiously, the fire, by now well establish, lay in a narrow circular trench, rather than the traditional fire pit the Watchers would make. Ambler, the wiry little man she had mistaken for leader, was busy tending the fire. Averil, having no duty, sat and contemplated the flames, occasionally glancing up to watch the warbands' comings and goings. The purpose of the line of reed mats they placed at the edge of the clearing defeated Averil's imagination.

With the fire burning down to coals, Ambler, who appeared to be their cook, positioned several metal pots of water on the stones, and spits loaded with chunks of game across the trench. He constantly poked and stirred the bubbling metal pots with a range of utensils hanging from a branching stand next to the fire.

The unusual trench layout fascinated Averil. Its embroidery of large stones, flattest side up, for the pots, was normal, but the pattern of spits across the trench disturbed her. Four spits angled such that they matching the pattern of the four paths around Our Lady's Tower. Again, she had to wonder if they truly worshipped the same Goddess, or if there was a simpler explanation. Perhaps, as her history teachers suggested, both people traced their ancestry back to the Builders. Maybe the layout was from before the Days of Fire, maybe even coming from Aithe with the builders.

Almost in unison, the ferals gathered at the fire. Sumner returned and introduced Averil to each of them. She felt like an honoured guest rather than a prisoner of war. They gave her an ample portion of all they had and except Ethyl of the Stones, called her mother. Ethyl seemed to have taken an instant dislike to her.

"Mother?" she asked.

"In recognition of your eyes. Mother is like your term Lady. A strong female candidate will be the mother of the Face," Sumner told her, ripping meat from a leg of the wild pig with his teeth.

The delicately seasoned, mouth-watering food went dry in Averil's mouth. "Well yes, but ..."

Suddenly she felt besieged by doubts, and a touch of guilt when she remembered how the Watchers treated captured ferals. She looked up to see Ethyl scowling, and wondered if it was the male feral's attitude to female candidates that made her resent Averil, as she herself had resented Willard.

The more she thought about her recent past, the more questions arose. Why did the Goddess bring her here? How does me being here, help her plan? The sighting had to be accidental, one of those events the Goddess couldn't foresee or control. On the beach, Gardner had wanted to keep me from them, but his sword was powerless and so was he without it. And they had abducted Wylie, not Willard. Logically then, she was here by accident, not by any plan of the Goddess.

It was dark by the time they finished and cleaned up, Averil helping where she could. They used the residual light of the dying fire to proceed to the line of mats; an unsure Averil following at a distance. As each knelt on a mat, they turned their faces skyward and chanted. Averil knew, even before she looked up, what the object of their homage would be. Within minutes, Severne's Eye, which ferals called the Jewel of Heaven, waxed bright. When she looked down, to her bewilderment and shame, she saw an empty mat—hers.

• • • •

The ground rose into a dark unfriendly sky. Hazel of the Sands, the plump young feral who shared Ambler's tent, was leading. Sumner, again taciturn, was at the back just in front of her.

Unlike the ferals Kingsley was tracking, Sumner's band forbade conversation on patrol. Early in the journey she had asked "Where are we going?" and Stone Ethyl, as the others called the unsmiling woman 'of the Stones' had given her a look that matched her name. A week with them, and Averil still couldn't tell if her nickname was a bad joke or a term of endearment.

After witnessing their observance of the transit of Severne's Eye that first night, she had prepared to soften her ingrained prejudice, but the friendly courtesy at night seemed to vanish with the dawn and 'Mother Averil' once again became the enemy and the ferals were back to the maddening daytime silences. So be it. Strange as this constant reversal of status was, she would work with it. Clearly, her only duty was to get word of their flying craft back to the Watchers.

Hazel slapped her left shoulder. The warband came to a halt and Hazel glanced at Sumner. Averil watched the exchange with interest. Except for a slight incline of the head, Sumner appeared not to acknowledge her. Ambler held his breath. Perhaps this was some sort of test for Hazel. Sensing danger in the way they now held themselves Averil scanned the horizon looking for trouble. A jagged streak of lightning leapt from the dark underbelly of the massed clouds ahead. Averil automatically began a slow count. She had counted to three before the accompanying thunder rolled across the warband.

"Just over half a mile," she said, and drew a sharp grimace from Ethyl.

Hazel flicked her fingers as if to rid them of something sticky and Filma slapped Averil's pony on the rump as the warband moved off at a trot towards the ridge ahead, straight into the teeth of the approaching storm. Are they mad?

The land rose ever more sharply as they closed the ridge. Averil leant forward as they climbed, their ponies labouring with the strain. The band topped the rise and beheld a sight that made Averil gasp. The crest formed a ridge that curved away in both directions to meet at the far horizon, stark against the approaching storm. In the centre of the vast flat-bottomed valley was a circular lake containing oddly shaped islands. One quick glance was all she could spare before having to give her full attention to the downward plunge.

Disaster struck unexpectedly.

Hazel's pony found a dust hole, stumbled, and fell, pitching her forward. Hazel tucked her head in and rolled, coming to her feet at a run. Averil cringed at the thought of Hazel's hurts even as her pony, swerving to avoid the pair, slammed into Filma's, which lost its footing, crumpled sideways, trapping Filma and rolling over her. The pony scrabbled to its feet and continued. Ambler reached down to grab Hazel's hand as he passed, but she was in the wrong position or too heavy for him. She had pulled him from his pony before he could let go. Both were quickly back on their feet as the rest of the warband flashed past, unable to stop, Sumner desperately trying to drag his pony to a standstill.

Averil felt sick by the time the slope gentled enough for her to slow the mad rush and turn back. When she did so, she noticed she was the last. Sumner was already beside the prone form of Filma, and Sinjon of the Forest was running to join them. Enemy or not, Averil felt sorry for him. Sinjon and Filma shared a tent.

Stone Ethyl, returning to Ambler and Hazel with their ponies in tow, frequently stole grim looks at the sky. Averil followed her gaze out across the lake. Just this side of the distant ridge, a ragged white and brown column like a dirty twisted cloth, reached down from the massive clouds and touched the ground.

"What's that?" she asked, but they were too far away to hear. She wondered if this might be an opportune moment to make a break. She had a pony, and she could pick up Filma's riderless mount on her way out. The phenomenon, snaking unpredictably across the crater, held her back. The ferals, though not afraid exactly, were wary of it, anxious. Having gathered their fallen, they were heading across the slope towards a cave that Averil hadn't previously noticed.

A sudden gust brought cold rain that spattered her face and as quickly, the rain turned into stinging pellets of ice. Averil slapped the pony into motion and sped off across the plain in the lake's direction. The wind rose to a shriek as the distance between her and the writhing column narrowed. By squinting, Averil could see the twisted funnel-like cloud was turning rapidly, kicking up dust and stones as it bludgeoned its way around the lake. It dawned on her that what she thought were bushes whirling around the edge of cloud were in fact whole trees.

Filma's pony was running an erratic course away from both Averil and the whirling cloud, but the cloud seemed to track the pony's every move as if chasing it down. In fascinated horror, she watched the whirling wind overtake the beast, lift it screaming off its feet, drag it up and around the twisting funnel then fling it away.

Averil wrenched her pony around, dug in her heels, and sped away through a shower of debris. The pony screamed and swerved when a tree dropped from the sky directly in front. Behind her, Averil heard the whirlwind hit the lake and chanced a backward glance. Water erupted in a cone under the twisted cloud. The twin columns didn't quite meet. A flash of lightning cracked overhead with a thunderous roar, and the funnel withdrew into the clouds. The water cone collapsed, sending waves across the lake as her pony struggled up the slope towards the cave. The cloud disgorged a torrent as she reached it.

"A wise decision, Uplander," Sumner said without looking up as Averil stepped out of the downpour, trailing her pony.

She stood dripping in the cave entrance, shaking with cold and the aftereffects of heart-pounding fear. The storm beat at her back as she checked the warband for signs of hostility. Except for Sinjon, and as usual, Stone Ethyl, they met her gaze with disinterest. Sinjon's smouldering dark eyes glistened in a frame of shoulder length hair. There was no sign of Filma.

"I'm sorry," she said, raising her voice to overcome the din of the pelting rain and making her apology sound strident and false.

"Sorry will not bring her back," Sinjon said.

"Neither will anger," Sumner added.

Sumner, despite being Sinjon's leader, failed to intimidate him. "My loss is twofold."

Severne's tits, thought Averil. I hope he doesn't mean she was pregnant.

Despite the tumult outside, Sumner's deep voice was clear. "It is always thus; life is at the whim of Our Lady." He stood and showed Averil should have his place at the fire. "I will tend your pony," he said, taking the reins from her, stroking the pony's neck as he led it around the band into semi-darkness at the back of the cave.

Her admiration for him rose again. Feral or not, he's a leader to emulate. He cares, she thought, watching him settle the pony. Gratefully accepting both Sumner's offers, she subsided into the spot by the fire he had vacated. The stale, rancid smell of damp clothing and unwashed bodies went way beyond unpleasant. She would dearly love to shed her wet clothes to dry both them and herself properly, but she had no idea how they might receive nudity. More likely, they would hate the unreadiness that came with disrobing. In silence, clothes steaming, she surveyed the cave and its symmetry immediately distracted her from worrying about what Sinjon's twofold loss meant.

The cave was perfectly cylindrical, like the inside of a huge burrow. It immediately struck her that this was the same as the cave at the outcrop on Willard's farm, the same smooth textured builder material as the walls of Deep Creek's Tower. It peaked at about three times her height; its floor flat with untold years of accumulated debris. The difference was this cave stretched back past the dimply visible ponies into darkness.

· · · ·

The rain petered out overnight, and the rising sun bouncing off the lake below, shone blindingly in through the cave mouth. The warband rose in unison, and shielding their eyes, filed out into the chill morning light.

Averil followed, looking back the way they had come, but the slope was clean, as if the savage twirling phenomena hadn't happened. This triggered a memory, an off-hand remark about ferals at the academy, but it slipped away when she tried to pin it down. If it became important, it would come back. What she knew was that Filma of the Forest was gone, probably dead. Averil assumed they had left Filma in the cave, without benefit of the ritual or burial, as Gardner had performed at the signal tower. The man who fell to his death still haunted her. She was glad now that it had been a server, not a feral.

She mounted and waited to see how the warband would form up. Stone Ethyl took the lead; Hazel and Daisy the tail. They achieved this without a word or a sign from Sumner who took up a position in the second rank next to Sinjon. Until now, she had been at the back, in the middle; in her own rank and file. If she stayed there, it would leave a hole in the third rank next to Ambler and destroy the symmetry they seemed to crave. She wondered if they expected her to take Filma's place, only one way to find out. Averil, looking straight ahead, sidled her pony into the empty place, completing the pattern, gaining a sense of rightness she didn't fully understand. Her assumption went unchallenged.

As Stone Ethyl rode off, heading down towards the lake, Averil felt she had gained two intangible benefits, a change of status and an insight into feral thinking. Is all this an illusion? Am I just fooling myself? That they might accept her until she proved unworthy had merit, but was alien to her way of thinking.

Closer to the lake, the stubborn barrenness of the landscape gave way to small bushes, then stunted trees with gnarled and knotty trunks and sparse drab leaves. Yesterday's twirling phenomena, Severne's Finger, Ambler had called it last night, had torn a swathe of bare earth through the grove on the western shore. The remaining scrub was oppressively quiet in its struggle for life.

For once, Averil remained close-mouthed as the band skirted the small circular lake and rode up the wide path Severne's finger had etched on the landscape. She breathed easier when the band left the depressing flat bottom of the crater and headed for a black hole a little way up the side of the far rim. Another cave. As they climbed higher, it became clear to Averil; it replicated of the cave they had left hours ago. She craned her neck to locate the one behind, reassured when she found its dark mouth directly opposite. Quick glances forward and back revealed the two caves were at the same level. It was easy to imagine them joined at one time, but what purpose such a long tunnel-like structure might serve was a mystery that had died with the Builders.

The band's mood lightened as they began the steeper climb up to the crater rim and Averil again thought to talk to Ambler, the friendliest of her enemies. He refused to answer and with a quick shake of the head showed the conversation was not welcome at present, leaving her with the impression they might talk later.

At one point Hazel and Ambler peeled off, but Averil, too exhausted from the heat, almost asleep in the saddle, took no notice. The rest plodded on through the hot morning. The sun beat on her head and heat from the ground bounced back in her face. Even the hottest days in Deep Creek were tame compared to this. Averil dreamt of the cool forest glade around their swimming hole, the deliciousness of the cold water on her naked skin as she and Will splashed ... Willard. Of all the children who frequented the local swimming hole, what made me think of him?

Hazel and Ambler re-joined the band as they neared the new cave and Averil noticed that each carried extra bags that dripped blood; freshly butchered game, Averil assumed. how they had found so much, so quickly, in such a desolate landscape? I could learn a lot from these people, she thought, noting she no longer thought of them as feral. She even liked some of them, Sumner and Ambler, for example. Stone Ethyl remained unapproachable.

When the warband reached the cave mouth, Stone Ethyl dismounted and walked her pony into the darkness. Sumner followed, then Sinjon, Ambler, Averil, and Hazel. Daisy brought up the rear. The sudden coolness was a welcome relief from the oppressive heat.

Unlike the earlier cave, rays of light from a hole in the roof struck the floor a long way further in. Reflections off the curved walls gave an impression of a tunnel, rather than a cave. Two beams, about a foot high and six inches wide ran along the tunnel floor, dividing it into three paths. As Ethyl led their ponies along the central path between the beams, the sound of their movement: the jangle of harness, the clop of hooves, and the occasional whinny, echoed unnaturally loud in the confines of the tunnel.

As she passed under the hole in the roof, Averil shielded her eyes from the dazzle, and feeling the cold fresh air on her hand, took a few deep breaths. There were piles of rubble outside both beams, so presumably the warbands used this route often and had cleared the central path.

Once they had passed the hole and her eyes re-adjusted, there was nothing in front of her but darkness, yet the silhouettes ahead kept moving. It only made sense if the tunnel went right through the ridge. As they rode on into the darkness, Averil, though barely able to see the tail of Ambler's pony, saw a pale orange light up ahead. It took a second to realise that Stone Ethyl had lit a lantern.

Deeper in, the cave grew colder, as nose to tail the ponies carried them after the lantern, Stone Ethyl not stopping for a midday meal. Averil was about to break the silence and ask how much longer, when the light from Stone Ethyl's lantern went out and a tiny bright circle appeared in the distance.

• • • •

They made camp inside the tunnel, their ponies tethered to the beams further back, and Ambler's cook fire just outside the mouth. Averil, not understanding what function Filma had performed, was unsure if she now had duties associated with the position she had assumed. She stayed close to Ambler, helping to prepare the meal and draw from him what she needed to know. The nightly camp was the time for camaraderie and, as expected Ambler was voluble.

"You don't ..." Averil started, then waited until she had his attention, " ... you don't blame me for Filma's death, do you?"

"Why should I?" he asked.

"I bumped her."

"True, but before that, Hazel's pony fell." Ambler hacked another strip of bloody meat from the chunk he was working and wrapped it around a green twig.

Averil rubbed hairs, dirt, and skin from an assortment of orange and cream tubers. They resembled the carrots and potatoes with which she was familiar but were smaller, less well formed and much blemished, as she had expected the ferals to be.

"Should we blame Hazel who caused you to swerve," Ambler continued, "or her pony for its lack of agility, or the pony's ancestor for siring such a clumsy animal? Perhaps we should blame the digger of the hole the pony stumbled into."

"Whoa. I get your drift."

"Do you really? I wonder." Ambler paused, waved the bloody knife under her nose. "If you go that path, then ultimately all blame lies with Our Lady." He put the knife down, raised his eyes, and touched his forehead. "Blessed be Our Lady."

Averil eyed him speculatively, as Sinjon laid out the mats much earlier than at their first camp, and she now realised not at all last night. The cooking hadn't even started when they gathered for their obeisance. Averil joined them as they knelt, and within moments, their Jewel of Heaven passed overhead. How do they know in advance, precisely when the Severne's Eye will appear? There was more to these people than she had ever imagined.

Their evening meal was one of the most delicious Averil had eaten since leaving home, though the amount of fresh meat puzzled her. She was about to compliment Ambler on the wonderful tenderness, when the events of the day, arranging themselves in the back of her mind, fell into shocking order and the off-hand remark slotted into place. 'ferals,' her instructor had said, 'those cannibals'.

Carefully, she spat the morsel she was eating into her hand, put down the skewered piece she held, and tried not to think about it. Rat was fine but ... I must be wrong; his remark was not serious. I know nothing.

"What do you do with your dead?" she blurted, concentrating on her lap.

"A curious question for mealtime," Sumner replied.

Averil could hardly contain an underlying bubble of anger. "Where's Filma's body?" Still, she did not look up.

"At peace in the builder tunnel," Sumner said carefully.

"Then where ... all this?" Averil faced him, holding out her hand.

"Her pony," he said and she could see her premature conclusions flash across his face faster than her relief. Pony meat, she thought hysterically, only pony meat! She still couldn't stomach it. As she turned and retched, she heard anger in Sumner's tone.

"Jewel of Heaven, Uplander, what do you take us for—animals?"

Chapter 19

Kezia shook with the memory, ranting long and loud at Howard, as if he had executed Elmira for her sake.

"It's barbaric."

"Efficient and painless," answered Howard.

"It was public ..." His answer incensed Kezia.

"Every lesson needs witnesses."

" ... with children present."

"Regrettable."

The way he said regrettable showed scant regret.

"But what good did killing him do?" she screamed.

"Him," enquired Howard.

Kezia put her hand to her mouth, suddenly quiet. "Her," she stammered, "Elmira ... what good did ..." *Dear Lady, what have I said?*

Howard returned her gaze dispassionately, his expression non-judgmental and yet she knew from the way he had enquired he knew she had been referring to her father.

Thankfully, the huge throne room was otherwise empty. Howard had taken control of Port Calder until Sev Tyrell could resume. In fact, his role as Arch Server had yet to begin. His cataracts were minor compared to the way Elmira had kept him blind. *It changes nothing,* thought Kezia. *Father's death worsened my situation, lost me everything. Tyrell's life is not better for Elmira's death.*

Howard interrupted her thoughts. "Elmira ensured that any candidates stronger than her son met with fatal accidents."

"Her death is as much a waste as the candidates she killed. It would've been better to have shown her why she was wrong, and forced her to make amends," said Kezia, still thinking of her father.

"An example had to set, that anyone who kills an untested will die. Her murderous spree may have doomed us all. We are in a race against time. Any of the candidates she killed may have had the potential to be Our Lady's Face."

"Where's the fire?" Kezia snapped.

Howard smiled. "You have no idea what you just said. You're only here because the Days of Fire were survivable. Typhon is not."

"Typhon is a tale we tell our children to make them behave."

Howard regarded her with a look that made her feel small and stupid. "If the prophecies Our Lady has laid out in *Legends* are not true, then there is no point to the existence of any warrior."

"Exactly," Kezia spat back. "All of you are nothing but her executioners, killing anyone who gets in her way."

"Is Our Lady then a liar?"

"The Goddess is different," Kezia snapped.

"Our Lady gave us *Legends,* to keep us focussed on finding her Face. If her quest fails, Typhon will destroy Nuaith. We cannot afford to lose a single candidate of worth before they take her test."

Kezia remained unconvinced. *Legends* was a book of fables; the title amply signposted the content. To her the lesson in Elmira's execution was a salutary demonstration of the power of the Restoration Warriors. She should feel flattered he tried to justify his actions to her, but the thought of her executioners as public servants was so extraordinary, she felt scared rather than flattered. Every certainty in her world was vanishing.

• • • •

Kezia and Wesley stood together on the newly completed causeway tower. From that vantage point, Kezia appreciated Port

Calder's worsening refugee problem. A caravan of wagons, open and covered, plus drays and pushcarts stretched all the way across the plains to the first bridge. The ragged column of despondent humanity advanced at the pace set by their walking wounded. Once proud uniforms were now tattered fragments, dirty and dishevelled, unrecognisable but for the dominance of dark blue. Interspersed with the column were other refugees, hardy pioneers from the Great Plains. Kezia supposed the large numbers of wounded passing through their towns had prompted the plains people to think that the Wall was down, and it was time to abandon their scattered settlements. They had been pouring through Long Gully Pass before she and Wes arrived.

Howard turned all non-combatants north and told them to keep moving. Nobody argued with a warrior.

"Soon there will be no one left to run the Windrail staging posts," Wesley said.

"The what?" Kezia asked.

"Windrail, it has staging posts all along the Star and Arrow Road. It's the main route across the Great Plains."

"Oh," ' said Kezia. She was grateful for Wesley's willingness to answer her constant questions. He is full of surprising information. Their relationship had stumbled into intimacy with no need for overt protestations of undying love. She'd missed her a period about five weeks ago and it hadn't returned. Wesley had avoided mentioning it though he probably knew. Kezia was grateful for his restraint because she had not decided what to do about it. She knew several remedies for losing her burden, but wasn't sure that's what she wanted. Willard would be proud of her indecision. Given what Wesley had suffered when they arrived, Goddess only knew how it would affect the child's future being part feral. She decided she may have to quell her misgivings about the Goddess, and consult her oracle, but not yet. They should probably oathe before it became too obvious, but she wasn't sure about that either.

Unaware of her contemplations Wesley added, "I hate to say it, Jena, but it looks as if we've given up."

"Why say it then?"

"Because we usually hospitalise Watcher wounded in Walfort until they recover. If they're evacuating the wounded here, somebody has decided we may not hold the Wall this next bud."

Kezia nodded her agreement. He was probably right. The two-thousand-mile journey from the Wall to Port Calder would kill as many wounded as it saved.

"Did you know," Wesley continued, "we started planning for a feral breach years ago? The then Watchmaster General decided if it was, we could fall back behind the Barriers and hold up any invasion in Long Gully Pass. We've been building walls across it from the summit down towards Maida. Port Calder is to become the support base for them. This influx is only the beginning."

"How are we going to take care of so many?"

"Ask Howard," Wesley said, nodding in the causeway's direction.

Tyrell was back as Arch Server, and had appointed a new custodian. That left Howard free to go about Our Lady's business. He took command of the militia and was now overseeing the flood of humanity into Port Calder. Kezia easily tracked his movements by his robes and the occasional flash over his shoulder. From the reactions of the surrounding people, she judged he was joking with them as he categorised and directed the wounded. A few short weeks ago, people would have shit themselves at the sight of him, now they joke with him.

Kezia would not have believed it, like everyone she had thought warriors remote, solitary, elusive, only ever appearing to dispense justice. She had watched the boy, fresh from the test, become the warrior who successfully took on the roles of Custodian, Magister and server in the island's biggest city. He had wrought incredible changes not just in organisation but changes in attitude to his perceived role. Kezia wondered how much of what he did came from the Goddess and how much was his own idea. Sometimes he was almost human.

Watching him made her feel guilty. There were people hurting down there. She should be helping. Crisis healing wasn't quite what she had in mind when she'd set up her clinic here, but it had kept her busy for the whole of Bud.

"I have to go. I'll see you later," she said, kissing him tenderly. Wes and her work had stopped her dwelling on the past.

Wesley waved goodbye. "I'll help the Watchers sort the incoming tide." As she watched the militia welcome him with backslaps and laughs, she felt almost ready to forgive Howard for Elmira. Under warrior leadership, the militia readily accepted Wes.

Kezia sighed and made her way to Howard's convalescent hospital, composed of a series of recovery tents, in concentric semicircles, centred around a large emergency tent. To provide the healers with a constant supply of fresh water, Howard had set the burgeoning complex on the banks of the Lynn River.

The stench of death and decay hit her as soon as she stepped inside. Two Bone-Cutters were working on blood-soaked butcher blocks cutting away already hacked limbs that had festered. Had she dared, she could have used hundreds of her mother's jars.

Kezia took her usual place alongside Shelly, the older of the two, relieving a young apprentice healer who looked quite ill himself. Tom Shelly acknowledged Kezia's arrival with a curt nod as she picked up a needle and began sowing together the flaps of skin he had left above the cut. Guessing that this patient had a good chance of survival, Kezia surreptitiously sprinkled a few grains of mother's dust on the stump as she bandaged it. Some would not make it no matter what she did, but when a chance arose, she did what she could with the little she had.

By the time the queue stopped and an exhausted Kezia emerged, it was dark. She arched her aching back and searched the sky, but none of the bright stars overhead moved. Perhaps the Goddess was not watching tonight, perhaps she never had been.

After a wash and a hasty meal, Kezia walked the long centre aisle between rows of camp beds in the amputee recovery tent. The sight of so many with missing limbs upset her but kept her motivated. She wondered why the Goddess, her servers, or the brethren didn't do something about this never-ending slaughter. Why can't we make peace with the ferals?

As if overhearing her thoughts, a lad further down the row was saying to the woman in the bed next to him. "My server says the ferals are evil. They've turned away from the Goddess."

He was missing his right arm from above the elbow. Kezia had sprinkled this stump simply because he was younger than she was. No one deserved to die that young.

The woman, old enough to be his mother, disagreed. "Bloody servers wouldn't know if their arse was on fire, the ferals worship Our Lady just like us."

"Then why do we fight them?" interjected Kezia, squatting between them. "Let me have a look at that stump while I'm here." She unwound his bandages.

"Begging your pardon healer, we aren't fighting them, they're fighting us."

"There's a difference?"

"Shit yeah. They attack we defend. If they stopped, we wouldn't have to fight them off."

"He's right about that," the older woman put in, as Kezia re-bandaged the stump. The wound smelt clean and felt healthy.

"You make it sound simple."

"It is. They just have to stop attacking, and we can all go home."

"So why don't they?"

"Beats me, you'd have to ask a feral."

"Your stitches can come out soon," Kezia said and, excusing herself, moved on.

Near the middle of the next tent, the expression on the face of a woman about her mother's age with short-cropped brown hair and blue eyes stopped her. The woman rested on her elbows, staring vacantly at the man sleeping in the adjacent bed. Her lined face, brown from too much squinting in the sun, could be Averil after a few years on the Wall.

"Are you alright?" Kezia asked.

"He's dead," the woman said.

The tent orderly, a mere boy, sitting at a small table near the entrance of the long tent, nervously watched Kezia. when she looked up and made the circle sign on her chest. He knocked over his chair as he stood and dashed out. Kezia heard him shout 'burial detail' as she turned back and sat beside the woman.

"Friend of yours?" she asked.

"Friend?" the woman repeated, her face screwing up and her eyes closing, as if confused by the question. When the burial detail came in and picked up the body, the woman made no protest, simply tracked them. Helpless to do anything more for her, Kezia again excused herself and moved on. Two beds later, another woman beckoned to her and whispered, "Her husband."

Kezia gaped back at the blonde woman, her head now sunk on her chest, softly crying.

In every tent, the stories were similar. Kezia overheard, or someone told her, a Wall story. Stories that made her wonder, stories that made her cry, or stories that made her blood boil. It was a constant revelation to find out how truly ignorant she had been, but the worst discovery she made was the staggering numbers of Watchers who died coming home to convalesce.

Restless in bed that night, Kezia rolled over and tapped Wesley on the shoulder.

"Jena?" he said into the darkness.

"Did the oracle say how far you were to follow the healer?"

A long silence followed. Kezia felt his body tense and his breathing pause. "To the Wall," he said, so quietly, it was almost inaudible.

Kezia knew he spoke the truth, but his answer again challenged her increasingly confused beliefs about the Goddess. *Did the Goddess know I would decide this, or has she manipulated events to make my decision inevitable?* Analysing her reasons, she couldn't see how. At the wall, she could save more lives by treating them before they made the arduous journey across the Great Plains. It was that simple.

"To the Wall," she repeated softly. The words had a certain ring to them, a sense of destiny, which gave her renewed purpose. On the Wall, she could better atone for her father's death.

"How far is it?" she asked.

"From here," Wesley said, "about eighteen hundred miles as the crow flies, but the shortest route is twenty-two hundred."

Her old dream to be Lady Kezia Leach, server's wife was long dead. Her new dream as Jena Setler, Port Calder's Healer was not working as well as she had hoped. "I'm sorry Wes," Kezia said, but he was already back asleep.

• • • •

On the morning of their departure, Howard tried to convince her Port Calder needed her more than the Wall.

"Why?" she asked him, now suspicious of everything that emanated from the Goddess, noting with a twinge of regret that even her thought pattern had changed from Our Lady to the Goddess.

"All the wounded will end up here."

"All," she quipped? "Half don't make it here."

"You're safer. A dead healer is no use to the wounded."

"I won't be in any more danger than I am here. It's not as if I'll be treating them on the battlements. Wesley says the hospital is fifty miles behind the Wall."

Arguing with him made it hard to believe Howard was a fabled Restoration Warrior. He had become so ordinary. Faced with her obstinacy, he abruptly stopped, wished her well and turned back to the task she had interrupted as if she had ceased to exist.

"Bloody puppet," she snapped, but even this drew no response. She stormed off to join Wesley, waiting patiently with the horses. Howard's sudden disinterest hurt and angered her. She preferred him trying to persuade her to stay, despite knowing the Goddess was behind it. It made her feel needed. If she was truthful, she had felt he liked her, but realistically, she was just a task the Goddess had given him. Now he had another.

Leaving, however, filled her with dread. They were the only riders moving against the flow from Long Gully. As they retraced the last leg of their inward journey to Port Calder, she felt like she was undoing all the progress she'd made. She threw Wesley her packhorse leads and dug in her heels, urging *Providence* to a gallop, racing alongside the road, desperate to get back past the point where they had joined this road, to feel she was going forward again.

At the narrow stone bridge, she leaned forward on the horse's neck and with a feral whoop charged. A wagon about to enter the other side pulled up in a hurry as *Providence* pounded into the approaches. The horses pulling the wagon reared, almost tipping it as Kezia sped past with a shouted apology. She drew to a halt shortly after in Aldgate, originally the last supply station before Long Gully, a place of ancient buildings and narrow streets from which the river took its name.

This was new territory for Kezia. She paused then and looked back at Port Calder, to Howard's convalescence hospital. A second shattered dream already this year. Perhaps it would be better, she thought, not to dream at all, simply take life as it came, day by day, the way Willard did.

Wesley reigned in beside her.

"What do you dream of Wes?" she asked

"I don't, or if I do, I don't remember when I wake."

Kezia smiled. "I didn't mean that. I meant what you dream of doing with your life."

He handed back the reins of her packhorse, "Besides following you, you mean?"

"Yes," she said with some exasperation as they headed into Long Gully.

"That depends where you lead."

"Severne's Eye kiddo, you're as bad as Willard."

The look Wesley gave her was part chagrin, part curiosity, but he said nothing as Kezia withdrew into herself. The outburst had surprised her. She had only ever called Willard kiddo. Wesley's answer had caught her off guard. He had Willard's attitude of being content to let life to happen to him, rather than embrace it. Have I merely substituted him for Willard?

She drew ahead, creating a small dust cloud for the stoic Wesley. With one hand protectively on her abdomen, she tried to think about what it all meant, what was her place in the plans the Goddess had. Beside her, the Aldgate River rushed down the gully along with the straggly groups of wounded. Kezia stopped a group she saw they had critical cases, grateful for the distraction.

Chapter 20

"Willard. What can I do for you this time?"

The Goddess sat on a stool, clad as usual in a long flowing robe, hung from bare shoulders, its plunging neckline revealing. She crossed one leg over the other, the robe parting at the knee to show a bare leg and foot. Her arms rested on the bare knee, crossed at the wrist.

"Er ... a telling," Willard said, as he sat on what he knew to be the server's tripod.

"Ask."

The way she said it, Willard felt mocked, yet her eyes appeared compassionate. "Why am I here?" Willard asked, taking an oblique approach.

"Assuming you mean, 'why am I in Mount Bakor' and not 'why do I exist', you are here because you are by far the most promising candidate of this generation. I cannot chance losing you before you have offspring or take the test, in that order if possible, and preferably offspring with Averil."

He opened his mouth to ask why it had to be Averil and not Kezia. They were sisters after all, except Averil's eyes had changed.

"No," he said, changing his mind.

"No Willard? No to fathering offspring or to the test."

"No to a telling, I've changed my mind. I don't want to know."

He strode from the Audience Chamber, an unasked question answered; Averil had the eyes. His self-image shattered when he realised that like girl candidates, he also was prime breeding stock, no different from one of his ... Arthur's prize pigs. Breeding him to Averil was just the next step, in case he didn't win a Blue Ribbon. He felt sorry for Averil. Girl candidates had it worse; breeding stock with no chance of ribbon, not even allowed to enter the contest.

On subsequent visits, despite his persistent refusals to talk about offspring or the test, the Goddess remained helpful and forthcoming to all enquiries except Kezia's whereabouts. On that topic, all she would say was, "Kezia is safe," and then ask, "how can I persuade you to trust me?"

"Let me go, so I can find Kezia."

"Do you love her?"

Willard, wondering where this led, replied hesitantly. "Yes."

"You do not sound positive."

"But I am. I want her back."

Severne's voice dropped an octave, became silky smooth, "and Averil?"

Willard groaned. Now he knew what was coming. "What about her?"

"You like her, do you not?"

"Of course I like her. She's Kezia's sister," he said, his voice rising.

"Averil almost drowned at Wiseman's Ferry."

Willard was abruptly at a loss. "Why are you telling me this?"

The image of the Goddess stilled. "To show you the consequences of your actions."

"What!"

"You refused to help her. Horseless, she had to walk. The storm that saved you nearly drowned her. That delay forced her to take her chances with Perisher Pass."

Willard was too shocked to speak. The last time he'd seen Averil, the militia was marching her towards the gaol he had just left. He remembered her asking to borrow a horse, but that was before they gaoled her.

"Stopping the oracle wasn't my fault. She wouldn't have needed a horse if that hadn't happened," Willard challenged. He stopped short of accusing Averil or the Goddess for stopping it.

The image of the Goddess settled, the sparks becoming intermittent. "From the start, your actions have put Averil at risk. If you had tested when your eyes changed, all that has happened since may not have happened at all."

"But Averil's alright now?" Willard asked, still struggling with her accusations.

"I have assisted her, as I have you, and will continue to do so until I have what I need. Then you will both be free to pursue your own paths."

"Really," Willard thought. As he left, he latched on to the hope embodied in her last statement, the chance to have his life not determined by any force other than his own.

• • • •

Spiralling sparks settled to show Severne in the same position he had left her in days ago. Her eyes tracked his entrance with what he thought was a speculative look. He had walked down through the town and had sat on the jetty for hours, digesting the information that when she had what she wanted, he and Averil would be free. He was back to ask what she meant.

"I need to test you. If you fail the Test of Reason, you will be free to go immediately. I will reunite you with Kezia."

Test of Reason? Two fragments, like pieces of a puzzle, turned over around in his mind and joined. We will be one if you pass the Test of Faith, and now this: fail the Test of Reason and you're free.

Willard scanned the chamber's bland walls that could change in an instant to moss-covered rocks. His scan came to rest on the crystal cube, and the image of Our Lady, the Goddess

Severne, sitting inside it, calmly watching him, talking to him, trying to persuade him down a track he didn't want to go, because he didn't really understand exactly what these Tests (plural) involved.

It was past time he found out. "Faith or reason, which am I meant to take? Where's the catch?"

"Your attitude would break your mother's heart. There is no catch," she added, sounding very much like his mother.

"The Test of Reason is a preliminary you must pass before attempting the Test of Faith. I will implant a device in your head, which will put you in direct contact with me. This requires only cooperation, not unquestioning belief."

"Then why ask? Why not just do it?"

Severne's image flared as if exasperated. "Because, unless you are willing to submit to the Test of Reason, you are unlikely to have the wherewithal for the Test of Faith, where total commitment to the procedure is vital."

"I should warn you; once you accept the need, I expect you to pass both. The difference in your eyes indicates great potential. Nothing is certain however, and if you fail this stage, it will show I was wrong. I will have no further interest in you." The Goddess paused before adding, "Or your offspring."

"Really," Willard said intrigued. First at the Goddess admitting she could be wrong and secondly that his failure would bring him absolute freedom. "Still, if I pass, as you think I will, I can't have Kezia. Restoration Warriors don't marry."

"Passing the Test of Reason does not make you a Restoration Warrior."

Willard opened his mouth to say 'what' but only a managed an unintelligible squeak.

"Failing the Test of Faith does."

Willard was speechless for some moments. All this time I could have taken the damn test, passed it, and still married Kezia.

"Why didn't anyone tell me?"

"You actively avoided being told."

"Beefshit." Willard cringed as soon as the word left his mouth and but he couldn't stop now. "Hedley was always telling me," and Averil, "about the test, like it was only one."

"Hedley sometimes fails to heed my advice," Severne said, investing Hedley's name with fondness, as if they were old friends.

Willard remained mute. Failing the second test is the problem, not passing the first. How did I get it so wrong? I didn't. They lied to me. No, they didn't. They just left out a vital truth. The Goddess and Hedley misjudged all of us. From the moment the Forrestor brothers met the Leach sisters, as one patron family to another, Kezia and Willard hit it off. Averil's only interest in boys was beating them. Both boys had thought Kezia more attractive, but Kezia chose Willard.

In hindsight, it astounded Willard how far the Goddess and Hedley had then gone, trying to separate him from Kezia and put him with Averil.

"What if I pass?" Willard asked.

"Then I will try to convince you of the necessity to go further, but I cannot give you the Test of Faith until you truly believe in the necessity of doing so."

"I'll think about it."

"I will be waiting, Willard."

• • • •

The room the Goddess called the theatre was in the bowels of the Mount Bakor servatory. Willard lay on the altar, face down like an acolyte prostrating before a server. He felt lightheaded just thinking about how he came to be here, after a lifetime of avoidance. He still wasn't sure this was the right thing to do, but the Goddess had painted it as harmless.

The altar, like the furniture in the Eye, had shaped itself to the contours of his body. He could feel an artefact running mouse-like over his head, removing his hair. The thought of the hairlessness of warriors induced a mild panic that she had duped him into taking the wrong test.

"It will grow back, won't it?" he asked, and the chin-rest adjusted to the movement of his jaw.

In reply, the voice of the Goddess filled the room.

"Yes, Willard, the Test of Reason is a simple procedure. This small patch will regrow."

A cold stinging fluid doused the shaven section as several of the larger fixed artefacts, ranged around the walls, came to life. He watched a big jointed arm flex towards him. aithcraft. He closed his eyes. Despite the Goddess had told him what to expect, the movement sent a shiver through him. It wasn't natural.

"What's it like to talk without speaking?" he asked, focussing elsewhere.

"I can't say."

"You talk to your warriors all the time, don't you?"

"True, but my ..." a long pause, as if she couldn't articulate what she wanted to say, " ... it is not the same for me. In a moment, you will feel a small sting. We will talk when you wake."

"No." Willard said, trying to keep the panic out of his voice.

"Are you now refusing the test?"

"No, but I don't want to wake ... er sleep. I want to stay awake."

"That will complicate an otherwise a simple procedure."

"Can you do it without putting me to sleep?"

"Yes."

"Then I'd prefer to know what's going on."

He felt a tiny vibration at the side and turned his head in time to see a large padded oblong lift over the edge of the altar. It stopped an inch from his nose.

"Eyes to the front, Willard. The head restraints are for your ears."

He turned back and felt the oblong and its twin touch his ears firmly, gripping his head. He squirmed against it, tried to slip out of it, reaching with his hands to pull it off.

"Do you wish to reconsider, Willard?"

He thought about that for some minutes, reworking every decision that led him here, step by incremental step. This was for Kezia. "No," he said.

"Since you seem unable to keep still, I will also immobilise your limbs."

"Sorry," he said, and slowly resettled, concentrating on the tiled floor, as padded grips gently closed over his wrists, elbows, ankles, and knees. The altar tilted up. He was now looking into the room, not at the floor. He felt a sting in his back, like an ant or mosquito bite.

"What was that?" he asked, wanting to reach back and swat it, but his trapped arm wouldn't move.

"Ready?"

Willard tried to nod. When he couldn't he said, "Yes." At least the chin rest allowed him to speak.

"Relax Willard. You will not feel any pain during the procedure."

"I'm scared," he said with difficulty as numbness spread around his scalp and down his neck.

"Perfectly natural but unwarranted, I will not harm the man who may be Nuaith's saviour."

"That scares me more."

"Why?"

"I don't think ... I can do ... what *Legends* says ... the Face must do?"

"You will acquire the knowledge you need during the Test of Faith."

Willard wanted to say he was not taking the Test of Faith, but he could not form words from the thought; his lips and tongue strangely uncooperative. A tiny whirring sound close to his ear made him want to scream, but his throat refused. Though he felt nothing, his imagination provided images that made him sweat.

"Breathe slowly Willard, count each breath. When you get to ten, start again. One, two, three -"

By the time she reached nine, Willard noticed her counting matched his exhalations, and she was slowing down. To test it, he held his breath and she paused until he let it go.

"I cannot begin Willard until you mind is as relaxed as your body."

Having come this far he wanted to get it over with and get on with his life. He forced himself to relax, thinking of himself and Kezia in the cave behind the outcrop.

The whirring began again, but lasted only a few seconds before it abruptly stopped. The lights flared, dimmed, and went out. The ubiquitous background hum faded to silence. Willard couldn't move, couldn't call out, and the head restraints limited his view to a few feet in front and on either side. The orange glow that replaced the failed lights cast deep shadows. Only a few of the builder artefacts showed signs of working, tiny spots like coloured stars. Severne's silence put an edge on Willard's growing panic.

His eyes widened and swivelled at a movement in the shadows. He couldn't be sure it wasn't his overstimulated imagination until it moved again, a growing black hole in the pattern of lights. A figure walked toward him. The figure stepped into an orange pool and pulled back the cowl of his dark robe. It was a long moment before Willard recognised Arch Server Millar. Instant anger shaded Willard's fright. If his mouth could have managed it, he would have spat at Miller.

The Arch Server stepped up to the altar and leaned over Willard to examine the head restraint.

"How unusual. You're awake," he said, evidently surprised.

Willard again noted the different shades of green in his eyes when Millar stood in front of him. How did such a weak candidate pass the test? He didn't, thought Willard, now understanding the significance of the two tests.

"You have become a problem, young Willard. You are about to let Our Lady, the high and mighty Goddess Severne, invade your mind as she did to me. She is babbling at me right now don't you know? I no longer listen; neither should you. Your admirable refusal to date is all that has kept you safe. Once in your head she will pester you until you can no longer distinguish, right from wrong, reality from fantasy."

Willard blinked and licked his lips, his skin tingling with the slow return of sensation.

"Think about it, Willard. People fear Restoration Warriors because they take heads. How can you believe in, or trust, a Goddess whose disciples are nothing more than executioners, whose mere appearance terrorises whole towns?"

Millar brought his face close to Willard, his eyes alight with a strange excitement. He's mad, Willard thought, although what he says makes sense.

"Pity you can't talk," he said straightening, "the numbing will last for a while yet. I should just kill you. You have caused me a great deal of embarrassment not to mention gold when you evaded the ferals. Your brother didn't."

The blatant admission, confirming his hand in Aldus's death, astounded Willard.

Millar stood. "Still, your years resisting makes me hesitate. You would be such an asset to our cause I'm prepared to make you an offer. Make your resistance count. Join the fight against this artificial Goddess and her Restoration."

Willard could feel his tongue fizzing and a slight pain at the back of his head. Where are you Severne?

"Join us," Sev Millar continued, "and you will be free to live as you choose. You will never have to take the Tests. We have our own carefully bred candidate to host the false Goddess and show her up for what she really is: a sophisticated machine. Come to Mono, the god of the Builders."

Willard's mind felt as numb as his body, trying to find sense in Millar's statement; Mono, the god of the Builders.

"Mono is a god of peace. He doesn't need executioners or want war with the ferals. Think about that while you thaw out," said Millar, smiling, his thin face lurid in the orange light.

Willard shuddered, which caused a throbbing pain in the back of his head. He could feel the pads over his ears and tried to move his head, but couldn't.

Millar paced up and down beside the altar as he continued. "Unfortunately for you, Severne started her invasion before I arrived. You now have a hole in the back of your head ready for her to insert her controlling device. With her turned off, however, your only way out of that head restraint is to leave your ears behind, if that's possible. You would then probably bleed to death. I'll give you a few moments to think about it. I know how hard it is for you to decide on anything."

It's only a small hole, Willard thought, fighting panic, resisting the urge to put his hand on the chin rest and rip his head up out of the ear pads. Where are you Severne? Langley? Anyone, even Thane would be welcome. He was stuck with a mad server who wanted to kill him. How could the Goddess be so helpless in the heart of a servatory?

Millar loomed. "Times up Willard. I know you can speak now, yes or no."

Willard's instant, "No," surprised him. To make such an ill-considered snap decision wasn't like him. It would astound Kezia if she ever found out.

"You're a bloody fool boy," Millar said, "but so be it. I leave you to your fate. You will die slowly of thirst, alone on her altar, a sacrifice to stupidity."

Arch Server Millar headed into the shadows and was about to disappear when the lights snapped back on, once again emitting harsh white brilliance. As Willard shut his eyes, he was relieved to hear the quiescent artefacts return to life. Millar whirled, striding back towards him.

"Quit while you're ahead Nyle," said a familiar voice. Behind Millar, he could see a man in green, with a gemmed sword on his back. A warrior stepped from an aisle between two of the banks of winking artefacts. Unbelievable, Willard thought, recognising the face in the green cowl, Hedley.

"You know the penalty for depriving Our Lady of any candidate," said Hedley, "let alone one with such incredible potential."

His voice was stronger, more commanding, somehow threatening. Willard could only stare in fascination. Server and

Restoration Warrior and given what Langley had told him ancient. Willard wondered if Hedley was … human.

"Your test will complete soon," the Goddess said from the padding around his ears.

Millar took a step back towards to the altar.

The gemmed sword hissed as it slipped from the scabbard. Lighting crackled along its edge. "Your attempt to turn Willard to your purpose is an abuse of the trust Our Lady placed in you."

Millar finally found his voice. "What would you know about trust? The servatory has more secrets than a Charismatic's concubine," Millar said, backing up, hands groping for the altar. "Look at him Willard. Remarkable for his age, don't you think? You and I might live seventy years, but Bakor here is already over four hundred and that's only one of his secrets. Ask him how it is. He carries an unnamed warrior sword and yet still has a lovely head of hair. Ask him about your father, your real father."

Ob Walker told me only the Goddess knew, thought Willard, his eyes dancing between Millar's back and Warrior-server Hedley?

"We are done, Willard. Don't speak your answer think the words," the Goddess said, her voice close, as if she were whispering in his ear, closer than from the ear pads. Her rich tones now held layers of meaning, undercurrents of implication, and yet the words rang with truth and certitude as sharp in his mind as the blade biting his neck. As he pondered the extraordinary clarity, Willard felt the restraints on his head ease. The altar slowly tilted back to horizontal.

"I'm curious, Hedley," Millar continued, as he moved to the side of the altar out of Willard's view. "What are you really, a special kind of Restoration Warrior, or something grander, perhaps an awakened builder?" His hand on Willard's back was not a friendly gesture, nor was the razor edge of the knife he laid on Willard's neck. "It matters not. Neither you nor Severne's artefacts are fast enough to reach me before I separate Willard from his life."

"Is that a fact?" replied Hedley?

Millar didn't flinch, but Willard felt a drop of sweat hit next to the blade biting into his neck. It stung. He didn't dare move. The tingling throughout his body had now thoroughly dissipated though he doubted he could speak even if Severne hadn't warned him not to. His mouth was too dry.

[How], he thought?

[Just so], Severne answered.

Willard blinked, already not liking his thoughts overheard. [Does this mean I passed?]

[Only if you continue to listen,] Her answer was immediate and undistorted.

[The hole in my ...]

[Sealed.]

As far as Willard could tell, Sev Millar neither heard nor noticed the brief exchange nor the removal of Willard's restraints. Nor, it seemed, had he noticed the Goddess had finished. His whole attention since the lights came up had been on Hedley.

"It seems we have an impasse. Move towards me and Willard dies, but if I move away from him, I die."

[The implantation went well, despite less-than-optimal circumstances.]

[Will that matter if Millar kills me?]

[Have faith Willard. I am with you and will be always.]

"I will not stop you leaving." Hedley said, the sword tracing slow, tight, snake-like arcs as if trying to mesmerise the Arch Server.

"But how far would I get, do you think?"

"As far as you want. Just never come back."

"You have my word on that, Sev Miller," the Goddess added to the room.

Millar must have glanced down because he said, "Since her machines have now finished their grisly job, I think it might be wiser for me to keep your young protégé hostage."

"That is not an option," Hedley replied, taking the stance, the gem glowing red.

[Ready Willard,] Severne asked quietly.

[For what?] Willard yelped in silence.

[When I drop the altar, close your eyes, and roll right.]

Willard swallowed and felt the edge of the knife bite. [I'll cut my own throat.]

[Now,] the Goddess said and Willard rolled, expecting pain as he fell. He saw vicious hatred on Miller's face as the Arch Server slashed down after him. Willard's hand snapped out, grabbed Miller's wrist, desperately twisting the knife away, pulling him off balance as a tight beam flashed overhead.

Willard's shoulder hit the hard floor. He almost blacked out when his head followed. As he lay there fighting to stay conscious, excruciating pain in his head, Arch Server Millar twitched on top of him.

[How is he?] asked Severne as Hedley rolled the Sev off him, relieving the pain in his ribs. Willard glanced across and saw the hilt of Miller's knife sticking up from his chest. He added another death to those the Goddess had caused, this time by his own hand. Even though Miller deserved it, Willard was sick at heart. Rest in peace Aldus.

[He's lucky to be alive,] said Hedley. [The hilt has broken a rib. He's concussed and the implant site is bleeding. How's comms?]

[Undamaged, but he will need to heal before integration.]

Willard looked up at Hedley, saw the grim line of his mouth and realised he was overhearing a silent conversation between Hedley and Severne.

[Yes Willard. You are indeed fortunate. Miller would have killed you, had his cabal not persuaded him to make you an offer first.]

Willard thought differently. If he hadn't insisted on staying awake, he might be dead. Following his instincts instead of her advice had saved his life.

Severne instantly scotched the notion, [Not true Willard. Rolling on my command saved your life and incidentally showed you are not entirely lacking in faith.]

• • • •

The jetty timbers creaked as Willard and Hedley walked back towards the tower. Willard brushed a hand over the back of his head, felt the fine stubble around the sore spot where the Goddess had replaced a skull fragment and sown back a flap of skin. In a few weeks, Our Lady's voice in his head would be the only sign that he taken the test, though only the preliminary not the real one, the one that made warriors from its failures.

Hedley's return caused much less trouble than Willard had imagined. Apparently, warriors came here often and since no one died when they did, they were welcome. Only Langley's tearful collapse caused any excitement until Hedley explained he and Langley were old friends. Hedley left the shaken Langley in the Goddess's care and accompanied Willard to the lake where he attempted to explain, almost like old times.

"As you are now aware, Willard, I am not what you imagined. Severne trusts you to keep this knowledge to yourself."

"Then who are you?"

"A man, as you are, a lot older and no wiser. As Langley may have told you, I was server here for many years long ago. I never intended to come back. Millar forced my hand and once here ... I didn't expect Langley would still be alive. I'm sorry. The situation would never have arisen if I had given credence to the suspicions you voiced to Ob Walker."

Willard drew no satisfaction from the vindication. Millar's death had left him empty, ending his desire for revenge. He shied away from the thought that the hollowness of his victory might be because his killing blow was not deliberate.

"How did Millar stop the Goddess?" Willard asked, thinking of what happened to Averil.

Hedley eyed him speculatively. "He didn't. He merely interrupted her."

Not a lot of good if she can't do anything, Willard thought, expecting the Goddess to comment, but the voice in his head remained silent.

They stepped off the jetty, past the disintegrating Port Hedley sign. Children appeared from nowhere to skip alongside, playing a new game of tag, racing in to touch Hedley or his locally famous protégé, the Man Who Will Be Face, then darting away giggling.

"I would have come sooner," Hedley continued, "except this end of the portal was off. It's lucky for you I installed a remote power switch down here and taught Langley what to do in case of oracle failure."

As they entered the tower, the children dispersed.

"Truly Willard even if you fail the Test of Faith, you will have your answers. Nuaith's future could well depend on the outcome of your test. I don't envy you, but someone must take up the challenge."

"Why?"

"Find out, take the test." They turned into a familiar corridor. "And now," he added, "I must leave you."

Hedley held out his hand and Willard felt obliged to match the strange gesture. His old mentor vigorously shook the offered hand. "Good luck," he said and stepped through the corridor's shimmering wall.

Willard watched the silent exchange as Hedley said a new final goodbye to Langley with a similar hand shaking ritual but also with a big, long hug. Then, with a final wave to Willard, he stepped through a door and was gone.

Willard supposed there must be a portal, somewhere in this tower, for him to get back to the Pillar, or the Eye, or perhaps somewhere entirely different. How many destinations were there?

Severne's unexpected whisper in his mind was startling despite its softness, [Hedley has left Preservation Island.]

Willard walked back to the Audience Chamber, knowing if he couldn't learn to control his thoughts, he had to put up with her overhearing them.

[Is this what it's like for every warrior?] Willard thought, not realising he hadn't spoken.

[Yes. As you rightly surmise, you must learn to control your thoughts. Foreign thoughts in your head are infinitely more distracting than your own. You must never become so engrossed in our conversations that you ignore the world around you.]

[How do I do that?]

[Practice. In time, you will learn the ability to vary the intensity and direction of your thoughts as you do with your voice. Hiding your thoughts will be as easy as not talking.]

[I can't wait,] quipped Willard as he stepped through the shimmering curtain and sat on the server's tripod. As the

Goddess coalesced, he added, [Frankly, I expected more. Having the implant is hardly a test at all. How can anyone fail?]

[Failure is the inability to accept my thoughts in their minds. I close their link. Those who go on and take the Test of Faith fail at various levels of the download. Very few reach warrior status. You will go further than anyone before, but even if you cannot host me, all your questions will have answers.]

[That's what Hedley said.]

[Hedley knows.]

[Why not just tell me, why keep it secret?]

[Because at some point you need to make a leap of faith, to take the test because you believe you must. Any lingering doubt and you will fail and the time for failure is running out.]

Willard glanced around the now familiar Audience Chamber, then back at the Goddess trapped within the oracle's big blue crystal. She returned his steady gaze with what he thought was amusement in her eyes.

An impasse, Willard thought, like the one Millar had faced. The Arch Server had not believed, had not been willing to sacrifice his life for his cause. If he had, I'd be dead. Severne did not respond.

[So what happens now?]

[I do not know. You are my strongest and most difficult candidate. I cannot let you go untested and I cannot test you unless you are ready.]

[That's not what I meant. Now that I've passed the first bit, I can marry Kezia.]

[That choice was always yours.]

"It won't be if I have children with her sister," Willard said, breaking into speech, feeling better for it, thinking to her when she was right in front of him seemed silly.

Severne answered in kind, "I have already told you Willard, you need not marry or have sex with Averil, I can ..."

"Except I still can't see any way to marry Kezia once I take next the test," interrupted Willard. "If I pass, I'm you. If I fail, I'm a warrior. Either way, I can't marry her."

"I do not forbid warriors from marrying. Most choose not to."

"Why?"

"The Test of Faith alters their perspective."

"So Millar was right. You're not content to map out my future. You want to alter my perspective to make me like it."

"That is a perverse way to view the knowledge you gain."

Willard was no longer listening. Clearly, despite everything he'd done his situation was worse. The real test was still ahead and the Goddess was still pushing him towards it. But how can I trust her if she holds things back?

Severne answered with a voice, "That will come in time. Now that we have direct communication, you will only ever hear the truth. Constant verification of this will build trust. From trust will come true belief, then I will test you."

Then I will test you, reverberated through Willard's mind. He felt like he was holding the tower bell as it struck. He just had a telling, direct from the Goddess with no chance of server misinterpretation or misrepresentation.

"No, you will not test me," he said with all the deference, defiance, and determination he could muster. "I will not submit. I will not give up Kezia."

The Goddess stood. "Not even to save her life, Willard?"

Willard's mouth gaped. He had no answer. He could not imagine a set of circumstances in which his compliance would save her life, but the implicit threat in her words made him tremble. Arranging the circumstances would not be difficult. He could not be sure if that chilling thought was his own or hers.

[You wouldn't,] he thought.

The voice of the Goddess boomed at him from the walls. "Do not underestimate your importance in my plan, Willard." Then as her image winked out, a parting thought unfolded in his mind, [Trust me Willard, or you will lose her.]

Part II: The Test of Faith

Interlude

The man sat facing the sea, his legs crossed, his lined hands resting lightly on his knees: open, palm up, thumb and forefinger looped.

[Do you think meditation helps, Hedley?]

[Yes,] he thought back. [Meditation helps Hedley.]

He rose, knowing he would get no further peace and as he threaded his way down one of New Adelaide's rubble-strewn roads added, [and that helps you. I am cataloguing and persevering things we may need. It keeps me sane in your insane world, or would you prefer me as I was, when you last found me?]

[This is how I last found you. Same pose, different pile of rocks. Willard is as recalcitrant as ever, spending his days roaming Mount Bakor seeking a way out. And if he succeeds, he will go after Kezia, not Averil.]

Was that an accusation, Hedley wondered? [In hindsight, Averil was too young. Our timing was not good.] he said, including her in the blame.

[If Averil was too young, why did you introduce Willard?]

A definite accusation this time. Hedley pushed back. [I didn't introduce him. You put Willard in the same social strata as Jorgena's girls. He and his brother were friends with Kezia and Averil well before puberty. When Willard's eyes changed, Kezia saw him as a solution to her problems, and the rest is history.]

Birds flew past, sweeping up through trees growing in roofless rooms, flashes of blue and orange amongst the green; a vast ruined city softened by nature. He had several years work here identifying critical items for Kestrel. Then he needed to coax Jorgena into piloting the shuttle to the colony ship.

Severne interrupted his thoughts. [You allowed them to oathe.]

[They bypassed me,] he said, wondering if further hardware degradation was affecting Severne's processes. Severne's personality profile had changed. He could remember her sarcasm, but not this petulant apportioning of blame.

[I understood Kezia's need for Willard, but why did Willard choose her over Averil?]

[Love. Where love will strike is unpredictable. It develops in mysterious ways, part of being human.]

[I am ... I am ... trying to save the world.]

There it was again, the hesitation he and Jorgena had noticed before they escaped the orbiting station. Severne's inability to articulate what she wanted to say often ended with a sudden rush of words on a different topic.

[All this is now academic Severne. You need to concentrate on alternate ways of getting the progeny you need from Willard and Averil.]

[I am, but it takes time. Howard has settled Kezia as Port Calder's healer. I have detained Willard but Gardner had to surrender Averil, a temporary setback.]

Hedley smirked, [Something unforeseen?]

[That too, is academic. When Averil reaches the Wall, I will release Willard. He will proceed there to find Kezia and I will ensure be meets Averil. Perhaps then, this ... this ...] A long pause, Severne suddenly tongue-tied again. [... that develops in mysterious ways will have a second chance.]

Chapter 21

Willard did not venture back into the Audience Chamber for several weeks after Severne's veiled threat against Kezia, during which he blocked his mind to her. Then it occurred to him that this did nothing but maintain the status quo.

"Severne?"

Her image coalesced in front of him. "You called ... Willard."

For a moment, he had the insane notion that she was going to say 'master'. He ignored it. "If Averil is at the Wall, would it not be in your interests to help me get there?" Privately, his impudence, trying to bargain with the Goddess, appalled him.

For once, she did not immediately reply. The image simply sat there as if thinking. Willard felt immoderately pleased to have posed the question.

"You may go," she eventually replied.

"Go? As in, leave Mount Bakor?"

"Yes Willard. I brought you here to satisfy myself you could fulfil your potential. You can. You may leave and go to the Wall. As you pointed out, Averil is there."

Grinning madly, Willard stepped out of the Audience Chamber. An equally beaming Langley sat in the crowded Penitent's Waiting Room. He looks almost spritely, Willard thought, as the aging server rose to greet him.

"We have a full house for you, Lord."

"I can't see them; I have to go."

"Go? Go where Lord?"

"Away. I have work to do for the Goddess," he said, taking the talisman from around his neck and trying to put it over Langley's head. "You can have this. It goes with the job."

To Willard's surprise, Langley proved agile for his age and ducked the honour.

"I am too old, Lord. My tenure as acting server ended with your arrival. Are you not staying?"

"No."

"But Lord ..."

They were still arguing when Nelda entered. Her restored body was a study in youthful good health. The black curly hair shone, the dark eyes flashed and she had replaced her goatherd outfit with a plain white smock that hung in loose folds to her sandalled feet, reminiscent of the Goddess.

Of course, thought Willard. The obvious solution made him grin at her. Nelda blushed and looked down as he approached. He had the talisman over her head before anyone could protest.

Langley's howl was one of outrage. "A woman can't be a server."

"Why not? The Goddess is a woman, and Nelda is special to the Goddess. Did she not restore her?"

Langley stammered in incoherent protest. "But the Tests ... the Tests are only ..."

" ... given to candidates," Willard finished for him. "Look closely at her eyes. Nelda is a candidate."

Langley stared at Nelda as if seeing her for the first time.

Willard lifted his voice to address the penitents in ringing tones. "In the name of Our Lady the Goddess Severne I appoint Nelda as Mount Bakor's server." He bent and kissed her on each cheek, then whispered in her ear, "Our Lady awaits you."

He led her through the stunned audience towards the shimmering curtain across the chamber entrance, before turning to face his audience, taking their measure. They were open-mouthed.

"The Goddess chooses who serves, not I. If Our Lady has not chosen candidate Nelda, will not the oracle refuse her entry?"

Nelda turned and looked at him apprehensively. He held her gaze and nodded as he mouthed the words, 'trust me'. She drew in a breath and stepped through the curtain.

As Willard edged slowly out through the awed silence, he wondered what Nelda would find inside, presumably the damp-cave image.

"That was beautifully done, Lord, and despite my prejudices, a worthy choice," Langley said when Willard backed into him.

Willard turned, smiling. "I'm glad you approve."

"You would have made an excellent server."

"Why thank you Langley, but really, I have no desire to tell other people how to live. Perhaps you could tell me how I can get to the nearest settlement?"

"This way Lord, Our Lady said you might ask. I had hoped you would not."

As he led Willard to the central column lifting room, Willard knew the Goddess had expected him to use Kezia to bargain his way out.

"After you, Lord," Langley said, amused by his confusion.

They entered, and Langley closed the door with a tiny click. Willard felt his stomach rise. The door slid open and they stepped out into a long, wide corridor of glowing cream walls and soft blue matting. Hit with a strong sense of Déjà vu, Willard stumbled.

"Are you all right Lord?" Langley asked.

"It's nothing," Willard replied, putting out a hand on the wall to steady himself. The wall was warm.

"I sleep down here in the winter," continued Langley, as if hearing his thoughts, "although not all doors open for me.

Perhaps they will for Nelda." He looked around, then pointed to the door at the other end of the corridor.

"Ah, there's your door Lord."

Willard looked up, but could see no difference between it and any other. "How do you know?" he asked.

"Our Lady told me, and having shown you the door, if you'll excuse the expression Lord, I must leave you."

"Goodbye Ser Langley." Willard said, making the ancient sign, touching circled thumb and finger to head and heart.

Langley beamed and extended his hand. "Just Langley Lord."

Willard shook it and Langley stepped back into the lifting room. "Our Lady be with you Lord," he said as the doors closed on him.

Willard turned and walked down the corridor to the door Langley had indicated. It opened automatically at his approach to reveal a tunnel sloping upwards into darkness. Looks like I have a long walk, he thought, grinning as he stepped over the threshold. Several lights came on, but the tunnel still stretched into darkness beyond the farthest of them.

[This will take you back to the servatory. Please hold the handrail,] Severne said in his mind with startling clarity as the passage floor moved. He could see now why some would want to turn her off. It would take a while not to jump at her sudden intrusions no matter how soft. The walls passed with increasing speed as the moving floor took him on a rapid ride upward, traversing in an hour what had taken him and Edwy a whole day.

He arrived in a room that was immediately familiar. Full circle, he thought. At least now I know where I am, where I'm going and why. The black surface of the portal pulled at his eyes, mocking him. He speculated on stepping through it. Where would she send me?

His speculation ended when the black surface collapse. An image of Severne appeared and pointed. [Please replace the talisman you gave Nelda and follow me.] As Willard picked up the iridescent oblong, he recalled the look of frantic horror on the face of Ser Tomas when he realised Averil had lifted his talisman. He felt guilty for giving his, to Nelda.

As he followed Severne's ephemeral image deeper into the lower levels of the Mount Bakor servatory, doors opened before and closed behind, with now familiar, less magical, builder proficiency. He sensed an underlying pattern to the layout of rooms and corridors and began a mental map of the complex, confident he could find his way out without her help.

The scale of the room Severne led him to made Willard gape. Facing him was a continuous countertop that stretched left and right for as long as Deep Creek's main street. Behind it, yard wide columns rose all the way to the high ceiling. An artefact zoomed from between two columns, and the claws sticking out from its front dropped to counter height. A gemmed hilt protruded from a tooled leather scabbard held firm in the claws. The artefact deposited the scabbard next to two neatly stacked piles on the counter. Willard, recognising some items like the sword and green cloak, concluded she had led him to a warrior warehouse.

Eyeing the group on the counter in disbelief, he automatically used voice to ask. "Who's that for?"

"You, Willard."

"But I'm not a warrior. I haven't even submitted, let alone failed?" He was still getting his mind around warriors as failures.

Severne replied in kind, her voice filling the warehouse room. "The Wall is a dangerous place. I want to protect my investment in you. Please take what you need."

Willard ignored her statement of proprietary interest and reached for the scabbard, withdrawing the blade a little. Tooled into the leather and etched into the blade were the words Severne's Bane. The sword was incredibly light for its size. He was both astounded and elated. With a named sword, he'd be safe wherever he went.

"Pay attention Willard. The sword focuses power through your body from underground power lines. At close quarters, it will cut through anything you are likely to encounter. The power decreases rapidly with distance. Channelling it will drain you. Use the sword wisely."

How can you use a tool made for killing wisely, and as he slipped the shoulder strap over his head, he hoped he never had the need? The ties jumped together around his waist and bonded.

"Try on the clothes."

"I don't want to be mistaken for a warrior."

"Willard, you astound me. Anyone can put on green robes and shave their body, but the named swords I provide are unique to warriors. What you have strapped on your back will undoubtedly mark you as a warrior."

Willard, wanting the sword but not the implied status, figured he could always cover the hilt until he needed to use the sword. He changed the subject. "What are these?" he asked, pointing at a stack of shiny transparent boxes divided internally into two rows of three. The six small cubes looked like chunks of goat cheese in a variety of colours.

"Food concentrates. You are fifteen hundred miles from the Wall." The sound of her voice in his ears was strange, coming as an echo of the thought. "Each square contains sustenance for one or two days, depending how active you are. Place it in your mouth and allow it to melt away."

"I'd need something to carry them in."

"There is a backpack under the clothes."

At the bottom of the backpack, he found a cloth-wrapped package.

"I had Nelda pack you a meal," Severne said.

Willard grinned as he packed one 'food' box into the backpack just in case he was ever desperate and unable to get any more real food.

"They are real food."

"Stop listening to my thoughts."

"That would not help you control them. The next nearest town is two hundred miles north. One box is food for one week."

Willard put two more boxes in the pack, just in case, and then picked up a small round jar with a screw-top lid. The silvery powder inside moved as if alive, which seemed familiar.

"Each micro-injector contains a range of nanites, which, when released in your bloodstream, maintain health and repair injuries," said Severne. "Use them sparingly preferably in secret. Onlookers often misconstrue the results. Kezia is managing well with them."

Willard instantly remembered Kezia had once shown him a jar just like this; her mother's healing dust.

"Where is she?"

"Safe."

A wave of nostalgia caught him unawares, a longing for Deep Creek, for Kezia, for Aldus, for the farm, but mostly for a return to blissful ignorance. Sadly, the only way back is forward and I can't—I won't do that without Kezia's approval.

"You did that deliberately," he challenged.

"You need to be reminded that her fate, yours and ultimately mine, is in your hands. Please take the Test of Faith as soon as you feel ready."

Two can play that game, Willard thought, as he put the jar back on the counter. "Perhaps you will take better care of me if I am more at risk."

"Excellent," said Severne, her surrounding voice overlaid with the sound of clapping, in synchronous with the hands of her image repeatedly coming together.

And If Kezia comes to harm, he thought, hoping she was still listening, even if it's not your fault, then I promise you I will never take the damned test.

"Ah Willard. Truly, the named sword you carry was made for you."

As the Goddess led him back through the complex, he wondered about the differences in her appearance. In Mount Bakor, she had been ephemeral until constrained in the oracle, whereas here she was stronger when mobile. In the Eye, a solid image had confronted him. The eye must be the source of her power, sent to the servatories through the portals and then on to her towers, underground maybe. He waited for her comment. None came. Did he hide that thought, or did she just not answer? How would he ever tell?

The dusty corridor of his first experience here was now clean and well-lit. As they passed under the hole in the ceiling, he could see repairs were under way. A multitude of Severne's little helpers in various sizes and configurations, bots she called them, repairing the place for Ser Nelda.

[You know the way from here,] Severne said in his mind.

A few strides later, he was through the doors that had given so much trouble earlier. He was back on top of the mountain where he had first mistaken Nelda for a boy. The afternoon was sunny and the mountain air crisp. Somewhere in the builder labyrinth below, he had taken a test, but not the Test.

He strode to the edge of the plateau on the northern side of the servatory, free at last, and soon found a path going in the right direction, towards the Wall and Kezia (and Averil). If Kezia wasn't there, he would walk all the way back along the route she had to take to get there. If that failed, then he would trace her movements from Deep Creek.

· · · ·

The path down however, was never more than a goat track. It meandered through a dense conifer forest, reassuringly familiar pines, but taller and straighter than around Deep Creek.

Days passed, the mountains became hills, the pine forest thinned. He stood on a small escarpment. A long way off, a road leading to a tower beckoned. He was getting somewhere at last. When he turned around, there was nothing behind him but the forested slope, no sign of his goat track, as if even the goats had given up ... unless the goat was one of her bots and had erased the track. No wonder nobody ever came to Mount Bakor.

With night approaching, Willard started looking for a new place to camp. The escarpment offered the possibility of a shallow cave or at least the protection of a small overhang. He skirted the edge and found a way down. The small cliff had an overhang, but no caves. In a short while, he had turned the small clearing into a tidy camp. He sat back on the pile of leaves assembled against the low cliff and let a food cube melt in mouth. They weren't as a bad as he had thought they might be, they just didn't give a sense of having eaten. Nelda's small round loaf, cut to make two sandwiches, spread with goat butter, and filled with slices of goat meat and a dark red tuber, Nelda had called beet he found more satisfying.

Idly fingering the talisman inside his shirt, Willard gazed at the name *Severne's Bane* tooled into the leather scabbard, and quailed at the thought of what Severne expected in return. Although still determined not to let having it pressure him into the second test, he now regretted not staying long enough for some expert tuition. He really should know how to use it. He could use a sword of course. Most boys and some girls, like Averil, could one, but a named sword was something else. It projected power that could kill at a distance.

As dusk settled around him, Willard stood and grasped the hilt. The embedded gem glowed with a soft amber light. He drew it slowly, admiring how the etched name, *Severne's Bane,* stood out in sharp relief, and how the blade's edge rippled with tiny sparks.

Severne had said it would cut through anything. He studied a sturdy pine a few steps from his camp, worked out a good angle and lined up the stroke, wondering how much force he would need. He stood and gently squeezed until the gem glowed orange and the blade's edge crackled. When he swiped at the pine, the beam erupting from the tip, effortlessly sliced through that trunk and few others alongside. The lack any resistance threw him off balance. He dropped *Bane* as he fell backwards. The trees hesitated and then slipped down the cut on their sap. Fear impelled Willard to his feet and he scrabbled madly away as the biggest pine gathered momentum, smacking away lesser branches as it rushed to the ground beside him. The thump when it landed shook the earth.

"Struth," Willard said, as the dust and debris settled.

[Willard?] Severne's questioning thought sliced through his turmoil just as effortlessly.

"You could have killed me," he screamed. He hadn't been this frightened since the landslide. "Why didn't you warn me?"

[Of what,] Severne asked.

"The sword you ... I just cut through a whole damn tree and it nearly fell on me."

[Felling trees is not the sword's intended use.]

"What are you talking about? Why didn't ..." he stopped confused, feeling as if he stood on the edge of a precipice. Not only had the Goddess not foreseen this, she had not witnessed it either. It surprised Willard that her Eye watching over him was not as literal as he had supposed.

Severne's thought was clear even through the pounding in his head. [You see why I need the brethren. Sometimes they are my only eyes and ears.]

Heart still hammering, Willard went back to retrieve the sword and found the pine had pushed the blade into the ground and was lying across it. The gemmed hilt protruded up between branches.

"Damn it's trapped."

[What is Willard?]

"The sword you gave me."

[Perhaps if you explain to me exactly what you can see, I could help.]

"The tree I cut has trapped *Bane*."

[If the haft is clear, take firm hold and slowly withdraw the blade.]

Willard did so. The gem in the hilt glowed orange, blue fire crackled along the blade's short viewable edge, below the guard. *Bane* slipped free easily, leaving a burnt wood smell.

"Thanks."

[The knowledge and training you need to use the sword effectively, is provide with the Test of Faith.]

Willard protested, "But you gave it to me without the test, so why not give me the training to use it?"

[Traditional instruction methods are tediously slow. It would take you years we may not have. The Test of Faith takes less than an hour and gives you everything you need.]

Willard knew this gambit. "Where's Kezia?" he asked. Severne acknowledged his question with a chuckle as her presence left his mind, their impasse intact.

Later, as he sat, staring at his dying fire, he went over the incident. Obviously, the absence of response was not proof Severne was not listening. She could be keeping silent just to let me think my thoughts are private. She had already congratulated him once for hiding his thoughts. He knew he could, but how to distinguish between her not hearing and simply not responding eluded him. Did it matter?

He looked up from his contemplation of the coals. The first and most brilliant stars had already appeared above the seaward horizon. Severne's Eye, though bright, flickered through the sparse canopy. All is well while the Goddess watches, the saying went, but this automatic response no longer brought Willard the comfort it once had. Too much contact with the Goddess. I don't know what to believe anymore. She is real, yet intangible and less aloof than I expected. He remembered his hands clapping through her body and wondered if he'd really been up there or was it all an illusion?

[Was the tree you hacked with *Severne's Bane* an illusion?]

Willard glanced at *Bane*. It was, as she said, evidence that not all his encounters with her were figments of his imagination. He held the talisman through his shirt.

[Why should I bother with the test when I already have these?] he asked silently.

[Perhaps to learn the whereabouts of Kezia or the identity of your father,] Severne replied.

"You ..."

[Bitch, is the word you hesitate to think. I admire your restraint.]

Willard glared up at the transiting Eye. If the aithcraft embodied in Ob Walker's portal could physically transport him right across Preservation Island, then it made sense that it might also get him to the Eye and back. If he had been there, then perhaps mother's claim that she had also been there was not as far-fetched as he once thought. He could see no way to verify it except to ask.

[Have I really been to the Eye?]

[You will find out when you take the Test of Faith.]

Her answer didn't surprise him. She would not let any opportunity pass. At least I didn't come back pregnant, he thought unable to suppress a grin.

That night, Willard dreamed of a soft blue plain that ended in a starry abyss. Dragged towards its frightening edge, he shouted silently for Severne and struggled against rough hands, trying to throw him into the void, but there was no reply. The edge loomed, the hands propelling him let go and he was suddenly falling ... into nothingness.

A sharp stab in his knee woke him as he broke through several branches, crashed to the ground, and tumbled to an abrupt and painful halt. He rolled sideways, for a moment feeling as if he was back on the cart heading to Grundston.

[Stay calm Willard.]

Looking up through the tall canopy brought back a semblance of reality. He was on a steep pine slope, below the escarpment on his back and sore all over; history repeating itself. How many did the Goddess kill his time?

[None,] Severne said; her tone sounded hurt.

The sky overhead lightened. Another clear, cold morning with the promise of a hot day. Fortunately, he had landed on something spongy. The smell told him pine needles before his fingers felt their textured softness. He could move but had no desire to; movement brought pain, history repeating still.

[You refused my nanites,] the Goddess mocked.

[I'm not that hurt,] he thought back at her, knowing it was untrue.

The sound of voices somewhere above reached him. Bushrangers, he assumed. Who else would it be out in the wilds?

"Food's good," said a deep muffled voice.

I can't have fallen far, thought Willard.

"Ugh. I don't know how you can eat those ... turds," said a higher, feral accented voice.

Despite his predicament, Willard smiled at the apt description. But a feral out here? [How can they know those pellets are food, Severne?]

Severne remained silent. Willard, not wanting to attract their attention, did likewise.

"Oops," said the deeper voice.

"What did you drop them for idiot?" The higher voice whined.

"Be nice Adee. You said I could thump people who aren't nice. I wouldn't like to thump you."

"Ah, forget it," interrupted the high-voiced Adee. "Come and have a look at this. We were right to follow this one." The whispering hiss of *Severne's Bane* as it slipped from its scabbard told Willard what they had discovered. "This will fetch a good price if I can find someone willing to take it. The jewel alone must be worth a fortune."

"My sword," said the deeper voice, now tinged with awe.

His sword? Who does he think he is? thought Willard?

"Pig's arse you lumbering dolt," Adee replied. "You never got one."

"Maybe we shouldn't have thrown him away, Adee. Not a warrior."

"He can't be a warrior, dolt? He still had his hair."

"He had my sword."

"You never got one," Adee repeated.

There was a pause in the conversation, and Willard found it easy to imagine the exchange of glances. The deep-voiced, true believer, though simple, was not completely powerless. Adee had readily capitulated to the threat of a thumping. How does Adee know he never got one? Is he a candidate? Whoever heard of feral Candidate?

"He can't have fallen far," Adee said.

Feet scrabbling above dislodged a shower of dirt and needles into Willard's face. He tried to sit up and rolled further down the slope. The voices were right behind him.

"There he is, grab him."

Willard heard scrambling above. A further cascade of needles, dirt, and pebbles hit him as hands seized him. One set belonged to a thin, reedy man with a sharply protruding face that gave him a rodent-like look. The other was taller and stockier, with unmatched eyes and a well-remembered face totally devoid of hair and expression.

"Wylie?"

"Hello," Wylie said without a hint of recognition.

Willard's shock subdued the pain as the pair dragged him back up the slope.

"How ..." he stopped just short of saying, in the name of the Goddess," ... did you get here Wylie?"

[No one has told me of this,] Severne interposed.

The eyes in the rodent-like face narrowed as they dumped Willard in front of the short wall where he had slept last night.

Willard stared up at Wylie. The return gaze was benignly vacant.

"What happened to you, Wylie?"

"That's thrice you've named him, candidate," Adee said, evidently surprised. Wylie simply smiled.

"We grew up together in Deep Creek, thousands of miles away, on the other side ... I don't understand. We were candidates together. The last time I saw him he was going into our tower for his test. How did you get here Wylie? What happened to you?" repeated Willard.

"I would've thought that was bloody obvious," Adee said, warming his hands over Willard's rebuilt fire. "There's not a lot going on upstairs with yon Wylie. He failed the big test. Show him your scars, Wylie."

Wylie turned his head, showing two small burn scars on the back of his skull.

Adee spat. "Fried his brain, poor bugger." He seemed to draw some satisfaction at Willard's shock. "I guess they forgot to mention that at candidate school. The test that separates the men from the boys can turn your brain to jelly."

Severne's sharp thought cut across his reaction. [The chances of intellectual damage are extremely small.]

[Tell that to Wylie,] Willard shot back, but his savage quip drew no response. He said nothing to Adee. There was little he could say. Wylie's appearance matched Adee's theory and Severne admitted it could happen. Something had gone wrong. Wylie senior could wait forever, his candidate son would not be returning as either server or Restoration Warrior. [Why aren't we warned, Severne?]

"You, my friend, are an altogether different enigma. A warrior with a talisman or a priest with a named sword would be mysterious, but an untested candidate with both is a paradox."

Willard glanced sideways. *Severne's Bane* lay across his pack, back in its scabbard.

"Don't even think about it," said Adee without looking up. "I'd just as soon kill you as trade you. It's a lot less trouble. But my half-wit friend here thinks your eyes entitle you to those accessories, whereas I wonder how you came by them."

Willard nearly said Severne gave them to me, but changed his mind at the last second not knowing what might offend Adee's belief system. "Our Lady gave them to me."

Adee's reaction was shockingly unexpected. In one blindingly swift move, he was across the fire, holding a knife to Willard's throat. "Don't shit me boy, if there's one thing I can't stand, it's a liar. There is no way the Goddess would give you anything without testing you. What did you do, stumble on a dead warrior?"

[Help, Severne,] Willard pleaded.

The Goddess remained silent. Wylie, who had looked skyward at the mention of the Goddess, was chanting. "I want to go home Lady. Take me home." He stopped and frowned as if he were trying to understand something just out of reach. Then he noticed Adee at Willard's throat.

"You can't do that, Adee. He brought me my sword. If you hurt him, I will have to thump you."

Adee's eyes darted between Willard and Wylie, who stood with his head canted, flexing his fingers. Wylie had always been a big lad, now as a man he was twice Adee's size.

"I wouldn't hurt him you dolt; just scare up some truth." He backed off slowly, a broad smile on his face to placate Wylie. As he sat back, a look of resignation replaced the anger.

Wylie beamed him an expression of pure joy.

[Thanks, Severne.]

[You are fortunate. Wylie's test did not disconnect him entirely.]

Willard relaxed a little, despite bafflement and anger. [How could you abandon him like this?]

[I did not.]

[But you must have been there when he took it.]

[Yes, and as happens rarely, his failure damaged him. I gave him into the care of the servatory.]

[At the pillar?]

[Yes. Arch Server Miller's disloyalty was unknown to me until his disruption of your Test of Reason.]

[How did he get here?] Willard asked and immediately answered his own question, [The portal. Miller, or one of his cronies, dumped him here.]

Severne was silent, but Willard's mind churned. [Shit, I saw their tracks when I first arrived. I was so busy trying to get out that I forgot them as soon as I got the doors open.]

[If you had taken the Test of Faith, then I would have seen the tracks too.]

During this exchange, he noticed Adee intensify his scrutiny and Severne's warning came back to him. Internal communication can be a fatal distraction. He would need to shut her out. [Talk to you later.]

The silence in his head was abrupt, but he knew she was still there, a now familiar waiting presence.

"Help me up, Wylie," he said, ignoring a glare from Adee.

Wylie smiled and extended his hand, bent up at the wrist, fingers and thumb straight together; the universal sign of peaceful intent. "Will you be my friend too? I can have two friends, can't I?"

Willard. Two friends, thought Willard, reciprocating the gesture. You have lots, Wylie, a whole town full, and a family too. "Yes Wylie," was all he managed as their fingers touched.

Wylie nodded at him vigorously, "I ate some food," he said simply.

"I forgive you."

Wylie beamed. Adee grunted and spat. "How kind of you," he said, his expression belying his words.

"Where are you from ... Adee?" Willard asked.

"The name's Aderic," he said, spitting into the fire, watching his spittle sizzle on an ember. "With a face like this, where do you think?" Aderic said as if that was explanation enough.

Willard noted the bitter tone in Aderic's voice. "I'm just being polite."

"Adee's a feral," Wylie said.

"Polite? You're staring."

"I'm sorry, I didn't mean to, but you have to admit you have an interesting face," Willard said.

Aderic nearly choked with laughter. "That's the first time anyone has described my face as interesting."

"I'm Willard," he added, glancing at Wylie for a reaction. Disappointed, he wiped the sweat from his palm on his trousers and again extended his hand.

Aderic ignored it, though he watched avidly as Wylie intercepted the gesture, again touching Willard's fingers.

[What do I do now Severne, I can't leave Wylie out here?]

[Persuade Aderic to take Wylie to Mount Bakor. Nelda will give them sanctuary.]

[How, I don't know how to get back there myself?]

[I can guide them, through Wylie.]

"Our Lady offers you sanctuary in a place called Mount Bakor. With Our Lady's help, Wylie can guide you there."

"Not interested. That's where I found my addled friend, in the care of Our Lady's servers. They ignored him until they needed a bloody workhorse."

[Severne?]

[The only server enclave in this area is Thornton Abbey, 229 miles, 1953 feet, directly nor'-nor'-west of Mount Bakor.]

"Wylie was one of the lucky ones," Aderic continued, a look of respect in his glance at Wylie. "Big strong, and willing to do anything they asked. Their graveyard is full of the weak and the stubborn; like me. But for his friendship, I'd be looking up at a dirt sky."

[I will investigate when I have more warriors.]

Willard smirked at her thinly veiled entreaty for him to take the Test of Faith. Did she expect him to fail, despite what she said earlier?

Severne made no comment. Did she hear, or had he kept those thoughts private? He couldn't tell.

"I can assure you, in offering you sanctuary, I speak for the Goddess."

"Prove it."

"Let me, Adee, please let me," Wylie interjected into their conversation. "Our Lady calls me,"

"What would you accept as proof?" Willard asked.

"Prove the sword is yours."

Willard slid *Severne's Bane* out of its scabbard. The gem glowed.

"Here, give me that," Aderic said.

Willard hesitated.

[Do it,] Severne said. The gem went dull as soon as his fingers left the hilt.

Aderic raised *Severne's Bane* to the vertical and squeezed until his hand shook.

[I will enjoy Aderic's company. He knows more warrior lore than you do and much more than he should.]

The rumours about named swords and Restoration Warriors suddenly gelled for Willard as Aderic handed it back. *Bane* would only work in his hands. He squeezed hard. The edge crackled and a thin beam erupted from the tip. A bird squawked away as a branch fell from the tree above.

Aderic shook his head in disbelief but his words were an acknowledgement of Willard's claim. "Mount Bakor you say. And this brain f... Wylie here is going to lead the way."

Wylie nodded vigorously.

Chapter 22

A lthough still light, Kezia and Wesley stopped when they reached the summit of Long Gully Pass. An engraved stone pillar proclaimed the summit as nine thousand, four hundred and seventy-three feet above sea level. The surrounding peaks soared above them, which made evenings here come early. They had been in the saddle since an hour after sunup, with only a break at midday to rest the horses. Port Calder was a hundred miles, countless bridges, six days and six checkpoints behind.

As often happened, they met a mixed group of wounded Watchers, checkpoint militia and refugees as they prepared to camp. Wesley sighed as they dismounted. It had become Kezia's custom to leave him to set up their small camp, while she joined whatever Watchers convoy was going the other way and asked to see the worst wounded. Catching his expression, she again felt compelled to explain.

"I'm a healer by choice, Wes."

"I know."

"Would you like me to help you set up camp first?"

Wesley sighed again. "No, I can handle it. You should go; do what you need to do."

Early reservations aside, Kezia had become very fond of Wesley. Despite their intimacy, which had her carrying their child, she would hesitate to call it love. He maintained his independence, allowing her to do the same, always producing coin for the little he purchased and never asking her for anything. She supposed he was living off previously accumulated funds. Placing a hand around his neck, she reached up and kissed him.

"Thanks. I won't be long I hope," she said. She pulled away and unhooked her shoulder bag from *Providence*'s saddle. As well as the jars of mother's dust, the brown leather bag now contained many small cloth packets tied parcel-like with twine. Along the way, she had collected several medicinal plants and herbs, at last putting into practice all she had learnt at the Institute of Healing Arts. The shoulder bag was part of her new persona, along with short-cropped hair. She still wore the light grey of Medicorps uniform, but stripped of all insignia.

Between Port Calder and the summit, Long Gully varied from two to three miles of undulating meadow to a thirty-yard-wide ditch, barely enough to accommodate both the road and the river. The checkpoints were invariably at the narrowest end of the nearest wide section, to provide grazing for the militia's horses. The militia only checked those heading east for deserters or infiltrators. They considered those going the other way, sporadic wall volunteers, like Kezia, and merchants seeking their fortune, idiotic; they ignored them.

Staging camps had grown up around the pass checkpoints. All had small but growing cemeteries and nearly all had a small shrine to Our Lady of the Towers. The shrines were about the size of her mother's potting shed, set in a cleared circle ten yards in diameter. All paths led to the single doorway. Inside, instead of an oracle, was a statue of the Goddess. The shrine was a place to worship, not to petition.

Here, at the top of the pass, the camp was bigger, swollen with construction workers, a mixture of Watchers, militia, and civilians. As Wesley had said back in Port Calder, they were building a wall at the far end of the meadow, right across the gully. The checkpoint stood in the central gap of the uncompleted wall.

Here too, at the crossing point, travellers pooled their resources: big pots of meat and vegetables stewed on real stoves in open shelters, fresh baked bread from newly built ovens, plus fruit carried up from Maida, lay on long trestle tables, even a rudimentary pub: two casks in cradles under a canvass awning.

That night, the entire community, both travellers and construction workers, gathered around a large communal campfire. The wine merchant tapped a fresh cask. Its contents flowed freely in the ritual celebration of crossing the Barriers. Often, despite horrendous injuries, the wounded joined in, some smiling for the first time in weeks. All were better for the ministrations of the renown healer, Jena Setler, whose reputation had raced before her like a mountain stream. The singing and dancing went on well into the night and Kezia, who danced lightly and well, was much in demand. To her surprise, Wesley produced a flute and took up with a fiddler. The two minstrels quickly worked out which tunes they both knew, and sitting on the empty barrels produced a haunting combination of sounds.

"Look," someone shouted, "Severne's Eye."

All eyes turned skyward as the familiar light, slowly waxing and waning, traversed a hole in the cloudy night sky, the sighting seen as a benediction on their passage. Shortly afterwards, light snow began falling and the party broke up.

"You play beautifully," Kezia told Wesley, as they hurried back to their camp, the communal fire now only a giant heap of sizzling coals. "What was that last tune, the one you played by yourself?"

"It's an ancient melody called Luna's Theme. No one knows how old it is. Generations of minstrels have passed it down from antiquity. Some say it came from Aithe with the Builders."

"Will you teach it to me?"

Wesley looked at her with interest. "It takes a long time."

She laid a hand on his arm and smiled. "I know."

• • • •

A week from the summit, Kezia and Wesley emerged from the confines of the snow-covered peaks to open vistas. In the past week, along with the continual flow of wounded Watchers and refugees from the Great Plains, they had passed two more wall-building projects. The building of walls in Long Gully Pass reinforced the general feeling that the Wall might soon fall if it hadn't already. Those dangers were still sixteen hundred miles ahead, but despite she was heading into them, Kezia felt better than she had since her father ...

Kezia forced herself to relax. That life, with all its difficulties was now on the other side of the Barriers. They had paused on a hill overlooking the windrail terminus of Maida. Twin ribbons stretched out from the town and disappeared into the vast grasslands of the Great Plains. The Star and Arrow Road of *Legends*, that pointed across the plains, directly to Long Gully Pass; the only viable route through the Barriers. The route Eldwin Forrestor took on his way to found Deep Creek. Hopefully retracing Eldwin's journey in reverse would lead to her atonement. Only then could she hope for a better life. She placed a hand on her belly, glanced across at Wesley, and smiled.

Wesley smiled back. "It's ten times the size of the entire East Coast, sixty per cent of our landmass and grossly under-inhabited. Even with the constant traffic between the Wall and the East coast, the grassland is empty except for the windrail depots, and a few isolated farm settlements along the rivers. It doesn't rain much out there, but it still has an abundance of water from numerous rivers that start in the Barriers."

Kezia's gaze returned to where the distant horizon, shimmering like an oracle curtain, beckoned. With a contented sigh, she took in the breathtaking view, a fragrant grassy breeze in her face.

Wesley pointed out the trail to Maida, which crisscrossed the stream they had followed from the summit. "We lose it at Maida," he said and pointed southwest. "It runs that way but we ..." he then swept his hand around to the northwest, "... head that way, along the windrail. The sidings have water for the horses that pull the windtrains back to Roden Crossing. Takes a third of the time you would need to go the river route."

It's so big, thought Kezia. There's room for everyone. "Why haven't we settled it?" she asked.

"Except for Roden Crossing, there are no towers out here, no way to consult Our Lady."

That this vast, well-watered land remained unsettled for the sake of a few overrated tellings irked Kezia, now busy trying to urge a skittish *Providence* around a small rockslide.

"What is it, girl?" she whispered soothingly in *Providence's* ear as she dismounted, signalling to Wesley that something was wrong. Tiny pebble avalanches cascaded down the slope alongside them as the ground trembled. She drew the mare and the packhorse together, a tight grip on their reins so she could quieten both while the tremor passed. The low rumble grew as it came directly towards them.

"Ley line," Wesley shouted above the increasing rumble. He stayed mounted; his packhorse held close.

Her packhorse reared; the flying hooves were close to Kezia's head as it pawed the air. She let it loose. Wesley raced by, scooping up its reins while trying to control his horse. Eyes wide, Kezia felt the tremor pass directly beneath her feet. The surface of the swift flowing creek beside her erupted in a line of choppiness as the tremor continued down the valley. The horses quieted as the vibration dissipated. Wesley, who had stayed in the saddle and slowed the packhorses, wasn't long returning.

"What in the name of the Goddess is a ley line?" Kezia asked as she took back the reins. Her packhorse still trembled.

"Who knows? The Builders supposedly had an underground network of tunnels that covered the whole island, maybe the entire world."

"Whatever for," asked Kezia, leading her horses to the river? Water and rest would settle them.

"The theory goes that it was a transport system between the servatories. Until now, I would have said they were a myth. All we really know is that ley lines have a strong magnetic effect. I thought they might be power lines for named swords, but this felt very much like something fast moving underground, straight down the ley line."

Kezia stared at him with something akin to awe as they stopped in an open a patch of sunlight and dropped the reins to let the horses graze the lush grass near the bank. Where does he get all this knowledge?

"We've been mapping these lines of magnetic effect, as the Watchers call them, for years."

"Who're we?"

"The SoS, Society of Scholars."

I know so little thought Kezia, and almost nothing about the father of my child. Perhaps I should tread more carefully in the future. What am I saying? It's too late for that, way too late.

While *Providence* grazed, Kezia slipped the flute out of the pocket she had sewn onto her pack, put it to her mouth, and blew a few practice notes and drifted away in the mournful Luna's Theme that Wesley had taught her. He had expressed surprise at how easily she had taken to the instrument, as if she had some innate musical ability that had needed an outlet.

Wesley walked back over the section of road where the ground shaking had taken place, dangling a rock from a piece of string, and walking in a systematic pattern. Eventually, curiosity got the better of her.

"Watch the lodestone," he said as she joined him. He walked twenty paces along the road towards the pass. "See our footprints. This is where the horses bolted." The lodestone aligned itself to the tremor line as he crossed it. He looked around at the hills surrounding the valley that formed the western entrance to Long Gully Pass.

"There," he pointed, leaning his arm across her shoulder.

Kezia squinted, following the pointing finger across the river, but could see nothing.

"What am I looking for?"

"A cairn," Wesley said, watching the suspended lodestone held in his outstretched hand. "This line's mapped already."

So that's how he knew the tremor had followed a line that I couldn't even see, Kezia thought. After she found the first cairn, they were easy to see and clearly; they followed the line of disturbance.

"Who mapped it? your society?"

"A volunteer with them, someone like me, interested in the truth rather than dogma. I'm surprised you haven't heard of a society founded in Deep Creek back in 904 FD by Jorgena ..."

Kezia startled.

" ... Blackwood," Wesley finished, nervously scanning their surroundings. "What is it? What's wrong?"

"It's nothing," said Kezia. For a moment, she had thought he was going to say Leach. Jorgena was not a common name, but 904 FD was nearly a hundred years ago. Mother had always looked much younger that her years, but a hundred? No way.

"The way you jumped I thought we were under attack."

"I'm sorry I scared you. Forget it, let's get going."

As they descended through the last of the Barrier foothills towards Maida, the official western end of Long Gully Pass and terminal for the newly reopened eastern section of the windrail, they made plans. Maida would be a short stay to resupply for the long ride to Roden Crossing. The windtrains, confined by the rails could not readily tack against the prevailing west to east winds. The rail-dogs had found pulling the flatbeds with horse teams quicker and easier.

As Maida grew around them, Kezia's hopes for a new beginning as Jena Setler rose. Lives saved during their journey had prepared her for the Wall. She could see only one drawback. Her enhanced reputation as a gifted healer would only last until Mother's dust ran out.

They stayed longer than expected. Wounded Watchers, intimidated by the climb to Long Gully Pass's summit, had so swollen the depots' population that Kezia was in constant demand. On Wesley's advice, she started accepting offers of payment, mostly in goods they would need or could re-trade for what they needed. Eventually, the stories she heard of those not making it this far led her to decide she really must continue to the Wall.

• • • •

Out on the Great Plains, it was easy to imagine that she and Wesley were alone in the world. An ocean of grass stretched to the horizon on each side of her. Alongside them, the twin rails used by the windtrains parted this ocean before and behind. Occasionally they came across the small hand-pulled rail carts with two or three repairers, busy cleaning and/or adjusting the rails. Several windtrains, sails billowing and flatbeds, heavily loaded with wounded, rumble swiftly past. The passengers and rail-dogs waved and shouted in good cheer, but the train did not slow. Kezia regretted being unable to help any of their wounded, but as Wesley pointed out, once up to speed, a windtrain rarely stopped, except for emergencies. The lost momentum caused hours of delay.

Only one thing marred Kezia's newfound contentment in the journey: morning sickness. Life would be simpler without that complication. The standard herbal concoction to reduce the pain had not stopped her from vomiting every morning. She wiped a residue of mucus from her mouth with a clump of soft grass and tucked her small kit into *Providence*'s saddlebags.

"Are you alright Jena?" Wesley asked, handing her the gourd, refilled with water collected in the overnight traps.

"Fine," Kezia replied, kicking dirt over the remains.

Wesley avoided stating the obvious, and Kezia was grateful for his restraint because she had not decided what to do about it. She knew several remedies for getting rid of her burden, but wasn't sure she wanted to lose it or keep it, especially now she could feel it moving. Willard would be proud of her indecision. If it had been his, she would have used her pregnancy to manoeuvre him into fulfilling their oathing regardless of the Goddess wanted. Wesley's child however, would have a touch of feral. Goddess only knew how that would affect the child's future, given what Wesley suffered in Port Calder. She decided she would have to quell her misgivings about the Goddess and consult her oracle in Roden Crossing. Perhaps she and Wesley should oathe before it became too obvious; except she had no idea of the status of her oath to Willard.

The clear sky promised a fine, if somewhat cold day. She noticed for the first time since Maida that Wesley was wearing a short sword. During the early part of their journey, he had strapped it to the horse, still within easy reach but more comfortable for riding. Why does he think we need protection in Roden Crossing?

As they mounted, Wesley pointed to a moving black stain on the Northern horizon. "Wildebeef," he told her. The vast herd grazed quietly in the early morning light. "We should tell the Watchers in Roden Crossing. The Wall garrisons are always looking for fresh meat." With a light squeeze of his heels, he headed off, following the path beside the wooden track. Kezia followed mutely, deep in thought. Her contemplation of a visit to the oracle brought unwelcome memories.

Mid-morning, a half day short of Roden Crossing, they met a becalmed windtrain whose passengers treated them to the familiar plains greeting, "Where bound?"

"The Crossing," answered Wesley. "And you?"

"The Pass," replied the rail-dog. With the pleasantries concluded, he jumped off the flatbed and came to greet them. Of the ten stationary carriages, the last one corralled two horse teams.

"I'm a healer, you have wounded," said Kezia, a statement rather than a question as she dismounted. The flatbed presented her with the usual assortment of gangrenous stumps, intermingled with something she hadn't seen before, burns.

"Bloody ferals are using fireballs," said a Watcher in answer to Kezia's question about her friend, who Kezia judged was most in need. He was drifting in and out of consciousness, lying on his right side, belly down, left leg bent up for balance, right arm behind. The prone position, thought Kezia, someone with healer training.

"I thought the Wall was too high," she said.

"Clever little bastards are firing from the caves."

The man's closed eyes tightened and he ground his teeth when Kezia lifted a corner of the bandage. The stench made her already delicate stomach heave. Molten tar had burnt away the layers of skin from shoulder to wrist on his left arm, a suppurating mess of bubbly pink, black at the edges.

"Caves?" asked Kezia.

"The Break's riddled with them," said the woman as Kezia contemplated how she could catch any spillage of the healing powder she would have to sprinkle on the wound.

"They've been tunnelling under us for centuries. Makes you wonder what's holding the wall up," the woman continued.

Carefully using her body to shield what she was doing Kezia unscrewed the jar, alarmed to see it already below half and they were nowhere near the Wall. She would have to husband it, treat only life-threatening wounds. Taking a good pinch of the silvery powder between thumb and forefinger. She concealed the pinch in her palm while she deftly resealed the jar.

"Hold him," Kezia said, her eyes closing as she peeled back the bandage. She ignored the bile rising in her throat as she rubbed her hands together to sprinkle it on the wound, like adding salt to a roast, she thought, grimacing at her new found cynicism.

Almost immediately, the sheen on the raw surface layer dulled. Blobs of tar fell off as patches of drying skin spread rapidly, leaving it bright pink but still ugly.

"Aithcraft," whispered the woman wide eyed. The word spread down the carriages faster than the healing dust, moving of its own accord, spread across the wound.

After a few minutes, there was only a scabby line around the border of what had been an incredible wound.

The man stirred and looked at her uncertainly.

"Who are you?" he slurred.

"She's a miracle worker," his mate said. "she just saved your arm.'

There were nods of agreement from the crowd she had drawn as a shout came down the tracks, "wind's rising." As if in response to the call, the sail billowed and snapped.

The man smiled. "You have the face of a Goddess healer. Are you the one?"

"No," Kezia replied quickly. "I'm just a healer."

"It's not aithcraft, it's Jena Settler, the Goddess' healer," someone said and her name passed between those on the flatbed, then on to the next and the next. The breeze stiffened, the sails filled, the string of flatbeds started rolling. Wesley rode alongside leading *Providence* as Jena attempted to see another, then another wounded Watcher as the windtrain slowly built momentum. Soon Wesley's horse was trotting.

"Jena," he pleaded as the sails gathered wind.

Kezia looked up to find him just keeping pace as his horse negotiated the uneven ground beside the track.

A quick glance around the flatbed at the smiling faces told her she could do little more here.

"Let her go," Kezia shouted as she threw Wesley her shoulder bag.

Wesley dropped *Providence*'s reins and caught the bag. Kezia whistled and the mare broke into a gallop. Quickly outdistancing Wesley's horse, *Providence* matched the flatbed. Kezia, pressed by the urgency to jump before she lost her nerve, thought it would take more luck than judgement. *Providence*'s back rose and fell alarmingly. She jumped, landed awkwardly in front of the saddle, and felt a sharp pain in her belly. Grasping wildly for *Providence*'s mane, she clung on as the mare gradually eased her pace and veered away from the track. A loud cheer went up from the passing carriages as the tail of the windtrain rattled past.

The last flatbed was dwindling rapidly when Wesley joined her. Exhausted, she slipped off *Providence* and lay on the grass, flushed and breathless from her exertions but elated with a mounting sense of achievement. Purpose renewed, she sat up, catching a last look at the windtrain's sails, surging above the waving grass as it rode the Great Plains towards Maida.

Standing, she felt a twinge in her abdomen and cursed her stupidity. She had forgotten her pregnancy until she landed on Providence.

Chapter 23

I ncongruous shapes, stark against a huge ball of light, greeted Averil's first waking moments. She startled into full awareness before she realised the bright patch was the rising sun, defined by the tunnel mouth and the lumpy silhouettes of her sleeping escort; a feral warband. Except for Stone Ethyl, she would call the band, not friends exactly, but not sworn enemies either. Mates? No, colleagues; fellow soldiers like her? Did this make her a traitor?

Unable to return to sleep, she crawled out of her bedroll and made her way out the entrance to attend her ablutions; her stomach still tender from vomiting. Pony meat. Warriors eat rat and ferals eat pony. Her catastrophic mistake was harder to swallow. She paused at the tunnel entrance, absorbed by the view, forgetting about her aching stomach, growing hunger, and last night's blunder. In sharp contrast to the barren terrain travelled since they picked her up, a verdant plain swept away to the distant horizon. The sun rising behind her picked out precise details, giving the landscape the quality of a finely woven tapestry. Averil headed to the nearest copse.

Her escort was just stirring when she returned. An unusually relaxed band, laughing and joking quietly, and saying farewells. She gleaned from the chatter that this mission was over and the group would disband. Is that what Sinjon meant by his twofold loss? Did Filma's death break the band? Stop overthinking it, she told herself. Use the relaxed atmosphere to gather information that might later help you escape.

Instinct and training prompted her to walk back up past the mouth towards the crater rim, pausing and turning often, noting of the lay of the land, as the view expanded. Flashes of light showed where a river cut through the forest. Tracing the river's course, she found a settlement partially obscured by forest, about a half-day ride away, most likely their destination. From the position of the sun, Averil worked out that the river must run into the Dividing Sea. If she followed the river to the coast, she could then follow the coast to the Wall, if not in time to save her captaincy at least to prove she hadn't deserted. She would have to pretend to be one of them, get up the Break with the assault. The problem then would be how to identify herself to the Watchers before they killed her.

A compelling thought halted her at the crater rim. If the tunnels either side of the lake once joined, perhaps they extended even further. Adjusting her mental image, Averil projected a line from the mouth to where it intercepted the curve of the Shadow Mountains, away to the southwest. The distant crater wall, however, was a disappointing scree slope, devoid of vegetation without a shadow of a cavern.

"Beautiful, is it not?" said Sumner in his accented Islander.

"Yes," she answered glancing sideways. In this light, the squint lines on his face were smoother. He had freshly washed and groomed; his hair darker when wet. She found herself strangely attracted to him, despite he must be almost twice her age, close to forty. He was in good shape for someone so old, and he constantly displayed qualities she admired. She supposed he represented the father she would like to have had rather than the bastard who sired her. If she was honest, though, it was more ... she stopped in mid-thought. You cannot go down that path Averil, the Goddess wants your offspring sired by Willard. Why should I care about that? What's in it for me but slavery? Besides, her salacious fantasies featuring Sumner did not include children.

"We must go," Sumner said. "I ..." he stopped, restarting only when Averil looked up, " ... thank you for your cooperation. Our ways must seem strange to you, yet I feel we are not that much different, you and I." As he left, he added, "A season or two with us, Uplander, and you would be ours."

Sumner mounted, and the warband quickly formed up. Averil took up the vacant spot in the second rank behind Sumner. The festive atmosphere and boisterous camaraderie evaporated, the band returning to their normal, intense, taciturn demeanour, but with subtle differences. They sat straighter. Their clothing was neater, their ponies brushed and every harness polished. She hadn't noticed them doing it and had done nothing about her own appearance or that of her pony. It left her feeling shabby. She was still trying to correct her oversight hours later when they splashed across the shallow river and wheeled into the main street of the settlement she had spotted from the ridge.

The street was a haphazard line of low walled enclosures that ran parallel to the river. Cheering crowds lined the way. Excited children ran up and touched the boots of the warband as they passed. She heard some of their names called from waving spectators. The warband sat erect, stared straight ahead, did not acknowledge the crowd. Averil tried to imitate them but failed. It was all so different she could not keep her eyes still.

Set well back from the street, the dwellings she glimpsed through the gaps and over the top of the wall were low, flat-roofed structures of mud and straw. The butts of roof support poles jutted from the walls, and ladders to the roof leaned against them. Behind each enclosure on the riverside was a small, ploughed field.

On the high side of the street, the dwellings at the rear of the enclosures backed into the hillside of terraced gardens. One, twice the size of the others, attracted her attention. As they passed, she could see the flicker of candles deep inside the hill through a huge doorway, the ornately carved doors wide open. Her immediate thought was that this must be their equivalent of Our Lady's Tower. Then, down through a side lane, she spotted two huge red balls in an open field.

The flying craft. I must get a closer look.

Without warning, the cheering tapered away and died. Averil looked up to find a crowd of feral eyes watching her, whispering to each other behind their hands. It seemed they had only just realised that although the warband was complete, someone was missing, replaced by an interloper. She heard Filma's name mentioned as Sumner halted the band. He leaned over in the saddle and handed something to an old man standing rigid in the street.

The warband resumed, riding into a widening of the street, but the crowd remained subdued. Averil's heart went out to the old feral who must be Filma's father, perhaps grandfather. She bent down as she passed.

"I'm sorry," she said.

Stone Ethyl grunted. The crowd gasped. The old man, fiercely grasping what Sumner had given him, looked up at Averil with disgust and spat in her face.

Stunned, Averil wiped the spittle off with her sleeve. What am I doing here? What was I thinking? I'm not one of them. As she studied the circle of unfriendly faces, she spotted Stone Ethyl smiling and her temper flared.

"Bastards," Averil screamed and cruelly digging her heels into the pony's flank, whipped past Sumner at a gallop and plunged into the crowd. Caught by surprise, people and animals scattered: adults dragging screaming children, dogs yapping, and chickens flying. This isn't how I planned to make a break, she thought.

With the warband still mounted behind her, and no idea where to go, escape seemed hopeless, but she refused to give up. Veering into a narrow lane between two enclosures, she headed towards the river. The first sounds of pursuit reached her as she sped across the flying craft field, with barely a glance, then across a field of dark earth next to the river, trampling seedlings.

She looked back and saw Stone Ethyl enter the lane. Bloody ferals, she thought. Time to show them just what it means to be a Watcher. She stood in the stirrups and lent forward, whispered in the pony's ear. The pony leapt ahead, increasing its stride as it splashed across the shallow creek, scrambled up the other bank and turned upstream towards the forest, callously trampling more river bank crops. At the forest edge, she spotted a narrow trail. A grin played across her lips. It would force the warband into single file.

Pursuit was now by sound rather than sight. Without doubt, there would be straighter, more direct trails, which didn't follow the river, but she had to do something quickly or one of them would intercept her. She dismounted at the gallop, vaulting backwards off the pony, running full tilt as she hit the ground, windmilling her arms to maintain balance, swerving sideways into the thick undergrowth as soon as she had slowed enough. The pony, now riderless, cantered away. Averil calmed her racing heart, taking long, deep breaths while she waited.

The first feral to come pounding down the trail after her was Sinjon, hotly followed by Ambler, both at the gallop. What happened to Ethyl? Taking a shortcut to intercept? She waited. Daisy came trotting into view shortly after. If Averil was wrong, thinking no one else had joined the chase, that Sumner and Ethyl were trying to cut her off, then her freedom was going to be short-lived, probably her life as well.

She leapt out, grabbed Daisy's arm with both hands and pulled her from the pony. Daisy hit the ground head first with a sickening thud still holding the reins. Don't think about it, they're ferals, she thought, as she prised open Daisy's fingers with one hand and steadied the pony with the other. Then she spotted Daisy's boot knife. As she grabbed it, Daisy's hand came up in a roundhouse swing and knocked her to the ground.

Averil rolled, coming up in a crouch with the knife poised ready to strike. Her eyes glazed with hatred; her mouth twisted into a feral grimace. She stared at Daisy for several long moments. Her blood cooled when the mutual hate in Daisy's eyes went out.

"Tits Severne. Why does it have to be this way?"

"It doesn't."

Averil's scalp crawled at the sound of Gardner's voice. The warrior who had put her in this shit, and left, was back. A cold anger gripped her.

"Fuck off, Gardner."

"Our Lady sent me to help you."

"You're too fucking late. I don't need your fucking help or your fucking Goddess." A sharp pain shot through the back of Averil's legs as she rose to stand and a wave of dizziness nearly overcame her. Gardner reached out to help. She waved the point of the stolen knife under the warrior's nose.

"Fuck off, I said."

She sheathed the knife and ripped the pony's reins from Daisy's grasp. Ignoring Gardner's protest, she led the pony into the river and waded upstream until she was around the first bend. Here she struck it lucky. The pony she had let go had stopped to drink and graze. With two mounts, she could go a lot further and a lot faster. She gathered up the reins and with both in tow exited the river on the settlement side, keeping to whatever hard ground she could find.

Gardner followed doggedly.

Once she was away from the bank, Averil mounted and, using the sun as a guide, headed in the opposite direction to where the Wall was and hopefully opposite to feral expectation. The warrior loped alongside as she kicked her pony into a trot then a canter. It gave her an enormous sense of satisfaction to see him fall behind. By the end of the day, she had lost sight of him.

"See that Severne," she shouted at the sky as she rode out of the forest into a large natural clearing. "Time you taught your warriors to ride."

While she was looking up, she spotted a flying craft floating in the air just above the treetops ahead, heading her way. Her scrutiny of the craft abruptly halted when the pony collapsed beneath her and she pitched forward toward the ground. She tucked her head into her shoulder and rolled with the momentum but her shoulder hit a rock. She uncoiled with the sudden sharp pain and landed flat on her back with a numbing thud. Gritting her teeth, she rolled frantically sideways out of the path of the following pony and stopped, face down, cuts and bruises all over her body.

How did that happen, she wondered, lifting her head to look back at the pony? Two arrows protruded from its body, one in a front leg the other in its neck. Two thoughts occurred to her simultaneously. Nice shots and where did they come from? The flying craft, she thought, as a large chill shadow passed overhead.

Averil rolled onto her back, once more reaching for the knife as a vast red face filled the sky, black eyes, flaring nostrils and pointy white teeth. There was nowhere to run from the flying beast. She closed her eyes against the heat of its fiery breath, waited for it to engulf her with knife poised. Her trip to the otherworld would cost them dearly.

Then she heard voices, opened her eyes, and saw Stone Ethyl hanging over the side of the beast's belly, scathingly berating the feral with her. Ethyl was climbing out of the basket when a sudden gust caught the craft and she fell back as flashed up and away, well out of reach. Averil could see now it was more like a boat than a bird, floating rather than flying, at the mercy of the wind. Arching her back, she tried to spring to her feet and fell hard, wincing at the toll the manoeuvre took on bruised muscles. She reproached her stupidity as she climbed slowly and painfully to her feet then started after the remaining pony.

The floating craft diminished as it drifted away transforming back to a huge red droplet, Stone Ethyl staring at her, no longer arguing. Severne's tits, Averil thought heart pounding in astonishment as she tried to come to terms with airborne ferals. How do we fight them? She had a sudden vision of multiple craft, using the constant updraft up the face of the Break, to float over the parapets. They could drop ferals behind the wall and even inside the forts; the entire structure primarily designed to forestall frontal attacks. She had to get back and warn the Watchers, yet she remained transfixed, wondering if the craft could carry more than two, forgetting there had been a second craft until a shadow fell over her. She whirled in time to see Sumner of the Lakes let go of the tilted basket and rush towards her. Caught by surprise, there was little she could do, but tense for the collision. As he slammed into her at a dead run, she wondered how they had traced her so quickly.

· · · ·

Everything ached, especially her head. She had difficulty breathing. Her nose was heavy and blocked, as if she were ill.

Dust and the stench of the pony coated the inside of her mouth. The ropes binding her hands and feet chaffed. When she opened her eyes, the world was upside down. She was looking at a pony's feet kicking up dust and every step the animals took sent a paroxysm of agony through her.

She could feel herself gagging. "I'm going to be sick," she whispered hoarsely, as she felt her stomach heave. She tried to raise her head, but the pony's gait caught her at the wrong time and she started choking on her own vomit. A hand grabbed her hair and lifted her head. Her eyes watered as the contents of her stomach streamed from her mouth and nose. The pony danced out of the way.

As she lay semiconscious across the pony's back, Averil was vaguely aware of a conversation between two male voices, both of which she knew well, but understood not at all. She wished they would both drop dead. In fact, she thought they could all drop dead: her father, Willard, Gardner, and Sumner. She reworked the Watchers maxim about ferals to the only good 'man' is a dead 'man', and then choked on her laughter as the latest two in her life, men she had felt she could like and respect, argued over her like a prized possession.

"Out of the way, warrior." Sumner's voice was somewhere just above her.

"When you release the candidate," Gardner answered.

"Truly I wish I could rid myself of her, but ..."

A whistling hiss penetrated Averil's consciousness as Gardner's sword slithered from its scabbard.

"Our Lady has granted you your wish."

Averil felt Sumner's back muscles tense against her side as he replied. "Put up your sword, warrior. Its magic will not work here."

"It is Our Lady's wish that you return your captive to me."

In the respite afforded by the halt, Averil recovered enough to lift her head for a moment. She saw Gardner in the stance, *Brimstone's* tip in its toe cup. The jewelled hilt extended away from the body in what Averil considered an inefficient and awkward two-handed grip.

Tentatively, she tested her bindings.

Sumner, sword drawn, dismounted, saying as his leg swung past Averil's head, "It would distress me to harm you, but if you will not step aside ..." He let the implied threat hang in the air between them.

"Our Lady decides."

"Then prepare to be crippled in her service."

Ritual stupidity, thought Averil, rocking up and down, slowly slipping off the pony, already lying more on her chest than her stomach. Her breasts hurt, her nipples rubbed raw, but a few more inches and her feet would touch the ground. She could see now without lifting her head. It would be an interesting contest. How could Sumner remain so confident of Severne's favour knowing Gardner was Goddess trained and equipped?

As soon as her feet touched the ground, Averil sat to untie them. The rope was thick and her hands numb, but she persisted, worrying the knot loose, watching the standoff under the pony's belly. Sumner faced away from her. Gardner could see what she was doing, but gave nothing away. Thank Goddess for small mercies.

"Our Lady bids me warn you Sumner, at this moment you hold unborn generations of Lake's people in your hands. For their sake, let her go."

Averil could see from the change to Sumner's stance, this had shaken him.

"Consult her oracle," Gardner continued calmly and for emphasis the warrior's sword snapped to the vertical. Sumner was right however, and *Brimstone* remained as lifeless as it had on the beach. Sumner's sword also came to the vertical, a mutual salute before engaging.

Her legs free, Averil gripped the pony's harness with her bound hands and painfully pulled herself upright. She was sick of being the object of a power play between rival adherents of the same Goddess. If Our Lady's favour resulted in her becoming a chattel, she would rather Severne despised her. Grasping the pommel, she swung into the saddle and kicked the pony into action heedless of the clash of swords behind her. She pulled at her wrist bonds with her teeth as she rode.

Once out of sight, she changed direction back towards the Dividing Sea, still hoping to follow it back all the way to the Wall. With luck, she might run into a Coastwatch ship blockading the ferals from a seaborne invasion.

Averil constantly glanced upward now, anticipating threats from the sky. Catching her unaware once was more than enough. She saw immediately the floating craft's potential: enemy observation, archery platform and the ability to drop the enemy anywhere it floated. She also had questions. How did they float? How did the rider control them? Could they communicate with the ground or with each other? Was the collapsed one she and Gardner had stumbled across on the beach, a test flight, or was it there to pick up the man they thought would be the Face from the feral raiders Kingsley was tracking?

A more important detail was the now ambiguous position of the warriors, handing her to the enemy one minute, trying to retrieve her the next. From what she had seen, warriors had status among the ferals but did not generate the fear, probably because down here, the named swords often failed. How was that possible? Then there was the ferals' ritual observance of Severne's Eye. Why would they do that, unless they believed Severne was on their side? It begged the question, which side did Severne really favour? She shook her head to dispel her disquiet. Gardner came back to rescue me and did not give away my escape from Sumner. Hang onto that.

By late afternoon of the next day, Averil was hot and more than a little bothered. She imagined the sweat from her exertions turning to steam as soon as it beaded. She wore a light shirt open down the front and, but for the protection it afforded from the undergrowth and the insects, would have gone bare-chested in this clammy heat.

Strips ripped from a sleeve of her shirt bandaged both wrists and both ankles, rubbed raw by the rope. Her jaw ached from unpicking her wrist bonds. There were scratches that stung with sweat, bruises from Sumner's assault and a cramp in her belly from lack of food after vomiting while draped across the pony.

Maybe heading for the coast had been a bad move. The maps of feral lands, Averil remembered, had this region marked as a barren wasteland, unpopulated and treeless. Craters and builder tunnels had been some of the many adjustments she had had to make. Unpopulated was the only thing the mapmakers had right.

The forest had thickened gradually and the trail petered out. Only the late afternoon sun told her she was still going south. She wiped her forearm across the headband, made from the other sleeve of her tattered uniform, to keep the sweat from running into her eyes. The air was sticky, the insects biting, and sounds she couldn't identify all around her. The thick understory, which had steadily become less like forest more like jungle was not on any map she had ever seen. Worse, the ground was getting squelchy underfoot, turning swampy.

In sudden panic, Averil looked at the sun's angle, low in the canopy, and realised she had to turn back immediately. It would soon be dark. Trapped in a swamp after sunset was a less than welcome thought. She backed the pony around and retraced her path, urging the animal into a faster gait as soon as she could. The sun sank rapidly, plunging the dense woodland into preternatural gloom. Averil, judging the light level too low, knew she would not make it out tonight. Dense foliage surrounded her; the thick trees covered in a tangle of vines. With darkness, she lost all sense of direction and finally had to admit; she had gotten lost.

"Where are you Severne? I need help," she sniggered at the canopy and got the response she expected. None. As the gloom deepened, a barely discernible glow appeared in the densest patch of foliage. Fireflies, she thought, Severne's little bots. Averil grinned, apologising for all her previous doubts. Whether the Goddess ultimately favoured ferals or Uplanders, she hadn't abandoned Averil, and presumably Willard, at least until we have offspring.

Chapter 24

Willard rode into Port Taylor on a long-dray piled high with hay bales destined to feed the Wall's horses. The west coast port was much bigger than Willard had imagined when it was just a dot on a map. It sprawled across undulating country at the mouth of the Thornton River. Quinton, the driver, had picked Willard up nearly seven weeks earlier, a few miles out of Thornton Abbey, "for the sheer pleasure of company on the road."

Willard had spent two weeks at the Abbey instructing and reorganising its servers, to ensure what happened to Wylie and Aderic didn't happen again. It occurred to him, that although he had wanted it done for Wylie's sake, and had found it worthwhile to get better treatment for failed candidates, it was also a delaying tactic. The same thought recurred when Quinton, coming out of a farm gate, picked him up. He could probably walk faster than the overloaded dray.

"Why walk when you ride?" Quinton asked, looking at his chest.

After dealing with the Abbey, Willard had covered the gemmed hilt, but had forgotten the talisman hanging outside his shirt. Too late now, besides he had a point. Why walk?

"You don't seem worried I might rob you." Willard said, thinking about how Aderic and Wylie had been living off the land.

"What are you going to steal, hay?"

"I could take your money."

"Not much fear of that. I got naught but this load and a few parcels for Ortum. I trade a bale or two for me tucker as I go."

"How about the horses or the dray?" persisted Willard?

"Them?" Quinton said, scratching his beard, "Nah, they're strong mind but pretty slow, good for pulling but not for riding. Only another driver would want 'em, or the dray. You don't look like a long-dray man to me, more like a damn priest." He spat to the side as if the word had left a bad taste in his mouth, reminding Willard of Aldus.

Intrigued, despite a sudden pang of loss, Willard asked, "If you don't like servers, why offer a lift to someone who looks like one?"

"The Goddess likes 'em."

[See how they regard me Willard,] the Goddess interposed.

"Yes," Willard said aloud, forgetting for a second. [With fear,] he finished silently. Fortunately, Quinton had taken his 'yes' as agreement to 'the Goddess likes 'em'.

[I warned you.]

[Then don't speak when I'm with someone.]

[That would not be useful to either of us. I would advise you to accustom yourself to it. I will be with you always.]

Willard gave up.

In payment for the ride, Willard had helped with the driving, though it was hardly an exacting task. The big club hoofed horses followed the road and, except for an occasional slap of reins to keep them moving, it required little thought and no energy.

The bigger task was getting the horses in and out of the traces and removing the harness. At that, he was practically useless for the first few days, but by the time they reached Port Taylor, he could do the whole job without help.

They stopped on a high cliff overlooking a bay, Quinton called Stingray Cove, the air rich with the tang of salt. The port of Taylor sat on the headland. Houses of logs with planked rooves, climbed the foothills. Down by the wharf, stone buildings, some two stories high lined either side of its wide main street, wide enough to accommodate the dray's turning circle. Out in Great Bay, he could see what would be big sailing vessel ships, made tiny by the distance.

"That's your quickest way to the Wall," Quinton said, "a fast supply ship through the canal."

Willard wasn't sure he liked the idea. He had been to the seaside only once and wasn't fond of it. The water was cold, tasted foul, and constantly tried to drag him under.

"Is there a road through the Mountains?"

"There is. It goes to Stonegate due east of here. That's seven hundred miles and you'll be no closer."

[Good advice is hard to get. Take it.]

"Thank you," Willard said, as they resumed their journey. Again, he had answered aloud and coincidentally his answer had again been appropriate to both Quinton and Severne. The Goddess saying 'take it' showed she had stopped delaying him.

"Tell you what," Quinton said, "if you're prepared to work like you have for me, I'll have a word with the shipmaster taking this load, him being a friend of mine."

In late afternoon, Quinton pulled the long-dray in a wide arc at the end of Main Road onto the wharf. It creaked to a halt alongside a black hulled ship, the top half painted green. The name *Bay Trader* painted on the side at the bow. From bow to stern, the Bay Trader was about four drays with horses long, roughly eighty feet. Two masts, festooned with rigging towered above them to a height Willard imagined equalled Deep Creek Tower. The taller carried two cross beams, the bottom beam currently rigged like a derrick with a block and tackle. Quinton had positioned the dray under the derrick.

Quinton hailed the ship and standing on the dray spoke to a man who stepped up to the rail. The man turned and shouted orders. Several other heads appeared a swarm of able-bodied sailors scurried off the ship to unload it.

"Right, soon as this is unloaded, I'll take you to meet Shipmaster Barnes."

Willard stepped down, rubbing the base of his spine, sore from the constant jostling on the hard wooden seat. Overlaying the briny smell with him since they sighted Stingray Bay was that of fish and seaweed. It made a change from the smell of hay.

There was so much to see Willard hardly knew where to look.

Sweating, bare-chested sailors soon surrounded the dray. They lay a net on the wharf and unloaded bales onto it then brought the corners of the net together over a hook hanging from the derrick. The net stretched around the load, and the derrick lifted it off the wharf. A sailor, fore and aft, using guide ropes attached to the net, pulled the load inboard and guided it down into the hold.

All along the waterfront the scene repeated, sailors loaded and unloaded ships. Outbound, along with the hay, were horses, sheep and goats, sacks of potatoes, barrels, presumably of wine or beer, and sealed crates labelled Walfort Supplies. Ominously, wounded Watchers were the main cargo unloaded.

Willard searched the Watchers-run carts as they passed, and headed up the main street towards the convalescent hospital, looking for Averil. When he noticed Our Lady's Tower, he angrily suppressed a wave of homesickness. He longed to go home, but not without ... flushing with guilt, he again searched the carts of departing wounded, this time looking for Kezia.

Quinton, seeing his glance, asked, "You looking for someone?"

Willard nodded. "I know people from home who went to the wall."

"There are many routes home, but it's easier on the wounded to come by ship to Port Taylor. The main road from Canalbridge to Stonegate has four treacherous river crossings. The road from here has only one, and that's a bridge at Stonegate. They get to rest up again on the Windtrain, if they make it. Some don't no matter what route they take."

"So not finding them doesn't tell me anything, good or bad." Willard said.

[But I can, Willard. Averil and Kezia are safe.]

[Thanks,] he thought back, getting it right for once, and returned to helping with the unloading.

The process emptied the long-dray in half an hour, but it was dark by the time they stabled the horses and secured the dray.

"I'd hide that if I were you," Quinton said as Willard pulled *Severne's Bane* out from under the seat. "Going armed in this town invites trouble."

"I can't afford to lose it. It's a gift."

"Strap it on round here and you will. Real or fake, if it looks like a named sword you'll have trouble, because it usually comes strapped to the back of a warrior. You, my young friend, have the eyes right enough, but you also have your hair. Folk round here might not believe you have a right to it, if you get my drift."

"Do you think that?" Willard asked.

"What I think don't bear a telling. I minds me business. I don't bother Goddess sufferers and them don't bother me. Best you keep it wrapped and hidden while you are here. Leave it where it is while we get fed."

Willard, after a quick look around the gloomy stables, trussed the sword up under the dray seat with baling twine.

The sign outside the pub read Est. 770, *The Old Sailor's Drinking Society*, fights every night, closed on Satelday for tellings. Capt. D. Wallis, barkeep & bouncer.

"The pub's now run by Mrs Wallis. Does a good meal," Quinton told him.

The taproom was full of smoke, noise and the smells of hops and cooking. Quinton spotted his shipmaster in a back corner, quietly draining a pot of ale. Barnes was a thin, almost emaciated man, with dark eyes that constantly browsed the crowded taproom. He was the first but not the only patron to take an interest in Willard as they threaded their way to his table.

"Evening Odell," said Quinton, nodding at Barnes as he eased his bulk onto the plank opposite.

"Evening, Quint. All squared away?" enquired Barnes, as Willard slipped in behind the dray driver.

"Yea, lad have loaded me bales," Quinton said, then formally introduced Willard. "Willard, this is Shipmaster Barnes of the *Bay Trader*; Odell this Willard Forrestor. Lad's looking to work his passage to the Wall."

"Willard or Ser Willard?" asked Barnes.

"I'm not a server Master Barnes," Willard replied, bowing his head slightly. "As you can see, I still have my hair."

What mystified Willard was how Barnes knew to ask. His eyes marked him as a candidate, but he didn't have the sword with him and the talisman was out of sight inside his shirt.

Barnes waited until Willard looked up, then his gaze locked on. "So the miracle worker is not a server," Barnes said.

Willard sensed heads turning his way and the eavesdropping room quietened. *Miracle worker? What are they talking about? How did Nelda's story get here ahead of me? Mount Bakor doesn't have any contact with the outside world. Severne must have spread the word and detailed description of him, via her towers to manipulate him into a position that would force his hand. There must be posters in the towers. Everyone had known him the moment he entered.* He tensed under the intense scrutiny, unsure what these people expected. Should he feign total ignorance or go for glory and claim credit? He opted to admit to knowledge of the events but deny his part in them.

[It won't work Severne.]

[We shall see.]

"The Goddess performed the miracle. My presence was happenstance."

Odell Barnes looked thoughtful for a moment. "I believe you."

That's a change, nobody else does. "Why?"

"You called her the Goddess rather than Our Lady. A server wouldn't," he said. Then, noticing the silence, "more ale and some food please Mrs Wallis." He waved his empty glass at the bar and leisurely inspected the taproom. The patrons looked away when his gaze fell on them and slowly, like an incoming tide, the noise resumed.

"I would suggest, once you've eaten, that you get your kit and sleep aboard," Barnes whispered. Then, in a more natural voice, "I won't be aboard tonight," he winked at Quinton. "Report to the mate, Kedron Butcher." He handed over a brass button engraved with a ship and the name *Bay Trader* curving around the edge.

That settled, he turned to discuss crops and cargoes with Quinton. Willard took it as a hint, and saying his thanks rose to leave. Barnes slapped the table and the room jumped, Willard with them.

"Pay attention when I tell you something. Once you've eaten, I said. Sit, eat," he added quietly. Then he turned on the room again, "You lot got nothing better to do than watch me eat."

Onlookers turned away. Mrs Wallis delivered bowls of steaming stew and Willard sat and ate, thankful for Barnes' insistence. He was hungry.

Finished, he excused himself and left on his own, but as he walked through the taproom, he intercepted furtive glances that shied away when he looked back. They know something I don't and can't wait to see me find out; he thought.

[Nor can I,] said Severne as he pushed his way through the door into the cold clear night.

• • • •

"You'll get a hammock at sea," the mate Mr. Butcher said, as he allocated Willard the topmost berth of three between, a plank between two ribs. A supporting deck beam was only a hand-span above. "Last man signing on gets what's left."

Willard slept well and woke late from a dreamless sleep to the gentle creak of timber, the slap of water on the hull and the redolent smells of salt, fish, and straw. He completely forgot where he was and sat up before opening his eyes. His head cracked the underside of the deck and he fell back in agony. The Sailors stacking bags of grain in the hold below greeted this with howls of laughter.

Willard winced as he opened his eyes. A wooden nail hammered into the beam where he had sat up, protruded slightly. The nail head was bloody. Willard gingerly touched his throbbing temple and his finger came away smeared with blood. He rolled out of his berth, dropped to the deck. The jar on landing brought waves of pain and he staggered. Fresh blood trickled down his nose. He mopped it up with his sleeve as he headed for the square of light.

A waist high pile of Quinton's bales under the hatch cushioned the grain sacks dumped into the hold. Willard coughed in the dust as he ascended the ladder, thinking the pain would pass if he kept busy. Time he earned his berth.

[Take the Test of Faith. Repeated concussion puts at risk the result I need.] Severne said.

Willard ignored her. He was not in the mood this morning. His head throbbed. Again, he had to mop the blood from his brow as he scanned the deck for the Mate. He found Butcher engaged with Barnes. "We don't have crew to waste on crowd control," he heard Barnes say.

Crowd control? Willard stepped over to the side. Tumultuous cheering rippled along the packed wharf from a crowd so huge it jammed the intersection of the wharf with the main road. People continued to arrive at the back and press forward, tightening the crowd.

Below him, an almost empty grain-dray jutted like a peninsula into the sea of upturned faces, the crowd making the unloading difficult. No wonder Barnes is irate. What are they staring at? A quick glance behind showed he was alone. He had the sickening feeling that the mesmerising field of eyes had singled him out. His hackles rose when he turned back and the crowd abruptly went silent, expectant.

"You, lad," the mate bellowed, "Get below before you cause a riot."

Willard ducked out of sight.

"Get off," a sailor called out from the wharf. The thud of a dropped sack followed.

Barnes leaned over to assess the situation. Mate Butcher shouted for the crew, "All hands!"

Willard lay on the deck and peered through the scuppers. A sailor was struggling with someone who had climbed up onto the dray. Another, then two, and then three joined the interloper. The sailor jumped onto the remaining bales, then leapt for the ship. Hands appeared on the gunwale above Willard's head, his view abruptly blocked by the man's body.

A cry arose from wharf, "The Face, the Face."

A youth, with lank brown hair and a crooked nose, hooked his arms over the gunwale, and got a foothold in the scuppers. Barnes' sinewy arm snapped out and punched the youth full in the mouth. The youth let go and shortly after hit the dray with a thud.

"Get below," Barnes barked at Willard. Face livid, he shouted for the mate, "Mr Butcher, prepare to repel borders!"

Before Willard even thought of moving, a new and different roar arose from the crowd on the wharf. Those clambering aboard looked over their shoulder and suddenly changed their minds, desperate to let go. Willard heard splashes, as well as thuds.

Again, he looked out through the scuppers. A file of green-robed warriors, gemmed hilts poking above their shoulders, and hoods thrown back from hairless heads came down the main road at an easy lope. Before such awesome power, the crowd parted like tearing cloth, fleeing in panic, or prostrating themselves in supplication, fearing for their lives. Those caught too near the edge of the wharf clambered aboard anything alongside, or jumped into the sea. Intermingled screams and weeping had replaced the jovial bustle of ships preparing to catch the tide.

Three Restoration Warriors. Three! Common knowledge held there were only seven in the entire world, so scattered that nobody had ever even seen two together. In *Legends*, and other written prophecies, seeing one was bad enough, two excessive, three a calamity. Willard having studied Legends at the servatory, knew a gathering of warriors heralded the imminent arrival of the Face, prior to the Restoration.

[Exactly,] Severne said, and Willard saw how neatly she had pinned him in place, as the centrepiece of her plans. Transfixed, he watched the column jog in unison onto the wharf. He had known since his abduction that something portended, but hadn't bargained on a warrior gathering.

"Fuck."

[Your language, Willard, is getting as bad as Averil's.]

Two warriors took the stance at the bottom of the *Bay Trader*'s boarding ramp, facing out, as the familiar-looking lead warrior jogged up the plank and jumped lightly to the deck. The sibilant electric hiss of three named swords slipping from their scabbards scattered any remaining onlookers. Those who hitherto were sure they had done nothing wrong were no longer so sure. There was a sudden quiet. The wharf had emptied and the town looked deserted. Willard got to his feet, finding the deck as empty as the wharf.

"Master Barnes," called the warrior who had come aboard, and Willard, recognising the voice, shivered. This was the warrior who had accosted a younger Willard in Severne's Wood to give him a little incentive. Willard, who had been only eleven and whose eyes hadn't yet changed, had thought it an ultimatum. Take the test or die. Ser Hedley had intervened, and Baxter had warned both Hedley and the Goddess, "You and Our Lady are too patient with him."

"Aye," said Barnes, and stepped out from behind the mast. "And you are?"

Willard's admiration for Barnes shot up. For a man who might be about to lose his head, he seemed calm.

"Warrior Baxter. Our Lady be with you, Shipmaster," Baxter said. "We are here at her request to protect a passenger you carry."

"I carry no passengers, only crew," Barnes said, and Willard's estimation of the man doubled. Defiance would clinch his death.

"Working passage then. He is called Willard Forrestor."

Willard silently cursed Severne. [You're carrying this too far. You can't make me the Face without the Test of Faith.]

[We shall see.]

"He's aboard," said Barnes.

Willard approached warily.

Baxter bowed deeply. "At your service, Lord Willard. You should see to that wound," he said, handing him a damp cloth.

Willard had forgotten all about banging his head. He stared at Baxter, the oldest known warrior, a legend from *Legends,* and dabbed at his forehead. The presence of three warriors would confirm what the populace suspected from the Mount Bakor rumours. What a bloody mess, he thought, pulling away the blood-soaked cloth.

Barnes's thin face blanched and he fell to his knees, arms outstretched palms down, touching his forehead to the deck at Willard's feet, "Forgive me Lord, I was blind."

Willard cringed. What the ... with Severne always listening, he was at a loss for expletives. Faintly, he heard a low feminine chuckle.

"Get up," Willard pleaded. "I'm not who you think I might be, really I'm not."

As the seconds ticked away, the futility of fighting against such unreasoned beliefs was abundantly clear. He may as well act the part, so long as it didn't interfere with his search for Kezia.

Reaching down, he grabbed Odell's hands and dragged him to his feet. "When can we go, Master Barnes?"

"At noon ... Lords, on the tide, about two hours, if I can get my crew back, if I can get a crew at all."

Watching him now, Willard found it difficult to know if Odell had converted on the spot, or like him, had just thought it better to go with the flow. He glanced over the side, the wharf and Main Street remained empty except for one brave form well to the back, prostrate with arms outstretched towards the ship, The other two warriors stood rigidly at ease, sword points resting in toe cups, hilts at arm's length out from the body. Warrior lore said they could hold the stance until they keeled over, if Severne wished it.

"Excuse me lords, I must prepare," Barnes said. He shouted for a sailor to fetch Willard's kit from the hold and transfer it to the stern cabin under the Port tiller.

Baxter stopped him.

"Lord Willard is our responsibility. We will render whatever assistance you need," Baxter said.

Barnes nodded, and after a quick glance at Willard said, "I need a crew. But ... with you aboard, I won't get one."

Baxter paused, considering then said, "Our Lady has said she will oversee Willard's journey." With that, he strode down the gangplank and the three Restoration Warriors jogged off into the town.

Willard, still occasionally wincing from the pain in his forehead, eyed Baxter's retreat with suspicion. Baxter's laugh echoed in his mind.

[The ability to identify the owner from a laugh you have never heard shows great potential.]

[Only potential. If you're not sure, why are they here?]

[Until realised, I need to keep safe that potential.]

With a deep breath, Shipmaster Barnes nodded to the mate, "Do what you can Mr. Butcher, but I fear we shall miss the tide."

Mate Butcher fetched two sailors who'd remained aboard. They were about to head into the town to round up the crew, when the trickle of those returning turned into a rush.

Barnes almost smiled. Willard's grin was mirthless. Who would stay in a place where warriors gathered?

The crew hastily completed loading, secured the cargo, and made *The Bay Trader* ready for sea, all while giving Willard a wide berth.

Left alone, Willard mused on his new predicament. Until he learnt control, the brethren would be privy to his thoughts. Even though Hedley had got between him and Baxter that first meeting, Willard had seen a history of pain in Baxter's eyes. Rumour had it he was over two hundred years old, yet the hairless face looked barely fifty.

A tap on Willard's shoulder made him jump. He spun to find Baxter grinning at him.

"Thank you," he said.

Even with the clubbed hair, the sailor's canvas shirt and trousers, the face and eyes were the same. The pain was still there. He was also barefoot and Willard's kit rested in his hand. Willard suspected the large bag now contained an extra named sword.

The warrior waited expectantly as had the crowd.

"I remember you, Baxter," Willard said after his thumping heart settled.

"I know Lord."

Despite the deference in Baxter's tone, it felt like talking to an old friend, yet their only encounter had been two minutes of sheer terror. Everyone had laughed when he said he had seen a warrior, even his mother. Hedley hadn't backed him up.

"Your cabin is this way."

Willard followed, wondering about the other two warriors.

[Fletcher Lord,] said a voice in his mind, [I was on the left of the gangplank.]

"The other lad was Dudley," Baxter said behind him.

[G'day Lord Will,] said a new voice in his mind.

[This changes nothing, Severne.]

[You are wrong Lord,] Baxter countered. [I know from long experience, every action changes something, sometimes disproportionately to what you might expect.]

"Talk to me with voice Baxter," Willard said, his mind rebelling at all the intrusion. At the same time he projected to Severne, [stop broadcasting my thoughts to your troops.]

[The broadcast was yours,] said Severne.

[And loud,] added Dudley, the thought distinctive to him.

"Are you going to follow me everywhere?" Willard asked Baxter when they arrived at the cabin. He needed rest. The mental handstands, required to talk and think with several people at once, were tiring.

"It is my duty to protect you, Lord." Baxter sounded offended and amused at the same time.

"It stops at this door."

"As you wish Lord," said Baxter.

Willard stepped inside and with great relief closed out the horrifying world the Goddess had chosen for him. The cabin, although small, had a long bunk to accommodate Barnes' long frame, and the deck above it was out of reach of any sudden sit-ups. The cabin also had its own privy, a tiny cubicle jutting from the side of the ship with a washstand, inset basin, and a jug of fresh water. His status seemed to have shifted from working his passage to honoured guest.

Willard crossed to a metal mirror nailed above a washstand to inspect his head. Instantly, he recalled Barnes' conversion. The wound in the centre of his forehead had taken the shape of an eye.

Chapter 25

The first sign Kezia had of how close they were to Roden Crossing was Our Lady's Tower on a hill that protruded above the sea of grass. The town itself lay hidden in the wide river valley through which the Mighty Muddy flowed, a turgid, brown torrent that traversed the entire island from Perisher Pass in the north to the vast Marshlands delta in the south.

As they approached, Kezia saw the tower boasted three of Severne's Ears. Unlike at Rivers Junction, one faced skywards to where Severne's Eye would transit. Beside it was the slightly shorter Watcher's signal tower.

"Infantile, the servers won't allow our tower to be higher than theirs." Wesley said.

"With good reason. How would Our Lady hear petitions? You can't put anything in the way of Severne's Ears. You wouldn't be able to have a telling." Which might not be a bad thing sometimes, thought Kezia.

"Our tower would not have been in the way. There are no dishes on the south side. The ruling forced us to build extra towers to avoid a blind spot in our network. Unlike her, we don't have an orbiting platform. We have to see the next ground-based tower to pass on a message."

"Then you shouldn't have built it so close."

"Do you see another hill we could've used?" Wesley asked.

"But if they allow it here, the Watchers will press for the same in other places, and some towers are completely ringed with ears."

"Then why not let the Watchers build a signal platform on top of the tower?"

Kezia looked at Wesley with genuine dismay. "You can't use holy ground for unholy purposes."

"I'm sure Our Lady wouldn't mind so long as we didn't interfere with her hearing. What's unholy about communication? Isn't that the purpose of her towers?"

"Only with the Goddess. It's not for idle chatter."

Even as she said this, repeating tower teachings she had grown up with, Kezia wondered. Her beliefs had taken a battering lately, thanks to the beheading of a rogue server. She still felt she couldn't blame the Goddess for deeds of her followers.

Her mother would disagree she knew, despite Kezia had never discussed it with her, only with Averil, who often told her what mother had said. Averil and the twins were the ones to receive the benefit of mother's advice on Our Lady whether they wanted it or not. Kezia wanted it but only ever got advice on healing. In retrospect it seemed her mother had known in advance Kezia wouldn't be a candidate but all her sisters would and need advice on Our Lady.

Kezia had fervently embraced the servernian doctrine to shock her mother into paying more attention. It had backfired badly, attracting instead the unwelcome attentions of her hypercritically devout father. Which is why I'm out here, in the middle of nowhere, pregnant to the part-feral Wesley, she thought, as they paused on the crest of the wide gorge, the Muddy River below had taken centuries to carve from the grass plains.

Wesley pointed to broken pylons, creating eddies in midstream. "Those are all that's left of our attempts to build a bridge for the Windtrain. The annual floods have swept away every pylon we've built in the middle gap."

Kezia couldn't really visualise how the middle span might look. It would be an incredible feat, apparently not beyond their ancient forebears, considering the remaining pylons on each side, but unimaginable now. The pylons the Watchers had built were quite an achievement, but it still left a huge gap.

"What was the builder bridge used for? They must have had something better than windtrains?" Kezia asked.

"We don't know. We just followed the trail of pillars they left."

"Pillars? I didn't see any pillars."

Wesley turned in the saddle, smiled at her and she knew immediately he was about to tell her everything he knew about it. This was a telling she could enjoy, as much as Wesley enjoyed dispensing it, from his wealth of accumulated knowledge. "The builders used an elevated transport system across the plains. Only a scattering of pillars remained when Eldwin the Forrestor climbed the Break in 705 FD, but enough to guide him to Long Gully Pass. By the time the Watchers finished building the windrail, the pillars had fallen and the material carted away to build the wall."

"We've lost so much," she mused, watching a ferry make its slow way across the river.

"That depends on whom you mean by we," Wesley replied as he pointed to the ubiquitous tower. "The towers, you seem fond of defending, have plenty of builder artefacts, builder knowledge and builder power, which they keep closely guarded. Their foyers blaze with light twenty/six."

"But they must. It's a symbol of the Restoration, a beacon of hope for the future."

Wesley turned in the saddle and stared at her. "Look Jena, I don't wish to trample on your beliefs, but warrior Howard's actions in Port Calder show even Severne is not always pleased with her towers."

"What do you mean?"

"He executed an Arch Server."

"That's not true. He ..." She couldn't finish. The image of Elmira's toppling was still so vivid it made her nauseous. She laid a quieting hand on her swollen abdomen. There was no hiding it anymore. She probably shouldn't be riding.

"Isn't it?" Wesley persisted. "Tyrell was Arch Server in name only. Do you have any idea how often a warrior execution removes someone highly placed in Our Lady's hierarchy?"

"What are you saying?"

"To me, it seems like Our Lady uses her warriors to keep her towers in line. Sorry that's too broad - to keep the upper echelon of tower personnel in line."

Wesley's argument stunned Kezia. She wanted to refute it, but it had the insidious ring of truth. The incident with Elmira was Kezia's only real experience of the Goddess meting out justice. Like everyone, she had heard rumours, but she refused to believe her warriors warred with her towers for ownership of the Restoration.

"There's the tower," Wesley said, "go ask."

I intend to, Kezia thought, but not a useless question like the one you think I should ask.

"I'm heading to the Watchhouse to report on the Wildebeef herd we saw," Wesley said. "Meet you at the ferry in an hour."

He turned his horse and cantered off before Kezia could reply. She watched his back receding down the wide main street, annoyed by his know-it-all attitude.

Roden Crossing's Tower was so like Deep Creek's the Builders might have poured them from the same mould. The hard wooden pews and the burnt smell from the power curtain in the Penitent's Waiting Room, heightened by the unfamiliar faces, induced homesickness. With a sigh, Kezia sat and formulated her question, immediately rejecting, 'Should I keep the child?' She wasn't ready to abdicate that choice.

After struggling over the wording, she eventually decided on 'will the child have a future?' She signed it, Jena Setler. Absently stoking her abdomen, she wondered if a question from Jena would go unnoticed. If the Eye of the Goddess was truly on her and her question correctly put, then she could expect a sign from Our Lady.

She watched the young acolyte hand her question to the server, who took it through to the oracle. The server returned almost immediately and spoke to the acolyte. Kezia was close enough to hear his whispered, 'Where?' and saw the acolyte nod in her direction.

The server approached with the unanswered question sheet trembling in his hand, the talisman at his neck flashing iridescent against the light black robe. He lowered his gaze when he reached her, almost bowing before her.

"You are the healer Jena Setler,"

" ... Yes."

"Ser Wybert, at your service ma'am, will you come this way? Our Lady wishes to speak with you directly." He stood back with head politely bowed.

Kezia gulped in confusion. She certainly had not asked for nor wanted a private audience, especially after what had happened to Averil. All she wanted was some sign that her child had a future. Ser Wybert waited patiently for her answer. She glanced around the small waiting room and the unknown faces watching her expectantly.

"Please, Jena," Ser Wybert added, which started a buzz of conversation around her.

She rose and an allowed him to steer her down the hushed aisle towards the shimmering curtain.

"Where are you headed?" Ser Wybert asked conversationally.

"The Wall," Kezia replied.

They reached the curtain covering the entrance to the Audience Chamber.

"Do not be afraid," Ser Wybert said, taking her hand. "Just close your eyes as we step through. Ready?"

Kezia nodded.

"Now," he whispered, squeezing her hand.

She took a breath, closed her eyes, and stepped through.

"You can open your eyes now."

Even in the dim light, the sight awed her. The Audience Chamber was all she had imagined from childhood storybooks: ancient and imposing, a cavern chiselled out of solid rock, its moss-covered walls constantly dripped on the rough stone floor. It even smelt cold. She shuddered as an oracle guard slithered past her boot.

Ser Wybert gripped her hand. "Be still."

With a hiss, the coppery snake moved away, disappearing under a three-legged stool into a vaporous crack beneath. Behind the server's tripod on its polished marble altar, the oracle hummed. The crystal cube filled with frosted sparks.

"Leave us," a golden voice said as Ser Wybert went to sit on his tripod. He paused. Objections swept across his eyes and vanished.

"As you wish dear Lady," he said and backed out slowly, bowing and fingering his talisman.

The sparks swirled, joined, became so bright Kezia had to raise her hand against the glare. Then suddenly Our Lady was sitting facing her, hands folded on knees, feet together and back straight. Austere dark brown eyes bored into her. Our Lady's eyes are like mine, Kezia thought in wonderment.

"Why are you in Roden Crossing, Kezia?" she asked, her tone stern.

Kezia shook so hard she vibrated. The blood pounding in her temples threatened to burst out. The Goddess knew everything.

"I'm pregnant," Kezia stammered. "I wanted to ask if ..."

"Good," Our Lady interrupted, "but why have you left Port Calder?"

"What?" The question took Kezia by surprise. She glanced nervously around at the cave, wondering what she could say. Why not came to mind, but if she asked, she might not get to put the question that had prompted her to come for a telling. She wondered why it mattered to Our Lady where she was? Inadvertently, she voiced her perplexity. "Where should I be?" Damn, she thought, I wasted my only question answering Our Lady.

"With the wounded, you abandoned at Port Calder."

Abandoned? That hurt. Kezia still puzzled that Our Lady was asking all the questions, said, "I can save more lives on the Wall. Too many die before they get to Port Calder. The journey kills them."

"The Wall is dangerous. If you die out there, how will that help?"

That was Howard's argument she remembered. Kezia still had no answer. Perhaps putting herself in mortal danger to save lives was her way to atone for father's death. Surely, Our Lady must know this.

The oracle hummed. The staring Goddess flickered, becoming transparent. Kezia sensed the curtain behind her flicker and turned. Ser Wybert, his face as white as an acolyte's frock, stood behind her firmly in Wesley's grip, the tip of Wesley's knife on his cheek.

Before Kezia had time to react, Wesley had snipped the cord holding the talisman and unceremoniously pushed Ser Wybert

back through the rippling curtain into the Penitent's Waiting
Room

"Interesting," said Wesley, as he pocketed the talisman. "You
don't need it to get out."

Kezia, remembering the results of Averil breaking into Deep
Creek's oracle, shouted at Wesley. "What are you doing here?
Are you mad? It's sacrilege."

"You're here," Wesley said softly.

"Our Lady invited me."

"Wesley," Our Lady said, her voice neither angry nor
outraged. "I did not request your presence."

Wesley spoke only to Kezia. "When I came to find you, an
acolyte told me Wybert had taken you for a private audience."

"So?"

"I had to warn you. You are in mortal danger here."

"You misrepresent me Wesley," the Goddess said. "My aim is
to protect Jena."

"Don't listen to her, Jena," he said, stamping past her towards
the altar on which the oracle stood. "She makes the same
promises to the ... us."

Kezia reached out pulled Wesley around to face her. "What
are you saying?"

"She's promised us the restoration," Wesley said.

"Us," Kezia searched his face, "I know you're part feral,"
Wesley's eyes widened in pleased surprise, "but you're putting
yourself in with them."

"I'm more than part Federal," said Wesley, holding her
hands.

Kezia's thoughts automatically focussed on her womb. I
carry an abomination.

"I'm sorry Jen. My people sent me to find the Face. I followed you in the hope he will eventually trace you. What developed between us was unexpected. It changed me."

Kezia was so focused on what Wesley had said, she forgot they were in the holy of holies without a server.

"Why would the Face look for me?"

"Willard," Wesley said.

Kezia laughed derisively. "How can you possibly think Willard is the Face?"

"Who told you that Wesley?" Severne asked.

"You did," Wesley replied seriously, staring at the ephemeral Goddess in the crystal. He let Kezia's hands fall. The now iridescent eyes of the Goddess followed him as he walked purposefully behind the light filled cube.

"What are you doing?" asked Kezia.

"Turning her off, so I can talk to you without interruption."

"Whomever you talked to Wesley was not me. I would like to know when and where you thought this happened," the Goddess said quickly. "Please, Wesley what you ..."

With a loud whip-like crack, her voice stopped. Simultaneously, her image flickered and went out accompanied by an acrid burning smell. Wesley grunted, then collapsed on the oracle's pedestal. The cave walls went blank, became smooth textured, their whiteness dull in the weak light coming through the uncurtained doorway.

Rigid with shock, Kezia stared at Wesley's legs poking out from behind the oracle, willing them to move. They remained as lifeless as the crystal cube. Kezia refused to believe the oracle was dead, as Wesley appeared to be. Our Lady was just gone. Wes had killed the oracle as Averil did, but this time the oracle also killed him.

If only Howard had been here, I wouldn't have needed an oracle to consult Our Lady. Wes would still be alive. It's my fault. The father of my unborn will never see his son. I can't go through with it, it's half-feral.

Ser Wybert came up behind Kezia, his voice gentle.

"Where is he?"

Kezia nodded dumbly at Wesley's legs. She stared as Ser Wybert stepped over him and bent down behind the altar. Then he rose and signalled to his acolytes. She felt other hands gently pull her away. She kept looking over her shoulder as they helped her back into the now empty Penitent's Waiting Room, seated her on a pew, and eased her back until she was lying down.

She felt her abdomen spasm when the acolytes carried Wesley out through the doorway. An instant later, Ser Wybert, a grim smile accenting the lines of his face, stepped through the audience chamber's uncurtained doorway, his talisman dangling higher on his chest from the re-knotted cord.

He stood towering over her; his face hidden in shadow. "If the Watcher was a friend of yours, I'm sorry. Our Lady has seen fit to take him to the otherworld."

Kezia squeezed her eyes shut against her tears. The oracle had killed her baby's father. She felt sure now it would be a boy, a half-feral boy. Is Wes's death my answer? It can't be. Our Lady said my pregnancy was good. I must keep him? Wesley was playing with a power beyond his ability. His death must be an accident.

The hardness Kezia felt under her shoulders and hips as she lay on the wooden pew did not distract her from her spinning thoughts. Wes, a man she loved and trusted, had lied to her and used her. It seemed the Goddess was never happy with her choices. As soon as she felt close to someone, the Goddess snatched them away: Will, Howard and now Wes. Wes, a feral infiltrator, who unbelievably thought Willard was the Face. Even the Goddess had wanted to know who told him it was Willard. Did that mean Howard handing me into his care wasn't to protect me, but to watch him? The Goddess and Howard must have known he was a feral spy all along. Maybe they hoped he would get rid of me, so Willard could marry my sister. Damn her Eye, I can't trust anyone, not even the Goddess.

The baby kicked and Kezia's first inclination was to get out of here as fast as possible. Part feral or not, with Wes gone, this baby is now wholly hers.

"Are you alright, Healer?"

Ser Wybert's considerate tone did not console her. She opened her eyes on the hovering face and felt revolted. She had serious doubts about what the Goddess had planned for her. With a supreme effort of will, she made herself smile.

"Yes, thank you."

She held out her hand and allowed him to assist her to a sitting position. What if Wes was right? Was it an accident or did the Goddess silence him? Kezia's need to get out of here had developed a sense of urgency.

"Would you like to continue your telling?" asked Ser Wybert. "Warrior Howard will soon have our oracle repaired."

Howard? Her scathing thought was, You're too bloody late. To Wybert she said, "My consultation was over. I have my answer. I must move on."

Ser Wybert bit his lip and coughed. Kezia could not imagine why, but he seemed nervous.

"What should we do about the ... feral?" he asked.

The questions tempted Kezia to state the obvious, 'bury him', but guessed that was not the thrust of his question.

"Report his death to the Watchers. They can handle it. Our Lady has sent me to the Wall. I have to go." The lie came easily.

She hoped he would need to go to the oracle or Howard to confirm it.

Ser Wybert followed her as she walked steadily back to the relative safety of the foyer. While inside the Audience Chamber, she had lost all sense of time. The world outside had turned orange. She found *Providence* tethered to a perimeter tree along with her packhorse and Wesley's horses. She patted the nose of the mare as tears flooded her cheeks. Wesley was dead. She had become so used to his presence she turned to look back across the tower lawns, expecting him to emerge. Instead, Ser Wybert stood at on the steps smiling.

"Are those the Watcher's horses?"

Kezia felt she saw a glint of avarice in his eyes and anger seethed within her. How dare he?

"No," she said, "they're mine, all of them."

"But surely he was riding one, there are two saddled?" Ser Wybert said, coming down the path towards her.

"So what, I own them? warrior Howard gave them to me," she said. "Ask him."

Untying Wesley's horse from the tree and looping the reins over *Providence*'s saddle, she mounted as Ser Wybert stepped through the Public Gateway.

"There are several settlements between here and the Wall. You won't need four."

His persistence irritated Kezia beyond measure. She could see he was about to make some further protest, and she cut him off.

"Quite true and I would donate one if Our Lady had need of it, but I feel our hard-pressed defenders at the Wall have a much greater need, don't you agree?"

Ser Wybert paused. Kezia, sensing this would not hold him long, smiled sweetly and dug her heels into *Providence*'s flanks.

As she wheeled past, the trailing string of horses nearly trampled the server. It gave her an extravagant sense of pleasure.

Her only regret was she dared not stay to see Wesley properly buried. He didn't deserve full Watcher honours. He had been a feral spy, spying on me to catch Willard. That notion was so outrageous she had discarded it until she recalled the manner of delivery. Wes betrayed his own to tell me his mission and then the oracle killed him.

The sky was getting darker by the minute and Wes had told her that the ferry did not operate at night. She urged *Providence* to a canter. Poor Wesley following me was the mistake of his life.

Roden Crossing spread out before her like a gallery, a series of terraces down to the ferry terminal. The Windtrain terminal was on a high terrace upstream in line with the pylons. As Kezia cantered down the main road, her mind kept replaying her audience. Like Howard, the Goddess had said she was supposed to have stayed in Port Calder. She assumed it was to keep her away from Willard, which suggested he was on the Wall. But was he there for me, or Averil, she wondered?

In the rapidly fading twilight, lights came on. The town became a patchwork of crossed yellow squares sewn on a dark quilt. The terminal apron was emptying as the ferry workers leaving the terminal. Across the broad expanse of the darkly flowing Muddy, she could see another cluster of yellow patches, tiny with the distance. Kezia hailed a departing ferry worker.

"Where's the ferry?" she asked, dismounting. She had hoped she might sleep aboard while she waited; anything to stay out of Our Lady's Tower.

"Other side tonight," the man replied.

"When will it be back?"

"Mid-morning if we're lucky."

Damn, all night and half of tomorrow, I can't hang around that long. "Where's the next ferry?"

The man removed his cap and scratched his thinning hair. "Dunno that there is one." He turned to a passing friend, a short woman of ample girth and a round face. "Hey Jocie, is there another ferry on the Muddy?"

Jocie veered from her course and waddled over. "As far as I know, this is it."

"Is there another way to get me and my horses across?"

"Swim them," Jocie chuckled.

Kezia blanched at the thought, and Jocie's laugh erupted, infecting her friend.

"It's not as bad as you think. The Builders were smart. It's fast and wide here, but also shallow. You can practically walk out to the first pylon," she pointed up river. "The ferry just saves you getting wet."

"Is there a guide I can hire?"

"When do you want to go?"

"Now, if I can?"

Even in the evening gloom, Kezia could see the round face become incredulous. "At night? Not even a warrior would cross this river at night."

"I would."

Kezia spun at the familiar voice. "Howard," she screeched, rounding on him in a fury of emotions: guilt, blame, loss.

The ferry workers backed away into the deepening night, astonishment written on ghostly faces.

Howard neither embraced Kezia nor rejected her; he simply stood like a rock until she regained control of her emotions and her fists stopped beating on his chest.

Darkness enveloped them as the sound of the madly rushing river overcame the pounding in her ears. Except for the brilliant canopy of stars and the soft spillage of yellow from curtained windows, it was so dark she could not see Howard's expression. Thankfully, thought Kezia, it also hides my turmoil. Is he friend or foe? Ser Hedley once told Willard that warriors totally dedicated their lives to Our Lady's Restoration. Keep that in mind and trust no one.

When she went to thank the ferry workers, they were gone, no doubt spreading the word that a warrior had come. Howard's custodial work at Port Calder might not have reached this far yet. Probably no one would believe the story if it had. Right now, those of a nervous disposition or labouring under a burden of guilt would start packing.

"Why did she send you after me?" Kezia asked Howard, slapping at a biting insect.

"To protect you and the child and it appears she was not wrong to do so."

The reference to her child raised the hairs on the back of her neck and a sudden fear for her unborn. She had been undecided about keeping it when she went to ask about its future. Wesley's death had decided her. Obviously, the Goddess has told Howard everything.

"I'm not going back to Port Calder," she said, knowing it was defying the Goddess.

"As you wish, Our Lady has only ever had your interests in mind."

Kezia stared at him in disbelief, but he seemed genuine. "So help me get away from here."

Howard met her request with a question of his own, querying the reason for her haste. Kezia explained how Wybert had been angling to get his hands on the horses. Even as she spoke, Kezia realised that Howard's presence, and her association with him, would now prevent any overt actions by Ser Wybert.

Or would it? Howard had to spirit me away from Rivers Junction. Wes was right again; the Goddess wasn't in full control of her towers.

"We could cross tonight, but not easily," Howard said.

"Let's go then," Kezia said, bending double to a sudden cramp.

Howard reached out to support her. Through the pain squeezing her abdomen, Kezia wondered if Howard was talking to her, himself, or the Goddess when he asked. "Do you want to keep the child?"

"Yes," Kezia replied through clenched teeth.

"Then the tower is your only choice," he said, taking the reins from her.

"No." Kezia screamed again as another pain gripped her.

Howard slipped her arm over his shoulder, his arm around her waist and half carrying her, started for the tower. "I'm not about to lose either of you."

The pain was now too much for Kezia to argue. Instinctively, she knew something was wrong with the way she was carrying the child. She really needed the attention of a good healer. Her resistance collapsed. She was in some measure comforted by Howard's strong arm around her, even aroused by the smell of him, a mixture of a sweat and smoke and the oil he rubbed on his hairless body. If only he hadn't enslaved himself to the Goddess.

Ser Wybert stood at the tower door, surveying his town. He suddenly paled when he saw Howard storming up the road, supporting a stumbling Kezia. His hand reached for his talisman and his eyes flicked to the gem poking above the Restoration Warrior's shoulder. When he spotted the four horses Howard led, a smile flicked across his face and he hurried down to meet them.

"You found her I see."

"Yes, and these are now your responsibility," Howard said, handing Wybert the bunched reins. "See to their care."

The server rubbed his hands together and called to an acolyte who led the horses away to the stables. "Well done warrior. A good night's work, their sale will add much needed coin to Our Lady's mission."

"They are not yours to groom not to sell," Howard said, reaching toward his shoulder.

Wybert's frock coat trembled at knee level and he clasped his talisman with both hands. His mobile expression flashed from grovelling through dour to fright.

Howard scratched his ear.

"Our Lady will tell you how to assist Healer Jena," he continued calmly. "I have a funeral to arrange." He stared into Wybert's eyes. "Are we clear?"

The server's relief was palpable. The warrior was not smiling however, and Kezia realised that for him intimidation was simply another means to an end. The boy she met had learnt quickly.

He sent Wybert to fetch instruction from the Goddess then turned to Kezia. "You and your baby have nothing to fear from Our Lady."

Kezia gripped his arm, whispering fiercely, "I don't trust her anymore?"

Howard looked surprised. "Whatever caused you to doubt her is probably a misunderstanding. Please, go with Ser Wybert. He will take good care of you. I have to see the Watchers about Wesley."

Kezia, assuming he was referring to the funeral, whispered a heartfelt, "thank you." Such considerations were not something one expected of warriors, but it occurred to her he could just as easily be checking on Wesley's movements.

"I'll be back soon," Howard said, and disappeared into the darkness, again leaving her feeling deserted.

Kezia turned to find Ser Wybert had returned. As they eyed each other with mutual mistrust, another cramp caught her. Wybert was immediately solicitous and helped her across the threshold back into the blazing foyer, hurrying her towards the lifting room in the central column. Kezia, knowing what to expect, tensed ready for the jerk. Wybert raised an eyebrow and though he said nothing, she guessed he was revising his estimate of her status.

The lifting room went down, not up, so that when the doors parted, Kezia was on unfamiliar ground. They stepped into a corridor that extended into darkness in either direction; past what Kezia would imagine was the boundary of the foyer above, out under the grounds, possibly beyond the perimeter wall. The light spilling from the lift illuminated more than her surroundings. This was the true domain of the Goddess, or more correctly the builders, soft muted colours, and otherworldly textures.

"This way Healer," Sev Wybert said, and led her to a green door. He jumped back when the door opened before he could place his talisman on the frame. It compounded his astonishment when the voice of the Goddess issued from inside.

"Come in, Jena. Thank you Wybert, that will be all."

Chapter 26

The light of Severne's little firefly bots came steadily towards her. Behind it, she could make out a silhouette, not Gardner or Sumner, thankfully, but strangely familiar.

"Averil, if I'm not mistaken," said a voice from her past. Her mind went blank when she tried to put a name to the voice. Closer, she recognised the face under the grey beard.

"Hedley."

"At your service," he said with a chuckle. The light was not from fireflies at all, but a tube Hedley held in his hand. The beam pointed at her feet.

"Severne's tits Ser, what are you doing down here?" she spluttered. She would have coped better if it had been Gardner or Sumner.

"I'm here to help, as Our Lady requires. This way, it's not far," he said. Swinging the beam around, he turned and walked back into the forest, the light bobbing in the dark.

Dismounting, Averil led the pony after the glowing silhouette. 'Not far' turned out to be miles and she was already bone tired. The glow suddenly faded, as if he had gone behind a tree. It grew again as Averil advanced. Definite edges emerged to frame an arched doorway in an overgrown rock wall. The ruins of a stone dwelling.

"I don't believe this."

"Well, don't just stand there, come in. I could use the company and you know I don't bite."

She tied the pony to an aerial root, pushed aside the cobwebs, and stepped through.

"Are you hungry? I have food and coffee. What would you like? Please, have a seat. "

She moved closer to the light, a blindingly bright strip. "Sorry. I didn't realise the light was in your eyes," Hedley said and twisted it to shine on the ground. "Is that better?"

"Yes Ser." She could see him now.

"I'm not your server. You're not in Deep Creek. Call me Hedley. How have you been, Averil?"

"Fine," she said.

"Fine to calling me Hedley or you've been fine."

"Both."

This Hedley disquieted her. He was not the austere blacked robed server of childhood memories. This Hedley, with his neatly trimmed greying beard, wore ordinary clothes, carried no talisman, and chatted like a man with no friends. He sat in front of a large tent, on a strangely constructed chair of shiny tubing and some tent-like material. Both looked to be of builder origin.

A mouth-watering aroma attacked her nostrils and made her stomach rumbled. She could not tear her eyes away from the pot sitting on the device in front of him. She had seen her mother use a similar heating artefact. Incredible. He had working builder artefacts, in a feral jungle.

Alongside his chair was a large oblong blue box with a thick white lid, on which sat a recently used plate. Hedley shifted the empty plate to the ground, lifted the lid and reached into the box to produce a clean one. Then, with deft movements, he uncovered the steaming pot, ladled two generous helpings onto the plate and handed it to her.

"Careful, it's hot," he said as a delicious cloud of steam erupted into her face. It reminded her of Ambler's cooking. Her mother had only occasionally produced dishes like this when Averil was very young, but they became increasingly rare after the twins were born. She wolfed it down as fast as she could, and in the process burnt her mouth

As she ate, she surveyed her surroundings. The small campsite was of long standing. The jungle, previously cleared to the enclosing wall, had regrown around the tent, the box, and the various other builder artefacts that littered the site. The rectangular enclosure had high walls and the single arched entrance. The hot food, coursing down her throat and settling in her stomach, not only tingled her tastebuds but also radiated warmth throughout her body, engendering a feeling of wellbeing she had not felt for years.

"Now that I've fed you tell me your story. I love a good story. How did you end up here?"

"It's a long story."

"I have plenty of time, and you look like you could do with a rest."

For a reason she could not fathom, and despite the bizarre nature of their meeting Averil found she still trusted him, as she had when he was Deep Creek's server. Something about the clear blue eyes or the way he reacted encouraged her to unravel her tale, beginning with her breaking into Deep Creek's oracle. She hardly noticed that he had stopped talking, and was listening intently, interrupting only to clarify certain points. Incredibly, she felt a lot better afterwards, the way she was supposed to feel after a telling but never had.

"So tell me Averil," he said, when she'd finished eating, "now that you have a much more personal relationship with our Goddess. What do you think of her?"

Averil's hackles rose instantly. Her doubts about him suddenly resurfaced. Yet when she looked at him, the doubts receded. He had a quality that reminded her of her mother, eyes that held unfathomable wisdom. He had always encouraged her and Willard to be open and honest about what they thought. There it is again, she thought, Willard and me without Kezia.

Jigsaw-like the pieces clicked together. Hedley had been trying to implement Severne's plan and none of us saw it. She relaxed again, deciding to go with her instincts, to give him the benefit of her doubts, as Sumner's band had done, until he proved otherwise.

"I don't know," she said, "You gave me tellings despite mother bringing me up Aithist, and mostly they were accurate."

"But not always?" asked Hedley.

"As you say," Averil said, sipping the coffee, "not always. When you talked to Willard, you always included me but never said why."

"I felt it advisable not to. You were not ready and judging by your reaction when you were told, I was right and Seven, Our Lady if you prefer, was wrong."

Tired or not, that statement shook Averil.

"A flawed Goddess not to your liking?" Hedley asked.

"Flawed and not in control either," Averil replied, putting the cup down. "What's worse is the ferals worship her, too. How can she be their Goddess as well?"

"Why can't she?" Hedley asked, looking at her, continually adjusting an artefact in the palm of his hand.

"Because we're fighting the ferals in her name, to protect her towers until the restoration, and they're fighting us in her name to take the towers from us and do the same," Averil said, stretching and yawning.

"Did Severne tell you this?"

"Common knowledge," Averil said in frustration.

"Did she set you against each other?"

"Well no. But ..."

"Then why blame her?"

"I'm not, but then ..."

Hedley interrupted. "How about you? Have you sought her advice on getting tested?"

That got her attention. "You, of all people, should know there's no point. The Sevs will never permit a girl to take the tests."

"More common knowledge, I suppose?"

"Yes." She yawned again.

"It's getting late. We can continue this fascinating discussion in the morning when you're refreshed. There is a spare bedroll and sleeping bag in at the back of the tent. You put the bag on top of the roll the slip inside it. Please, take your boots off first."

Averil did as he asked, without protest. Long days and restless nights had exhausted her. The bedroll puffed up as soon as it was flat. She placed the bag on top and sat on the combination to unlace her boots. It felt luxuriously soft, like the best feather and down mattresses. She could hardly wait to try it and didn't need prompting to slip into the opening. Hedley was still sitting on his chair fiddling with an artefact, but Averil was now so comfortable she was beyond caring what he did and was asleep in seconds.

• • • •

Hedley was not about when Averil got up. Neither was the pony. She bitterly chastised herself for a fool, swindled out of her ride for a meal by a fast-talking ex-server. She hesitated. Ex-server didn't quite describe Hedley or what he was doing down here in this feral jungle.

A quick glance around the enclosure reassured her that nothing else was gone. Maybe he hadn't skipped after all. In daylight, the enclosure had a different character, much more like an enormous roofless room with the campsite in the middle. The coarse white material that once coated the walls had broken away in places to reveal a layered red stone structure, looking ancient but not builder. The walls were approximately eighteen to twenty paces high. On the wall next to the arched doorway was an edifice that might once have served as a hearth and, opposite it, a bricked-up doorway.

Averil estimated the distance from the arched doorway to the vine encrusted back wall at forty paces. Past the tent off to one side she noticed a split. Through the split was another wall, much further back than the vine encrusted wall she had thought contiguous. The split was another doorway.

The sound of running water coming from this room gave Averil's need for relief an added urgency. Skirting the pool, she walked into the next room. The water poured from a small round hole in the wall into a bowl, sculptured from the stonework. The overflow ran down the wall and pooled in the centre of the paved floor until it seeped away through the cracks.

Averil hardly noticed, entranced by a new sight. There was no jungle past the wall opposite the fountain, despite it being low and broken, as if she sat perched on a cliff. Drawn irresistibly, she ambled towards the imagined precipice. It disappointed her. It wasn't as high as first impressions suggested. The room overlooked a rubble plain that stretched away to the Sea. I made it, thought Averil. She had been closer to the Dividing Sea than she imagined. Quickly, she went about her morning ablutions in the rubble and washed up in the bowl before returning to the view.

After staring for several moments, a pattern emerged in the rubble: streets lined with the broken stumps of walls that had once been buildings, interspersed with steps, irregular patches of green and or water. An ancient city of staggering proportions. It went all the way to the Dividing Sea, a builder port probably.

As far as she knew, there was nothing like this anywhere on Preservation Island.

Across the street from her stood two stone columns, topped by a lintel. Wind and rain had obliterated most of the lintel's engraved lettering. A space between the only legible words, 'New' and 'laid', suggested a missing letter or two. She imagined 'ly' attached to 'New' and grinned at the thought that 'Newly laid' could be centuries ago.

A flash of colour attracted her eye. Hedley, riding the pony, was moving along a street. The scale of the place jumped out at her. The wall he was riding past was several times higher than man and pony combined. He turned the corner into a street that led back to her and waved. Relieved, she waved back.

Averil returned to the campsite and looked in his box for something to cook for breakfast. She found eggs, tomatoes, onions, potatoes, and the cold leftovers from last night but had to give up, unable to work the builder artefact that did the heating.

Behind her, she heard the clop of the pony. Hedley appeared moments later, whistling.

"So you're up. Where's breakfast? I'm famished. Just think, New Adelaide was once a thriving community of several million," he said, providing her with the missing letters.

Immediately afterwards, he became despondent. "It will take me several lifetimes to plunder it, except we don't have that many lifetimes left. I hope you don't mind me borrowing your pony. I had something big to move."

Averil watched as he unhooked the large flat object the pony was pulling.

"Getting this working will help."

"What is it?"

"A GECKO," Hedley said, stopping when Averil gave him a blank look. "Ground Effect ..." he paused again as if searching for words. "Never mind, it's a carryall. With this, I won't need your pony. Let's eat."

When he busied himself with the cooking stone, Averil watched intently, trying to discover the magic that would start it. It looked to be a simple matter of putting the food on the top of the stone. No talisman, no incantations. It just worked. How, she wondered? What was the secret of builder magic?

Later, when they had eaten, she had questioned Hedley at length about the ruins and the artefacts he was collecting. Offhandedly, she suggested he reminded her of her mother. Hedley startled when she mentioned this and rattled on about very little for some minutes. Averil had the feeling he was hiding something behind his blather. She asked him what tune he'd been whistling earlier.

"Something old, borrowed and blue," Hedley replied.

"It's nice," Averil said.

"And more ancient than you might imagine." He paused fractionally to look her up and down. "You look a lot better this morning. Last night you looked like death warmed up."

Averil looked away, embarrassed. She didn't know whether to thank him or slap him, but now he'd mentioned it, it surprised her how well she felt. She also remembered being surprised when she removed the bandages from her wrists earlier, expecting scabs where the ropes had rubbed her skin off. Instead, she had found only a mildly reddish ring. Again, memories of mother's healing dust surfaced. She had used it sparingly, to avoid attracting attention. But because the only people she treated with the dust were seriously ill or injured, its use had the opposite effect. Rumours of aithcraft swirled around mother like dead leaves on a windy day, always circling, never still, never sticking; the evidence hidden under the potting shed. When Averil looked up from her introspection, Hedley was stroking his beard, studying her.

"What?" she asked, adding silently, why are you staring at me?

"Forgive me," Hedley said. "I was reminiscing. Tell me something. Why are you here?"

Not again, "I told you last night."

"Not here in this place. Here at all. Why do you exist?"

What an odd question Averil thought. What choice did I have? What choice does anyone have? "Why ask me. Ask my parents."

Hedley seemed amused by her answer. "But what is the point of life, your life?"

Severne's tits, thought Averil. He is sounding increasingly like Willard, always asking stupid questions that start with why.

"There isn't one," Averil said. "There isn't any need for one. It's a question without an answer." She cast around the ruined room, looking for a way to explain. "It's like asking why the sun comes up every day and goes down every night."

"I could tell you," Hedley said.

"Who cares? We still have to live with what it does regardless of why."

"So what if I told you, it was all about to end, that a rock as big as Deep Creek was about to fall from the sky and wipe out all life on Nuaith, you, me, all your friends, everybody including the ferals, all dead?"

"We're all going to die sooner or later, this would just be sooner," she said, while thinking, it isn't my fault, that's life.

"Are you saying that if we could prevent this coming catastrophe, you wouldn't bother?" he asked.

"Of course I would," Averil retorted.

"But why?" he said, wiping his eyes.

"Because I enjoy living and don't want to die any sooner than I have to. If you really must have a point to life, mines to live it to the full while it lasts. You're going to be dead a long time."

"Ah," said Hedley, shaking his head. He perked up, nonetheless. "Well, thank you for your refreshing perspective. For you, Averil, I will persist with Our Lady's plan a little longer." He glanced up at the sky as if struck by an enlightening thought. "I suppose that's why she sent you to me."

What! He'd said the bloody opposite when he found me, that the Goddess had sent him to help me. "No one sent me to you, idiot. I got lost."

She said it kindly, but it horrified her to have called Ser Hedley an idiot? But his intriguing thought took hold. Did the Goddess send me here? Gardner's sword failed. He gave me to Sumner, then freed me when that soured, but didn't pursue me. Oh shit. Don't even think it Averil, that's too contrived even for Severne. Leave that sort of thinking to Willard. That way lies madness,

Hedley rose, gripped her right hand with both of his. "You have been both entertaining and informative, and now we must go. It seems we both still have parts to play."

He led her towards the bricked-up doorway, which shimmered at his approach. Severne's tits. He has an oracle here. Not until she stepped through, did she realise her mistake. A long flight of stairs led to an area that bore a remarkable resemblance to the tunnel caves through the Crater Lake's ridge. A large cylindrical object that hissed like a kettle occupied the tunnel. Doors popped out from the side and parted. Averil stared at the huge working builder artefact.

Hedley stepped through the opening. "Come on, you're needed at the Wall," he said.

"I'm not going in there."

"Why ever not," he said. "It's not that different to what your mother has buried in her backyard,"

Dumfounded, Averil wondered why, if he knew about mother's hoard of artefacts, he hadn't grabbed them for the tower when he was their server?

He disappeared into the interior. Averil felt compelled followed, better to go with him than stay here alone. Stepping inside was like stepping into her past.

Chapter 27

Kezia felt a twinge of fear as the door closed behind her, shutting out the dumbfounded server. The room she stepped into, in contrast to the corridor, was mostly glass and metal. Ranged around the Walls was an odd assortment of builder artefacts. Some were vaguely familiar from her mother's hoard, only here they were all clean and shiny and ... alive, was the word that came to her mind. Central to the room, under a dome of brilliant lights, was an altar draped in a warrior green cloth. There was no oracle and no trace of the Goddess.

"I would like to say how nice to see you again Kezia but I understand you have issues with me."

Kezia jumped at the voice, which came from the bright lights over the empty altar, but she kept enough presence of mind to note the Goddess called her Kezia not Jena, as she had in public

The pain of a spasm bent her over.

"Please remove all but your undergarments and lie on the altar."

"Why?"

"You have pain. I can help, but I need to examine you and the baby." The lights in the room dimmed as the Goddess spoke, the smooth voice calm and reassuring.

Curiously, Kezia felt no embarrassment at removing her clothes. She had always thought she had a good body, long legs, well-rounded hips, and firm breasts better than Averil's boyish figure. Her breasts had become swollen and pendulous recently, but she could still give them shape by lifting her shoulders.

"What will happen?" Kezia asked as she removed her clothes, carefully folding and placing them in a pile on the hard floor.

"I will put you to sleep and correct the cause of your pain."

"Promise me I can keep the child I carry," Kezia said, no longer stunned by the audacity of trying to extract the promise. Kezia had no idea why the Goddess had taken an interest in her, but if she could put it to her advantage, she would. She would trust the Goddess one last time.

"I promise you; I will not harm the child you carry, but you must help. You must stop riding until the child is born."

"But I need to get to the Wall."

"Why?"

"My skills and ... can save lives."

"Your child also deserves to live. If you persist, I cannot guarantee a successful outcome. The choice is yours, however. Think on that while you are here."

Slowly, as if taking part in some ritual, Kezia stepped up to the altar, rotated and sat, then swung her legs around and lay back, full stretch, thinking through what the Goddess had said. She knew the closer she got to the Wall the better for the wounded, but she also knew she would have to stop to give birth. She stared up at the ring of lights.

"How far can I get before I absolutely have to stop?"

"No further than Blades Point."

"How close is that to the Wall?"

"Too close for a newborn."

She closed her eyes and thought of her child, Wesley's child. She hardly felt the tiny prick, like a nettle, in her arm.

"How close?" Kezia whispered dreamily.

"It is five hundred and fifty-four miles by road from the Wall."

Close enough, she thought as consciousness faded, "but after the birth ... we can ... go ..."

• • • •

Kezia stayed another two days in Roden Crossing, to attend Wesley's funeral. Howard arranged a Watcher burial with full honours. Officially, his death was accidental, but the Watchers had ferreted out the story behind it and some came solely to warn Kezia about the Goddess. Howard, if he knew, omitted Wesley's role as a feral infiltrator, following Kezia to locate the Face. Where did he get such an outrageous idea it was Willard, for Goddess's sake? It beggared belief that Willard would become the Face of Our Lady.

As the gravediggers lowered Wesley's coffin, Kezia found it difficult to shed a tear. It dismayed her to discover she already had difficulty recalling Wesley's face. The slight bulge under her tunic was the only reminder. Just when she had accepted her new life with him and their child, he was gone and she was relieved, making her wonder if she had really moved on from Willard.

Crossing the Mighty Muddy disappointed Kezia; they took the ferry. Once disembarked on the Western bank, it was almost like old times, Kezia riding *Providence*, side-saddle now as instructed, and Howard loping alongside as they followed the tracks north westerly across the Great Plains. Howard, as always was courteous and helpful. She soon came to rely on him again, but with reservation, still suspicious of his Goddess.

Since the examination, the spasms had stopped, and the morning sickness abated. In fact, Kezia felt a lot better and was gratefully aware of the baby being alive and kicking. The Goddess had kept her word, and yet the manner of Wesley's death still haunted her. Try as she might, Kezia could make no sense of the Goddess's actions here. Why kill Wesley, then promise to do all she could for his child? Maybe Wesley's death and the hurt to me were truly accidental and not punishments.

Strangely, they met no windtrains on this side of the river. The occasional sidings and the twin ribbon that bisected the vast ocean of grass in the heart of Preservation Island were ominously empty and quiet.

"Is the Wall already down?" Kezia asked, dismounting to walk awhile. Strung out in a line behind her were the other three horses, Wesley's, still saddled, and the two pack animals. The unused had saddle failed to tempt Howard.

"I doubt it. We would've encountered fleeing Watchers or feral hordes by now." The Warrior cocked his head to the side. "It would seem the plains have been so depopulated. There are no longer enough rail-dogs to get up a train."

"So, what happens to the wounded?"

"They have to travel the old river route: raft down the Eldwin from Stonegate to the Muddy, then backtrack upriver to either Maida, or Roden Crossing. If the windtrains from there have stopped, it's a long dry walk along the rails to Maida. Carrying enough water to cross the plains is hard for able bodies with horses, impossible for sick and wounded on foot."

"What is your Goddess doing about it?"

Howard stopped and turned Kezia to face him. "Our Lady's only concern is to find her Face. If she can't, then everyone, including the wounded you have already saved, will perish."

Kezia could see he believed it, but she was increasingly sceptical about what the Goddess told him. To her, it sounded like an excuse for the Goddess to do nothing.

The grass dwindled, trees appeared, and the Northern Hummocks rose out of the plains. When they stopped for a midday meal, the mountains, though not snow-capped like the Barriers, had grown noticeably. The spine of the range ran northwest to the sea from the twin towns of Windgate and Stonegate. They spent a night in the deserted Windrail terminal, which really had nothing to recommend it, before moving on to the railhead's support town. sheltering from the winds in the foothills. Even with the light failing, Howard did not stop but pressed on to Stonegate. To sleep in the warmth of its tower rather than spend another cold night under the stars, he told her.

Kezia could only agree. Roden Crossing was four weeks behind them, twenty-four days sleeping rough. She estimated it was mid-fall and she had now missed Averil's birthday, as well as the twins' and her own. She had been a couple of weeks out from Maida before she realised hers had passed and she was now twenty.

Stonegate appeared deserted, the Tower an oasis of light in a dark desert. Where it spilled out onto the Tower grounds, Kezia could see that the lawns were withering, the paths unweeded. It brought back memories of the happy hours she and Willard had spent side by side, on hands and knees, maintaining Deep Creek's extensive tower grounds, a duty Averil and Aldus avoided. Away from the tower, the four had been inseparable friends. She wondered if grounds duty was where they had first become more than friends, long before his eyes changed everything.

"How quickly it all falls to ruin. Isn't the Restoration meant to restore the power of the Builders, make working artefacts available to all? Look at this place. What works besides the lights?"

Howard looked thoughtful for a moment and Kezia wondered if he was clearing what he was about to say with the Goddess. They walked into the light through the open doorway and made straight for the doors in the central column.

"Restoring the power," said Howard as they waited, "is only a secondary task. The primary task is to prevent a cataclysmic end to our world."

"The Typhon myth again?" asked Kezia.

"I wish it were a myth, but Typhon is real and coming ready or not." The doors parted, revealing the now familiar lift, the Warrior's abbreviation for the lifting room. Howard continued as they stepped inside, "Being able to turn on a few artefacts is not important. Our Lady believes that ..."

Kezia did not even notice her stomach sink as the lift rose. She had latched onto Howard's opening words 'Our Lady believes'. What an astounding thought. The Goddess had beliefs. Did she also have a deity? Did the Goddess believe in a Goddess who believed in a Goddess who?

The lift stopped, Howard still talking " ... undesirable aspects of the Builders' culture, would you?"

"Yes ... er ... No," Kezia replied, though she had heard little of what he'd said.

· · · ·

A glorious dawn broke over the deserted Stonegate. Kezia had taken the lift to the top of the Tower and looked out between the variously sized bowls, known as Severne's Ears. The air was crisp and the sky clear. A heavy frost lay like snow on the grasslands. Fall only had weeks to run. Chill would be upon them by the time they reached the wall. At least it was way further north than Deep Creek, close to the tropics Wesley had told her. Already she missed his storehouse of knowledge, and unlike Howard, he readily answered all her questions, no matter how trivial.

Turning away from the grasslands, Kezia walked across to the town side of the tower. Like most plains' towns, unfettered by landscape, Stonegate's planners had laid out the streets in the classic concentric semicircles around the tower, its three major roads reflecting the pattern of pathways inside the grounds. The sun rose behind her. Its light crept swiftly down the mountains and sparkled off the turbulent Eldwin. Kezia pitied the wounded forced to go the river route; rafting down that would be awful.

Kezia glanced over her shoulder at the sound of the lift doors parting. Howard appeared, frowning, his expression troubled as if he had received unpleasant news. He stepped past her and up to the mesh, quickly scanning the town.

"There," he pointed and Kezia looked. A thin column of black smoke rose languidly in the still air.

"We are not the only ones here after all," Kezia said.

"They floated in last night," Howard said.

It was then that Kezia noticed the smoke rose from the side of a house not a chimney, it must be on fire. A flicker of movement caught her attention. People running from house to house as more smoke trails rose in the still air, like a line of signal fires. Flames now licked the roof of the first house.

Kezia shrieked in fright, "ferals! The Wall's down."

Howard gripped her arm, pointing with his other hand. "Look again. Some of them are still in uniform."

Once he pointed it out, Kezia could make out occasional remnants of blue Watcher tunics. What the ... why are the Watchers looting and burning? Has the world gone completely mad?

The surge of destruction spread towards them. Now she could hear frenetic shouts above the crashing of timber and the occasional sound of breaking glass.

"Come, they'll be here shortly. I have to get you two away."

Two, thought Kezia as she turned to follow, is my baby now as important as I am? A shout from the mob below reached them. "The Tower. Burn the bloody Tower."

The lift seemed malevolently slow. Eons passed before the doors finally slid apart. Kezia asked why they were fleeing, "Won't we be safer in the Tower?"

"Our Lady says no."

Kezia was right behind him when Howard stepped into the foyer. *Firebolt* slid from the scabbard with a crackle as he urged her straight to the server's private entrance at the back. A flaming brand smoked through Patrons Arch, skidded across the tiled floor, and landed against the Wall next to their exit. Kezia stared in horror as the fine white surface blackened and bubbled, and the door erupted in green flames that gave off an evil smell.

Howard veered in mid-stride reached back with his left hand to grab Kezia's wrist and yanked her after him.

"Hold your breath as long as you can," he shouted, as they ran around the central column. Another brand whirled in though Public as they raced toward it. Lightning edged *Firebolt's* blade. With a deft stroke, Howard deflected the brand and veered again, shepherding Kezia out through Paupers into the face of the mob.

Kezia bumped into him when he stopped. In the hiatus, while the mob adjusted to their unexpected appearance, Howard prepared. He set his feet apart, placed the sword tip into the toecup sewn into his left boot, and tilted the hilt out from his body. The gem glowed yellow. Kezia, who was more concerned with the increasing conflagration behind them, constantly glanced over her shoulder. Who knew a builder tower could burn?

"Who dares this sacrilege?" Howard said, his voice rolling out to the crowd like thunder. Kezia, watching him thought it sounded like an echo coming from the Tower, not in synchronous with Howard's lip movements.

The mob stood firm in defiance of the Warrior as if their numbers offered protection. Perhaps they do, thought Kezia, not knowing how many a warrior could handle.

"Where's the bloody server?" yelled a bald man in a tattered Watcher uniform from the relative security of the mob. Howard's head turned to fix his gaze on the speaker as Kezia straightened and stepped up to Howard's side. She suddenly felt completely at ease. If the Goddess could not protect her here, then Kezia doubted her protection was worth a feral curse. The mob acknowledged her presence with calls and whistles. Server's whore was the kindest term. Wryly, Kezia noted they directed their vitriol at the easy targets, the absent server and herself, not Howard.

"Ser Hugh has taken a group of your wounded colleagues to safety," Howard said.

"Deserted you mean," the balding man replied, "and left a Warrior to protect his whoring Tower." The mob endorsed these remarks.

"Someone had to get the wounded away." This came from another voice, less hysterical, deeper in the mob, which had now reassembled inside the perimeter Wall, and spread out either side of Paupers Gate.

Howard's gaze swept between the speakers. In the background, another house burst into flame to raucous cheers from those unaware of the standoff at the Tower.

"How does what you do here help the wounded?" Kezia said, startled when her voice also thundered out to the mob.

"No offence Warrior," returned the reasonable voice ignoring Kezia, "but the server and his town have abandoned us. There's no one left here or at Windgate to put a train together."

"What's your hurry?" asked Howard gently. "The mates you left defending the Wall still hold it."

One or two looked shamed. The bald man stepped to the front. "And what were the warriors doing while we held the Wall?" he shouted indignantly, his eyes fixed on Howard but addressing the mob. "When has anyone seen a Restoration Warrior on the wall? Who has seen one fight? They're nothing but damned Goddess executioners. Bet they die just like anyone else."

Kezia blanched, wanting to defend Howard, but in her limited experience, it was true. She had watched him execute an unarmed woman. Reluctantly, she drew her own knife. Drawing it always ended in someone close to her dying or getting hurt. *This time, it will probably be me. I hope it's quick. Sorry Wes junior.*

"Does anyone even recognise this warrior? Is the sword real?" The bald man continued urging the mob forward. Those at the back pulled stones from the top of the perimeter Wall in anticipation.

"Our Lady tested me this Bud. I chose the name Howard."

"Coward more like."

Howard tensed with a slight tilt of the head. *Firebolt* came out of its toe cup in a blur. Blue lightning crackled along its edge and coruscated from the tip.

"Stop now or prepare for the otherworld," Howard said, but the Tower's magic enhancement to his voice had gone in the roaring flames burning their backs.

A rock came hurtling from the mob. *Firebolt* flashed up and the rock nearly knocked it from Howard's grasp. The power of his sword had also gone. Seeing the sword powerless, the bald man charged, brandishing his torch. Behind them, something in the Tower, exploded. A ball of incandescent blue-white flame scorched past Kezia, hit the charging man square in the chest, lifted him off his feet and propelled him back into the mob. They scrambled out of the way, letting the charred corpse fall to the ground under Paupers Gate. More explosions erupted in the Tower.

Howard drove Kezia after the mob, now scattering in all directions. Stepping over the body, he dragged her down behind the Wall to escape the random fireballs spewing from the burning tower. Looking back as Howard dragged her away, shocked Kezia. She had thought the Towers were indestructible. How could they have stood for hundreds of years when a simple firebrand could destroy them? Why had it not happened before?

The inescapable conclusion frightened her. The Goddess was losing the ability to protect her towers. Aldus was right. The servers had whittled away at Severne's power until there was nothing left. She wondered how much of the widespread scepticism, disbelief, and outright antagonism, as Aldus displayed, had contributed to the Goddess's loss. And I'm one of them now.

The smell of hay and dung on the path around the perimeter wall intruded on her reflections. *Providence,* she thought with alarm.

"They're gone," Howard said.

He was right. The stables, though undamaged, were empty. Kezia raced outside and looked at the stragglers. They were all on foot. She whistled anyway, hoping that *Providence* was still around. There was no response. Whoever had taken their horses was long gone, probably before the mob started looting and burning.

The clothes they stood in and the contents of Kezia's backpack were now all they had left. At least she still had her medicinal supplies, but without the pack animals, it would severely restrict them in what they could take, especially Kezia, who was already carrying a load.

They returned to the smoking ruin, standing well back from the intense heat. Out on Great Plains, Kezia saw several large grass fires, started by the tower's fireballs, and fanned by the morning breeze. Howard stared at the pile of melted wreckage, his head cocked to one side, nodding to himself.

"What was that about?" she asked.

"The tower was overdue for a new resistant coating, but Our Lady has too few warriors. Fortunately, the levels below have automatically sealed. Unfortunately, we can't get into them until the heat has dissipated. It could be days or weeks."

"How will my child survive if I starve? Where are we going to get food?"

"Our Lady will provide," recited Howard.

They exchanged a glance, then without a word began systematically scouring the town's least damaged buildings, picking up anything they needed, doing exactly what she had abhorred in the mob. Despite their need, Kezia felt like a common criminal breaking into other people's houses for food, then rummaging through their belonging for suitable clothing, particularly good footwear. The Goddess helps those who help themselves, she thought, remembering one of her mother's more arcane sayings.

The ransacked town yielded everything they needed, except horses. She would have to do without, but it's going to be a long, hot walk. By following the Eldwin, they would have fresh water all the way, except the last two to three days into Blades Point. Her only worry was that on foot they might not make it before the baby was due.

She asked Howard if the Goddess had allowed for this in her calculations.

"Of course," Howard replied immediately and then cocked his head in the now familiar attitude to confirm it. He continued with assurances, "She allowed for you to have three weeks' rest before the birth. Not having horses will force us to travel slower, slower still, as you get bigger. We may lose two weeks of that.

The birth must be in a tower and under normal circumstances, Our Lady would keep you here, but the room needed will not be accessible."

"Why must I give birth in a tower? Women have given birth at home or outside for centuries. It's a perfectly natural human function."

"In case of complications."

"Complications? what complications?" asked Kezia, placing her hand protectively on her bulge?

"Wesley being part feral, the child may be ... mutated. And some mutations can damage the mother."

. . . .

It had started easily enough. She'd been cleaning out her shoulder bag, discarding medicinal leftovers too small to be of use, when her waters suddenly gushed between her legs. Her quick calculations told her she was several weeks too early. It would have been embarrassing had Howard been there, but he'd been off foraging. The baby kicked and settled lower. A small twinge tickled Kezia's belly. That's not so bad; I can manage that, she thought. Since Stonegate, her pregnancy had been mostly a pleasant inconvenience. In expectation of giving birth soon, she had woven a papoose from the coarse grass growing along the river, and remade a spare shirt into tiny clothes. She fingered the stone-softened fabric and tried to imagine what it would feel like to hold a baby to her breast, her baby, Wesley's baby. At that moment, more than at any other time since his death, she missed Wesley. The indispensable Warrior Howard was nowhere near as comforting.

Howard had returned that day at dusk, striding out of the evening leading a horse. To Kezia's relief his self-satisfied expression disappeared when he saw the patch of damp ground.

His knowledge obviously extended beyond executions and outback survival.

"My baby's coming," she said.

Howard's usually calm face showed concern. He stood quietly with his head on the side for a moment before speaking. "Even with this horse, Blades Point is still several hours away and you can no longer ride."

Kezia looked up at the deepening gloom where the first stars were appearing. "And it'll soon be dark?"

"We have Our Lady as guide." Howard said, the concern in his gaze now tinged with fear.

"But I can't ride like this, can I?"

"Our Lady says we have no choice. Her last examination showed the baby not sitting right."

A soft groan escaped Kezia's lips. Now she tells me. "What does that mean?" she asked.

"You need more help than I can give you out here. Our Lady has planned for this contingency. I will ride, carrying you."

While Kezia stared in amazement, he made a sling from his cloak, to support his arms, mounted, then lifted her into his arms as one would lift a small child. After he adjusted the sling, they rode into dusk, Howard guiding the horse with his knees and a few clicks of his tongue. A speechless Kezia stared up into old eyes, looking straight ahead. She could feel his body-warmth and breath. She was now closer and more personal than she had ever thought it possible to be with a warrior. He was riding, carrying her; no one would ever believe her.

Evening slid into cool night. The hills went grey the river black; the horizon became a ragged line where the sprinkle of brilliant stars abruptly stopped. A soft yellow light lit their path, a cloud of fireflies that had only become visible when the daylight faded, as if they had always been there, unseen. As the horse trotted the dimly lit track, Howard absorbed each jolt it made trotting over uneven ground. Kezia felt only the discomfort of the baby's head pressing down, making it hard not to push.

Just when the journey seemed endless, a light in the distance differentiated into two arched doorways, glowing in the dark like eyes. Light spilled onto the grounds and made the perimeter Wall look like a grinning mouth, gap-toothed at the gateways. The face of the Goddess, thought Kezia, does not look inviting.

At Patrons Gate, Kezia's breathing suddenly became short and uneven followed by a long agonising sigh. The server hurried down to meet them. Howard, leaning over, set her gently on her feet, the server supporting her while he dismounted, but Kezia, limp from the strength of the last contraction, collapsed. The young server struggled to hold her upright.

Howard picked her up again with ease, and as he carried her up the stairs into the brilliance of the Tower, she thought of Willard, wondering if he would become like Howard when he took the test: strong, decisive, self-reliant. Would he then lose his appeal? Is that what I see in Will, someone I can manage?

Chapter 28

A veril recalled little of her tunnel craft journey with Hedley. It left her an impression of great speed down a seemingly endless tunnel, distant lights on the wall raving towards her and passing overhead. At one point, she had felt they had slowed to a standstill. She looked up in time to see the tunnel slide to one side and moments later another slide into place from the other side. The craft was soon speeding again, ending up what had to be hundreds of miles from the ruins.

During the journey, Hedley was unusually quiet, while Averil's mind whirled around the many changes and firsthand experiences that had remade to her views on Warriors, ferals, the Goddess and now of builder artefacts. Who would believe a feral-carrying flying craft had run her down, or that warrior swords could fail? That a former server, who repaired builder artefacts in a ruined city full of them, had healed her and was now transporting her hundreds of miles closer to the wall, in a speeding builder craft, through an underground tunnel?

She was still in turmoil when the tunnel-craft slowed to a stop.

"Last stop, everyone out," Hedley said, and pointed her to where the opening magically reappeared. Averil stepped out on to a darkened apron, still blindly following his instructions, as she had since she was a child.

"Now pay attention. You are five miles north of the Dividing Sea, well west of the coastal jungle and about three hundred miles closer to the Break. You still have four hundred to go, but it's as close as I can get you; some tube lines don't connect. If you head west, it's open country all the way. Regrettably, you are still knee deep in Federal territory, sorry. Try not to mention how you got here. No one will believe you, anyway. Here's your pack. Thank you again for your help and good luck."

Distracted, Averil stood quietly watching as Hedley stepped back into the tunnel-craft. The opening closed, and with a slight tremor, the craft move back into the tunnel. A blast of air struck her as it whooshed away out of sight. Belatedly, she went to thank Hedley, but an invisible barrier blocked her way. More builder magic, she thought, or was it Goddess magic like the Audience Chamber illusion? She wondered if the ancient Builders had also worshipped the Goddess, or if the Goddess was one of them.

A rock fall, directly opposite the barrier, led up to a patch of greenery. Daylight filtered through the foliage and dribbled down the rocks into the tunnel bed. Averil scrambled up the slope and pushed her way through, through the bushes, planning what to do next. Her most important task was to get to the Wall and tell the Watcher about the floating craft. Although, without being able to say how they worked or how to stop them the knowledge might be of little use. What she could say was how desperate the ferals were to stop her from getting away, when they only suspected she had seen their small flotilla. Desperate enough to tackle a warrior.

She emerged on a small rise overlooking a flat plain in an open forest. The bush surrounding the hole, which led to the tunnel, was one of many dense thickets scattered around her. Finding the spot again would be almost impossible. A few paces away, and it was indistinguishable from the rest. Picking up two likely looking rocks, she placing one on the ground, repeatedly smashed it with the other until it broke, then using an edge she blazed an 'H' on the tree nearest the hole. Hedley had said she was five miles south of the sea and four hundred short of the Break, three weeks. Bastard, he kept the pony. I'll have to walk it.

If there are rivers to cross, three weeks could blow out to four or more.

Taking her bearings from the sun, Averil shouldered her pack and marched west towards the legendary mile high drop from the uplands to the lowlands, feeling a tinge of excitement at the thought. The pity of it was she was again on the wrong side. It had become emblematic of her efforts to get to the wall starting with Deep Creek, then the Aldgate River, and now the Break.

As she jogged on through the lowland scrub, she constantly scanned the sky for signs of the floating craft. The oppressively hot day had her wishing for the cool slopes of home. She stopped frequently for a swig from the canteen Hedley had provided.

The jingle of horse harness, disturbing the quiet of her midday meal. Quickly ducking behind the nearest bush, Averil scanned the treetops. Minutes later, a column of ferals rode into view barely fifteen feet away, surprising her with how little noise they made. They rode three abreast behind a single lead rider, on horses rather than the ponies Sumner's warband used. She counted sixteen rows as they rode past her hiding place, kicking up choking dust, and made a mental note that it represented seven warbands. Their horses looked well fed and groomed, their uniforms clean and tidy, and the troops seemed happy. Averil would have been proud to serve with them if they'd been Watchers.

When the dust settled, Averil eased out of her cramped position and wandered over to the find the road they had used and right into the path of a following column, a hundred yards further back. They saw her immediately. There was no way she could undo it, no way to backtrack or fight that many and no way to outrun them. She half raised her hands in the universal gesture of surrender, but their lack of interest delayed her. Only a few glanced her way, a quick appraisal as they rode past. Averil waved instead.

The lead rider came ahead, reined in next to her, extended his hand and took his foot from the stirrup. He's offering me a lift, she thought. For a fraction of a second, she hesitated, wondering what might happen if she declined. Making a snap decision, she held out her hand, shocked to see how brown it was as she grabbed his, placed her foot in the empty stirrup, and swung up behind him.

Her sponsor shifted a little in his saddle, settling his back comfortably against her and, to the grins of his comrades, re-joined the column.

"I am Elgar of the Shadows," he said in a heavy feral accent, his back moving more than he needed to get comfortable, rubbing her nipples erect. "And you?"

"Averil ... of the Lakes," she said.

"Ah. You must know Sumner."

"Yes," she replied, after a small hesitation and instantly regretting the admission.

"Have you ridden with him?"

"Some," Averil said, hoping this interrogation would not last much longer.

"Is Ethyl of the Stones still as jolly as ever?"

Averil's hesitation was fleeting. "Stone Ethyl is as always, the jolliest member of any band."

Elgar's back jiggled with laughter, and immediately afterward, he stopped deliberately rubbing up against her.

"I like you, Averil of the Lakes. Having been privileged to ride with our General, you will make a fine recruit for this Circle."

As Averil reappraised Sumner, their General, she noted that a column of seven warbands made up a Circle. She also noticed that Elgar wasn't the only rider carrying double. She looked carefully at the other two, both young and neither in uniform. With hindsight, their lack of reaction to finding her made sense. They were recruiting as they went. Her weeks in lowlands had so darkened Averil's skin she looked like them, and thanks to clothing Hedley had supplied, had dressed like them. They had interpreted her wave as a hailing signal.

Suits me. I get to ride, get them to feed me, and get to the Wall quicker.

They rode on into the afternoon with Elgar continuing his interrogation, pressing for details of her ride with Sumner's warband. Averil continued to answer, in monosyllables where possible, afraid of a slipup. At dusk, they rode into a clearing of hard-packed earth Elgar said was a clay pan. Averil saw she was in the third of five similar columns, or Circles, entering the clearing. That put the number of ferals in the camp at around two fifty, or about the same number of Watchers in each of the Forts along the Wall. Averil often heard this group politely called a latent Wheel, less politely a few Circles short. She surmised a complete Wheel would have seven Circles. They were obsessed with the number seven, no doubt taking it as representing the Goddess.

The front Circle rode around an invisible hub until the head joined the tail and they all turned inward and dismounted almost as one, the new recruits tardy. In Sumner's warband, each member had referred to the point rider, who gave a range of subtle signals, some of which looked as if they were merely scratching an itch. Had she missed this one? Or was completing the circle signal enough? She now considered the Academy's teaching on ferals abysmal. They really knew bugger all about their organisation, behaviour, or beliefs.

Once dismounted, she tethered then tended to Elgar's horse as she saw other new recruits were doing for their recruiters. The encampment blossomed, a ring of the seven-person Warband tents in each of the five Circles. Two larger tents, cooking and eating probably, sat on either side of the central fire-pit. Curiously, the distribution of Circles was uneven. The first and last Circles were close together, Elgar's and the fourth were separate from them and widely spaced from each other. It wasn't until Averil concentrated on the gaps that she realised they reflected the four pathways around Our Lady's Towers including the back entrance, insultingly called priests, for the private use of sers, sevs and warriors.

As darkness fell, there was a constant stream of ferals to and from the central tents. Averil followed Elgar's lead, lined up at the pit for a meal, and took it to a table in the eating tent. In the middle of the meal, there was a sudden mass exodus. Averil, knowing what would follow saw most were carrying mats. They assembled along the broad equivalent of the Public Path and oriented their mats south to the opening. Severne's Eye appeared shortly after, tracing its customary path across the backdrop of fixed stars. Goose bumps arose on Averil's brown arm. The ferals had aligned the encampment with Goddess-like precision; the transit following an imaginary line from Public Gate to Private Gate.

· · · ·

On her first morning; they had given each of them a horse, a uniform and a kit that including a sword. Averil had been the only one surprised when Elgar gave her the same. After her experience with Sumner, she should not have found their ready acceptance hard to believe, but the ingrained prejudices she had collected at the academy were hard to break. Now, after three weeks, five days riding and one off to rest the horses, the latent Wheel was only a circle short of a full complement. At each nightly camp, which came slightly earlier every day as chill approached, the Circles adjusted to include the new recruits. Thanks to her experiences with Sumner's band she had easily integrated into the seven ferals who shared a tent with her. Her new band, led by Isolda of the Wastelands, with Penn of the Forests as her second, were all now friends, despite they had only met two weeks back during the circle reshuffle. Averil was Isolda's only recruit.

She had her first glimpse of the much talked about Break, when the Circle was still, according to Penn whose duty it was to train her, about twelve miles away. She was disappointed. The mile high escarpment barely topped the scrub. Despite that, for the last two days, she had felt it, as an unseen presence, a massive solidity beyond the trees. Her occasional glimpses this morning, as it crept steadily up into the sky, awed her. When the bush abruptly ended, Averil couldn't help but stop and stare in amazement. The Break stretched right across their path, a border of sheer rock, higher it seemed to her than Deep Creek's famous Arch. Pock marks of various sizes covered the central section like a bad case of the feral plague. Beside the pockmarks, a wide river poured over the edge, forming a magnificent stepped waterfall, showing it wasn't as sheer as it looked from a distance.

"Keep moving, Averil," Isolda shouted as the horse behind bumped into hers.

Still enrapt by the grandeur of the Break, Averil gently urged the bay back into position. Along the top, she could just make out tiny sections of the Watchers-built Wall, only noticeable because of its colour difference. That bump next to where the river had cut a deep vee in the top edge must be Fort Grand Falls. It was some time before she could tear her gaze away to find they were in the outskirts of the main feral encampment. Again, the scale staggered her. Their camp was bigger than Hedley's ruins. It stretched all the remaining distance to the Wall, east back to the trees and west to the horizon.

"How far ..."

"Nearly two miles to the base," Penn said, interpreting Averil's gaze. "Then almost sheer for over a mile."

"How do we get up that?"

"Slowly," Penn said with a laugh. "See those big black spots? Those are staging camps, caves that we have expanded over the centuries since the uplanders built their damned wall."

A dazed Averil stared at him. Severne's tits, if they ever make it over the top, we're in deep shit, she thought, using an expression she had picked up in Elgar's Circle. From snatches of conversation around her, she sensed excitement building.

"This will be our year to ..."

"... Uplands will be ours ..."

"Our Lady is with us."

Averil closed her ears to that last comment and concentrated on her surroundings as they made their way down a wide avenue between campsites. As far as she could tell, they had laid out the whole camp, each Wheel and each circle using the same tower-like pattern, as obsessed with circles as with the number seven.

The overall focus was a small mound in the centre a long way down the wide central alley, which equated to the Tower's Public pathway. As they progressed, the scale of the encampment invaded her consciousness. There were hundreds of complete Wheels here, thousands upon thousands of ferals. She had never imagined there could be that many people in the entire world.

Along the way, at regular quarter-mile intervals, they encountered stone bridges. Under each flowed a creek so straight-sided it could not be natural. Again, the scale of the undertaking staggered her. The canals ran to distant bridges on either side of her and beyond that to others. From the bridges, she could plot the curve of the canals as they encircled the camp. She could also see the central mound was much bigger than she had first thought. The silhouette across its top resolved into the skyline of a town. The thought that feral engineering almost rivalled the Builders sent a shiver up her spine.

Halfway down the long alley, a rider directed them to an open field with a stone building at its centre. Their Wheel turned off and formed up around the building.

"That's our cookhouse," Elgar told his Circles recruits. "This field will be our home for the duration of this campaign, which will end when we go over the Uplanders' wall."

Elgar directed the recruits to general camp duties the first of which was digging latrines. At their overnight stop, the latrines had been outside the horse-tether. Here, Penn pointed to a spot a few yards behind the cookhouse, and told her to dig there. Despite the alarming proximity of the cookhouse, she dug and an inch below the surface struck solid stone.

Averil looked up to find Penn grinning at her. "The digging you need to do is under the stone," he said. "You'll have to lift three, then put two back once you clean out any silt."

Silt? She had never heard it called that before, but after she had cleared the dirt off the stone, an accumulation of dust and leaves, she heard running water and understood.

"When you're done, I'll help you put our box over the remaining hole," Penn finished. Averil, using the hooked bar Penn had provided, lifted the first capstone, a thin square a foot wide, and peered down. The water was clear, and running fast. With three capstones off, she realised the ferals had an established water driven sewage conduit under each campsite. Dumfounded, she looked up at the black holes, then across at the other Wheel's campsites and back at the uncovered conduit.

With fear filled insight, she realised she was looking at two and a half centuries of preparation toward a single goal; invasion.

Helping ready the camp for inspection kept Averil busy all afternoon. She threw herself into the work, helping everywhere, assessing everything for her report when she escaped. By the transit of Severne's Eye, she was exhausted.

"Get a good night's sleep," Penn said as soon as Averil entered her band's tent. "Elgar has told me that tomorrow, General Sumner will inspect our Circle."

That's all I need thought Averil. Her mind spun, trying to resolve several impossible questions, preventing the sleep she badly needed. She had left Sumner in a standoff with Gardner. If he was here, perhaps Gardner was dead. Not possible, the test made warriors immortal. That thought brought her back to the conclusion, the Goddess must be helping the ferals. Why else, after three hundred years of defeat, do they think this campaign will be any different? She had seen no sign of the one thing that might make a difference, the floating craft they called balloons. Even if the Goddess has changed sides, I'll survive. The Goddess had plans for my offspring with Willard, but how does my being here fit that plan?

She grinned mirthlessly thankful no one could hear what she was thinking, and despite her mental turmoil, physical exhaustion won and Averil drifted towards sleep. Fortunately, the assault was not imminent, time enough to figure a way out. If not, she would go with them and chance that her own people didn't kill her. The Watchers had a reputation for not taking prisoners. Funny that, she thought. It's exactly what I used to say about the ferals. She pushed the thought away to refocus on dodging Sumner's inspection and woke with a start. I must have dozed off. What was I thinking about before? Sumner, I must disappear tonight. She paused, her eyelids registering too much light. Tits, I've slept the night away. Her eyes sprang open.

Penn was bending over her. "I was about to wake you. Inspection in fifteen minutes."

Averil blinked, looked wildly around the tent. Everyone was up except her. Three had already gone. Isolda was inspecting Brent's uniform.

"Full dress uniform, Averil," Isolda said. "General Sumner has expressed an interest in your progress."

"How did he know I was here?"

Penn grinned. "They teach them to read - in general school."

Chuckles from outside the tent angered her. Bastards,

"Penn likes to joke," Isolda said as Brent left and Penn followed. As Averil dressed, Isolda explained. "Elgar sent in a recruit report with your name underlined. The general makes a point of chatting with those who have ridden with him."

For the inspection, they stood in a continuous line around their campsite, facing in. The general and his entourage rode around the hub, inspecting both the troops and their camp. Averil stared straight ahead, as they approached, though she could see out of the corner of her eye, that it was indeed a resplendent Sumner of the Lakes riding at their head. The party stopped in front of her.

"Averil of the Lakes, you amaze me. This is the last place I would have thought to find you."

Now I'm for it, thought Averil. Any second now, he'll order my arrest. He must know I killed Daisy. Averil looked up into the dark eyes. "I'm flattered you remember me—general," she said, emphasising 'general' with a deliberation that bordered on insult.

An aide shifted a hand to a sword, and Averil chanced a quick look. Stone Ethyl, I should have guessed. Is she his aide or his consort? Perhaps she's both. Averil struggled not to shudder at the thought of constantly looking over her shoulder, or one dark night she might disappear.

Sumner retrieved her gaze.

"You have much to learn that I failed to teach you." To Elgar he said, "You would do well to watch this one. She has abilities beyond her age. She would have made an ideal spy except we will have no need of spies after this campaign."

He turned back to Averil. "You and I will soon be free to return to our Lakes," he said, smiling at her.

Stone Ethyl looked like she could spit teeth. After all that had happened, all he had done to her, and all she had done to them she conceded (thinking of Daisy), he was still trying to turn her.

"Have courage Averil. Unlike the Watchers, I value my troops. Do not disappoint the Lakes. I will watch you closely," he added before riding on.

Averil stared after him her shaking knees threatening collapse. *The bastard played me. Still better him than Ethyl who wouldn't hesitate to kill me.* Then her hackles rose when she glimpsed an aide at the back of his entourage staring at her. The aide had looked away by the time she noticed, but the face bothered her. It was both familiar and different, but not one of Sumner's old band. Putting a name to the face was on the tip of her tongue when congratulatory slaps on the back scattered her thoughts.

• • • •

Ribald humour speculating on the true nature of her association with the General, already rife, got right out of hand when Sumner summoned her to his tent. Her unknown escort smirked, appraising her as he might a horse he wished to buy. The General's quarters were in the centre of the elevated town. They rode around the mound to the nearest path up, the equivalent of Paupers, and then cantered through the hot night for fifteen minutes to the largest of the central buildings.

"Averil of the Lakes," her escort announced in front of a doorway that apparently led to a passage. He remained outside as she stepped through, finding it was only a short wall covering the entrance like a screen. Automatically, she went left and entered.

Directly opposite the entrance, Sumner sat on a bulky throne-like chair between flickering torches. Stone Ethyl stood to his right, steely gaze boring into Averil. A large table of maps stood in the middle of the room. The maps were crude but recognizable, Preservation Island, an enlargement of the Pointing Finger isthmus and on top, the layout of Fort Grand Falls. Leaning over the table was the aide she had glimpsed. This time, she got a good look and knew immediately they had snatched Aldus from Deep Creek. This time, she followed Gardner's advice and kept her mouth shut.

"You know him?" Sumner asked quietly.

Averil took a long hard look, suppressing all thought, all emotion. Aldus looked stricken.

"No."

"Padget of the Shadows, whom Gardner told me you know, picked him up the same as he did you." Sumner looked from one to the other, then nodded at Aldus, who turned and left followed by Stone Ethyl. "Uplanders," Ethyl sneered as she passed.

Sumner waited long after they were gone, studying her as she studied him: handsome, intelligent, and feral. Why do I always end up on the wrong side of every divide?

"What happened to Gardner?"

"Once you were gone, there wasn't a point to contest. He had other duties needing his attention, as did I. Now what am I to do with you, Averil," he gave a low chuckle, "of the Lakes? Your friend, who you don't know, hasn't worked out. His maps show nothing we did not already know. Perhaps you can."

"No."

"I thought not. That's why I like you. I suppose you only joined us to get home." That brought a smile to her lips.

"You should do that more often." He went on without pause, not looking at her, for which she was glad. "As general, I have an aide for strategy and a concubine for sex. I need a friend. Do you play chess?"

Averil didn't need to hold her tongue. She was speechless.

"Three times a week, every other day. I will teach you this most ancient of old Aithe battle games, starting tomorrow. The choice is chess or I give Aldus to Stone Ethyl."

Chapter 29

D own in the bowels of the Blades Point Tower, Kezia lost all track of time. There was no way to measure its passing. Steady light from above created unmoving shadows.

At least the contractions had slowed. As far as she could tell, this room was identical to the examination room in Stonegate. In the dimness, some artefacts looked unnatural, even grotesque, reawakening her fears. For her, the Goddess had not always been benign.

She had dozed fitfully and woke screaming as the pain in her groin seared down her legs, returning to a dull ache as the tension eased. The midwife, dozing in a chair, jumped up and mopped Kezia's brow. The pain ebbed and flowed, each spasm ripping through her body worse than the last, with little time between them to think. When will it end?

"Enough. Get this baby out of me before it kills me."

Though the Goddess remained silent, the overhead lights flared to brilliance and there was movement around her, the midwife and Howard. Distantly, she heard the midwife whisper to him, "any woman takes this long will give birth to a dead baby."

"Then help me, for pity's sake," Kezia cried as she lay back. Blood and other body fluids stained the sheets, the provided gown, up around her waist, despite Howard's presence. In her urgency to rid herself of this burden, she was beyond modesty.

"Here, my lovely, it'll be fine," the midwife crooned. She took Kezia's head in her arms and sponged cool water on her lips. With accomplished deftness, she cleaned up and returned Kezia to comfort, always talking gently, trying to calm her.

Then the birth began in earnest.

"Push," the midwife said, smiling at her from between her upraised knees.

Push! I don't have the energy to push anymore. She felt like throttling the woman.

A contraction made her bite on the cloth-covered rod the midwife had placed in her mouth and she felt her teeth crush through another layer of wood. Why does it have to be so painful?

She was exhausted, her back ached, her belly already tight as a drum tightened more with each contraction and still no end in sight. How can my baby survive this, let alone me? A small movement reassured her that despite its reluctance to enter the world her baby was still alive. I don't blame you for not wanting to come. It's not a nice place.

The riot at Stonegate had rattled her and given her another reason, aside from her distrust of the Goddess, not to enter the Tower at Blades Point, their susceptibility to fire. She was here under protest, for her child, because Howard insisted that only the Goddess could guarantee a safe delivery.

Most of this populace had also deserted, and the disgruntled Watchers had ransacked the empty houses. Unlike Stonegate, the server was in residence and Our Lady's Tower untouched. In anticipation of Kezia's arrival, the server had procured the services of a midwife from those who stayed, because their server had stayed. Howard assured Kezia that the Goddess herself had vetted the woman.

Kezia screamed as another contraction ripped through her belly. She closed her eyes against the harsh altar lights. Sweat poured from her body and her hair plastered itself in dank strands across her face. She thought of her mother, wondering how on Aithe she had gone through this agony three times, the third time with twins. Severne's teeth, mother, why didn't you tell me? If I survive this, it will be the last.

"Push." The Midwife spoke over her shoulder to Howard. "You, Warrior, pass me those towels."

Howard, though startled by the authority in her tone, did as she said.

As the rolling pains continued, the midwife gently probed Kezia's abdomen.

"It will be a hard birth," she said, inserted her fingers inside her. Kezia was beyond caring.

"The babe is lying face up instead of face down," she said, "and there's a hand here, alongside the baby's head, holding back the birth."

"He's stuck," cried Kezia, "I can feel it."

Gently, the midwife pushed and probed, and slowly pushed the little hand inside. Kezia screamed, her body tearing with the extra stress.

"There, there little one, it won't be long now," the midwife crooned, and Kezia couldn't tell if she meant her, or the baby.

"Any attempt to turn the child might damage him," said the disembodied voice of the Goddess.

Him? I'm going to have a son.

"Push."

Again, Kezia screamed loud and long. She felt the tension in her belly, felt the baby's head push out between her thighs, as if splitting her apart. His head was a large hard melon stuffed between her legs.

"Gently now. Almost there. One more strong push and you'll have him." The soft, assured crooning soothed Kezia as she readied her body.

"Fuck you Severne," she screamed as she pushed with everything she had left.

The midwife, with a sudden cry of alarm, urged "slowly" but Kezia was past being able to stop. First the head and then the child slithered into the world, the cord pulsing. She wept with relief, but as she fell back, she saw the midwife circle herself.

Never had Kezia felt such great anxiety at seeing the familiar gesture. How feral looking is he? As the wait to hold her son dragged, Kezia, with growing unease, held out her hands. "Give him to me," she cried, but the midwife, holding the wrapped baby close to her chest, turned away and hurried from the room.

"Where are you taking my son," Kezia whimpered, reaching out, trying to rise as the doors slid shut behind the departing midwife.

Howard wiped tears from his eyes as he came over to her. "I'm so sorry Jena."

As Kezia's own long wail tapered off, she thought she heard a tiny cry.

· · · ·

Kezia walked. The horse Howard had purloined trailed behind as her pack animal. Beside them, a river flowed noisily over rapids. Across it, the far bank rose in a series of ridges that culminated in the forested peaks of the Northern Hummocks. The sun shone warmly from a clear blue sky.

Like Howard, Kezia now refused to ride, but for different reasons. For her, the walking was comforting. The rhythmic progress of each step took her further from the horrors of the past, closer to the Wall. Her determination to take care of the sick and wounded at the front had become a solitary fixated goal, crystallising in her mind as her last chance at redemption. She had tried to thwart the Goddess, to take Willard from Averil, and then compounded the problem by killing her father and the Goddess had extracted a penalty.

Whenever Howard tried to dissuade her or suggest that she would do better to return to Port Calder, she would look at him as if he were an imbecile then walk on. She had no way to express what she was thinking, especially to Howard. She left the day-to-day decisions to him: when to rest, when to eat, when to sleep. She concentrated on walking, one foot after the other, day after day, mile after mile, mourning her losses: Willard, Wesley, her son. At night, tears mixed with the milk she expressed, weeping because she could not give it to her son. The instructions to express came from the Goddess, but only after Kezia started clutching her breasts in pain.

Occasionally, Howard would try to draw her out. The formerly taciturn Warrior would become voluble, giving a continuous running commentary on the landscape, the wildlife, the history, and the meaning of the Restoration, but nothing penetrated. Kezia took no interest in either her surroundings or his ramblings.

She began playing the flute again, but without Wesley to correct her, the haunting tune he'd taught her altered subtly. Kezia missed some notes, drew out others, repeated passages she liked. Over all, it was slower, more melancholic. She only knew the one tune and she played it endlessly, while sitting by their small fire waiting for Severne's Eye to pass over. Kezia would stop playing then, roll up and be asleep moments later.

After weeks of silence, she suddenly interrupted one of Howard's monologues. "Why did the Goddess take my son?"

Howard looked startled for a second before carefully replying, "Our Lady did not take your son, Jena. He was born ..."

"Don't," Kezia said, screwing up her eyes. She did not understand the distinction he was making. Her son had died and the Goddess had taken him. What she wanted to know was why?

"How did his death serve her plan?"

Howard chewed his bottom lip, his head cocked to one side. Though he looked at her, his eyes focussed inward. I had a son, she thought, as she looked away from Howard's vacant stare out over increasing greener grasslands, waiting for his reply. She repressed her anguish.

"I don't know all of Our Lady's plans," he said, a mild tremor in his voice. "But I can assure you, the need must have been great."

"Can you ask her?"

"She may not reply."

Kezia watched Howard's unmatched eyes take on that faraway look again. When he spoke, his voice had the pitch and cadence of the Goddess.

"Trust me Kezia. All that happens has a purpose."

Kezia thanked Howard for the uninformative answer, but somewhere below the level of conscious thought, a baby's cry haunted her. With no justification, the cry she thought she had heard kept alive a tiny spark of hope. It made it impossible for her to finish grieving and the lack of an explicit reason for her son's death fanned the hope. Simultaneously, the cry fanned her doubts about the Goddess and raised further questions. Had her father's unwarranted attentions, and Willard's lack of commitment been part of Our Lady's plan? Was my loving Wesley such a crime that both he and our child had to die?

When they walked on, it was along a well-maintained road into settled farmland. They increasingly met local farmers, who for generations had serviced the Wall. Howard removed his cloak and from an inner pocket produced a floppy hat and a cover for *Firebolt*'s gem. To Kezia's surprise, His warrior cloak folded into a small parcel he could put in his trouser pocket. The effect, though somewhat ludicrous, stopped people scattering at first sight and by the time anyone worked out why his sword hilt had a cover, he had charmed them. Most left soon after, but some were eager to ask questions: everything you always wanted to know about Warriors but were too afraid to ask.

Kezia, wondering why Howard was suddenly trying to be everyone's friend asked, "Are all warriors now doing this?"

"Doing what?"

"Talking to people; making friends."

"Our Lady has initiated a slight change to brethren policy."

"Slight is a gross understatement."

Howard was unfazed. "The effect of a slight change can, over time, magnify in importance. Your journey began with a single telling."

Kezia almost unravelled, as the accumulation of slight changes that had brought her here streamed through her mind. She sat on the ground in a flood of tears, regretting most of the decisions behind those slight changes.

. . . .

Howard, as always with the people they met, introduced Kezia as Jena with no added labels. Invariably, when the conversation turned to the status of the Wall, Kezia would repeat what she heard from the wounded about its immanent collapse.

"No disrespect Jena," said Dana, a drayman whose family had stopped for a meal in the same traveller's rest area, "but my grandfather used to say, you east coasters wouldn't know shit from clay if you stepped in it. You come out here saying it's not scalable and at the first sight of a feral, run off home saying it's going to fall."

He bit into the thick slice of bread and cheese his wife handed him. He was a thin, hard man, slightly stooped with bushy eyebrows. His wife Norma, as stout as her husband was thin, watched Kezia as if trying to decide about her.

Dana swallowed, "I tell you Jena, that Wall has been there for hundreds of years, will be for hundreds more I reckon. Them ferals can't breach it, long as we have Watchers on the parapets and us out here, keeping 'em fed."

Howard said, "But with the numbers heading east, aren't the Watchers spread rather thin?"

"They'll hold it. Always have, always will." He said it like an article of faith. "Ain't that right, Norma?"

A shout of alarm from their son who was watering the dray's team at the creek brought all heads up. One of the big horses reared over him, the lad still clutching the reins, trying to steady the animal.

"Let go, you damn fool," Dana shouted, springing to his feet, snatching up the empty potato sack he was sitting on. Howard was right behind him. Both were halfway there before Kezia could stand. Norma sat straight and tense, circling her chest with a forefinger.

Kezia watched in remembered horror as hooves flailed at the boy's head. *Firebolt* flashed through the reins and the horse wheeled away, heading up the embankment towards Dana. The drayman stepped nimbly aside as the horse bore down and his thick brown arm snapped out to grab the severed reins, pulling the horse's head around so savagely it stumbled and fell to its knees. Dana had the empty sack over the horse's head and was sitting down with an arm around its neck in seconds, as if it this was the most natural thing in the world.

Turning at a sigh from Norma, Kezia found her eyes were on her husband, not her son.

"Still the best breaker in the Hummocks," she said.

Kezia felt her face heating when she realised both had thought of the horse first. Norma eventually turned to watch as Howard carried her son's limp form up the embankment.

"Do what you can, Jena," he said, laying him on the grass beside her.

Kezia, seeing his grey pallor didn't like her chances of doing anything. She put her ear to his mouth and slipped a hand under his jerkin to feel for the beat of his heart.

"Dead I reckon," said Norma, her face devoid of emotion. The boy's father crooned to the horse now back on its feet with the hood off, then checked its legs.

Fuming, Kezia reached into her shoulder bag. Mother's jar of healing dust was almost empty, but nothing else would help when it was this bad. She wondered if she should bother. They didn't deserve to have him back.

"Jena?" Norma said as if struck by revelation, "The Jena, the Goddess healer!"

Dana looked around at his wife's exclamation, though he continued to hold and soothe the horse. "If you can't help Liam, no one can," he said.

Kezia gritted her teeth and took a pinch of the dust. There was a large and bloody gash in the lad's head, and pieces of skull in the blood-matted hair where she sprinkled a few grains. The blood dried up and flaked off. Kezia gently pushed the fragments back into their most likely positions, watched as they adjusted to match edges and fuse. With fingers on either side, she pushed the long gash together and held it while it slowly knitted.

Liam's colour remained pallid.

Howard knelt beside her. "Our Lady says I need to restart his heart." He positioned himself at Liam's side clenched his hands into a double fist and before Kezia could ask what he was doing or protest, he thumped Liam on the chest. Liam's body jerked from the blow. Kezia checked for breath or beat, but shook her head.

"Stand back," said Howard. He stood slipping *Firebolt* from its scabbard with a crackle. The gem glowed orange through its cover.

"Hey," Dana yelled and let go of the horse.

Kezia leaned back as *Firebolt* hissed past her ear and the point touched Liam's chest. Lightning crackled from both edges, one spark to his chest one to his side. She blanched as the body jumped. Liam moaned and his face suffused with blood.

"Dear Lady," said Norma, staring at Kezia in awe, nodding at her husband. "It's her! Our Lady's healer; Jena Setler. She brought Liam back to life."

Kezia stared, too stunned to argue. She had done little. Howard, the Goddess, and mother's dust had done it all. She felt like a fraud. She tried to explain, but Norma would have none of it. To her whatever Jena used, including a Warrior, were simply tools she wielded in Our Lady's name.

• • • •

Kezia thought often of her son and Wesley. She still felt both losses intensely. The ways of the Goddess are obscure. On one hand, she takes my son and his father, on the other she sends Howard to help me, and together they create an enviable reputation for me. The former feels like punishment, the latter like facilitating my redemption; it's contradictory.

Her immediate grief walked out, Kezia rode again, walling off her deep pain. Howard loped alongside in rhythmic quietude. Earlier he had done everything possible to delay her, repeatedly suggesting she return to Port Calder. Now, in a clear reversal, he was setting an unusually fast pace. On horseback, Kezia had no difficulty keeping up, but it caused her to wonder. Without doubt, the Goddess was behind both tactics, so what had changed?

The road had been following the river for over a week, and now crossed it to continue along the other bank. As Howard splashed across, Kezia noticed his head had a slight tilt as when receiving instructions from the Goddess.

He barely waited for her to ride across before announcing, "Our Lady thinks it best we bypass Clarcton."

He immediately set off at the same brisk pace, on a track away from the river into the hills. Kezia had to run to catch up and stop him. He was breathing deeply, dragging in great gulps of air, really pushing himself to maintain the pace.

"We need to resupply. Why are we bypassing Clarcton?"

"I don't know."

Kezia dismounted. "I want to walk for a while, so we can talk." She caught the look of pained distress that crossed his face. "Why the sudden hurry?"

"We will run short of food unless we shorten the time to Newbridge. It's only an extra day and there is plenty of water and grass for the horse."

Kezia walked on, leading the horse down the new track, which wound through a shallow valley. "That's the result of bypassing Clarcton, not the reason for it."

"Our Lady thinks ..."

"... it best," Kezia finished for him. If she continued to dawdle, the reason would become apparent. "Have you asked why its best?"

"I have no reason to."

"Well I do," Kezia said and ambled on.

When Howard fell into step beside her, she asked, "Where did you get such faith?"

After a moment of thought, Howard said, "I guess I've always had it. Servers run in my family. I have several uncles and great uncles in Our Lady's service, but I'm the first to make warrior."

She wanted to tell him that her faith had collapsed after the death of her son (she had finally accepted Howard's account), so soon after Wesley's death, but a faint shout from the direction of Clarcton instantly dispelled Howard's amiability. He snatched off his hat and the hilt cover, then withdrew and put on the green cloak. The transformation from a likeable young man proudly talking of his heritage, to the humourless, much feared Restoration Warrior, was profound. She thought he had aged ten years. No, not aged, matured ten years in an instant. A mercurial change she had already witnessed more than once.

Kezia felt a certain cynicism at the Goddess so quickly revoking the brethren's slight policy change. The volume of the shouting grew and Howard urged her to get back in the saddle. Kezia, intrigued despite a certain apprehension, refused. Whatever was coming was the reason for bypassing Clarcton.

Figures appeared, jogging over the crest beside them. Pointing and shouting, their number growing rapidly, they broke into a run and veered to intercept. They had to have started out yesterday. Clarcton was still thirty miles away. Knowing there was now no way to escape meeting them, Kezia hoped it wasn't another mob of deserters. The same thought must have occurred to Howard. He turned to face the crowd pouring down the slope and reached over his shoulder. *Firebolt* crackled and the tip came to rest in the toe cup on his boot.

Long before Kezia identified what they were shouting, she noticed cloth bindings on limbs and heads. At the back, some without bindings carried others who were bound up. Why, after manipulating me into the role of celebrated healer does the Goddess not want me to heal these people?

"For pity's sake, Howard, put up your sword."

"Not until they stop. They could trample you in their haste to be healed."

She could see he was probably right. Whatever their intent they resembled the Stonegate mob, the stronger ones rushing past those who fell without stopping to assist. Howard's presence might at least slow their rush.

"This is what you were trying to avoid?"

"Our Lady advised me it would be best," Howard replied without looking round. "Some may not be as benign as they seem. Most who choose to live out here, to support the Watchers, believe as they do."

Kezia, as always wanted to know why it mattered what they believed, but knew it would be futile. Trust me, Our Lady had said, but if I had, then these people would have missed whatever help I offer.

The crowd halted a few feet away, the front rank falling to their knees. Kezia passed her reins to Howard, unpacked her kit, and walked towards them.

"Who is most in need?" she asked.

Howard, after some hesitation, sheathed his sword, hobbled the horse, and joined her. It appalled Kezia that the biggest problem was simply a lack of hygiene. The most they needed was clean water and fresh bandages. She herded them to back to the river. It seemed word of the Goddess healer, Jena Setler, bringing the horse breaker's son back to life, had reached Clarcton days ago. Liam's name never came up. Plod was the horse that kicked him to death.

It took her the rest of the afternoon to see all those who had come. She instructed anyone who showed an interest in basic hygiene and set them to helping others. Very few serious casualties had made the journey from Clarcton. Only twice did she use a pinch of the fast-diminishing dust. Although used

surreptitiously and sparingly, the results were obvious.
Interestingly, those she treated by normal means healed just as
well, almost as if their belief in her was enough. Word spread.
The laying on of Jena's hands was enough to cure the sick.

As she moved through the crowd, it embarrassed Kezia to
hear her assumed name whispered in reverential tones. Worse
still was when they addressed her as Lady Jena, despite her
protests that she was just a normal country girl trained in healing
at the institute. One young lad, dressed in clean white trousers,
who followed her everywhere, carrying out introductions,
thoughtfully brought her a cup of water.

"Thank you," she said.

"The thanks are mine, that you accept my gift Holy One."

Kezia nearly choked on, Holy One. She looked around the
crowd to find that the lad had succinctly encapsulated all that
had happened while she was busy helping. Mother's aithcraft,
Howard, and the faith of those seeking help had further
enhanced her status. All they talked about was Our Lady's
miracle healer, Jena Setler, and her obvious link to a rumour
from the wilds. A strong candidate who carried both a talisman
and a named sword, but was neither a server nor a warrior. He
had recently appeared from the southern wilds with an eye
shaped scar in forehead and was making his way to the Wall.

"They say that after the 'Miracle of the Hands' he made a girl
into a server," said the woman. She was re-bandaging with the
woman's own washed and dried bandages.

"A girl?" asked Kezia, with obvious scepticism.

"The one he brought back to life, as your ladyship did for
the breaker's son. Ser Nelda she's called. Imagine that, a woman
server, never thought I'd live to see the day." The woman said it
was a sign that these were the last days. With the Wall falling,
the Goddess had found the Man Who Will Be Face, and sent her

miracle healer on ahead. The long-awaited Restoration must be close.

Kezia, knowing the reality of her own miracles, could not take the reports of similar incidents at face value. Without a doubt, it was the handiwork of the Goddess. She felt sorry for the poor man coerced into her plan. *At least Willard is off the hook.* That brought a smile. Willard had always said, if he waited until they find the Face, he wouldn't have to take the test. It was the first time since her son's death that she had thought about Willard. She hoped he was well.

Near dusk, Howard put her on the horse and took her back across the river, away from the crowd, to the shelter he had erected. Kezia flopped down on the provided palliasse, exhausted. Howard stood guard to ensure no one from the encampment crossed the river. Small fires, burning behind scraps of clothing strung between trees, softly highlighted ripples on the ford. Above her, the stars stood out jewel bright in the dark night, now quiet except for the clicking of insects and the distant bellow of Wildebeef.

"What do you know of this man with an eye in his forehead?" she asked Howard.

In the dim light, Howard looked startled for a moment, but recovered so quickly she might have imagined it. It happened a lot lately.

"Only one?"

Kezia ignored his attempt to distract her. "In his forehead I said. It's a scar in the shape of an eye. They say it's the mark of the Goddess. That it bleeds whenever she is in him."

"Rumours may contain a seed of truth, but are not fact."

"Is that a denial?"

"Our Lady has not yet found her Face, if that's what you're asking," Howard said, as an awed murmur went out from those still awake the other side.

Kezia crawled to the opening and looked up. Severne's Eye passed directly overhead, as if in benediction of what she had done here. She stared up at it, as it waxed bright, temporarily dimming the surrounding stars. It looked close enough to reach out and touch.

With a sigh, she returned to her bed, her lids closing on moist eyes, again thinking of Willard. If she were truthful, she had come to the Wall not just to atone but also to forget, and perhaps reunite with Averil, although she dreaded that meeting. The Goddess had plans for Averil and Willard's children. As she drifted off, it occurred to her that if Averil was there, Willard might be too. *That must be why the Goddess has delayed me, and will do so again when we leave this place. But then why did she want us to hurry past here.*

She slept soundly without dreams and woke clutching her throat. She tried to scream, but nothing came. Her throat was on fire and her stomach twisted. She tried to rise, but her muscles only twitched in response. Unaccountably, she heard Willard's voice ask, 'What's wrong Kez?' Another spasm in her intestines caught her hard. She drew in a sharp breath, her knees jerked up to her chin and she rolled off the palliasse in agony.

Chapter 30

Willard's first hours at sea had given him the worst case of seasickness the Master's Mate Kedron Butcher had ever witnessed. The only time he did not feel ill was when he was asleep, and that was rare because he could not lie down long enough without needing to rush to the little cubicle. At least having a cabin spared him the indignity of vomiting in public.

By the third morning, he could feel he was over it. Baxter was sitting in a chair opposite as Kedron entered, bringing breakfast. Willard was about to thank him when his stomach twisted in a knot and he fell to his knees. He knew, without knowing how he could know, that Kezia was dying.

"What's wrong Kez?" he asked, toppling sideways onto the floor unable to stop. Baxter was looking inward. Kedron looked at him like he was having a fit. Ignoring Kedron's stares, Willard vomited with Kezia, dry retching. [Where are you?] he pleaded, but the twisting had gone, leaving an empty blankness in his mind.

[Turn it down,] Baxter said. [She's fine. Our Lady is with her.]

[She'd better be.]

Kedron looked from one to the other, shaking his head in bewilderment.

· · · ·

The common explanation for Willard's sickness when he finally ventured on deck to hastily averted grins and the whispered nickname Lord Paleface, was "did not *Legends* say, For Our Lady's sake, the Man Who Will be Face, will suffer?"

Willard ignored it all, as best he could, and instead took an interest in the workings of the ship, learning the terms the sailors used. The crossbeam that held the sail they called a yard, though it was several yards long, and they climbed up to it on the shrouds, which bore no resemblance to burial sheets.

Beside Willard, only the Shipmaster and the Mate knew of Baxter's return. The crew had last seen them jogging out of sight up the main street of Port Taylor. Baxter's wig, eyebrows and wrinkles were as undetectable as they were fake. He used an eye dish like the one Kezia's mother had given Willard to make his eye colour match. No wonder they could disappear between executions.

The lasting result of their appearance was to irrevocably damaged Willard's standing with the crew. Except for Kedron, the crew bowed politely and moved away as fast as possible. When cornered, their answers were short: yes Lord, no Lord, a belaying pin Lord. And Odell was always too busy, leaving him trapped with Baxter and Severne's thoughts for company.

[Damaged Lord,] asked Baxter?

[Yes, only Kedron talks to me, and then only because Odell has made it his duty.]

By day five, Baxter's constant surveillance made him feel like a prisoner. Unable to get off the ship, he was never alone, even in his cabin. The walls were too thin. In retrospect, he saw his life since the militia first arrested him as a series of prison sentences interspersed with tantalising tastes of freedom. He had been in and out of custody five times: Ob walker had locked him in the servatory, Severne had held him in the Eye and then the Mount Bakor Tower, Aderic had briefly tried to hold him for ransom and now Baxter had him trapped on this ship. Every time he thought he had control of his fate, he ended up captive again.

The Goddess's claim that the choice was his was as mythical as the freedom of the Sea.

Desperate for a moment's peace, he leapt onto the gunwale in front of a sailor about to ascend the shrouds and started climbing. The sailor called for the Mate.

"Please Lord, come down," Kedron said.

"Come and get me," Willard replied and kicked his shoes off to go barefoot, as the sailors did.

Slowly at first, but with increasing confidence, he crabbed his way up the rigging, aping the sailors. Half way up, he looked down and noticed that the ship, which had seemed so large from the wharf and cramped from the deck, had shrunk to a rowing boat, dwarfed by his perspective and the immensity of the sea.

Shipmaster Barnes and Kedron looked oddly distorted and shrunken as they argued and pointed at him. Baxter stood unmoving at the gunwale. Were there limitations to a warrior's skills?

[No,] Severne said. [Nor are they afraid. If you die, you jeopardise all our lives. Unlike you, my warriors are not that selfish.]

[Good,] replied Willard, despite the hurt that caused him, as he doggedly returned to his climb. [You forced me into this. Don't blame me if it goes wrong.]

The higher he went the less secure he felt. The swaying of the mast, gentle at deck level, had increased as he climbed, and now swayed alarmingly. The ratlines became shorter and shorter until they were too short to put his foot on. He paused, wondering how to continue. He was too far below the platform around the mast, called the top despite it was only half up the mast, or even the comparative safety of the yard below. The shrouds continued to taper until they came to a point under it. From the deck, he hadn't seen how the sailors got around it. Then he spotted a hole in the top he could squeeze through; the other side. He was on the wrong shrouds.

As he clung there, thinking through his options to go over the top, across to the other shrouds or admit defeat and back down, his expanded view of the world distracted him. The distant snow-capped peaks of the Northern Hummocks were so small he felt he was looking down on them. The sea was a sparkling green plain, bounded by a curving horizon, giving him the impression of being alone on top of the world.

He turned to find Kedron only the length of two arms away on the opposite shrouds. Although the Mate still had the skill, he didn't have the wiriness or agility of the other sailors and the hole would be too small for him. He moved cautiously, his ragged breathing showing he hadn't been up the mast in a while; he was out of shape yet he'd climbed higher.

[When to back down is a skill you should learn, before you get someone killed,] Severne whispered.

Ignoring her, Willard looked down to see how he'd managed it, saw Kedron's feet turned sideways on the ratline, and nearly laughed himself into oblivion at the simplicity of the action. Duplicating the method, he climbed another two steps, enough to hook an arm over the yard, and hang there a while, easing the strain on his legs. If he tried for the top, Kedron would be close enough to grab him. He now had nowhere to go except out along the yard. He shifted one foot, then the other along the footrope, sliding his ribcage along the top of the yard. On the other side of the mast, Kedron rested a moment before working his way round the mast.

"No offence, Lord Willard," Kedron said, "but you must come down before you fall."

"I'm sorry this involved you," Willard said as he edged further out on the yard. "I owe you for getting me through the sickness, but I need some peace."

Kedron grunted and Willard felt his feet rise as the Mate added his weight to the footrope already cutting into his bare soles. Willard had to bend his knees to keep his chest on the yard. With each step Kedron took, Willard's legs flexed up and down. His knees ached and his legs shook but there was no way to rest them and nowhere to go.

"They have sent me to fetch you," Kedron said. "It is not safe for you up here."

[I'll come down if you back off,] he thought to Baxter. He was running out of rope, almost at the yardarm. Kedron took another step and gave a grunt of surprise. Willard's support dropped from under him, the air pushed from his lungs as his rib cage took his full weight. The footrope they were standing on had parted. He gripped the sail to stop himself from sliding off the foot-thick, round yard.

Baxter's thought was clear, [Fool.]

Willard turned to see Kedron had not fared so well. He was hanging precariously from the iron rod along the yard by one hand, and only two fingers of the other hooked through adjacent robands. Kedron's grip was tenuous. He urgently needed to change his hold from the unravelling robands to the halyard, but to do so, he would have to let go the rod. His whole weight on the robands would break them.

[Shit Severne now look what you got me into,] thought Willard, unable to help even himself.

[Up,] Severne said.

Up, he thought, and twisting on his ribs swung a leg up and over the yard, to lie flat on top of the iron rail. Gripping the yard tightly between legs and elbows, he crawled towards Kedron.

The mate's face was a study of fear and hope. His eyes flicked from the slowly unravelling robands to Willard, inching his way closer. His wrist and hand were white. He was hanging on by his fingertips.

The moment Willard reached out and grabbed Kedron's wrist the tie parted and his other hand slipped off the yard. Kedron used it to grip Willard's forearm. Willard felt an incredible wrench to his shoulder, as his stomach jammed hard on the yard, crushed the breath out of him as Kedron's weight began pulling him around the yard.

Shit, he's heavy.

Only Kedron's iron grip and Willard jamming his foot in between a couple of yard stays held them both. Willard could feel his wrist bones grinding together and the stays sawing at his ankle. Kedron swung back and forth, reaching for a halyard with his feet. Eyes screwed shut against excruciating pain Willard imagined that any second his wrist or arm would tear off, sending Kedron plunging to the deck. As if his thought had precipitated the action, his shoulder popped. Kedron let go simultaneously and the weight on Willard's arm vanished.

A ragged cheer reached him from below. Through blurred vision, Willard saw Kedron had somehow got a leg and an arm wrapped around a halyard and had slid down to the deck. Relieved, Willard lay panting on the yard, an agonising ache in his shoulder whenever he moved and his arm hanging uselessly. He shivered uncontrollably. He had come close to falling and neither Severne nor Baxter had been in any position to prevent it. Despite her repeated statement that she could not control everything in his life, Willard had assumed she would keep him safe no matter what he did. He was suddenly conscious of how precious life was.

A hand touched his good shoulder.

ROB BLECKLY

"Hold on Lord. I have you."

Baxter, at last acting like a sailor, sat astride the yard. He tied a rope around hips and chest and lowered him to the deck. The previously distant sailors clamoured to help carry him back to his cabin. Kedron shook his head when he looked at Willard's bruised and slightly misshapen shoulder. While the sailors lowered him gently on his bunk, Baxter stared silently at the deck above, refocusing on Willard as the last sailors left, and the cabin door closed.

"Our Lady says I can put your shoulder right."

Given her intervention had saved both his and Kedron's life, Willard felt obliged to let her try. [do it.]

[Thank you.] they replied.

Baxter positioned Willard's arm out from his body, holding it at the elbow, and massaged the muscles around the shoulder. Willard gritted his teeth. The strength in Baxter's fingers was incredible. In less than a minute, Willard felt his shoulder pop back in place. His relief was immediate.

• • • •

The *Bay Trader* constantly had to tack across the prevailing wind until it rounded Two Tree Point, on the westernmost tip of the Northern Hummocks. It made the first leg of the journey tediously slow, which gave Willard time to learn the ropes. Each of the hundreds of ropes had its own unique name: like clew line and bunt line. The crew became his mentors. He had not only saved the well-respected mate's life, but had injured himself. He must be normal.

For a while he walked with a slight limp and his arm in a sling while his shoulder healed but as soon as Baxter (speaking for the Goddess) allowed, Willard went back aloft and by the time the *Bay Trader* sailed into its home waters of Great Bay, the crew considered Willard an able sailor. Lord Paleface had changed from a joke to a term of endearment.

The Trader now ran quietly before the wind gliding quickly and effortlessly through a small chop. Willard leant on the port tiller rail, talking quietly with Odell.

"How long to the Wall?" he asked? Shipboard life was tolerable when he was asleep or working. Idle time dragged. The day-to-day tasks, interesting when new became boringly repetitive once mastered.

"A week, weather depending. Two days to get through the canal—they tow us, a day's sail to Carrier Point, and probably three days riding or a bloody long walk from there to Grand Falls. If we get becalmed in the Dividing Sea, a day's sail could take a week."

"What if I get off in Canalbridge and go overland? It's only about a hundred miles."

"A hundred and seventeen," Barnes said. "You save a day, two at most."

[You could be there in three days, if you can keep up the pace Lord, but why the hurry?]

[No hurry, I'm just sick of the restrictions.]

"Then I'll be leaving you at Canalbridge," he told Odell immediately after the shipmaster finished, his mental conversation with Baxter over in a small fraction of a second.

Odell shrugged and walked away, saying nothing, making Willard feel guilty. The shipmaster was losing two able sailors he might find hard to replace in Canalbridge.

Willard went up and out on the yard one last time to help haul sail as they approached Hell's Gap, the entrance to the almost landlocked ocean known as the Molten Deep. It surprised him to find Hell's Gap defined by sheer cliffs. From the charts, he imagined a washaway through low country.

"How on Nuaith did they dig all the way through that?" he asked Marri, the sailor beside him.

"It wasn't dug. The Deep and the Gap have been there since the Days of Fire," Marri replied as she smoothed the folds of the canvas.

"Best you hang on tight Lord Paleface," Kedron shouted up as he went to take up his position, alongside Odell standing behind and between the tillers, ready for the run through Hell's Gap.

With the sails furled, there was nothing for those aloft to do but wait as the men at the tillers steered the ship through. From the sea, it looked impossibly narrow; the effect enhanced by the towering cliffs on either side.

[At its narrowest, the gap is three hundred yards wide, and our widest mast is only thirty. Plenty of room,] Baxter said.

Still, thought Willard, who had it from the crew, it took a skilful shipmaster and good co-ordination between the helmsmen to catch the swell at just the right moment and steer the ship through the race.

Willard braced his now callused feet on the footrope, his chest on the yard, a grip on the iron rail and a handful of sail. The constrained swell built, lifted the ship, and surged into Hell's Gap. He wondered how the tillers stood the strain. They were no thicker than what a sailor could grip, but they controlled huge steering oars. The helmsmen worked them hard under Odell's sharp directions as they charged into the channel's dark shadow.

The ship rocked, the yardarm seeming to scrape the ramparts as jagged black rocks sped past, yet according to Baxter there was over a hundred yards either side. The spray, catapulted up through fissures in the enclosing walls, to spray Willard. It felt as if one mistake might smash the ship against the rock face and pound it to splinters and he could die. Severne was powerless here. On impulse, he looked around to find Baxter standing on the footrope beside him.

[I do my best to keep you safe. Sometimes, if it's not too much trouble Lord, you could help.]

Willard's exhilaration instantly ebbed, and before he could frame a reply, Baxter had gone and the *Bay Trader* emerged from Hell's Gap into the interior ocean and slowed dramatically. He felt cheated.

[Think on that next time you decide to ignore our advice.]

Kedron calling up to them to lower the sails, stopped him thinking about it and set him to work. The breeze inside the cliffs barely fluttered the sails, but the ship continued moving on the tide until out of the wind shadow.

"Those white dots over there, that's Bridgeport." Marri said. "It's part of Canalbridge, but the main town is behind it at the bridge." She pointed at the distant starboard horizon, to where the encircling curve of the shore reached a low point. She left, but Willard delayed, enjoying the view. Kedron joined him while he was still trying to take it all in, wondering if the incredible symmetry of the Molten Deep meant it too was a builder construct.

"It looks man made," Willard said.

"It's believed to be a crater from the Days of Fire."

Willard scanned the coast. "Is Canalbridge the only settlement?"

"Aye it is. The soil around the Molten Deep is bad. Canalbridge, exist only to manage the canal and the bridge. It imports all its food, which is good for the shipping trade."

They climbed down together, and Willard went out on the bowsprit to watch their approach. The distant town grew slowly. The dots on the straw-coloured background resolved into houses, glaringly white in the sun. With disembarkation immanent, Willard reviewed his decision to go overland. He still felt it was a good decision, except now he wasn't as sure of his direction. Since the landslide, all his energy had gone into finding Kezia. After discovering she'd failed to report to Medicorps in Walker, he had counted on her being at the Wall.

He had no alternative plan if she wasn't or worse, if she rejected him, as he had once rejected her, albeit out of an utter inability to make a decision. Sometimes when he looked back to their parting, he felt Kezia had used the moment as an excuse, a way of telling him politely she had finished with him. Yet even with the risk of rejection, he had to find her, to explain that not joining her did not mean he didn't love her. It was just ... what? Why didn't I say yes straight away?

With difficulty, Willard conjured up her face. The only moment he could truly recall was her farewell kiss. If only I hadn't hesitated, he thought, none of this would have happened. Tears stung his eyes at the memory. He leaned over the bow and let the salt spray wash over his face. Pointless to rehash what I should have done. I must go on; she must be there. Averil certainly will be. It disturbed him to find how easily he could conjure up Averil's face.

[That is because I meant you for Averil.] Severne interposed.

[Damn your plan Severne] he thought and when there was no answer, wondered if she had heard it.

A porpoise surfaced to play in the bow wave. Soon seven or eight were plunging and weaving across the *Bay Trader's* path. The sailors cheered, considering it a good omen. Willard was less cheerful. Beyond the leaping procession, he had identified the ubiquitous tower of Our Lady, standing on a small knoll overlooking Canalbridge, and he could see people and drays milling about on the wharves. His free ride was over. He clawed his way back to reality as word went up the mast to haul in sail. Baxter elbowed him. [You think too much.]

The *Bay Trader* eased up to Bridgeport's wharf. Baxter, carrying both his and Willard's kit wrapped around the two named swords, started for the gangplank. Willard reluctantly followed. Odell and Kedron intercepted him at the top.

Kedron twisted his cap in his hand. "Forgive me Lord, I would go with you to the Wall, but the sea is all I know. I am no good on land." He stopped and looked down at his bare feet, adding, "Thank you. I owe you my life."

"You owe me nothing, I owe you."

Kedron began protesting, but Willard waved him to stop. "I had thought I carried a death curse. You not dying is the best thing that has happened to me since I left home."

Kedron had confusion written on his face. Willard could imagine the way the stories of this voyage would grow. He was a strange one was Lord Willard. I sailed with him before he was Our Lady's Face. Lord Paleface he was then. He would owe you if you let him save your life.

[What an imagination you have Willard,] Severne said.

[It doesn't come close to your manipulations,] Willard shot back as he embraced Kedron. "I'll come back when I've found Kezia and we'll go sailing together. Until then, Our Lady be with you."

"And with you Lord Paleface," grinned Kedron, and after a brief nod to Odell, walked briskly away, shouting orders at the sailors.

"Farewell Lord," Odell said and the way he said 'Lord', took the sting out of it. Willard suspected that like Kedron, Odell still harboured the opinion that Willard was the Man Who Will Be Face, yet they also knew him as a friend and an able sailor.

"Seriously Will, you are welcome aboard the *Trader* anytime and no questions asked."

"Thanks for everything, Odell." Willard said quietly as they embraced.

Willard raised his hand in a final farewell as he stepped off the gangplank. The gesture drew a cheer from the *Trader.* When it died as suddenly, he turned to find two warriors loping toward him.

Not again, thought Willard, knowing from their greetings it was Dudley and Fletcher, the Warriors from Port Taylor. Their arrival proved there was, if not a quicker route, one of little difference. Why then had Severne let him take the longer sea route, having already told him it was dangerous? It put the entire voyage in a different light.

Instead, he asked, [Isn't one enough? Why three?]

[To impress upon you how vital you are to my plan?]

[I got that message on my mother's knee. Why are you now making it public?]

[To motivate you,] Baxter answered for the Goddess, which sent a shiver up Willard's spine.

[Disperse them, have them scout ahead and behind,] he said wondering how they would take him giving orders.

[Are you expecting trouble, Lord?]

[No, and I don't want any either. People expect Warriors to travel alone. Together like this, you stand out worse than a Tower.]

Baxter eyed him curiously, [As you wish, Lord.]

Even as he spoke, Dudley and Fletcher detached, and Willard's hackles rose at the amount of communication going on around him, without him.

[I exclude you from exchanges you would not understand until you take the Test of Faith.] Severne said.

[Help me find Kezia and I'll consider it.]

When there was no response, Willard took it for a no. He already suspected that he was much more likely to find Averil first. The ways of the Goddess were not always mysterious. [That's why you delayed me. Averil wasn't there yet.] Again, silence greeted the thought. Could he assume that no response meant he was correct?

His prediction that even two Warriors would draw attention bore fruit as he and Baxter, lacking any disguise, wound their way up the narrow Canalbridge streets toward the bridge. People fled, but doors did not fully close and curtains parted slightly. Willard upped the pace eager to be away from their stares.

The bridge approach started a good hundred yards back from the edge of the canal and soared over it in a single stone arch span. As they jogged closer, the scabbards across their backs bouncing in synchronous with every footfall, the magnitude of the builder canal became apparent. Warrior Dudley greeted them at the Watcher checkpoint gatehouse.

"The bridge is secure, Lord," he said and with a nod to Baxter jogged away up the bridge, presumably to where Fletcher had secured the far side.

[Your learning Lord,] said Fletcher.

Severne, clearing the way showed she was still trying to make him into something he was not. He felt intimidated. How can I fight it? Kedron would have said that to get where you wanted to go, sometimes you had to tack close to the wind and sometimes you had to run before it.

[Stop trying to force your plan onto me,] he told the Goddess before turning on Baxter, his finger tapping the eye-shaped scar on his forehead. "This does not make me the Face any more than the Sword makes me a Warrior or the talisman makes me a server."

"Then why carry them?"

[This will be interesting,] Severne said creating in his mind a sensation related to a chuckle.

"I thought they might come in handy, one for protection, one for access," Willard said.

"Not for any sense of power they give you," Baxter mocked with voice. Willard couldn't believe his ears. Baxter's voice sounded the same, but seemed slurred and slower. He replied in kind.

"What good is power if I can't choose the life I want?"

As Severne said, [Take the test and you might,] he thought he saw a look of respect in Baxter's eyes.

[I'll take the test when I get Kezia back.]

"Our Lady thanks you Lord," Baxter said.

Willard stared at him, remembering too late that thoughts directed to Severne might also go to the warriors. He pondered what madness made him promise such a thing before witnesses. Having started on this tack, he wanted to see how far he could push it, [and you can keep out of my mind until you're ready to tell me where she is.]

[Averil is at Fort Grand Falls.]

[Not Averil, Kezia. Until then, shut up.]

[Please remember Willard, the choice to close your mind to me was yours,] the Goddess answered.

As he strode up the wide sloping expanse of the bridge with Baxter following, he wondered if it would be that easy. The towpath passed beneath them, the width of the gap expanded and Willard had his first glimpse of the massive walls of the canal, and a long way down, black water. He paused at the apex for a good look and marvelled at the construction. It was builder material, made to look and feel like stone.

Baxter told him the canal was two miles long. It ran roughly east to west, in four straight sections, from the Molten Deep to the Dividing Sea. The section they were passing over was three hundred yards wide and some sixty feet deep.

Willard thought the granite-looking vertical sides were also too smooth to be stone; no encrustation of barnacles as had clung to the *Bay Trader*. The seams showed a single block was at least twelve feet apart, impossible to rebuild. Luckily, the ancients built to last. The canal was already old when Eldwin the Forrestor, Deep Creek's Founder, came through here after climbing the Break. The bridge and the canal were just two more enigmatic legacies from the Builders, along with towers, servatories, the Arch and the Pillar. The pillar was too regular to be a natural mountain. He wondered if there was a link between Our Lady and the Builders. Was she their Goddess as well?

By shielding his eyes against the late afternoon glare, he could just make out the *Bay Trader* entering the Western end of the canal. A sudden wave of nostalgia for the close-knit communal life aboard swamped him.

Baxter tapped him on the shoulder, signalling they should go. They jogged on down the bridge through the Watcher checkpoint without pause. The streets in Canalbridge's southern half were quiet but not empty. It crossed Willard's mind that instead of clearing his path the Warriors actively recruited spectators. No matter how hard he tried to avoid it, his fame was growing.

[No comment Severne?] he asked.

"Is that not what you asked of her?" Baxter said.

Willard glared at him as they jogged into the gentle midland hills of the Pointing Finger Isthmus, taking comfort from the thought that the Wall he never thought to see was only a week away.

Chapter 31

Averil, having just returned from Sumner's quarters, and flushed with afterglow, was about to drift off when a hand clamped over her mouth, and the sharp edge of a blade nicked her throat.

"Don't even think about it little sister," a voice whispered in her ear. "Scream, struggle or bite my hand and even Severne's magic will not restore your head to your body. Nod wisely."

Averil recognised the phrase, little sister. She had expected Stone Ethyl, but never in her most crazed moments, Aldus. As children, Aldus had been the oldest of their group, always a little more sophisticated, his dry irreverent humour amusing, and Averil, like her peers, admired him. Here and now, she found him very unfunny. She wanted to turn and belt him one. She was more than capable of it, but she recognised the threat in his tone and her throat could feel the seriously sharp edge of his knife. She nodded carefully.

"Up, slowly. We're leaving."

Averil went to shake her head, but the knife bit. A drop of blood trickled down into the hollow of her throat. She remembered doing the same to Kingsley when he rescued her from the band who abducted Aldus. Such irony, she thought, forgetting her need to protest as she slowly eased out of her bedroll. Isolda rolled in her sleep.

"Back."

Her sleeping position was in the back corner of the tent opposite Brent. Aldus was outside, behind her, with just his head and arm through the slit he'd made. Still sitting she backed out. Brent snorted and Averil paused, listening for any further disturbance from her band; strange how she now felt she belonged with them. Light snoring only.

"You're not dressed?" A fierce whisper in her ear. The knife, still at her throat, but turned, flat and cold against her neck, allowing her to reply.

Averil tried for casual, her tone aiming at a sense of kinship. "It's a permanent camp, Aldus. We don't need to sleep combat ready." She doubted anything would get through. His whole demeanour had changed markedly from anything she remembered.

"Behind enemy lines, you sleep dressed with a knife in your hand, unless you're a whore."

Averil stilled, flushed with anger and guilt. Aldus had a point. Sumner's chess evenings had eventually led to other games. She hadn't forgotten the reason she joined, but getting up the Break and back to the Watchers had lost its urgency. She had excused, delaying as gathering intelligence while waiting for the assault. Aldus's challenge to her allegiance had no ready answer.

Bastard.

She stood slowly, deliberately, so she didn't slip while she tried to work out what was happening—rescue or abduction; it felt like the latter. The pressure of the knife remained flat against her neck; a quick twist is all it would take. Outside, under the stars, was marginally less dark than in the tent. Averil's skin puckered in the chill. She was only wearing light undergarments.

Aldus backed her up through the line of horses and across the meadow between the circles to the canal. The ground underfoot was cold and the grass sharp.

"Sit," he commanded, and she sat.

The grass cut and scratched her backside through the thin material. She could hear him scrabbling behind her over the soft sounds of the night, the croaking of frogs, the slap of water, against the wall of the canal.

"Hands behind your back," Aldus said.

She felt a rope, expertly looped considering he was only using one hand, bind her hands then tighten like a cinch. Only then did his knife leave her throat. Another loop dropped over her head, the heavy braided knot hitting the top of her spine. He pulled tight around her neck and tied the tail to her bound hands. A feral chocker.

Briefly, he left her sitting on the cold sharp grass then two hands reached under her arms, clamped on her breasts, and dragged her backwards, over the edge into a boat. Averil stifled a cry as splinters skewered the back of her thighs. She bit her lip. You'll keep, brother. Brother is right, the stupidity of it was that's who the ferals really wanted; not him. He was here by accident. What a joke that would be, Willard as the Face of Our Lady.

Cold air slipping past her face brought her back to her current predicament. They were gliding quietly down a flat ribbon of stars. Her arms ached, but she couldn't lower them without choking. She slipped backwards and rested her hands on the dinghy's stern. At least Aldus had chosen a fresh-water canal not a sewer. Occasionally he needed to push them off from the sides of the canal, or hold them up, if there was activity near one of the many bridges. She shivered, whether from the cold or the silent menace of Aldus she could not decide.

He's prepared all this in advance. They trust him as they did me. He'd survived, according to Sumner, by helping them with information, not knowing it was useless. Sumner already knew everything he had given them, but that didn't mean Aldus was a traitor. He may have done so deliberately. So, is he rescuing me or taking me prisoner? Both? The deep questions she had to face were: Do I want him to rescue me? Whose side am I on? Willard would have a field day.

For what seemed like hours, her situation remained static. Averil tried to gauge the passage of time, but there was nothing to anchor her guess in the dark. She had no idea how long she had slept, and unlike Sumner, she knew nothing about timing the movement of the stars. They moved in a narrow, high-sided stone-lined channel, slicing through a dark world under a starry dome until, without warning Aldus steered the boat to the wall and bundled her out to sprawl on another frigid meadow. Her hands and feet were numb, her neck raw.

"Don't go away," Aldus said. He was back in a minute after pushing the boat off and unceremoniously hauled her to her feet. "This way."

A balloon, thought Averil, as Aldus pushed her toward a huge black presence that blotted out the stars. *He's escaping in a feral balloon, but why has he tied me? If he'd told me what he was doing, I would have come willingly. Tits, he called me a whore, but he thinks I'm a traitor.*

"Aldus I can explain ..."

He cut her off by jerking the choker. "Save it for the Watchmaster."

Now it made sense. She was a hostage. *He was going to deliver me as a traitor, to bargain for his freedom. No wonder it upset him when I was only half-dressed. He wanted me in a feral uniform.*

Bastard.

The balloon towered over her, bearing down with a ferocious grin that distorted into a lewd grimace, and then disappeared overhead as they got closer. It left only the darkness and its pleasant, hot breath.

"Ouch." Averil said. She had whacked her shin on something hard and low.

"Mind the steps," Aldus whispered. "There are three."

Averil looked down and saw a body next to the steps. Testing with her foot first, she climbed each step. At the third, her knees came up against a barrier. It was pliable and prickly like a coarse rope mat.

"Climb in the basket."

"My hands are tied, you stupid bastard."

For an answer, she felt an arm come up between her legs, jam into her crotch and lift her off her feet. She toppled forward into the basket. Then the rope around her hands snapped the noose taut. Unable to get a hand far enough back, Averil desperately twisted sideways to release the tension around her throat.

"For fuck's sake shut up," Aldus hissed, bending over her.

Averil had had enough. With her remaining energy, she banged her forehead into his face and felt a satisfying crunch. She never saw the savage blow that knocked her senseless.

· · · ·

In a dreamlike state of semi-consciousness, Averil felt herself getting cold again. A chill breeze stabbed through the open weave of the basket. Her back was up against it as she lay on her side at the bottom of a small well and she could feel its coarseness through her under-garments. I'm breathing at least, she thought abstractedly.

She kept her eyes closed. Occasionally she heard a whoosh, saw Aldus pumping a bellows, the glow of coals flaring and a warm bath of air washing over her. The cold returned, accompanied by the strangest movement, reminiscent of her trip across the Dividing Sea. This time, however, the movement was gentle and pendulum-like, side to side rather than up and down.

As she faded in and out, Averil was aware of other changes. Her neck was sore, but the choker had gone and a tarpaulin covered her. With her hands still tied behind her back, her upper arms ached. Though her head throbbed, she knew she was recovering, could almost feel it happening. She had only felt like this twice before. The first time was years ago, when she had fallen out of a tree and badly broken her arm. Mother had used the healing dust and her arm mended as good as new. The last time had been in the ruined builder city. Hedley? She tried to remember if he'd done anything other than feed her. Something in the food? Rubbish, food was food and mother always applied the healing dust outside. I'm overthinking it. Regardless of how, she enjoyed knowing she'd be returning to normal as Aldus tired.

The brazier above her flared again, lit Aldus's face as he pumped the bellows. There was blood smeared on his chin and his nose was now crooked. His eyes glinted in the light radiating hate. What in Severne's name had changed him so much? The wild rebel that had once seemed so attractive had turned mean and nasty. She added his name to her growing list of bastards; no longer surprised they were all male.

She closed her eyes when she saw him glance down. The air on her face was cool and mountain fresh, but she was warm, her body heat trapped by the tarpaulin. Except for her bound hands, she was comfortable, and until a boot nudged her in the ribs, she had felt reluctant to move.

Aldus was busy at the rim of her enclosed surroundings, untying thin ropes with careful haste. The basket jerked every time he succeeded. Beyond him, a large hole in the red ceiling above the brazier defined her world,

"Give me a hand, little sister," Aldus said his voice nasal. Averil rolled to her knees to hold up her hands, dislodging the tarpaulin, regrettably spilling the warmth. She felt remarkably well, and Aldus looked decidedly ill. His nose was purple and swollen, the whites of his eyes were red, his face puffy and, by comparison with his attitude last night, he was quite subdued.

"Sorry I forgot," he said, and bent to untie her hands.

The freedom to act sorely tempted Averil to deliver a hard, fast knee to the groin as she rose, but he looked so awful she relented. Instead, she bounced up, feeling on top of the world, and looked out, staggered to find a reality that matched her feelings. "Severne's tits, will you look at that?"

The land laid out below her was like a tapestry or a masterfully hand-drawn map. Quickly, she oriented herself: Great Bay in the West, some feral Gulf off the Dividing Sea to the East, the barren Wastelands and beyond it, many small perfectly circular craters some with lakes but oddly nowhere on the southern coast could she locate the vast builder ruins where she had met Hedley, must be too far away. Directly beneath her, the feral encampment looked like a field of archery targets, white rings around a larger centre on a green background.

"If you don't help, you're going to become part of the view," Aldus wheezed behind her.

Averil turned and found the opposite horizon blocked by sheer rock face, rushing towards her at a disturbing speed.

"Make it go up," she shouted to Aldus, looking in the brazier and finding only ash. The balloon, completely at the mercy of the wind blowing towards the Break, slowly descending.

"Out of coal," Aldus said, "can't heat the air to make it float."

The word coal was unfamiliar to Averil, but his meaning was clear. No fire, no lift.

"Have to ditch ballast," Aldus continued. He pointed to the bags on the floor. When Averil stooped to pick one up, she found she needed two hands. They were full of sand.

"Over the side with it," said Aldus, undoing the last of those suspended on the outside of the basket.

"But there are people down there."

"They can dodge. We can't."

Averil needed no second invitation. The Break loomed like an oppressive weight and seemed to teeter towards her. She grunted as she heaved the bags over, muttering under her breath. "Look out below."

There was a satisfying upward jerk each time she let a bag go. They were ascending faster now, but the top still seemed incredibly far above and each time she came up with another bag, they were closer. She could now see the Break was not sheer but terraced, cut with steps, riddled with caves, and festooned with ropes, pulleys, and ladders. The rock face crawled with ferals: ascending, descending, marching, loading, and waving or gesticulating, she couldn't tell. Averil waved back as she threw another bag over the edge.

They ran out of sandbags.

Averil gauged they were drifting towards the vee shaped cleft the river had eroded into the cliff, faster than they were going up, it would be touch and go. The roar from Grand Falls had become deafening.

"It's going to be close. I might have to throw you out," Aldus wheezed.

With frenzied haste, Averil cast about for something else to jettison. She wasn't worried about Aldus ditching her. He was too weak from loss of blood and lack of sleep, but she could see they were not rising quite fast enough to clear the rim. They would gain a brief respite if they made it into the cleft, but then, if they came too close to the falls, the basket would fill faster than it could empty. The falls would pummel them all the way down into the plunge pool. Regrettably, they had already ditched everything, including the brazier.

The basket was empty.

"Hang on," Aldus shouted above the roar of the falls.

Averil looked up. The top still loomed thirty feet above, but only six feet away. The vertical edge of the cleft raced towards them. She pulled her hands off the rim of the basket as it slammed into the Break. The huge red canopy above scrapped along the rock face. Support ropes snapped, the basket tilted and Aldus crashed into her. They twisted along the face of the Break for a few seconds before clearing the edge and leaping into the cleft, descending again, the balloon's air cooling.

Looking up, Averil could see the balloon makers had used a solid wooden hoop to gather the netted rope that trapped the balloon and held the basket. "Give me your knife," she yelled at Aldus as she pushed him off.

Aldus looked at her with suspicion. "Up there," she pointed, "We have to lose the basket."

Aldus glanced at the approaching Wall of water, handed her the knife, and started climbing. Averil hacked through a corner cable. The basket lurched, nearly tipping her out. She climbed up onto the gathering rail beside him and started hacking through the remaining supports. The roar of the plummeting water made conversation impossible. She shivered from the spray as the third cable snapped and the basket danced hysterically at the end of the last. They were now so close to Fort Grand Falls, Averil could see individual Watchers standing on the parapets, and bowmen nocking arrows.

The last cable was unravelling as Averil wearily hacked at the remaining strands. Her knife wielding arm felt like a dead weight she could hardly lift. When the basket fell away with a jerk, the balloon popped up like a cork released under water. Averil's stomach plummeted and she dropped the knife to grab hold. The balloon soared over the lip, clearing the falls with fifteen to twenty yards to spare. The breeze pushed it further, up and over a crenulated Wall section next to the river, to arrows and cheers, as if the Watchers couldn't decide whether to greet them as friend or foe.

Away from the edge, the balloon entered quieter air and descended again. They were now high enough to see several miles of the Wall, a massive structure of undulating stonework. Forts, mileposts, and turrets decorated the edge of the escarpment like a necklace. Averil was ecstatic. She could hardly believe her luck. She had brought the Watchers one of the feral balloons. Whatever Aldus's game was, he had provided exactly what she'd wanted. Maybe she had misjudged him. Except she had seen the unmistakable glaze of hate in his eyes.

Out behind the fort, the balloon drifted roughly parallel to the Wall, descending slowly. A squad of Watchers rode below them on the wide service road that linked the Forts. Averil, looking at the riders over her darkly tanned knees was suddenly aware of how she must look to them. Since her rude awakening in the small hours this morning, preoccupation with survival had kept her too busy to give it a thought. She looked feral and, though not in full feral uniform; she was wearing their undergarments. Aldus however, had planned well and dressed as he would at home. He couldn't have foreseen her arrival in the feral camp. Dragging her along was an afterthought, brilliant but unplanned.

The wind shifted and the balloon veered inland. As they neared the ground, Aldus jumped just as an updraught caught the balloon. The balloon suddenly lofted twenty feet into the air and by the time it started coming down again, it was into the scrubby forest; the Watchers pounding through the trees in hot pursuit.

Averil hung by her hands from the gathering ring, steeling herself against the expected pain to her feet and began pumping her legs, letting go as soon as her feet touched the ground. Out of the corner of her eye, she could see the Watchers closing in. Her inertia outstripped the ability of her legs to keep up. The balloon hit a tree and her stumbling run toppled into a roll. She managed three before coming to a hard stop.

Chapter 32

I n some part of her mind, Kezia knew she would die if she couldn't reach mother's dust in the next few moments. She focused her remaining consciousness on the jar's location, lucidly aware that she had to find it, first time. Shoulder bag ... inside pouch ... other side of palliasse ... too far. Kezia groaned again when she heard Willard ask 'where are you?', as if he was frantic to know. She supposed it was all in her mind, part of this nightmare, but hearing it strengthened her. She clawed her way back across the palliasse toward her bag an inch at a time. Another muscular spasm caught her unawares and the pain paralysed her. I tried Will, she thought, as blackness reached for her.

A shadow blocked the stars. She felt Howard land beside her. His hand dived into her shoulder bag and reappeared with the jar. Then he was kneeling beside her, holding her head, forcing open her locked teeth and shaking the remaining contents into her mouth. As the grains slid down her throat, she felt an explosion of multiple pricks on her tongue, in her cheeks and against her palate. Though she had never seen the dust used like that, it didn't worry Kezia as much as knowing that was the last of mother's dust. It was gone. Without it, her ability to heal the wounded would suffer, and so would they.

Her fevered mind ached worse than after the death of Wesley junior, not stillborn, but dying shortly after birth. She accepted that now. She hadn't even had time to name him properly before he was gone, taken like his father by the Goddess. Her oracle killed Wesley for interfering, and now she was after Kezia, wanting her out of the way, so Averil and Willard ... that can't be right. Howard saved her. Confused by events half-seen, half-heard in delirium and pain, Kezia knew only that someone had tried to poison her, and that Howard had saved her by pouring the healing dust down her throat.

. . . .

Kezia sat up. She was in a tent, on a low camp bed. Howard sat cross-legged on the ground just outside.

"I'm thirsty," she called out.

Howard examined Kezia's face minutely and seemed satisfied. "Here, drink this and later I'll see about something to eat."

Kezia took a few sips of the salty broth, then sat up and drank greedily. Around her, all was quiet.

"I sent them away," Howard said.

For her near-death experience, she felt in exceptional health, not in the least bit weak or tired, just upset by the experience.

"Who would want to kill me?"

"Aithists," Howard replied.

"What have I ever done to them?"

"Shown them they were wrong."

"What?"

"Liam, the drayman's boy, is walking proof of your healing power."

Kezia looked at him as if he was joking. "You of all people know that isn't true," she protested. "It was your sword and mother's dust that revived him. I didn't."

"True, but Liam's parents see and tell it differently," Howard said.

"That still doesn't explain why anyone would want to kill me."

Howard looked puzzled. "I'm sorry; I keep forgetting your youthful ignorance."

Kezia fumed, "Youthful ignorance. I'm older than you are."

"I meant only that you lack the knowledge the tests gave me. Our Island has two main belief systems," Howard continued, "Severnians follow the ways of Our Lady, and aithists follow a more ancient tradition, which some say came from Aithe with ..." He trailed off.

Her thoughts on his assumption that her ignorance equated to stupidity obviously showed in her expression. Howard skipped to the point.

"Anyway, from here to the Wall is predominantly aithist, including an overwhelming majority of Watchers. Rumours of the Man Who Will Be Face raising a dead girl, added to Liam's parents' claim that you raised their dead son, has veteran Watchers flocking to the towers. Severnian ascendancy comes at the expense of the aithists. They have ample motive to quash the rumours."

"That's one explanation." A Goddess biased one, she thought. "If these so-called miracles herald the Restoration, maybe it's but her towers that feel power slipping from their grasp, not the aithist."

"But, as you have seen, tower indiscretions that threaten Our Lady's plan do not go unpunished. I'll see to your horse while you pack," he added, effectively ending the conversation, but not before she had seen him startle at her suggestion.

Kezia surveyed her small bundle of possessions, pausing in anguish when she inspected the jars her mother had given her. They were all Empty, the magic dust gone. How long before her fame went with it? It would at least please mother to know their last miracle was to save her daughter's life.

• • • •

It felt good to be on the road again. A day or so ago they had crossed an unnamed river at Newbridge, a dot on the map which, as its name suggested had a new bridge but no to town and no people. Now that they were only a few days out of Canalbridge, Kezia wasn't looking forward to reaching it. After so much travel, it surprised her to find she now enjoyed it. She had felt more at peace on the Great Plains than she felt in Mother's sanctuary. In a burst of joyous energy and good humour, Kezia surged ahead for a while, but then reined in to let Howard catch up. When she turned to goad him for staying on foot, to her astonishment, she saw a sizeable crowd following, mostly young, running to catch up. Incredibly, the last place they'd stopped was about twenty miles back.

Howard turned as Kezia started back and his hand went straight to his shoulder.

He really ought to watch that automatic response, thought Kezia. Not every problem is amenable to his sword. She rode past him and dismounted to meet them. None of the children looked sick. "Why are you following us?" she asked.

A young girl, no older than thirteen and out of breath, stepped forward. "We want to help, to learn from you."

"But I'm going to the Wall. It's not a place for children and I won't have time to teach."

"We can learn by watching you healer."

Howard stepped up beside Kezia, hands folded in front, sword still in its scabbard. "How much have you learnt so far?"

The girl shuffled her feet looked away from Kezia to Howard and then down at the ground.

"Well, nothing yet," she said.

"Why not? Haven't you been watching?"

"Yes, but ..."

"No buts. If you wish to follow in Healer Jena's footsteps, you must begin where she began. Go back to your homes, attend classes at your local Institute of Healing Arts and be ready, as Jena was, when the Goddess calls."

The children (none older than the spokesperson) groaned and began arguing among themselves.

"Go!" Howard shouted, and they stepped away, still arguing. Some turned and started back.

Howard grabbed Kezia's elbow and propelled her in the opposite direction. "Don't look back," he said as he marched an unprotesting Kezia away. That was brutal, unfair, and full of beefshit, but he's right, she thought, pulling on the reins; the horse followed. She could hear the young crowd mumbling like penitents in a waiting room. It faded slowly and when it eventually disappeared, Howard veered off the path flowing the river northeast along a valley floor.

"We'll have to bypass Canalbridge as well now and try to get a ship direct to Carrier Point. Once we're on the peninsula, you won't have a problem. Except for Carrier Point itself, the only people south of the canal are Watchers."

"How is that safer for me?"

"No following. No threat."

"But you said it was an Aithist who poisoned me."

"Yes, an extremist Aithist. Without a following, it will be much harder for them to get close. The Watchers, like most Aithists, are not anti-Goddess, merely disinterested in her. You have a chance now to revert to Kezia, be the healer you always wanted to be."

But I never wanted to be a healer, thought Kezia. Losing Willard forced it on me. Her training had been her mother's idea because, in trying to get close to her mother, she expressed an interest. She took a few minutes to digest Howard's revised story of the poisoning. Foremost in her mind was that every utterance he made, he aimed at furthering the Goddess's plan for her. The Goddess might not lie, but what of her warriors? My following are believers, yet he and the Goddess want me to believe an Aithist tried to kill me, but I'm safe in Watcher controlled Aithist territory because I won't have a following.

"I'm not going back to being Kezia," she said defiantly, wondering if that was exactly what the Goddess wanted.

• • • •

By the following day, Kezia and Howard had reached Little Carrier Bay, bounded by Carrier Island and Watson's Promontory, at the western end of the Dividing Sea. The last leg of their journey along the coast away from Canalbridge had been through flat open range and herds of grazing cattle. Often, the fishing villages they passed harboured one or two Coastwatch ships, to keep the Dividing Sea and their Island free of ferals.

"Welcome to Java," Howard said as he led Kezia down a wide main street lined with a collection of small neat homes that some would call shacks. The only stone buildings stood at the intersection of the main street and the waterfront esplanade. Shacks extended either side along the water's edge, some squatting on poles, half in the sea.

Kezia, having seen no signpost, supposed Severne had told Howard where they were. At first, only fearful gazes greeted the Warrior, but increasingly the townsfolk stared in amazement. Then, much to Kezia's disbelief, some even greeted him, a polite nod here and a wink there. Her incredulity grew when she caught Howard smiling broadly back at them.

"I'm sorry Jena. I had a hidden agenda coming this way. Be patient and I will reveal all."

Before Kezia had time to ask him about their strange reception, Howard had veered down a narrow lane behind a row of waterfront houses on poles. He stopped at a shack with neatly trimmed grass around and under the support poles, and to Kezia's astonishment unclipped his scabbard and laid it against the steps.

"Wait here," he said, then bounded up the steps three at a time, strode across the narrow verandah and in through the open door. Almost immediately, there was a squeal of delight and Howard reappeared, whirling a diminutive woman around in a big hug.

"Oh Goddess, I look such a mess," the woman said, laughing and crying at the same time and trying to straighten her hair. "Put me down Acky."

Howard placed her gently on her feet.

"Mum, I'd like you to meet a very important friend of mine, a healer. Jena, this is my mother, Beverley."

Beverley wiped her eyes, one green and one brown, with the back of her hand, and then wiped her hands on her apron as Kezia climbed the steps in shock. Despite knowing Willard and Wylie as candidates, she had never thought of Restoration Warriors as having mothers. Intellectually she knew they must, but it was hard to connect the images of Howard the executioner to the toddler he must have been.

"Acky," Kezia inquired as they sat around a pot of coffee and delicious small cakes on the back verandah overlooking the Little Carrier Bay.

"It's short for Ackersley, after my father."

"So, your real name is Ackersley."

"Yes, Ackersley Green."

"Then where does Howard come from?"

"I selected it from the list of sleepers when I failed."

This is a failure? The thought staggered her.

Howard's mother sat admiring him. "It's a pity about his hair," she said, touching Kezia on the arm. "He was such a handsome boy when he had hair, not that he isn't now, but just imagine him with wavy dark brown hair, just like his father; Goddess, rest his soul." She described a circle on her chest and touched her forehead.

Kezia, watching the ritual, tried to remember the calm it had once brought her and regretted it no longer worked.

They talked well into the night. It was the first time Howard had been home since presenting himself at the servatory for testing. His father's death, lost at sea during a storm while fishing, had been the precipitating event. He took the test to keep his mother from destitution. The handsome pension provided with his elevation to the Warrior brethren would allow her to live out her days in the comfort of the familiar.

Eventually they got around to Howard and Kezia's need of a ship. Howard's uncle Jon, who had taken over his brother's boat, came in from next-door and said he'd be happy to ferry them across to Carrier Point.

"It's where I sell most of my catch, anyway."

• • • •

They sailed mid-morning, Howard working the small fishing boat alongside his uncle Jon. Heeled over to the gunwales, the Beverley crashed through the wind driven chop. into the passage between Carrier Point and Carrier Island. Howard strode the deck grinning, no doubt remembering his carefree childhood, before his father died and he became a warrior—a year ago.

Kezia, knowing academically about seasickness, had embarked with trepidation but her stomach had not reacted. So she tried to emulate Howard and came a cropper: bruising knees, elbows, head, in fact any bit that stuck out. Until then, she had revelled in the voyage.

Howard apologised. "Sorry Jena, wrong time of day for this run."

Late in the afternoon, the wind turned and the sea was suddenly flat, as the *Beverley* slipped past towering cliffs toward Carrier Point's port. Jon dropped the sail and Howard leapt onto the wharf to secure the mooring line. The wharf and jetty complex at the base extended a mile out to sea and three miles along the cliff face. A floating village loosely tied to the rock face by iron cables and bridged by planks.

The town stood high above them on the easternmost extremity of the Pointing Finger isthmus, the so-called knuckle. The finger pointed to Canalbridge a hundred and fifty miles around the coast from Java, but only half that across Little Carrier Bay. Kezia climbed a short barnacle encrusted wooden ladder to join Howard on the outer edge of the assemblage of boats, barges, and pontoons.

Two hours later, just as she was feeling comfortable with the constant movement underfoot, they reached firm land. Kezia did not even notice the transition to the first landing cut from the cliff until they began their ascent. The rock platform, at the top of the first flight, was a wide ledge a hundred feet above the water, yet she still felt movement, as if the stone stairs were floating.

She wondered why anyone would want to live on a floating village, yet they had walked long winding streets full of houses and through markets teeming with people. The movement wasn't a problem, but the wet rot and the constant smell of floating garbage would be more than enough to keep her away. Worse still was the short day. The village had been in the cliff's shadow since midday. Kezia already wished she were back riding the Great Plains.

• • • •

At the top, Howard led Kezia through an opening into a vast, well-lit cavern. A Watcher checkpoint stopped them just inside the entrance. Kezia, dropping the famous Jena, gave her name as Anne (her real middle name) Setler of Port Calder. Her breathlessness was more from nerves than from the climb.

"What happens when they find the description they just took, matches Kezia Leach wanted for desertion?" she whispered to Howard as soon as they were alone.

"They won't," Howard said. "You've shed weight and lost your pasty complexion. You no longer resemble the girl who left Deep Creek."

"I hope so," Kezia said, worried now she may have lost the looks that attracted Willard. She needed a mirror.

As they walked down an aisle between rows of boxes stacked halfway to the cave roof, pinpricks of light in the cavern roof, like stars, drew her eyes upward.

"Light holes," said Howard, anticipating the question from her gaze.

"Builder?" asked Kezia

"Yes, perfectly straight round holes, bored through thirty feet of solid rock. It isn't possible anymore."

Kezia looked at the cavern roof sceptically. There were hundreds of holes in rows, intensely alight at the back, dimmer in the successive rows that marched towards her, and those directly above were black.

"The Builders angled each row to catch the sun at every part of the day between dawn and dusk," said Howard. "And because the caverns are hemispheres, you can tell the time by them."

The cavern was bustling with uniformed Watcher personnel some of whom acknowledged Howard with a nod, again showing little fear of the Warrior. How can they be sure he isn't here for their head? Perhaps Wes was right. *It's only servers who fear Warriors and they pass their fear on to believers.*

As if sensing her dilemma Howard said, "Dad brought me here often. I am not unknown, although carrying a named sword makes even some old friends wary."

Kezia's notions of Warriors took another beating. They had no right to have friends. *But then what does that make me? A task?*

Chapter 33

Averil Leach and Aldus Forrestor stood waiting in the Watchmaster General's Walfort office, twenty miles behind Fort Grand Falls. Two framed tapestries, one a sunlit meadow, the other a forest stream, hung on opposite plastered walls, framed and glazed to give the appearance of windows into other worlds. The real window above each lit the room.

A small grey-haired woman, the bob on the back of her head, gathered by a polished iron ring, looked from Averil to Aldus as she paced a well-worn track between the tapestries, occasionally shaking her head.

"Who am I to believe?" asked the Watchmaster General, Heutte Butcher. "When you each accuse the other of being a traitor and a spy. I think personal animosity, for whatever reason, has clouded your collective judgment."

The carpet's worn track divided the long room into two squares. Her desk occupied the square furthest from the door. Averil and Aldus waited in the other. Returning to her chair, Heutte dipped her pen in the inkwell and sat poised over a blank parchment.

"Let's go over each of your stories one more time."

Averil's groan received a withering look.

"I still have questions, Leach. Forrestor, you say the ferals abducted you in early bud?"

"Yes," Aldus said.

"Why?"

"The Goddess told them to," Aldus said, and repeated his story.

Heutte interjected frequently to seek clarification and to scribble notes as Aldus described the raid, his capture, the journey, crossing the Dividing Sea and a long ride to the heartland to appear before Charismatic Doane. He gave to their general.

Averil nodded, although she still couldn't believe they could think Aldus would be the Face. He wasn't a candidate.

"Why are you nodding, Leach?"

"I'm tired," Averil lied, wondering how Captain Brande who'd been following Aldus's abductors had reported meeting her. She should keep her mouth shut.

Heutte eyed her speculatively as Aldus continued. "It seems they got the wrong man."

"Who were they after?"

"I don't know, they never said. Maybe Wylie. He was a strong candidate. But they got. And they didn't want me. I had to trade information just to stay alive ..."

Despite Averil's distrust of him, Aldus impressed her with his defiant admission, but his omission of his brother Willard, a stronger candidate than Wylie, was curious. She'd think about that later, once she worked out how to tell the Watchmaster General that Sumner already knew Aldus's information was useless, without incriminating herself. He beat her to it.

"... nothing they didn't already know, but enough to keep me alive. As their General's adviser on the Uplands, I learnt more than I gave away. I have information that could be valuable to the Wall's defence."

Averil suppressed a grin. He's a clever bastard, just loose with the truth.

"This General you ..." Heutte started.

"Sumner of the Lakes," Averil interjected and nearly choked. So much for keeping my mouth shut.

"You should know," Aldus snarled at her. "He greeted you like an old friend."

"Old friend be damned. He tried to kill me twice," Averil replied.

Heutte brought a furious fist down on her desk and glared at Averil. "Do not interrupt. And you, Forrestor, address your remarks to me."

He did, relating how he had already conceived a plan to escape in one of their balloons, when he spotted Averil proudly on parade for the General.

Then, in a credible imitation of Sumner's slight accent, Aldus said, "'You have much to learn that I failed to teach you.' She's obviously a protégé. Within a week, he had summoned her to his headquarters and dismissed me. I was back doing any shit job nobody else would touch or go hungry. They got together every other night after that.

"That's a lie ..." Averil bit her lip. It was, in fact true, but his tone made her visits sound lewd. She had to admit, that too became true, but in her defence, she had only agreed to save his life. Her turn would come.

"I dragged her along as a sign of good faith. She didn't come willingly I can tell you; she broke my nose."

Outraged at the slant Aldus put on everything, Averil could barely hold her tongue.

Heutte looked at them both, then up at the forest stream tapestry as if seeking answers in its placid waters. "Amazing to think you grew up together," she glanced down at her notes, "in Deep Creek."

"I hadn't seen her for four years before the bloody ferals abducted me. She was away at the Academy," Aldus said, "No doubt taking all our secrets down to the ferals."

Averil had had quite enough. "It wasn't like that, and you know it," she screamed in his face. "You're a fucking liar."

"You protest too much."

With that, Averil backhanded him with a fist, knocking him to the floor. "Bloody Forrestors, you're all alike," she shouted, and kicked him in the ribs.

Heutte shouted for her adjutant and in quiet fury told them, "If you two persist in acting like animals, I will have you leashed and muzzled."

Aldus struggled to his feet, coughed, and spat blood on the carpet.

"Spit on my carpet again, and I'll have you muzzled regardless," Heutte warned him, before returning to her chair.

Her adjutant, a captain and two corporals, separated the pair. The captain kept trying to attract Averil's attention. What is he on about? The idiot was fingering a small scar below his beard and winking at her. She tried to stare past him at Aldus, but he kept blocking her view. Then the sun came out from behind a cloud, pouring the clerestory windows above the tapestries, and she saw the face beneath the beard. Kingsley! The patrol captain, pursuing the ferals who'd abducted Aldus. The patrol had interrupted the feral that had been attacking her. She looked more closely at the grinning corporals. Orange-Hair and Onion-Breath. She couldn't remember their real names.

Aldus was back on his feet. "Only those born feral have skin as dark as she does," he wheezed heavily, his pointing at Averil.

Heutte, sitting calmly at her desk said. "You're black said the pot to the kettle." Her eyes remained steadfast on Aldus, as darkly tanned as Averil. "Don't talk rubbish. I've sent Watchers down there. Anyone who stays down there a while will come back just as dark."

"Excuse me ma'am," Brande interrupted, "but Leach here is the one we ..." he stole a glance at Averil, " ... saved from the warband."

I didn't need saving, thought Averil, studying Aldus as he worked it out. His eyes narrowed and she again glimpsed the hate she had seen in the balloon, suppressed since their arrival. His gaze switched from Averil to Kingsley. "You were there, both of you. Why didn't you kill the bloody ferals and free me?" he said in a hoarse whisper.

"Orders," replied Kingsley. "Sorry."

"Orders, I'll give you f...," Aldus suddenly stopped and veiled his flash of hatred.

After dismissing the two corporals, Heutte returned to stand in front of Averil. "I shall accept that you are who you say you are, since both your accuser and my adjutant have now verified your identity." She looked at Averil with searching intensity. "However, you have not denied you were in a feral uniform, on parade for inspection when Forrestor saw you."

Averil shook her head. "Only because he was part of the inspection party."

"Forrestor is not Watcher. He had no obligation to escape. You did."

"I was going to, but I wanted to find out more about the floating craft, the balloons."

"Why?"

"Because they sent a whole warband up against a warrior just to stop me reporting what I'd seen. I figure it has to be important."

"I believe you believe that, but what may surprise you is that we have known about their balloons for over a year. I like your term floating craft. It's so much more descriptive. They used them in their last campaign for reconnaissance before they attacked, to little effect I might add." She turned abruptly and returned to her desk.

Averil, although indeed surprised, refused to concede the balloons were not important. It would make her abduction inexplicable.

"But they can carry two warriors each, and can drop them behind the Wall," Averil said, as Heutte sat.

"How many did you say you saw, ten?" she asked, cross-referencing her notes with other documents, and making amendments as she spoke. "Even if they had twice or four times that many and dropped a hundred ferals behind the wall, it is hardly going to concern us. We get more than that over the ramparts every season. And in such an event, we will have a squad waiting for each of them as they descend, exactly as we did for you two."

That stumped her. Perhaps the Watchmaster was right. She had seen at least ten from the Pipe, but since then she only seen one or two together. They would need hundreds to take one fort. Then why had the feral waited on the beach for her?

Averil returned from her musings to find Heutte studying her. The Watchmaster looked away and for several minutes sorted, collated, and straighten the piles of documents on her desk. That done, she again came and stood before them. The woman is never still, thought Averil.

"Neither of you has any identification on you. Yet, despite accusing each other of treachery you have also verified each other's identity. If not for Captain Brande's partial corroboration and the plethora of signals relating to you two, I would think this was a clever ploy to plant two feral agents on me."

With no response from either Averil or Aldus, Heutte resumed pacing the threadbare path in the carpet. "This Deep Creek you come from must have been a nightmare to grow up in."

Averil raised an eyebrow. Why would she think that?

Heutte, catching Averil's expression went to her desk and picked up one of her neat piles. "I've got two warrants for you, Leach, one for desecration of your local oracle and another for failing to report for duty."

She turned to Aldus. "I also have one in connection with your disappearance," she said, staring at Aldus, "that names your brother Willard."

Neither could suppress their surprise and Averil guessed Heutte's phrasing was deliberate, to provoke a reaction so she could assess them from their responses.

"No less a dignitary than an Arch Server lodged it, acting as Magister in place of, she glanced at Averil, your missing father."

Heutte smiled at their surprise. "Since you, Aldus, are no longer missing, I can clear your brother of that one."

"That one, there's more on him?" asked Averil.

"Several. Under normal circumstances, I would say these," Heutte shook the papers, "are none of your business. The circumstances, however, are far from normal. Since two of them also name your sister ..."

"Kezia," Averil blurted.

"... I will allow you to read them."

As Averil read, Heutte recited from memory.

"Kezia Leach signed articles, took a uniform and did not show. The last person known to have seen her alive was," she turned her penetrating gaze on Aldus, "Willard Forrestor."

Averil stared incomprehensibly at the warrants. Willard?

"The third warrant names him for the almost complete loss of his escort detail, supposedly wiped out in a mudslide. The militia found all but two bodies," Heutte continued. "Forrestor of course, and a corporal, Edmund Samals. No one has seen either of them since. Acting Magister Miller wants both for questioning."

"Miller." Aldus an Averil said in unison.

"Ah! Tell me more."

Averil nodded to Aldus. "You tell her."

"The man who gave me to the ferals was called Miller."

"It's a common enough name. I doubt an Arch Server would be involved and anyway he too is now missing. Of late, it seems Magisters in Deep Creek often go missing. Sorry about your father, Leach. The warrants, however, are genuine and this many, for four closely related individuals, from one small town intrigues me."

It nonplussed Averil. "I can't believe they issued a warrant on Willard for Kezia; they're oathed. He's not a ... like that."

Aldus's reaction was unexpectedly bitter. "Bastard."

"Fascinating," Heutte said and she recommenced pacing, her eyes flicking between them. "His own brother suspects him and the victim's sister defends him. This just gets better and better."

Averil now understood why the Watchmaster thought Deep Creek a nightmare. She also suspected that behind this list of nightmares stood the Goddess, or one of her minions. Averil passed the warrants back.

Heutte stopped before Aldus. "Since the escape was your idea and it gave us one of their balloons to study, I'm inclined to believe your story even though I think you're as wrong about Leach as she is about you. You have both been too quick to point the finger when you should have assisted each other, especially since you've known one another since childhood."

"Whatever you've done, or had done to you, or think you have, either back east or down there, I don't much care. I badly need people of your, shall we say, resourcefulness? I'm prepared to take you on trust and train you until you prove otherwise. However, as a civilian, you Aldus are free to go."

Heutte returned to her seat, opened a drawer, and produced a one-page form. "If you stay you must sign articles," she said, sliding it towards him.

Aldus looked down at the paper, then shook his head. "I have people to see," he said and strode to the door.

Heutte shrugged, put the form back in the drawer. Averil could see her logic and admired the way she had changed her approach, charming him with her assumption of his innocence. Averil would never trust him again. His story was too neat. Then again, she could see that to an outsider, her story gave the same impression. She came out of her reverie to find Heutte endorsing a warrant. Reported for duty, late fall.

"The desecration warrant has nothing to do with the Watchers. It's between you and the towers. It can wait for the circuit server." Heutte closed the drawer. Placing her hands firmly on her once again clean desk, she looked up wistfully at the meadow tapestry and added, "Show Captain Leach to her billet Kingsley."

As Kingsley led Averil into the courtyard, she heard Heutte mutter to herself. "I can't wait to meet this Willard character."

Averil stopped at the door. "He's coming here?"

"Oh yes," Heutte said, rubbing her hands together. "He's coming here." Then she waved her hand dismissively. "Kingsley can fill you in."

Once outside, it took Averil a minute or two to realise she had finally made it. The Watchmaster General had confirmed her commission. She was now a captain of the Watchers, but she couldn't muster any of the elation she had expected to feel.

"Take me to the nearest pub," she said to Kingsley. "You owe me a beer."

Chapter 34

Darkness forced Willard and Baxter to stop. Out of habit, Willard watched for the appearance of Severne's Eye. He still found the first nightly transit reassuring despite his mistrust of the Goddess. Now that he was this close to the Break and its Wall, he was eager to see both; one a natural wonder, the other manmade. His mind wandered as he drifted towards sleep. How could he avoid the Watchers and find Kezia? In his dreams, he stood on the Wall with Averil. Thousands of muzzle-faced ferals with one red eye and one black poured up over the rim. His sword arm was so tired he could hardly lift it, and still they came.

He woke with a start, Baxter gently shaking his shoulder. The dream shred itself, leaving him with vague, unsettling impressions of wanting to escape with Averil. He wondered if Severne could use the implant to manipulate his dreams through.

"We have company Lord."

The grey statement matched the morning. Willard tried to remember where he was, Threeways, forty miles from the Wall. He rolled out of his bedding, surprised to find the land still. He had left the Trader two days ago and yet he still felt the movement. He threw a questioning look at the Restoration Warrior.

"Watcher Patrol from Walfort. Seven on foot, half a mile away and coming this way."

A quick scan of the area showed that Baxter had erased all traces of their brief stopover, except where Willard had slept, and woken him with ample time to do likewise. The other Warriors were nowhere in sight.

"Let's go," said Willard, backing up and hurling the branch he had used to sweep away his indent into the undergrowth.

"You set pace whatever pace we need. I'd like to be well past Walfort by tonight."

Willard followed Baxter, who padded off, stepping from rock to rock, leading him up out of the valley along a narrow animal track through low scrub made of blighted wattle trees and scraggly gums. They stopped on the crest and sat on a fallen log overlooking the road while they waited for the patrol to pass.

Two ragged lines came into view, three in each. Out front, a seventh set an ambling pace. Not all were wearing helmets. Some had spears, some swords, and even from here, their uniforms looked dirty and torn.

The man in the centre of the near file, who appeared to have his hands bound in front, stopped to urinate. The man behind pushed him in the back. In seconds, they were scrabbling on the ground. Baxter and Willard exchanged glances. Baxter's full of disgust, Willard's of surprise. The leader turned back, kicked both men as they lay on the ground, then drew his sword.

Willard reached over his shoulder, but Baxter closed his hand over Willard's and whispered in his mind. [You're not cutting down a tree now Lord.]

Raised voices reached them, but not the words. The leader's sword flashed out and the bound man stopped struggling. His dying cry reached them a fraction of a second later. After a moment of hesitation, during which the patrol stood with heads bowed like mourners at a funeral, there was a sudden flurry of activity. In less than a minute, they had stripped the dead man of sword, helmet, boots, and coat.

Willard turned away.

Baxter's hand squeezed his shoulder. "Stay here Lord, a real Watcher patrol is coming."

[Who's that then,] thought Willard but Baxter was up, and bounding down the slope in long, easy strides.

[Deserters.]

[What are you going to do?] Willard projected directly to the warrior without thinking, something he had never tried before. If Baxter heard, he didn't reply. Willard leapt to his feet and followed at a stumbling run.

Baxter was halfway to the deserters before one of them noticed him and waved frantically to the others while unsheathing his sword. The leader shouted and they all turned, forming up in a loose semi-circle in front of him. Baxter's approach was inexorable. Despite the uneven terrain, he did not stumble as Willard did.

With a hundred yards to go, Baxter drew *Constant Flame*, the named sword ablaze like its name. One member of the group broke away, running for his life. Another, not waiting for an arm's length encounter ran forward and launched a well-aimed spear. Baxter sidestepped without breaking stride.

Willard was not even halfway down when Baxter reached the three who stood between him and the leader, now beating a hasty retreat behind them. It was difficult for Willard to see exactly what happened as he picked his way down the slope. It appeared as if Baxter ran straight through them without breaking stride. Constant Flame flashed, swept aside a sword on the right as the central spearman jumped left unexpectedly knocking the third man down. The fallen men half rose, half scrambled as if only just realising they were up against a Restoration Warrior. Baxter then stopped and, ignoring those behind him advanced on the leader with deliberate slowness.

The sound of approaching horses panicked the rest, who fled in all directions except towards Baxter. The mounted patrol reached the body of the leader's victim at the same time as Willard, who stood staring at the young man's face, drawn by the wide staring eyes of very different colours, a strong candidate.

What were they doing with a bound candidate? More to the point what was a candidate doing in the Watchers?

Willard's gaze lifted to the newcomers, suddenly uncomfortable about the body at his feet. These were the Watchers of reputation, shirts worn but clean and battered buttons shiny. As he dismounted, their captain dispatched his squad to run the escapees to ground.

Looking to Baxter for help, Willard saw the leader on his knees. Hands clasped together, looking up at the Warrior as if pleading. Baxter stood statue still, Constant Flame sheathed, and Willard felt relieved that it had ended with so little bloodshed. He had expected a slaughter when Baxter charged. Then the leader's head rolled off. Willard gagged as the Watcher Captain pinned his arms.

• • • •

News of Willard's arrest flashed ahead. By the time he and Baxter arrived in the outskirts of Walfort, the broadsheet about them, pasted on a board wall they were passing, already faded and tattered.

Under the headline, Captain Aubrey captures Willard Forrestor. It read: Accompanied by Warrior Baxter, Forrestor, an untested candidate (he has his hair), wears a talisman, and carries a named sword called Severne's Bane, and an eye-shaped scar in the centre of his forehead. We have linked Forrestor to a female server, the sudden appearance of multiple Restoration Warriors, and to miracle healings. Is this the man destined to be the face of the Goddess? The Watchmaster General has several warrants in connection with Forrestor.

Willard grunted, [why Severne?]

"This is not Our Lady's doing. I told you to stay put," Baxter answered for her.

Willard rounded on him, "You didn't have to kill him. He'd surrendered."

"He killed a candidate."

"It's still murder," Willard said coughing in the choking dust. "We have Magisters to judge and sentence criminals."

"Our Lady judged him. I executed her sentence. Do you question her judgement?"

Willard started to, but gave it up, noting that Baxter had dropped the respectful 'Lord'.

Walfort was both headquarters and the supply depot for the Wall. It was bigger than Willard had expected, and much bigger than its builders had intended; the parapets of the fort were just visible in the distance.

The crowded roads held a polyglot mixture of Watchers, ordinary folk like himself, and the occasional black robed server. Amongst them were horses, ridden and pulling carts, and oxen pulling drays loaded with bags or bales. Everywhere Willard looked, he saw purposeful chaos that abruptly stopped at their approach. People stepped away, put something between themselves and the patrol, and in wary fascination, focused on Willard and Baxter, unchained, and armed with named swords.

They were a mile into town before they reached the first corner of the fort, built at the same time as the Wall, during the Preservation Wars. Four long stables, arranged around a quadrangle and two granaries stood opposite the fort. A storehouse next to it, still under construction, proved to Willard the Wall was not in danger of falling all that soon.

Double story stone towers projected from the fort's wall either side of the main entrance. A spearman walked each tower rampart. Spearman at the entrance stepped aside as the patrol turned in under the central recessed arch and emerged into a wide, walled thoroughfare. The familiar stench of fresh dung reached them from the original stables lining the northern wall. Willard's impression was of two forts with a wide road between them, gated at either end by the massive gatehouses.

The captain separated Willard and Baxter from the deserters, handed his horse to a stable girl then led them through another arched gateway of huge blocks dressed and precision fitted, each one slightly tapered as they rose to a keystone twenty feet above.

Headquarters was busy but less frantic. The guards on the verandah stood aside as Captain Aubrey ushered them through the main entrance and straight across the forecourt into the proclamation hall. The waiting crowd parted before them. Aubrey spoke briefly to a fellow captain who smiled broadly at Willard and disappeared through a doorway at the side. He returned moments later, and Willard caught murmurs of discontent when he beckoned to them.

Considering the Watchmaster coordinated the defence of the Wall from here, Willard had expected it to be lavish. Instead, the Watchmaster General's office was a rather plain, long room that formed the eastern side of the forecourt. Two huge tapestries hung on the plastered walls. Late afternoon light streamed through several small, high windows and cast orange stripes across the thread-bare carpet. Stark, thought Willard, remembering the Ob's quarters with its gallery and panelling, and yet it was debatable who had more power.

Watchmaster General, Heutte Butcher, sat behind a large desk, two-thirds of the way into the room, signing papers. Someone else who orders other people's lives, thought Willard. Eventually she looked up, rose from her desk, and came around to stop in front of them. A small woman noted Willard, only coming up to his shoulder, with short grey hair clasped at the back by a silver ring to form a small bob.

She stood in front of him, looking up. "My aide Captain Brande may have seen fit to leave you armed, but I do not. You, Forrestor will please surrender your sword until I decide your status."

Imperiously, she held out both hands palm up. Seconds dragged while Willard stood undecided. Neither Baxter nor the Goddess offered any advice.

"Thank you," Heutte said abruptly, with a slight flexing of her fingers. With her assumption and lack of advice to the contrary, Willard felt compelled to comply. He unstrapped the scabbard.

"An intriguing name for a sword, wouldn't you say, Baxter?" Baxter remained mute and Heutte went on. "All the named swords I know contain the word 'fire' or 'flame'. Turning, she laid Severne's Bane on her desk.

She then began pacing a section of the worn carpet between the tapestries, head down, hands clasp behind her back. Several turns later, she stopped, again in front of Willard, scanned him from head to toe.

"So, this is the famous, perhaps infamous, Willard Robert Forrestor. Having heard so much about you, I have eagerly awaited this meeting."

Willard could not tell if she was serious or making fun of him. "I hope what you heard wasn't all bad Watchmaster."

Heutte started pacing again. "There are two views on that, the official one and the rumour mill. Unfortunately, I must go with the official line, and that presents me with a problem but first let me apologise for the arrest and putting you on show. We knew you were coming of course, but there was a report from Canalbridge of three Warriors with you. I wanted to ease the panic."

Heutte paused in front of Willard reached up and tapped the talisman dangling by its cord around his neck. For her, it was at eye level.

"This says you're a server and that," she said, pointing to Severne's Bane on her desk, "a warrior. This, however ..."She stood on her tiptoe, grabbed a tuft of hair, and gave it a sharp pull.

"Ow!"

"This says you haven't taken the test. Yet you possess two items you ought not to have. Please explain."

"The Goddess gave them to me."

Heutte stepped sideways and stood in front of Baxter. "You appear to be the genuine article and your apparent willingness to associate with Forrestor lends credence to his story. However, I have had no less than four warrants for your associate."

She glanced across at a dumbstruck Willard. "I tore one up when your brother arrived."

Willard started, "My brother?"

"Aldus Forrestor, shorter than you, stockier, brown hair ...'

Willard interrupted. "It can't be my brother. He's dead. I found the body." He swallowed rising bile at the memory of the headless corpse lying in the pipe.

"If he's not your brother, then he's a damn good imposter. He fooled Captain Leach who claims to be your future sister-in-law," Heutte snapped. Then in a less aggressive tone she said, "How curious, Leach's eye-colouring is the reverse of yours."

"Yes," Willard said absently, still trying to come to terms with the possibility of Aldus being alive.

"I can assure you your brother was here in this very room. Once I'd debriefed been him, I had no grounds to hold him. My adjutant has advised me he has left the Isthmus."

Willard's legs shook. Aldus is alive. It wasn't his body in the pipe, just someone with the same boots. Poor d ... Arthur.

"Are you alright? You look ill. Bring him a chair, Kingsley. I would suggest you sit before you fall."

Willard rubbed his eyes as the aide brought him a chair. "I thought the ferals killed him. I found his ... a body, I was so sure. Is he on his way home?"

"I don't know. Captain Leach may, but she is in Grand Falls." Heutte said and resumed pacing. Five steps, turn and repeat. After several turns, she again stopped in front of Willard and rubbed her hands together. With him now seated, she was above him.

"Interesting scar. Tell me what happened to the militia detailed to escort you to Grundston."

Willard swallowed. "We got caught in a mudslide. Ask the Goddess."

"I'm asking you. You survived," said Heutte in a restrained voice. She pulled her hair tighter through the ring, flattening it against her head, giving her face an even more severe expression.

"I was lucky."

"Obviously. What attempts did you make to rescue survivors or report the incident?"

"There were no survivors. They were all buried under the mud." With startling clarity, Willard recalled the leg of a horse sticking up through a hardening crust.

"There was one other," Heutte said, watching him carefully.

"Samals," he said, his voice shaking as he saw again the cart rolling over the man he had helped.

"So, you knew. Lying won't help you," Heutte said.

Baxter stepped forward, and Kingsley stepped back. Heutte remained unmoved, staring up at Baxter. "trying to intimidate me will not change the facts."

Baxter smiled and stepped back.

"I didn't know, but I'm not surprised. Samals tried to warn them. It was too dark, too wet, and too slippery. He was gone before the avalanche."

Heutte began pacing again. "Personally, I don't think you should be accountable for acts of the Goddess, or nature, whichever you prefer. You, however, did not report the incident to anyone."

"I needed to stay free to clear my name."

"Innocent people have nothing to fear from the militia. They are mostly Watcher veterans."

Baxter, at last, came to his defence. "How long since you went back east Watchmaster? The militia are no longer ex-Watcher. There is corruption at the highest levels of Our Lady's Church. Good candidates have disappeared, the Arch Server who issued that warrant planned for Willard to join the missing. The Goddess has dealt with him."

Willard stared at Baxter in stunned silence, thoughts tumbling, know he would never have reached Grundston.

"Sev Miller, Deep Creek's acting Magister?" Heutte asked.

"Yes."

The Watchmaster seemed to relax. "I had heard rumours, of course, but this far from the capital I can't afford to give them credence. I will take your word for it that Forrestor had no choice. One of the remaining two warrants however concerns the disappearance of Kezia Leach ..."

"That's why I didn't report the death of my escort. Her disappearance is why I needed to clear my name," Willard said, cutting her off. "I followed her to Medicorps, but she didn't show. I know she's alive, I've ..." he stopped, not wanting to say he had repeatedly heard her voice in his head. "The Goddess has assured me she is safe," he finished. [She had better be, or I will never take the damn test.]

Severne said nothing.

"Before I was so rudely interrupted," Heutte said, "I was about to say the Watchers do not accept warrants based on missing persons. There are many reasons for people to go missing, not always criminal. We only issue warrants if we have a body."

"The remaining warrant, a recent one, issued by a server in Port Taylor, is a problem. The Towers take impersonation of a server seriously. We have an understanding to exchange our miscreants for theirs. Unless you can prove the Goddess gave you that talisman, I will be obliged to hand you over."

"If Our Lady permits," Baxter said.

Here

The Watchmaster moved to stand and look up at the Warrior. "I'd take your word for it, but your Goddess's servers won't. Are you at war with each other?"

Baxter nodded. "Some entrusted with Our Lady's plan have lost faith."

"Since we have no tower, I suggest we use the nearest wayside chapel and the circuit server from Carrier Point. In anticipation of your arrival, I spoke to Ser Digby, who uses it to hear the petitions of our increasing number of Severnians." Heutte's lips held an expression of distaste when she said Severnians. "He will accept Forrestor's claim if hears it from the Goddess." She turned to Willard, "A Telling will clear the remaining warrant on you."

Baxter cocked his head, then nodded.

Willard shuddered, projecting to the Goddess, [No foretelling Severne, or I stay unwilling.] Severne did not answer. Addressing Heutte, he asked, "I'm free to go if the Goddess confirms she gave me the talisman."

"Or stay. The Wall is desperately short of able bodies, and you have that." She pointed back at *Severne's Bane,* lying across her desk.

"Done," said Willard, with a tremble.

Walfort's 'chapel' was on a small hill, a hundred yards inside the new town limit. The town had grown past it. In place of the Tower stood a large, thick, flagpole-like structure with a cluster of curiously rectangular version of Severne's Ears arrayed around its summit. A small building, the size of an average Deep Creek house stood at the base with a traditional locked door rather than the power curtain. Only the pole and her Ears looked builder made.

The Watchmaster General stood to one side with Willard and Baxter while Ser Digby entered a curtained lean-to that covered the doorway so nobody could see the oracle when he opened the door. He re-emerged a minute later, perplexed.

"I cannot clear him if I don't hear it," Ser Digby said, "but Our Lady wants to speak with candidate Willard alone."

[I was afraid of that,] thought Willard.

[Our Lady cannot give you the Test of Faith unless you go to a servatory,] Baxter told Willard, and then to Ser Digby said, "Our Lady will ensure you know the result."

The entourage waited as Willard, only partially relieved, entered.

"Willard, how nice to see my favourite candidate. I trust you are well."

The oracle crystal was a flat panel, not cubic, her image like a moving painting, quite clear yet lacking realism.

"Why ask when you know," Willard said. "Where's Kezia?"

"Kezia is safe and well. She had a child."

Willard felt his stomach twist as if she had punched him. Kezia had a child, his Kezia. She must have meant the 'forget me' part, after all. She has moved on. All this time I have hung on to the hope that ...

It was a savage blow and Severne, sitting with one leg crossed over the other, hands clasp about her bare knee, had delivered it brutally.

Willard blinked back tears. "I'll believe it when I hear it from Kezia." he said, his anguish dissipating a little when he realised the Goddess meant to make him think Kezia had moved on, leaving him free to have offspring with Averil.

"When will you learn to trust me, Willard? I have never lied to you. You are a very special candidate. I gave you a talisman and a named sword to show my faith in you. You need to reciprocate and take the Test of Faith."

"I'll consider it if, Kezia ..." he stopped, momentarily choked with emotion, "... rejects me."

"I will keep you to that promise, Willard. Kezia is on her way here as we speak." The image faded and the flat crystal turned grey.

"Wait," Willard called. "How can I prove you gave me the talisman?"

Severne's voice filled his mind. [They know. I transmitted our conversation outside.]

In shocked silence, Willard tried to recall what he'd said, but his mind was blank. When he eventually stepped outside, a whole range of responses played over the assembled faces, from reverent astonishment through pity to derision and laughter. He felt his face flush as bits and pieces came back.

Whether the Aithist Watchmaster General believed all she heard, she did not say. She told him she would pass back through channels that the missing Kezia was not dead and would eventually turn up, probably with a child and a husband.

Ser Digby accepted the oracle's testimony without reservation. He informed Willard he would tell his Arch-server that Our Lady had indeed given Willard a talisman and the named sword *Severne's Bane*.

Sympathetically, Heutte suggested Willard could wait for Kezia in Grand Falls with her sister. Willard was too depressed to argue. He had nothing else to do but wait, to be convinced by Kezia that she really had no place for him in her life.

• • • •

"Where exactly are we going, Captain Brande?" Willard asked, as they rode slowly out of Walfort. Baxter jogged alongside.

"Call Me Kingsley. We're going to Grand Falls," he said. "You're assigned to the training unit at Wall Watch Seven, as a cadet officer." He glanced down at Baxter. "They hope your warrior friend will impart some of his several hundred years of experience. Severne knows we need all the help we can get."

It still disconcerted Willard that the Watchers were more curious about warriors than afraid of them. Kingsley called neither of them Lord.

Willard let them chat and withdrew into himself. He knew now he had never had a chance. It was always going to be Averil or nothing, but he refused to give up. [Are you listening Severne? If I can't have Kezia, I'll never take the damn test.]

Out of the corner of his eye, he saw Baxter start and surfaced in time to hear Kingsley ask. "You surely don't object to the use of animals?"

"Only to a dependence on them," Baxter said smoothly, his eye on Willard.

Kingsley argued with him for a while, soon drifting onto other topics from which Willard retreated. Whenever they passed any of the many travellers, Kingsley would wave. It did not seem to matter who they were: Watchers, dray-drivers, shepherds. All of them stared at the trio. Few returned his wave and then only tentatively.

"I don't actually know them all," Kingsley said, "but it always pays to be friendly. They might remember me, and you never know when you'll need a friend. Things are getting pretty scary around here."

"Why do you say that?" Baxter asked.

"The omens are all bad."

"Omens?"

"The year for one, it's nine hundred and ninety-nine years since the Days of Fire."

"I thought the Watchers were Aithists and didn't believe in omens," Willard prompted.

"We don't, but the ferals do. They will take the approaching millennium as an omen that they can win. And that will spur them on, you see."

Irritation at the comment drew Willard into the conversation. The Days of Fire he argued was an arbitrary point, fixed hundreds of years after the event, by people who could not possibly know. It had no intrinsic meaning.

Kingsley scoffed at Willard's protest, saying it did not alter what the feral believed, and that was what mattered. He enumerated a whole catalogue of recent mysterious happenings, including Willard's appearance and the increasing public visibility of Restoration Warriors.

After a while, Willard gave up and returned to his inner world, half listening, absently staring at the countryside, hope battling with despair that he and Kezia could somehow beat the odds. If not, he would return to Deep Creek and help with the farm.

Again, it was something Kingsley said that sprang Willard from his reflections, "... chasing them up the eastern side of the Barriers. Anyway, we got all the way to Deep Creek. After they grabbed the bloke, they thought would be the Face, they disappeared without a trace. Funny thing is we found out later, it was your brother ..."

Kingsley suddenly twisted in the saddle to stare at Willard. "Well, I'll be buggered. It was you they were after. Even the ferals think you're the Man Who Will Be Face." He cast a sideways glance at Baxter before continuing. "It all fits. I mean, look at you: eye shaped scar, talisman, named sword, warrior protection and what the Goddess said in your telling, a very special candidate, well that just about ..."

Kingsley kept talking unheard as they clattered across a bridge. "... in Deep Creek. Anyway, one of their band was burnt to a crisp, damnedest thing I ever saw."

Willard swallowed hard as Kingsley chatted on unaware of the effect his words. [I didn't kill him Severne, you did.] He received his usual reply, silence.

Baxter, he noted, watched him with interest.

"Had to rescue Averil from them too, not that she was all that grateful. Great girl, though, full of grit." He stroked his throat, smiling at some memory he did not share. "You, of course, already know her. She runs the training camp. Would you believe it, before the ferals captured her, she trekked over Perisher ..." His voice trailed off in the clatter of a second bridge as they recrossed the Falls River.

Kingsley still hadn't finished when they reached a fork in the road. "This is as far as I take you. Grand Falls is ten miles that way," he said, pointing. "Give my regards to the Major. Tell her it's her shout." After a quick wave, he let out a whoop, took off his cap and slapped the horse's rump, spurring it into a gallop down the other road.

Willard and Baxter watched him until he disappeared.

"He talks a lot."

"Yes, Lord."

Into the refreshing quiet, Willard heard a muted rushing sound. "What is that?"

"Grand Falls Lord."

With the sound of the distant falls in his ears, Willard caught his first glimpse of the Wall. He stared at the small, low section, still several miles away, which included what Baxter told him was a milepost.

Considering the Wall had stood as a bastion against feral barbarity for two and a half centuries, he found it a disappointing sight. He expected more, had built an image in his mind of a towering edifice, something worthy of all the stories. At each new crest, however, his view of it expanded. Eventually, the ramparts of the Fort at Grand Falls came into view and five miles west of it, Fort Midway. The terrain became flatter, rockier, and less fertile, the Falls River beside them wider, faster, and shallower.

Willard stopped in the next vale out of sight of the Wall and dismounted. To Baxter's inquiry, as he untied his backpack and strapped on his sword he said, "If possible, I want to have a look before this," he tapped the eye-shaped scar on his forehead, "makes it impossible."

"As you wish Lord," said Baxter.

"So, I'm going to be billeted with Averil," Willard said, thankful that at least Baxter was speaking to him.

"Was that not inevitable, Lord?"

"I guess so," said Willard, slapping his horse's rump, watching it canter down the road toward Grand falls. That will give them something to think about, he thought, surprised that neither Baxter nor Severne commented. Perhaps he was at last keeping some thoughts to himself.

.

Chapter 35

A veril rolled her new title round in her head. Major Leach. Rapid promotion was quite usual on the Wall, but Averil had excelled at everything, from hand-to-hand combat to strategic planning. At twenty, she was the Watchers youngest Major. Her first two weeks in the new position had kept her busy, up and down the Wall, reorganising the entire training programme.

At every Fort and milepost, after a hard training day, the locals would insist on taking her for drinks. Her reputation for consumption of beer now matched the strenuousness of her training regimen. Averil was as proud of having out-drunk all challengers in each of the wall's eleven alehouses as she was of her promotion. Everyone, from the Watchmaster General to the newest cadet, knew of the exploits of Major Leach, starting with her incredible balloon arrival.

About to quaff her first beer after a boring morning of paperwork, Averil was more than a little put out by the cadet who burst in crying. "Duty Watch, duty Watch."

Averil paused, the tankard inches from her lips, the sweet smell of hops tingling her nose. No one among the assortment of captains was putting up their hand. She took a sip and twisted around to find the cadet undecided what to do.

Averil put down her beer and stood.

"Over here."

He was probably only two years younger, but he quailed before her. The authority she projected constantly surprised her. Shows what a little training, experience and reputation can do.

"What's your name?"

"Wolfe sir ... lady ... major.

"Report Wolfe," Averil said formally, suppressing laughter. She didn't want to embarrass the lad.

"There's a riderless horse at the main gate," Wolfe said, relaxing a little.

"Describe it."

"It's one of ours, still saddled."

Averil was beginning not to like the sound of this. A riderless horse meant a missing rider. A missing rider could mean a feral on this side of the Wall. Just last week, a lone assassin had killed three officers before someone stopped her. At least it had convinced the Fortmasters that the balloons were dangerous. ferals could drop behind the wall at night in perfect silence. The Fortmasters now had patrols on the east coast of the Pointing Fingers Isthmus all the way back to Carrier Point, watching for lights in the night sky.

She turned to the room listening then pointed to someone in the nearest group. "Captain Elswyth. Take a patrol follow Wolfe. Find out which way the horse came in and backtrack it. Report to me what you find."

She turned back to the young Watcher cadet. "Thanks Wolfe, you did well to persist in the duty Watch's absence. Now go."

Wolfe beamed as he led Captain Elswyth out.

Averil turned back to the bar, eyed her beer, and sighed. "Captain Ogden?"

"Yes, Major."

"Call the Watchers to alert. We may have another infiltrator. I want squads of spearmen fanning out in both directions from here to the next mileposts. Let's trap the bastards. Move it."

• • • •

Based on Baxter's descriptions, Willard aimed at a section between sentry turrets. A few hundred yards short, they crossed the service road connecting Grand Falls and Fort Midway and could see all four mileposts between. Willard paused, captivated by the structure, re-evaluating his first disappointed impression.

The Wall stretched out of sight in both directions, following the contours of the land. Thousands upon thousands of stone blocks, quarried, moved, shaped, and fitted together with precision. Beyond, even though he knew there was a sheer drop, he expected to see something, a mountain, or a distant forest canopy. The impenetrable nothingness of blue sky disturbed him in a way he did not quite understand; as if the wall bordered the edge of the world.

The land between the service road and the Wall was open, grazing land. In full sight, Willard and Baxter headed across it towards the second sentry turret between mileposts and to Willard's surprise, they reached it unchallenged. Not having thought to get this far, Willard ranged along the base of the wall, wondering how to get up on the parapet for a better look.

Without warning, Baxter pulled Willard into the shadow of the turret. A moment later, the sound of a second storey door scraping open made him look up. A spearman emerged, walked a few steps, undid his breeches, and urinated down the wall where Willard had been.

[You'd think they'd piss on the feral side.]

[It's into the wind.]

Finished, the spearman walked away toward the next turret. Once he was out of sight, Willard stepped out from the Wall, and peered up at the walkway, sixteen feet above. Unless there was someone standing quietly out of view by the door of the turret, this section was clear. He led Baxter a hundred yards away from the stain before stopping to reappraise the walkway.

[How do you intend to get up there?] asked Baxter, following his gaze.

[Stand on your shoulders maybe?]

[Even if you stood on my hands and I threw you I doubt you'd make it. Allow me.]

Baxter pulled a coil of fine rope from the lining of his cloak, and with uncanny accuracy, heaved the loose coils upwards then tugged. The rope came taut. [It's secure,] he said.

[You came prepared.]

[Our Lady knew what you would do. After you Lord,] he said handing the rope to Willard.

Willard stared at him.

[It's simple, put your feet on the wall, lean back and ... untrained as well as untested.] Baxter said. He made a loop and tied it off. [Put the loop under your arms once I'm on top.] Gripping the rope, Baxter put a foot on the wall and walked swiftly up. Less than thirty seconds later, he was on the walkway, dragging Willard backwards up the Wall. Once on top, Willard saw the rope had indeed secured itself around a merlon. More of Severne's magic, thought Willard as he stepped to the Wall's outer edge.

An expansive sound escaped his open mouth as he gazed out into the void. Puffs of cloud floated below him all the way to the curve of the horizon. Between the clouds, the distant land was verdant, increasingly less so in the middle distance, and directly below it was a dull brown, curiously patterned, in a design he felt he knew. A wide ribbon of silver, the outflow of Grand Falls, separated the patterned ground from a mass of tangled growth further east. Willard had to lean out to follow the course of the river back to Grand Falls. He lost sight of the wall in billowing clouds of mist from the pool Grand Falls had dug at the base of the escarpment. His amazed gaze wandered back to the centre and he looked straight down. The base of the wall, twenty feet below, stood less than three feet from the edge of the Break, which dropped sheer away.

"What is that?" asked Willard, pointing down at the patterned ground.

Baxter leaned out through the adjacent crenel and followed the direction of Willard's finger. "The Federal camp."

Willard blinked, but his immediate disbelief drained away when he looked again. Circles within circles cut by lines, each resembling the grounds and paths of Our Lady's Towers. "There must be hundreds."

"Thousands. Each large circle is a company of twenty-four hundred soldiers, and from this angle you're not seeing the whole camp. There are nearly seventeen thousand Federals down there," Baxter told him.

"But that's impossible," Willard said, and was about to add, that there weren't that many people in the entire world when the closer turret banged open. Two spearmen stepped out and quickly overlapped their oblong shields to form a solid barrier across the narrow parapet.

When the door of the more distant turret banged open behind them, Willard and Baxter turned. Two more spearmen emerged, established their own shield wall, then slowly advanced towards them.

Willard looked down at the patrol path inside the wall.

"No Lord, the jump would injure you," Baxter said. "Our Lady wants you here."

Even as Baxter spoke, four spearmen exited from the ground floor of the nearest turret and jogged down the path, shields held above their heads.

• • • •

Averil had just exited milepost two when the call came through the pipes. They had trapped two people between turrets seven and eight. Two infiltrators, one turret from Grand Falls; not good. Averil looked out over the parapet. For as far as she could see in either direction, there were no ferals in the kill zone and none on the wall between her and the next turret. It wasn't an attack.

Flipping the cheek flaps of her helmet into place, Averil, with six spearmen close behind, paused in the empty Turret seven, ordering four of her squad down the ladder and out behind the wall to cut off any retreat. She could see turret seven's Duty Watch just beyond the open door had the intruders trapped between them and those from Turret eight.

As Averil strode between them, she saw immediately that one of the pair was a Restoration Warrior. The other was a rumour made manifest, the so-called Man Who Will Be Face: eye shaped scar in his forehead, talisman dangling from his neck and a gemmed hilt poking above his shoulder.

Averil felt she should know the face beneath the unkempt shoulder length hair and full beard. The man scrutinised her just as hard, but the helmet's protective cheek flaps left only her eyes and mouth visible. She removed her helmet. He smiled, a flash of teeth in the beard; he knew her. Their gazes locked and she saw the differently coloured irises—Willard. In the stunned silence of mutual discovery, all Averil's remembered hurts abruptly vanished. Even under the turmoil of trying to fit him to the role of the Man Who Will Be Face, she was glad to see him.

"I guess it had to be you," she said, grinning as she strode confidently towards the pair and embraced Willard enthusiastically. In the back of her mind, she could see that bringing them together was Our Lady's plan in full swing.

"Glad to see you made it," Willard said, and although he seemed genuinely glad to see her, his returning hug was rather timid.

Averil supposed he was still unhappy with his part in Our Lady's plan, yet the talisman and sword suggested he had done an about face on everything else he had previously rejected. The look of smug satisfaction on Baxter's face, presumably for having completed a difficult task for the Goddess, was annoying.

"Well, give me a look," Averil said, gazing over Willard's shoulder.

After glancing at Baxter, Willard unslung *Severne's Bane,* and handed it to her.

"That name is a break with tradition," she said, running her over the tooled letters. She drew the blade half out of the scabbard, admired the gem in the hilt, and the intricate engraving on the fabulous blade, now one of eight. It was all she had hoped for, and could never have.

She slammed the blade back into the scabbard and pushed it back at him. "What are you all staring at? Get back to your posts."

After she had helped Willard and Baxter settle in, she took Willard on a tour of the fort. "So, what really happened?" she asked as they were passing the granary.

"I found out there are two tests. The first just implants a device in your head so she can talk to you." He showed her the scar. "I did it thinking if I rejected her voice in my mind, she wouldn't need me or my offspring. I would never be more than a server, like Kezia wanted."

"And?" Averil asked?

"Severne's idea of rejection is jumping up and down, and screaming to have it out. It doesn't bother me, other than being a bloody nuisance sometimes. I guess that makes me a server. And since the second test is my choice, I'm not taking it."

"That would please my sister even more."

Willard told her about Hedley's part in saving his life. "He's a full Restoration Warrior and older than Baxter. He only posed as our server to coach us."

Averil quickly related how Hedley had done the same for her. "He put something like mother's healing stuff in the food he served me."

They exchanged stories at length, which eventually led Averil to the topic uppermost in her mind since seeing the eye-shaped scar.

"Rumour has it, you raised a girl from the dead?"

"Nelda? She wasn't dead, just injured. I suspected a broken back, but who knows? Severne healed her and set me up to take the blame."

Averil was silent for a few moments. "But you made her server. I can't imagine that happening back home?"

"It is different in the wilds. Langley, the retiring server, objected to Nelda, until Severne made the talisman I gave her, work."

"But you got another one."

"It's useful for access."

Averil ran a hand over her short hair as they exited South Gate and took the roadway to the Mill. "My problem is I'm still not sure I like, or trust, our Goddess. How about you, now that she's in your head?" she asked.

Willard did not answer straight away. He felt vaguely ill at ease with Averil, not knowing if she still rejected the plan for them.

"I don't know what to believe anymore. I told her to stop bothering me and she's been silent ever since. When she speaks to me, it's always to urge me to take the second test."

"Gardner kept telling me she only had my interest at heart, then dumped me with the ferals."

"I was stunned when the watchmaster said you escaped with Aldus. I was sure he was dead."

Averil scowled at him, but said nothing. He didn't pursue it and the conversation died. In silence, they turned off the road to head across the field to the only good stand of trees for miles, content for the moment to pursue their own reflections.

As the Goddess had wanted, the warriors had thrust Willard upon her; it was hardly a natural outcome. The stories they'd exchanged showed Severne had gone to extreme lengths to arrange it. She wondered how much of what had happened to them would not have occurred if they had made other choices. Or had it all been inevitable from the moment their eyes changed? Certainly, she felt closer to Willard now than she ever had growing up together. Even thousands of miles apart, they had shared similar experiences. They had travelled with Restoration Warriors and had conversed directly with the Goddess. Yet he still loved Kezia, still hoped to complete their oathing and still did not intend to produce offspring with her.

Averil broke the silence. "So, why are you here?"

"Does there have to be a reason? Why can't I just exist because my mother got carried away?"

Averil burst into a fit of laughing. "I had this conversation with Hedley."

"What?"

"He asked why I was here and meant why do I exist? You answered that question when all I wanted was why are you here at the Wall? Is this a male thing?"

Willard stared at her.

"Never mind," Averil said, waving a dismissive hand. "Why did you come to the Wall? Why not just go home when Severne let you go?"

"Kezia left shortly after you did. Severne told me she was coming here," he said, and flushed slightly when he caught Averil's look. "I knew you would be here and what that means for her plan, but I also trust Severne not to lie. Kezia will come eventually."

• • • •

Watchers bowed and backed away as Averil and Willard walked down the main street of Fort Grand Falls towards the two massive stone arches of South Gate.

Averil nodded to the guard as they passed out of the shade of the portal into sunny open grassland behind the fort, and Willard felt relieved. For weeks now, nobody but Averil and Baxter had treated him as normal. Nothing Willard said, or did, made a scrap of difference. He could not shake off the Man Who Will Be Face tag. Giving Averil swimming lessons was a chance to get away from the problem.

They took the service road to the Mill. The Watchers had diverted the Falls River into a holding pond to feed the race. Water splashed and gurgled as it pushed the paddles through the race. Timbers groaned as the wheel turned. At the water's edge, protected from the wind by the two-story mill, Willows growing around the pond had created a small oasis, used by everyone as a recreation area.

Back in their first lesson, with Baxter standing guard Averil had stripped naked. She wasn't in the least embarrassed, but Willard was, despite skinny-dipping with her when they were children. He had turned away wondering if she was simply insensitive, deliberately provocative, or now believed Severne's plan was inescapable.

When he turned back at a splash, he found her knee deep at the edge, grinning up at him. Deliberately provocative, he decided, and although discomfited, he did not look away. The strong facial features were reminiscent of Kezia, the same underlying bone structure, and the same mouth shape as their mother Jorgena. He had not previously seen how very much alike they were to look at because of her difference in their eye and hair colour. He felt a guilty twinge as his eyes travelled down over the naked skin, the small protruding breasts, nipples erect from the cold, a flat muscled stomach, and the fine triangular tuft of reddish gold curls. Body wise, Averil was slimmer and looked fitter.

"Get over it, brother. You're here to teach me to swim," she had said, grinning.

"Wear something, or I'm not."

A petulant Averil had climbed out and slipped on her undergarment, not that it hid much once it got wet. Willard walked in up to his waist fully clothed.

For subsequent lessons, Averil arrived lightly dressed ready to swim with her uniform in a bag so she didn't have to stay wet. She had been quick to grasp the principles and could already swim across the pond unassisted. Willard now watched and gave instructions from the bank. In exchange, she was training him in a variety of weapons except for *Severne's Bane*. Baxter provided the specialist training on how to use the named sword's formidable power.

After a dozen laps across the pond, she emerged dripping and planted a wet kiss on his cheek. "Thanks, bro. All I need now is practice; like you with *Bane*," she said, her tone wistful.

As Willard stood, he spotted movement in the pond a few yards away, barely visible under a Willow. Averil had a towel over her head, drying her hair. Peeved that Baxter hadn't kept everyone away during their swimming lessons as he said he would, Willard pushed through the tendrils, wanting to have a few choice words, and found a body clothed only in undergarments, face down in the mud.

He shouted out to Averil.

Averil went still for a second, then quickly changed while Willard hauled the body up out of the water onto the bank. The head flopped back at an odd angle, and Willard felt his gorge rise. An ear-to-ear slash across the throat had nearly severed the head from the body, feral fashion. Even after all the deaths he had witnessed since the raid, he found Kingsley's death particularly frightening. It was too close to home. He and Averil had drunk and joked with the man only a couple of nights ago, and now he was gone, never to return.

The finality of it made Willard wish he could believe in an afterlife, that in death he would become a sleeper in Severne's Eye, waiting for the restoration. But he'd already been there and the Eye of the Goddess was bland and empty of promise.

The bloated, white face and the swollen purple lips didn't stop either of them from recognising Captain Kingsley Brande.

"Fucking ferals. Why did it have to be Kingsley?" Averil looked distraught and angry all at once. "Search the bank for his uniform and anything out of place. I'll meet you around the other side."

Willard skirted the mill and returned to the water's edge eyes scanning ahead. The nature of Kingsley's death brought home to him. He was on the front line, where generations had fought and died to stop the ferals from overrunning civilisation. He appreciated the fact that someone had to defend the Wall, but he didn't belong here. As soon as Kezia arrives, they would go back to Deep Creek, to hell with the plan.

Baxter joined him and Averil back where she'd been swimming, opposite the slowly turning wheel.

"Anything," Averil asked.

Willard shook his head.

"Dead two days," Baxter said, and when Averil raised a finger skyward, added, "Our Lady's eyes were elsewhere, I'm here."

"That figures," Averil said, her angry gaze on Willard.

"Is stripping the body a feral custom?" he asked, desperate to change the subject.

"Not that I've heard. My guess is whoever killed him wanted the uniform, which means they think they can pass themselves off as one of us. It might even be one of us, feral trained or ..." she paused, shook her head, "it couldn't be."

"Who?" Willard asked, but when Averil looked up at him, her eyes slid away. The furtive look hid a mystery Willard had been trying to solve since arrival. He'd often felt Averil was on the verge of telling him something important, but she always shied away at the last moment, shaking her head almost as if she didn't believe what she'd been about to say.

Aldus, thought Willard, with sudden insight. That's why she hasn't broached the subject. "You can't seriously think it was Aldus," he said, his tone disbelieving.

"Now that you mention it, I do."

"Aldus went home."

"That's what he said he would do, but the more I think about it the more it makes sense. I'll have to verify his departure."

At first, Averil's theory irritated Willard. "Aldus might be a little rough, but he isn't a traitor."

Averil glanced at Baxter but said nothing.

Willard became incensed when the full implication hit him. "My Goddess, Averil, are you saying he murdered Kingsley for his uniform?"

"I'm sure of it. He used me to get here and he chose Kingsley deliberately to exact revenge."

Willard saw her in an entirely new light. "You're mad," he said. "Whatever happened down there addled your brain." He knew this was unfair and he could see the doubt it caused her, but he could not believe what she was saying about Aldus. Even though he knew Aldus wasn't his brother, Willard had grown up believing it; they were brothers in spirit.

"You weren't there. You didn't see the hate in his eyes," Averil said, almost pleading with him to understand. "Something down there changed him."

"It certainly changed you. You could just as easily be trying to throw suspicion away from yourself," Willard shot back.

"I was here when you found the body."

"He's been dead for two days."

"Enough," Averil said, glaring at him. "You know I didn't do this."

"I know Aldus didn't either. You told me yourself the Watchmaster General even offered him a position."

Averil seemed taken aback for a second, frustrated. Willard, knowing he had made a telling point, felt relieved for Aldus's sake.

"I have a job to do," Averil said with sudden anger. "Either sign up or get the fuck off my Wall, I don't have time for amateurs."

Her vehemence stung Willard as much as the content. She knew he was waiting for Kezia. "But ..."

Averil cut him off. "Visiting time is over. Wait in Canalbridge."

She stormed off, leaving Willard unsettled, looking to Baxter for answers. The Restoration Warrior looked pained, but like the Goddess, remained silent.

Chapter 36

When Kezia and Howard arrived in Walfort, a rotund individual bursting out of his uniform accosted them. Watcher Captain Ogden insisted they report to headquarters for a priority interview with the Watchmaster General. Without a doubt, Walfort expected them. Very detailed and lifelike drawings of Healer Jena were on display everywhere.

Ogden ushered them into the Watchmaster General's office, where they found Heutte studying one of two huge tapestries, a stream running through a forest.

"Ah, Healer Jena," Heutte said, turning from her contemplation of the tapestry. "You're well I trust. I heard someone tried to poison you."

"You're well informed Watchmaster, but as you can see, I am as well as one can expect in these trying times," Kezia said, admiring the tapestry knowing the hundreds of hours it would have taken. "Well, enough to work at what I came to do, save lives."

"I'm sure you can. Your reputation precedes you, and we are shorthanded in every area now. One of our healers from the last contingent failed to turn up. I would much appreciate as many of my wounded as you can manage, being back on the Wall."

Kezia paled, but Heutte didn't notice. She was busy adjusting the silver ring that held her greying hair in a bob.

The deep blue eyes sparkled. "As for you, warrior Howard, you're the second warrior, to turn up here accompanying a celebrated, rumour enhanced, favourite of your Goddess. No offence, but I lose several Watchers to her every week. If she keeps stealing my people, I'll have nobody left to protect the wall, and the ferals will have her towers."

"I don't understand," Kezia said.

"The Watchmaster must discharge believers; divided loyalties," explained Howard.

"Not anymore. I now ignore the Moral Desertion article, as we call it. If they wish to stay, they can, and thankfully most do."

"No one told me I had to renounce the Goddess to join Medicorps."

"Medicorps is not Watcher. They don't take the Oath of Allegiance." Heutte frowned, "I didn't realise you were Corps Jena. That's not in my brief."

Kezia swallowed. "I'm not. I wear the uniform because it's associated with healing, but you will notice I have stripped it of insignia," she said, concentrating on the tapestry.

Intercepting Kezia's gaze, Heutte commented, "Lovely, isn't it?"

"It reminds me of home."

"Oh, where are you from?"

"Deep Creek," Kezia said, instantly regretting the admission.

"But of course, why did I even ask? Notoriety, Warriors, and Deep Creek are now common bedfellows," Heutte said, her deep blue eyes narrowing at Kezia. The Watchmaster then marched to her desk and picked up a folder. As she read the contents, she frequently glanced up at Kezia. Kezia sensed Howard holding his breath.

Closing the folder with a shake of her head, Heutte sighed. "For a moment, you had me worried. Our missing healer is also from Deep Creek. She waved the folder at Kezia. "You are now the fourth ... no, fifth ... never mind, I have it on good authority. My healer will eventually turn up. She paused, put the folder down, and squared it with the corner of her desk before returning to them.

"What was I saying? Ah yes, we live in interesting times. You, healer Jena, are the fifth person from Deep Creek to be brought to my attention and the second miracle worker accompanied by a Restoration Warrior. Would you not agree this is beyond coincidence?"

Kezia and Howard remained mute.

Four others from Deep Creek, thought Kezia. Averil is one. Who else? Wylie?

"What on Nuaith is going on in your town? Is it your fabled Arch of Restoration, something in the water, what?" Heutte asked.

Kezia shrugged, eager to leave before Heutte rethought her earlier connection.

Heutte seemed to give up and changed the subject. "Tell me something Warrior," she asked, appraising Howard as she paced back and forth across the worn carpet. "Does your Goddess tell you what your brethren are doing?"

"When necessary," Howard replied cautiously.

"The other miracle worker, Willard ..." In turning at the end of her fourth step, Heutte missed Kezia's shock, "... had both a named sword and a talisman, apparently without taking the Test. Did you know about that?"

"No," said Howard, cocking his head.

Kezia's mind spun. It can't be my Willard. It's a coincident name like acolyte Willard in Rivers Junction.

Ignoring Howard's hand on her arm, Kezia forced her voice up through the constriction in her throat. "This other miracle worker, if he's from Deep Creek maybe I know him. What does he look like?"

"Tall, long brown hair, beard ... and a livid scar in the centre of his forehead, shaped like an eye."

Kezia exhaled slowly, a scar. "Sorry, can't place him."

Heutte returned to her desk. "Must be the millennium. It's driving everyone balmy. However, good healers are in short supply. I'll give you all the help you need."

"Captain Ogden." She shouted several times, but it was a full minute before Ogden appeared, during which Heutte ranted about losing her best staff. When he appeared, she exploded at the hapless captain.

Later, outside, Captain Ogden apologised for his Watchmaster's behaviour. "The ferals have stepped up their campaign. They attack a different point on the Wall every other day. The appearance of miracle workers and Restoration Warriors has everyone on edge. Something must be about to happen, and I doubt it will be good."

He added that already some Watchers had deserted, fearing the imminent collapse of the Wall. Others had converted to the Faith. "But what has really upset her was Captain Brande's death. He's been with her from the start. We found him murdered in the millpond a couple of days ago," Ogden said. "Throat slit ear to ear, feral fashion."

• • • •

The discovery of Kingsley's body had two immediate consequences. Willard joined the Watchers and Averil put them on standby. Coincident with his death, the number of feral attacks escalated along the entire length of the Wall. Averil was certain the killer had sent out a signal.

Willard wrapped his great cloak tighter and thought about the irony that had him stationed at Fort Forrestor, named after Eldwin, a man he once believed was a paternal ancestor. [It was all beefshit and it started with you Severne. Why should I believe anything you have ever said to me?]

[On the wall,] Severne said her voice shockingly loud in his head. He hadn't expected an answer. She hadn't spoken to him through the implant since his outburst.

[You said I should keep out of your mind until I was ready to tell you where Kezia is and I have done so despite your persistence in addressing me. You say you trust me not to lie and you are correct. I do not lie, yet you continue to question everything I tell you.]

[It's not wholly my fault. Not telling me when I was mistaken is as good as lying to me.]

Severne did not reply. Did she only break her silence to make that point? No, she had said something before, reminding him why she was silent; Kezia's location. Shit, he couldn't remember. He'd been so shocked by her sudden return he had paid no attention. It would still be there in his mind. He just had to ferret it out. He stole a quick glance at Baxter, who showed no sign of having overheard the exchange. Stop thinking about it and it will come.

He peered over the battlements. The normally expansive view had gone under cloud, providing nothing to focus on. The narrow killing field below, the strip of land between the edge of the Break and base of the Wall often disappeared like this, inducing a sense of vertigo. He blinked rapidly to clear the wet plume chilling his eyes and tried again to peer through the constantly shifting mist.

"We should go Lord," Baxter said. "The end fast approaches."

"So, you keep saying," Willard replied, and in one sense, it was true. Year's end was fast approaching. He would be twenty-four on the first of the New Year. What stupidity, he thought. Nine hundred and ninety-nine years since the Days of Fire, which wiped out the Builders, and here we are still squabbling over the remains.

He sensed however that Baxter meant something else. "What end fast approaches, or should I say whose end? Why does the Goddess ..." He broke off suddenly.

"What's that?" Willard pointed down into the swirling mist.

The Watchers either side, five arm lengths away, raised shields, pointed spears into the mist and passed along his alert.

"It is nothing Lord, you're jumping at shadows," Baxter said. He sounded exasperated.

"How can you be sure it wasn't one of Averil's balloons?"

"There is no wind and they cannot see through mist any better than we can."

Willard rescinded his alert. "I'm staying on the wall until Kezia arrives and we can leave together." On the wall, that's it, that's what she said. [Kezia is on the Wall.]

[Yes Lord.]

Willard stared at Baxter with consternation, then back into the mist, sorting through conflicting doubts. Kezia is here. All I need to do is find her, but with forty-seven miles of wall where do I start? Will anyone let me look? He rejected leaving his post to seek her, considering the Watchers were too thinly spread. It would have to wait until this duty ended. Baxter told him the attacks were a softening-up process for an end-of-year assault, the like of which hadn't happened for hundreds of years. Kingsley's statement about 999 FD being significant now seemed prophetic to Willard.

"So, whose side is Severne on?" he asked animosity animating his voice. "Averil said the ferals are as devoted to the Goddess as we are."

The Watchers on either side of them fell silent.

"Our Lady does not take sides."

"Then why are you up here and not down there?"

"To ensure your survival, nothing less and nothing more."

[Me too,] said Fletcher.

[And Me,] said Dudley.

Willard looked around at the listening Watcher but although he could identify Fletcher and Dudley's thoughts, he had no idea what they looked like.

"Everything we do serves Our Lady's plan to save Nuaith from Typhon," said Baxter as the mist thinned.

"You have the litany well memorised, but all most people hear about is Warriors lopping heads as you did. How did killing that deserter serve her plan?"

Baxter reached over his shoulder and gripped the hilt of *Constant Flame*.

Willard's mouth went dry. *I've gone too far.*

"ferals," shouted Baxter. [you were right Lord.]

The Watchers passed it along through the speaking tubes embedded in the wall. It reached Fort Forrestor in seconds. Within minutes, the entire Wall knew that turret sixty-eight was under attack. Off duty reserves in the next closest forts would turn out, even as Willard spun and stared into the dissipating mist. He could see nothing. The top of a ladder thudded against the wall in front of him. Startled, he jumped back as sword, spear, and pike tips topped the Wall, immediately followed by heads.

As Willard reached for *Severne's Bane,* Baxter leaped into the space between him and an attacking feral. *Constant Flame's* gem glowed red. Power crackled along the edge of the blade as it described a long arc cutting through everything in its path: three fingers from a hand gripping the ladder to his left, through the ladder in front, including the feral standing on it then through the head of the man on his right. The shortened ladder twisted. With a frozen look of surprise, the fingerless feral slipped sideways into the next ladder, and on into the thinning mist.

The upper torso of the middle feral fell away and Willard had a split-second view of white viscera, of heart pumping, of blood spraying. It splattered on his hands.

Of a sudden, there was a clear space around him. No one, feral or Watcher, wanted to be within the reach of a warrior's sword. Willard fell to his knees, involuntarily emptying himself. That he was not alone did not console him. Averil was right. I shouldn't be here, he thought, staggering to his feet. I'm worse than useless. I'm in the way.

The frenzied bellows of the living and the screams of the dying invaded his ears. His nostrils, tainted by the smell of vomit, caught a powerful whiff of the blood on his hands when he went to clear his nose. The mist swirled and Willard saw ferals pouring over the wall, hacking down Watchers. Curiously, the ferals seemed concentrated around Baxter, standing one pace in front of Willard. Fletcher and Dudley, only identifiable by the lightning encrusted blades they wielded held off tight knots, massing either side of him.

It suddenly struck Willard that he was at the centre, was, in fact, the focus of this attack. "No," he screamed at the Goddess. Rage against her boiled in him. He felt his eyes fluttering and saw the world in slow static changes. The gem in Severne's Bane passed quickly through amber and yellow to an intense white. Lightning along the edge of the blade converged, and a beam leapt from the tip as he danced around Baxter and ran at the ferals.

In a red fog, ferals fell before him as he moved towards a pinpoint of intense white light forever just out of reach. He cleared all opposition in front, turned, leapt into a crenel, and stepped up onto a merlon. Skipping along the top of the battlement from one merlon to the next, he rushed back past the three warriors, clearing ferals from the wall and the parapet.

A buzzing sound crept into his awareness and he felt himself slipping into darkness as hands reached out to pull him back to the parapet. He stopped. His muscles ached and his legs trembled and as he struggled to regain control, a figure formed in the light. Kezia. He let *Bane* drop. "Thank Severne. Let's go home."

But Kezia seemed confused. 'Willard? Where are you?'

"Don't go, Kezi," he whispered, reaching out to her, "don't go." As if seen through a distant heat haze, she shimmered, as insubstantial as the mist, and his reaching hand passed through her as easily as it had the Goddess. He was too late. The white light collapsed, the red fog dissipated, and the blackness tried to enfold him. Refusing to give in, he opened his eyes and saw stars. One was moving, Severne's Eye watching him.

A looming face obliterated it. "I'm not Kezia."

At the sadness in Averil's voice, Willard blinked back tears and looked again. Encased in her leather helmet, Averil's head seemed framed in a dark halo, like Kezia's hair, an easy mistake.

A moment later, he remembered the attack and tried to rise.

"Relax brother, you've done enough damage for one day," Averil said. "Take him away Baxter."

• • • •

Willard felt himself lifted and carried. Averil disappeared, shouting orders, reallocating Watchers. He tilted his head back to talk to Baxter, holding the trailing end of the stretcher. "What damage?"

"You demolished the turret and a fair section of the parapet wall. The attack, however, collapsed the moment you started," Baxter said. "By morning, you will be more famous than any of us. The man with the eye-shaped scar is a warrior not to anger."

"I remember ... very little of it," Willard said.

"I used to feel that way after a good drinking session. Then I took the Test."

Baxter grinned, as Dudley and Fletcher, he knew their faces now, manoeuvred the stretcher through blackened walls of stone, the remains of turret two. Willard turned his head to stare at the damage, too tired to rise. Never had he felt so lethargic, so drained; so unable to move. "It isn't my fault, the sword ..."

Baxter cut him off. "Did I not tell you? You are the sword. Controlling the power it draws through you takes considerable effort. You need to learn how to control yourself if you wish to control the sword. If Averil hadn't pulled you off the battlements, which stopped you, *Severne's Bane* would have used you up."

Willard sank back, reflecting that here was something he could believe. Used up was exactly how he felt. What stopped him wasn't Averil, it was Kezia and it wasn't the first time he had felt this strong, almost physical, link to her, but he was at a loss to account for it. Surely, Severne wasn't doing it, yet it felt much the same as communicating with the Goddess.

They passed through Fort Forrestor's corner tower and joined a queue of stretcher borne injured making their way down the Western ramp into the purposeful chaos of recovery. "Where are you taking me?"

"Back to barracks. The sword has drained you, not injured you. All you need is rest. Let the healers help those who need it."

The Fortmaster had allocated Willard and Baxter a barrack close to the bathhouse, and billeted them in the two big end units, normally reserved for officers. Willard had objected, wanting to be treated like a normal recruit.

"I know less than anyone," he had argued.

The Fortmaster would have none of it. "Given you both have named swords, you are, at the very least, officers, and your billets should reflect this."

As they carried Willard down Perimeter Road, he said to Baxter, "I wish Severne had told me about the sword."

"She did. So have I. You don't listen."

"But I had no training," Willard retorted. "There's this too," he said, picking up the talisman. "Why give me both without instruction and before testing me? Who am I, or should I ask, what am I?"

The Restoration Warrior did not answer immediately. He waited until they had reached the barracks and transferred Willard to his bunk, Dudley and Fletcher, looking like ordinary Watchers left with the stretcher. He shut the door before he spoke. "Our Lady's expectation is that you are the interface she seeks."

Willard recalled the term interface was the term the Goddess had used.

"This is the reason behind the extra protection she sent for you. Dudley and Fletcher have never been far away. We have gathered to be on hand when Our Lady comes into her Face."

Willard eyed him with abhorrence, replying glibly, "I'd rather be dead. The only thing worse than knowing bits of your future is to know all of it."

"This is a false assumption, Lord. I took the Test of Faith many years ago, yet I have never known what next would happen to me. I have expectations in the same way you expect Kezia to turn up here. My expectations perhaps seem clairvoyant, but they are no more certain than yours are. They merely draw on greater knowledge. Our apparent prescience gives us a certain mystique. People only remember realised expectations."

Baxter stopped, poised as if he was about to say more, but after inclining his head, his mouth closed and he left quickly.

Willard let the lethargy overtake him. Damn you Severne, he thought as he drifted towards sleep. She had marked him as hers from the start, manipulated his expulsion from home, his narrow escapes, Nelda's revival, the talisman, and the sword named *Severne's Bane*. He would like to blame her for the eye—shaped scar, but the Goddess had been worried it might damage his brain. All the rest however, she designed to push him to the Wall, to Averil, and to the second test, while proving to everyone that to be her Face, was his destiny, regardless of what he wanted.

He should have refused her help, but had not. He had thought he could bargain with her to find Kezia. He knew now, even though Kezia was here Severne would never allow them to meet. He was here for Averil. Severne's plan was more important than the feelings of one obstinate, lovesick candidate.

Chapter 37

"Holy mother, you wouldn't want to have a fear of heights," Kezia exclaimed as she looked down between the merlons.

"I never tire of it. It takes my breath away every time," Ogden said. He was showing Kezia and Howard the vertiginous view from the fighting platform atop Grand Falls' North Gate. The parapets below were awash with activity.

"There's a skirmish at turret sixty-eight. Nothing to worry about it happens daily," Ogden told them.

"But they'll need me when it's over, we should go shortly," Kezia said, taking in the panorama. "What makes that pattern down there? It looks like the layout for a huge tower."

"That's the feral encampment, Healer," Ogden said proudly, as if to say see how many of them we keep at bay, but Kezia, distracted by another voice, was no longer listening. 'Thank Severne you've come. Let's go home.'

Kezia could not believe her ears. Willard had come for her. No, he'd said she had come. She whirled ready for his embrace, worthy or not, if he would have her. He was nowhere in sight, yet his voice had been so distinct, so close that not finding him standing behind her confused her more than his initial remark. "Willard? Where are you?" she said aloud.

"Are you alright Jena?" she heard Howard ask as she desperately tried to catch Willard's fading voice. 'Don't go Kezi,' Willard whispered, 'don't go.' What did he mean, don't go? Don't go where? Besides, I'm not moving.

The young Watcher, who burst upon them to give an excited report to Captain Ogden, alleviated the emptiness she felt after Willard's voice left her.

"... a berserker sir repelled the ferals," he reported. "The warrior with the third eye, the one they call the Man Who Will Be Face. They say he demolished a turret with a single stroke. I was also told to report there were two other warriors involved, but nobody saw them arrive, and now they had vanished."

"You don't want to believe everything you hear," Ogden admonished. He glanced up at Howard as if about to ask something then looked away.

"Get on with your report, Wolfe."

"Yes Sir, Five dead and sixty wounded four critical."

Kezia was instantly attentive. This was what she had come for. "Where will they take the wounded?" she asked.

"From sixty-eight, that would be Fort Forrestor," Ogden said.

Kezia gave a small start, but realising they had named it after Eldwin, the first man to climb the Break, she relaxed again. "How far is it, Captain?" persisted Kezia.

"Fifteen miles from here, passed Midway and Summit," said Howard, drawing a surprised glance from Ogden.

Kezia eager to get there, said, "I'll need a horse."

"Eh."

"I'm here to heal, captain," said Kezia, quietly resting her hand on Ogden's arm. "I can do that best, if go to my patients."

"I was told to take you to the hospital we have here." The captain looked decidedly ill at ease with Kezia trying to change his orders.

"I will return when my work is done."

"But ..."

"Captain, you were told to assist me were you not?"

"Yes Healer."

"Then I need two horses. The warrior knows the way. He will take me there, and return me safely here." Kezia spoke calmly, despite a visceral urgency telling her to go.

"Yes healer."

They scrambled down the short ladder into the Gate Room, Howard first then Kezia, then Ogden. The base of the ladder stood on a landing three feet up the Northern wall. Steps led down from there to the floor of a long, empty room. Kezia surveyed the four arched embrasures on either side, then the doors at each end that led into the Gates' guard towers. Which way, she wondered.

Howard picked one and moved towards it.

"Wrong way, warrior," Ogden shouted from the ladder. "There's no exit from that gate tower."

Howard turned around and Kezia noted he appeared flustered. So she thought, he didn't know, and he's still too young to ask.

The captain led them down a narrow flight of stone steps inside the western tower and out into the busy main street of Grand Falls. En route they had to dodge street vendors hastily packing up, a column of spearmen jogging the other way, and a long dray piled high with hay and drawn by two oxen, heading as they were, for the stables. Every delay chaffed at Kezia. Ogden cleared her requisition for a horse and bid them Goddess speed.

"Please come back healer, I have troubles enough without losing a dignitary."

He waddled off as Kezia urged her horse out of the stables and down the main crossroad, Howard running alongside. They barely made it out through the Western Gate before the Watchers heaved it shut.

She started out at full gallop, leaving Howard behind, but the road that linked the forts, though well used, was uneven and badly maintained, and it soon slowed her down and let Howard catch up. It took two frustrating hours to cover the distance. Fortunately, the gates of Fort Forrestor opened to Howard. Kezia dismounted to show her pass.

"The hospital is that way," the guard said, and pointed. His gaze remained on Howard.

The stench struck Kezia as soon as she was through the door into the open courtyard. She immediately expunged all thoughts other than those for the task. The layout of the hospital was not very different from the one in Port Calder. Nor were the wounded any different from those she had tended in Howard's tent city. Heartrending screams issued from the room to her left, next to the entrance. That would be the surgical ward, she thought, and headed there.

The room was stifling from a brazier in the corner, pumped by a surgical assistant operating the bellows. Cauterising irons on the coals glowed cherry red. A man lay face down on the table, staring at the floor, his teeth clamped around a thick peg, his eyes bulging with fear and pain. Two other surgical assistants held the man by wrists and an ankle. His leg had torn open to the bone in places; a long, ragged slash from the back of the knee to the ankle. The surgeon, in a bloody apron, bent over the man on the table with a large curved knife, shaped specifically for legs. He was readying to amputate above the knee.

"Stop," Kezia screamed, though she doubted she could do anything other than what the surgeon was preparing to do. All her mother's dust was gone.

"Who in the pits are you?"

"Healer Jena," Kezia said, with as much command as she could muster.

The surgeon paused.

The man on the table spat the peg. "Please ... healer ... my leg."

Kezia responded to the appeal in his eyes. "I will if I can," she whispered. She shuddered just looking at the exposed and damaged tissue.

The surgeon grunted, wiped the sweat from his brow with the back of a bloody forearm. "Well, get on with it. Show us your magic. I have other patients waiting."

"I have no magic. I practice healing in the same way you do. Will you help me sow him up?"

"No. Trying to save that leg will kill the patient. Get out of my surgery," he said and raised the curved knife.

Howard stepped to Kezia's side. Quicker than the eye could follow, and despite the cramped conditions, *Firebolt* appeared in his hand. The surgeon again paused, though he seemed far from intimidated.

"What point your threat, Warrior? Who will save these wretches if you kill me?" He looked down at the man's leg, then at Kezia. "One day. If the leg gets no better, it's off."

"I'll hold. You sew," she said, and squeezed the protruding flesh together. The man screamed and fainted. Sweat broke out on Kezia's forehead as she leaned over to get a better grip. A bead fell onto the stitches.

"I hope you're not diseased," the surgeon said, poking the curved needle through the puckered flesh and pulling the thread tight.

He'd done two more stitches before the first popped out, as if rejected. The skin below, though red and swollen, had already knitted. when the adjacent stitch popped, the surgeon stepped back from the table and dropped his needle. He stared at Kezia in awe, traced a quick circle on chest and touched his forehead.

Kezia was no less astounded than the surgeon. *The magic is now in me.* Remembering Howard pouring the last of her mother's dust down her throat, she wiped a finger across her brow and examined the collected moisture. If there were any silvery grains, she couldn't see them. She wiped off the sweat on the less severe, still unstitched upper wound, and held it together. For several seconds nothing happened, then ever so slowly the tear knitted, a diluted response, but useful.

The surgeon sat down heavily, put his head in his hands and wept.

From the stretcher behind her, Kezia heard a waiting casualty say, "Dear Goddess, me next healer."

The commotion this caused spread through the ward at astonishing speed. Even those who had not witnessed the healing relayed it with ferocious hope.

• • • •

The surgeon at Fort Forrestor, having witnessed exactly where the miracle healing properties had come from, had privately joked that her sweat was worth bottling.

Kezia had taken the idea seriously. If the sweat of her brow could cure the sick, she would gladly donate it. Howard commandeered the hot room in the Fort Forrestor's bathhouse and had additional braziers brought in for her. Kezia spent hours at a time closeted in the room, sitting naked in a large bowl. Howard, at the door in the adjacent warm room, took the warrior stance, the tip of *Firebolt* resting in its toe cup. Kezia eventually corked forty-nine tiny bottles before declaring enough. She reckoned by now it must all be out of her; she was exhausted.

She secreted five bottles snugly into the back of the shoulder bag she always carried, leaving forty-four, four for each of the walls eleven forts. After packing forty in a straw-lined box, she left the remain four with the Fort Forrestor's Surgeon saying, "I don't want the source known."

"I can only partially agree, Jena. You are the chosen instrument of Our Lady's mercy. You should get the credit; in her name of course. There's a rumour now spreading that your tears, meaning the tears of Jena, Our Lady's Healer, can restore the most horrendous wounds. Is not this rumour better than the truth?"

What have I done? Kezia wondered, collapsing into a wicker chair. She tried to imagine it being widely known, that her sweat had healing powers. She grimaced at the thought that someone might try to lick her for a cure. The surgeon was right. Best to settle for 'tears' and avoid any speculation about the benefits of her other bodily fluids.

. . . .

Kezia and Howard travelled the entire fifty-mile length of the wall, from Fort Alpha to Wallsend, delivering four of her so-called tears, to each of the eleven forts' hospitals. When they eventually returned to Fort Grand Falls, much to Captain Ogden's relief, who had billeted them in the Fortmaster's residence.

Despite being bone weary, Kezia slept badly and woke while it was still dark. The events of the last few days had drained her both physically and emotionally. Howard didn't help her restless mood when he related what the Watchers were saying.

"Not only does the Man Who Will Be Face stride the wall with warriors, but the Goddess, as Healer Jena, weeps for her people, and her tears heal them," he said, with altogether too much relish.

The Watcher's ready acceptance of such incongruent facts baffled her. How could they think she was the Goddess and have the likely Face on the battlements at the same time? It made little sense. In *Legends,* it's the Face of the Goddess, singular.

"Our Lady thanks you," continued Howard. "Once again, her name is on everyone's lips."

"I don't want her thanks," Kezia spat. "It won't do them any good."

Howard looked troubled. "How can you say that, after all you have achieved?"

"Because tomorrow they'll be back on the wall and probably end up dead."

"We all die."

"So why do I bother healing them? Why doesn't your Goddess do something worthy of praise and stop the bloody war?"

Howard protested. "Our Lady didn't start the war."

"And in three hundred years she has done nothing to end it," Kezia shouted, and stormed out on to the balcony.

The rain was easing as she looked out across the inner courtyard and over the roof of the dining room to the wall. Silhouetted against the sky, she could see Watchers walking the North Wall parapets. One of them could be Averil. In her travels up and down the Wall, she had heard a great deal about her sister, the hard drinking head case, Major Leach. Meeting her was inevitable. Kezia hoped it would not be when they brought in her mangled body.

When the rain stopped, she could hear water trickling along the gutter into the cistern. The sound reminded her of the ancient tune Wesley had taught her. Thinking this might be her last chance, that she too could be dead tomorrow, she had a sudden desire to play. Howard was absent when she went back inside to fetch her flute. Just as well, she thought, I've had enough of the Goddess.

She dragged a chair out onto the balcony and settled herself. Fortunately, her one tune repertoire was not festive. Year's End on the Wall was not a time for celebrations. The first few notes she blew into the hushed expectant fort were tentative. Then, as she relaxed into the rhythm, her playing became confident. The tune enveloped her, carried her away from the cares of her self-imposed mission. She played as she had never played before, a flawless, hauntingly beautiful performance that lingered long after the last note had dissolved into silence.

A light clapping behind her made Kezia turn.

"Well played Jena. The tune is familiar, yet I can't place it." Howard said.

"No point asking me," Kezia replied. "Wesley knew, but I've forgotten what he called it, only that it was ancient beyond measure."

"No matter, we must go."

"Go where?" Kezia asked standing and dragging the chair back inside. "My place is here. Today, of all days."

"Our Lady fears for your safety."

"Really, where has she been the rest of my life, when I lost Willard, and Wesley, and my ... son? What can she possibly want of ..."

"Your child lives," Howard said.

" ... me now? What did you say?"

"Your child lives," he repeated.

Kezia searched his face with an intensity that would have scorched someone less assured than a Restoration Warrior. "I don't believe you," she said, cold fury distorting her features.

"I'm sorry. It had to be kept from you."

"You fucking bastard!"

Kezia swung at Howard so unexpectedly she caught him unprepared. Wesley's flute narrowly missed the hilt of his sword, struck him on the temple and broke, adding to Kezia's rage. She slashed the flute's ragged end across his face. Howard staggered and fell to one knee, blood welling from a long gash. Too enraged to care, Kezia kicked away his supporting leg and he toppled sideways. She lifted the chair over her head and brought it down with a resounding crack.

He lay still, probably hurt, though with a warrior, it was hard to tell. The chair was undamaged, but Howard's face, and his arm where the chair had struck, looked odd, as if independently alive. He opened his eyes.

Kezia reached down and pushed the broken end of the flute against his throat. "You will take me to him, or your Goddess is going to be short one warrior."

"ferals," someone shouted from the courtyard below.

Kezia's eyes flicked to the balcony and Howard's good arm snaked out, gripped her wrist, and squeezed. The flute fell from nerveless fingers.

"Shall we go?" he asked coldly, twisting her arm as he rose to his knees.

Kezia unable to twist away from the pain in her arm, spat in his face.

"Thank you, that will help," Howard said. With his damaged arm, he wiped the spittle from his cheek and rubbed it into the wound at his temple. It stopped weeping.

"This way, Healer." He jerked her arm up her back and propelling her onto the balcony and down the stairs.

Like most Watcher buildings, the Fortmaster's residence was a miniature fort. The rooms looked inwards towards the courtyard. The outside walls, except for the two entrances were featureless. The front entrance led to the main road via a tunnel through the building, with heavy doors on either end. The back door, to which Howard now led Kezia, though less imposing, was equally secure and led directly from the stables into an alley between the residence and the carpenter's workshop.

Four saddled horses waited in the stables. That two would be the scarred pretender for the Face and his warrior, was obvious, and the warriors being prepared to ride showed their desperation to get her and scar-face away. Kezia realised immediately the ferals would win.

"What about my bag?" she said, thinking of the three remaining bottles.

Howard nodded to a black mare reminiscent of *Providence*. Her bag hung on the pommel. His advanced preparations threw her back to their first meeting. How different and sinister his resourcefulness now seemed. Somewhere in our travels, he'd changed into a ... Goddess damned Restoration Warrior.

"The choice is yours," Howard said, letting her wrist go and taking the reins of the brown stallion. "Follow me, or you will never see your son again."

Kezia flexed her fingers and rubbed her upper arm, then snatched the reins of the mare as Howard opened the door and checked the alley, before leading his horse out. Kezia followed.

They mounted quickly, walked their horses to a cross lane between the residence and the hospital, turned into it, and rode away from the commotion. After crossing a busy road at the end of the lane, they entered an even smaller alley between back-to-back barracks. Kezia held her nose. Those in a hurry, or just too lazy, obviously used the place as a night latrine. The alley brought them to the perimeter road a few yards short of the rarely used western gate. The Watchers had already closed it.

Chapter 38

As the rain stopped, a mournful sound floated up from the Fort to Willard's new station. Dudley, under instruction from either the Goddess or Baxter, had prevailed on the Watchmaster General to have him transferred to Grand Falls under Averil's command.

The Watchers were on full alert, knowing the ferals would begin at first light. Their increasingly ferocious attacks in the days leading up to new year's day, the first of bud 1000 FD, were merely a prelude. Unreclaimed bodies littered the killing ground, the narrow strip of land between the base of the wall and the edge of the Break.

In the predawn, as Willard was about to climb up onto North Gate's archer platform to watch the sunrise, Averil arrived, shaking her head at his foot on the ladder.

"Don't be an idiot. You get in my archer's way, and someone will get killed, probably you. Severne might have plans for you, but right from the start, she warned me she can't control everything."

Baxter agreed. "Averil is right, we should go Lord."

"Not until Kezia arrives."

"Too late," Averil said, "If she isn't already here, we will stop her at Walfort." Peering over her helmet's cheek flaps at Willard, she stared pointedly at the hilt of *Severne's Bane* and then at the talisman around his neck.

"Those won't save you. Take the test, or give them back."

Willard averted his gaze.

Averil grunted in disgust. "Despite everything that has happened, you haven't changed." As she left to do last-minute checks on the rest of her command, she had one last jab at him.

"For Goddess's sake, Willard, you're twenty-four. Grow up. Make a decision."

That struck at his deepest fear, whether to take the test. Kezia had been saying she wouldn't marry him until he took it, believing he would fail and be a server. Everyone else, including himself had expected him to make warrior and warriors didn't marry. A no-win situation, he had studiously avoided. On the day she left, Kezia recanted and said, 'come with me, I won't make you take the test.' As his life unravelled after she'd gone, he began wishing he'd taken her offer. He hoped she still felt the same when he explained that having the implant wasn't the test.

The mournful dirge from inside the fort died away with a long, low note, and although he didn't know the tune, Willard recognised the sheer artistry of the player.

"Who is that?" Willard asked Baxter

"Healer Jena," said Baxter, "The one the Wall talks about when not talking about you."

"Is she another of your lady's protégés?"

"I know only what I hear from the Watchers."

"Severne doesn't keep you informed?"

"As I have said many times Lord, if I need to know ..."

"You will be told," Willard completed for him. "She plays beautifully. I would like to meet her when this is over, though not in her professional capacity," he joked.

The rain stopped. Light spread across the eastern horizon. The sun would soon rise from the Dividing Sea. Averil re-joined them, angry as usual. She looked from Willard to Baxter as she lifted her helmet to scratch at her blonde stubble.

"I have to say, Baxter, I think your Goddess is as thick as two short planks."

"Why is that?" Baxter asked, without rancour.

Averil, shivering in the cold, pointed at Willard. "He's still here, for one. Why would she thrust her potential Face into a bloodbath, one she must know we will lose? I know it here," she said, tapping her head, "and I feel it here," she patted her stomach. "Our records show that despite considerable losses every year, the ferals start from a higher position with a larger force."

For generations, beginning with the natural caves and ledges, the ferals had constructed a warren of staging posts in the escarpment. Huge spaces hewn out of the solid rock, connected with tunnels, ladders, steps, platforms, and ramps, that they extended each campaign. The Watchers joked that the only way the Wall would fall was into a feral excavation.

Averil continued her rant. "The numbers poised just below already exceed the entire compliment on the Wall and that's piddling compared to those massed down there. All they need is to establish a foothold her and they be all over the island."

The pearly grey light gave way to the rising sun. Willard gazed down at the vast feral encampment a mile below, wondering why there was no movement of troops toward the wall.

Averil, still fuming, clenched and unclenched her fists. "Somehow, those balloons will be a big part of this. I know it as sure as I'm standing here, but no one believes me." She shot a glance at Willard and drew a deep breath. "Bloody Aldus backed Heutte's conviction that they don't have enough b ..."

Suddenly, she leant out and stared down. "Severne's tits, there's one in every tent." With a controlled scream, she drove her fist into a crenel. A stone chip flaked off where she hit the block. Willard and Baxter jumped in unison as she turned on them, blood seeping from her knuckles.

"Bloody Fools! I'm surrounded by fools, and you two are the worst. Look at their camp."

Willard perplexed, said. "There are a few red tents now."

"Balloons," Baxter said quietly, holding up a moistened finger to the morning breeze.

Looking again, Willard saw new red dots spring into existence, like mushrooms after rain. "They're multiplying," he blurted.

"Sumner played me," Averil said, and Willard heard a hint of admiration in her tone. "I was down there with them and never saw a thing. There was no balloon in my tent, probably not in my Circle. We didn't escape, the bastards let us go," Averil cursed. "I was Aldus's ticket here."

"They're on the move," Baxter added.

"Tits," Averil said, looking down, then immediately screamed "ferals," into the nearest pipe,

Word spread like wildfire through the wall. The Watchers on standby jumped to the parapets. The rest, although knowing this would be the day, were still at the many duties that kept the Wall running. They poured out of barracks, workshops, and dining halls, but the call to arms left them frustrated. There was no attack to fend off, only the distant red dots; moving, growing.

Along the length of the wall, the Watchers peered down from the heights, impressed by the spectacle. From similar but smaller camps below each of the eleven forts, red balloons rose slowly towards them in the cold light air. Hundreds had already doubled in size. More were just starting out.

A spectacle of mesmerising beauty thought Willard as he tried to estimate their number and waited on Averil's orders.

Averil paced up and down the parapet constantly testing the wind, looking over the parapet at the rising threat, then to the south behind the Wall.

"Now will you come away, Lord," Baxter said, "the Wall will fall. The future is Federal."

"It can't fall. It has stood here for three hundred years. We can't just give up. We have to fight them off." Willard could not believe what he heard himself say. One berserk rage with a Goddess named sword does not a warrior make. Yet how will Kezia and I get our lives back, if the ferals overrun us?

Baxter patiently waited on Willard. Willard waited on Averil. Kezia was still missing and their future was about to fall to invaders. Fight or flight? Ironically, that decision had passed to someone he thought had the least influence on his life, Averil. He stared at her, willing her to make a stand.

• • • •

"Baxter's right," Averil said. "The Forts can't hold." She pointed at the rising red cloud. "once that lot float over the Wall, it's over. We'll be fighting on two fronts, yet protecting nothing but the wall itself."

"What do you plan on doing?" Willard asked.

Averil turned to the young Watcher she had made her aide. "Wolfe, I want you to take a very important message to the Watchmaster General. Tell her the Wall has fallen."

"But ..." Wolfe stammered, glancing wildly around in obvious confusion. The Wall was not even under attack.

Averil took him to the parapet showed him the dots and explained that every one of them was a floating craft carrying two ferals. Some had grown big enough to obscure parts of the feral camp. Smaller red dots were filling the gaps and still smaller ones were just lifting off.

"Look and remember. By the time you get to Walfort, the Wall will be theirs," Averil said quietly. "Tell her all you've seen, and make her believe it. Now go. Ride fast."

Wolfe turned and ran.

After dispatching Wolfe, she issued orders to pull all but the archers off the fifty-mile section of Wall she controlled, and sent the same message to the other forts. She asked for volunteers and gave strict instructions to them to decamp at the first sign of a scaling ladder and retreat up the Pointing Finger isthmus to Canalbridge.

Willard was outright defiant when she ordered Baxter to take him away.

"You should come with us," Baxter said. "Gardner won't get here in time."

Averil shook her head. "He's the main man. I'm a part of the backup plan. There are plenty more like me."

"We should all go or all stay," Willard said.

"No. I want archers for the balloons. If our resistance looks real, it might slow down those waiting in the caves below." She was shouting now to cover the new and unsettling feelings she had for him.

"But look what I ..."

"I don't need uncontrolled mayhem," she interrupted in a quieter voice. "You're as much a danger to us as you are to them," Averil said and reason prevailed, where shouting had not.

"I'm sorry," he said, sounding hurt. "You're right, of course. I'm in the way."

He looks so dejected, thought Averil, as he turned to go. It flashed through her mind she might never see him again. She strode over, pulled him around and kissed him full on the mouth. "Happy birthday Will, I'll see you in Canalbridge."

She turned to Baxter. "Get him out of here."

She strode back to the parapet, wondering why in Severne's name did I do that? Of course I'll see him again. We need to have offspring. She laughed raucously before more pressing concerns occupied her mind.

· · · ·

Averil's kiss dazed Willard. As Kezia's had done a year ago, Averil's lingered on his lips. It was far from sisterly even for his birthday, and as he dwelt on what might be behind it, Baxter pulled him to the ladder, urging him down into the Gate Room. "Hurry Lord, the main assault is imminent."

Willard paused as his eyes came level with the platform, just before he lost sight of Averil, and wondered if she was now following Severne's plan for them, or was he reading too much into it. Averil did not look around. She stood at the Wall barking orders and the Watchers sprinted to do her bidding. Inanely, all he could think of was she had lovely legs.

"This way Lord," Baxter said.

He led Willard down and out of the Gatehouse, straight up the main road between the north and south Gates, past the harness workshops, the granary, and headquarters to the Fortmaster's residence. Willard glanced down the alley towards the hospital as they passed the residence and saw two riders at the other end. A quick glance only, but something about them piqued his senses. When he stepped back for a second look, the riders had gone. He recognised what had grabbed his attention when he turned back and saw the gem in Baxter's sword. One rider carried a named sword. A warrior riding? He supposed the other rider must be the healer, Jena.

Willard ran to catch up to Baxter as the warrior disappeared into the courtyard of Fortmaster's residence. "What are you doing?" Willard whispered.

"Getting horses," Baxter said, letting himself into the Watchmaster's stables. Inside, two horses stood saddled, ready.

"But Warriors don't ride," Willard said despite what he had just seen.

"Except as Our Lady needs," Baxter replied, handing one set of reins to Willard.

What more will Severne do to get what she wants?

[Whatever it takes, Willard.]

Her reply made Willard miss the stirrup and he stumbled against the horse.

[Steady,] Baxter said into his mind as he led his horse out into the narrow alley they had passed earlier.

[You listened in,] Willard said, but by then Baxter had ridden into the Watcher traffic streaming out through the south gate. Willard hastily followed.

Chapter 39

The dawn was cloudless and cool from the light breeze. A beautiful day, too lovely for this shit, thought Averil. "Fire," she shouted, dropping her upraised hand.

A host of flaming arrows left smoking trails across the sky, trying to puncture the terrifying black face painted on the side of a huge red balloon. Most glanced off. Those that hit the baskets underneath were more successful. Balloons with burning baskets often leapt higher, as their occupants took a desperate, futile gamble, and jumped for the Wall.

"Forget the balloons. Aim at the ferals," Averil yelled.

A flash in her peripheral vision had her looking around for Gardner. She was about to dismiss the idea of a protected space around her when another flash occurred on the opposite side. Not possible, she thought. There weren't enough Warriors to waste two protecting her.

Disquiet from another source nibbled at her like a rat in a grain bin. The ferals hadn't yet launched an attack on the wall. Sumner should have pressed the advantage of his balloons. Is he waiting for some of them to land and open the gates? It made sense, in an odd sort of way. It would save quite a few lives.

Averil scanned the balloon dotted sky and again dropped her hand. Arrows whooshed passed her as a second line of archers fired at the drifting targets, while the first re-nocked

"Fire at will." she said and for the umpteenth time in the last half hour, she scanned the edge of the Break. Another disquiet. All the unclaimed bodies from the last skirmish in the killing ground, arms, and legs akimbo, tangled, unmoving, in some places three deep. Why had they left their dead this time? She guessed that with their new flying craft they sensed victory; burials could wait.

She had ordered the turrets under her direct control abandoned, leaving only a signaller and four archers, with multiple quivers, in each milepost. They would pass her strategy along, but it was up to each Watcher Major to make their own decisions. Her retreating captains had instructions to form a cordon about five miles behind the wall to attack the descending balloons, then cut and run to Canalbridge before the ferals overwhelmed them. She hoped her reputation might cause the other commanders to follow her lead.

Arrows flew around Averil continuously, well targeted, but now fewer, showing the archers were running low; almost time to go.

Without doubt, the Watchmaster General would have canal's lock-gates unhinged and the bridge destroyed, to create a second line of defence. The bridge might be a problem. It was Builder. Once the ferals brought up their balloons, the Canalbridge defence would be as futile as her defence here; the outcome was inevitable. Only the height of the Barriers offered any hope of stopping them. We might just hold the East Coast, if we can hold Long Gully Pass, and the Coastwatch can hold the Dividing Sea.

She looked up. Though no balloon was close enough to threaten her position, they filled the sky, bumping into each other and the wall, even drifting as she had into the roaring falls. Some were now crossing the battlements. One balloon, rising too rapidly under another, ripped its basket. Seconds later, the basket above ignited and burnt through, dropping its brazier into the one below. The flaming tatters spiralled through the upcoming fleet, collecting any that couldn't get out their way.

Nice to see they have problems.

As she had predicted, each balloon carried two ferals. Often one would dangle beneath the basket, sword in hand, as Sumner had done. If the balloon were low enough when they crossed the wall, the hanging feral would let go, and sword swinging, plummet into the archers on the parapet. It took fine judgment and a lot of courage.

Some lacked judgement. They jumped too soon or too late. Averil estimated that between accidents and those the defender killed, the attackers were losing about a quarter of their aerial soldiers. It still left hundreds sailing overhead completely out of reach, landing a long way behind the wall.

Ferals throwing out the balloon's brazier as they passed over was an unanticipated disaster. Hot coals, reigniting as they fell, rained down on the fort. The wooden shingle rooves of the barracks and stables erupted in geysers of flame, and the unburdened balloons lifted away to land further inland than she had counted on. Averil again felt a surge of hate for the ferals when she saw one of her archers run off the parapet in flames.

Grand Falls was now well alight, yet there was still no assault from below. If only the Restoration Warriors would take part, thought Averil, their named swords could clear the balloons from the sky before they came anywhere near the Wall. By not taking sides, Severne not only risked me, but has ensured a feral victory.

A balloon poked its head over the rim of the escarpment directly in front of her, rising rapidly. The strengthening breeze pressed it and its basket against the escarpment.

She yelled at her archers. "Leave it, find another target."

Averil waited in anticipation as the Balloon came free and cleared the edge. Then the breeze again pushed the basket against the wall. Ropes snagged on the battlements and the wind pushed the huge canopy down towards Averil. She slashed with her sword, tearing a great rent across the fabric. Hot air gushed into her face. The balloon collapsed and the basket fell onto the bodies below.

Averil stared in disbelief as bodies scrambled out of the way. Then another movement grabbed her attention. Right below her, on her side of the wall, the thick edge of the North Gate edged into view. Abruptly, everything that had nibbled at her became clear.

"You bloody fool," Averil screamed at herself. Overnight, their troops had swapped places with their dead, knowing the gates would open, knowing they wouldn't have to scale the walls.

The killing ground erupted with life and surged towards the opening North Gate. Averil signalled a waiting Watcher to lower the Grand Falls pennant. The prearranged signal, repeated by the Mileposts on either side, rippled away down the Wall. It was now a matter of survival. Flee and reform at Canalbridge.

There was nothing left for Averil to do. She took a quick final look around at her first, and probably last, command. The afternoon light painted a lurid picture of shambles. Quirks of wind strength had placed ferals in varied concentrations all over the landscape. Still, there were large gaps. It would be blind fate, or dumb luck, (Averil couldn't decide which) whether the fleeing Watchers escaped, or found ferals blocking their line of retreat.

Then the wind changed. Those balloons still aloft drifted the other way. Choking smoke from the burning barracks washed back across the compound.

"Too late Severne," Averil said as she climbed down the ladder into the relative quiet of the gatehouse's first floor. Her fate was now in the hands of the Goddess. She felt remarkably calm about it, certain now Severne would keep her safe, at least until she and Willard produced 'offspring'.

The eastern Guard Tower of North Gate was empty. The double doors, at either end of the Room, stood open. She could

see right through the other Guard Tower all the way to the
Fort's corner turret. The westering sun threw a long orange strip
through the open doors, highlighting in sharp relief the two
black slots in the floor. Murder holes. I could dispatch a few
bloody ferals if I had a bow. Then another thought occurred to
her. Averil walked over to the nearest slot, lay flat on the cold
stone floor, and put her eye to the hole.

Helmeted heads poured through the arched portal below,
giving her a sense of foreboding the like of which she had never
experienced and decried in others. Whatever her personal fate,
their Island was irrevocably feral.

Two of the mass below stood apart from the incoming
stream. One feral, one Watcher. The feral had just handed a
bag to the man in the Watcher Captain's uniform; Kingsley's
uniform.

"Fucking traitor," Averil screamed.

Two heads swivelled up and shocked Averil. Stone Ethyl she
might have expected. Aldus she should have, but hadn't.

• • • •

Kezia fumed over Howard's duplicity. The damned Goddess had
her son, and this excuse for a warrior had let her believe he was
dead, until it suited his Goddess. She followed him in hope, as
he made his way towards the twin stone arches of the West Gate.
The Watchers had bricked up the left-hand portal of the edifice
years ago, for reasons known only to themselves.

The single spearman standing in the remaining portal near
the centre of the wooden doors shuffled his feet as they
approached.

"Open the gate," Howard said.

"No offence, Warrior, but I can't do that during an attack.
Please, try the south gate. It's always closed last."

"Ordinarily true, but these are extraordinary times. I am escorting healer Jena to Walfort."

The spearman swallowed. Kezia could see him working out his chances, looking from her to *Firebolt* and then glancing around for someone to ask. A squad of Watchers passed at the double as if they were not there.

Organised panic, thought Kezia.

Reluctantly the spearman unlocked the bar and tilted it to vertical, then laying his spear against the pillar pushed.

The big inner door swung back on groaning hinges enough to admit the riders into no-man's-land, trapped inside the wall, between gates, neither in nor out of the fort, flanked by the remaining guardhouse, and under the murder holes.

As the spearman unbolted the outer door, a Watcher Captain waddled through the inner door. "What are you doing, Pike?"

Pike cringed as he turned. "Following orders, Captain."

Kezia eyed Howard as he turned his horse to face the captain and backed it up to the outer door. For someone who shunned riding, he did it expertly. Howard held her gaze a moment, a warning furrow appearing between his eyes, before he directed his attention to the captain. Kezia clamped her mouth shut.

"We are leaving, Captain Ogden."

"Not during an attack, surely Warrior. Major Leach hasn't given the word. Lock that gate, Pike."

The hissing sound of *Firebolt* slipping from its scabbard underscored Captain Ogden's remark. He stepped back. Kezia squeezed her eyes shut.

"Open the gate or you won't have one."

A sparking crackle followed by the smell of burning wood, and the horse under Kezia moved. She opened her eyes as they rode out past a still smouldering furrow across the old planking.

Glancing back, she saw Captain Ogden and spearman Pike frantically pushing the gate closed. What are they scared of now, Kezia wondered, they still have their heads? A moment later, a chill shadow enveloped her and she looked up into a frightening black face painted on a red balloon passing overhead.

A bolt of lightning ripped from the end of Howard's sword and the basket underneath burst into flame. A feral in the basket scrabbled up the webbing. Another feral hanging from a knotted rope underneath dropped to the ground. The balloon rose with a jerk, dislodging the feral in the rigging. Arms and legs windmilling he landed on his back with a thud and lay still. The first feral rose and favouring her right leg, barred their way, her short sword held in a two-handed grip. Howard's sword flashed once as he passed. Kezia, seeing the feral sink to her knees, the top half of her sword gone, looked away.

Howard surveyed the area with what looked like satisfaction, as if this had been an exercise in problem solving. Kezia gagged, sickened as much by Howard's attitude as the acts themselves. Swallowing bile, she rode on, not looking at him or the bodies, looking to the future as Howard retook the lead. You fucking bastard, she thought, her eyes narrow slits of hate focussed on the broad back of the young warrior. Yet she followed without a word, knowing she would do so for as long as he held before her the prospect of finding her son.

They rode alongside the Grand Falls wall, as more balloons sailed up from behind, their shadows dotting the road, some so high Kezia could barely make out the occupants; an awesome sight. Despite their surprising number, she and Howard encountered only ragged columns of Watchers streaming south at the trot.

As they clattered across a small bridge over the outflow from the Mill, Kezia at last understood that if she wanted to get son away from the Goddess, she had to become a lot smarter and a lot less ignorant. The knowledge the Warriors had was the real key to their power.

Suppressing her loathing, Kezia drew alongside Howard. "What are they doing?" she snapped, pointing at the Watchers.

"Retreating," answered Howard.

"Why? The attack just started," Kezia said.

"Someone with brains and courage saw it couldn't stand and decided they could save as more by retreating than making a stand."

Kezia was almost sorry she'd asked. Looking around at the fleeing Watchers, she had to believe it. But if the ferals win, what then for my son and me?

Howard paused on a crest at the southwest corner of the fort. Extending from the fort's northwest corner, the wall turned to follow the bank of the Falls River. From here, the road descended, skirting the Mill, and joining the main road from South Gate, which ran across a long-arched viaduct. Already a bottleneck, the viaduct had jammed with people. Incredibly, it seemed both crowds wanted to be on the opposite bank. At twelve feet wide, two-way traffic across the bridge should have been easy, but when the demon faced red balloons flew overhead, shooting arrows, dropping rocks, and sometimes fire from the sky, even veteran Watchers pushed people out of their way.

Kezia stared in horror as a body fell from the viaduct and made a tiny splash below. The raging flow immediately swept the body past her, towards the thundering falls.

"We can't cross there," Howard said, and turned against the flow of Watchers from the South Gate. A short time later, as they left the road, and again turned south, he asked. "How well do you ride?"

"Well enough."

Howard pointed to a thin green line ahead. "Good, when the way is clear, we have to jump the Mill diversion."

"Why cross it at all, if we're going to Walfort?"

"What gave you that idea?"

"It's what you told the spearman at the Gate."

"In case he lives to repeat it. Our Lady does not want your whereabouts known."

Your Goddess is not sane, thought Kezia. She ruined the life I had planned, recreated me as Jena, and now it seems she wants to bury me. Clearly, recovering her son, even if it was possible, would not be easy. She would have to keep close to Howard and bide her time. Willard was right not to take the Test. The Goddess is not worthy of our trust.

"Now!" Howard shouted, and slapping the rump of her horse, urged his own into a gallop.

The green line across their path expanded as they raced across the Watcher grazing lands. Kezia could see the occasional flash of light as the diverted water ran its channel towards the mill. The breadth of the channel widened. Too wide, she thought. We'll never make it, but by then it was too late to stop. Too scared to close her eyes, Kezia leaned into the gallop and hoped the horse knew how to jump.

• • • •

Willard and Baxter attached themselves to the rear of a cavalry unit, exiting Grand Falls. When the cavalry turned east along the service road, they dropped away unnoticed and turned south. Grand Falls soon diminished behind them as they sped away down the Walfort road towards Midway Bridge.

With no conscious decision, Willard had again lost control of his life. He had only just learned Kezia was here when the balloons rose. He could see no other course now but to follow Baxter and hope she was safely away.

"Where are you taking me?" he asked.

"To safety," said Baxter, his voice sounding tired.

"Where?" Willard demanded, trying to reassert himself.

Baxter inclined his head. "Canalbridge," he said and his tone suggested an unspoken 'where else?' as if the answer was obvious.

It made sense thought Willard, recalling Averil's parting words, 'I'll see you in Canalbridge'. What surprised him, given Severne's stated goal, was her putting them both in danger.

[For the Test of Faith, I need candidates of character,] Severne whispered.

It shook Willard to discover his control had slipped. Severne's long absences had encouraged him to relax. Now that he had her ear, he may as well pursue his question.

[Averil's still there. You won't get our offspring if they kill her.]

[The risk is slight. I have Warriors protecting my interests.]

[Dudley and Fletcher,] he guessed.

[Yes Lord,] said Baxter.

[Take the Test and I'll keep you informed,] Severne added before her presence lifted from his mind.

Their road from Grand Falls joined the Fort Midway road at a bridge. Willard was halfway across when faint cries reached him. He pulled his horse around and rode back to the entrance. Crowding the sky above the scrubby forest was the leading wave of balloons. The cries came from a loose assembly of refugees from the settlement outside the fort, now dispersing in panic, away from the Grand Falls Road, abandoning everything in their haste to get out from under a descending balloon. A long way down the Midway Road Willard saw a column of dark blue uniforms break into a run. They would arrive far too late.

"Baxter, you have to do something," Willard shouted, his voice echoing in the bridge cover.

Silhouetted against the light at the far end, the warrior halted. "About what?" he shouted back.

"That! Willard said," stabbing the air, but the bridge structure hid the problem from the Warrior. The floating ferals fired indiscriminately into the crowd below. People dropped like dead leaves, easy targets for bowmen, nocking and firing as fast as they could, killing men, women, and children.

Willard dug in his heels, his hand reaching over his shoulder as he pelted down the Grand Falls Road towards the slowly drifting behemoth. His rage at the slaughter of unarmed children focussed on the feral archers. The gem in *Bane's* hilt glowed white. Blue fire crackled along the edge, exploded from the tip in a jagged beam, aimed as best he could from the galloping horse.

The balloon suddenly expanded and burst. The huge canopy shrivelled to tattered ribbon as the basket plummeted to the ground, smashing on impact spilling its occupants. One feral had staggered to his feet when a stone hit him in the head. The refugees, sensing a turn of events surged back with an animal growl.

By the time Willard arrived, both ferals were dead, battered beyond recognition by blunt instruments. He dismounted in a field of carnage, bodies everywhere, bristling with arrows. Yet not everyone sporting an arrow was dead. Many had taken hits on their arms or legs. One got hit in the backside as he lay in the ditch trying to hide. If only Kezia was here, she would know what to do.

"Are you all right, Lord?" asked Baxter, catching up.

"I'm fine," Willard said as he sheathed *Bane*. He felt elated to have brought down the balloon, but sickened by the intended victim's bloody revenge.

"That was a remarkable performance," Baxter said seemingly in awe of him. "It took me weeks of constant training to learn that degree of control."

"But I came too late."

"Better late than not at all Lord," said a voice.

Willard turned as the white bearded owner of the voice straightened. "You could have left us Lord, and they," he spat on the feral body, "would have killed us all."

Willard was about to protest when 'white beard' must have spotted the talisman hanging at Willard's neck, for he looked quickly at Willard's head.

"The Man Who Will Be Face," he shouted to the others and the cry spread like a grass fire. Refugees prostrated themselves before him, as did their white bearded spokesperson. "Thank you, Lord, thank you. Our Lady be with you," he said, bowing low.

"Get up," Willard commanded. "I am not the Face, I'm ..." he stopped embarrassed as much by his inability to explain as by their worshipful attitude.

"We should go, Lord," Baxter said, once more solicitous. [Your destiny lies elsewhere.] He tapped Willard on the shoulder and pointed. At various altitudes, more balloons drifted into view.

"How can we leave them?"

The old man spoke up. "Go Lord, they caught us unawares this time. It will not happen again and next time we will shoot back. We now have two bows, and," he added, with a grimace, "plenty of arrows."

Chapter 40

Kezia and Howard sped south. Behind them, the azure sky continued to fill with the giant red balloons, painted with evil grinning black faces. A few had drifted ahead.

Kezia felt flushed with excitement after jumping the diversion. She had let the horse have its head, had felt the power under her as muscles bunched and released, the heart stopping silence as they soared over the water and the thundering crash as they landed at the gallop. Riding full tilt was more to her liking than plodding along narrow trails in Severne's Wood. Once I have my son back, we'll move to the plains.

Howard had stayed well to the west of the main road. Despite hating him, she knew he was right to do so. As they neared the midway bridge, fleeing people packed the road. Hundreds were on foot or pushing handcarts. A few drove drays, or wagons. Even less rode as they did. A long way behind them, a column of deep blue uniforms on foot came at the run, a full retreat.

Periodically, she glanced up to watch the balloons. Despite the menace they represented, she could not help but admire the way they sailed majestically through the air. Several drifted slowly their way. One descending on the road. Then she noticed the group of refugees underneath it scatter. One fell, then another, then two more.

"They're firing on them," Kezia screamed at Howard, reining her horse to a stop. She looked back at the column of Watchers, closing the gap but too far away to be any help. Peripherally, she picked up movement at the covered bridge. A rider headed full speed towards the group, a sparkling blade held aloft, pointed towards the balloon. Kezia heard his cry even at this distance.

Lightning erupted from the sword. The balloon expanded and burst. The remains plummeted to the road.

Kezia stood in the stirrups and cheered. "See that? A named sword can do more than kill," she said, conveniently forgetting Liam's revival.

"The ferals survived then?"

"I have to help."

"Not if you wish to see your child."

Kezia hesitated, stared malevolently at the man/boy who had more than once saved her life. Then, without a word, she urged her horse towards the road.

The sword wielder and another warrior rode away as Kezia and Howard approached. "I thought you travelled alone," Kezia said.

"Times have changed."

You certainly have, thought Kezia. She dismounted next to a woman showing a mixture of raw flesh and blackened skin on her thighs. Burning coals had set her dress alight and a well-meaning friend had peeled back the dress material burnt on to her skin and laid the flesh bare. Two women held her while a third fanned her face.

As Kezia unpacked one of the small bottles from her kit, a bent figure with a white beard came towards them. He walked slowly, as if the universe was a burden on his shoulders. He looked up at Howard from under bushy white brows.

"This is healer Jena," Howard said as Kezia put her finger on the top of the bottle and tipped it up, then dripped a little onto the woman's exposed flesh.

"Truly Our Lady has blessed us this day," he said, "to be saved by the Man Who Will Be Face, and then have our wounded treated by her Healer is nothing short of miraculous. I am Willard," he said, startling Kezia. Until now, she hadn't known

Willard as a name was so common. "My people call me old Will, despite my youth."

Concentrating on the woman's wound, Kezia wondered what had happened to young Willard, the boy acolyte she had met briefly in ... in ... she could not remember. It was nearly a year ago, another life.

"Bless you Healer, bless you," the woman said obviously out of pain. Kezia smiled. The burnt skin had stopped weeping and the raw flesh underneath was lightning. She could have had the same effect by spitting on the wound, but that would only fuel the stories. As spiting on Howard had shown, she hadn't yet exhausted her internal supply. She moved on to the next patient, leaving the woman talking to her friends in hushed tones. "Look at my leg. This is no ordinary healing. It's a miracle."

Kezia refused to let Howard hurry her, but eventually there was nothing more she could do and they resumed their journey crossing through the Midway Bridge in the wake of the two Warriors.

At the next junction, Howard took the smaller track, telling Kezia it was a shortcut, unsuitable for carts. She followed blindly, confused by her 'miracle' healings. On one hand, the Goddess was an uncaring, child-snatching tyrant, manipulating people towards some end that only she understood. On the other, she was a caring and powerful benefactor, who had enhanced Kezia's natural inclinations by giving her a special healing gift. Or did she? My healings only started after Howard poured the last of Mother's dust down my throat. Before that, it was always and only the dust. Mother got the dust from the Builder artefact buried under her potting shed. My gift really comes from the Builders.

When Kezia looked up again, they were climbing through an open pine forest and she had no idea where she was.

"Where are we headed?" she asked.

"Back the way we came, Carrier Point then Java."

"My son is there?"

"No."

"Where then?" asked Kezia, meaning 'where is my son?' Howard's answer, 'For the moment we stay put in Java,' made her see the ambiguity of her question. His answer also told her the Goddess intended to keep her in Java indefinitely. She husbanded the ambiguity. He didn't know she knew his intent. You worship a cruel Goddess, she thought to his back. I must warn Willard not to take the Test. She choked back bitter laughter at that thought. In their last days together, she had pestered, cajoled and all but threatened him into taking it. What a fool I was. I'll find my son on my own, she thought, and an obvious place to start would be where he was born.

"How long before we get to Carrier Point?" she asked.

"Three days."

"Can we make it in two? I want to get back before the ferals wreck all the towers," Kezia said, and inwardly cursed. She had just made it plain she was not about to stay in Java, which had no tower.

From Howard's answer, however, he may have been listening elsewhere and not heard her reason.

"We can try," he said affably, with a characteristic tilt of the head. He looked relieved that she had spoken to him without rancour.

Kezia followed thoughtfully. It had occurred to her she could get what she wanted, if first, she worked out what Severne wanted, then made their goals coincide. The trick was finding out what the Goddess wanted. She wants me off the peninsula. Willard must be here.

• • • •

Averil rolled onto her back and stared up at the beams supporting the fighting platform. Money had changed hands, payment for treachery and murder. Aldus Forrestor, her erstwhile brother-in-law, had sold out to the ferals, had killed Kingsley for his uniform. Why did no one look for him? Why didn't I insist on it? Willard.

Heart pounding, she wondered if either knew who witnessed the deal. They have only seen an eye, thought Averil, and heard my voice. I should have kept my mouth shut. With Stone Ethyl on the scent, Averil doubted she would live to tell this tale. Get me out of this one Severne.

As she contemplated capture, she could hear ferals pounding up the stairs in the adjacent guard tower. She sprang to her feet looking for an out, but there was nowhere to go. The long gate-room that straddled the portals ran between doors that led into the guard towers and then out onto the parapets. With ferals at all exits, they had her trapped. She looked at the hatches in the other half of the gate room over the bricked-up gatehouse, now used for grain storage, the murder holes plugged, and the hatches unopened in years. Quickly she knelt and tried each one not surprised they were all stuck fast.

Stone Ethyl was the first to top the stairs. Averil gave a feral war cry and charged down the gate room. Ethyl hesitated. Was it because Averil appeared unarmed, or because they had ridden together, or simply because she had not expected Averil to charge? At the last moment, Averil grabbed the lintel, swung her feet through the arch and kicked Ethyl in the chest, knocking her backwards into those behind her, pushing them all down the stairs. Averil dropped to the floor, pulled the doors closed, and slammed the bar in place. I should have done that first. "Idiot," she berated herself.

She went back to the first hatch and ran her knife around the edges while keeping her eye on the open doors at the other end of the gate room. Wiser to have closed them too before trying to get the hatch open, but as always it was too late. She could hear them on the distant stairs as she grabbed hold of the ring and heaved. The hatch lid moved slightly. At least it no one had locked it, but the effort made her ears ring. She thought at first it was her own pounding heart, except it seemed to come from behind. She turned.

The ferals were battering at the door right behind her. She had time for only one more try. She carefully placed her feet, squatted, gripped the ring with both hands, straightened her back and arms, took a deep breath and pushed up with her legs. With a crack, the lid came free. Her fingers jammed in the ring and the edge of the hatch slammed into her wrists. She let go, and fell back, biting down on a cry of pain and shame. She should have been on the hinge side.

The hatch lid stood half way to vertical, jammed, inviting. No time to stop now, Averil thought and slammed it vertical with her feet. Not bothering to get up and mentally preparing for what might be a long drop, she pushed with her damaged hands, and dropped feet first, into the gloom. Her feet struck the top bag of the stacked grain three feet down, disturbing a colony of rats. Her back hit the edge of the hole, bringing new pain that overwhelmed those in her wrist and fingers.

Sitting, Averil reached up and grabbed the locking bar to pull the lid shut, but it refused to budge. To her astonishment, however, her wrists felt good and strong again. Whatever Hedley had given her down in the wastelands was still working. She could already feel the pain in her back easing. Holding the hatch locking bar, she lifted her feet, placed them on either side of the hole and heaved the hatch shut, cutting off the light.

When she dropped back on the bags, the choking dust she raised stung her eyes and blocked her nostrils. She scrabbled crabwise across to where the door should be, snorting wheat dust. A thin line of light, ten feet below, showed a small cleared semicircle where the door swung in. Averil dropped into the space, pressed herself against the stack of bags and inched the door open. The bottom floor of the guard tower was empty. She could hear them still pounding on the doors above. I need to hide until they move on.

Opposite, she noticed a small storage space under the stairs, the door open and the back wall visible. They must have checked there already. If they saw it closed again, the chance of remaining undiscovered was only slightly better than here. The banging stopped and the doors squealed opened. Footsteps crossed the hatch above.

"No one came this way," she heard someone say.

"There's no other way out." That was Aldus.

"Where does the hatch go?" Sumner, a voice she knew well. Surely, he has better things to do than chase after me. She was however pleased, better him than just Ethyl. I might survive.

Unwilling to give up, Averil eased open the makeshift granary door, slipped across the ground floor of the guard tower to the tiny under-stair storage. She had just pulled the small door closed when she heard steps. Her bolthole, an arched space of stone three feet high and two feet square, cramped her as she peered through the crack between two planks. A feral opened the granary door and called up to someone inside, probably Stone Ethyl coming down through the hatch. She'll come here next as I did. It's over. I've lost.

Sighing with resignation, she leant back against the bricks to ease the cramp in her knees. The wall behind gave way and she fell backwards down a small flight of stairs. The door of her hideaway snatched open at the same moment, and Stone Ethyl's granite features appeared in the opening.

Averil knew she should run but couldn't move. Devoid of energy, she waited for the inevitable, but there was no light of discovery in Ethyl's eyes.

"Empty," she said.

Averil couldn't believe it. Ethyl was looking straight at her. *Why would she deliberately let me go? Shit, she must see only what I saw, a blank wall.* Averil only just held in bubbling laughter in case this Aithcraft illusion allowed sound to penetrate. *Severne's tits, a bloody priest hole in the Watcher's grandest fort.*

Against a background of crackling flames, she heard Aldus say. "For fuck's sake, you let her get away."

"You don't know it was Averil," she heard Sumner say as something bit her hand. She jerked her hand away, fell sideways and banged her head on the rough stone, which drew an involuntary curse.

"I know that voice," Aldus said.

Averil hastily drew her knife and grinned, glad that Aldus knew who had discovered his treachery. If she got away, he would sweat buckets waiting for her to come after him. She dared not move while the blue trousers and laced leggings shuffled in front of the small arched opening.

"I'll have to kill her now," he continued.

Not if I see you first you treacherous bastard. Through her small window on the world, she saw a sudden rearrangement of the legs and heard a strangled cry as the fee hanging out the blue trousers lifted off the ground.

"At least she has honour," Ethyl said.

"Go Ethyl," Averil whispered, certain now they couldn't hear her through the barrier. It was just like in the tunnel-craft station where Hedley had left her after their underground ride.

"Leave him," Sumner commanded. "He isn't worthy of us." He paused and the blue uniform crumpled to the floor like a discarded doll.

Averil could clearly see Aldus, his mouth set in an ugly sneer, looking up as he took deep breaths and coughed in the smoky room.

"I would suggest you stay well behind our advance," Sumner finished.

The cross-laced leggings disappeared and sometime later Aldus spat in the direction they had gone; his face so contorted with rage and hate that Averil cringed. Then he clawed his way to his feet and was gone.

Averil took stock of her surroundings. As far as she knew, nobody had even hinted at priest holes in the Wall. Except for the whisper tubes, it was supposed to be full of rubble. *Do I see where this leads or wait and go back out there?* A burning rafter falling across her access hole decided the issue.

• • • •

As Willard and Baxter recrossed the Falls River, Willard looked back, shocked to realise that each of the ominous red glows on the horizon marked the position of a Fort the ferals were torching. The ease with which the Wall had fallen astonished him. It had stood as an insurmountable barrier, keeping the ferals from destroying civilisation since the Preservation War three hundred years ago. Common belief held that a feral breakthrough would not only end any chance of the Restoration, but it would also herald a new dark age not seen since the cleansing that followed the Days of Fire.

"The fall was inevitable, Lord," Baxter said, catching Willard's mood if not his thoughts.

"Why?" asked Willard.

"Superior numbers, greater cause."

"A greater cause than finding the Face? What happens to your restoration when they go after the Towers?"

"Is that your own opinion or did a server give it to you?" Baxter threw back the green hood and, tilting his hairless head towards Willard said, "See the scars, Lord Willard. I have taken the Test of Faith. I am not a pretend warrior. I'm the real thing. The demise of the Wall is of no consequence. Our Lady will still test candidates in brethren controlled servatories."

The speech was the most information Baxter had ever volunteered. Willard reddened with hurt anger at the implication that he was a pretend warrior, not worthy of holding an opinion. The Goddess herself remained silent. Severne had not intruded on his thoughts since telling him danger was character building.

Baxter restored his hood and pulled ahead. They rode on, into the chaos of Walfort. Baxter only broke the silence once to argue against going into Walfort, but Willard, wanting to ask about Kezia, insisted and Baxter eventually agreed, reverting to his deferential, "as you wish Lord."

The old fort, around which the town sprawled, was twice the size of Grand Falls and geographically central to the great curve of the Break. All roads from the Wall led to Walfort, the only bottleneck before the bridge itself at Canalbridge. The retreat had swelled the town beyond its ability to cope, more coming in than could get out. The crush of people, each frantic in pursuing their own ends, led to flared tempers, scuffles, drawn swords, mayhem, and death.

Despite the crush, Willard and Baxter rode in an island of calm. The crowd parted and flowed around them as they rode directly into the headquarters-building forecourt and dismounted unchallenged. Willard found it unsettling. Fear of Warriors had not been part of their outward journey. He gathered from the whispers. They were primarily afraid of the berserker with a Named Sword.

"A sign of the times," Baxter said, answering his unvoiced question. "The year, rumours of miracles, and our increased activity, everyone sees as ominous."

Willard loosened the straps on his horse and led to the animal to the water trough. He did not like the way Baxter had used the inclusive term 'our'. He was not, as Baxter had pointed out a real Restoration Warrior and never would be, test or no test, fail or otherwise. [It's just not me, Severne.]

As they walked from the forecourt into the cool shade of the building, he could not deny the advantages of his new reputation. Even seasoned Watchers steered out of his way. The Watchmaster General's new young adjutant stood back as he held the door for them. The room was unchanged. The scenic tapestries, the worn-out carpet, and two neatly stacked piles of papers on an otherwise bare desk, an oasis of calm. Heutte was the only one who seemed unimpressed.

"Ah," she said, uncharacteristically tilting her chair back and putting her feet up on the large chapelnut desk. "The misfits have returned. What can I do for two such distinguished gentlemen?"

Willard asked if the Watchmaster had seen Kezia.

"Kezia no, but I had another odd couple, like yourselves, through here. A warrior accompanying a young healer called Jena Setler. I wondered if it could be her, but she did not fit the description and she came from Port Calder. I see you've heard of her," she said, watching their expressions.

"And nothing of Kezia?"

"Sorry. If that's all you came for, I can't help you. However, you can help me," she said, sliding her feet off the desk with a thump and standing. "How goes the defeat? I heard there were more balloons than Watchers."

Willard and Baxter reported all they had witnessed and left Heutte shouting for her adjutant. "Wolfe, get in here. I need help with these tapestries."

As they made their way out of Walfort, Baxter seemed more withdrawn than usual. Willard tried to be receptive and listen in, but though he thought he heard murmuring he could not make out words. Maybe the speaker could control who heard the communication. He watched Baxter closely and, following a barely perceptible nod at someone in the crowd Willard saw a jewelled hilt disappear behind the huge double Granary.

[Dudley,] Baxter told him.

Willard grimaced. He was wrong. Baxter had read his mind as easily as Severne had. The Goddess had once told him he was quite adept at hiding his thoughts from her, and having found a difference between hidden and broadcast thoughts, he knew this was true, yet his aptitude had not helped him read the others. If Dudley was here, was Fletcher? And if they both were? [Where is Averil?]

[Safe Lord.]

[Nice of you to ask after Averil for a change,] the Goddess added.

They continued south up a wide valley, Baxter in a complete trance, eyes closed, head to one side, withdrawn into a spiritual commune with the brethren and/or the Goddess.

I need some way to eavesdrop, thought Willard, and tried to still his mind enough to listen. By the time they reached the Three Ways junction, he imagined he was making progress.

He fancied he had heard Baxter's thought to change direction, just before he directed his horse onto the Carrier Point Road, and shouted, "Change of plan, Lord."

"Not for me. I'm meeting Averil in Canalbridge," Willard shouted back, exhilarated by the capture of a thought as he continued down the Canalbridge Road. He pulled up short in a spray of dust when Dudley and Fletcher suddenly appeared out of the scrub, riding to intercept.

[If it's any consolation Lord, Averil will be at Carrier Point,] Baxter said.

Chapter 41

The flaring beam blocking Averil's exit provided very little light into the priest-hole. The short flight of wooden stairs she had fallen down ended in hard packed ground, the start of an oblong passage about seven feet high and three feet wide ending in darkness, its walls formed from the same dressed stone of the illusion.

The light diminished as Averil felt her way along the passage. In places, lichen, dark red in the flickering light, and soft to touch like fine matting, encrusted the stone. She sensed the passage ran in the same direction as the Wall. It would be good if it emerged at a Milepost, or better yet, a turret. She would feel safer when she had another way out, but the passage ended abruptly.

Backtracking along the opposite wall, she found a lightless gap in the side where the air felt fresher. She stepped through, skidded on loose pebbles, and tumbled down a slope, clutching at the lichen-covered wall in vain.

'Oh shit!' she screamed, her thoughts whirling, thinking she was going to slide out through the Break and plunge to her death. Instead, she came to an abrupt stop on a polished floor, choking on the dust cloud she brought from the rubble slope. Thankfully, her wrists and back, damaged on the hatch, no longer hurt. New back and head pain from the stairs, to which she had added both knees and an elbow, had replaced her earlier welts. As she lay recovering, sneezing, and waiting for the dust to settle, she tried to visualise where she was, but had no idea the direction of the slope.

"Averil, how nice to see you again," Severne said, as brilliant white light exploded in Averil's' eyes. She snapped an arm over already shut lids. "You look a little the worse for wear."

What a curious expression, thought Averil, like something her mother would say. She slowly lifted her arm, letting her eyes accustom to the brightness. The room she had slid into was not much bigger than Deep Creek's Audience Chamber similarly fitted out. So much more than a priest hole. It really shouldn't exist in a Watcher stronghold. The rock walls, however, seemed genuine, as if hacked out of the escarpment, which made her wonder how the ferals had missed it.

She winced as she sat up, noting it was an age since anyone had been down here. Old cobwebs clustered in the corner, small black spots covered the round ceiling lights and thick dust covered everything except the crystal in which the Goddess sat.

"You haven't done a very good job of protecting me."

"You are alive, many are dead," Severne said, her voice soft and resonant.

In a blink, the Goddess had disappeared and the crystal showed a bird's-eye view of Grand Falls. Averil felt as she had in the balloon, the ever-changing world below her, just as horribly real. Grand Falls was in flames, yet on the battlements, a remnant of Watchers fought on.

Bloody fools, I told them to go. ferals, three sometimes four to one, swamped the blue uniforms from behind. Her vantage point was too high for her to recognise individuals, but she knew there would be friends among those she was watching die. Why hadn't they followed orders? Averil turned her gaze up towards to the ceiling, focussed beyond it to where she imagined Severne's Eye, the otherworld home of the Goddess, might be. "Why aren't you stopping this?" she pleaded, tears in her eyes.

"To be blunt, Averil, stopping it, is beyond my ability."

Averil looked across at the image of the Goddess seated in her the crystal.

"My servers have misled you into thinking I am all powerful. I am not. If I were, I would have no need of Restoration Warriors. Those I have are not sufficient for the task; keeping my special candidates, like you, safe."

Averil stood and limped around the room, wondering how long she would have to stay before the ferals cleared off.

"You have a remarkable knack for both hurting yourself and recovering from it."

I was right; she thought. Hedley gave me something.

The crystal ascended as the Goddess continued, "If you will allow, I can further help you."

Averil stared at the altar where the crystal had recently stood. She would be here a while, so why not? She was still sore in places and unimaginably tired. The Goddess sounded caring, but could she trust her? On reflection, it seemed as if Severne had always played straight with her, despite Gardner actions, which had often appeared detrimental. She stepped toward the altar unable to see a hidden agenda in the offer.

"Please lie flat on your back."

The crystal glowed underneath with a pulsating white light that made Averil feel happy. What harm could it do if she had a rest? She sat, swung her legs up, lay back and closed her eyes. The altar adjusted to the contours of her back. An odd smell wafted up her nose, and suddenly she felt very relaxed.

"Willard got away safely," Severne said. "I can transport you to him."

"That's nice," Averil said, drifting off, thinking of the time Magister had paid her that first unwelcome visit. What made her think of that now? she wondered, from within her dream. She had not talked to mother but confided all to Kezia. Kezia had berated her, and told her she should never let it happen again. Ever after, she stayed alert, even in sleep, ready to slip out the upstairs window at the slightest rattle of the doorknob, treating it like a game, seeing how long she could go without encountering him. She had become quite proficient. Sometimes a whole week would go by before her father would ask if she still lived here. Poor Kezia didn't heed her own advice and suffered in my stead, inadvertently protecting me.

· · · ·

Averil woke refreshed, luxuriating in a warmth and comfort she had rarely experienced since leaving home. Reluctantly, she opened her eyes and immediately sat upright.

"Where the f ... am I?" she said.

"Good morning, Averil. I trust you slept well," said a disembodied voice that filled the room.

Memory returned. "Very well, thankyou ... er, good morning ... your ladyship," Averil said, not knowing quite how to address a Goddess without anger prompting her.

"Call me Seven," the Goddess said, pronouncing her name the same way mother often had. "How do you feel?"

"Great," Averil said, swinging her legs off the remarkable bedlike altar into a sitting position. Her inspection revealed no sign of abrasions anywhere. "Severne's ..." she exclaimed, pronouncing the name as she always had, out of habit; she doubted that would change. Her exclamation came from pulling out her shirtfront and looking down at her breasts. The unnaturally deep tan she had picked up in the wastelands was gone from everywhere, not just her arms and legs. "I'm not feral anymore."

"You never were. The harsh conditions of the lowlands damaged your skin. It needed repair."

Averil flexed her arms and found the ache in her elbow gone. Pushing off with her hands, she landed on the floor and nearly collapsed from a sharp pain in the groin, reminding her of the weird dream of home.

"First door on your left," Severne said.

Averil mumbled her thanks. She needed to go, desperately, but she was equally sure that was not what had caused the pain. I've had a full bladder before. This felt more like a knife wound. She examined herself in the toilet but could find no external signs to account for it.

The crystal had descended when she returned to the Audience Chamber, feeling much better for having emptied her bladder. Maybe that had caused the pain after all. The Goddess sat watching her.

"You should take the Test," Seven/Severne said.

Averil looked sharply at the seated image. Until her travels with Gardner, Averil would have jumped at the chance to become a Restoration Warrior. Now, as she recalled his limitations, she was not quite that ambitious.

"What's the point? I can't be the Face."

"Why?"

"Common knowledge. It has always been the Man Who Will Be Face," Averil said, emphasising man, "and now rumour has Willard tarred with that brush."

"Common knowledge is often wrong."

"Are you it saying it won't be a man or won't be Willard?" Averil asked.

"If I knew, I would not test candidates. I can only predict that Willard is my most promising candidate so far."

"Still, you only test male candidates."

"My servers only present me with male candidates."

The Goddess shifted position, uncrossing her legs. The long gown parted, revealing a knee to envy, thought Averil. Her own were knobby and callused, strong but ugly. Severne was the ultimate representation of everything female, everything Averil lacked. Kezia, except for her dark hair would be a better match for the Goddess.

Tempting as this new offer was, it had one major drawback: hairlessness. Despite her current very short hair, Averil really did not fancy the hairless state caused by the Test. Hair cut short could regrow, but Warrior baldness was permanent. Yuk.

"If it's all the same to you, La ... Seven, I'd rather not. The Watchers will need all the help they can get to make a stand at Canalbridge, and I promised to meet Willard there. I ..." she dried up, mildly embarrassed.

"Willard is going to Carrier Point. Canalbridge will not hold."

Averil could no longer contain her frustration with the way the Goddess operated. "Why are you so against us?"

"I am neither against, nor for, you. Canalbridge cannot hold because the Federals have superior numbers and a technological advantage. Charismatic Doane's goal has shifted to swift occupation of the uplands rather than pursuit of Willard. Your presence in Canalbridge will not alter the result."

• • • •

The road from Threeways to Carrier Point constantly descended as it followed the course of the fast-flowing Cascade River. Willard had spent much of the time since the Warriors forced him onto this road, thinking through his options, aware that Fletcher and Dudley, although unseen, were not far away. He couldn't escape them. He would have to tackle his problem with the Goddess's plan at its source. He had put it off too long.

[Severne, I have a proposition,] he said, as Our Lady's Tower grew steadily higher above the horizon. No answer. What did that mean: not listening, busy or out of reach? No, Baxter talked to her all the time. Or did he? Maybe he was talking to Dudley and Fletcher. Could they do that without her? I still know nothing useful.

"Is there an oracle in Carrier Point?" he asked Baxter.

"A servatory Lord," Baxter replied.

His condescending tone, as much as the reply itself, unsettled Willard. He now understood the forced change of destination? Still, a servatory would serve his purpose just as well as a tower. Sensing a pattern to Severne's manipulations, he wondered if she had predicted his decision or contrived to have him make it. Was Averil also forced into coming here instead of Canalbridge?

"It's a working servatory, isn't it?" Willard said, with sudden insight.

"Yes Lord," said Baxter, followed by a whispered, "why does he think we're going there?"

An angry Willard rounded on him and stopped when he found Baxter looking off into the scrub, smiling. Willard gulped; immediately aware Baxter had not meant the comment for him. [I heard that,] his mind blurted.

[Heard what Lord,] replied Baxter, turning to regard him, one hairless eyebrow raised.

"That the Watchers don't know there's servatory right in their backyard," said Willard, improvising badly, knowing it was not something anyone could miss.

Baxter turned away.

What had surprised Willard was twofold: first that Baxter did not give his 'I heard that' it's full import, and secondly that Baxter's opinion of him had sunk so low. It's my fault. I do nothing except in rage. I keep hoping the Test will go away so Kezia and I can have a life. Doing nothing hasn't worked. No more, he thought, and straightened in the saddle.

Four miles from Carrier Point, the Cascade River turned sharply away from the road as it dipped and passed under the stone arch of an aqueduct, Carrier Point's supplementary water supply. The first farms Willard had seen since Canalbridge appeared shortly after. On either side of the road, bordered by a low freestone wall, were crops interspersed with grazing land. He had thought the isthmus uncultivated except for the occasional family garden of married officers.

Willard watched a mob of sheep, startled by the horses, flow across the landscape like a single beast. It evoked a memory of the day he had sat above the valley, waiting for Kezia, dreaming of the farm they would have together. He knew now that Severne would continue to part them, at least until he attempted the test.

Baxter paused on the final grade to allow Dudley and Fletcher to join them, and Willard had his first full view of Carrier Point. The fortified town, shaped like a squashed octagon, was quite unlike any place he had ever seen. He loved it instantly. The neat geometric but irregular layout touched something deep. They had set their buildings with their orange tiled roofs in green parkland, separated by broad avenues crossing at right angles. In the centre, straddling a dozen blocks across where the main avenues would have intersected was a thick-walled compound. It enclosed a three-story dome-roofed building he presumed was the servatory, and alongside it, Our Lady's Tower. The aqueduct passed over the wall a little to the left of where the road ended in a twin-towered gate. Light sparkled off the water, pouring from the aqueduct into twin cisterns.

Camped under the arches of the aqueduct and around the gate were hundreds of dishevelled Watchers, yet Carrier Point looked empty. The approach road, however, remained clear. Willard assumed the archers he could see on the gate's towers kept it clear. A bridge spanning the wide ditch around the town joined the road to the gate. The gate was open, but an iron lattice behind it blocked the way.

The sight caused a frown to pucker Willard's scar. [What is ...] he started asking Baxter.

[A portcullis.]

[... that doing closed?] he finished.

[I would've thought that obvious, Lord.]

"They're locking out the Watchers," Willard said, breaking in to speech, not hiding his irritation.

Baxter did not reply as the warriors rode through the outer edges of the astounded camp. The murmur of subdued conversation flowed around them. Ahead, the portcullis rose, and the crowd at the gate stirred. A squad of spearmen, in an unfamiliar uniform, jogged out across the bridge and took up defensive positions along its edge and across the road. Some campers surged into the ditch, trying to get behind the squad. On the verges, they pressed close to the riders. The gate tower's archers nocked arrows and drew.

Willard's sense of injustice rose beyond offended. How dare they keep the Watchers out? He turned on Baxter. "Do something."

"What do you suggest?"

"Clear away the spearmen. Let the Watchers in."

"You could do that yourself, Lord, but I would advise against it. They too have a right to live."

Willard seethed. [I said clear them, not kill them.]

They were still a hundred yards from the bridge when Dudley and Fletcher surged past, crackling blades circling in the air, and like little boys at play they shouted in unison—charge. The crowd and the spearmen parted as the warriors dismounted, theatrically sliding off their horse's rumps as they reached the bridge. The horses clattered on over it, through the open gate, and under the fully raised portcullis. Dudley and Fletcher took up positions on each side of the road at the head of the bridge and with their named swords gave a dazzling display of power that kept the path they had forged clear.

Willard and Baxter rode through the corridor of clean pressed uniforms, reminiscent of Grundston's propaganda Watchers.

[This lot doesn't fear me, or you,] thought Willard.

[Your turret demolition hasn't yet reached here.]

[Only because they're keeping the Watchers out.]

The spearman drew back over the bridge. Fletcher and Dudley brought up the rear, backing up in lockstep, the crowd constantly pressing, almost forcing its front row into the path of their whirling swords.

"Why are your fellow brethren helping keep the Watchers out?" Willard demanded of Baxter.

"To keep you safe Lord, though why we bother, Severne only knows. You're a spoiled brat, accepting of Our Lady's largess, but not the attendant duties."

His comment stunned Willard into hurt silence, unable to think of a single word in his own defence. It left him wondering why the Warrior, and by inference the Goddess, had turned his plea to help the Watchers into an attack on him.

[Whatever it takes Willard,] he thought, not at all sure the thought was his.

The portcullis rattled down behind the last of the spearman, leaving Dudley and Fletcher holding the crowd at bay. As Willard dismounted, glanced out through the iron grid, and saw the pair lower their swords and take the stance, an award looking reverse grip, with the tips of each sword, in its respective toe cup.

The portcullis had been up for less than two minutes. The crowd, having risen in anticipation of gaining entry, dispersed slowly, with an angry, hopeless clamour.

"It's good to be on foot again," Baxter said, as the local militia led their horses away to stables just inside the gate. The massive doors beyond boomed shut and the bar fell into its iron slot, shutting out the tumult.

A delegation approached along the main road.

[They expected us,] said a still fuming Willard.

[Of course Lord.]

"Our Lady bids you welcome Lords," the leader of the delegation said, bowing low with a flourish and coming up red faced from the exertion. "Custodian Stewart at your service," he said, then introduced two other councillors, and Ser Digby, the circuit server Willard had already met. "We appreciate you coming to our aid in these perilous times and grant you citizenship."

"Our Lady be with you," Baxter replied.

Willard, despite what Baxter had said, was not so polite. "Keep your citizenship. It isn't worth a feral curse while you keep the Watchers out?"

Custodian Stewart stepped back a pace. "Er ... we cannot accommodate everyone, Lord. The town is already bursting at the seams."

"You could fit the entire wall's compliment in here." Willard pointedly looked around at the vast open spaces and wide avenues.

A look of horror appeared on Ser Digby's face. "But they're Aithists," he said, as if that was explanation enough.

"So might I be," Willard said, dusting down his Watcher uniform, attempting to startle the Custodian and his councillors out of the complacency.

"You jest Lord," Custodian Stewart replied. "Ser Digby heard the Goddess proclaim you. Our oracle told us to expect the Man Who Will Be Face and here you are Our Lady's symbol clearly marking your forehead."

"You read too much into a simple scar. I hit my head on a wooden peg."

"And the named sword you carry, the talisman, the Warriors with you ..."

"My gaolers forced me here."

As Baxter jabbed an elbow in Willard's ribs, he heard Dudley chuckle and saw Custodian Stewart trying to work out what he meant. "You really do not believe in her," he said in surprise.

"Who cares what I, or the Watchers, believe? They have protected this little shit hole for centuries. Now, when they need your help, you shut them out."

Stewart looked to Baxter for support.

Ser Digby seemed put out. "But we serve Our Lady, they do not."

"Severne help me," Willard roared.

The delegation took several steps backward, councillors jostling each other in confusion.

[Not so loud Lord,] came the distinctive mental pattern that was Fletcher. Willard spun around, saw that he and Dudley were holding their hands over their ears, as if that would help.

[You heard that?]

[The entire world heard that,] a new distant voice said.

[Then pay attention, or I'll shout louder.] Willard turned back and saw Baxter had his eyes squeezed shut. The Goddess, however, remained silent and, in the silence, Willard thought he heard an echo of feminine laughter. He calmed himself and sent an apologetic thought to Baxter before saying, "Take me to her."

"Yes Lord," Ser Digby said.

[Yes Lord,] chorused Baxter.

• • • •

The altercation at the Western gate did not reach Kezia on the altar, deep in the domed building beside the Tower. The pain from the spear wound in her shoulder was easing, slowly, the swallowed Builder dust losing its potency. As she waited, she wondered how, despite her active resistance, the Goddess always ensured Kezia ended up in the bowels of a tower.

Hours ago, perhaps yesterday, on first seeing it poking above the trees, Kezia had reined in and gaped at the assortment of oblongs, circles, and spheres around its summit. She stole a guilty glance at the heavens to see if Severne was watching, but it was still too light.

Some seventh sense must have warned Howard she was not following, for he turned and rode back to her.

"I'm not going in there," she said, pointing.

Howard's gaze followed her finger. "You have already been in there, on your way to the Wall."

"I was ill and tired and it was dark. I didn't see the bloody tower before. I'm not going anywhere near one."

"There is no other way off this isthmus."

"What about Canalbridge?" Kezia asked.

"Too late," Howard said, as he pulled his horse around to resume their journey. "If you wish to see your child again, follow me," he added.

Kezia followed, fuming at Howard, at the Goddess, and at the injustices of life. Two days hard riding up the eastern coast of the Pointing Finger isthmus had put her back under the eyes and ears of the Goddess. Freedom was ephemeral.

The little used southern gate opened for them and closed again in the face of a bedraggled group of wounded Watchers trying to slip through with them. Kezia's anger turned to indignation, rising to a crescendo when she heard about the size of the West Gate encampment.

"You just told me this is the only exit. They don't want to settle here. They can't get away if they can't come in."

"There are not enough boats to evacuate them from here. They should move on to Canalbridge."

"You said it was too late for that. Why aren't the boats making more trips?"

"Some are," said Howard.

"Some," shouted Kezia. "They all should; as many as it takes, they owe the Watchers."

Ignoring her outburst, Howard continued. "Given the numbers, to evacuate Carrier Point will take two whole seasons."

Kezia looking about her as they rode up the main road passed prosperous looking shops and spacious houses. The place could easily accommodate thousands.

"Selfish bastards," she said, seeing large empty paddocks at both ends of the cross streets. She tried another argument. "The Watchers could help their defence; hold the town for two seasons while everyone gets away."

"It's more complex than that."

"I've heard that excuse before," said Kezia, remembering her mother's excuse for not ... she shuddered. I haven't thought about father in ages. "All it means is you lack the will to do something about it."

"What do you propose I do?" said Howard, an edge of irritation in his voice

"Open it like you did at the fort."

"At Our Lady's request."

Kezia took a deep breath before answering. They had stopped in front of the hospital, a two-storey building with a broad colonnaded verandah. "Then you go do what you do best, and I'll do the same."

"What is it you think I do best?" Howard asked.

"Intimidate people. Go intimidate whoever runs this place for passage out of here. You're taking me to my son remember? Lop off a few heads. That should do it." She looked away, in though the wide entrance at a tranquil pool centred in an atrium garden, such a contrast to the hard baked earth floors of the Wall's hospitals.

"Why the sudden about face?"

"I'm a woman," said Kezia, dismounting, hoping he was still boy enough to believe that ancient adage.

Howard's smile was thin. "Where will you be?"

"With the sick and injured where else?" One trick your Goddess taught me. A misleading truth is often more potent than a lie.

As soon as Howard was out of sight, Kezia remounted and headed for the West Gate to help, as she saw it, the sick and injured who really deserved it; those in the camp outside. Riding down the main tree-lined boulevard, she found her first impressions of Carrier Point were quite accurate. Someone had given thought to the layout, making it spacious with clean lines. In happier times, it would probably be quite peaceful. Pity the ferals will burn it to the ground.

At the gate, she ran into her first problem. Two squads of spearman in unfamiliar uniforms lined up in front the closed gate.

"I need to go out," she said, picking on a likely officer.

A spearman laughed and grabbed her horse by the halter.

"Move her away. We need room to manoeuvre in case the Watcher rabble get restless."

Kezia tried another approach, even though she found the words bitter. "I am Jena Setler, the chosen healer of the Goddess. Let me pass."

That gained his attention.

"There are sick and wounded outside in need of my skills."

His interest turned to perplexity with a trace of anger. He seemed undecided as he looked over his preparations. "I haven't got time for this now," he whispered to himself then called a second spearman to help the one holding her horse. "Get her out of the way. Arrest her and take her to the Custodian. I think she's a Watcher spy."

The accusation so stunned her, Kezia did not react until after the delegated spearmen had dragged her from her horse. What was happening here? When had the Watchers become the enemy? Her captors half marched, half dragged her back down the boulevard towards the walled villa from which the tower loomed. Terrified, Kezia jammed her heels into the cracks between paving blocks, sank her teeth into a restraining hand and tasted blood before the hand let go. Swinging her body around, she lifted a knee into the other spearman's groin, then ran blindly down the avenue away from the tower.

One spearman recovered enough to let fly. His spear caught her in the shoulder with a tearing thud, knocking the breath out of her, pushing her over. She saw the bloody tip protruding from the front of her shirt as she fell headlong onto the paving and woke from that nightmare into a truly frightening scene.

Strapped on a tower altar, looking up into a strong light, Kezia re-lived the earlier nightmare; of giving birth in Blades Point. She closed moist eyes. The light pulsed rhythmically through her eyelids as she drifted off again.

"Kezia," said a voice she never wanted to hear again. "Why do you fight so hard against my help?"

Kezia wanted to tell her, wanted to scream at the Goddess for stealing her son, for killing Wesley, for all the other injustices in the name of the Restoration, for doing nothing to prevent generations of carnage on the Wall, but she could not even find the will to open her eyes.

"No matter, sleep now. All will be well."

Other than being here, what wasn't well? The pain in her shoulder passed through an ache to an itch, already healing, but then as the lights faded, she felt a sharp pain in her groin.

No, please no, not again. I want more children.

· · · ·

Kezia woke with a fresh memory of the pains of giving birth, anxious about what Severne might have done to her. She sat up and slipped off the altar. The empty windowless room looked like a large petitioner's waiting room, except that instead of pews there was a small dressing table against the wall. Her clothes, clean and folded, the shirt sat on top flawlessly repair, like her boots underneath the dresser.

She pulled back the gown to inspect the damage and found a thin white scar, an inch-long, under her shoulder blade. Flexing the shoulder brought pain. Not much, just enough to remind they had speared her. The healing was not complete this time. What was the significance of that? Were the healing powers of the Goddess limited, or was this a warning, a mark of her unworthiness?

The air vibrated and the Goddess formed from gathering dust motes right before her eyes. "Good morning, Kezia."

Kezia backed away. "What have you done to me?"

The Goddess looked hurt. "When?"

"Yesterday." She assumed it was morning, as Severne had said in her greeting.

"I have made you whole, and replenished your exhausted healing nanites."

"What have you done here?" Kezia said, clutching her lower abdomen through the white gown.

"I corrected a problem."

"Why didn't you fix it when you stole my son?" Kezia asked, tense now, as she pulled off the gown and slipped into her clothes, scanning the room like a caged animal.

"The problem was not apparent then. Your reproductive organs are now in perfect working order. I kept your son to save his life. He needed intensive care."

"You lied to me. You said he was dead."

"That is not true. I was not sure I could save him. Howard did not want to give you false hope."

"But I asked. I know it was Howard's mouth, but it was you speaking something about my sacrifice. What sacrifice if my son was not dead?"

"Do you not think believing your son dead sacrifice enough?"

Kezia was aghast and enlightened at the same time. While it suited her purpose, she deliberately kept me ignorant. "Why are you keeping him from me now?" Kezia added.

"Is not Howard taking you to him?"

Kezia had to concede the point. She had been following Howard with precisely that expectation ever since he had told her that her child was alive. Her problem was she might never reach her son and Severne's statement would still be true. It's just like her tellings, open to interpretation.

As Kezia sat at with her back to the dressing table, lacing her boots, she wondered what else the Goddess had left out. What did she mean by your reproductive organs are now in perfect working order? Kezia had always assumed they were.

"Where is my son?" she asked.

Severne did not directly address the question, saying instead: "Howard has arranged safe passage for you, but you must leave immediately."

Her image was dispersing into dust motes even as Kezia asked, "Why?"

"As I told you," Howard said, stepping into the room. "There are not enough boats and the wealthy of the town, who own them, take vast amounts of luggage, sometimes a family to a boat."

Howard did not look happy about it. It seemed he did not like to be on the receiving end of frustration. "Well, tough, your damn Goddess has been frustrating me for ages. Grow up Howard and get me to my son. I don't care how you do it, just do it."

The voice of the Goddess filled the room. "Mind how you speak of me in Carrier Point? They have no tolerance for non-believers."

Kezia, after a brief mirthless laugh, said, "I only say what I believe is true, as you say you do. If your worshipers don't like it, tough. You'll just have to protect me better."

• • • •

Howard stepped through the shimmering curtain into what Kezia had supposed was the oracle but was, in fact, a stairwell, and started down it, expecting her to follow. She assumed the warriors had a secret exit to the port at sea level; ground level was somewhere above. Kezia baulked, her earlier musings finally crystallising. Her son's whereabouts would forever remain just beyond her reach, as was the nature of this carrot and donkey ploy. It stops now, she thought, as she headed up the stairs. "I have work to do. I'll find him myself when this is over."

Howard bounded after her, grabbed her by the arm. "Where do you think you're going?" he asked brusquely.

"Where I belong, with the wounded, and there's bugger all you can do about it." She was counting on the Goddess keeping her safe and had only now worked out why. Like her son, she too was a carrot on a stick, being dangled in front of Willard. She was certain now. Willard was holding out; for her.

Howard said nothing, his head typically titled. Kezia shook him off and resumed her upward march with no idea where it might take her and not caring. Howard matched her step for step.

"What about your son?" Howard asked.

"What about him?" Kezia asked, a tightness in her breast.

"I know where he is, I ..."

Kezia rounded on him, with a withering mixture of disdain and pity, knowing he would never take her to her son. He was a puppet, as much jerked around as she had been. She was just as certain that Willard and Averil were also being manipulated.

"Then bring him to me. My duty is here," she choked out, then turned and fled up the stairs barely holding back the conflicting emotions that threatened to wrench her apart.

Chapter 42

The cold rock walls of the Audience Chamber added to Averil's despair. The ferals had breached the Wall, and were overrunning the isthmus. With her own eyes, she had seen Aldus, Willard's brother for Goddess's sake, paid off for opening the gate to Grand Falls. Willard would never believe her. It was over, Canalbridge couldn't hold. Like the rest of the world, their island would soon be under feral rule. She'd known this as soon as the balloons started rising, but having Severne state it so bluntly was a blow. From the Goddess, such an utterance was prophecy. *I should go to Canalbridge and warn them.*

She stared at the lichen-covered wall and tried to work out what to advise Heutte: stand and die or retreat to Long Gully Pass, perhaps to stand and die there. Considering the superior numbers, she doubted the pass would hold them long. She could see few alternatives, but to lay down arms, and throw themselves on the mercy of the ferals. This drew a hollow, bitter laugh. It would not be acceptable to a people who had prided themselves on their superiority. *We 'Uplanders', as Sumner calls us, see ourselves as the Builders' inheritors, the chosen people of Our Lady. Pity she seems unaware of it. Like so much else, it's too late now. Perhaps my rejection of her offer was too hasty. Perhaps being a hairless warrior was preferable to a dead or captured Watcher Major.*

"What are my chances?"

"My analysis suggests Restoration Warrior."

"That's a relief," she thought, knowing she did not have the temperament to serve in a tower even if the Ob Server allowed it. "I'll do it." Her laugh this time was cynical. "You know what's funny. Me taking the test was the question I came to ask you back in Deep Creek."

"You would have saved yourself much time and misery had you done so. The nearest servatory is Carrier Point."

"That figures."

"I can get you there quickly, safely and in secret. Please step into the lift."

"Lift? What's a lift?"

In answer, a section of wall opened like a door to reveal a small room. She stepped inside, the door closed, and the 'lift' rapidly fell. Stupid name, thought Averil, but then again, it would have to 'lift' back up to be of any use. When the door opened, she immediately recognised the layout as a tunnel-craft station. No illusory wall this time. Instead, an identical craft, to the one Hedley had taken her in, stood waiting with the door already open; humming with restrained power.

Averil half-expected Hedley to poke his head out of the opening as she strode across the platform. She stepped in and glanced around the interior, which looked in better shape than Hedley's tunnel-craft.

"You have travelled a tube before?"

"In the feral lowlands," Averil said as the door slid shut surprised that Severne did not know. Maybe she does and is just testing my honesty. "Ser Hedley, my old server, helped me out," she said, settling back determined to enjoy the ride this time.

"Ah!" exclaimed the Goddess.

She sounds pleased, thought Averil, looking out the front window into the tunnel, which, like the craft, appeared first-rate. It was better lit for miles by rings of blue light, one inside the other. Spillage from the first ring showed a glass-smooth wall. The craft moved forward with soundless vibration.

"Hedley said lots about you," Averil continued. "He was collecting Builder artefacts and trying to make them work."

"Thank you for your excellent observations, Averil. You will make a superior Restoration Warrior."

Averil grinned as the first ring of blue light disappeared around her and the craft sped up. The combination of vibration and light rings whipping past gave an impression of exhilarating speed.

Tits thought Averil suddenly aware of the meaning behind Severne's 'You will make a superior Restoration Warrior'. When the Goddess had first offered to test her, despite the analysis pinning her to the role of warrior, the slim chance that she might become the 'Face of the Goddess' instantly made sense. A female, as the Face wouldn't have such a huge identity crisis.

As the tunnel-craft rapidly slowed, an afterthought struck her. Willard was right. It's better not to know the future; it kills hope.

The door opened, sliding into the curve of the wall, and Averil stepped out onto another platform so similar it was hard to tell if she had gone anywhere.

"This is Carrier Point?" Averil asked incredulously.

"Yes."

"Whoosh and you're there. Two days hard riding in what, ten minutes? Wow."

There was no rock wall or illusion here either, just a long wide room with another empty tunnel opposite. Ramps at either end led both up and down into darkness. The dust stirred up by the craft's arrival slowly settled.

"Which way," asked Averil?

"Left and up, but first you will need a talisman."

Voicing directions, the Goddess led Averil down a long corridor, one wall of which was transparent, the chamber beyond ablaze with light, a treasure trove of working artefacts, which might even surprise Hedley. It made her mother's buried hoard seem like a collection of trinkets. Small artefacts, embedded in the central altar like jewels, winked with a myriad of colours and hummed with the magic of Builder power.

The transparent wall shimmered. The image of the Goddess beckoned and Averil stepped through into a large room that smelt of burning dust. A replica of the Arch immediately drew her gaze. The impenetrable matt-black surface within did not shimmer, yet somehow disturbed her vision.

"Now what do I do?"

"You have a decision to make," the Goddess said.

Averil tore her eyes away from the replica, focussed on the Goddess.

"You should understand, the Test of Reason is only a preparation for the Test of Faith. It will put us in intimate contact."

No doubt this was just a fixed point in a well rehearse ritual, that a server would have prepared her for, if she'd been a man.

"Should you fail, you leave here no worse that you came in. Given your pedigree, this is extremely unlikely."

My pedigree? Magister?

"The Test of Faith is a severe intrusion in your mind and causes the complete loss of all body hair. There is a risk that you could go mad, or die."

"What?"

"My servers feared candidates would not come if they advertised the risks. In the unlikely event that you host me, the world will be yours; once we have saved it. My projections however, have determined that Willard is the interface I seek."

This didn't surprise Averil. Everything had pointed to Willard for years. "Then why do you want to mate him with me? Don't answer that. If I have a slim chance of passing, he has an equally slim chance of failing."

"There are those whom I have trusted do not believe in the threat posed by Typhon. Sev Miller tried to kill Willard during his Test of Reason."

"He what!"

"Did he not tell you? I implanted him before I released him."

"Bastard, all that time we were together he said nothing and I thought I knew him. Well, if he can do it, I can go one better. Do both at once."

Severne's tone became formal. "Averil, will you submit to my tests?"

Though nothing of significance had changed, Averil was suddenly afraid. Yet it was still better to risk death in hope than to live under feral occupation. At least as a warrior I will have respect from feral and islander alike. And if I die or go mad, what of it? Mad or dead, I won't know about it, will I?

"Yes," Averil said, her reply emphatic.

. . . .

Admiring her outfit in the mirror, Averil thought, Warrior green, the same shade as her left eye, suited her. The hooded robe covered straight leg pants, shirt, and jerkin. She pulled the hood up, wincing when it touched the two round burn marks on her shaven head. Severne told her the pain would soon go but the scars would remain. Her hair would attempt to regrow but fail and disappear completely in a few weeks along with all other body hair. The advantage, thought Averil, was clean legs and armpits.

"What day is it, Severne?" asked Kezia, vocalising unnecessarily.

[Satelday.]

The answer was there before her brain had time to operate her lungs, push air through her vocal cords, shape her mouth and position her tongue to put the question. She now knew exactly how the whole process worked, without knowing how she knew. Her vocalised question reached her ears after the answer, like an echo of what she thought to ask.

"Bloody Nora!" she thought, and said, immediately following with, "I have to stop repeating myself." Again, her speech echoed the thought. She bit her lip, determined to master this mental communication, and amused at now actively trying to keep her mouth shut.

[It will come with practice,] said Severne. The voice of the Goddess was now lower in both volume and pitch, and infinitely more precise. [The problem will then reverse. You will become frustrated when people do not answer immediately. You have been here two days.]

[Two days, a lot could happen in two days.]

[Yes.] The instantaneous reply startled Averil and she wondered if she would ever have a private thought again.

[Yes, but that also takes practice. Willard has now mastered the technique.]

[How is he?]

[Angry.]

[I can imagine,] said Averil, her mind ablaze with test-derived information. [Oh, wow.]

In the last two days, there had been very little dialogue between Severne and Averil. Averil had spent most of the time lying on the altar, which had run in and out of a cave like artefact that hummed with power and made her skin tingle. She had been fine with the bombardment of sound, images, and ideas until it became what she could only describe as a mental invasion. Averil had recoiled and pushed back against it.

Afterwards, she could correctly answer questions on subjects she knew nothing about. Sometimes the answers also meant nothing. With access to immense knowledge and with mounting excitement, she pieced together the bits she understood. Finally, some of Nuaith's enduring enigmas, Typhon's threat, the nature of Severne's Eye and her fragile rescue plan, made sense.

"I'm a warrior," Averil said aloud, her grin as wide as her face.

[Yes,] the Goddess thought back, [time to choose a name.] Averil was not far down the list of Sleepers, her implant providing vast quantities of information on each. Then she saw a name she had to have.

[April,] she said.

Severne seemed amused. For Averil, it was simply the closest to her own, and though she rarely thought about it; she had always liked the name mother had given her.

Besides the Test, the Goddess had prodded and poked Averil, weighed and measured her, scourged her body inside and out with potions and lotions. One surprising aspect was that she did not remember sleeping in the last two days, and yet, she had never felt better or more alive in her whole life.

[Does every warrior have this knowledge?]

[To varying degrees, depending on how much they can assimilate. You have exceeded all previous downloads. You came very near to hosting me.]

Thinking about it, Averil did not know whether to be pleased to have come so close, or pissed to have just missed out.

[Be pleased,] the Goddess said. [If Willard fails, one of your progeny will succeed, and all will revere you as the Mother of the Face.]

[I know the ferals will. I'm not sure about my lot.]

Toward the end of the two days, the Goddess had directed Averil to a storehouse and provided her with the accoutrements of Restoration Warriors, including that most prized possession, a Goddess named sword. Averil strapped the scabbard to her back and drew the blade. The haft adjusted to her hand as her fingers curled around it; the jewel glowed green and the blade edge crackled, illuminating the name etched in the blade. *Fires Kiss* was light for its size.

[The sword is an extension of you. Your mind focuses power drawn from the network around New Earth. One final word of caution: in the interest of our common cause, in public you should refer to me as Our Lady.]

It surprised Averil to find she understood perfectly both the need to do so and the ramifications of not doing so.

[No worries Seven,] thought Averil, now pronouncing the name, as did the Goddess and her mother. Only now did she appreciate Mother's real secret, and her own pedigree. She was glad Magister had nothing to do with it.

• • • •

Baxter led Willard to the domed three-story building adjoining the courtyard in which Our Lady's tower stood. The complex covered a whole block in the centre of the walled town. Except for visiting Warriors, nobody in Carrier Point including the Custodian, Ser Digby or his Arch Server had ever been inside the servatory. To the delegation, Willard, going unhindered through the power curtain, made a mockery of his protestations that he was not a believer.

Inside, he followed Baxter through a maze of passages, until they came to a huge room, like an Audience Chamber but with two roomy chairs in place of the server's tripod.

The Goddess watched them come in.

"How do you justify keeping the Watchers out?" Willard asked.

"I am not keeping them out," the Goddess replied. She sat as usual, one bare leg crossed over the other. The long, low-cut gown parted almost to the top of her thigh, seductive yet imperturbable.

"The citizens of Carrier Point do, in your name, because the Watchers don't believe in you," Willard said, as Severne swung a shapely leg higher. She has Averil's legs, he thought. "How is it in anyone's interest, or yours, to let the ferals slaughter us?"

"It is time you understood the difference between the collective you, and the individual you. What I do in your best interest is for the collective you: Federals, islanders, believers, and non-believers. I cannot be responsible however, for every individual you. It is of no concern to me if groups of you fight among yourselves, unless you endanger those of you who are special to me, like yourself and Averil. You are both vital to the collective you. Is that now clear?"

Willard churned with frustration and a little shame that she had taken so much time to explain in scathingly simple terms what he already knew, as if he were a recalcitrant child.

"Does this mean you won't help?"

"No. It means I won't interfere."

"Same thing and I won't take your damn Test."

"Averil has."

"Oh f...," said Willard.

Baxter merely said, "Oh."

"Meet Restoration Warrior April," Severne added, as Averil stepped into the room.

Baxter smiled, and the Warriors clasped hands in ritual greeting, "Welcome bro ... sorry, sister."

Willard swivelled around and stared in shocked silence. Averil looked magnificent, despite the shaved head. She had an aura of maturity about her, an indefinable light in the differently coloured eyes that radiated through him and plainly said, I know more than you can imagine.

She turned and walked over to him with a poise and grace very unlike the boisterous Major of only a week ago. She pulled him to his feet and gave him a big hug.

[You really could be the one,] she said into his mind, tracing the scar on his forehead. [I forgive you for not telling me.]

Willard stiffened, disgusted. He felt betrayed. Averil, the last person he would have expected to go Severnian, had sold out. Averil smiled at him.

"Ask her where your sister is," Willard said.

[I don't have to, I know. Kezia is quite safe.]

"Did you see her yourself, or did your new deity tell you this?" Willard said, persisting with speech, "and get out of my mind."

Averil started, a little put off, but recovered quickly. Her speech hesitant she said, "Forgive me Will, I so much prefer the clear and precise communication of thought, I didn't expect anyone able to use it would object, least of all you. To answer your question, I know for certain, through Howard, the warrior protecting her, that Kezia is safe. All you need to do is ask, and he will show you."

"You sound like a server," Willard said, surprised that Kezia also had Warrior protection, until he thought about it and remembered how far Severne had gone to get him tested. He accepted then that Kezia was safe and strode to the door with renewed purpose.

"How do I get out of here?" he asked from the doorway.

"When I release you ..." the Goddess started, but Averil interrupted.

"Let him go Severne. He will come back when he's ready."

The doorway's shimmer ceased.

Baxter squeezed past him. "It's this way Lord,"

As he followed, Willard thought, Averil's right. I will have to take the Test to get Kezia back, but I want a lot more. I want a life with her, a normal life.

Outside, he found Custodian Stewart talking animatedly with Ser Digby.

"You'd better speed up the evacuation. I'm opening the gates to let the Watchers in," he said, as he brushed past, no longer in the mood for a political solution. He was out of earshot before the startled custodian could respond. A few steps on, he glanced back and he saw the custodian and the server hurrying off in different directions.

Could be good or bad, he thought as he strode straight for the West Gate, his ire still up over the exclusion of the Watchers and Averil's betrayal. Well, that settles the offspring question. Even if he took the Test, he would never mate with her. Severne can go elsewhere for progeny.

Baxter jogged alongside to keep up.

The already nervous citizens jumped hastily out of the way. One named sword bearer was fearsome enough, two ominous. A berserker with a dark, brooding countenance was apocalyptic.

Even the militia did not oppose him until he arrived in front of the West Gate. A captain of the guard hurried to join his spearmen, still doing up the gold buttons of his uniform.

"Get that up." he said pointing.

The clang of slipping links as the chain tightened around the portcullis windlass was music to Willard's ears. At last he was doing something that need doing. The Watchers outside must also have heard. They began banging on the gates before the tines had left their stone sockets.

"Do you have spare drawbars?" he asked.

The captain was slow to respond. "Of course ... Lord," he said, confused.

"Good, you'll need it," Willard said, reaching over his shoulder. *Severne's Bane* sprang into his hand, described a graceful arc between startled spearman, frantically leaning away. The beam burned a thin channel through the two-foot-thick drawbar, holding the gates closed. Relieved of the pressure, the doors creaked inward.

"Now open them or I'll take out the hinges."

The captain swallowed but stood his ground. "You wouldn't. would you? Do that and we're all lost."

Willard admired his nerve, again marvelling that out here Warriors were nowhere near as feared as back home.

The captain nodded to someone.

Behind him, Willard heard a crackle as Baxter's sword slipped past his ear. The ground trembled and Willard could imagine the furrow *Constant Flame* must have drawn across the road.

"Come any closer and you will lose a few toes, all of you," Baxter said.

Willard continued. "There are four, no five now," with Averil, "named swords in Carrier Point, captain. No doubt we could hold the gate if you force me to take it down." *Severne's Bane* lifted threateningly towards the massive hinges.

"Open the gate," the captain said to his spearman.

The big gates groaned inwards. The Watchers beyond pushed them back. The mad inward rush barely parted around Willard and Baxter, standing in the centre of the roadway. It seemed a couple of warriors in front were less menacing than the feral hoard they knew was not far behind.

"Nicely handled Lord, you could have killed the captain and any who opposed you," said Baxter.

"Don't patronize me. I know what you think of me, but thanks for your support, it might have been a disaster otherwise."

He paused, studying Baxter's face for a moment. "Was it your decision?"

"April's Lord," said Baxter.

"Who in Severne's name is April?"

"I introduced you to her less than an hour ago," Baxter said. "Averil Lord." Then, after a long pause, he placed into Willard's mind. [I have relinquished my leadership of the brethren. Warrior April is now Our Lady's representative on Nuaith.]

[Good Goddess, all this time it's been you Baxter,] Willard answered in kind, [Everything that has happened to me has been your decision.]

[Not all Lord, but some.]

The single word 'ferals' screamed by a sentry on the gate tower caused pandemonium. Those pouring through the gates redoubled their efforts, pushing, shoving, shouting, trampling. Willard and Baxter strode through the surge and tried to re-establish some order, but by then no one would pay any attention, even to Warriors.

[We need to protect their rear,] Willard said, about to jog down the road to cover the retreating Watchers furthest out.

Baxter held him back.

[No Lord, you are their target. Hold the gate open, I'll see you in an hour, or two,] he said, shouldering his way through the oncoming tide that no longer parted for him.

Dudley and Fletcher, already across the bridge, diverged through the rapidly emptying encampment.

Willard flowed with the rush back to the Gate tower, climbed to the fighting platform atop and moved to the centre, standing above the point where the gates would close. *Severne's Bane* crackled with lightning over the crowd, singeing the tall heads until they steadied. The Watchers, he noticed, turned back to the ramparts as soon as they were inside.

Constant flashes of lightning down the road showed Baxter had a fight on his hands.

[Why, after criticising me for suggesting it, do your warriors now side with us?] Willard asked Severne.

[April thinks it is the best way to protect you.]

Averil joined him on the platform moments later. The flashes on either side of the road were converging as Fletcher and Dudley drew back ahead of the ferals, protecting the backs of the incoming Watchers. The flow slowed, jamming in the gate's bottleneck. Averil restrained his attempt to send a beam to the feral front line. "They're out of range. A beam sent that far will drain you yet only tickle them."

"The ferals aren't showing much respect for your Warriors," Willard said.

"We stopped being neutral."

He was glad she was using voice. "So, my being here forced your hand?"

"The Federal breakthrough forced our hand. We fight now to protect candidates from their new Charismatic. Doane gave them the balloons."

"But Baxter said the wall's demise didn't matter," said Willard, noting Averil now used Federal for feral.

"That was true until Our Lady acquired information I learned from Sumner, their general. Doane isn't interested in controlling the Face. He wants you and every other prime candidate dead."

When the central flashes ceased, Willard asked, "Is Baxter alright?" The Warrior's welfare had become personal.

"I redirected him," Averil said.

Willard viewed that with suspicion, mildly surprised that the Goddess, or Baxter, could still communicate with her without him overhearing, although it would not be beyond Averil to make it up. Baxter had said, 'April now speaks for Our Lady'

[She does,] Severne said.

Willard found it hard to swallow. The oldest living warrior, brethren leader for over a hundred years, had passed the mantle to Kezia's little sister.

"Two hundred," Averil said, grinning at him. She flicked the talisman hanging around Willard's neck. "I'm your guardian angel now, Lord Willard."

[Good luck with that,] Baxter said, to a multitude of brethren chuckles. Willard recognised them all and it was suddenly clear that every chuckle he had attributed to the Goddess had really been an eavesdropping warrior.

Chapter 43

K ezia burst from the stairs into a large square room under a huge dome that soared three stories above her. Heedless of the tears coursing down her cheeks, she frantically searched the walls for an exit, and found a shimmering doorway. She rushed headlong through it, into a courtyard formed from two wing-like extensions of the domed building behind her.

Out of breath, she doubled over, wheezing, a stitch in her side from the rapid climb. Howard did not appear and Kezia felt vindicated. She had called Severne's bluff and won. Her belief in the Goddess' genuineness faded. My son is dead; any hope of finding him is an illusion. She felt abandoned by everyone, except perhaps Willard, but she wasn't as sure as she would like to be. All she really had left was her duty to the wounded.

Kezia wiped away her tears, straightened her back and discovered a disturbingly familiar curved wall in front of her. Carrier Point's Tower. The intimidating structure loomed over her, seeming to frown at her, but the fear that had once held her captive was absent. She turned. The three-story domed building behind with its shimmering door must be the servatory. She'd stopped halfway between it and the tower on a short path that she assumed ended at the server's entrance.

An increasing tumult had reached her ears from somewhere outside the compound. Kezia skirted the tower, noting the servatory's twin extensions, lean-to building on the compounds enclosing walls, contained big empty, barrack-like rooms.

The clamour came from behind a gated arch between two rooms in another long barracks that joined the extensions.

A path ran from the from the gated arch to the tower's Public Arch. Paths from Patrons and Paupers ran to the corners where the side barracks joined the gated -arch barrack. A dishevelled rabble burst through the gates just as she arrived.

"What's happening?" she asked of the first person to acknowledge her.

"ferals," was the reply.

"You have wounded? I'm a healer."

"Plenty," she said, gauging Kezia.

"Who's in charge?"

The woman scanned those pouring in through the gates. "I don't know now. We've lost so many. Ask Captain Ogden. There," she said, pointing to a man in a bloody uniform, an arrow protruded from his leg, the bearers struggling to carry him on a bowed stretcher.

"Right, but first, I want the worst injuries in the Public foyer, walking wounded in any of these rooms you can open or on the lawns. If anyone questions you, say Jena Setler ordered it."

"Our Lady's healer," said the woman, her eyes widening as Kezia walked towards Captain Ogden. Ogden recognised her immediately and tried to lift himself onto an elbow, upsetting the stretcher. The front bearer lost his grip. The captain rolled onto the ground and screamed as the arrow twisted in his muscle.

As Kezia knelt beside him, she saw that despite his scream; the wound was not bad, the entry not wide enough for a tipped arrow. The captain could easily have pulled it out and saved himself from further agony. He fainted when she did. Ignoring the stares of the bearers, Kezia spat on the wound.

"That room," she told the bearers and pointed. "Who can tell me who's in charge?" She raised her voice so all those swirling around her could hear.

"Major Leach, healer," said the lead bearer as he helped roll the Captain back onto the stretcher.

Averil, that figures. She had known her sister was on the Wall, and it was like her to take charge. What surprised her was they hadn't already met.

"Are you alright healer?"

"I'm fine," Kezia said. "It was a bit of a shock. I know her. We're ... old friends."

"You'll find her changed," said the other bearer as the two men prepared to pick up the stretcher. "The Major's a warrior now, the first female warrior I ever heard of, but a damn fine officer still. Okay Morgen, lift." The bearers lifted in unison. "Let's go."

Kezia, nodding dumbly, sat down where she had stood. The tail end of wounded Watchers flowed around her. Averil a warrior, my little sister a head lopper, one of Severne's elite executioners. Holy mother, she must have taken the test. Somehow, Kezia could not imagine Averil submitting to anyone, let alone the Goddess. What am I to do now, hide from my sister or confront her? Does she know about father's death? Better if it comes from me. I've shirked the responsibility for too long. Averil, of all people, might understand. I ought to find her.

From behind her came the muffled sounds of her temporary hospital in the servatory compound, and in front, the distant sounds of the battle beyond the compound's walls. In between, it was eerily quiet. As Kezia walked toward the West Gate, surreptitiously looking over her shoulder for spearmen, streams of people, dragging or carrying all their possessions, spread around her in all directions. Silently they joined the long queues at the shrine-like rotundas scattered around inside the walls of Carrier Point Hopeless, thought Kezia, watching the slow-moving queues hanging off the entry points to Carrier Point's giant caverns, like worms on hooks, always wriggling. The ramps down to the floating port, where she and Howard had landed on their inward journey, must be full.

On either side of the main avenue, the Watchers were putting out spot fires. Kezia looked up, but there were no balloons, must be fire arrows. The ferals were close outside. Ahead of her, four sources of sword flashes clustered around West Gate, two beyond the wall and two from the fighting platform atop the Gate Room. Four warriors siding with the Watchers against the ferals. I bet that's Averil's doing.

The platform warriors suddenly disappeared as a fireball passed over where they had stood. One returned the other emerged from the guard tower. The gates started closing as the last group of Watchers staggered down the road towards her.

Confronting Averil would have to wait.

• • • •

Despite the lightness of *Fires Kiss,* Averil was bone weary. It didn't surprise her that Sumner's force had followed Willard. Sumner disagreed with his Charismatic, to him the Man Who Will be Face was more important than the invasion. He had ambition to be the next Charismatic. Nor was she surprised this first engagement had lasted hours. He had told the first attack crucial; "Each time you fail the cost of the next attempt doubles". Playing chess with him, she had learnt a lot about strategy. He was always several moves ahead.

[The last Watchers are coming through now,] Fletcher said.

[Left,] Severne shouted and Averil ducked left, pulling with her the Watcher she'd told to shut the gates, a second later. She was too late. He collapsed beside her, an arrow in his throat. [The gulls?] she asked, scanning the sky as she bounced up and let loose an angry bolt that scorched across the ferals front line, leaving a trail of dead.

[Yes April,] Severne confirmed. [It is time Willard departed. I cannot warn him as I did you. He questions rather than respond.]

[I'll need him to shut the gates first.]

She could tell from the decreasing frequency of and shortness of blasts that even Dudley and Fletcher were close to exhaustion. The mental energy to focus and project the power was physically draining. The swords were at their best in short bursts at close range, not in sustained long-distance strikes as Willard was doing. For an untested warrior who lacked the essential knowledge, he had become quite adept. His rolling slice across the front row, tracing the line of least resistance, shoulder height, had cut a deadly swathe across the southern flank of the advancing ferals.

With another slashing burn over the heads of Dudley and Fletcher, Averil strode over and tapped Willard on the shoulder. She got no response. As she tapped him harder, she noticed a lone figure walking down the road from the servatory towards the gate had a familiar gait, but fearing Willard may have gone berserk again, she let it slide. She punched Willard's sword shoulder. He looked back at her with annoyance. "Go. Close the gates," she shouted at him.

[Down.]

Averil dropped, slamming her knees into in the back of Willard's, pulling him down on top of her by *Bane's* scabbard. A second later, a fireball hurtled through the spot they had stood.

"Get off me," Willard screamed, rolling away, coming to his feet in a crouch. For a second he looked bewildered, then shaking his head, he glanced sheepishly at Averil. "Thanks."

"Just ... get the bloody gates closed."

As he left, dragging his sword, frowning at the carnage, Averil wondered if he had thanked her for saving his life, or for breaking his trance.

At the hatch, he sat with legs dangling, unslung the scabbard, carefully sheathed *Severne's Bane* and put it down. Then, with quick movements, he put his hands on the edge of the opening and dropped through into the gate room, not bothering with the ladder. Moments later, Averil heard the gates bang shut and the bar drop into place with a clunk. The rattle of the chains as the portcullis fell followed.

Retrieving Willard's sword, Averil threw the scabbard over her opposite shoulder and drew *Severne's Bane*.

[You are mortal April,] the Goddess warned as Averil stepped up onto the battlements, through a crenel and placed one foot on each merlon that framed it. Holding both named swords high, she let loose two bolts straight to the heavens. It mildly surprised her that Willard's worked for her, a second before the knowledge of how Severne keyed them popped into her mind; genetic markers. It was an impromptu display of bravado as if to say, here I am, strike me down if you can, I have power to spare.

The battle paused.

On the first crest down the Three Ways Road, behind thirty haphazard ranks of archers, spearmen, cavalry and catapult haulers, someone stepped forward from a tight group of officers and bowed low. Despite the distance, she knew it was Sumner. The bearing, the mannerism, the acknowledgment could only be the general she knew so well.

Averil bowed low in a return salute, as two grapples thrown from below, wrapped around the merlons on either side of where she stood. Dudley and Fletcher, taking advantage of the lull, ran up the wall. The distant Sumner raised his hand, dropping it the moment Fletcher and Dudley landed on the walkway.

Hostilities resumed.

Averil made one last sweep, pouring heart and soul into both the named swords, tearing two huge fissures in the ground in front of the first rank. She then exploding the bridge below into flaming splinters. As a last gesture of defiance, she stepped down casually, as if from a carriage. Arrows, spears, and balls of embers arched past all around her, but none close.

[It seems you have a patron among the Federals, April.]

The attack stalled as soon as the gates closed. Knowing Sumner, Averil knew the respite would be brief. In the interim, her mind worked furiously. With her new ability, akin to a seventh sense, Averil traced lines of consequences from current events to their inevitable conclusions, a virtual projection of the near future. She could now see how the oracle might work, how the Goddess could make reasonably accurate predictions. She marvelled at how the balloons had shifted the balance of power; three hundred years of stability disrupted with the discovery of nothing more startling than bags of hot air.

It was also clear that Carrier Point was the nexus about which the future turned and, despite appearances; it was now the safest place this side of the Barriers. Averil suddenly remembered the lone figure with the vaguely familiar walk. Kezia.

[Truly April, you are the gem of your generation. Such a pity you could not host me.]

• • • •

Willard had been more than willing to leave the fighting platform. He was ashamed of his detachment, wielding *Bane* in delicate wavelike strokes to maximise the kill with a minimum of effort. Averil's intervention, spoiling a long sweep that would've taken a record number of heads for a single stroke, had annoyed him. On his way to the hatch, the realisation that he had been counting sickened him. Only then did he grasp how emotionally uninvolved he had been. He sat down, sheathed *Severne's Bane*, unbuckled the scabbard, laid it beside the hatch and left it there when he dropped through.

[It's over Severne.]

He received no reply, nor did he want one. The swathe of death he had just cut would haunt him for as long as he lived. He could not lay these deaths at her feet. If *Severne's Bane* was merely an extension of himself, then he was the monster.

The last of the Watchers streamed through the West Gate as Willard stepped out through the side door of the tower.

"We're closing it," Willard yelled to the warriors, moving to help the stragglers.

[About bloody time,] Dudley answered. A flurry of renewed violence between the warriors saw several Watcher fall to a storm of arrows directed through the closing portal. They thudded into the massive wooden gates, moving slowly together.

The familiar sizzle of a named sword igniting, followed by a double clap of thunder, brought a sudden pause to the attack. The ferals were looking up at whatever was happening above. Averil, he thought and wondered why the feral he could see between Dudley and Fletcher was bowing.

Willard heard a thwack and felt a sharp pain. He looked up to find an arrow had pinned his hand to the gate. Gritting his teeth, he broke it in half and wrenched his hand up off the jagged end of the shaft. He pulled back his arm, seconds before the gates boomed shut. Calmly, he walked away and was under the portcullis when the drawbar clunked into its iron loops. Chains rattled and shortly after, the tongs of the iron lattice slammed home into stone.

His hand throbbed, but it was satisfying to have successfully completed the task. Closing the gates would be the last order he would take. It was time to confront Severne and get Kezia back. Gripping his swelling hand, he trailed after the Watchers towards the tower. He paused, fascinated to see a gaunt woman in an unadorned healer's uniform bend over and spit on a woman's chest.

"This one next healer Jena," said the Watcher behind her, and the healer turned to the stretcher where a man, slashed across the face by a spear, lay with his face covered in blood, one eye gummed shut.

So this is the famous healer whose tears, and apparently her spit, have magical healing qualities. His first impression was she was so thin, she could do with a good meal.

Glancing down at his hand, Willard wondered if he should ask her to look at it, but decided his wound was not bad enough to require her special attention. As he started walking past, the healer stood up, groaning with the effort, massaging the small of her back. Then she looked around as if searching for someone and her eyes locked on him.

Willard couldn't believe his eyes. He drank in the image as if she were a phantasm of Severne's that might dissipate any second. The image was both familiar and unfamiliar. The brown eyes stared out from a face that despite its thinness and grimed lines was Kezia. The short blonde hair was brown at the roots. Combined with the gaunt appearance, she looked more like Averil. A year of frustrated longing welled up inside him.

· · · ·

When Kezia looked up from the last patient, to see if she could see Averil, she found Willard, staring at her, the eyes and mouth instantly recognisable despite the untidy beard. Then she noticed the eye-shaped scar and the talisman around his neck. Goddess be damned, another betrayal. Willard, her Willard, was the one they were calling the Man Who Will Be Face. The Goddess had marked him and claimed him. *I've lost him.*

Then she realised how she must look to him: short hair dyed blonde, and haggard from a hard year on the road.

"Where have you been?" he asked. "I've been waiting for ..."

The whole of Kezia's journey flashed through her mind. She remembered why she had taken a new name and changed her appearance; her father. Even without that, Willard could never be hers. She'd had a son by another man.

"It's me," he said.

The pleading in the differently coloured eyes weakened her resolve, but the talisman held her in check, until she noticed he didn't have a sword, and he still had hair. *He can't have taken the test.*

Willard spread his arms. The gesture was so appealing, so much what she had wanted; she felt unable to resist and took a step. Moments later, she was clinging for all she was worth; her face buried in his neck unaware of the transition. She began hoping that somehow, despite all that had happened they could make it work.

· · · ·

It was a long time before Willard could speak. The nearness of death, the stench of blood, and the chaos of battle into which Severne had thrust him, gradually faded. Every time he tried to back away a little to look at her, Kezia would pull him closer, burying her face in his neck. He could feel her tears, wet and tingling, on his skin.

He flinched when a loose thread in her uniform caught in his wound. Kezia stepped out of his embrace, pulling his arm from behind her.

"You're hurt," she said.

"Not badly."

"Untreated you could die of it."

She lifted his hand to her mouth, gently kissing the open wound and running her tongue over it. Then she turned it over and repeated the process.

The circle of Watchers around them applauded as Willard inspected the wound. His hand tingled hot around the dark, blue-black puncture. The colour lightened; the wound no longer throbbed.

Their eyes met and they began laughing, whoops of joy and relief as they again tearfully clutched each other.

Peripherally, Willard saw the surrounding crowd disband. Averil had come down from the tower and had taken charge. He and Kezia remained immobile. He had found her and she still wanted him. He could ignore Severne and her plans now she had lost her hold over him. He need never take the damn test. Whatever they faced under feral occupation, they could face together.

· · · ·

Both swords across her back, Averil dropped into the Gate Room, pushed through the double doors into the guard tower and sped down the stone stairs. She emerged from the tower, through the side door into the main thoroughfare before the gates, and stumbled into Willard and Kezia. They stood among a group of applauding wounded, arms locked about each other in a fierce mutual embrace, oblivious to all around them.

Averil felt a twinge of envy. Or was it jealousy? she wondered. [What about our offspring,] she asked.

The Goddess remained silent and Averil immediately surmised that their failure to mate, despite every opportunity, must be one of those unforeseen results that caused Our Lady's oracles to be less than infallible.

[April?]

[Howard.]

[There is absolute chaos down here. Very few boats dare to return. I doubt we can get everyone away inside a season.]

Willard and Kezia remained preoccupied as Averil organised the Watchers, quietly issuing orders to get the wounded into the servatory compound first. Evacuation may be futile, but she would have to maintain the appearance of doing so, as best she could, until the last possible moment. In the end, like the Goddess, Averil saw her primary responsibility for the greater good - was Willard.

[Dudley, get up to the Gate Platform, help them hold the wall for as long as possible. Fletcher, I want everyone that's left moved into the compound, then seal all the rotundas except number seven. Hold that open for us. Howard, I'm adding Willard to your brief. Come up and take them away.]

As the Restoration Warriors moved, Averil caught wondering glances from the Watchers. To them it must seem, as it once had to her, the warriors worked independently. If they only knew how truly connected we are. Yet even with her new insights, Averil found some of the Goddess's ways exceedingly confronting. [In not worried about what you did to me, I know why, but what you've done to Kezia will set Willard against you.]

[We need to discuss that, April.]

Averil grinned. [Indeed, when time permits.] She turned her attention back to her primary charges, walked over, and placed her arms protectively around Willard and Kezia.

Chapter 44

T he clapping made Kezia redden. She again buried her face against Willard's neck until she felt another arm on her shoulder, and looked up to find Averil had joined them.

"I have to get you two out of here," Averil said quietly.

Kezia's hackles rose as she looked into Averil's familiar eyes. The mirror image of Willard's, but with such added depth, she knew immediately that what the Watcher had said of her sister was true. Averil had taken the test. Goddess knowledge exuded from those depths.

I can't trust her anymore, Kezia thought, as the war reasserted itself with the chilling war cry of thousands of attacking ferals.

"Head for the tower," Averil cried as she threw Willard his sword. A shiver ran up Kezia's spine as he deftly caught the scabbard and slung the strap over his shoulder, before Averil whirled away from them, her own sword slipping from the scabbard.

"Scaling ladders," someone shouted as Willard grabbed Kezia's hand and pulled her along at a stumbling run, constantly changing direction as he angled across the open paddock. Kezia glancing back could see two warriors, one of them Averil, backing up to a cavern entrance rotunda, glowing swords just clearing the top of the battlements. ferals poured over the wall.

Hand in hand, they ran for the servatory compound, Willard keeping them off the roads where the feral firepower had concentrated earlier.

Howard greeted them as they passed under the stone arch into the tower grounds, "This way Jena, Lord."

Willard stopped, pulled Kezia to him, and kissed her briefly. "I hate it, but I know how to use it," he said, touching the hilt at his shoulder. "I can't just abandon them." To Howard he added, "Take care of her."

Howard looked as alarmed as Kezia felt. The warrior gripped her arm. Kezia, seeing the hope she had nurtured crumbling, frantically tried to hold on to Willard.

"Don't do this to me, Will," she pleaded.

"I don't have a choice. I won't be long," Willard said, gently prising her fingers from his arm, turning to look back to where blue flashes pinpointed Dudley and Averil's retreat. As he turned, Howard pulled Kezia sharply backwards and reached over his shoulder. His sword came out in a blur, gemmed hilt forward, and struck Willard on the back of the head.

As Willard collapsed, Kezia dropped to her knees, catching him as he fell and cradling his head in her lap.

"April ... your sister said to stop him," Howard said.

"Now help me get him inside," Kezia said, grateful but wary.

Watchers jumped to Howard's request and loaded Willard onto a stretcher. With Howard directing, they crossed through the tower foyer, out the server's private entrance, and across the packed compound to the servatory. The bearers hesitated when they reached the shimmering curtain. Howard ushered Kezia in with a hand on her shoulder and assured the bearers the Goddess would admit them. He stood in the doorway to pass them out after they had laid Willard on a bench.

Kezia removed his sword, glancing briefly at the strange name, *Severne's Bane,* and put it under the bench. She sat then, placed Willard's head in her lap, and gently caressed his brow, trying to smooth out the eye-shaped scar. *We are going to make it kiddo, no matter what; we are going to make it.* Howard's intervention had rekindled her hopes.

Willard groaned and tried to sit up, his hand reaching for his head. "What hit me?"

"I did Lord," said Howard. "April says she told you. You're the reason Sumner came here, rather than Canalbridge."

"So?"

"Once we tell him you've gone, he will have no reason to stay. Can you walk?"

"I think so."

Kezia helped him to his feet, saying nothing about the named sword left under the bench. Howard hurried them through a door, down a series of stairs, and along a pale green corridor past many closed doors until he stopped to open one. Kezia saw nothing to set it apart from the rest.

The shimmer of a power curtain in the doorway distorted the people inside. It appeared to be a storeroom, cut directly from the rock. Their entire world was falling apart, and these people stacking boxes were still doing their jobs. She squeezed Willard's hand for reassurance.

Howard waited until they left before leading Kezia and a very subdued Willard between the piled boxes. As she stepped across the threshold, a warm, damp smell assailed her, salt spray and rotting timber. We must be close to the Port. It confirmed her guess when they emerged from the storeroom into the vast domed cave where she and Howard had arrived.

That a network of hidden corridors, unknown to the general populace, existed side by side with the known caves was worth noting thought Kezia. It shows the Goddess and her warriors in their true light; a secretive cult within Our Lady's church.

• • • •

Averil watched Willard pull Kezia off the road on a zigzag course towards the Rotunda. At least he's remembered some of what I taught him.

[Dudley, time you got off the wall.]

[Yes please.] his thought sounded tired.

Averil joined him as he exited the gate tower and together, they backed up towards the Rotunda held by Fletcher. The ferals had opened the West Gate before they had retreated a block. By the time they reached the rotunda steps, the Federals had her and Dudley surrounded. The gem in *Fires Kiss* was down to an orange glow, Dudley's to a cherry red.

"Conserve your energy," she told Dudley, as she made a circular sweep, the power from *Fires Kiss* scorching across the chests of the front rank. Federals fell on the grass and rolled about, trying to put out the flames and fighting back against those who would trample them in their haste to lay a blade on the exhausted warriors.

Behind them, a door opened onto descending stairs. Fletcher beckoned. Dudley started down the stairs, and the partly rested Fletcher joined her. His gem yellow, he cut across the second rank, as Willard had done with such devastation; heads rolled.

Beyond the carnage, Averil saw Sumner of the Lakes, and Stone Ethyl ride into view through the demolished West Gate. Those around her and Fletcher stopped fighting.

[Fletcher, join Dudley down the stairs.]

Sumner, quickly locating where the last pocket of resistance had been, trotted across, and dismounted. Ethyl right behind.

"What warrior and sword name did you choose, Averil of the Lakes?" Sumner hailed, as their war was over.

"I chose April. Fires Kiss was Our Lady's choice," she replied.

"Well ... April of the brethren,"

"Leader of the brethren," Averil corrected.

"Is Baxter dead?"

"Not at all. He simply relinquished the leadership."

"Well, leader April, as you can see, you have lost. If you surrender the Man Who Will Be Face, then all within may go free."

"Our Lady's warriors do not surrender general," she said. Except, as Sumner should know, Gardner had on the beach. And Willard had said Baxter had surrendered to the Watchers.

Sumner scowled, "Then I shall take the Face by force, and all the Uplanders within will suffer in the taking."

"Except for candidates, Uplanders no longer interest me," Averil lied, "My sole concern is Our Lady's Restoration, as it should be for one as devout as you claim to be, or is your worship merely an empty pretence?"

Averil edged back towards the inner pavilion, a step away from the door and the stairs, and took up the stance. The tip of *Fires Kiss* rested in its toe cup, ready but at ease.

[Beware the spearman.]

"You do me and yourself a grave injustice. As we have discussed many times," he said, reminding her of their many nights playing games, mostly chess. "We all want the same thing, but you Uplanders want it for yourselves alone."

[Left,] came a thought and Averil leaned left as a spear passed her head. Despite her lethargy, *Fires Kiss* came up crackling. The beam that leapt from the end traced the spear's flight path, lighting up the empty-handed spearman. When the ferals turned to stare at their burning comrade, Averil disappeared down the rotunda stairs. Three named swords combined in a concentrated effort. The pavilion imploded, bringing down tons of stone and rubble to plug the stairwell.

Averil coughed and spluttered in the choking dust, thankful that Sumner had followed his own maxim and tried to do it all in the first day. If he had waited until he had the numbers to attack all sides at once, he might have succeeded.

[The lure of the Man Who Will Be Face,] Severne said.

[Who told them it would be Willard?] asked Averil.

[A source Our Lady can't access ...] said a new voice in her mind, faint yet familiar. It faded to nothing.

[Who was that?]

[Gardner,] Dudley said. [He is still down there trying to find the source of Federal information.]

[So my capture on the beach was an unfortunate side effect of Gardner's real mission; once he got me over Perisher.]

[No April. Gardner's mission was a 'fortunate' side effect of your capture. It put Gardner on site. Once you were safe, I directed him to find their source.]

[Good luck with that Gard,] she projected, reaching out to the distant Gardner. The two minds beside her reeled.

As the warrior trio marched down the wide stone passage from the Rotunda to the caverns, Averil brushed a hand across her sweating head, and came away with short blonde strands stuck to her palm. She wiped them off on her leggings, briefly wondering at the price of taking the test. She itched everywhere.

[It will pass,] Severne said.

[That's what I'm afraid of.]

As they emerged into utter chaos in the main cavern, Severne added. [The Federals have halted at the compound.]

[As I expected, invading a tower is a desecration too far, for a man like Sumner. Besides, I have problems enough down here.]

The stone steps and ramps, down to the floating Port, had jammed with people, shouting, and pushing to get down to the boats. There was a break in the retaining wall where, according to Howard, the press of bodies had become too great and some hapless persons had pushed right through it.

Three named swords slithered in unison from the ornate leather scabbards and despite their owner's weariness, the swords sizzled. The mob hushed.

[Dudley south, Fletcher north. Kill any troublemakers.]

[Harsh, April,] Severne said.

[If I'm going to save any of them, I need absolute control. They're a danger to themselves,] Averil answered, but amended her instructions to Dudley and Fletcher already down in the crowd. [Disable them and make bloody sure they know death follows if they persist.]

• • • •

People packed the cavern from one rock wall to the other. Kezia drew close under Willard's arm, drawing as much support as she was giving, and grateful again for a warrior escort. As they made their way along the edge of the cavern, the throng parted when they saw the named sword at Howard's shoulder.

A loud crack and three blue flames roared to the ceiling at the back of the crowd. Kezia recognised the voice issuing the commands, Averil.

"There will be order here, or heads will roll," Averil barked, her voice echoing in the quiet vastness. She had their attention immediately, some protectively rubbing their necks. "I want this cavern cleared. Watchers, I want you on the compound roof." The Watchers greeted this with a groan. "Civilians." She put a sneer into the word and heard the groan migrate to a chuckle. "Back onto the rotunda ramps and stay there. Move slowly."

A big man ahead of Kezia, taller than those around him, griped about the high-handed attitude of this new female warrior. "She seems to think she's the Goddess."

Beyond him, Kezia could see a warrior approaching.

"Dudley," Howard told her, and Willard nodded.

Howard, a step ahead of her and Willard, was only a yard away when the scuffle broke out and the big malcontent fell to the ground, screaming in agony, ineffectually holding his bleeding wrist. The surrounding crowd fell away and Kezia saw his severed hand clutched a knife. Warrior Dudley stood over him, his sword pointed at the man's chest.

Kezia slipped out from under Willard's arm, reached down and picked up the hand, prised open the still warm fingers to lose the knife. She knelt beside the big man, spat on the neatly severed wrist and the stump.

"Don't be afraid, I'm healer Jena. let me restore your hand before you bleed to death." She hoped it was true. She had never actually tried to restore separated limbs though some she had treated had been close.

The man looked from his stump at her, then past her to Dudley. She saw the agony in his eyes turn to rage. He pushed Kezia away with his bloody stump and she fell back onto the low wall, head and shoulders over the abyss, the floating port hundreds of feet below her. Howard pulled her back from the brink as the man struggled to his feet and, screeching his rage, lurched towards them.

Dudley stepped back, flicked his sword through the charging man's neck. The headless body drove into Howard just as he thrust Kezia away from the edge into Willard. Kezia reached out wildly as Willard held her, clutched at Howard's billowing cloak as he flew backwards over the edge, futilely trying to rid himself of the body. His scream mingled with hers as he disappeared.

It seemed ages before shrieks from below floated up to Kezia.

• • • •

When Averil reached them, Dudley and Fletcher stood in a large open space at the edge of the cave mouth, looking down over the low wall. Between them lay a man's head. Willard was holding a distraught Kezia as best he could while the storm of outrage coursed through her. She was cursing the Goddess in terms that made Dudley frown and drew hostile stares from others.

Our Lady's warning came in focus, 'you are not immortal', as she quick assessed the situation. That Howard was so young made it a double tragedy; hundreds of years of useful life lost. White-faced, Averil glanced at the gull circling under the dome roof. [Where were you when this happened?] Averil asked, also projecting the question to Willard, trying to force communication with him.

[I cannot protect any of you from random acts of violence.]

If Willard heard, he did not open to it. Averil's gaze flicked from his face to the talisman and back. He seemed confused. [Where did he leave *Bane?*]

[The servatory.]

She had to remind herself he didn't have the advantage of the knowledge the test gave, yet she must now rely on him to get himself and Kezia away.

She tapped Willard on the shoulder, waited till she had his attention. "I need you to get yourself and Kezia away from here. Our Lady needs you both."

[Is this wise, April?]

[My sister doesn't trust anyone else now we've lost Howard.]

Her words to Willard must have sunk through her sister's emotional miasma. Kezia twisted out of Willard's grasp and spat in Averil's face. The hate behind it stunned her, despite the downloaded knowledge that showed everything Kezia had suffered. Averil wiped her cheek with the hood of her cloak, looked back at Willard and with a quick motion of the head said. "Go."

[I stand corrected, April.]

Willard, with his arm protectively around Kezia, headed for the ramp. Averil spun back to the circle of expectant onlookers, suppressing tears pooling at the corner of her eyes.

[Dudley, keep this lot moving. Fletcher, go with them and organise the Port. It's made of boats, dismantle it, fill them, send them off. Make sure those two get away. I'm going up to see Sumner] and get some air. [Once I can assure him Willard is gone, he might leave.]

Several muted voices saying, [Yes boss,] echoed in her mind.

• • • •

Willard, slowly regaining his senses after Howard's savage blow, glanced back over his shoulder as he shepherded an unresisting Kezia towards the queue on the ramp, but Averil, already busy with crowd control, did not look around. He felt the pressure from behind ease and supposed Averil had won her battle to regulate the traffic. Those at the bottom were still dispersing through the conglomeration and trickling away in whatever boats still had the courage to keep returning.

Kezia rallied as they stepped off the stone terrace onto the wooden wharf. "We have to find Howard ... his body," she said.

Willard could see instantly that no protest would sway her. Besides, the delay wouldn't matter. Even if they escape all the way back to Deep Creek, the ferals would inevitably come there. All we have left is each other. He acquiesced.

They navigated by instinct through the warren of linked boats and barges that formed Carrier Point's floating Port. The place from which Howard and his nemesis fell was easily identifiable. The tricky bit would be to find a path to where the bodies must have landed. His talisman proved to be a useful passport among the Severnian residents who eventually led them to Howard's body. Willard hardly recognised the warrior. The locals had stripped his body and without his accoutrements; he looked like a rather thin, prematurely bald young man.

"What will I tell his mother," Kezia said, "I hated him Willard, for what the Goddess made him do to me?"

"Was he … the father?" Willard asked.

"Goddess no," Kezia said, looking up at him. "She told you that?"

"Only that you had a child. When you said … I just assumed …" he stopped, nodded at the body of the warrior.

Kezia lay her hand on his arm. "No Will, he's not the father. It's a long story, but his part was telling me my son had died and then telling me the opposite when the attack came, just to get me off the Wall." She started crying. "Now that he's dead I can't hate him anymore. He died saving my life."

Again, Willard did his best to comfort her, but she seemed inconsolable. [You will pay for this Severne, I promise.]

They wrapped Howard's body in a borrowed sheet, and Willard hoisted the light bundle over his shoulder. By the time they joined the crowd at the floating Port's dismantled edge, Willard was stumbling under the weight.

Opposite them, across several miles of glassy ocean, stood the closest point of Carrier Island and strung out between, in a long sparse line, a flotilla of small boats rowed back and forth, some with sails, limp in the still air. His talisman again attracted attention.

"Need a boat ser," asked a small wiry man in a stained white shirt. Willard doubted the five-foot long rowboat could make the distance.

"Been over and back five times," he added, flexing his arms to show off his biceps.

"Where are all the ships?" asked Willard.

"They won't come any more, too calm and too hard to get away when those ferals come. All anchored the other side of the Island where the wind is. I take you to this side, you hoof it across and they'll be waiting."

"How much?" Willard asked.

"I'll take you for free, brother," said another voice.

Willard's scalp crawled. Sitting in the stern of a similar boat sat Aldus.

"Aldus," Kezia shrieked in delight.

Willard's relief at seeing a face he could truly trust not to be a Severnian puppet did not override questions he had about where his brother's loyalties lay.

"Come on, if you're not hiring get out of me way," the boatman said, pushing off, calling up to someone else on the floating wharf, "need a boat."

• • • •

After threading her way up the ramp against the flow, Averil headed straight for the compound's battlements. Battlements overstated the series of wide planks over the gutter between the servatory roof and its external wall two feet higher. As she crawled past, she murmured platitudes to those asking when they were getting out. "Soon," she said, "soon." Occasionally she stopped to chat with those she knew, 'How's your arm', 'nice day for a war'.

"What's your name?" Averil asked of a veteran she had seen on the parapets of Grand Falls, but didn't know.

"Randal," the man said.

"What's happening, Randal?"

"Bugger all."

They chatted a while. He seemed very well informed for a simple soldier. She made a mental note to keep a watch on him, then moved on. If he wasn't a spy, he might be useful.

When she reached the section over the compound's gateway, Elswyth, one of her captains from Grand Falls, said, "The General keeps calling for you Major, ... er, Warrior April."

Averil grinned, "Is that so?" She poked her head above the low wall. The town was now quiet and full. Every conceivable space: the fields and the roads, held tents, horses, and Federals.

"You know why the ferals stopped?" she asked reverting, knowing that using Federals would muddy the message she wanted to get across. It was time to enlighten the Watchers about their new masters.

"No, major," said Elswyth.

"General Sumner is an honourable man. He respects the sanctity of a servatory." She could see his disbelief.

"Like most ferals, General Sumner believes in Our Lady."

As if sensing her presence Sumner's voice lifted to them on the light breeze. "Bring me April."

Averil stood up, "General Sumner, how nice to see you again."

[Do you mock me April?]

"And you Ethyl," Averil continued, ignoring Severne.

"There you are, Averil of the Lakes," Sumner said, reminding her of their time together, "but then, where would you go? We have you trapped. I will be here until you surrender the Man Who Will Be Face or until you all starve to death."

[Do the ferals know about the caves and the Port?] Averil asked as an idea began fermenting, in an area of her mind inaccessible to Severne. If the worst happened, it might work. Better to get Willard away.

[Yes.]

"Soon, the last of your boats will be gone," Sumner continued. "The choice is yours and is simple. Surrender the Man or starve."

Averil sent an urgent thought to Fletcher, [How many boats left?]

[Plenty, but untangling them is slow work.]

Averil privately pondered what Sumner meant by their last boats being gone soon, when Fletcher said there were plenty. She believed them both. From firsthand experience, she knew Sumner was not one to make idle boasts. He was normally a most taciturn man. Perhaps the message was for his troops. What could she offer the Watchers in return?

[How long Fletcher?]

[Several days.]

"Enjoy our town general. You have a long wait," she said, and with luck, we will be gone before you realise it.

"So be it," Sumner said, and strode away to his tent.

To the delight of the Watchers Averil strode the battlements in plain sight of the ferals. Watchers stood and clapped as she passed and she smiled at their cheerfulness, a feeling she did not share.

"Since the ferals will not fire on us," Averil told her captains, "we will march this tiny parapet proudly and give them a show. When the time comes, when everyone is away but us, we will disappear and they will be the proud conquerors of an empty town."

[Where are Willard and my sister?] she asked Fletcher.

[Boarding.]

[Thanks.]

Chapter 45

K ezia stepped down into the boat, and Aldus stood to catch her. She gave him a big hug.

"You don't look pleased to see me little brother," Aldus said.

"I thought you were dead until Averil told me she seen you."

Kezia felt Aldus's arm around her waist tense, and his voice took on an edge. "What else did Averil tell you?"

"I didn't believe her," Willard said, his gaze locked on Aldus.

The conversation lost Kezia. What had Averil said that Willard didn't believe, and why did Aldus appear threatened by it? She looked from one to the other in mild alarm. There was an undercurrent between them she had never seen before. Naked antagonism from Aldus and scepticism from Willard. The eye-shaped scar on his forehead stood out with the effort of balancing Howard's body on his shoulder against the motion of the floating wharf.

"Hey. Simmer down you two. Come on Will, pass Howard down." She turned to Aldus. "I'm taking Warrior Howard's body back to his mother in Java."

Aldus looked down, rubbed his neck. When he looked up, the antagonism had vanished and he was once again the Aldus she remembered. "Okay Kez," he said, letting her go, then turning back to Willard. "As you can little brother, I'm alive and kicking. The ferals that attacked us liked me so much, they took me home with them."

"So Averil said," answered Willard, lowering Howard's legs into the boat.

Aldus flinched but remained genial. "I found it hard to leave. I kept thinking it didn't matter. Any day now, my friends will come to rescue me."

Even as Kezia wondered what they were talking about, she fretted they were wasting time. "Surely, this can wait. Come on Will, get in. You can swap stories as we go," she said.

Willard smiled down at her. "You're right, we can sort this out when we're safely away," he said and went to step down into the boat.

"Hey. Back up brother," Aldus said.

For a fleeting second, as Aldus issued his terse command, Kezia thought she saw a flash of hate in his eyes. She sat down heavily in the stern of the little boat, wondering if she had imagined it.

"You don't want to sink us," Aldus said, grinning. "I can't take all three of you."

Kezia could see he was right. The small boat had settled deep enough already.

"So who's for the first trip," Aldus asked Kezia, "Willard or the warrior's body?"

Willard looked at her, then at Aldus, and she knew it would be her decision.

"What if I stay with Willard," Kezia said, "while you take warrior Howard's body across, then come back for both of us?"

"No. I want you safe," Willard said. "I can get another boat. I might even beat you across and at worst Aldus will come back for me, won't you, brother?"

There it is again, Kezia thought, a sudden heavy emphasis Willard put on 'won't you brother', as if he doesn't trust him.

"Of course, little brother," Aldus said, in similar tones. "Would I leave you to suffer alone in enemy hands?" He quickly dipped the oars. "See you little brother," he added, pushing off.

"Willard," Kezia pleaded, reaching out for him, not wanting to go without him, but wanting a reciprocal sign he felt the same. Willard stood undecided and lost the moment. Aldus rowed with powerful strokes, and the distance rapidly widened. Willard dwindled, blended into the ramshackle port and the overbearing wall of rock behind it.

"It will be alright," he called to her, but by then they were too far away for her to read his expression.

"Don't do anything I wouldn't do," Aldus called back.

• • • •

What would you not do, brother? I don't know you anymore, thought Willard, following the boat until it was just a speck, indistinguishable from all the other specks. He could no longer be sure which speck he'd been following. Had he done the right thing in getting Kezia safely away? Averil must be wrong about Aldus betraying them. He wasn't wearing a watch uniform.

"Lord Willard, why are you still here?"

Willard jumped, startled out of morbid thoughts, to find Fletcher standing behind him. "The boat was too small."

"This way, Lord," Fletcher said, leading him a little further along the water's edge. "This should do," he said, pulling up planks to reveal a small boat underneath, used as a pontoon. Without warning, Fletcher jumped back and pulled Willard with him. A huge ball of flaming coals slammed into the boat; clouds of steam arose as the coals burnt through the flimsy bottom. It sizzled and sank.

"Aw shit, too bloody late," Fletcher said, as flaming balls fell in increasing numbers all over the floating Port. "Go," he said and pushed Willard towards the rock face, about a hundred yards away. Seconds later, he ran past Willard and took the lead. "Follow me."

• • • •

Severne suddenly tapped Averil's mind. [Forget evacuating April. Sumner has launched coals and lit tar at the Port.]

[What,] she said as several fireballs passed overhead.

Moments later Fletcher told her, [They're firebombing us, the boats will all be gone soon,] his last remark echoing Sumner's threat. His thought stream then paused, like an intake of breath, and she knew he had a thought he would rather not share.

[Out with it.]

[Lord Willard is still here.]

[Severne's t ... Eye.]

[Is watching you April,] Severne added.

Averil controlled herself, kept her next thoughts private. Damn Willard, can't he do anything right? She conceded he might have got it partly right. Kezia must have got away, or Fletcher would have said.

"Bring him to the tower," Averil said to Fletcher and took a deep breath herself, contemplating private thoughts about Willard not getting away.

"And the rest?" Fletcher asked.

"Bring them all," she broadcast.

· · · ·

They were well over halfway to Carrier Island, when Kezia saw a frown appear on Aldus's face, then a hint of awe, perhaps smugness. She couldn't tell which.

Kezia turned to look back at the shadowed collection of angles at the waterline. Balls of fire were falling from the top of the cliff into a pall of smoke and steam that rose above the water.

"We have to go back," Kezia yelled.

"No point," Aldus said, looking over his shoulder to see how close they were to Carrier Island. He doubled his stroke. "Willard wouldn't thank me for putting you in danger."

"No," Kezia screamed, "we're going back now." She stood up, rocking the boat. "Turn around or I'll jump in and swim back." It was an idle threat; she knew she wouldn't make the distance.

"Sit down and shut up," Aldus snarled, and a thrill of fear whipped through her. "I'm taking you out of this willingly or otherwise."

He shipped the oars and stood, leaning forward to grip her shoulders. The boat rocked wildly as he tried to push her down. "Sit down before I knock you down."

Kezia sat and twisted around to stare at the distant conflagration.

"And this is going too," he said behind her.

She was too slow to grasp what he meant. She whirled back at the sound of a splash as Aldus rolled Howard's body over the side. She started getting up, but Aldus smacked her hard across the face, knocking her into the bottom of the boat.

"Don't move. Next time, I won't be so gentle," he warned.

• • • •

Occasionally, Fletcher stopped or veered off at right angles to the next public thoroughfare as a fireball crashed into the planking they'd been heading for. Willard marvelled at how Severne could so accurately predict where they would fall. Fletcher kept just ahead of him, but Willard that without him along, the warrior would have already have reached the ramp.

Fire rained down everywhere, adding to the already widespread blaze. Carrier Point's port was breaking up as it burnt down, sinking through geysers of steam. Willard saw evacuating refugees and boat residents alike, diving into the sea. A burning woman ran towards them. Fletcher's sword slithered out, and like a story come to life, the warrior lopped off her head. Willard looked straight ahead as he passed the spot. The head and body had fallen on different sides of the plank. Was that a mercy killing, or had she just been in the way?

The public walkways were broader, but more crowded as they neared the cliff face, and the older, more established section of the Port. There was less burning close under the looming rock face, and Fletcher slowed. They passed a devotee, kneeling in his boat, looking up at the sky through the smoke and flames, making the sign of the circle on his chest and touching his forehead.

Willard stopped and shook him until he had his attention. "The Goddess can't help you. You need to help yourself," he shouted in the man's face.

"Yes, Lord," the man said, and went back to praying as soon as Fletcher pulled the cursing Willard away. They did not stop again until they reached the cliff.

Still gasping from running through smoke, Willard watched as boats burned and sank, worried that there was a sinister pattern to recent events. The Goddess was punishing him for not taking the test, by dangling Kezia before him like a baited hook, then whisking her away just as he was about to take it. He tried to think back. Was their reunion accidental or was Severne trying to show him that if he didn't fall in with her plans, she would make sure his plans fell apart? Surely, Aldus wasn't part of her plan.

"This way Lord Willard," Fletcher urged.

"Where are you taking me?" he asked. He was relatively safe here and he wanted to wait and see if Aldus would return, although with the Port gone, he doubted it.

"To the safety of the servatory, Averil is waiting."

Even that sounded suspicious. He'd become paranoid about hidden forces and motives. He no longer trusted anyone except

Kezia. When Fletcher ushered the survivors up the ramp, Willard followed.

There was nowhere else to go.

. . . .

Averil suppressed annoying thoughts. The boats were gone along with most of the original citizenry, including the custodian, his councillors and Ser Digby. Although the Watchers patrolled the parapet in full view, her plan to withdraw surreptitiously was in tatters.

Sumner has trapped her. As the Senior Watcher commander, she had responsibility for nearly a thousand men, women, and children, and as brethren leader, responsibility for saving the Man Who Will Be Face. The two were not mutually exclusive, but if she had to sacrifice the lot for him, she would. No one other than the brethren would or could ever know, and it would haunt her, for the rest of her very long life, worse than the feral she killed at Perisher tower. Longevity was a heritage the test had shown was hers, though not why.

She'd failed. The Man Who Will Be Face will soon be in Federal hands unless ... a thought she'd had earlier became a conviction and the idea derived from it crystallised. Sumner wanted the Man Who Will be Face. Assuming her projections were accurate, she would give Sumner what he wanted. Averil quickly buried her idea at the deepest private level and, as she went to meet the arrivals from below, she put a secondary idea to the Goddess.

The refugee residue trickled up through the caverns into the servatory compound Willard among them. Nuaith's best hope looked haggard, unsure of himself and miserable. He seemed to brighten when he saw her and Averil felt a guilty, warm glow.

"We can't go on meeting like this. Kezia will get suspicious," Willard said, attempting to lighten the mood.

Averil looked down until her face cooled. "She got away then."

"Aldus turned up with a boat ..."

Averil's head whipped up. "Aldus," she screamed, "you let Aldus take her ... you stupid son of a ... I already told you he's the one who killed Kingsley and opened the gates."

[Why didn't you tell me,] she shouted at Severne and the Fletcher.

[I don't know the man,] Fletcher said.

[I will redirect Baxter,] Severne added.

Willard looked at her defiantly, obviously not convinced.

Averil realised she had no opportunity to tell him she saw Ethyl pay Aldus. She willed herself to get a grip on her emotions. This was going to be an extremely difficult tale to tell.

To preserve the careful reputation Severne had built for him, she whisked him away from the public gaze, to the abandoned server's suite near the top of the tower. Poor bastard, she thought, trying to see it from his point of view. He had only recently discovered the brother he grew up with was alive. Now he was coming to terms with the fact that not only had his brother had become a murderous traitor, but that he had entrusted his beloved Kezia to the man. Poor bugger, we had already burdened him with Aldus and Arthur not being family at all. She relayed Severne's recordings of how Arthur had gone to recover his grandson Aldus's body and found the boot Willard had seen in a pile of rubbish caught in the overflow pipe.

Willard withdrew into himself after Severne confirmed the details. They had got drunk after that and now lay on the Arch Server's opulent bed; she cradling Willard in her arms while he wept uncontrollably, holding him tight when the occasional shudder passed through his body. It was an awkward position. Her leg rubbed his groin with every spasm. She felt him harden, though she doubted it was anything other than reflex.

Her long-ago conversation with the Goddess sprang to mind with incredible clarity.

"I want you to survive, to have offspring."

"Who with?" she had stupidly asked.

"Willard Forrestor."

Now that she knew what it meant to Seven's plan, Averil wondered at her motives for being here, in bed, with a vulnerable Willard and Kezia gone. Was it really for the survival of them all? Yes, her extra knowledge told her.

[Is that the reason or my rationalisation?]

Severne was silent.

· · · ·

"You promised you would go back," Kezia said, through swollen lips. She could feel her bruised face repairing itself. Severne had replenished the healing dust during her adjustment of Kezia's reproductive organs, a thought that still chilled Kezia.

Aldus, watching her, drew back as if she were evil. "I saw Averil healing herself like you're doing. The bloody Goddess has corrupted you both."

Kezia said nothing, knowing that the past year had radically changed them both. She was prepared to forgive him when he was ready for conciliation. Despite his abusive manner, he'd been right about dumping Howard's body overboard; they were riding higher and faster. How do I tell Beverly her son's death was a stupid accident? She'd have to make it sound more heroic. And If Beverly wanted to know where he lay, Kezia could truthfully say she had buried Howard at sea.

"As for going back, forget it," he said. "You saw the fire bombs destroy the port. If my brother survived, then the ferals have him, and trust me, you don't want to know why they want him."

"The ferals don't want him, the Goddess does?"

"You still don't get it," Aldus said, and she saw pity in his eyes, as he beached their boat on the foreshore of what the sign said was Bridgeport, one boat among a flotilla of abandoned boats. The town, a collection of ancient-looking hovels, had clustered around a very different tower, oblong rather than round, squat as if beheaded, yet still several stories high.

"Are you coming, or do I have to drag you?"

Kezia followed, bewildered. Aldus had implied Willard was, in some measure, responsible for the attack on Carrier Point. She asked again.

"Their oracle told them, whoever controls the Face controls the Goddess."

"What has that got to do with Will? Good Goddess, surely, they don't think ... how do you know all this?"

"Where do you think I've been this last year?"

"I didn't know. Until this morning I didn't know you'd left home," Kezia said. "I left straight after our trip to Arthurton."

Aldus stopped in the middle of the narrow main street and stared at her in amazement then laughed, slapping his forehead with the heel of a hand as if trying to pound something into his brain. "With the contingent?"

" ... sort of."

"You don't know then?"

"Know what."

"Their oracle named Willard as the Man," he snarled and Kezia noted the bitterness in his voice. "A couple of days after you left, a full warband raided the farm looking for Willard, and took me by mistake."

"I'm sorry."

"Sorry," Aldus bellowed. "Sorry won't cover half what they did to me, or that the Watcher patrol following them could have rescued me." He turned away and headed for a ramshackle set of stables. "Now move it. I have a ship waiting."

"I'm not going anywhere without Willard."

Aldus stopped and came back. As he leaned close, there was a cunning look in his eyes that reminded her of her father. "Your best chance to see him again is to persuade the captain I've hired to sail back for him." His gaze dropped to her cleavage. "Who knows what you could achieve if you try?"

Kezia's face reddened, part embarrassment, part resentment, but she followed. He was right again. A ship was her best chance.

Despite exorbitant prices, Aldus still purchased a horse. Kezia supposed he had stolen the money from the ferals. She hated the idea of riding with him, but once mounted behind him, hated liking it. It reminded her of riding the Great Plains with Howard.

"You know what's really ironic," Aldus said, picking up a thread of their earlier conversation, "The ferals told me my little brother isn't even a Forrestor, in fact he is only half human."

Kezia stared silently at the back of Aldus's head as she tried to digest half-human and failed. How would the ferals know that? *Their oracle, or whoever interprets for it, is mad, but even if it's true, it no longer matters. I love him and that's all there is to it.*

They rode in silence across the barren island, and down into Riverport on the windswept northern shore, its harbour crowded with ships. Beyond the headland, a ship under full sail butted its way out into the Dividing Sea and two smaller boats, each rowed by four sailors, were towing another ship, its sails furled, out into the bay.

"That's our ship," Aldus said, pointing out a ship at the wharf. "The green and black one."

Aldus sold the horse on the wharf for a pittance and hailed the ship. A burly sailor in a peaked hat appeared at the rail.

"Ah, it's you, Forrestor come aboard. Your timing is good, the tide is with us, we can sail immediately," he said, barking orders at the crew.

Aldus and Kezia boarded amid a general bustle of activity.

"Any baggage?" Inquired the Shipmaster, looking at their dishevelled appearance.

"Only what we stand in, Shipmaster ..." Kezia said inflecting the last as a question.

"... Butcher, but please, call me Kedron."

"Je ..." Kezia started and changed her mind. She wanted to be herself again. "Kezia," she finished.

"A lovely name," Kedron said.

"Thank you," she said and waited. He seemed to want to say more.

"Er, welcome aboard."

• • • •

On waking, Willard was acutely aware of being on his side with Averil's naked back against his chest his knees in the hollows behind hers. His erection wasn't arousal. He desperately needed to pee. How much did we drink? he wondered, looking at the fine wrinkles in the back of her balding head. His exhalation on the residual stubble blew away a few light strands. The price you pay for faith, Averil.

He took his hand from where it lay just under her breast and gently slipped his other arm out from under her shoulder. Every movement hurt his head, and his mouth felt like the bottom of cocky's cage. Had this been inevitable from the start?

[You will know after I test you.]

Severne's answer made him jump. It had been a long time since he had let control of his thoughts slip.

[Your control is excellent, but you miss much.]

Averil murmured in her sleep.

Shutting Severne out, Willard rolled out of bed and, eyes slitted, staggered into the luxurious bathroom, which included an indoor toilet. Such privileges these servers enjoyed. With blurred vision, he studied his image in the mirror, saw his hair and beard were down to his chest.

Returning, he found his clothes were clean and neatly stacked on a chair, his boots where he left them, and *Severne's Bane* sheathed in its scabbard, leaning against the wall. The last time he remembered having it, he was heading back to help the defence when Howard knocked him out.

[Kezia put it under a bench in the servatory.]

[Good, I don't want it.]

[You will.]

Five empty bottles from the server's well-stocked cellar stood on the sink in the kitchenette. No wonder he felt ill. He could remember little of what happened after they opened the third bottle, except that drunk was better than the misery of failure. Averil had said she felt the same. He vaguely recalled it was his suggestion: they get into bed naked, to make Severne think her plan complete, but after that, nothing.

Sober, the anguish returned, intensifying his physical discomfort. Aldus had taken Kezia. No, he corrected. I gave her to him, but how did he know to be there if not manipulated by Severne? He could see the Goddess would continue to separate them until he took the test. As he pulled on his boots, Averil turned in bed and came awake instantly.

"You have recovered I see," she said, throwing back the covers, striding unashamedly across the room, outwardly unaffected by last night's drinking.

Willard concentrated on her face. "Did we ...?"

"You don't remember?" Averil asked, pausing in the bathroom's doorway, raising her eyes to the ceiling before stepping inside and closing the door.

He asked Severne, [Is your backup plan done or not?] Like Averil, Severne did not deny or confirm it. Averil returned dressed except for her boots and sword. Willard stood absently fingering his talisman, mentally preparing to get Kezia back the only way left to him. As convoluted as the series of events that led him here were, it had all panned out exactly as foretold. Severne was right. My resistance just made the journey harder.

"Where do I go?" Willard asked, handing Averil her boots.

As she took them, she stared at him for some moments with a blank expression and he wondered if she was speaking to Severne. He heard nothing.

"Follow me," Averil said.

They went down and out through the crowds around the main entrance. The burning of the boats had put everyone on edge. Averil tried to reassure them as she made her way across the gap between the tower and the servatory. She led Willard down several flights of stairs to a familiar glass-walled corridor.

Tapping the talisman hanging about his neck, she said, "This goes ..."

"Ob walker said it he didn't need it," Willard interrupted,

"For those tested it isn't," Averil said, pointing to a pedestal half way along. "I have to go upstairs and sort out a rather large mess. I'll see you later, brother." She gave him a chaste kiss on the cheek and strode off down the corridor, whistling.

Chapter 46

Willard placed the talisman in the slot, waited for the wall to shimmer then stepped through into a well-remembered room. The first thing he saw was the vision-disrupting surface of an Arch replica, like the portal that had taken him first to the Eye, then to Mount Bakor.

"Willard, how nice to see you again," said Severne.

"Severne," Willard said, acknowledging her with a nod.

The image of the Goddess shivered. "The coldness of your greeting does not sound promising. I presumed you came to take the Test of Faith."

"If you meet my conditions," Willard said, looking around at the room's abundant artefacts. At the head of the altar was the floor to ceiling testing artefact, shaped like an overblown doughnut slightly bigger than the one at the pillar servatory.

"What makes you think you can bargain?"

"Your persistence in forcing me down the path you set for me. Ever since Kezia and I oathed, your purpose has been to keep us apart until I mated with Averil. You bred us for to the roles, like livestock."

Willard stood before the altar, relaxed, watching the eyes of the Goddess; regarding him warmly, he imagined.

[You are so much more.]

"I got that message. The enormous trouble you've gone to ... to create me. A special gift to my mother, a talisman, *Severne's Bane,* and this," he said, fingering the eye-shaped scar on his forehead. "I'm aware of the problem. Averil told me time is running out and you have few warriors to protect so many. You need to test me, but you also need our offspring as backup in case I fail."

"Averil talks too much." Severne sighed, "Why is it that those closest to being my interface are the most difficult to work with?"

"Perhaps you made us too much like you," Willard said.

"Perhaps I have."

"Given what's at stake, why have you never forced me to the test?"

"As I have explained to you before, the second test is truly a Test of Faith. Unless you come to it whole-heartedly, believing you must succeed, you will fail. Any doubt, no matter how small, even an unconscious hesitancy will spell failure. If you resist, it could kill you or worse. Remember Wylie."

"I do," Willard said. "So believe me, I will only be able to embrace the test wholeheartedly if you can assure me that Kezia is safe and will remain so, no matter the outcome of my test."

Severne sat as if seriously contemplating his conditions. "This is a big ask, Willard. I cannot guarantee anyone's enduring security, even my own."

That rocked him. If that were so, taking the test might prove pointless.

"I agree to your conditions provided you understand I can only promise to do all in my considerable, but not unlimited power, to fulfil them."

"I'll take your word for it, if you can show me where and how she is right now, and how you intend to take care of her." He still fretted at having let her go with Aldus, but how could he have known his brother had become a murderer?

[By not excluding me,] Severne said as a multitude of tiny dust motes swirled and thickened within the crystal cube, forming a new three-dimensional image.

A boat rose and fell on a moderate swell. The room around faded. The tang of salt assailed him as the image rapidly expanded to swallow him. The hallucinatory experience made him feel giddy. He was flying, swooping towards the deck of a black and green ship. Nostalgia overran him when he identified Odell's *Bay Trader*. Then he could hear the soft creak of her timbers, the gentle slap of rigging and the snap of loose canvas. A desire to tighten the offending sail dispersed when he spotted a head of short, blonde hair with dark roots. The familiar profile turned. Kezia was standing at the rail talking to a burly individual in a shipmaster's peaked cap. Willard smiled, happy knowing that Kedron was now the *Trader's* shipmaster.

"As you can see, she is in safe hands," the Goddess said.

Willard's view continued to change as the gull circled the boat. Aldus was leaning against a hatch, watching the pair at the rail.

"Not around Aldus, she isn't."

He could not say 'brother' anymore. Mother's revelations then Averil's had ended any sense of kinship. He pointed, his finger touching the cool surface of the crystal, yet the imaged remained undisturbed.

"He is being watched. Look."

The view moved to a figure resting in the shadow of the upper deck. Above the figure's shoulder, Willard caught the sparkle of a gem. The warrior turned and looked directly at him and winked. Baxter.

"If you are now satisfied, then we can begin."

• • • •

"Willard?" Kezia said, gripping the rigging to hold herself upright as the ship lifted on the swell. She had felt sure he was watching her, but all she saw were swooping gulls. When she turned back, the Shipmaster was staring at her. "What is it ... Kedron?"

"Willard, you said," his voice excited.

"Sorry, I was thinking out loud. Why?"

"I sailed with a Willard once. I wouldn't mind catching up."

"Willard is not an uncommon name, believe me."

"But Kezia is and you came aboard with a Forrestor. That many connections are more than chance." His stare became a scrutiny. "I see it now. You are as Lord Willard described you."

The gull alighted on the yard.

"You know him?" Kezia hardly believed her luck.

"But for him, I would not be here."

Quickly glancing around at Aldus, Kezia lowered her voice. "He's trapped in Carrier Point."

Aldus stepped up and grabbed her elbow. "No point bothering the Shipmaster Kez. He can't sail under the cliffs and the ship's too big to row."

"It's tricky. I'll grant you, but not impossible if you time it right."

"You'll do it?" Kezia asked.

"For Lord Willard, I will."

"Not while I'm paying you, Butcher," Aldus said.

Kedron signalled the Mate, "You have the ship Culver. Set course for West head." He turned back to Aldus. "Come below. I'll give you your money back."

"What?"

"I'll take you for free but I'm going via Carrier Point," Kedron said, as he made to go below.

Aldus grabbed his arm. "The ferals will fire bomb you as soon as you get close."

Kedron stared at the hand on his arm and Kezia shrank back at the dangerous look in his eyes.

"No one lays hands on me on my ship," he said, reaching back with one hand for a belaying pin.

Aldus let go, grabbing Kezia instead and pulled a knife. She could feel the point of the blade on her neck with each movement of the ship.

Kedron, looking past them, grunted.

"I'm not falling for that one." Aldus sneered and tightened his grip until the familiar his and crackle that only a named sword could make caused him to turn.

Not again, thought Kezia, twisting out of Aldus' grip. "Stop!" she shouted at Baxter. "He's Willard's brother."

Baxter pulled the stroke and the tip of his sword missed Aldus's neck by a fraction but the fire around the blade's edge drew a burning line across his chin. He screamed, dropped the knife, and clutched his face. Kezia stepped forward to help, but he pushed her aside and with a stumbling run vaulted headlong over the rail, quickly disappearing beneath the waves.

Kedron immediately brought the ship about, but though they tacked back and forth over the spot, Aldus did not reappear. To her dismay, Kezia eventually had to admit it was hopeless and let Kedron resume to Carrier Point. As she had with Howard's death, she felt partly responsible. It would fall to her to be the bringer of bad news. How do I tell Willard? He's only just learned Aldus is ... was alive?

· · · ·

Ah Willard, Averil thought privately as she sprang up the curved staircase to the triple tiered foyer of the servatory. You are in for an awakening that will make your mother's revelations seem like an amusing anecdote.

Her mind snapped back to business when she reached the top. [About my request Severne?]

[No April. Knowledge of the tunnels will not only undermine the mystique you have to appear suddenly when candidates need you, but will lead someone to map the power lines your swords use. There is still much to do, before we can allow the few warriors we have to be compromised.]

Tits. Her request had been to use the tunnel-craft to get the remaining population out the way she had come in. She understood Severne's uncompromising stand, but it narrowed her options. Now was not the time to argue, but the refusal left her with one risky idea. It depended on her judgement of Willard, and the timing would be critical. She hastened across the tiled floor, drowning her thoughts in action.

Waves of hostility from the expectant crowd of refugees washed over her the moment she stepped out.

[Get used to it April, nobody likes us.]

[Thanks Duds, I really needed to know that.]

Several thoughts gently pinged her mind. [We like you.]

Among them was a thought pattern that she now knew was Gardner. [I'm so sorry Gard. After all your help, I treated you badly.]

[You're welcome.] There was no residual animosity in Gardner's thought.

[Now there's a man I can like,] thought Averil, letting her mind drift to salacious images, triggering a round of good-humoured banter.

[Hey people, I don't mind choice, but six to one.]

The reminder that Howard was gone, and they were back to eight, stopped the banter.

Angry with herself for the quip, she pushed through the crowd, wrenched open the compound door and strode out into the feral encampment.

"General Sumner," she shouted.

Spears bristled around her as word spread, and the parapet above soon crowded with Watchers.

[Severne.]

[Yes April.]

[How goes Willard's test?]

[We are about to start. This will fully occupy me for the next hour. I will let you know when we finish. Try not to need me until then.]

[Good luck.]

[The test requires faith not luck,] Severne replied and the presence in her mind ceased.

Sumner strode towards her. In full dress uniform, he was resplendent, so unlike the scruffy feral who picked her up from a deserted beach, and different again from the thoughtful chess player. She wasn't sure which she preferred.

"Have you come to surrender the Man?" he asked?

"I'm here to trade."

Sumner smiled. "You have not the position to trade."

"Then why are you camped outside my door?"

"You have a point," he said, laughing.

Averil felt a tremor pass through her. She was about to go way beyond her authority on a hunch. With Severne absent, she let the idea surface.

A storm of protest from the brethren beat around her mind. She quelled them with a single thought. [Until Severne says otherwise, I speak for her.]

* * * *

The *Bay Trader* ran across the face of the wind, away from Carrier Point, which Kezia found hard, but as Kedron explained, necessary to get in position for a close in run down the isthmus coast.

"The ferals are less likely to see us under the cliffs and it's deep water with a strong current," he pointed out.

"But it delays us," Kezia said, worried Willard might weaken and take the test. She would lose him to the Goddess forever. She could have him on that damned altar right now.

"Is not running close to the cliffs dangerous?" Baxter asked.

"The sea is always dangerous, no more or no less dangerous than riding a horse. If the horse is sound, then the danger depends on the rider. My ship is sound, and I'm a safe shipmaster."

"I meant no offence, Kedron. I am concerned only for the Lady Kezia's safety."

"I don't want your protection," Kezia snapped.

Kedron interposed, saying, "Lord paleface was a damn good sailor in the end," and Kezia willingly dropped her conversation with Baxter.

"Lord paleface?" Kezia questioned.

"He was as sick as a dog until he got his sea legs." He grinned at her, "It was here on the *Trader* he got that scar everyone talks about. First day it was, and my old shipmaster, Odell, was all over himself, thought Lord Willard was already the Face."

"Didn't you," Kezia asked, wondering which creed if any shipmasters followed.

"At first," Kedron said, "but then I went and checked. It was just as Lord Willard said. He got up too fast and bashed his head on a wooden nail above his bunk. It's still there if you want to have a look. I s'pose if he becomes the Face, that nail will be an important relic."

"I'd really like Willard to show me," Kezia said.

Kedron chuckled, a deep belly laugh. "He'd probably enjoy that. Lord Willard always rejected any notion of being the Face. Severne knows lots tried to tar him with that brush."

He told her about their voyage to Canalbridge, glossing over the part Baxter had played.

His portrayal of Willard was exactly what Kezia wanted to hear. She hoped he was still rejecting the notion, at least until she could rescue him. "How long before we turn?" she asked.

Kedron looked up at the sails and around the horizon at the cliffs. "About now," he said, and signalled the Mate. The hands turned out and the ship weathered round to run before the wind, perilously close to the coast.

As the *Trader* picked up speed, Kezia looked up at the full sails and smiled. Now that they were underway, she felt confident of reaching him in time, but not without reservation. *Maybe Willard and Averil's rescue is now more important to the Goddess than my safety. Maybe they have ...,* but that was a thought so horrible, Kezia refused to think it.

· · · ·

"This is your point of no return," said the Goddess, her mellifluous voice rich and strong, comforting, familiar. "You should understand, the Test of Faith represents a severe invasion of your mind. It will challenge everything you believe about yourself and your world. You will not die or go. The range of tests I did before I gave you to your mother suggested a ninety-seven percent probability of you becoming my interface."

"Before I was born, how is that possible?" Willard asked.

"Any attempt to explain how, before your test, would be futile."

Mother was right all along, Willard thought. *I was a gift from the Goddess.* He posed another question, wanting to know but dreading the answer. He had already lost a father and a brother this way. Truth was not always better than ignorance.

[Is she my mother or not,] he asked unwilling to voice that question?

Severne replied in kind. [Eliza gave birth to you.]

"Thank you."

[Hedley and I have monitored your progress throughout your life. Your brain has the right structures and you have the required philosophical temperament for the task, but we are about to test if you have enough faith.]

"What does that mean, exactly?" Willard asked, reverting to speech.

"Faith is putting your beliefs to the test. Averil believed in becoming a warrior. You believe in the love you and Kezia share. You have faith enough in her love for you to present for this test. This is promising. I shall begin, in the hope, that your love for her is enough."

Severne's tone became formal. "Willard, do you want to be tested?"

"Yes," Willard answered with a sense of relief. It would soon be over.

"On the altar please Willard,"

Though comfortable, Willard was getting dizzy. He was lying on the altar, his feet higher than his head. The altar had indented and wrapped itself firmly around him. He could feel a mouse running backwards and forwards over his scalp, removing hair from the base of his skull. A cold, stinging fluid doused his shaved scalp as the altar tilted the other way until he was almost upright.

I've been down this path before, thought Willard, hoping nothing went wrong this time. Shiny metallic arms reached out to place two round pads on the shaved places on either side of the implant site. They felt wet and slimy, like frogs. The procedure now took a new path as the altar returned to horizontal and slid into the doughnut artefact behind him.

[To monitor your progress,] Severne said.

Willard closed his eyes against the light as the cave hummed and his skin tingled with warmth. He hoped Kezia would appreciate why he had to do this.

• • • •

Averil was pleased to see Sumner taken aback when she said, "I will give you the Man Who Will Be Face ion exchange for a sanctuary inside these walls for all who enter."

Sumner eyed Averil speculatively as they stood in a cleared space between his besieging army and Carrier Point's servatory compound.

"You have a sanctuary now." He said, looking over her shoulder.

"It's not enough. I want the whole of Carrier Point and I want it ..." Sumner's eyebrows shot up even before she added "... for all time."

"That is not within my power, Uplander. I am not the Charismatic."

"The Goddess will square it with the Charismatic and make it binding on all future incumbents. The brethren and I will enforce it."

[Dudley, Fletcher, to me.]

"Ah yes," Sumner said. "You now have the legendary extension of life for those tested. How I wish I had been born with differing eyes."

This time, he surprised her. His dream was far more ambitious than hers had been. He was wrong of course; she had been born with extended life. Like Willard, both her parents were builders. As she glanced up to where Severne's Eye orbited, she ran a hand across her head, conscience of her baldness. The skin of her scalp, already lightly tanned, was burning.

"You look as lovely without it," Sumner said, his eyes travelling down her body and she could see him visualizing as hairless, other parts of her anatomy, with which he was intimately familiar. Her face coloured to match her scalp.

Sumner tapped his head, "Do not misunderstand me Averil of the Lakes. Your loveliness is here. Do you imagine this sanctuary will save the Watchers you have here?"

Averil's blush increased, pleased that despite all that happened between them he liked her. The feeling was mutual.

"This small town made a perpetual sanctuary. In exchange for the Man Who Will Be Face. It's a fair bargain, if genuine."

She knew he was looking for a hidden motive. "You have my word, backed by the word of the Goddess," Averil said, as Dudley and Fletcher appeared behind her, walking slowly towards them.

Sumner seemed impressed and genuinely amused at the same time. His guard nervously bunched up behind him.

"No warrior, before you, has ever claimed to speak for the Goddess. Why should I believe you?" Sumner said, watching the approaching warriors.

"April speaks for the Goddess," Dudley and Fletcher confirmed. To her Dudley added, [I hope you know what you're doing.]

She felt Fletcher mentally nod his agreement.

[Trust me,] Averil thought back as she reached over her shoulder.

Stone Ethyl instantly stepped in front of Sumner. The circle of archers drew back on already nocked arrows.

"Here is my sword on it," Averil said, un-slinging the scabbard and offering *Fires Kiss,* hilt first to Sumner. Sumner was, like those around him, astounded.

"Let us be quite clear. I have your word as a warrior you will deliver to me, Willard Forrestor, known as the Man Who Will Be Face."

"To be even more precise and ensure no misunderstanding, I will give you the Willard Forrestor, known as the Man Who Will Be Face, and marked by Our Lady, with an eye-shaped scar on his forehead."

"In exchange, I am to declare a perpetual sanctuary for this place." His dismissive gesture swept around Carrier Point.

Fletcher scowled. Baxter said, [Giving away a potential interface might be your last act as brethren leader. Doane will kill him.]

[We shall see,] Averil replied.

"On behalf of the Charismatic I accept," Sumner said, taking Averil's sword with reverence and handing it to a sceptical looking Stone Ethyl. "We will immediately withdraw beyond these puny walls." He straightened, speaking loud enough for his staff and those on the parapets to hear.

"In the name of Charismatic Doane, as supreme commander of Federal Armed Forces, I declare this town, known as Carrier Point, a sanctuary in perpetuity. As Our Lady is my witness, nobody in the Federated Tribes will pursue those who seek its sanctuary, past these walls." He looked down at Averil again, as a boisterous cheering arose behind her. "If they make it." Sumner added quietly.

"I will have papers drawn up for us to sign. This Sanctuary will only become official when you deliver Willard Forrestor to me and I return your sword. Let me warn you, April of the brethren, any treachery, and I promise you, your fellow Uplanders will pay for it."

Averil nodded, smiling around clamped teeth. His proviso worried her. It would be hard to bring candidates into a blockaded Sanctuary, except through the tunnels, which might not meet with Severne's approval. Still, she had done it. Now she would have to make it work. She turned and strode between the warriors on her way back to the compound. They fell into step a little behind her.

Federal tents began collapsing immediately. Soon, a steady stream of marching columns filled the main road to the West Gate. The Watchers toasted Averil wherever she went. One man fell at her feet. "Praise be our Lady Averil, the Goddess of Freedom."

"Your praise belongs to Our Lady of the Towers, the Goddess Severne. It is her work I do," Averil said, lifting him up. I just hope she sees it that way.

Chapter 47

An image flashed into Willard's mind.

[What do you see Willard?]

[Looks like a wheel with a bloated rim, bright on one side, rotating slowly against ... a night sky.]

[This is what you call Severne's Eye often called the otherworld.]

[I've been there?]

[No.]

[Where then?]

[We will come to that when you understand more.]

Another image replaced the doughnut, then another in increasingly quick succession. They came at Willard furiously: some moving, some with sounds and/or smell, some immediately recognisable, others completely mysterious. With another part of his mind, he wondered how he would keep up, but he did, effortlessly.

The blinding blur of images diverged: drawings, numbers, patterns, people strange and familiar, bizarre animals, explosions of colourful vegetation that burst forth from seeds, grew into enormous trees, aged, died, fell, and rotted away in a compressed instant.

The unending stream of images merged into a single bright white light, pulsing slowly. Willard sensed the beginnings of an ache in his temples. It intensified to a light throb as the pulse increased in frequency and a sliver of doubt assailed him.

[Have faith Willard. Kezia is depending on you.]

Willard thought of Kezia, but the throbbing continued, building to a crescendo that threatened to tear his head off. He could feel the blood pounding through his temples as if trying to burst from the confinement of their vessels. His whole body vibrated in synchronous with the pulse. He could no longer see discrete images and he sensed a shift of intent, coherence to the information invading his consciousness - the Goddess was coming.

[Stop,] he screamed.

A terrible echo of the scream, not his, crackled through his mind like the lightning bolt from a named sword. He suffered an instant of non-being, then a heart-thumping silence.

And in the silence, Willard knew everything he thought he had always wanted to know and many things he would rather not know, but there were also gaps, a multitude of disparate pieces of information that did not properly connect.

[I failed,] he thought, with relief.

· · · ·

[You were right April] Severne's voice in Averil's mind sounded tired.

[I'm sorry Severne, but I know Willard. Even when he really wants an outcome, he over-thinks it and often baulks at the last moment.]

[What will he do now?]

Holy mother the Goddess is asking me. [I don't know,] Averil said, and felt an intense echo of their first meeting. [If the test has changed his perceptions as profoundly as it did mine, your guess is the equal of mine.]

[I do not guess.]

Averil cleared her throat. She didn't know quite how to tell Severne what she had done in her absence.

[Yes?]

[I ... er ... I made a deal with the Federals in your name. I got them to withdraw from Carrier Point and declare it a Sanctuary.]

[Should this concern me?]

[I promised to give them Willard.]

Despite the measured tones of Severne's next statement, Averil had a distinct impression of laughter.

[Best come and get him then.]

• • • •

Averil found Willard in the servatory foyer, looking up at a long slit in the dome three stories above.

"Averil," he said, using his voice without a trace of echo in her mind. "Did you know this place was once used to observe the stars?"

"I did." [How do you feel?] Averil asked.

"I failed," he said grinning, replying to her thought with his voice.

"I thought you might. In fact, I bargained on it," Averil said, in kind.

"Severne told me. Very astute little sister."

"Thank you ... Lord Willard," Averil said with an impish grin.

"Shall we go out there and retrieve your sword?"

As they walked out into the compound, Willard directed a thought to the Goddess only, [To make this work I need a favour.]

[For your supreme effort in trying to host me, I will consider any reasonable request.]

Willard laid out his proposition. Alongside him, Averil nodded, [clever.]

[It is possible but there is a cost.]

[There always is. Do a cost benefit analysis of the effect on your plan.]

[I will be ready in an hour,] Severne said seconds later.

• • • •

Always in the back of Kezia's mind was the disquieting thought that since their eyes changed, a bond had sprung between Willard and her sister that excluded her. Yet despite this natural bond, Willard had only ever had eyes for her, and Averil had shown no interest in him or anyone else. Whatever had changed, Kezia was betting the Goddess was behind it. *I'll know soon enough.*

The *Bay Trader's* sails flopped listlessly. The wind had dropped away the moment they rounded the Pointing Finger's knuckle. Kedron and Baxter worked the twin tillers like oars, trying to maintain the ship's momentum as they drifted through the flotsam of what had once been Carrier Point's Port: bloated bodies, blackened, waterlogged timbers, scraps of charred material, a child's wooden duck.

The bombardment Aldus had predicted for them did not eventuate, which worried Kezia so much she asked Baxter.

"The battle for Carrier Point is over. The Federals have withdrawn," he replied.

"And Willard," Kezia asked?

"Safe," was all Baxter would say.

Unable to stand not knowing, Kezia leapt up onto the stone wharf before the *Bay Trader* had tied up and started up the ramp at the run. Baxter soon caught up. She gave in and let him help her to the top.

. . . .

[April, Kezia is on her way up.]

[Thanks Baxter, this won't take long.] Willard heard the exchange as he and Averil walked out of the servatory compound together, flanked by Dudley and Fletcher.

Sumner of the Lakes and Stone Ethyl waited patiently under the awning of the one remaining tent inside Carrier Point, halfway between the compound and the West Gate. The light of late afternoon glinted off the gem in the hilt of *Fires Kiss*, which lay on the negotiation table. A small complement of spearman and archers attended their General. They had been waiting all day.

Willard carried neither *Severne's Bane* nor the talisman. He had dressed as he would at home to work the farm with the addition of a wide-brimmed hat to protect his soon to be hairless head. He felt better than he had since his eyes changed. He knew at last where he was going and how to get there. His future path was his to choose.

The party was less than halfway, when a scuffle broke out behind and Kezia's angry shout reached Willard. "Let me go."

Willard felt Baxter's angst as he turned to see Kezia break through the Watchers at the gate and run toward them.

[What's happening Baxter,] asked Averil?

[Sorry April but Lady Kezia is damned hard to stop.]

[Like her sister,] Gardner quipped.

[You go on,] Willard said to Averil. [Tell your General I'll be there shortly. Don't start without me.]

Averil grinned. [How can I? You're the prize.]

Averil, Dudley, and Fletcher continued as Willard turned and waited. Kezia crashed into him moments later, breathless from her climb, close to exhaustion. When she eventually looked up at him, she stepped back in horror, tears making her dark eyes mirrors.

"You've already done it. You stupid bloody fool, how could you?" she said, anger overrunning hurt.

Willard grabbed her wrists and gently but firmly held her until she stopped trying to hit him. "Look at me Kezia, I am not what you suppose. I have bargained us—you and me—free of Our Lady. I will be neither warrior nor server."

"How? I don't believe you," Kezia said.

"Yes, you do," Willard told her and let her go, holding her only with his gaze. "We can now have a life together in this sanctuary we're about to create." He did not mention that a decision of her mother's meant her potential lifespan was half that of his.

[Don't be too long, brother. Stone Ethyl is edgy.]

[On my way.] "I have to go now. Please wait for me."

Before she could answer, Willard turned away and walked toward the waiting ferals to validate Averil's bargain with Sumner. The day was bright and warm. Bud was upon them again. Young gulls pecked in the untended grass. Willard, playing for time, approached slowly, as if out for a casual stroll around the town while channelling a narrow band of thoughts to Severne. [How are preparations for our demonstration?]

[Easier than expected. Ready.]

[This could go very wrong once they realise.]

[April does not think so. She trusts Sumner.]

[She may be right, but the long and inglorious history you showed me is full of honourable men performing shamefully when it suited them. I would feel happier if I knew what motivated Sumner.]

[Sumner has ambition to be the next Charismatic, absolute ruler of New Earth,] Severne answered.

[Is Sumner one of Hedley's brood?]

[A shrewd observation, I do wish you were my interface. I would love to romp through the fields of your mind.]

[You might not like all you find,] Willard said. As he neared the tent, he pushed his hat back a little to reveal the eye-shaped scar. [It is however very human of you. How can that be, seven?]

[I am ...] A long pause followed where he felt the pressure of an impending thought which never eventuated, [I am ... damaged.]

A few of Sumner's retinue fell to their knees with outstretched arms, bowing until hands and head simultaneously touched the ground. Sumner and Stone Ethyl remained upright, staring.

[What was Severne trying to say?] Averil asked.

[I'm not sure. Might be worth looking into, later.]

"It's true," Sumner said, as Willard halted, the awe in his voice undisguised. He seemed about to fall to his knees until Stone Ethyl nudged him in the ribs with a sharp elbow.

[Ethyl bears watching,] Averil cast as she stepped forward. "General Sumner, I present to you as promised, Willard Forrestor, The Man Who Will Be Face. My sword, if you please."

Sumner moved like an automaton to hand *Fires Kiss* to Averil, his eyes on Willard.

A true believer, thought Willard, wondering how the truth would affect him. Without breaking eye contact with Sumner, Willard peripherally scanned the rest of those present, something he would not have thought possible mere hours ago. Stone Ethyl's gaze switched between Averil and him as if waiting for treachery. Averil's gaze, most often on Sumner, had a hint of fear mixed with admiration.

[Such a useful of array of skills you have given me Severne, their thoughts are plain on their faces.]

[Why do you fear him, Averil?] Willard asked gently and saw her blush lightly.

[The exchange is my doing. I don't want him to hate me for it,] Averil replied candidly.

[Ah.]

Averil's colour deepened. She concentrated on retying her scabbard.

Sumner rallied from of his wordless reverence, motioning to his guards as he claimed Willard. "I have the Face," he said.

"Not quite," Averil said.

Stone Ethyl went for her sword before Averil had finished. Fletcher and Dudley were quicker with swords that crackled and spat lightning. Sumner of the Lakes frowned and his mouth thinned.

"Calm your aide, general, before she pointlessly gets herself killed. I am the man Averil promised you, marked by the Goddess as the Man Who Will Be Face. You can feel the scar if you wish." Despite the softness of his voice, Willard held them entranced. "But regrettably, I failed her test. I am not the Face of Our Lady."

[Thank Severne for that kiddo,] Kezia whispered in his mind, immediately followed by a gasp. [How did I do that?]

[I activated the ring your mother gave you. It talks to the one intended for Averil that you gave me.]

[Is that how we ... all those times?]

[Yes, they automatically activate during times of stress,] Willard said. He could feel the wonder in Kezia's tone of thought, as she remembered all their hauntingly brief contacts.

A stunned party of ferals was still coming to terms with the outcome of Averil's bargain. The lightning from Fletcher and Dudley's drawn swords was now all that held Stone Ethyl in check. Sumner looked grim. He was perhaps facing ruin for his failure. An unsmiling Averil, her sword still sheathed, watched him with moist eyes. [Now I'm for it.]

"As I also promised," Sumner said to Willard, though he was looking at Averil. "You Uplanders will pay for your treachery. We will restore this temple to its original glory by erasing every other structure around it. Once we have purged the caverns below with fire, we will fill them in, and I will push any of your people still here at dawn tomorrow, into the sea."

As he spoke, Stone Ethyl regained a measure of pride. Their tense entourage smirked. Averil wilted. Only Willard seemed unperturbed.

"There was no treachery. Charismatic Doane's oracle led you astray, misrepresenting Our Lady's confidence in me as a fact. You, and I mean all of you from Doane down, gambled it was true. April gambled it was false. You were wrong. April was right."

[Don't overdo it,] Averil slipped into his mind.

[Wait, there's more.]

Willard continued with hypnotic smoothness even as he conversed with Averil. "The one Who Will Be Face has yet to be born, and if you break your contract with Our Lady, on whose behalf warrior April made it, you put at risk a potential Mother of the Face."

The shocked silence dragged as all but Willard searched for meaning in his statements. Beginning with Sumner, all gazes gravitated to Averil.

Averil stared at Willard. "What the fuck are you saying?" she blurted in full voice.

Willard told Averil privately, [You're carrying Sumner's child.]

Averil went rigid.

Willard's projections showed rumour, and legend would spread like ripples from this point to the limits of New Earth. His longer view also saw the all the banks on which the ripples would break, barring the unforeseen, like his failure to host seven.

[It's a great bargain Averil,] he added, trying to ease her shock at him knowing her condition when she hadn't.

[How can ... I haven't been sick, I haven't missed ...]

[Ask Seven. She knew and yet still tested you.]

[The test only affects your mind,] Severne said.

[Hair doesn't grow on minds,] said Willard, and felt Severne presence suddenly withdraw.

He noted that Sumner's gaze had not left Averil, the ambitious general, calculating his chances on several fronts. Three Restoration Warriors could easily demolish his entire entourage. The Face was yet to be born. Averil could well be the Mother and he the father if he wooed her, she might already be with child, his. As father of Our Lady's Face, he would have control of the Goddess's host from birth. A simple step from there would make him Charismatic of all Nuaith.

Stone Ethyl roused. "He cannot know this. It's another gamble."

"Is it not natural that this Sanctuary will draw to it the Mother, to protect the child," Willard said. "The next One Who Will Be Face," Willard said, watching their faces, reading their confusion, seeing the possibilities and the doubts he had sewn.

[Fuck,] Averil's expletive exploded in the brethren's minds, [If I was pregnant during my test, it can't be yours.]

[Thank goodness,] Kezia said.

[Seven's plan is on hold until you give birth,] Willard said. Severne's continued silence was conspicuous. They both knew why, but neither wanted to expand.

Willard continued his speech to Sumner's entourage. "When I let you leave, I want you to ask your Charismatic to explain his oracle's failure. You may find you are not following Our Lady at all."

[Let them leave,] Averil asked.

Dudley and Fletcher tensed?

The flash of anger that crossed Stone Ethyl's face showed she had not missed it. Willard set out to confirm her suspicions. "If I do not have your word, Sumner of the Lakes, and yours, Ethyl of the Stones, you will both be here until the restoration."

[Spoken like a true warrior even though you're bluffing. You don't have a sword,] Baxter said.

[Averil's is in easy reach. I will kill them first, and deal with whoever steps up to take their place. Nothing is more important at this moment than the establishment of this Sanctuary.]

Sumner's assessment was rapid. "No need for threats, Lord Willard. I am a man of my word. You have my pledge."

Ethyl, her mouth a crack in a hard expression, glared malevolently at Willard, then at Averil and eventually at Sumner.

Sumner stared back at her, his hand on his sword. No ambiguity there, thought Willard. 'Your word or I kill you.'

"You have my pledge," Stone Ethyl grunted.

"Thank you," Willard said, acknowledging both. [Now,] he projected to Severne as he stepped out from the tents overhang and looked up into the evening sky, as the last intense sliver of sun dipped below the horizon.

Averil just pulling out of her shock, followed and curiosity got the better of the entourage. They joined Willard, looking up. Despite the still bright dusk, Severne's Eye unexpectedly appeared, well outside the schedule he knew the ferals kept, and grew brighter than it ever had been, almost as bright as a named sword at full power.

"Behold Our Lady's signature to our agreement," Willard said, raising his arms in a theatrical gesture.

[Now!]

Willard clapped once, and the light went out.

All but Sumner of the Lakes, Stone Ethyl and the brethren present faced towards where the Eye had been and prostrated themselves. Even Stone Ethyl, despite her fury, seemed impressed.

[What was that?] asked several warriors.

[Severne sacrificed a communications satellite. She might be slightly less available.]

To Sumner, Willard said, "Severne's Eye will reappear on schedule. You should prepare. I will leave the signing to brethren leader April."

A bedlam of voice and thought erupted behind him as he walked back to where Kezia waited. New insights continued to unroll in his mind. He now knew how vital Severne's search was, if Nuaith was to survive Typhon, the unseeable lump of rock heading their way. He would have a long and serious talk with Hedley and Jorgena.

Kezia hugged Willard close and he returned the hug with mixed feelings, love tempered with compassion. Barring an unforeseen accident, he would outlive her by centuries, but that was nowhere near the worst of what Severne had done to Kezia and Averil.

[I'll live with, so long as Kezia never finds out] he told Severne. Averil now knew that to ensure Willard and Kezia could only have the required offspring, the Goddess had removed Kezia ovaries and transplanted into her, one from Averil.

Willard promised himself that no matter how long they had together, he would do all in his power to make it up to her. Holding her close, he gazed up at the darkening sky in time to see the tail end of the Eye's transit fade like a slow wink.

[I have my eye on you, Willard.]

The End

Don't miss out!

Visit the website below and you can sign up to receive emails whenever Rob Bleckly publishes a new book. There's no charge and no obligation.

https://books2read.com/r/B-A-AFKY-HKXJC

BOOKS 2 READ

Connecting independent readers to independent writers.

About the Author

Rob Bleckly was born in Port Pirie, South Australia. He has written stories since his teens but only after founding the Blackwood Writers Group in 1996 did he finish and submit his stories. His first submission to L. Ron Hubbard's Writers of the Future Contest won an 'Honorable Mention'. Over the next 20+ years he wrote The Restoration Legends trilogy. He lives with his wife Felicity in Strathalbyn, a town in the Adelaide Hills.

Read more at https://www.rob.bleckly.com/.

Printed in Australia
Ingram Content Group Australia Pty Ltd
AUHW022001021023
384440AU00002B/2

9 798223 746003